FLAME OF REQUIEM

FLAME OF REQUIEM

THE COMPLETE TRILOGY

DANIEL ARENSON

BOOK ONE:
FORGED IN DRAGONFIRE

ELORY

Blood.

Searing sunlight.

The *cracks* of whips on flesh.

With cries of agony, with sand and tar, with twisted shoulders and breaking backs, the children of Requiem toiled.

"Faster!"

The flaming whips flew, ripping through skin.

"Up!"

The chains rattled. Slaves fell. Masters roared.

"Toil!"

The sunlight beat down, as merciless as the whips. Across the pit, a nation broke. A people shattered. Thousands spread across the crater, hobbling forward, feet chained. The whips cut them. The sun burned them. The yokes hung across their stooped shoulders, secured with chains, bearing baskets of bitumen. The tar bubbled up from the wells, filling the pit, burning bare feet, churning the air, invading lungs with noxious fumes.

"Faster!"

Blood.

"Up!"

Whips ripping skin.

"Toil!"

Golden masters of light. Shattered, dying slaves.

Requiem—a nation broken. A nation in chains.

Elory trudged across the tar pit, chains rattling around her ankles. The seeping tar burned her feet. The yoke shoved against her narrow shoulders, cracking the skin, threatening to crack the bone. Sticky clumps of bitumen filled the baskets hanging off her yoke, the fumes filling her nostrils and lungs, spinning her head, leaving her always dizzy, always numb. The sunlight beat down, baking her shaved head, burning her arms and neck, nearly blinding her. Her collar squeezed her neck, leaving her wheezing, struggling for every breath.

"Faster, worm!"

She could not see the overseer, but she felt his whip. The lash slammed against her back, and Elory yowled. Even over the stench of bitumen, she smelled her own blood. She wobbled. She fell to her knees, nearly spilling her baskets, burning her knees in the seeping, sticky blackness.

"Up! Toil!"

The whip slammed down again. Elory screamed. She wept. She pushed herself up. She hobbled onward.

Faster. Up. Toil. The words rattled through her mind, an endless chant. The prayer of her people. The only words that would perhaps allow her to cling to this flickering life. A life of blood. Of pain. Of tar.

Of hope, Elory thought, eyes stinging with tears.

"Move, maggot!"

Her master's whip lashed again. Again her back tore. Elory shuffled onward, chains rattling, blood seeping, the ancient word on her lips.

"Requiem," she whispered as she struggled across the pit, carrying the bitumen. "Requiem. Requiem."

"Faster! Up! Toil!"

Requiem.

Tears stung her eyes. Elory looked around her. Through the fumes of tar, the blinding sunlight, and the sweat in her eyes, she couldn't see far. All around her, her nation broke. Men. Women. Children. Chains around their ankles. Collars, cursed with dark magic, keeping their old magic at bay. Slaves. Wretches. No more than maggots by the blinding light of the beautiful masters.

But once we were proud, Elory thought. *Once we were dragons.*

She shut her eyes, and tears streamed down her cheeks. She tried to imagine it. She tried to believe. Her father had taught her that five hundred years ago, their people—the Vir

Requis, an ancient race—had lived in a distant, northern land. Lived a life of peace and plenty. Lived in palaces of marble and forests of birches.

Lived free to fly as dragons.

Elory opened her eyes and looked over her shoulder. It still lay there. She had to believe. Past the tar pits. Past the great wall and the seraphim upon its battlements. Past the desert. Past the sea. Past the wilderness of forests and mountains. A realm lost but not forgotten. A realm where her people had flown. A realm called Requiem.

For thousands of years, Elory thought, *we flew free . . . until they came. The masters.*

She blinked tears and fumes out of her eyes. She saw them there, around her and on the wall. Beautiful beings of light. Towering men and women, their hair long and golden, their eyes shining with inner light, their pupils shaped as sunbursts. They wore gilded armor, carried lances and shields, and swan wings grew from their backs. Haloes shone around their heads, pale gold, barely visible in the searing sunbeams.

The destroyers of Requiem. The masters. The seraphim.

"Move, you wretch, or I'll toss you into the tar!"

Her own seraph, a beautiful deity who shone in the sunlight, swung his whip of fire. Again the lash slammed into Elory, knocking her down. Again she struggled to her feet. Again she shuffled onward. For ten years now—since she had been only eight—she had labored here in this pit. Carrying the bitumen, this black gold, the viscous tar that held the bricks of palaces and temples, that waterproofed ships, that glued mosaics to floors and gemstones to chains of gold, that gave Saraph its power and kept Requiem in chains.

"Requiem," Elory whispered. "Requiem. Requiem."

With every utterance of the word, her collar squeezed her neck. The collar that kept her in this form—a scrawny youth, her limbs bony, her head spinning, barely five feet tall, barely heavier than the yoke she carried, her back whipped, her skin burnt. The cursed collar engraved with runes of dark magic. The collar that let them rule her people. The collar that kept a proud nation enslaved.

The collar that chains the dragon inside me.

Elory looked behind her again. There, in the center of the pit, she could see them. A group of dragons. Only five. Vir Requis with their collars removed.

The great reptiles labored in chains. Seraphim stood around them, pointing lances and swords, swinging their whips. The five dragons dug with claws, ripping into the hard earth, seeking the reserves of bitumen within. Elory's own mother, the silver dragon Nala, dug there into the rock, her scales cracked, her wings wrapped with chains. Soon more of the tar would rise into the pit, filling the crater with its hot, sticky, precious gift. Soon the rest of Requiem, myriads of collared souls, would refill their baskets.

Day after day.

Year after year.

Generation after generation.

Five hundred years of blood. Of whips. Of prayer.

Once I too could become a dragon, Elory thought. She took step after step, feet burning, knees buckling. She tried to imagine that she was one of those great reptiles now, that she flew on the wind. *Once none of us had collars. Once millions of us flew in the north, proud and strong. Before the seraphim came with their chariots of fire. Before they toppled our temples, brought us to this distant land. Once we too were an empire.*

She stared up at the sky. The fumes stung her eyes. The sun beat down, a white inferno. She could not see the stars of Requiem, the Draco constellation that her father believed still watched over their people. But Elory still prayed to those mythical lights. The ancient prayer of her people. The prayer her people had been singing for thousands of years in the northern forests, for five hundred years in this desert of blood, of whips, of toil.

"As the leaves fall upon our marble tiles, as the breeze rustles the birches beyond our columns, as the sun gilds the mountains above our halls—know, young child of the woods, you are home, you are home." Elory's voice cracked, barely a whisper, and she tasted blood and tears. "Requiem! May our wings forever find your sky."

She trembled as she shuffled onward, carrying her

burden. She had to believe that those birches still grew somewhere. That leaves still fell upon marble tiles. That blue mountains still rose above marble halls. That Requiem awaited her, that she could see it someday, that she could someday tear off her collar, become a dragon, and find her lost sky.

"Silence, slave!"

No trees grew here in her captivity. The only palaces that rose were not the marble halls of dragons but the vicious fortresses of Saraph. The only wings here were the swan wings of seraphim. No dragons flew here in the south, only the whips of the overseers, and again those whips tore into Elory.

Again she fell.

"Bloody wretch." The overseer stepped closer, whip flailing. "Useless. If you can't stand up, I'm going to beat you into the tar."

As the whip lashed, Elory screamed.

Her back tore open.

She cried. She begged.

"Sir, please!" said another slave, hobbling forward, an old woman with gray stubble on her head. "I'll help her rise. I—"

The overseer swung his whip toward her, lashing the grandmother across the face. She fell, spilling her baskets of bitumen. The overseer roared with rage. Elory lay in the tar, unable to rise, her blood seeping, wondering if this was the day she would die here, die like slaves died every day in the pits, die without ever seeing Requiem.

She ground her teeth.

I must live. Tears burning, she struggled to her feet, limped toward the grandmother, and helped her rise too. Blood dripped from the old woman's cheek.

"We toil onward," Elory told the overseer. She saw her own blood boiling on her flaming whip. "Always. Always."

For that hope, Elory thought. *For that dream of dragons. For that dream that, after five hundred years of our backs breaking, we will someday fly again.*

"Requiem," she whispered as she made her way out of the pit.

Ahead of her, across the haze, sprawled the dry land of Saraph. No trees grew here. No rivers flowed. A barren, cruel land of sunlight, of stone, of gold, of tar. Across the rocky field, thousands of her people labored in chains. They mixed clay with straw and bitumen, poured the mixture into molds, formed bricks. In the northern distance grew the wall, eternal, towering, topped with seraphim, forever a cage around her. Far in the south, swaying in the distant heat, Elory could just make out the city of the masters. There these bricks rose into great palaces and temples, cobbled roads and bathhouses, statues that soared hundreds of feet tall. There the labor of Requiem raised wonders for the glory of the seraphim. There was a land forbidden to Elory, a land she built yet would never visit, a wondrous empire made from this bitumen, this clay, from the blood and tears of Requiem.

We will never enter the city of the seraphim, but someday we will fly into Requiem again, Elory thought. *Someday we will remove our collars, rise again as dragons. Someday the stars will guide us home.*

She was carrying the bitumen toward a squat stone refinery when the archangel arrived in his chariot of fire, forever changing Elory's life.

The chariot streamed across the sky like a falling sun, casting out heat and light. Four firehorses pulled the vessel, beasts woven of flames, their manes flaring, their eyes white stars. Shoulders stooped under the yoke, Elory stared up at the chariot, as lowly as an ant witnessing a swooping phoenix.

Five hundred years ago, Elory knew, an army of such fiery chariots had streamed into Requiem. Thousands of seraphim had fired their arrows, tossed their javelins, shone their light. The hosts of fire had felled the dragons from the sky, crushed the marble halls, burned the trees, collared the Vir Requis to contain their magic, and taken them south to a burning land. Thousands of such chariots had covered the sky that day, the Day of Burning. Today, here under the blazing sun of southern Saraph, it took only this single chariot to strike terror into the hearts of all who saw it.

A banner flared out from this chariot, wreathed in flame yet not burning. Upon it shone a sigil embroidered in gold, shaped as an eye inside a sun. Sigil of the Thirteenth Dynasty. Sigil of Requiem's ruin. Sigil of Saraph's royal house.

Across the tar pit, the refineries, and the rocky fields where brickmakers toiled, the Vir Requis slaves knelt. Even the overseers, seraphim in gilded armor, folded their swan wings against their backs and knelt in the muck. Even these towering beings of light, haloed and immortal, were as lowly as worms by this flaming chariot.

The light flared out, nearly blinding Elory as the chariot descended. Sweat washed her, stinging the open cuts on her back, dripping into her eyes, soaking her canvas rags. With shrieking fountains, the chariot of fire landed upon a hill ahead, and its rider emerged.

Now new sweat washed Elory—cold, sticky, trailing down her back like the fingers of a ghost. She stared, unable to look away, terror squeezing her heart.

A towering man alighted from the chariot and stood on the hill, staring down at the pit of despair. No, not a man. A seraph. An angelic being, closer to a god than a mere mortal like her. Elory had been laboring in the pits all her life, whipped, beaten, surviving on gruel and whatever brackish water the masters allowed her. At eighteen years of age, she was barely larger than the yoke she carried. Yet the seraph ahead stood seven feet tall, his shoulders as wide as Elory's burden of wood and chains. His hair flowed in the wind, and his eyes shone, just as golden and bright, the pupils shaped as sunbursts. He wore a gilded breastplate molded to mimic a bare, muscular torso, and he held a lance and shield emblazoned with the Eye of the Sun. His feathered wings spread out, purest white, reflecting the true sun. Upon his head, gleaming in the light of his halo, perched a steel crown.

Elory knew this seraph. All in this barren land knew him, the son of the queen, the god of the desert. Three years ago, when he had traveled south to fight the giants of the mountains, the slaves had sung and prayed in joy, finally free—if only for a while—from his terror. A month ago, when this seraph had returned from his conquests with fire and a vow to raise great palaces in his honor, the slaves had wept.

Here was the cruelest of the masters, the fairest, tallest, brightest, the golden son of Saraph. He was known by many names. The Sunlit Conqueror. The Son of Sunlight. The Blade of the Desert. Kneeling before him, her lips bloody, Elory whispered his true name.

"Ishtafel."

The Prince of Saraph stood on the hill, staring down upon the Land of Tofet, these pits of slavery. As lowly as the slaves were—broken, chained, collared, beaten—this idol of gold was lofty, a being of beauty, light, and eternal dominion.

Once we too were beautiful, Elory thought. *Once we flew free, beings of dragonfire and scales, gliding above marble halls. Now we toil. Now we serve. Now we pray to fly again.*

Her eyes narrowed. She clenched her fists, and she squared her shoulders even as the yoke threatened to crack them. She glared up at this beautiful being, and a new feeling rose in Elory. Not fear. Not pain.

Rage.

She raged against the brightness of his armor and the stripes across her back. She raged against his palaces and her pit of broken bones and sweat and blood. She raged against his beauty and her wretchedness. She raged for a nation stolen away, chained, enslaved, their homeland in ruins. Raged against a rising empire of light and sandstone built upon shattered spines.

One day we will fly again, Ishtafel, she vowed, staring up at his light. *One day Requiem will rise. One day we—*

Her heart clenched. Her breath caught in her throat.

Ishtafel lifted something from his chariot. At first Elory thought it a scrap of red cloth, then when she saw the draping limbs, she thought it the carcass of an animal. The corpse seemed so small in the seraph's arms, like a child in a mother's embrace.

Then red stubble caught the sun, growing from a caved-in head, and Elory knew it was her.

Tears filled her eyes.

"Mayana," she whispered.

The young woman had toiled in the bitumen pits with Elory until only a month ago. Ishtafel had landed his chariot here that day too, freshly returned from the war, seeking a house servant for his palace. He had chosen Mayana—young, fair Mayana with the red stubble on her head, green eyes, a rare beauty in these pits of ugliness.

"You will serve in a palace now," Elory had whispered to her friend last month, holding her close. "You will no longer have to haul bitumen, only jugs of wine. You will no longer wear a yoke, only soft livery of cotton. You're blessed, child."

Mayana had trembled against her that day, so afraid, tears streaming down her cheeks.

And now you return to us, Elory thought, shedding her own tears. *Now you're back among your people.*

Ishtafel raised the corpse above his head. His voice rang across the pit, deep, sonorous, a voice of dark beauty tinged with menace like a panther lurking in a shadowy forest.

"I took a slave from among you!" the seraph cried. "She is used up."

The slaves cried out as Ishtafel tossed the corpse down into the pit.

Elory winced and scurried backward, chains rattling. Her heart thrashed against her ribs. Her belly churned. One of her buckets tilted, nearly spilling the sticky clumps of bitumen.

Her friend's body slammed down onto the rock beside her, bones snapping.

Elory wanted to look away, to close her eyes, to do anything but look. And yet she found herself staring at that corpse, her eyes wide, her breath frozen.

Bruises spread across Mayana's face. Rough hands had torn at her clothes, and fingernails had dug into her flesh. The marks of fingers wrapped around her throat, leaving raw welts. Somebody had beaten her. Slowly. Inch by inch, finally strangling her. Elory had seen death before. When you worked in the tar pits, you saw death every day—death by whip, by starvation, by exhaustion. Yet here was a different sort of death, something more meticulous, something wrong, something that should never have been.

You will serve in a palace now! Elory's own voice echoed through her mind. *You're blessed, child.*

Elory forced her gaze away. Slowly, fists trembling, she turned back to stare at Ishtafel.

The Prince of Saraph still stood on the hill, but even from this distance, it seemed to Elory that his golden eyes stared into hers, his gaze haughty, amused. Across the pit, the slaves and overseers knelt as one, heads bowed, trembling in Ishtafel's presence. Yet Elory forced herself to stare into his eyes.

I am a daughter of Requiem, she thought, fingernails digging into her palms. *If not for my collar, I could become a dragon. I am descended from a great nation, blessed by starlight. I will not cower before you, false god.*

From the distance, it seemed as if he smiled—a thin, knowing smile.

"Slaves, step forth!" he cried, never removing his eyes from hers. "I will choose a new servant from among you."

Across the tar pit, the stone refineries, and the fields of brickmakers, the lesser seraphim—the overseers—straightened and cracked their whips.

"Up, slaves!" they roared. "Rise before your lord! Heads bowed. Rise! Stand still."

Elory struggled to rise to her feet. The noon sun blazed overhead, searing hot, burning her skin. She had been laboring in the pits since before dawn, and she hadn't eaten or drunk in that time. Straightening cracked her back and made her limbs shake with weakness. The yoke still hung across her shoulders, chained to her collar, its baskets of bitumen threatening to rip off her arms. Their fumes spun her head. But she forced herself to stand as straight as she could, to stare at the deity ahead. To hate him. Never to fear him. Hate was better than fear.

Yet as Ishtafel beat his wings, soared skyward, and then descended toward the valley, cold sweat washed Elory, and her heart twisted with that old feeling, the feeling that even now, broken and whipped so many times into this lingering wretch, she could not crush.

Fear.

The Prince of Saraph landed in the dust, yet it seemed that no dirt could ever cling to him. Not a scratch marred his armor. Not a speck of sand clung to his sandals, his flowing golden hair, nor his snowy wings. He walked among the slaves, towering above them, seven feet of light, of gold, of immortal beauty. They said that Ishtafel was centuries old, that he had lived and ruled even back on the Day of Burning, the day when Elory's ancestors had been captured and taken to this land. And yet, as he drew nearer, Elory saw that he seemed ageless. His face was smooth; at a glance, it seemed no older than the face of a thirty-year-old man, the skin bronzed, the lips full, the cheekbones high. Yet his eyes were old. Eyes with pupils like suns. Bright yet shadowed. Seeing all. Ancient eyes.

"These slaves are scrawny." Ishtafel frowned as he walked through the pit. "They stink of sweat and tar."

One of the overseers nodded. She was a cruel seraph named Shani of House Caraf, high ranking among the masters, her eyes and hair shining gold and her wings purest white. "They are weredragons, Your Excellence. Wretched beasts worthy of little more than crawling in the mud. Offensive to the nose and distasteful to the eyes."

Ishtafel grimaced and held a handkerchief to his nose. "And fragile. Discipline them and they shatter, their mortal life fleeing their frail forms."

Elory glowered at the seraphim walking before her. Frail? Wretches who crawled in the mud?

She placed her hands upon her collar. The iron ring squeezed her throat when she gulped. A dark light coiled within the metal, a magic only the seraphim held, a magic that crushed her own power. Without these collars, they could rise as dragons. Magnificent and mighty. Beings to soar, blow fire, as beautiful and powerful as any seraph. How dare these beings of light mock her people, the children of starlight?

Elory took a deep breath, trying to summon that memory—a memory passed through the generations, perhaps just a dream. A memory of Requiem. A memory of dragons.

For thousands of years, we flew above the birch forests of our home, she thought. *Our marble halls gleamed in the sunlight, and blue mountains rose in the dawn. We flew free, millions of dragons of all colors. No collars around our necks. No chains to hobble our wings. No seraphim to whip us, grinding us into the dirt. A proud, ancient kingdom, a land of beauty, of white halls in green forests.* Her eyes stung. *A kingdom of dragons, a home where we were free.*

She had never seen those marble halls, those birch forests, those blue mountains, those golden dawns. Nor had any of the slaves. Only their ancestors, beyond the generations, had ever dwelled in Requiem. Yet the tales had passed from parents to siblings. Her own mother—a dragon chained, whipped, forced to dig for the bitumen—had told Elory the tale a thousand times, the same tale her mother had told her. In her mind's eye, Elory could see Requiem, as if she herself had flown there. Every night before she huddled in her mud hut, before she fell into a slumber that would last only a few hours before the overseers woke her for more labor, she would imagine Requiem. In her dreams, no collar squeezed her neck, and she could summon her magic, grow wings and scales, rise as a dragon.

In some dreams, she was a dragon of gold, like the great Queen Laira, Mother of Requiem. In other dreams, Elory's scales were black—black like King Benedictus, one of Requiem's greatest rulers. In other dreams, she was red and fiery like the great Princess Agnus Dei, a heroine of Requiem who had defeated the griffins. Elory had never become a dragon before, for her collar had never been removed—only diggers were allowed to become dragons, their claws seeking the tar reserves, never the bearers of yokes. She did not know what color her scales would be, but the land below never changed in her dream. Requiem was always a realm of sprawling birch forests, of great marble columns, of statues and fountains in pale squares. Of beauty. Of peace. Of pride. A land whose sky she found every night in her sleep, a land she prayed every day to see with her waking eyes.

"This one does not cower like the others." Ishtafel's voice tore through Elory's thoughts. "Nor is she quite as wretched to behold."

Elory's heart thrashed. She realized that he was talking about her, that he had come to stand before her. Her head spun, and she gulped. She struggled to raise her chin, to square her shoulders, even as the yoke shoved down upon her.

She was scrawny, short. He towered above her, easily thrice her size, his shoulders broad, his chest wide. Her wings were hobbled, her magic hidden. His swan wings spread wide. She wore rags and chains. He stood clad in priceless gilded armor. She was a creature broken, whipped, her soul shattered. He was a being of pale beauty and light and dominion. And yet Elory thought of Requiem and stared at him, refusing to kneel again, refusing to cower, refusing to be a slave.

I stand in chains, the daughter of many generations of slaves, and yet I still remember Requiem. I am still proud.

Ishtafel's brow furrowed as he stared at her.

"Look at how she raises her chin, how she stares at me, not at her feet." Ishtafel tilted his head. "A proud one. Not yet broken."

Ishtafel's companion, Shani the overseer, snarled. "I will break her, Your Excellence."

The seraph raised her whip and Elory winced, expecting the pain, but Ishtafel reached out, staying Shani's hand.

"Wait."

Elory released a shaky breath she hadn't realized she'd been holding. She stared up at the seraph, her chest rising and falling, her arms shaking. Sweat dripped into her eyes, and she felt blood trickling down her back, and the damn fear wouldn't stop crawling along her spine.

Ishtafel stepped closer. Elory felt as small as a child before this giant of a god. He reached down his hand, a hand large enough to encase her head. While the rest of him was all wealth and might—the gilded armor, the pale wings, the flowing hair—Elory noticed that his hand was not soft. Calluses covered his fingers, and thin scars trailed across his palm. The hand of a warrior.

With that large hand, he rubbed tar off her brow, the movement almost like a caress. He stared down upon her, and in his golden eyes, Elory saw herself reflected—covered in tar, sweat, and blood, a young collared woman with a shaved head and dark eyes, a slave, only a slave with dreams of ancient glory.

"You do not look away?" Ishtafel said, his voice soft, his words only for her. "Most slaves avert their eyes from the sight of a god."

"I did not avert my eyes from Mayana's corpse," Elory said. "I will not avert them from you either."

"Impudent worm!" Shani raised her whip again, teeth bared. The seraph stood nearly two feet taller than Elory, her arms strong, her whip crackling with fire. "I'm going to flay you alive and toss your skinless corpse into the tar."

"You will do no such thing," Ishtafel said, voice calm. "Lower your whip, Shani. This slave intrigues me. Not yet broken. Still some spirit to her." He smiled thinly, and he stroked Elory's cheek. His fingers came back sooty. "Once the dirt is removed, and she's clad in livery, her hair growing longer, her body perfumed, she would do well in the palace. There's fire to this one. There's strength to her. I like that." His smile widened—a thin, predatory smile, the smile a wolf gives a sheep before devouring it. "She will last longer than the previous one."

Elory's eyes stung. Her heart felt ready to shatter her ribs and thump into the dirt. She turned her head and saw the corpse still there. Mayana's eyes were still open, staring at Elory, her face twisted with pain. Her teeth had been bashed in. Her eye socket had shattered. Drying blood soaked her fine cotton livery. The finger marks around her throat were long, powerful—the same fingers that had just caressed Elory's cheek.

"Sir, I . . ." Elory gulped. "I know not of the palace's ways. I'm only a yoke bearer, sir. I—"

"You will address him as 'Your Excellence!'" Shani said, and now her whip did lash. The fiery throng slammed into Elory's chest. Her rags tore. So did her skin. She cried out, wobbling, nearly dropping her yoke. If she spilled the bitumen, she knew the overseers would not allow her a quick death. Bitumen was the glue that held the empire of Saraph together. To lose buckets of the black gold meant a burning in Malok, the bronze bull on the hill. Recalcitrant slaves cooked within the belly of the idol, their screams flowing through pipes and rising from the bull's mouth as a melodious song.

"Shani!" Ishtafel's voice barely rose above normal volume, yet it carried the rage and authority of a great cry. His hand— that hand that had beaten Mayana to death, that had stroked Elory's cheek—swung and backhanded the overseer.

Shani hissed and clutched her cheek. Ichor dripped down her alabaster skin. Her golden eyes flashed with pain, with surprise, with rage . . . then dropped to stare at her feet. The mighty seraph, the overseer who had beaten so many slaves into submission or to death, knelt in the mud. She lowered her head, letting her hair hang down.

"Forgive me, Your Excellence," she whispered.

"Nobody will hurt this one anymore," Ishtafel said to the kneeling overseer, then looked back at Elory. That thin smile returned. "Nobody but me." He reached out his hand. "Come, child. Take my hand. Join me in my chariot of fire, and I will take you to live in a great palace, a place of jewels, of fine wine, of wealth you cannot imagine. A place away from the tar and filth and stench of this place."

But not away from the whip, Elory thought. *Not away from the rage of a master. Not away from my chains, my collar, and the threat of death every dawn and dusk.*

The fear grew in her. She had known nothing but the tar pits all her life. For eighteen cruel summers, the palaces of Saraph had been but a glimmer in the distance, a land of wealth on the southern horizon, a place whence came the masters, came death and pain. The place where the bitumen she mined held together bricks, roofs, jewels, mosaics, cobblestones, an empire. To walk upon those cobbled streets? To live in one of those palaces? To serve a seraph not as a yoke bearer but as a personal servant, a girl to wash his feet, polish his armor, pour his wine, serve his food, perhaps warm his bed at nights? To suffer his hand—stroking her, beating her, choking her when he pleased?

Elory glanced behind her. To leave her family?

Her breath shuddered. The land of Tofet, these pits of slavery, sprawled into the distance, a realm of nightmares, of sweat and blood and agony. Hundreds of thousands of slaves toiled here. Many, like her, bore yokes and baskets. A handful, like her mother, served as dragons, digging the wells of tar. Others, like her father and brother, labored in the rocky fields to form and bake bricks. Elory did not see her family much—only for five precious hours a night, a time to pray, to nurse one another's wounds, to huddle together, to sleep in their mud hut. And yet Elory could not imagine her life away from them. Her kind mother. Her wise father. Her strong and noble brother. How could she leave them here to a slow death while she flew off in this seraph's chariot to a new life—a life only a few miles away, yet a life different from any she had ever known, a life she would return from only in death?

She looked behind her. Across the torturous landscape, they were watching her. Men, women, children, elders, all in chains and collars. The yoke bearers. The brickmakers. Farther back, in the center of the pit, even the diggers—those few Vir

Requis allowed to remove their collars, to dig in dragon form—were watching her. Her own mother stared across the distance, a chained silver dragon.

Elory's eyes burned.

"I cannot leave," she whispered. The land of Tofet, home of the slaves, was a land of blood, chains, and endless death, but it was her home now. The only home she had ever known. Here was the only family she had ever known. She would not abandon her family, not even to escape the yoke and tar for a palace of gold.

"I cannot leave," she repeated, turning back toward Ishtafel. "Please, Your Excellence. Choose another."

Ishtafel's brow furrowed. A flash of anger crossed his eyes. He reached out and grabbed her arm, his grip like a vise. He tugged her forward.

"Do you think that I take orders from weredragons?" He stared down at her, his smile stretching wider, revealing his canines, a smile almost like a snarl. "Do you think that I crushed your kingdom, dragged your ancestors here, and chained you in the muck so that I, defeater of Requiem, slayer of giants, a god of Saraph, should take orders from a worm that crawls in the dirt?" He backhanded her, rattling the teeth in her jaw. "You will do as you're told, or you will end up like your friend, a crushed wretch in the tar."

Pain flowed across Elory's jaw. She tasted blood. She knew she should kneel in the dirt, kiss his feet, beg for mercy. She knew she must obey or she would be cooked in the bronze bull, dying slowly as she screamed. She knew she should cower, worship him, fear him.

Yet Elory stared into Ishtafel's eyes, and she spoke softly.

"Our name is not 'weredragons.' We are Vir Requis, children of Requiem, a great nation that still blazes in our hearts. Requiem still lives, even in chains. You cannot extinguish her light."

And now Ishtafel's smile stretched into a grin, showing more teeth. He grabbed her yoke, that hunk of wood and iron that had weighed upon her shoulders for years, and he snapped it between his hands. All her life, Elory had struggled, bound to this burden; the seraph shattered it like a man crushing twigs.

The baskets of bitumen fell to the ground, spilling their precious contents. Chips of wood and metal showered. Before Elory could feel any relief, he grabbed her, twisting her arms, nearly snapping her too.

"No!" she cried out. "No! I won't go. Release me! I won't!"

She kicked, but her ankles were still hobbled, and she could not reach him. She tried to strike him, but he held her wrists, laughing, mocking her resistance.

She growled.

I can become a dragon. I can fly, blow my dragonfire, burn him.

Elory sucked in air, trying to summon that ancient magic, the magic only the diggers were allowed to use, the magic that had once let millions of her kind find the sky.

She felt it deep within her, a reservoir of starlight, there since her childhood, waiting to tap into like the bitumen buried underground.

She let it fill her.

Held in the grip of this cruel angel, she felt the magic flow through her.

She felt the nubs of wings begin to sprout from her whipped back. Her skin thickened, hardened, began to rise in scales. Her fingernails lengthened into the hints of claws, and she felt her teeth bite into her lip, forming fangs. Flickers of fire filled her mouth, and her body began to grow, lengthening, ballooning into a dragon that could fly, slay her enemies, escape to—

She gasped for air.

As her body grew, her collar tightened further, constricting her, nearly snapping her neck.

Keep shifting! she told herself. *Tear through the collar! Fly! Burn him!*

She croaked for air, yet she clenched her fists and kept tugging on her magic, kept growing, and—

Something seemed to crack in her neck. Blackness spread across her. Stars exploded and spun. She lost her magic. Her body shrank, and she gasped for air, sucking it greedily. She would have fallen to the ground were Ishtafel not still holding her.

He dragged her across the dirt, then lifted her and slung her across his shoulder. Elory screamed, struggling against him, crying out to Requiem, to her stars, to her mother. He walked across the barren hill. They moved toward the chariot of fire, prepared to fly away from this place, fly to a palace of gold and danger and death. All around, the slaves knelt again, yet their heads were raised, and their eyes stared into hers. Those eyes shone with tears.

"Farewell, daughter," one old woman whispered, her shoulders stooped under her yoke.

"Farewell, Elory!" said a child, a young boy carrying a yoke larger than himself.

One slave broke free from the others, hobbled forward in his chains, and cried out for the camp to hear. "Requiem!" The man's voice tore with agony, a voice broken like the backs of a thousand slaves. "Requiem, may our wings forever find your sky!"

The prayer of their people. The ancient prayer of dragons, of starlight. A prayer for a home lost, a sky they must reclaim. The seraphim overseers raced forward, whips lashing, spears thrusting, cutting the slave who had prayed aloud, then dragging him off—to the bronze bull Malok, to a burning in the belly of the beast.

"Requiem!" Elory called out, answering the cry. Let them burn her too in Malok. Let them all cry out together, one voice, one prayer, one—

A roar.

A roar tore across the camp, rising louder, shaking the earth.

Iron chains snapped.

Leathern wings beat.

A dragon, silver and thin, scales chipped, wings punched full of holes, soared through the air.

"Mother!" Elory cried.

Nala, a digger of Tofet, a dragon of Requiem, flew across the sky toward her. Shackles still encircled her legs, their chains snapped and dangling. The marks of countless whips covered her scales and underbelly, and her horns had been sawed off, her teeth uprooted. And yet still fire flickered in her mouth, and still her claws reached out—claws sharp enough to dig through rock for bitumen, claws sharp enough to tear even through a seraph.

"Elory!" the silver dragon cried. "Elory, I'm here! I'm here, I—"

The javelins of the overseers flew. The shards of steel stormed across the sky, pale and reflecting the sun, to drive into the dragon.

Scales cracked. Blood spilled. The dragon cried out in agony, yet still she flew.

"Elory!" she cried. "Daughter!"

"Mother!" Elory shouted, still caught in Ishtafel's grip. She reached out to her mother. "Fly back, Mother! Back to the pit. Please!"

Tears filled Elory's eyes as she watched more javelins drive into the dragon. Seraphim beat their swan wings, flying around the silver dragon, thrusting lances, firing arrows, thrusting swords. The weapons cracked more scales, drove deep into the flesh, shed more blood. A lance ripped into Nala's wing, tearing through it, making a horrible sound like ripping leather. A cry, equally torn, emerged from the dragon's throat.

"Mother," Elory whispered, tears flowing. "Mother, turn back . . . please . . ."

But it was too late.

Laughing, Ishtafel spread his wings and took flight. The seraph soared, carrying Elory across his shoulder. They rose higher. From up here, Elory could see for miles—the tar pit, the field of bricklayers, the refineries, the limestone quarries, the city of huts, the endless agony of a nation forgotten.

And a single silver dragon, gazing at Elory with damp eyes.

"Remember Requiem," Mother whispered. "Remember that I love you. Always."

Gripping Elory with one hand, Ishtafel hefted his lance in the other.

He threw the weapon.

A shard of light, the lance streamed through the air, fast as lightning, slower than generations of slavery. It cut through a lost sky. It drove into the silver dragon with a blast of light and red mist. It tore into Nala's throat, emerged from the other side, and the dragon lost her magic.

Nala fell as a woman. A chained slave. Haggard. Torn with many blades.

"Mother," Elory whispered, shaking in the grip of the seraph.

The seraphim swooped. Their lances thrust. They ripped into the falling woman, tearing her apart, severing her limbs, gutting her innards. Nala thudded onto the ground in pieces and shattered . . . shattered like Requiem, like Elory's heart, like all her hope, all her prayers.

She closed her eyes. She wept.

I'm sorry. I'm so sorry, Mother.

She wanted to scream, to rage, to curse the stars that had abandoned her, to curse Ishtafel the Cruel. Yet her strength was gone.

The seraph's lips touched her ear.

"Remember what you saw here, precious doll." His breath brushed her head. "Remember what happens to those who defy me."

He carried her away from the camp. He took her into his chariot of fire. He cracked his whip, and his firehorses bucked and soared, carrying the chariot across the sky.

Elory sat in the chariot, chains around her ankles, the seraph's arms around her frail frame. They left the land of Tofet behind—left a place of screams, of endless blood and tar, of a memory that Elory knew would forever haunt her. Ahead, across the barren distance, rose the city of limestone, steel, and gold, a place of splendor, of might, of a new home.

VALE

Vale was chipping rocks in the quarry, cutting bricks for his masters' temple, when the chariot of fire flew above him with heat and light, and his world went dark.

He had been working since before dawn. The chains chafed his ankles, the sun beat down on his shaved head, and the whips had torn into his back. Blisters bloomed across his hands, but he kept working, chipping limestone with his chisel. The walls of the quarry soared around him, taller than temples.

Ishtafel, Prince of Saraph, had returned from war, and the empire celebrated. In Shayeen across the river, the city of the seraphim, feasts and dances were held all day and night. Parades would be marching down the limestone streets. Dancers and singers would be performing for the masses. And across the city, great monuments were rising for Ishtafel's glory: statues of the hero, obelisks tipped with precious metals, and a great temple to the Eight Gods bearing the prince's name.

And so Vale toiled.

And so thousands of his kinsmen, the men and women of fallen Requiem, swung their pickaxes, carving out bricks that would rise for their lord's glory. And so Requiem, a once-proud nation, cried out in pain, whipped, worked nearly to death, praying to stars that no longer shone at night.

Vale wiped the sweat off his brow. He was a young man, only twenty-one, but he felt old, weary, haggard. His arms seemed so thin to him, and his head swayed. The sun kept beating down. He wanted water—only a few drops to soothe his parched throat—but dared not ask. The last slave to have begged for water now hung upon the quarry wall, hands and legs nailed into the limestone, the crows pecking at his living flesh.

Maybe he's the lucky one. Pausing for breath, Vale flicked up his eyes. He saw them there. They stood upon the quarry's rim above. Twenty seraphim masters. As thin, dirty, and wretched as Vale and his comrades were, the seraphim were noble. The sunlight shone on their gilded armor and swan wings, and their golden eyes stared down into the pit, all-seeing.

"Work, worm!" one master shouted, raising his firewhip.

Vale returned to chipping the stone. Rage burned in his throat like the thirst. The collar itched around his neck, worse than the weariness, the thirst, the pain. More than anything, Vale wished he could take the pickaxe to that collar, break it off, summon his magic. With every swing of that pickaxe, Vale imagined that he was beating leathern wings. With every chip of stone that flew, he imagined claws lashing. As the sunbeams beat him, he imagined streams of dragonfire.

All around him, the thousands of slaves labored. Some fell with exhaustion, even the whips of their masters unable to rouse them. Others prayed under their breath—prayed to the Eight Gods of Saraph when the masters drew near, prayed to the old stars of Requiem when no seraphim could hear.

"Requiem," Vale whispered, swinging his pickaxe, the sun and dust and sweat in his eyes.

He tried to imagine it. His ancestors, millions of Vir Requis, no seraph masters to whip them, no collars around their necks. Thousands of men and women who could summon the ancient magic of starlight, grow wings and scales, breathe fire, and take flight as dragons.

We need to rise again. Vale clenched his jaw, banging against the limestone walls with all his rage. *We need to shatter our collars. To rise as dragons. To blow our fire, fight again, to—*

"Stop hacking like a butcher at a hog!" shouted an overseer. The seraph swooped, landed behind Vale, and lashed his whip. "These bricks are for Ishtafel's temple, not one of your wretched maggot huts."

Vale screamed as the whip hit his back, ripping the flesh, cauterizing the wound with a sizzle.

With a grunt, the seraph moved to swing his whip at another slave, a mere boy of ten years who had accidentally cracked a brick in two. The whip swung again and again, the boy screamed, and Vale's hands shook around the shaft of his pickaxe. So many nights he had tried to swing that pickaxe against his own neck, to shatter the collar, but couldn't break the ancient curse that held it together, that buried his magic—the magic of dragons. So many nights he had prayed for the courage to swing that pickaxe just an inch higher, to drive the blade into his neck, to end the pain.

And so many nights he had seen those who had fled this nightmare. Those who had summoned the courage to do what Vale could not—to end their lives.

Vale ground his teeth, slamming the limestone again and again, carving out the bricks, the stones that would raise great monuments for the seraph who had crushed Vale's kingdom.

I live so that one day I can drive this pickaxe into your throat, Ishtafel. He snarled as he worked. *I live to see that day when we rise in rebellion. When we do what our ancestors could not.* He drove the axe so deep into the stone the shaft cracked. *For the day we burn you all.*

Just as he was imagining dragonfire raining down on the masters, fire crackled above. Vale raised his head and saw him there.

A growl rose in his throat, and his knuckles whitened around his pickaxe's grip.

"Ishtafel," he hissed.

The chariot of fire streamed above the quarry. Its royal banner unfurled in the wind, displaying the Thirteenth Dynasty's sigil—an eye within a sunburst, the Eye of Saraph. Steeds woven of living flame pulled the vessel across the sky, heading away from Tofet, the land of slaves, toward Shayeen, the distant city of seraphim. Even from here below, Vale could see the tyrant's torso and head rise from the chariot—the gilded pauldrons and breastplate, the golden hair that streamed like another banner.

There he was, so close! The immortal creature who had destroyed the realm of Vale's ancestors, who had brought Vale's people here, who doomed him to a life in the mine, breaking the very stones that built temples in Ishtafel's name.

Vale tugged at his collar, wishing—as he had since childhood—that he could rip it off, summon his magic, soar, blow his fire, avenge his people.

But, like all others across the quarry, he only knelt. Thousands of quarrymen, scores of seraphim overseers—all bent the knee as the chariot of fire flew overhead.

But as the others all lowered their gaze, Vale stared up at the flames, eyes narrowed, stinging with sweat, with hatred. His pickaxe trembled in his hands—the axe he would someday drive into that tyrant's golden, beautiful flesh.

"Praise Ishtafel!" cried an overseer. "Praise the Prince of Saraph, the Slayer of Giants, the Destroyer of Requiem!"

Curse you, Vale thought. *Curse you, foul murderer, and curse your family, and curse your empire, and curse—*

"Brother!"

The cry rose from far above, torn in pain.

Vale looked back up at the chariot and his world seemed to crash around him. Were the walls of the quarry to tumble, the sky to fall, the ground to open up to swallow him, Vale could not have felt more shock.

Above in the flaming chariot, held in the tyrant's grip, was his sister.

"Elory," Vale whispered.

"Brothe—" she began, leaning over the edge of the fire, eyes wide, and for a horrible instant, Vale was sure she was going to jump, to leap from the flames and crash down dead into the quarry. Then Ishtafel grabbed her. The seraph pulled her back into the flaming vessel.

The chariot flew onward, vanishing from view over the quarry's rim, heading toward the city of seraphim.

"Go on, back to work, scum," an overseer said, cracking his whip. "Stop kneeling like worms, and get to cutting stones for your lord's temple."

Across the quarry, the slaves rose and resumed their work.

Vale rose too, but he couldn't bring himself to swing the pickaxe. His head spun. His breath rattled in his lungs. His knees felt weak.

Ishtafel, the conqueror, the son of Queen Kalafi herself, the creature who had killed so many Vir Requis . . . has my sister.

Vale could barely breathe.

He had heard tales of Ishtafel's bedchamber. Any man with a sister or daughter had. They said that Ishtafel's chambers made the quarry, the refineries, and the bitumen pit seem leisurely. They said that Ishtafel took pleasure from his slave's bodies, a pleasure so barbaric he snapped their bones, tore up their insides, later discarding the corpses and fetching fresh meat from Tofet.

And now he has Elory. Vale let out a strangled gasp. The quarry swayed around him. *Now he has my baby sister.* Vale had already lost one sister to the seraphim—a sister they rarely spoke of, only in whispers, in darkness. Losing Elory too was a pain too great to bear.

A seraph marched toward him, dust staining his armor and wings, a helmet hiding his head. His sunburst eyes flared through the eyeholes, and he lashed his whip of fire.

"Back to work!"

Vale grunted as the whip stung his arm. But the pain of that wound was nothing compared to his fear.

He has Elory.

Memories flashed before Vale's eyes: Elory as a babe, born in their hut, an innocent child who had never asked to come into this world. Elory as a toddler, fitted with a yoke, sent to the bitumen mines. Elory coming of age, turning eighteen, a young woman who would never know freedom, who would always know nothing but the lash, the tar, the old prayers of a fallen land.

And Elory above him, only moments ago, crying out to him, taken to the only place in Saraph worse than the bitumen pits.

The seraph master growled, lowered his whip, and raised his lance above Vale. "Gods damn it, maggot, I'm going to spill your guts."

"Wait."

Vale stared at the seraph, refusing to flinch even as the lance thrust forward, stopping only inches from his belly.

"You dare talk back?" The seraph cracked his whip in one hand and thrust the lance closer. Vale was tall for a slave, almost six feet, a rare height among the malnourished, weary Vir Requis, yet this seraph soared a foot taller. The tip of the deity's lance bit into Vale's side, scraping a red line beneath his ribs.

I have to do this. He forced in a deep, dusty breath. *I have to save her. Stars of Requiem, I have to stop this.*

"I want to serve Ishtafel!" Vale said, letting his rage fill his voice, twisting it into something he hoped sounded like religious zeal. His voice sounded too loud to him, torn with pain, a crazed voice. "I want to serve the golden god of Saraph!"

The seraph grunted and lashed his whip. The throng drove into Vale's side. "Worship him by digging limestone. Your bricks will form a temple to him. A temple you'll never worship at." The seraph barked a laugh. "You can pray to him as you cut into the stone."

Vale raised his chin, ignoring the agony of his wounds. "My mother is a digger. She digs for bitumen as a dragon. The claws in our family are sharp. I would serve Ishtafel as a dragon in the City of Kings, flying above the scaffolds of his rising temples, holding the stones in my claws." He forced himself to stare into the seraph's burning eyes. "I spent the past ten years cutting bricks here. Now let me bear those bricks into the sky."

His breath shook in his lungs, but he refused to look away.

If I can fly as a dragon, no collar around my neck, bearing stones to the tops of temples . . . I can break free. He clenched his jaw. *I can roar through the seraphim, charge through their lances and arrows, fly to the palace . . . and save my sister.*

The arrows would cut him, he knew. The lances would thrust into him. A thousand chariots of fire would charge against him. But he would take the pain. He had taken the lash so often, he could endure their blades. He would grab his sister from the demon, and he would carry her away, carry her into the wilderness like the hero Lucem who was said to have fled ten years ago. They would fly over the desert, over the sea, seek freedom in shadows from this empire of light.

I will save you, Elory. We will escape. Just like Lucem. I promise you.

The overseer stared at him, and those gleaming orbs of eyes narrowed, the sunburst pupils dilating. "And what makes you think I'll transfer you to the building crews?" He lifted his whip again. "What makes you think I won't whip you to death right here?"

"You could whip me to death," Vale said, taking a gamble now, his chest thudding, his fingernails digging into his palms. "But did you hear what Ishtafel's new slave called me? I'm her brother. The brother of the woman now sleeping in Prince Ishtafel's bed." He let a chaotic smile twist his lips. "My family was born to worship your prince."

She might be a slave, he thought, sweat dripping down his brow, tears burning down his cheeks. *But she's the slave who's sleeping with Ishtafel.*

At that thought, sickness filled his gut, so overpowering he had to struggle not to double over and vomit over the overseer's feet.

Before the seraph could answer, a voice rose behind Vale, soft yet cutting through the din of pickaxes and lashing whips.

"Vale."

Slowly, Vale turned around and stared.

For the second time that day, he lost his breath.

A tall, ragged slave came walking across the quarry. He was an old man, clad in rags, his thin ankles hobbled. His head was shaved, like the heads of all slaves, but his beard was long, brown, streaked with white. His name was Jaren. He was Vale's father.

"Vale," the old slave whispered again, eyes haunted, glassy. In his arms hung his burden—tattered, red.

This time Vale could not help it. He doubled over and gagged, losing the paltry gruel the overseers had fed him that morning.

"No." Vale trembled, fell to his knees, and tossed back his head and cried out to the sky. "No! No!"

He stared again, eyes burning, chest shaking.

"I'm sorry," Jaren whispered, and a tear fled the old slave's eyes.

In his arms, the old man carried a mutilated corpse. Two limbs broken. A leg and arm missing. The face still whole, burnt in the sun, finally at peace.

"Mother!" Vale cried, then lowered his head and wept.

ISHTAFEL

He flew in his chariot of fire, taking his new slave from a land of death to a city of gold.

As the flames roared around them, Ishtafel caressed Elory's head. She sat before him, ankles hobbled with a foot-long chain, a collar around her neck. Brown stubble covered her head, shaved only days ago. Ishtafel preferred his women with long, flowing hair, but his mother—the damn crone—insisted on keeping the slaves shaven. An easy decree for the old bitch to pass. She wasn't the one seeking the slaves' pleasures in bed.

Elory shuddered at his touch, still not daring to look at him. She was a pathetic little thing, raw welts across her back, her body sticky with tar, her rags torn. But Ishtafel had never lacked in imagination. He had imagined the world cleansed of enemies, and he had cleansed that world. He could imagine Elory cleansed of filth, and he would cleanse her. He would make her as beautiful as the empire he had built. And he would conquer her body as surely as he had conquered the world.

"Why do you tremble at my touch?" he asked, letting his fingers flutter across her ear, caressing, exploring the shape of it. A small ear, barely larger than the tip of his thumb.

"I'm afraid," she whispered.

Ishtafel's smile grew. "You should be."

He remembered a time, five hundred years ago, when he himself had been afraid. He had been only a young seraph then, no older than thirty summers—a mere child. He had led his first campaign, a great invasion of the north. With thousands of flaming chariots, he had flown into a land called Requiem. He had faced the dragons in the sky. He had seen their mad eyes, their sharp claws, their streams of dragonfire flowing toward him, felling his fellow seraphim.

And yes, he had been afraid.

But I overcame that fear. He ran his hand down Elory's spine, pausing at the small of her back. The girl had such a narrow waist; narrower than his arm. *I conquered Requiem. I slew those dragons who flew against me. I placed cursed collars around the necks of those I captured, forever crushing their magic. I lost a woman in the land of reptiles, and so I will claim women from among them.*

He leaned down toward Elory and inhaled deeply, savoring her scent. She smelled of tar, smoke, and fear. An intoxicating smell. For five hundred years, Ishtafel had kept his playthings here in Saraph, the heart of his empire, refusing to let them die. Refusing to fear them again. The weredragons, once proud warriors who could rise as fire-breathing reptiles, were now nothing but his toys.

They flew over Tofet, the land Ishtafel's family had given to the weredragons: the pits of tar where chained dragons dug and collared slaves hauled out the bitumen; rocky fields where men, women, and children labored in the blinding sun, forming bricks from clay and straw; fields where slaves labored, sweating and bleeding and dying to grow produce from the dry earth. The land of Requiem lay in ruins in the distant north across desert, sea, and forest; here the nation of Requiem languished in the dust.

The flaming chariot kept flying, leaving Tofet behind. A river snaked below, gleaming silver. Here was the Te'ephim River, blessed life giver, shimmering in the sunlight, lined with rushes, palm trees, and fig trees. Upon its waters sailed countless ships from distant lands, bearing spices and gemstones and exotic animals in golden cages.

Past the water, the landscape changed, and they flew over Shayeen, the City of Kings, capital of Saraph.

Ishtafel inhaled deeply again, letting the aroma of the city below mingle with Elory's scent.

"Look below, child," Ishtafel said. "Behold the glory of Saraph. Behold the land of gods."

Shayeen was built as a wheel. Eight cobbled boulevards spread out like spokes, stretching for miles, the eight Paths of the Gods. Each road was lined with statues of one of the Eight Gods—towering idols of limestone, gilded, jeweled, forever watching over their holy pathways. Eight archways lined the outer wall, hundreds of feet tall, topped with statues of ancient heroes and kings. Within this wheel of stone rose the marvels of the city: columned temples, manors topped with hanging gardens, fortresses whose towers kissed the sky, obelisks capped with platinum, marble bathhouses, and amphitheaters.

It was the greatest city in the world, Ishtafel knew. A place of wealth, power, a vision of lost Edinnu reflected upon the earth. Thousands of years ago, his people—the golden seraphim—had lived in the heavens, dwelling in a land of light upon a distant star. But the seraphim had grown too mighty in their own eyes. They had rebelled against their gods . . . and they had lost.

We fell from the sky, Ishtafel thought. *Lost children, cast aside from our gods. Yet we built here a new city of light. A new star to shine upon the cosmos. Here we will worship the gods until they forgive our sins. Until they call us home, until we ascend again to our lost paradise.*

As the chariot crossed the sky, Ishtafel saw a statue rise ahead, carved of limestone and gilded, a hundred feet tall. The statue of a woman, fair and fierce, clad in armor, raising a sword.

Reehan.

Ishtafel winced. He always winced when passing by this statue. It had been five hundred years, but the sight of Reehan still hurt him. The memories still would not let go. And the slaves would still suffer for what they had done to his beloved.

He looked beyond the statue. In the center of the wheel-shaped city rose the greatest building in Saraph, the beacon of the empire. The ziggurat soared, over a thousand feet tall, its sandstone surfaces engraved with scenes of the seraphim's wars, conquests, and the ancient banishment. Its crest tapered into a triangle, coated with purest platinum, and upon it blazed an eye within a sunburst—the Eye of Saraph, all-seeing, casting its gaze across the world.

Ishtafel whipped his firehorses, and the flaming equines pulled the chariot across the sky, heading toward the ziggurat. Two colossal statues, shaped as cats with women's heads, guarded the staircase that led to its gates. Shaped as La'eri, the goddess of royalty, the statues stood so tall their eyes were larger than the chariot. The firehorses descended and landed between the feline guardians.

Ishtafel grabbed Elory, slung her across his shoulder, and alighted from his chariot. He was tall even for a seraph, close to eight feet tall, and his shoulders were nearly as broad as this slave was tall. He carried her like he would the carcass of a pretty bird, perhaps a peacock with bright feathers. She made not a sound and did not struggle as he carried her across the flagstones and toward an archway, the entrance to his family's ancestral home.

A dozen seraph guards stood before the gates, clad in gilded breastplates, holding spears and round shields, their wings purest white. They knelt before Ishtafel and bowed their haloed heads.

"You." Ishtafel snapped his fingers at one of the kneeling guards. "Come to me."

The seraph straightened and stepped forth. A bronze helmet hid his face, and his eyes gleamed, somber, through the eyeholes. "My lord!"

Ishtafel unslung the slave off his shoulder and shoved her into the guard's arms. "Have this one delivered to the bathhouse. See that the other slaves have her scrubbed clean and prepared for me, then see her delivered to my chamber. Have her waiting there when I return from tonight's feast."

"Yes, my lord!" The seraph nodded, beat his wings, and took flight. He soared up the ziggurat's flank, holding Elory in his arms, ascending toward Ishtafel's chamber a thousand feet above.

Ishtafel nodded toward the other guards, who pulled open the jeweled gates to the ziggurat's base. Ishtafel stepped through the archway, entering the palace.

It was the Day of Rebirth, the holiest day in Saraph's calendar, and he was late for the feast.

A towering hall greeted him, a chamber so large that armies could have mustered within it. Golden columns rose in palisades, supporting a ceiling painted with scenes of lost Edinnu. A mosaic sprawled across the floor, displaying the hundreds of enemies Saraph had vanquished since its banishment three thousand years ago: the horned behemoths of the south, the wild demons of the east, and many more, including the weredragons, the cruel shapeshifters who now labored in Tofet. As Ishtafel walked across the mosaic, he stepped on these old enemies, smearing mud across their faces.

Thousands of seraphim crowded the hall already, the masters and mistresses of Saraph, lords of all seraphim, rulers of all conquered lands. They sat at ornately carved tables, turning toward Ishtafel as he entered. A feast steamed before them: roasted peacocks on beds of mushrooms and wild rice, their tail feathers reattached; entire roasted hogs upon baked apples, their crunchy skin glazed with honey; fruits of every kind, from sweetly scented persimmons to grapes the color of blood; endless pies of every sort, almost bursting with plums, savory duck, sweet peas, jams, and every other filling found across the empire; and finally wine . . . endless jugs, sweet chilled whites, delicate reds, deep strong crimsons, all pouring like rivers into mugs of ivory, platinum, and filigreed ostrich shells.

Not a single morsel had been touched. Not a single drop had been drunk. The seraphim, hundreds of them, had awaited him. Now they rose from their seats and knelt, wings folded across their backs.

Ishtafel took a step into the hall, and two young seraphim—mere boys—raised trumpets to their lips, and they blew a fanfare.

"Here enters Ishtafel!" one cried, lowering his horn. "Prince of Saraph! Slayer of Giants! Destroyer of Requiem!"

"And a bloody hungry bugger!" Ishtafel called out. "Let's eat."

Laughter rolled across the hall, and they ate.

Musicians, seraphim in flowing muslin robes, played lyres and harps upon balconies—the songs of old Edinnu, the Realm that Was. Dancers performed on a stage, wearing elaborate horned masks, depicting the beasts that had lived in the lost land. And everywhere scuttled the weredragon slaves—clad in simple livery, collars around their necks, their heads shaved, weak mortal beings, no taller than the seraphim's shoulders.

"Slave, here!" Ishtafel said, snapping his fingers at one of the beasts. The man rushed forth with a jug of wine and filled Ishtafel's cup. A second slave, a thin young woman with green eyes, approached with a tray of grapes. Ishtafel ate, pulled the slave onto his lap, and inhaled her scent until a third slave arrived with steamed shellfish, drawing his attention.

Since he had returned to Saraph a month ago, a great conqueror, the defeater of the giants, he had feasted here every day. The last enemy in the known world had fallen. Edinnu was lost, but Saraph—this new kingdom they had built in their banishment—now ruled the world they had fallen to.

After two more mugs of wine, he rose to his feet. He raised his mug, and across the hall, seraphim and slaves alike fell silent and turned to stare.

"Seraphim!" Ishtafel cried to them. "Raise your mugs with mine. Today is the Day of Rebirth. On this day, four thousand and four years ago, the Eight Gods punished us for our pride. They struck down our parents, those who had rebelled against them. They burned my own mother—your queen!—inflicting a wound upon her so dire that even today, so many years later, she languishes in pain rather than drinking with us here."

The faces grew dour. Seraphim lowered their heads. The banishment—it was an open wound upon his mother, the Queen of Saraph, but no less an open wound even to those, like Ishtafel, who had been born here in exile, who had never seen the lost paradise. The fall of Edinnu still cast a shadow upon all in Saraph.

"But we built a new kingdom!" Ishtafel said, louder now. "We fell to this world scared, scarred, cast out from paradise. But we fought. My father vanquished many enemies, building a great city in this land before his death. And I completed his work! Five hundred years ago, I crushed the kingdom of Requiem, taking the weredragons here to serve us as gods. Since that time, I fought every enemy that has risen against us, and I cast their bones into the dust. The last giant fell last moon, and now—now we in Saraph are masters of this world, gods of a new Edinnu!"

The seraphim roared in approval. Their eyes shone like their haloes. Their wings spread out. Only the slaves did not join the cheers; the little weredragons lowered their eyes, perhaps remembering their own fallen kingdom, a realm they would never more rebuild.

"So drink, friends!" said Ishtafel. "As my mother suffers from her wound, as our enemies lay dead around us, drink and be joyous, for we are gods. We—"

The hall doors slammed open with a clang.

Hissing in annoyance, Ishtafel spun to see who had dared interrupt his speech.

A woman stepped into the hall, clad in light, and Ishtafel's anger melted like snow under spring's dawn.

"Meliora," he whispered.

His sister was short for a seraph, no more than six feet tall, a childlike princess, cherubic and soft. She was not yet thirty, a babe among the immortals, the youngest in this hall. She gazed around with huge eyes like pools of molten gold—innocent eyes, eyes that had never gazed upon blood or war. She wore a muslin *kalasiri* dress, the white fabric embroidered with ibises, and a medallion of the Eye of Saraph shone upon her throat. Her hair flowed down to her hips, the color of dawn, and her wings were the white of purest snow. Her halo was so thin Ishtafel could barely see it, a ring of gold no wider than a thread.

Ishtafel paused, simply staring at her. Whenever he gazed upon his beloved sister, he lost his breath. Here was the purest among them—a seraph unsullied by war, by the fall from heaven. The most beautiful being on this world, a precious goddess to cherish, to worship, to forever protect. Ishtafel had lived for five hundred years, had hated many, had slain more. But since Reehan had died in the tunnels beneath Requiem, centuries ago, Ishtafel had not loved another soul. Not until twenty-seven years ago, when Meliora had been born.

It's not only the Day of Rebirth, he thought. *It's my sister's birthday. It's the holiest day of the year.*

"Meliora!" he called to her, holding out his hands as the other seraphim knelt before their princess. "Come to me. Dance with me."

A grin split her face, and she ran toward him across the mosaic, feet padding against the dragons of many tiles. Her two personal slaves followed—a pair of young, bald women whom Meliora took wherever she went like a girl with favorite pets.

"I love to dance!" Meliora said. "Can Kira and Talana dance with us?"

Ishtafel laughed. "Your pets are weredragons, my dear. Let them join the other slaves and help clean the empty plates."

Meliora bit her lip, looked at the two collared weredragons, then back at Ishtafel. "But . . . I want to teach them to dance too! I taught them already to sing the Song of the Silver Tree, and—"

"Meliora!" Ishtafel frowned. "That is a holy song of Edinnu. You had your slaves profane it with weredragon lips? Mother would have them burned in the bronze bull if she knew."

Meliora's bottom lip wobbled, and tears flooded her eyes. "No," she whispered. "Please don't tell Mother. Please! I'm sorry. Don't send them to the bull!" She lowered her head, tears flowing.

"Sister!" Ishtafel pulled her into an embrace. "Don't weep. I forget that you're but an innocent, silly thing with barely more sense than a child."

Meliora nodded. "I know that I'm silly, but don't scare me like that. I get so scared, Ishtafel! So scared of the bull. I dream of him sometimes, that he invades my bed, that . . ." Her cheeks flushed. "I promise not to teach Kira and Talana any more songs. I promise! I'll dance with you alone."

Ishtafel nodded at the musicians on the balcony, and they began to play his favorite song—the Burning of Requiem. It was a song of his first victory, a song commemorating that glorious war five centuries ago—he had been barely older than Meliora was now—when he had crushed the weredragons, toppled their halls, and brought them here in collars. Normally a robust marching song, the harpists played a soft, slow version of it, letting Ishtafel and Meliora sway gently in the hall. The other seraphim watched, heads bowed, giving their prince and princess the first dance of the night.

"When I was away in the south, fighting the giants, I missed you every day." Ishtafel tucked an errant strand of Meliora's hair behind her ear. "I thought of you every night before I went to sleep, and I remembered your face every morning as I slew more of our enemies."

Meliora's eyes shone. "I thought of you too, brother! I drew paintings of you, did you know? I went into the gardens every morning to paint you, and to watch the birds and the butterflies, and sometimes I'd try to count the flowers. I could never count them all, though. We have some new flowers this spring! I'll show you tomorrow, and there are some baby birds in the fig tree by the fountain."

He kissed her forehead. "Such a silly thing you are!" He laughed. "I speak to you of war and conquest, and you speak to me of birds and butterflies. But that's how I love you, sister. Pure. Your hands unstained with blood. Your eyes unsullied by the sight of death and war."

Meliora nodded, grinning. "War is for boys! I'm a princess of flowers. You can have the blood. I'll keep the baby birds."

The first song ended, and more music played, and more seraphim joined them in the dance. The sunbeams falling through the oculus gleamed on the golden tables, jeweled dishes, and the statues of gods that rose between the gilded columns. The birds painted onto the domed ceiling and the mosaic beasts glittered and seemed almost to be living things. The feasting, the drinking, and the dancing would continue all day and long into the night. By the time Ishtafel returned to his bedchamber and sought pleasure from his new slave, he would be well fed, a little drunk, and as weary as after a battle.

Yet despite the splendor of this place, despite the glory of his victory, a nervousness filled Ishtafel.

The time has come, he thought. *After five hundred years of war, the time is here . . . the time to tell my sister.*

He could hesitate no longer. He took a deep breath, cupped his sister's cheek in his palm, and spoke softly.

"Meliora, today is a special year for us. It's not only five hundred years since I crushed Requiem. Not only the year I defeated the stone giants, our last enemies in the world. It's also the year that I will marry. That I will give Saraph an heir."

Meliora's eyes widened, and she grinned and bounced. "A wedding! A royal wedding! Who will you choose? Perhaps Lady Teelan? She's very beautiful, and she loves baby birds too! Or—I know!—you can marry Lady Merishan! She's a friend of mine. She lets me play with her puppies sometimes. Oh, I can't wait! I can help her choose fabrics for her wedding gown, and—"

"Meliora." Ishtafel's voice dropped, grew solemn. "You've heard tales of the old dynasties."

Meliora tilted her head. "Of course." She recited as if reading from a book. "Ours is the Thirteenth Dynasty, the Dynasty of Kalafi. Twelve dynasties have ruled Saraph since our banishment. The first, the Telaka Dynasty, wandered the wilderness. The second, the—"

"Meliora, do you know how those dynasties ruled for thousands of years? With purity of blood. With a refusal to dilute their nobility. Those who failed at this task, who married for love or lust, saw their dynasties fall." He sighed. "If you ask me, that's foolishness. A mere superstition. In all my wars, I saw humble soldiers of low blood slay many beasts, while nobles of old families perished in the mud. A man rules by the blood he spills, not the blood in his veins. And yet Mother is a superstitious woman. All those who still remember Edinnu, who were born in our old realm in the heavens, are so." He stroked Meliora's hair. "It's Mother who commands this. You must understand that this is her wish, not my own. Yet she is our queen, and we will obey her."

A small line appeared on Meliora's brow. "What do you mean, brother? What . . . whose blood could be purer than the ladies of the court?"

"The blood of a princess." Ishtafel placed his finger against her throat, feeling her pulse. "Your blood."

Still Meliora seemed confused. "But . . . how . . .?"

Ishtafel sighed again. Meliora was beautiful, innocent, yet a silly thing indeed. "It will be for the good of Saraph, my sister. An heir of pure blood, a child purely of our dynasty, undiluted, will bring a glory to Saraph to last a hundred thousand years."

Slowly understanding dawned in her eyes. "You wish . . . to marry me?" Meliora gasped, stepped back from him, and blanched. "Mother commands us to marry, to . . . to make a baby?" Confusion and disgust battled on her face.

Ishtafel glanced around him. Damn it! Other seraphim had heard her. People were staring. Even slaves. He had hoped to break the news to his people on another night, but it seemed the secret was out.

He cleared his throat. He stepped toward the table, grabbed a goblet of wine, and raised it overhead.

"My friends!" he cried. "Hear me! My sister and I have an announcement to make." The seraphim turned toward him, and Ishtafel stared across the crowd—those he would someday rule as king. "For five hundred years, my family has ruled Saraph, a dynasty that saw us finally conquer this world we fell to, that brought us the weredragons to serve us, that saw us create a new kingdom of wealth and prosperity. The time has come to create a new heir, a third generation for our family. Our royal blood will be preserved for a hundred thousand years. On the summer solstice, two moons hence, I will marry my sister. Meliora and I will bear Saraph a prince!"

The seraphim cheered. Even a few of the slaves cried out his name. Many seraphim here had lived five hundred years ago, back when Reehan—his first betrothed—had died. They rejoiced that their prince found new love at last. Wine now flowed and the trumpets blew. All celebrated . . . all but Meliora.

The young princess stepped closer to Ishtafel, tears in her eyes, and slapped his cheek.

As he sucked in air and stared with shock, the girl spun on her heel, grabbed her slaves' hands, and fled the hall.

The cheering died.

Everyone stared.

Gods damn.

Fury—hot and unadulterated—filled Ishtafel. He forced it down with all his might.

He cleared his throat. "Well, my friends have warned me that wives are harder to defeat than dragons."

He forced himself to laugh. It wasn't much of a joke, yet the crowd laughed. He was their prince; they'd laugh at anything he himself laughed at. Yet as his laughter rolled across the hall, the rage flowed through Ishtafel, and his fingernails dug into his palms.

You humiliated me, Meliora. He drank deeply from his cup. *You will bear my child, and you will pay for your insolence.*

The feast continued. It would be a triumphant feast that never ended.

MELIORA

"I won't do it." Meliora pouted and stamped her feet. "I won't, I won't, I won't! I won't marry my own brother."

She stood in a chamber of opulence. A mosaic of precious stones covered the floor, depicting colorful fish swimming in a sapphire sea. Lines of silver and platinum coiled around limestone columns, rising toward capitals of purest gold. A fresco sprawled across the vaulted ceiling, recreating the lost paradise of Edinnu. And yet, despite all the gemstones and precious metals, despite the golden vases and ivory statuettes that covered her shelves, despite the scent of frankincense and the haze of wine, Meliora felt trapped here. A prisoner. Lower than a slave.

"Your Excellency, Ishtafel is most handsome." Kira, a young slave, looked up from painting Meliora's fingernails. Her eyes were large and dark, her skin light brown, and black stubble covered her head. She spoke with awe in her voice. "His eyes shine like suns, and his hair flows like molten gold. All the women of the realm whisper of his magnificence."

"He is most handsome," agreed Talana, her second slave, who was busy brushing Meliora's hair. While Kira was dark and demure, Talana had skin as pale as milk, strewn with many freckles, and stubble the color of fire covered her head. "You are most fortunate, Your Excellency."

Meliora fluffed her feathered wings and emitted a long, loud whine. "You don't understand, you fools."

She pulled her hands back, though only half her fingernails were painted. She leaped up from her bed, though her hair was only half-brushed. She whined again—a high, wailing sound, letting out all her frustration and pain. Those silly slaves would never understand! Their lives were easy. All they ever did was coo, gossip, giggle, brush her hair, paint her nails, wash her body, tend to her clothes, serve her wine—an easy life, a life free from the pressures Meliora faced.

My life is harder than that of any slave, she thought.

Meliora perhaps wore a platinum necklace sporting diamonds and pearls, but it was worse than any slave collar. She perhaps wore a *kalasiri* dress, the soft white muslin shining with sapphires and emeralds, but it was rougher on her skin than her slaves' coarse cotton.

My mother wants me to marry him . . . Ishtafel. My own brother.

Meliora shuddered.

She flounced across her chamber between platinum statues of ibises, jeweled vases blooming with orchids, and ebony tables topped with gold and silver mancala pieces. She came to stand before her bronze mirror, looked at her reflection, and felt like the poorest wretch to have ever crawled upon the earth.

She was still beautiful, Meliora thought. Wondrously beautiful. The most beautiful woman to have ever lived in this palace—no, the most beautiful to have ever lived anywhere, at any time. She was a seraph, an immortal being of light, a *princess* of seraphim—a deity among deities, a goddess of gods. Her golden hair flowed like molten dawn down to her hips. Her eyes shone, just as golden and bright, the pupils shaped as sunbursts. Her lips were full, pink, pouty. She was short for a seraph, standing just over six feet tall, but still tall enough to tower over her weredragon slaves. Most beautiful of all, she thought, were her wings. They spread out from her back, their feathers snowy white, gleaming in the light that shone through the windows.

I am magnificent, Meliora thought, gazing at her reflection. *Yet now this legendary beauty will be caged, broken. Now I will become but a womb, a garden for my brother's seed.*

Tears gathered in her eyes and flowed down her flawless cheeks, coming to rest on her flawless lips—lips her brother would soon be kissing.

"Your Excellence!" Kira cried. The slave rushed forth, her cotton shift rustling, and held out a silver jug and cup. "Would you like me to pour you more wine?"

"No," Meliora said. "I've had enough of wine. Enough of you. Enough of this life!"

Her lips quivered, and she swung her arm, knocking the jug and cup out of the slave's hands. They clanged onto the floor, spilling their crimson liquid. Meliora felt as if her own blood were spilling.

"Clean it up!" Meliora said. At once Kira and Talana grabbed towels, knelt, and began soaking up the wine. Easy lives. All those two had to clean up was some spilled wine—not the mess of a royal family. All they had to do was serve her, not serve a cruel brother, not serve an entire empire.

She was cursed, Meliora thought, fingers trembling. Cursed to be born to the Queen of Saraph. Cursed to be the younger sister of a prince returned from a war. Cursed to have this royal ichor coursing through her veins, pure blood that must be passed into an heir.

Those damn tears kept falling.

"Wine," she whispered. "I want wine. Bring me new wine!"

"Of course, Your Excellence," said Kira. The little slave— oh, so innocent, so sheltered!—rose to her feet, rushed to fetch another jug, and poured Meliora a cup.

Meliora drank. The wine was awful. Too acidic; it must have been sitting in the open for a day at least. But she guzzled it down until the warm haze coated her thoughts. When the cup was empty, she tossed it to the floor, wobbled forward, and stepped between porphyry columns onto the balcony.

The sunlight fell upon her, and Meliora gazed at her realm. She placed a hand on her belly.

They want my womb to produce an heir for this land.

The hot wind blew across Shayeen, scented of frankincense, sandstone, and the distant pits of bitumen that bubbled on the horizon. The breeze caressed Meliora's hair, kissed her lips like a lover, and ruffled the long white feathers of her wings. Her *kalasiri*, inlaid with jewels and golden disks, chinked like laughing spirits. The muslin caressed her skin, soft to the touch, almost sensual.

If my mother has her way, Meliora thought, *it will be my brother who kisses my lips, who strokes my skin, who removes this muslin from my body and plants his heir within my womb.* She clenched her fists. *I will not allow it!*

She studied the city below. Shayeen. City of Kings. Jewel of Saraph. The capital of an empire. Her birthright, the city this marriage would let her rule someday as queen.

The eight Holy Paths flared out like sunbeams, lined with statues of the Eight Gods. Between these cobbled boulevards rose columned temples, lush gardens, bathhouses, amphitheaters, and menageries. Here was a realm of opulence, of pleasure, Edinnu rebuilt upon this world of exile. Standing upon the ziggurat in the city center, a thousand feet above the surface, Meliora could see all the way to the city's outer wall. She felt like a goddess, a deity among deities, an immortal ruler . . . yet one who was afraid. One who felt chained—as surely as the slaves beyond the horizon were chained in the land of Tofet.

"I wish I were a slave," she whispered into the wind. "I wish I were not born into this bondage, the daughter of a queen."

She envied her slaves. Envied them! She had never been beyond the horizon to Tofet itself, the land where thousands of slaves dug for bitumen and built bricks. But Meliora knew that their lives were easier than hers. They walked free in the open air, basking in the sunlight, singing as they dug and built. How Meliora wished she could join them! How she wished to spread her wings, flee this palace, join the weredragons in Tofet, live free in the open air! Far from this ziggurat. Far from these golden chains, this gilded cage.

A long time ago, they said, the weredragons had lived in a distant realm, a place called Requiem, a land her brother had crushed. Back then, the weredragons had worn no collars, could become dragons at will. Millions of them had flown in the skies. Sometimes, on long dark nights, huddled under her silken blankets, Meliora would dream that she herself lived in Old Requiem, could become a dragon too, that she flew in a cold sky under distant stars. Sometimes, even during the days, Meliora remembered those dreams, wished they were real, wished she could become a dragon, fly away to a distant cold kingdom, escape this life of torment.

Her fingers curled into fists. A rage boiled within her.

"Why should I allow my mother to torture me?" Meliora snarled. "I'm strong. Wise. Fair. I'm the strongest, most beautiful woman in the world. I won't do anything I don't want to." She stamped her feet. "I won't! I'll tell her. I'll tell Mother I refuse. And if she doesn't like that, I swear I'll just fly away. I'll fly so far that I'll die of starvation in the wilderness, and then they'll be sorry." Her tears flowed. "Then they'll all be sorry for torturing me."

She turned away from the view. She left the balcony, reentering the ziggurat, the palace her dynasty had ruled since the great uprising five hundred years ago, the year her family had crushed Requiem, taken the weredragons captive, and overthrown the old dynasty to usher Saraph into its golden age.

I will tell her, Meliora thought, fists clenched. *I will tell Mother that I refuse. That I'll run away and die in the wilderness!*

She walked through the palace. Columns rose alongside, inlaid with silver and gold, their capitals jeweled. Frescos covered the ceiling, depicting scenes of Old Edinnu, the realm that was lost. Mosaics spread across the floor, forming a great blue river where swam stone fish of every kind. Ferns grew from painted vases, rustling in the wind that flowed through the skylights.

Seraphim soldiers stood at attention between the columns, clad in steel breastplates, their wings folded at their sides. Gripping spears and shields, they bowed their heads as Meliora walked by. Slaves scurried about the palace, bearing jugs of wine, trays of fruit, fresh linens, and ointments and spices. Clad in simple white livery and metal collars, they knelt before Meliora, whispering praises of her glory.

"Move!" she said. The damn slaves—such lazy creatures—were blocking her way.

The slaves scuttled back, letting Meliora pass. She left them behind, moving down the glittering corridors, seeking her mother.

Finally Meliora reached the Ivory Chamber, her mother's favorite place in the palace. A portico of columns spread across the northern wall, leading to a balcony lined with potted palm trees. Beyond spread the blue sky and distant, golden mountains. Light flooded the chamber, shining on a mosaic floor, walls painted with scenes of ibises and crocodiles, and vases full of sweetly scented rushes. Ivory statues of La'eri, feline goddess of royalty, rose along the walls, giving the chamber its name.

A heated pool steamed in the middle of the chamber, and in the water, facing the sunlight that streamed through the balcony, bathed Queen Kalafi.

"Mother," Meliora said.

The water rose to the queen's shoulders. Three slaves stood in the pool with her, young female weredragons, their collars gilded. Two of the slaves were filing and painting the queen's fingernails. The third was combing and oiling Kalafi's long, golden hair. The queen seemed not to have heard Meliora; she remained in the water, staring out at the sun and sky beyond the columns.

"Mother!" Meliora stamped her feet. "I will not be ignored."

Kalafi spoke softly, still not rising from the water, still not turning toward her daughter. "The turtledoves fly early this year. I can hear them from this chamber. It's strange, is it not, daughter? That spring begins with the song of birds, yet their melody heralds the cruel heat of summer. Thus did the gods curse us—to forever glimpse beauty, never to fully grasp it." She sighed. "It was always spring in Edinnu. There was no pain in Edinnu."

Meliora rolled her eyes. She was only twenty-seven, a babe among the immortal seraphim. She had been born and raised here in this exile, in this palace, within the reign of this very dynasty. Yet Queen Kalafi was thousands of years old, a seraph who had fought the gods, who had fallen from heaven, who still yearned for days long gone.

"Mother, I will not do this. I will not. I refuse. You cannot make me." Meliora's anger left her lips with a serpentine hiss. "Send my brother back to his wars. If you make me marry him, I'm going to run away and die of starvation in the desert, and then you'll all be sorry."

Slowly, Queen Kalafi turned and rose from the pool, climbing underwater stairs. The water ran down her lithe body in rivulets. Kalafi was perhaps an ancient being, thousands of years old, yet she looked no older than Meliora. Her eyes shone, two suns. Her hair cascaded down to her hips like molten gold. Her wings unfurled, the water gleaming upon their white feathers. The sunlight shone upon her nude body.

She was a being of light, of perfect beauty—perfect but for the scar on her side.

The burn spread beneath her left ribs, down toward her navel and across her hip, raw and red, an oozing sash. The ancient gods had given her that wound thousands of years ago, searing her with godlight. That had been the Day of Banishment. The day the seraphim had lost their rebellion, the day the gods had exiled them down to the earth.

The wound will never heal, Meliora knew. Only the hot, salty water could soothe the pain, giving relief between bouts of flaring agony. Most monarchs ruled from thrones; Kalafi ruled from pools and baths.

Slaves rushed forth and clad Kalafi in an embroidered robe, hiding her nakedness, hiding the wound, the ugly reminder of their failed uprising.

"Daughter," Kalafi said, stepping toward her across the mosaic. "For thousands of years, Saraph's dynasties have wed brother to sister to preserve the royal blood. My own husband, may the gods forgive his soul, was also my brother. Only thus can we remain pure beings."

Kalafi reached out to caress Meliora's cheek.

"Don't touch me." Meliora shoved her mother's hand away. "Pure beings?" She barked a laugh. "When Ishtafel brings weredragon slaves into his bed, is he a pure being? When you soak in water to hide that ugly, dirty wound of yours, are you a pure being? I refuse to marry any man, least of all my brother." Meliora let out a whine, almost a scream. "Bed him yourself if you wish to keep the blood pure. I will not! I—"

Kalafi struck her.

White light flashed across Meliora's vision. She hissed and clutched her burning cheek.

"How dare—" Meliora began.

The queen struck her again, a blow to the second cheek. "You will not defy me, child." Kalafi's eyes flared like exploding suns. "For five thousand years, I roamed this earth. For five hundred of those years, your brother fought wars to conquer this world, to give us—to give *you!*—a home of light and splendor. You are but a child. Twenty-seven summers old, a mere babe, spoiled, impudent. What do you know of pain? What do you know of the agony of our long banishment, of the fires of war, of the triumphs your brother gave our race?"

Meliora held her burning cheek, struggling to keep the tears from her eyes. "I *will* defy you! Yes, I am young. No, I never knew our fall from paradise, and I never knew our long exile in the desert. Yes, I was born into a life of splendor, slaves to wait upon me. But that doesn't mean that I will serve you as a slave. I—"

"Slaves?" Kalafi laughed. "You take them for granted, as if they're as inherent a part of our lives as our wings. It's thanks to Ishtafel, the conqueror of Requiem, that slaves now serve you. Yes, thanks to this brother you spurn. And so you will learn to live without them." Kalafi's lips stretched into a thin grin. "Your two house slaves will die tomorrow. Come see them burn in the bronze bull, daughter. Come hear them scream, then return to your chambers where you can make your own bed, pour your own wine, and wipe your own backside."

Meliora gasped. "Mother!"

She thought of Kira and Talana, her two slaves, young women who served in her chambers. The two were meek things without sin—aside from the sin of their lesser race. To burn them in the bronze bull?

Meliora had heard Ishtafel speak of the bronze bull before—of Malok. Her brother used to terrify her with those stories. As a child, Meliora had believed them and would cry and cower. Ishtafel had described how soldiers pulled an unruly slave into a great, hollow statue of a bull. Fires were lit under the bull until the bronze heated, boiling the slave within. The slaves' screams would rise through a network of pipes, emerging from the bull's mouth in a melodious song.

If you're a bad girl, Ishtafel had once taunted her, *I'm going to toss you into Malok's belly and dance to your screams.*

Meliora had cried so much that Ishtafel had hugged her, soothed her, confessed that he had lied. Yet now her mother resurrected that old threat. How could Malok be real? How could the cruel bronze bull truly exist in Saraph, this realm of light and beauty?

"You lie," Meliora said. "Those are just stories Ishtafel invented. There is no Malok."

Queen Kalafi laughed. "Yes, daughter. Mere stories. And little fairies conjure up our bitumen with the snap of their sparkling fingers, and unicorns bear us the tar on their backs. I have sheltered you for too long, girl. You will accompany me tomorrow at dawn to see your precious slaves sing in the bull. And then you will return to your chambers, where you will pray to never see true horror as I have seen. And in two moons, on the blessed summer solstice, you will marry your brother. And nine months later, you will bear me a pure heir. You will do this or it will be you burned in the bull."

Meliora's chest shook, her head spun, and her eyes burned with tears. She spun and fled the chamber.

VALE

He stood in the blood, dust, and agony of Tofet, burying his
mother.

My people languish in chains. Vale's eyes burned, and his fists
trembled. *My sister was taken captive.* His breath shuddered, and
the chains around his legs rattled. *My mother is dead.*

For all his twenty-one years, Vale had labored in this place,
making bricks with his father while his mother and sister mined
the bitumen that would hold those bricks together in palaces and
temples. For all those twenty-one years, Vale had sweated, wept,
screamed when the masters whipped him, yet still clung to
hope—clung to a desperate dream that someday Requiem would
rise again, that someday he would fly free with his family.

Now that family is broken. Tears burned in his eyes. *Now I
bury my hope along with my mother.*

The grave yawned open before him. A pit. A mass grave
for all the slaves killed that day, over a hundred souls. A hundred
slaves worked, starved, beaten to death. Some mere children, the
whips of their masters too cruel for their frail bodies. Others
were elders, slaves who had toiled for decades under the sun,
clinging to a hope to see Requiem again, finally to end up here,
bodies in a land of despair.

And one woman, torn apart, her severed limbs and
battered torso wrapped in a shroud. A woman who had dared to
fly, dared to fight. A lost light of Requiem. A mother.

"I'm sorry, Mother," Vale whispered. "I'm sorry I wasn't
there, that I couldn't fly with you, fight with you."

A soft voice spoke at his side. "Her soul will rise to the
celestial halls of Requiem. She will shine there in palaces of
starlight, drink wine, and sing among our ancient heroes. She is
at peace now. She is at peace."

And yet pain filled that voice. Vale turned to see Jaren, his
father, standing at his side in the crowd of mourners.

"There is no such thing." Vale's voice was a hoarse whisper, yet the pain of an anguished cry filled it. "Celestial halls? An afterlife of starlight? Just dreams. Just stories." His tears burned in his eyes. "Maybe Requiem itself is but a dream, a land that never was."

He saw how those words wounded his father. Jaren winced and his lips tightened into a line. Dust coated the priest's long grizzled beard, and chains hobbled his ankles. Years of brickmaking in the sun had weathered his face; Jaren was only in his fifties, yet he looked like a man of eighty——wrinkled, weary, his hair gray. Despite the chains, despite his rags, despite his years of labor, Jaren still clung to the old stories. Still called himself a priest of the Draco constellation, the stars that supposedly had once blessed Requiem, that would someday save them again. Still believed in that lost, distant realm the seraphim had burned five hundred years ago.

But Vale no longer believed, no longer cared if he hurt his father. There was so much pain in this place, so much anguish. What was more pain? Why even live on, why linger, why cling to stories? Perhaps his mother had taken the only sensible path. Perhaps it was best to rise up, to fight, to die in battle rather than linger here in chains.

Vale expected Jaren to argue, to insist that Requiem was real, that stars truly blessed them, that a dragon constellation truly shone in the northern skies. But the old priest merely lowered his head, and tears streamed down his cheeks into his beard.

Vale felt all his anger fade. He stepped close to his father, his own tears falling, and embraced the old man. They stood together, crying together, their chains rattling, watching through the veil of tears as the corpses were lowered into the pit.

Several dragons, their collars removed but their limbs chained, pulled forth the wagons of corpses. Upon a hill, an old slave with a white beard chanted prayers to the Eight Gods, the vengeful deities the seraphim worshipped, the religion forced upon the Vir Requis slaves in the land of Tofet.

"Praise the Eight!" the white-haired slave cried upon the hill. "Blessed be their light! Praise the seraphim masters for their mercy, and may their light guide the souls of our dead to rest."

"Praise the Eight!" answered slaves in the crowd, hundreds come to see their dead buried, as the dragons tilted the wagons, as the dead spilled into the mass grave.

Curse the Eight, Vale thought, staring at the bodies sliding into the pit. One among them was his mother; he didn't even know which one anymore. *Curse the foul gods of this place. Curse the seraphim. Curse the land of Tofet. Curse these chains. And curse Ishtafel.*

The memory filled Vale, burning inside his skull. It had happened only hours ago, yet it seemed eternal, an event ancient and current, a flame consuming all time, a terror that he knew would always fill him. His father stepping into the quarry. Mother dead in his arms.

Vale closed his eyes, and his fists shook at his sides.

"You killed her, Ishtafel," he whispered. "You killed my mother. You kidnapped my sister."

I should have been there, Vale thought. *I should have flown with you, Mother.*

He should have flown, blown his dragonfire, lashed his claws. Yet this collar kept him chained. Kept him in the dust, a worm, a wretch.

"Praise the Eight!" the priest on the hill cried. "May the gods bless their souls."

At Vale's side, his father closed his eyes and whispered so softly Vale could barely hear.

"As the leaves fall upon our marble tiles, as the breeze rustles the birches beyond our columns, as the sun gilds the mountains above our halls—know, young child of the woods, you are home, you are home." Jaren took a shuddering breath, raised his head, and gazed up at the sky. Tears filled his eyes, and awe filled his whisper. "Requiem! May our wings forever find your sky."

The ancient prayer of Requiem. The words that, the stories claimed, King Aeternum had sung six thousand years ago in a distant land, forging a home for the Vir Requis. A home for dragons.

Vale raised his eyes, seeking the Draco constellation, seeking those stars his father claimed blessed Requiem. But he saw no stars that looked like a dragon, only a field of cold lights like so many dead eyes.

The stars had abandoned them. His mother was gone. His sisters were gone—both Elory and the sister they never spoke of. All hope was gone.

The wagons dumped the last corpses of slaves into the pit. The dragons—the few slaves allowed to shift into their ancient forms—began shoveling dirt into the grave, hiding the dead, hiding the shame. Soon Vale would return to his hut with his father, but his mother won't be there, nor his sister, and in a few hours he would rise, and he would toil in the sun, and the chains would chafe his body, and the whips would cut his back, and it would continue. Year after year. Generation after generation. Endless pain in the land of Saraph as Requiem remained but a memory, fading to myth.

"Come, son." Jaren placed a hand on his shoulder. Tears still streamed down his lined cheeks to dampen his beard. "Let us return to our hut. Let us pray. Let—"

Laughter.

Laughter rolled across the darkness, interrupting Jaren's words.

"Mother!" A voice rose in mocking falsetto. "Mother, please!"

Slowly, his chains rattling, Vale turned around.

He saw them there on a hill. Two seraphim, a woman and a man. Both wore gilded armor, the breastplates curved to mimic bare torsos. Both carried round shields and lances. Vale was tall for a Vir Requis, almost six feet tall—a giant among the malnourished slaves—yet these seraphim dwarfed him. The immortals were beings of beauty, hair long and lustrous, pupils shaped as sunbursts in their golden eyes, lips full and pink, wings the color of milk. Fallen angels. Masters. Destroyers.

"The little whore whined like a babe," said the male seraph. He raised his voice to falsetto again. "Mother, Mother, please don't let the bad seraph take me! Don't let him spread my legs and thrust his holy spear into me!"

The female seraph laughed. She raised a flaming whip. Vale recognized her. Here stood Shani, an overseer of the tar pit, a woman who had beaten Elory with her whip too often to count. So many nights, Elory had lain shivering on her straw bed, feverish and moaning with pain, as Vale rubbed ointments into the wounds on her back—wounds Shani had inflicted.

"Ishtafel's new whore was in my work team," Shani said to her companion. "Worked as a yoke bearer. I striped her back many times. Squealed like a pig every time."

Rage flowed through Vale, a fiery explosion. His fingernails drove into his palms, shedding blood.

They're talking about Elory. About my sister.

"Come, son," Jaren said, voice still choked with grief. He placed a hand on Vale's shoulder. "Let's go. Leave them be."

But Vale could not look away from the laughing seraphim on the hill. The pair were still talking, laughing as they stared into the grave.

"Little harlot will be back in Tofet in no time." The male seraph snorted. "The weredragons never last long with Ishtafel."

Shani barked a laugh. "Not weak as that one is. I beat her bloody too many times. She'll be back as a corpse soon. Next time the wagons roll around, we'll spit on her body."

Jaren was speaking behind him, urging calm. But Vale could no longer hear. The fury blasted through him, shaking his limbs, constricting his chest, painting the world red.

He could not fly as a dragon, not with the cursed collar around his neck, the metal engraved with runes to crush his magic. But he could still fight with tooth and nail.

Better to die fighting. Better to end this now, to die young rather than languish into old age. The pit awaits us now or after years of pain.

With a roar, Vale raced forward.

He charged uphill, fists raised.

In the old stories, the ones passed from father to son, the Vir Requis would rise as dragons, fight in great armies in the sky, blowing dragonfire. Vale had never become a dragon; the collar had constricted him since birth. But in his mind, as he charged forth, he was a dragon roaring, a beast of fury and fire.

The two seraphim turned toward him, eyes widening.

"For Requiem!" Vale shouted. "For stars and dragonfire!"

He leaped forward, fists swinging.

He was weakened by years of servitude, feeding on gruel while building bricks for eighteen hours a day, but the wrath of an ancient nation burned within him, and he moved fast. He reached the seraphim and landed the first blow, driving his fist into the male's chin.

It felt like punching a cliff.

Vale's knuckles cracked, and pain blazed through him.

"Rabid dog!" Shani shouted. The beautiful seraph, her blond hair flying in the wind, swung her whip.

The lash of fire slammed into Vale, tore across his back, and wrapped around him to sting his chest. His skin tore, and the fire cauterized the wound, burning his blood.

"Vale!" Jaren shouted, racing uphill. "Vale, no!"

But Vale ignored his father. Too much pain. Too much fury—the fury of a dragon, dragonfire blazing even within his famished human form. He roared and attacked again, driving his fist toward Shani.

Smiling savagely, Shani grabbed his fist in her hand. She squeezed, her grin stretching into a rabid, toothy snarl.

Vale screamed, his hand crushed.

"Yes, you will scream like she did." Shani tightened her grip. The seraph was taller than Vale, stronger, ancient beyond measure. Vale howled and swung his other fist, only bloodying his knuckles against her.

Agony exploded across his back. He screamed, falling to his knees. Another blow hit him, knocking him down. Vale tried to turn around, glimpsed the second seraph raising his fist, and then another blow slammed into him. Light flared. Vale hit the ground.

"Cease this!" Jaren cried somewhere in the distance—miles away. A fading sound. Vale could barely hear his father, barely hear anything but his own screams. The blows kept raining onto him.

"Father!" he cried. "Father! Requiem!"

"Enough!" Jaren shouted, but the voice was a muffled cry from another world, a whisper, then nothing. The world washed away under the blood.

"Wait." Shani spoke somewhere in the haze. "Stop. Keep him alive. We'll burn him in the bronze bull tomorrow." She laughed. "I'd like to hear the bull sing."

The blows stopped but the pain still bloomed across Vale. In his memories, he could see that bronze bull again, the fires burning below it, the screams rising through its pipes to emerge as a melodious song—a song of burning flesh, burning souls, of his death in the forge.

So I will burn. A thin smile stretched across his lips, and he tasted blood. *It's a good death for a Vir Requis.*

So hurt he could barely see, barely hear, he managed to spit blood onto Shani's feet.

The seraph cursed and drove her foot forward. Light exploded, then died to darkness, and Vale felt no more.

ELORY

She knelt in the dark, chained, shivering, the fear like a living beast coiling within her.

He's coming for me. He's coming to hurt me. The man who killed my mother.

She tried to stop the tears from falling. She tried to be brave, to be like the old heroines of Requiem from her father's stories. To be brave like Mother had been, defying the masters with her last breath. Yet still those damn tears fell, and still Elory trembled.

The past few hours were a blur, a dreamscape of color and sound, so hazy and surreal Elory wondered if it hadn't been a true dream, if she wouldn't soon wake back in her hut in Tofet. She recalled the heat of the chariot of fire, a flight over the desert, the smudged glimpses of a great city below. And then jeweled columns shining with light. Mosaic floors depicting all the fish of the seas. The labyrinthine corridors of a palace, a realm as confusing as another world.

And she recalled other slaves too. Other Vir Requis. But not ones like those from Tofet. Here, in this realm of gold and jewels, the slaves' skin was paler, for the sun did not burn them. Their shoulders did not stoop under a yoke, and their legs did not bend under baskets of bricks, and no hot tar stained their feet. Elory flushed to remember them stripping her naked, scrubbing her tarred skin until it reddened, shaving the downy hair that grew on her body, soothing her wounds with ointment, and finally cladding her in this cotton shift.

She knelt now in the dark chamber. Cleaned. Bandaged. Shaved. Perfumed with a hint of frankincense. Yet still her ankles were hobbled, and still the collar encircled her neck.

Still a slave. Still a daughter mourning.

Elory lowered her head. Still that vision played in her mind, again and again. She knew it would never leave her. Her mother, a silver dragon, calling her name, flying toward her . . .

and the lances, the arrows, the swords . . . the blood raining . . . the severed limbs, the anguished eyes, and . . .

"No," Elory whispered. She bit her lip so hard she tasted blood. *I will not let that vision fill me. I refuse.*

Instead, she conjured up older, kinder memories. Her mother comforting her after the overseers would whip Elory's back. Her mother holding her, singing to her the old songs of Requiem, whispering of the day when the dragons would rise again, overthrow their masters, and fly home. Elory would remember that woman instead: the kindly mother, face sunburnt and weathered but still beautiful, eyes still dreaming, still hoping, loving her.

You rest now in the halls of afterlife, Elory thought.

Requiem had fallen; the cruel seraph Ishtafel, her captor, had burned down the forests and toppled the marble halls. But a Requiem woven of starlight still shone above, Elory knew. And in that Requiem all the dragons from Mother's stories—King Aeternum, the founder of Requiem, and all those kings, queens, and heroes who had followed—lived there in the starlight. One could not see the Draco constellation from so far south, here in the empire of Saraph, but Elory knew that those stars shone beyond the horizon. That the celestial halls shone among them. That her mother was at peace.

I have to believe. I have to or my will to continue would flee me. I have to believe that the celestial Requiem shines above, and that we can someday rebuild the earthly Requiem in our fallen forests.

It was only hours ago that a guard had led her here in a blindfold, chaining her in the shadows, then leaving her. Elory had removed the blindfold, but she might as well have kept it on. She looked around her, trying to see through the shadows, but it was too dark. She could make out only the blobs of furniture. A chain ran from her ankle, securing her to a bedpost. She dared to walk a few steps back and forth, to hear the chain clank, to feel around her.

A bed topped with the softest fabric she had ever felt, even softer than her newly scrubbed, lotioned skin. A table with a bowl of grapes she dared not eat. A mosaic on the floor. Beyond that she couldn't reach, only gaze into darkness.

For a long time, Elory simply waited.

He'll come for me, she thought. *Somebody will.*

She shuddered to think what Ishtafel would do to her. Would he force her to pour him wine, file his nails, comb his hair? Or would he desire more from her—desire to know her . . . as a man knows a woman? Elory swallowed. She had never known a man. The thought of the tall, golden-haired seraph claiming her body, claiming her virginity, perhaps even planting a child within her womb—it made her shiver. Ishtafel was a creature of beauty, his eyes bright, his shoulders broad, a god of grace, yet the thought of him touching her sickened Elory. She would give up all the beauty in the world to return to her hut in Tofet.

She tried to think of that clay hut now, to think of her family. Was Jaren, her wise father, thinking of her now, praying to the stars of Requiem to protect her? Was Vale, her angry and torn brother, railing against the masters, speaking as always of rebelling?

More than she wanted water for her parched throat, more than she wanted food for her tight belly, Elory wanted to speak to her father and brother again. To tell them she was all right. To say goodbye. Tofet, realm of the slaves, was a land of sweat, of breaking bones, of breaking dreams, yet now Elory missed it. Her yoke was gone, her body cleaned, yet she felt more lost, more afraid than ever. She missed her family.

And there is more to my family.

"I have a sister too," she whispered in the dark, tears flowing down to her lips. "A lost sister I've never met. A sister in this very palace. A sister who can help me, who—"

Before she could say more, the door opened.

Lamplight flooded the chamber.

Elory winced, staring into the light. Her heart burst into a gallop. Her instinct was to cower, to cover her eyes, to hide behind the bed and beg for mercy. She resisted that urge.

I am a daughter of Requiem, heir to a proud race. I will not cower.

She squared her shoulders, raised her chin, and stared into the light.

He stepped into the room, a towering seraph, his wings as white as purest snow, his armor a priceless work of gold and jewels, a silver lamp in his hand. The destroyer of Requiem. The heir to Saraph. The murderer of her mother.

"Ishtafel." The word tasted foul on her lips.

The seraph placed his lamp on a table, and for the first time, Elory got a look at the chamber. The place glittered. Murals of seraphim battling sea serpents and demons covered the walls, inlaid with gold and platinum. Gemstones shone on vases, tables, and armchairs. Platinum statues of jackals and ibises glared at her with diamond eyes. Swords hung on racks, and massive skulls—each one so large Elory could have climbed into the jaws—stood in alcoves. In the center of the room rose a canopy bed; the chain from her ankle ran toward its ebony post.

It was a chamber of opulence, every inch of it priceless, yet to Elory it seemed more like a mausoleum.

Wordlessly, Ishtafel approached a table and poured himself a mug of wine. Elory stared at him, wondering why he was pouring his own wine. Was serving him wine not to be her duty? Did this mean she was here for another purpose?

She wanted to speak, to break this silence, to ask him what he wanted of her. But she dared not. She merely stood chained, watching him drink.

He lowered his jeweled cup and began to remove his armor. Again, as he worked the clasps, he asked for no aid. Again Elory's fear grew.

I'm not here to pour his wine. I'm not here to remove his armor. She glanced at his bed. *Am I here to service him in that bed?*

She glanced back at him. He had removed his breastplate now, and he was working at unstrapping his vambraces. His bare arms were massive; each one seemed larger than Elory's entire body. His chest was wide, muscular, the skin tinted gold; he seemed like a gilded statue brought to life. But he was not perfect, she saw. Four scars, as from claws, ran across his chest, old and white.

Dragon claws, Elory thought.

Still he did not speak. Still he did not glance at her. He removed his greaves off his legs, his last pieces of armor, remaining in a cotton skirt that fell halfway down his thighs. His hair flowed down his back between his wings, a mane of dawn, and Elory was reminded of the flaming manes of the firehorses that had borne her here. The seraph acted as if she were another piece of furniture. Ignoring her, he returned to his mug of wine, drinking as he gazed out the window at the night.

Finally Elory could bear it no longer. She raised her chin and stood straight, trying to stand as tall as she could; she still didn't even reach Ishtafel's shoulders.

"Why did you bring me here?" she said. "How am I to serve you? Will you not speak, will—"

He spun around. She felt his hand before she saw it move. His palm slammed into her cheek, and she cried out and fell to the floor. Blood filled her mouth.

She coughed, struggling to breathe, and stared up at him. He had returned to the window. Once more, he was calmly sipping his wine.

Slowly, Elory rose to her feet. Her chain clanked. She glanced toward the table and she saw Ishtafel's sword there. The blade was longer than she was tall, and it looked heavy, but Elory had been raised bearing yokes and baskets of steaming bitumen. She was small and thin but strong. She could lift this sword, drive it into his back, slay him, and—

And what then? she thought. Remain chained here until the guards entered the chamber, found Ishtafel's body, and dragged her to the bronze bull?

She swallowed, eying the blade. Perhaps there was another path. She could kill Ishtafel, then fall upon the sword. She would have her revenge, then her soul would rise to join her mother. What else did she have to live for? Why even draw breath? She would never see her father and brother again, never see the stars of Requiem or her fallen halls, and—

But I can still see my sister, whispered a voice inside her.

Elory's throat clenched.

My sister.

She did not know if she believed those stories. Stories of a sister who lived here in this palace, who could help her, who could help all the children of Requiem. A lost light.

She looked away from the sword.

I will live. I must. I will find her.

Finally Ishtafel spoke, his back to her, still staring out the window. "You will address me as 'Your Excellence' or 'my lord.'

You will remember this or my next strike will not leave you as pretty. Do you understand?"

Elory touched her lip. Her fingers came back bloody. "Why am I here, *my lord?*" She couldn't help but add a hint of scorn to those last two words. She would do what she must to survive, but she would defy him when she could, even with just the hint of an insolent tone. "What do you want, *my lord?*"

He turned toward her. He stared down from his height, eyes gleaming. Those eyes were inhuman. Eyes like those of a bronze statue with fire within its shell, casting out their own light.

They were gods once, Elory thought. *Angels in the heavens, fallen, cast out. Broken gods.*

In her mind, she saw the Requiem that had been. The Requiem from the old tales. A kingdom where the Vir Requis wore no collars, where they could fly freely as dragons. A kingdom of marble columns in a birch forest. That Old Requiem, fallen five hundred years ago, was a realm of ancient legend, a realm past great distances of time and space, a mere memory of myth. Yet here before her, here in this very chamber, stood the same seraph who had led that old charge, who had crushed Requiem and borne Elory's ancestors to captivity.

"What do I want?"

Ishtafel's voice was soft. He stepped toward Elory. She felt the heat of his body. She struggled against every instinct not to flinch, not to flee. He stood only inches away now, and again she was struck by his size, and how small she felt before him, a mere child. He lowered the hand that had struck her, and she saw droplets of her blood on the palm. Gently, he tugged at the lacings on her cotton shift, undoing them.

"Do you not know, child?"

Again, his voice was smooth, barely a whisper. Her shift fell to the floor, and she covered her breasts with her hands.

"I know of such things." She stared into his eyes; staring at them was an act of defiance. "I know of—" She bit her lip when he raised his hand, then spoke again. "*My lord.*"

"Then come into my bed," he said, "and pleasure me tonight, and sleep in my arms, and I will not hurt you again. Do your duty, daughter of Tofet, and you will find a life of wine, food better than gruel, a roof to shelter you from the sun, perfumes and ointments to smooth and scent your skin. Grant me pleasure or I will grant you pain." His eyes narrowed, burning with just the hint of menace. "Now lie on the bed."

She glanced at that bed. She swallowed. She had endured years of slaving under the sun. She had endured countless lashes of the whip. Why was she so afraid of this?

Perhaps Elory, with her dreams of Requiem and old heroes, had also clung to a different sort of dreams. Dreams of romance. Of love. Dreams of someday meeting a man—even just another slave. Of falling in love. Of living together in a home of their own—even just a hut in the land of Tofet. A fool's dream. Those days of love had ended five hundred years ago; Ishtafel had ended them.

Yet Elory had been raised on stories of old lovers in Requiem: the great King Aeternum and Queen Laira, founders of Requiem; the hero Kyrie Eleison and his beloved, the fiery Agnus Dei; even the stories of the doomed love of King Elethor and Queen Lyana who had led Requiem in war against the phoenixes. Elory wanted such a love for herself. A love of passion and fire and triumph over evil. How could she debase herself here, give her body to this murderer?

The anger grew in his eyes. She saw that. His hand rose again, prepared to strike her, and an image flashed through Elory's mind: the battered, strangled corpse of Mayana, a slave who had failed to please this god of wrath. How could Elory defy him? How could she, so weak, the collar stifling her magic, hope to resist him?

"You tremble." Ishtafel stroked her cheek, then wrapped his hands around her wrists. He lowered her arms, exposing her bare breasts. Elory felt her cheeks flush, felt goose bumps rise across her.

Again she glanced at the sword on the table. No. Even should she grab this sword, she could not hope to overthrow this cruel empire. Even the hero Lucem, the only slave who had ever escaped, had been unable to kill any seraphim. Perhaps only one person could still save Requiem—only her sister. But Elory could still fight, with words if not with the blade.

She looked at Ishtafel, having to crane her neck back to stare into his eyes.

"My lord, I don't know how to pleasure you. But I would learn. There are pleasure slaves in this palace. I know that the seraphim collect fair maidens from the lands of Tofet, take them here, and they are trained in the arts. I'm a virgin, my lord, and my gift of virginity can be given only once. Let me give you this gift not as I am, uneducated in the ways of the flesh." She bit her lip. "Send me to the pleasure slaves, my lord. Let me learn from them the secrets of pleasuring a man. Then I'll return to you, learned, experienced in their ways, and you can claim the virginity of one who can make you cry in pleasure, not one who is meek and afraid."

He frowned. Elory's heart thrashed against her ribs so madly she thought it would leap onto the floor.

Please say yes, she thought. *I need time. Time away from this chamber. Time to find my sister. Time to find hope.*

"What makes you think I cannot use your body to take my own pleasure?" he finally asked.

"You could conquer me," Elory said. "You could take me roughly, and I would lie beneath you as you groan above me. I know what sex is. I've seen it enough times in the dust of Tofet. But you would gain only the briefest pleasure, the briefest conquest." She kept staring into those golden eyes, though they burned her. "But if I were to learn the true ways of pleasure, my lord, you would find me a gift far greater than Mayana was. Let me go to the pleasure slaves, and let me learn from them. Let me feel their lips against mine, their hands upon my body, and let me learn how to pleasure them so that I may pleasure you."

There. She saw something new in his eyes. Not merely menace, not merely anger, but lust. She had made him desire her, more than he had before. With only a few words, she had kindled new fires inside him.

I have some power over him. He chained me, struck me, rules over my life and my nation, yet I have power over him.

He stared into her eyes as if searching, seeking deceit. He was an ancient being, a god fallen to the earth, and for a moment Elory's breath trembled, and she was sure he could read her mind, see right past her ruse. But perhaps his lust was too great, her naked body too alluring to those scrutinizing eyes. He nodded.

"I will have a man lead you to the pleasure pits," he said. "You will have one week there to learn the art from its mistresses. Then you will return here to this chamber, and you will prove yourself useful to me, or the next pit I toss you into will be a grave in Tofet."

Elory nodded. "I will learn well, my lord."

She closed her eyes and took a shaky breath of relief. She had one week—one week to learn how to love . . . one week to find her sister.

MELIORA

On a spring dawn, Meliora left her palace, flying in a chariot of fire to see her beloved slaves burn.

She didn't want to be here. She wanted to leap out of the chariot, beat her wings, and fly far away—fly to the desert and die of thirst, and let the vultures eat her flesh. That would teach her mother. That would teach them all! If she died in the desert, fleeing her family, they would finally realize what monsters they had been. They would cry and cry, and Meliora would just laugh from the afterlife.

And yet she flew here in this chariot of fire. Because Meliora had to see. She could not believe that Mother's threats were true, that . . . that this bronze bull truly existed. That Mother could truly be so cruel.

She's only trying to scare me. Meliora raised her chin and sucked in air, putting on a show of bravery. *I'll show her that I'm not afraid of her. That I don't believe her silly stories.*

She looked around her. In all her twenty-seven years, Meliora had never flown this far from the palace.

Several other chariots of fire flew around her: her mother in one, her brother in another, and lords or ladies of Saraph in a dozen more. The firehorses galloped across the sky, a great cavalcade, their manes scattering sparks. Below, Meliora could see Shayeen, the capital of Saraph—the City of Kings. Its eight boulevards spread out like spokes, lined with statues of the gods. The Temple of Kloriana, the Goddess of Wisdom, rose directly below her, columns capped with gold. Farther east, she could see the Temple of Bee'al, god of victory and war, its towers like blades. Soon the chariots flew over the Te'ephim River, and Meliora tried to count the ships below but could not; hundreds were sailing here, returning from distant lands with the sweets, spices, and perfumes she craved.

When Meliora looked behind her, she could see the ziggurat, growing farther and farther—the only home she had ever known. The palace soared a thousand feet high, dwarfing even the city's temples. Two massive statues, shaped as cats with women's heads, guarded the staircase that led to its gates. Each of the statues, depicting the goddess La'eri, stood so tall their eyes were the size of chariots. The ziggurat tapered into a triangular tip, covered in platinum, and upon it shone an eye within a sunburst—the Eye of Saraph, sigil of the empire.

A prison, Meliora thought. *No better than the huts of slaves.*

She returned her eyes to the north. The chariots were nearing the city's outer walls now, and soon, for the first time in her life, Meliora would fly above them. For the first time, she would leave this city. She would see the land of Tofet, the land her slaves came from.

Meliora took a deep breath. Tofet! So many times she had wished to fly there. To doff her painful, squeezing sandals. To remove the damn golden necklaces and bracelets that always clinked and got in the way. To live free. Free of her mother's incessant brooding about the lost old days. Free of her brother, the man she was to marry, to bear heirs for. Free of all the pressures of the palace. In Tofet, Meliora knew, the weredragon slaves lived a humble yet joyous life. Singing in the sun as they drew from rivers of flowing bitumen. Dancing upon grapes to make wine. Living like birds or butterflies, beings of no wealth yet a rustic happiness.

Meliora scoffed. *My mother thinks she can scare me with stories of bronze bulls. I'll show her I'm not afraid of anything.*

"Are you ready, daughter?" Queen Kalafi asked, riding in the chariot beside her. "Ready to see your slaves burn in the bronze bull, a punishment for your defiance?"

The queen had put on a show, sending troops to grab Meliora's slaves from her chamber. Meliora had not seen the pair—the dark, demure Kira and the pale, petite Talana—since last night.

"I'll see what I'll see," Meliora replied.

She did not believe this theater for an instant. Oh, perhaps Mother would arrange some fake bull. Perhaps she would even have Kira and Talana waiting there in chains, soldiers guarding them. A show, that was all.

Mother wants me to cry, to beg, but I won't. I'll force her to keep going, to keep performing this theater, until she's forced to stop, forced to admit I'm brave. She balled her hands into fists. *I'll never marry my brother. Never. Not even if Mother steals away every last slave in the palace.*

She was going to tell Mother that, to tell her that she'd run away if forced to marry, to scream and cry and stamp her feet, maybe even hold her breath until she turned purple. But before Meliora could speak another word, the cavalcade of chariots flew over the outer walls of the city, and Meliora found herself staring at the land of Tofet on the horizon.

Meliora lost her breath.

The land of slaves still lay beyond several miles of wilderness, but every heartbeat, it grew closer. Every mile the chariots crossed, Meliora's brow creased further. Whenever she had thought of Tofet, this land whence the palace slaves came, she had imagined a great garden. A place of brooks bubbling through meadows, of fig and palm and apple trees to shade resting slaves, of gleaming orbs of bitumen that shone like jewels in carts, the miners whistling joyously as they rolled forth the treasure. But ahead of her, Meliora saw no trees or streams, heard no singing or birds, smelled no sweet perfume of flowers.

Ahead of her, she saw a nightmare.

There were no jolly, bearded miners, whistling as they wheeled carts of black gemstones. Instead, she saw dragons—real dragons, the weredragon slaves without their collars on—digging in a massive pit nearly the size of the entire city behind Meliora. Meliora had only seen dragons several times in her life before, chained beasts who hauled great stones while building temples in the city. As the dragons below dug with claws like swords, tar gushed up from the depths, seeping across the pit. Even from up here, still flying in the distance, Meliora could smell the stench.

Thousands of skinny oxen moved about the pit, yokes around their necks, hauling the bitumen in baskets. Seraphim stood around the animals, lashing whips of fire at any who dallied or fell. Meliora rose in her seat, inhaled sharply, and balled up her fists. No animals should be treated so! Animals were made to be patted, cuddled, kept in the gardens, not whipped and forced to labor in the blinding sunlight. Meliora would speak to these seraphim below, she would—

She lost her breath.

Gods.

She stared down, eyes burning. Her hands loosened.

Those poor, whipped creatures below, laboring under the yokes, weren't oxen.

"They're slaves," Meliora whispered. "Weredragon slaves."

Countless weredragons covered the land of Tofet below. They hauled bitumen from the pits, the sticky tar that was used to caulk ships, form bricks and mortar, and hold together jewelry and mosaics. They labored in rocky fields, shaping clay into bricks using wooden molds. They dug irrigation ditches and plowed fields, no animals to help them, the masters whipping their backs every step. And they died. Everywhere Meliora looked, they were dying. Their corpses stank in wagons. The whole place reeked of death, of sweat, of blood, of terror.

"No," Meliora whispered, tears in her eyes.

How could this be? She knew weredragons! She herself owned weredragons! In the palace, they were meek little things, a foot or two shorter than the seraphim, slender little servants with shaved heads and collars to keep their dragon forms at bay. Not . . . not these filthy, beaten creatures, covered in tar and sand and blood. Not this hive of agony.

"You grow pale, daughter." Queen Kalafi smiled thinly, flying her chariot closer to Meliora's. "Finally, the pampered child of the palace gets a whiff of the world. Are you going to cry, little girl?"

Meliora growled at her mother. "You think I'm weak because I'm young? Because I didn't fight in wars like you and Ishtafel?" She snorted. "I'm stronger than you know."

The queen nodded. "Aye, very strong, child. So strong you think you can defy my wishes, throw tantrums, and refuse to bear me a pure heir. We'll see how strong you are when your little slaves sing in the bull. Ah!" Kalafi pointed. "There it is. We draw near."

Meliora stared back down at the land of Tofet, and she saw it there. For the second time since leaving the city, she lost her breath.

The bronze bull. Malok.

The idol stood on a hill, twice the size of a regular bull, its head lowered, its horns raised, a beast ready to charge. Its bronze body gleamed in the sunlight, blinding. Firewood and kindling were arranged below it, soaked with oil. Meliora had seen statues before—the City of Kings was full of them, idols far larger than this one—yet this bull filled her with dread. Its red eyes seemed to stare at her from below.

The stories are true, Meliora thought, trembling. *They cook people inside it, they*—

She tightened her lips.

No. Foolishness. She wouldn't let her mother win this one. Meliora tore her gaze away from the bull and glared at the queen. This was all a ruse. All a show. No doubt, Kalafi had placed the yokes on these slaves, covered them with fake blood, placed this silly bull here to torment here, and had arranged the whole thing. It was just bad theater, that was all. Just some elaborate punishment concocted to terrify Meliora into marrying her brother. The slaves below were just actors. As soon as Meliora turned and left, they would doff their yokes and return to their songs.

Meliora nodded. *I won't be fooled.*

"Let's hear the bull sing, Mother." She forced herself to laugh. "I'd love to hear it."

Meliora swung her lash, and her firehorses began to descend, pulling her chariot of fire down toward the bronze bull. She smiled thinly. Mother would be forced to stop this charade soon, forced to admit that she had lost. And Meliora would only laugh, proving her strength.

I will trick the trickster.

As she descended, she saw that many slaves were gathering on the hill around Malok. All were hobbled and collared, and seraphim overseers stood among them, flaming whips in hand. Most of the slaves wore rags, but a handful were naked, standing together in a wooden corral beside the bronze bull. Their backs were whipped, their arms shackled.

The condemned to be burned, Meliora realized.

Across the hill, both the weredragon slaves and seraphim overseers knelt as the royal chariots descended. Meliora's chariot landed first, and she emerged from the flames to stand on the hilltop by Malok. The bronze idol shone above the pyre of wood and kindling, and still its eyes seemed to stare into Meliora. Cruel eyes. Carved of metal yet somehow living, taunting her. She could see that a door was fitted onto the bull's flank.

They burn the prisoners within. Meliora remembered the stories. *They cook them in there, cook them until they scream, and the screams flow through pipes to make the bull sing melodiously, and—*

She shook her head wildly and forced herself to laugh. She was not fooled by this fake idol! It probably wasn't even made of real bronze, just painted wood. As for these slaves around her, kneeling and broken? Actors! That was all. Fake blood taken from a troupe of performers.

The other chariots landed around her, and the lords of Saraph emerged. Ishtafel inhaled deeply as if savoring the scent of blood, and a smile stretched across his face. The golden prince gave Meliora the slightest of winks. Queen Kalafi winced as she alighted from her chariot, sudden pain twisting across her face. Too far from her salted baths, her wound always began to ache.

"Nice try, Mother," Meliora said. "But I'm not scared of this place. I—"

"My lady!" rose the anguished cry behind her. "My lady Meliora, please!"

Meliora spun around and felt the blood drain from her face.

"Gods," she whispered.

Kira and Talana, her dear palace slaves, stood in the corral with the other condemned weredragons. Meliora had looked past them only moments ago, not recognizing them. The two had been beaten. Their faces were swollen, the skin purple with bruises, cuts bleeding on their lips and foreheads. Firewhips had striped their backs, tearing into the skin and cauterizing the wounds. Kira—sweet little Kira who had painted Meliora's fingernails so many times—was shivering, her arm hanging at an odd angle, dislocated and swelling.

"Please help us, my princess," Talana said, voice slurred, barely seeping past her swollen lips.

Even with her limbs chained, Kira managed to kneel. "We're sorry, my princess! We're sorry for our sins. Spare us the bull."

Meliora trembled. Cold sweat washed her. She panted, her head spun, and blackness began to spread across her vision. No. No! How could this be real? This *had* to be an act, just a show, but why did the blood smell real? Why was she trembling so? She was going to faint. Going to faint right here, but she had to save them, had to help her slaves, had to—

"Soon they will scream," Kalafi said. The queen approached and placed a hand on Meliora's shoulder. "Soon the bull will sing."

Meliora gasped for breath, forcing herself to suck in air. The world kept spinning around her. She was going to faint, here before her brother, before her mother, before the watching slaves. She couldn't. She had to stop this! This had to be fake, *had* to. How could this be real?

Meliora was consumed with the overwhelming urge to flee. She wanted to rush back into her chariot, to fly home to her palace, to never emerge again—to hide among her statues, her jewels, her mosaics and murals, her gardens and her libraries, to never return into this world. To never see the yokes, the whips, the blood. She was princess of Saraph. She could leave this place. She could escape all this pain. She could marry Ishtafel as Mother had commanded, return to her gilded cage, and—

"No," she whispered, breath shaking in her lungs.

She could not abandon Kira and Talana. They were only slaves, it was true. Only mortal weredragons, creatures no more important than cats or dogs. But they were *her* slaves. And Meliora could not see them suffer.

Though the sight shot terror through her, Meliora forced herself to look back at her slaves. At the bruises swelling across their faces. At the burnt welts on their backs. At the chains cutting into their limbs. This was real, Meliora realized. Her mother's soldiers had truly beaten her precious pets.

But I'm going to save you, Meliora thought.

She took a step toward the slaves.

A hand gripped her shoulder, stopping her in her tracks.

"Wait, daughter!" Kalafi tightened her grip, holding her from behind. The queen stood several inches taller than Meliora, stronger, thousands of years older, her hands like vises. "Wait and listen. The first slave is about to sing!"

Meliora stared, cold sweat dampening her jeweled muslin dress, as seraphim dragged forth one of the naked, chained slaves from the corral. He was an old man, haggard, shoulders slumped and back crooked. One of his eyes vanished into an ugly scar. The seraphim manhandled him toward the bronze bull.

"Do you know what his crime was?" Kalafi leaned down to whisper into Meliora's ear. "He failed to make two thousand bricks a day. He made only half that many. Now he will sing for us, and you will listen."

Meliora wanted to flee, wanted to leap forward to help, wanted to do anything but stand here and watch, but her Mother's grip was iron. Meliora stood, tears in her eyes, watching as the seraphim opened a bronze door on the bull's flank.

The old weredragon stared into the bull and tried to resist, tried to free himself from the seraphim soldiers, but he was so frail he could barely even stand. He tossed back his head and opened his mouth, revealing toothless gums. He cried out, voice torn, hoarse, cracking, yet loud enough to roll across the hill.

"Remember Requiem!" The slave raised his manacled arms toward the heavens. "Requiem! May our wings forever find your sky."

"Impudent reptile!" One of the seraphim guards kicked the man. Meliora grimaced to hear the *crack* of a snapped rib. The soldiers gripped the slave, lifted him into the air, and shoved him into the bull. They slammed the bronze door shut, sealing the slave within.

"He tried to sing to Requiem," Kalafi whispered, lips touching Meliora's ear. "Now he'll sing the melodious song of Saraph's glory."

The seraphim guards held a torch to the pyre beneath the bull's belly. Soaked in oil and stuffed with kindling, the wood burst into flame at once. Sparks showered out, logs crackled, and the heat bathed Meliora, so potent she winced for fear of her eyeballs burning.

The bull's underbelly began to redden. The heat spread across the flanks, down the legs, across the lowered head. Malok's eyes burned, and the bull began to sing.

The slave inside was the one screaming, Meliora knew—screaming as his flesh boiled. But the screams, passing through the pipes inside the bull, emerged from its mouth in a beautiful, astral song. The music of flutes, ethereal, a sound like the song of the seraphim back in the heavenly realm of Edinnu.

And across the hill, the seraphim began to sing with the bull. Their voices rose together—the queen's, Ishtafel's, the dozen nobles, all singing to the music, their voices fair and sad. A song of their lost realm, the paradise their gods had banished them from. A song of lost fields of clouds gilded in the dawn, of rivers of silver that flowed through meadows, of trees that bore a thousand kinds of fruit, of fields that yielded endless crops, a land with no pain, no toil. A land lost. A prayer never forgotten.

"Beautiful, isn't it?" Kalafi whispered to Meliora. "The song of our people."

Yet Meliora did not sing with them. She stared, tears on her cheeks, as the fire burned, as the bull's song died. When the last note had sounded, the seraphim opened the bronze door.

Bones and red-hot chains spilled out onto the pyre.

Meliora looked away, wincing. Her fists trembled at her sides.

This was no show. The god Malok. The brutality of Tofet. The looming death of her slaves. It was all real.

Meliora felt as if her own ribs were shattering.

Something changed in her life this morning, Meliora knew. Even if she returned to her palace, to her life in that gilded cage, she would never forget this place, never forget that song of her people—a song woven from the screams of Requiem.

"Cook the next ones!" Kalafi cried, voice shrill. The queen grinned madly, a grin that showed nearly all her teeth down to the molars. Her cheeks flushed; whether from the heat or excitement, Meliora did not know. "Toss in the pair! Make them sing."

The soldiers grabbed two more slaves—Kira and Talana.

Before she even realized what she was doing, Meliora tugged herself free from her mother's grasp, leaped forth, and shouted for the crowd to hear.

"No!"

The soldiers froze, holding the beaten slaves a foot away from the heated bull. The other slaves, thousands across the hill, turned to stare. The noble seraphim, standing before their chariots of fire, whispered amongst themselves.

"No," Meliora repeated. Her chest shook, her knees knocked, but she forced herself to raise her chin, to square her shoulders, to keep speaking loudly. "Stop this. Enough. Enough!"

The soldiers stared between Meliora and the queen. Tears were flowing from Kira and Talana's bruised eyes, along their broken cheeks, and to their bloody mouths.

"I'm going to save you," Meliora whispered to them. "I'm going to bring you home." She spun away from the bull to face the queen. "Mother, enough of this. I've learned this lesson you tried to teach me. Release them and end this."

The queen was resplendent in the sunlight, clad in a kalasiri woven with precious gems and golden beads. A tiara topped her blond hair, shaped as a serpent with ruby eyes. Her wings spread wide, blindingly white in the sun. Kalafi—Queen of Saraph, fallen angel—smiled in delight.

"You would have me renege on my promise?" Kalafi tilted her head, jewels jangling. "I vowed to teach you a lesson, daughter. You defied me. You refused to marry Ishtafel. You robbed our family of a future heir. So I will rob you of your slaves. Sing with us this time, Meliora! Sing with the bull as the weredragons burn!" The queen nodded at the soldiers who held the slaves. "Place them in the belly of Malok."

The guards began to drag the slaves back toward the bull.

"No!" Meliora shouted.

She raced across the hilltop, leaped forward, and placed herself between the bull and the slaves. Her heart thrashed. Her hair whipped in the wind. The sparks from the flames bit her ankles, and the heat of the bronze bull—only inches away— baked her back. She glared at the seraphim before her.

"Return these slaves to their homes," she told the seraphim, then spun toward the queen. "I refuse to let this happen. Yes, I defy you again, Mother." Her heart seemed ready to escape her throat, her knees shook wildly, and breath rattled in her lungs, but she refused to back down. "End this."

Kalafi's smile vanished. She stared at Meliora, and the amusement died in the queen's eyes, replaced with cold, murderous venom. Here was a woman who had defied the gods themselves. What chance did Meliora have facing her?

And yet Meliora faced her. She stared into her mother's eyes, refusing to look away. Something had broken inside of Meliora today, an innocence had shattered, and she was a different person. She had never fought against the gods like her mother, had never conquered realms across the world like her brother. Here was her war: a war against her family, a war to save only two . . . two slaves who had been with her for years. Two slaves who needed her.

"Back down, Meliora—" Kalafi began.

"I will not!" Meliora shouted. She knew her mother. Kalafi lived for her vainglory, to present herself as a goddess, infallible, perfect in her grace. More than anything, her mother feared this image shattering.

So let me humiliate her, Meliora thought. *Let the people see that she cannot control even her own daughter, let alone an empire.*

"I will not," Meliora repeated. "Do you hear me, Mother?" She raised her voice to a shout. "I will not let you burn them! I will not marry Ishtafel. I will—"

"Meliora!" Kalafi thundered, and flames burst out from her wings and haloed her head, white fire of her rage. Her voice tore across the land, booming, impossibly loud. "Stand back, daughter, or I will—"

"Or you will what?" Meliora shouted. She had never seen her mother so incensed, never seen the white fire of fury blaze across the queen. But it was too late to back down. "You lied to me, Mother. You lied!" Meliora trembled wildly, tears in her eyes. "You never showed me this land. You never told me the truth about this place. You raised me wrapped in silk, and now try to shatter my innocence by burning my own slaves? No. I will not allow this. I will not be a pawn to you, not be your slave, not be an incestuous womb for your heir. I would rather burn myself!"

"Then burn!" Kalafi roared. The sound tore across the land, shook the bull, scattered smoke from the flames, sent slaves falling to the ground. It was a cry louder than crashing temples, than falling nations, a cry that echoed across the land of Tofet.

Then burn! Then burn!

Meliora stared at her mother, silent. Suddenly her trembling ceased. Her tears dried in the heat. A calmness fell upon her, and her fear burned away like the flesh of the old man.

"So I will burn," Meliora whispered.

All my life I've been sheltered. Lied to. Deceived. So let me sing. Let me sing to save them.

She turned to look at the guards. "By the ancient rites, I give my life to save theirs. I will burn in their stead to appease Malok." She turned back toward her mother. "Sing with me, Mother. As my screams rise through the bull, sing with me. For your lost home in the heavens . . . and for your lost daughter."

Meliora stepped toward the bull and climbed inside.

"Daughter, stop this!" Kalafi shouted . . . but Meliora barely heard anything above her own screams.

The heat baked her. The bronze burned her feet, legs, knees, shoulders, every place it touched. She screamed in agony. Her wings caught fire. She heard her screams rising through the bull as melodious music, and she wanted to escape, but she would not, she would *not*, she would not live this life, not serve her mother anymore, not let her slaves die, not—

All thought faded as she let out a howl, the fire engulfing her.

Then burn! Then burn!

Another scream rose. Hands reached into the bull, grabbed her, pulled her out. She stumbled. She fell. The sunlight blinded her, and the fire still roared, and somebody was shouting and other people crying out in terror. Feet stamped on her wings, and Meliora cried out again.

The fire died.

She lay trembling on the ground, the bull rising above her, her feathers burnt. The tips of her hair still crackled. Her brother and mother stood above her, pale, shouting at soldiers, shouting at her, but she could hear only muffled sounds, see only mottles of light.

"Let them go," Meliora whispered. "Let my slaves go."

Through the ringing in her ears, she thought she could make out her mother's shouts. "Take the slaves to the tar pits! Slap yokes on them! Put them to work instead of wasting time here. Malok is appeased. Now go!"

Meliora's eyelids fluttered. A soft smile rose upon her cracked, burnt lips.

I saved them. I saved them.

Her ears kept ringing, and people kept shouting, and it seemed to Meliora that the sounds rose higher, softened, turned into the music of pipes. A song of old homes lost. A song of nations falling. A song of truth in a burning world. Her eyes closed, and she slept.

ELORY

Elory had spent her life in the bitumen pit, extracting the precious substance that held the empire together. When she stepped into the pleasure pit beneath the palace, she found a world just as dark and dizzying.

Here is a different sort of mine, she thought. *A mine for human flesh, perhaps just as precious to the seraphim as bitumen and brick.*

The chamber was buried deep beneath the ziggurat, a glittering cave carved from the living rock. Rugs and tasseled pillows hid the floor, and curtains hung everywhere, some woven of silk and muslin, others formed of thousands of beads. Incense burned in iron holders shaped as phalluses, and obsidian statues seemed to dance in the flickering candlelight, shaped as nude people with the heads of beasts. Hookahs bubbled, their glass vials filled with *hintan*—a spice of the northern deserts. The purple smoke swirled through the air, already spinning Elory's head, as intoxicating as the bitumen fumes.

But stranger than the smoke, the rugs, or the statues were the slaves.

A score of Vir Requis lounged here, collared like Elory, yet different in every other way. She gasped to see these young women. She wanted to look away but could not. While her body was scrawny, the skin bronzed, the hands and feet callused, these slaves were pleasantly curved, their skin pale, their hands soft. Long hair grew from their heads—real hair, not just stubble. Henna darkened their eyelids, and the red of crushed raspberries painted their lips. They wore naught but flimsy silks, the fabric revealing more than it hid.

Pleasure slaves, Elory thought. *A pit of them, mere flesh waiting for the seraphim to consume. How will I find my sister here?*

Yet what choice did she have but to study in this place? Aboveground, in Ishtafel's chamber, he would claim her body, brutalize her if she resisted, then discard her corpse with the others. Here she would live—for a week at least. A week to try to find her sister. To try to find help.

Elory cleared her throat. "I . . . I was told to come here. To . . . to learn from you."

Across the pit, a few of the slaves turned to look at her. One lounged on a pile of pillows, smoking from a hookah. She gave Elory a dazed glance, then turned toward a statue, jangled a bracelet that hung from its arm, and giggled as the jewel flashed. Two other slaves lay together, holding each other, sharing a pipe. They blinked at Elory, then returned to smoking the spice. Other slaves ignored Elory flat out, their eyes glazed. A few drooled on the floor.

"I . . ." Elory gulped. Was this the right place? "I've come here to join you. To become a . . . a pleasure slave," she finished with a whisper, her cheeks heating.

One of the slaves leaped to her feet. Her eyes flashed, and she marched toward Elory. She was Vir Requis too—no feathered wings grew from her back, no halo topped her head, and a collar encircled her neck—but fairer than any slave Elory had ever known. Her hair was long and brown, her eyes dark. She wore baggy silken pants, slippers, and a top that revealed a jewel shining in her navel. She seemed young, perhaps only a year or two older than Elory, short and slender but without the hard, famished look of a Tofet slave.

"You are nothing like us." The young woman's eyes flashed with anger. "You will never be like us. We don't want more goddamn filthy Tofet rats here. Last one infected the place with fleas."

Farther back in the den, the hookah smoker laughed hysterically, then hit the jangling bracelet and laughed again.

"She got fleas, Tash! Fleas! Fleas everywhere." The smoker hit the bracelet, gasped to see it glinting, and laughed again. "Fleas, fleas, fleas, glinting in the smoke."

Elory returned her eyes to Tash, the angry, brown-eyed woman. "I have no fleas. I was told to come here. I'm no longer a Tofet worker, I—"

"I said rat, not worker." Tash grabbed Elory's ear and twisted it painfully. "Are there fleas on that head of yours? Fleas can hide in stubble too." She groaned. "By the gods, you stink."

"Ow!" Elory winced. "Let go."

Tash groaned, released Elory's ear, and turned toward her comrades. "Why do they send these rats over?" She raised her arms. "What have I done to deserve these rats invading my cave?"

The smoker took another puff on her hookah, then laughed again. "Maybe you forgot how to smoke a seraph's pipe." She sucked deeply on her hookah, puffed out smoke, and tittered again. "Lost your touch."

Tash groaned again, even louder this time, and tugged her hair. "You lot are just as useless as the rat." She spun back toward Elory. "Well, rat, stop standing there like a goddamn statue. I take pride in my pit. The masters might show up any time, and I'll not have you scare them off." She grabbed Elory's wrist and tugged her. "Come on."

Elory stumbled in pursuit. Her ankles were still hobbled together, but the pleasure slaves wore no chains, only their collars and silks. Tash dragged her through the chamber, between the statues of the nude women with animal heads, around live women lounging on pillows while smoking hookah, and past several walls of curtains.

Finally, past a curtain of beads, they entered a little nook at the back. A rug hung across one wall of stone; the other walls were simply formed of curtains. Candles burned in alcoves, their wax dripping toward the floor, and many silks spilled from three open chests. A mattress lay on the floor, topped with pillows. A woman slept here, snoring by an empty hookah.

"Gods above!" Tash gave her hair a mighty tug and rummaged around the chamber. "They even left your goddamn shackles on. I try to run a quality establishment down here, and those dung-sucking guards give me nothing to work with. Nothing but rats! Now where's the damn key?"

Elory glanced down at her hobbles. Rings of iron circled her ankles, and a chain connected them, only a foot long— enough to let her walk but not run or kick. She had worn these iron shackles around her ankles since her second birthday; they had been opened only several times to be replaced with larger shackles.

"Only the masters of Tofet carry the keys." Elory shuddered to remember the cruel overseers with their whips of fire. "These are my permanent shackles. I've reached my full size. I—"

"Ah, there!" Ignoring her, Tash dug under a pile of silks and pulled out a key. "Haven't had to use one of these since the last rat scurried in here."

Elory gasped. Her eyes widened.

"A . . . key?"

Tash rolled her eyes. "She has the sense of a baby! Great." She pointed around the room. "Curtain! Bed! Wall!" She pointed at the sleeping woman on the mattress. "Useless lump of smoke-addled dung! There, now you can talk." She knelt and placed the key into Elory's shackles. "Maybe now you'll walk properly too."

The key turned.

The shackles fell off.

Elory's eyes dampened.

Trembling, she took a step. Another step. She blinked, eyes full of tears. She froze.

I can run. I can jump. I can kick if I want to. I—

"Well, don't just stand there like a statue," Tash said. "Stretch a little, for pity's sake. You're going to have to stretch those legs in the seraphim's beds." She rolled her eyes. "You Tofet rats. Useless, you are."

Slowly, Elory stretched out one leg, moving it a few inches forward . . . then another few inches . . . then farther than it had ever gone. Pain flared across her muscles, driving up to her hip, and she winced and her tears fell. It hurt. And it was wonderful.

"Thank you, Tash," she whispered. "Thank you so much."

"Don't thank me." Tash glowered, but then her eyes softened. She ran a finger down Elory's cheek. "You got good cheeks. Good lips. Good eyes. Thank your mother, not me. She gave you that pretty face."

Suddenly the pain was too much.

Mother . . .

The memory rose in Elory again—her mother flying toward her as a dragon, the arrows piercing her, the chariots of fire surrounding her, burning her, and then Mother losing her magic, falling dead as a human, and . . .

It was all too much, too soon. Elory's tears streamed and she trembled.

"Oh for pity's sake!" Tash groaned. "Will you cut out the waterworks? If the seraphim come, they—"

"I'm sorry." Elory wiped her eyes. "It won't happen again. It's just that . . . my mother. She died, and . . . and I'm so scared all the time. I feel so alone. I miss her so much and—"

Tash reached out, and Elory thought that the young slave would stroke her cheek again, but instead Tash slapped her. Hard.

The pain flared across Elory's cheek. She gasped.

Tash glared at her. "Shut your mouth." She jabbed Elory's chest. "If there's one thing I won't tolerate in my pit, it's self-pity. You won't shed tears here. You won't blabber on about how miserable you are, how alone you are." Tash's voice rose to an exaggerated falsetto. "Oh, I'm so alone in the world! Oh, my dear old mamma is dead!" She snorted. "Guess what, rat? Everyone here is an orphan. Everyone here is alone, and everyone here is scared. We're all slaves, if you haven't noticed the collars, and we're all bloody miserable. You're not special here. If you cry again, I'm going to bash out your teeth."

Elory wanted to cry again, to cower, to submit. But instead, she found herself staring back steadily into those angry, brown eyes.

"And we're all Vir Requis." Elory squared her shoulders. "We're all children of Requiem. We're all dragons, not rats. Did you forget that, Tash? Did you forget who you are, where we come from?" Her voice dropped to a whisper. "Did you forget Requiem?"

The rage in Tash's eyes only grew. "I forget nothing. Requiem?" She scoffed. "A dead land. As dead as your precious mother. Dragons?" She tugged at her collar. "Not so long as we wear these, my darling, and there's only one key in the empire that can open this lock. And that's one key I don't own."

The Keeper's Key, Elory thought. A key imbued with ancient magic. The key that had removed her mother's collar, letting the woman shift into a dragon to dig for bitumen. The key that fit into no padlock, but whose runes of power could unlock the collar around her neck. The key that removed the collars of the brick lifters, those who hauled stones as dragons, carrying them to the tops of temples. Just a single key, only one ever made, the most precious one in the empire.

If Elory could somehow steal that key—surely it was kept here in this palace!—and if she could remove enough collars . . . if enough dragons could fly against the chariots, blow their dragonfire . . .

But no. Elory dismissed that idea. Back in the war, five hundred years ago, tens of thousands of dragons had fought Ishtafel and his chariots. Tens of thousands had fallen from the sky. Even an army of dragons could not stop the seraphim. They were a race of immortal demigods. To them, even dragons were no more dangerous than animals were to men. As men in olden days had ruled beasts several times their size, so would the seraphim forever rule the Vir Requis, collared or not. Even should Elory find the Keeper's Key, it would not save them.

"Stop daydreaming!" Tash said. Her eyes rolled so far they almost looked into her skull. "Gods above, a simpleton, this one is. Now get out of my room. Go!" She pointed at the curtain of beads. "Go, go! Out with you."

"But . . ." Elory hesitated. "I was told that I'll learn the ways of . . ." She felt her cheeks flush, and she couldn't speak louder than a whisper. "Of pleasuring a man."

She glanced around her. Between the curtain's beads, she could see the rest of the pit. The women slumped across pillows, smoking the hintan that muffled their minds, waiting for men to claim them. Did Elory truly want to join them, to learn from them? She had come here to gain time, to hope to find a way to sneak through the palace, to contact her sister. Not to learn how to become a . . . pleasurer.

Yet if I don't learn, Ishtafel will know. He'll send down his men to check on me, or he'll come down himself. She gulped. *I'll have to learn this trade or I won't even last a week here.*

She looked back at Tash. "Will you teach me?"

Tash let out a groan so loud it was a wonder the sleeping woman in bed didn't wake. "Does a tigress teach a rat to hunt? Get out of my room. Go ask one of my girls to mentor you. I can't be wasting time on a hopeless cause."

Elory glanced through the curtain beads again. The other women barely seemed conscious enough to breathe, let alone teach her the skill. The one by the statue was jangling the bracelet again, laughing hysterically as it chinked.

"I'll try to learn from them." Elory sighed. "I promised Ishtafel that I would. The prince said that I have only a week here, and then I'm to return to his chamber in the ziggurat's crest, and—"

Tash grabbed Elory's cheeks and tugged her face toward her. "What did you say?"

She gulped. Tash's fingers were digging into her cheeks, as painful as talons. "I said that I'll try to learn from them. Maybe once the smoke clears, they can teach me, and—"

"Not that part!" Tash's eyes flashed. "What you said after that."

"That I promised Ishtafel that I'd study here for a week, that—"

"Liar!" Tash shouted, raising her hand to slap Elory again.

"I tell the truth." Elory pulled the scroll from her pocket; it bore Ishtafel's seal. "I bear a letter from him."

Tash snatched the scroll, examined the seal, and blanched. The slave could almost certainly not read—virtually no slaves could—but all knew Ishtafel's seal, the eye within the sunburst. Tash shoved the scroll back at Elory, unopened.

"Bloody stars," the pleasurer whispered. "Oh bloody stars above." She stared at Elory, eyes narrowed. "It's true. He chose you. A rat." Suddenly her eyes softened. "You poor thing. You poor, poor little rat."

Elory remembered Ishtafel returning her friend to the bitumen mine, how her friend Mayana had slammed down at her feet, beaten, strangled. She wondered how many other slaves Ishtafel had stolen from Tofet, how many of them Tash had trained, and how long they had lasted.

Elory gulped. She turned to step between the strings of beads. "I'll find a little spot of my own, I'll watch what the others do, and—"

Tash grabbed her arm, pulling her back. "No you won't." Her eyes flashed again. "Ishtafel himself chose you. Prince Ishtafel, the Fire of Saraph, the Breaker of Worlds. Do you know what this means? Do you know how dangerous this is? Do you know what would happen if you don't please him?" Tash shuddered. "He'd blame me. Me! I run this place, and you're my responsibility now. I will teach you. From now on, you follow me everywhere. From now on, you are my ward." She sighed—a huge sigh that flowed from head to toes. "Why do the gods curse me so?"

One week, Elory thought. *One week to linger here in smoke . . . to find a way out.*

She lifted one foot, placed it down, and lifted the other. No more shackles. Free to walk, to slink through shadows, to roam the palace . . . to find her sister. To find hope for Requiem.

ISHTAFEL

He walked through the shadowy halls of his palace, feeling like a wolf trapped in tunnels, hungry for flesh, thirsty for blood, ravenous for a mate.

He was not meant for this. Not for dark halls, gilded and jeweled though they might be. Not for languor, for splendor, for the pampered idling away—the languishing!—that his sister favored. No. Ishtafel had been born, bred, breastfed for conquest. For the conquering of lands. For the conquering of women. For the conquering of a world and all that was in it.

I should not have let the slave leave. Roaming the shadowy halls, Ishtafel clenched his fists so hard blood dripped from them. To let her learn how to pleasure him? Was he some weak king who lies on his back, like a turtle unable to right himself, seeking a harem to deliver their pleasures upon his withering flesh? No. He should have taken what he wanted from the girl, shattered her body if she resisted. He should shatter them all. Reptiles. Sick, disgusting, slithering snakes who hid in human forms, who—

"My lord!"

Several of the slaves—young women, collared, barefoot—appeared in the corridor before him. They knelt in the shadows.

Ishtafel did not slow his step. "You, up!" he barked, pointing at one.

The woman rose to her feet, quivering. "My lord? How may I—"

He shoved her head against the wall, a movement so fast she never saw it coming. Palm open, he grinded her skull against the limestone, crushing the bone, sending the blood and brain spurting out like juice from a shattered melon. The stone cracked, and still he grinded the mush of flesh and bone fragments until nothing was left, nothing but a body topped with ruin.

"Clean it up!" He walked onward, leaving the corpse to slump to the floor. "Slaves, clean!"

The other women screamed. Shrill sounds. Infuriating. Screaming and weeping, fretting about the hall, crying out wordlessly—terrified animals, that was all. No more than livestock.

Hand dripping, Ishtafel walked on, leaving them behind. The dark halls spread before him, and as Ishtafel kept walking, he imagined that he was back in Requiem, back in his first great war. A young man—not much older than Meliora was now. Many of the glorious battles, the famous ones, the ones engraved onto walls and columns and sung of in glittering halls, were the battles in the sky. Battles of countless chariots of fire flying against countless dragons. Battles of fire, rain, lightning, glorious battles for tapestries, paintings, epic poems. But the true battles, Ishtafel remembered, the true horror that had tested his mettle, had happened in places like this. In dark halls. Surrounded by stone. Underground.

In the last days of the war five hundred years ago, in the tunnels of Requiem, he had roamed like this in darkness. Battling the weredragons' human forms in their burrows, claiming step by step, life by life. Trapped in darkness, shining out his light, tasting their blood.

Watching his beloved Reehan die.

As Ishtafel walked in his palace, he raised his fingers to his lips, and he licked them, tasting the blood of the weredragon he had killed. Coppery. Sweet. An intoxicating wine, finer than all the vintages that poured from the jugs of the empire.

There is nothing sweeter than death, Ishtafel thought. *There is no finer nectar.*

Finally he paused by a portico of columns that afforded a view of the city beyond. Ishtafel stood here, staring out at the night, at his empire.

Saraph.

Ishtafel had been born on this world, this desolate rock floating in the darkness. He had never lived, killed, conquered back in the fabled realm of Edinnu, had never seen its fields, meadows, its trees that gave forth endless fruit. He had never fought the gods, never suffered their wounds, never been cast out from paradise.

But I built a new paradise here. I built a new realm with us as the gods. He clenched his fist, feeling the blood and brains squishing within. *Where we are the masters.*

And Ishtafel knew why he felt trapped.

After five hundred years, his war had ended. His paradise had been a paradise of blood, tunnels, death, and now—with the giants fallen, his last enemies slain—he too had been cast out from his realm of endless delights. He too was lost.

"I built this empire, but do I have a place within it? How do I live without killing? How do I stay strong in a realm of peace?"

There was only one answer, he knew. Had always been only one answer.

"With you, Meliora," he whispered into the night. "With the heir you will bear me."

He would not see himself soften, grow weak like his mother, a decadent queen who languished in a salted bath, a pathetic strip of meat still dreaming of the olden days. No. He would seize Meliora's womb. He would plant his seed there. He would grow a son within her, and he would raise a great prince, a great heir, a god.

"You will be mine, Meliora." He bared his teeth, sucking in the hot night air. "I conquered the world for our dynasty. Now I will conquer you."

ELORY

"No, rat!" Tash's brown eyes flashed with anger. "You have to ease into it. Slowly. To stroke him . . . gently."

She grabbed Elory's wrist and lowered her hand. Guided by her mentor, Elory stroked Tash's thigh, slowly running her fingers up and down.

"Like this?"

Tash groaned. "You're moving like an automaton! You have to relax. To be like a musician. A musician doesn't just play the notes rigidly, she feels the music. Feel me."

"I am!" Elory kept stroking the woman's leg.

"I don't just mean feel me physically, I mean . . . feel *me*. Who I am. Who *he* will be." Tash moved closer to Elory. "Let me show you."

They sat on a bed between the curtains of beads. The candles burned in their alcove, wax dripping. The hookah smoke flowed through the pleasure pit. On the bed beside them, two women lay asleep, drooling, deep in the slumber of hintan. Elory didn't know the hour. There was no sunlight here, only the candlelight and the light in Tash's eyes.

Slowly, the dark-haired pleasurer ran her fingers along Elory's body, trailing them up her legs, up her back, toward her ears, along her shoulders.

"See?" Tash whispered. "I want to explore you. To know who you are. To see all the little places where you're sensitive." She let her fingertips stroke Elory's earlobes, then move down her neck. "I want to know you. That is what lovemaking is. Any brute can thrust into a woman, and any woman can grab a man's stick and make him feel good for a moment. That's not art. What we do, my little pet, is *music*."

Tash's hands moved down her body, and Elory closed her eyes. She had to admit that it felt good. She had never loved anyone before, not a man or a woman. In the pits of bitumen, who had time or strength for such pursuits? Yet now, as Tash stroked her, new feelings awakened in Elory, then grew inside her, trickling across her body—her legs, her lips, everywhere that Tash touched. The woman's fingers were indeed the fingers of a musician, playing her every part, igniting her, lighting the notes upon her.

"I don't know if I can do this." Elory opened her eyes. "I feel so clumsy."

Tash nodded. "You are. Your hands are used to hauling buckets, not awakening fire in flesh. Try again."

Elory nodded and tried again, running her fingers along Tash, but she felt like a lumbering brute who had stumbled upon a lyre, unable to produce any chord.

"Oh, stars above." Tash groaned. "You really are useless. I'm doomed. Doomed! The seraphim will have my hide. Have you ever even kissed a man?"

Elory shook her head.

Tash rolled her eyes. "They sent me an idiot." She scuttled closer. "I have a lot to teach you. When you kiss a man, you have to start slowly. Not just leap onto him. First . . . you kiss his ear. Nibble it a bit. Blow on it. Move down to kiss his neck, just brushing your lips along, so lightly. Just like this. Slowly. Tease him until he's mad with desire, but let him linger." Tash moved her lips up, whispering now. "Kiss the corner of his mouth, and then—"

Elory kissed her, just a peck on the lips, that was all, then pulled back, blushing. "I'm sorry." She gasped. "I don't know what I did."

Tash laughed. "Gave me a little bit of hope."

That night—at least, Elory thought it was night—the pipes and hookahs were laid down, and the pleasurers slept. Some lay on mattresses, others on the floor, and some slept sprawled across piles of pillows.

A few times, bells rang on the doorway, and a seraph or two wandered in, sometimes drunk, always loud. They never lingered. They chose a woman. Sometimes they took her back to their chambers, sometimes they bedded her right here in the den, and the cries and groans kept Elory awake until the men were done, until the slaves all slept again.

Not that she would have slept much even in silence. Her mind was a storm. Over and over, she kept seeing it—her mother dying, torn apart. Over and over, she kept remembering them—her father and brother, wondering if she'd ever see them again. Over and over, she kept feeling it—Tash's hands and lips upon her, the fire it had kindled in her, that she couldn't extinguish. How could she hope to sleep when her world collapsed around her?

Finally the stream of seraphim died down. Elory lay on the bed, waiting for more to arrive. Yet they never did. Tash slept to one side, and two other pleasurers slept on a mattress a few feet away, one of them snoring, the other drooling. The candles burned low and guttered out, and darkness filled the pit.

Finally, when nothing stirred, when all the world was stillness and shadows, Elory rose to her feet.

She left the bed.

She tiptoed in the darkness.

I still wear a collar and I can't shift into a dragon. But my legs are free. I can walk, climb, run.

She inched between the sleeping women, hands held out before her.

I will find her—my half sister. She swallowed the lump in her throat. *I will find the child my father created before he met my mother, the child who had grown up in this palace, the child of Queen Kalafi.*

Tears filled Elory's eyes as she found the exit, as she crept into a corridor, as she climbed a dark staircase that rose into the ziggurat.

I will find my sister. I will find Meliora.

JAREN

Night had fallen, and the toil of the day ended, yet the Draco constellation did not shine above. Not in this distant land. Not in the land of Tofet in the empire of Saraph. Not here in the dust, captive, forgotten, in the dark.

The huts of Tofet spread around him, simple clay dwellings, their walls a mix of mud, straw, and bitumen. Unpaved roads spread between them, and the stench of tar rose on the wind; the pit lay only a mile south. Just over the horizon, only a quick flight for a chariot or dragon, rose the City of Kings—the jewel of the empire, a wondrous realm of soaring temples, golden palaces, lush gardens, wonder and wealth. Here in its shadow lurked the underbelly of Saraph, surrounded by walls, the realm of a broken nation, of dragons collared into human forms. Of death. Of loss. Only shadows and no starlight to light them.

"But we still remember you, stars of Requiem," Jaren whispered, kneeling in the dust. "The memories of your light have passed through the generations. As my forebears worshipped you in Requiem, as our first king prayed to your light thousands of years ago, so do I pray." He looked up toward the sky, seeing only the stars of a different land. "Requiem! May our wings forever find your sky."

For thousands of years, he knew, the Vir Requis had sung that prayer. It never had more meaning, Jaren thought. Throughout all of Requiem's wars—against the demons, the sphinxes, the griffins, the phoenixes, the thousands of others who had risen to slay Requiem—the Vir Requis could always look up, see their sky above. Yet now that very sky was lost. Those very stars, which had blessed Requiem for millennia, shone across the horizon, invisible to him.

"But your light still shines within me." Jaren clutched his amulet, a simple piece of tin. Upon it he had engraved a constellation shaped as a dragon. Brightest among its stars was the dragon's eye, Issari's Star, its light woven from the soul of an ancient princess of Requiem. "I still remember you, stars of Requiem. I will find your sky."

"The stars are only a myth." The voice rose behind him, hoarse, torn with old pain. "Requiem itself is only a myth. Only a story slaves tell to cling to a fool's hope."

Jaren rose to his feet, turned around, and saw his son walking between the clay huts toward him. Manacles encircled Vale's ankles, the chain between them only a foot long. The collar circled his neck. His tunic was ragged, reduced to little more than a loincloth. Ugly, charred lashes striped his chest, arms, and shoulders, and bruises covered his face.

The seraphim had beaten him. They would have burned him in Malok had Meliora not climbed into the bull, aborting the day's burnings. Yet Vale looked little better than a burn victim, a flicker of life in a raw shell.

Such pain filled Jaren that even the memory of starlight could no longer soothe him.

My firstborn daughter lives in a great palace, pampered, surrounded by gold and jewels. My son barely clings to life, and all his hope is lost.

Jaren lowered his head. The memories seemed too great to bear. Twenty-eight years ago, he had worked in the palace, a house slave, a young man to tend to the queen in her pool of heated, salted water. A young man to brush her hair, paint her nails. A young man she had taken into her arms, had loved.

A young man who had given her a daughter. A young man she had cast out into the heat, the dust, the agony of Tofet.

A young man who had grown into this old, weary man. A father mourning. For lost Meliora, unaware of her heritage, raised as a princess of Saraph. For lost Elory, kidnapped, taken to serve the cruel Ishtafel. For Vale, his son, perhaps more lost than even his sisters.

"You must believe." Jaren hobbled toward his son. "That the stars still shine beyond the horizon. That King's Column, our most sacred pillar, still rises from the ruin. That we can return to Requiem someday. That we can be saved."

They stood together on the dusty road outside their hut— the home that only the two of them now shared.

Vale's eyes were as chips of heated stone. "We've waited for five hundred years in Saraph for salvation. The stars have abandoned us, if they ever existed at all. No savior will rise to lead us back to Requiem. We must save ourselves. Or die." He took a step closer to Jaren. "Father, I leave before dawn to work in the city. The masters will transfer me. I will work on the new Temple of Ishtafel, hauling limestone in my claws." His eyes blazed with fire. "I will fly as a dragon."

Jaren had not thought it possible to feel more pain—not with his life shattered. Yet now new fear flowed through him. He gripped his son's arms.

"Vale, you must always obey the masters." His eyes dampened to see the wounds still covering his son. "You were saved once from the bronze bull. If you defy the seraphim again, they—"

"—will kill me." Vale nodded. "Good. Maybe I want to die fighting. Better than this. Better than to die as a slave in chains. But no, Father. I won't die." A chaotic smile stretched across his lips. "I must stay alive for Elory. To save her."

Jaren stared into his son's eyes, and he saw the desperation there, and iciness filled his belly.

"Son," Jaren whispered. "You cannot do this. You cannot hope to fly to her, to find her in the palace, to save her. They will kill you, son. I cannot lose you." Jaren dropped to his knees, shaking. "I already lost a wife. I already lost my daughters to captivity in the palace. I cannot lose you too."

Vale only stared at him, eyes hard. "You already lost me," he whispered. "We've all been lost. Always. Since we were born into this cursed land. But I will not fade into shadows. The fire of Requiem will rise again . . . one last time."

Fists clenched, the young man turned and walked away.

"Son!" Jaren cried. He tried to follow. His legs were too weary, too old. He tripped. He pushed himself up, elbows bloody. "Vale!"

He tried to find his son, but Vale disappeared into the labyrinth of huts, dirt roads, and chained slaves. Gone into shadow. Gone to fire.

Finally Jaren could walk no more, his legs too bent, too weak from a lifetime of toil. He fell to his knees in the dirt between the huts, despair coursing through him.

I lost my wife. I lost my daughters. Do I lose you now too, my son?

Chest shuddering, Jaren raised his head. He had reached the edge of the camp. From here, when he stared at the horizon, he could just make out the tip of the dynasty's ziggurat. The rest of the City of Kings lay hidden, but the ziggurat soared, its top coated in platinum, gleaming, displaying the Eye of Saraph—an eye within a sunburst. Always watching over him.

You're there in that palace, my daughters. You fly there now too, my son.

Jaren raised his eyes to the heavens, and he prayed, and he did not know if any gods heard, if any light but the light of Saraph could ever shine upon him.

KALAFI

She lay in her heated pool in her chamber of gold and jewels, the candles burning low.

Her slave blood is rising. Kalafi winced as the burn across her belly flared, even in the salted water. *Already Meliora sees the slaves as her people.*

Kalafi's memories rose like the steam. Long centuries of enduring her husband in bed, praying every year for another child, a child that never came. For centuries, her husband had railed against her, had railed against Ishtafel, claiming that his son had sucked Kalafi's womb dry.

How he raged!

For so many years, King Harash—her husband, her brother—had sunken into his wine, his stupor, his hatred of his son, his hatred of his wife's womb that would not bear him a daughter, a woman to mate with his son, to preserve the blood.

Lying in her pool, her walls of opulence glittering around her, Kalafi clenched her fists.

"But my womb was not barren. Your seed was as weak as your mind."

It was here in this very chamber. In this pool. Nearly thirty years ago, the slave Jaren had tended to her, a young man, handsome, tall for a slave, and she had taken him into the water. She had loved him. She had fostered his seed in her womb, growing a daughter, the daughter her husband could not give her.

Lying now in the same pool, the water soothing her wound that would not heal, Kalafi passed her hands down her legs, remembering his touch, the forbidden pleasure of slave flesh. She knew that her son took slaves into his bed, that many of the seraphim did, plucking beauties from Tofet and hiding them in the den beneath the ziggurat. Kalafi had succumbed to her temptation just that one time, then cast the man aside, let him grow weary and old in Tofet, to die far from her sight.

But her husband . . .

A smile rose on Kalafi's lips.

"I wanted to *see* you die."

She inhaled sharply, remembering how wonderful it had felt, seeing the king eat the poisoned fig, hearing him choke, watching him fall to the floor. A child in her womb—a slave's child—Kalafi had laughed as her husband died, and she had spat on his body. She had taken his throne. And now, under her reign, Saraph rose to its greatest glory—the empire's last enemies defeated, the world theirs, Edinnu reborn in exile.

Kalafi rose from the pool. Her wound, the ugly burn she had endured falling from Edinnu, bubbled on her side, rising like a red serpent from her waist to her ribs. The pain was a dull throb now, but she knew that within hours, it would flare again, never healing, fading only when she soaked in the hot water again. Alone, her slaves dismissed, she stepped out of her pool and walked toward the balcony.

She stood between the gilded columns, naked in the night, the warm spring breeze drying her. From the height of her ziggurat, she gazed at her city. Lanterns burned in the night, a field of stars, their light falling upon the Paths of the Gods, the temples and palaces, and the desert beyond. There, in the land of Tofet on the horizon, he still lived. She had seen him at the bronze bull.

"Jaren," she whispered.

Kalafi winced.

She too had wanted a daughter—a woman to breed with Ishtafel, to give her an heir of pure blood. Yet now the blood of weredragons flowed through Meliora. The girl did not know her heritage; she thought that her father was the fallen Harash, that the king had choked on a fig, not that Kalafi had pumped the fig fill of hemlock.

"But something inside you calls out," Kalafi whispered. "You saw the slaves . . . and you saw yourself. You burned yourself to save them."

Kalafi's fists clenched. She spun around from the balcony, pulled on a muslin robe embroidered with golden sunbursts, and strapped a dagger to her side. She left her chamber.

She walked through the palace, still wet, water dripping from her wings onto the mosaic floor. Oil lanterns glowed on the wall, illuminating ivory statues and murals of the gods. Finally she reached a door of giltwood. Armored guards knelt before her, and Kalafi stepped into the room.

She walked between jeweled vases and statues and stood above the bed, staring down at her slumbering daughter.

A rich, embroidered blanket covered Meliora, but Kalafi could see the burn marks stretching up to her exposed shoulders—the burns endured in the bronze bull to save her precious slaves.

You are beautiful, daughter, Kalafi thought. *Your hair is a river of gold, your lips are ripe fruit, your wings are clouds in sunrise. I thought that my purity would sear away the slave's blood, that you would be as I am . . . yet his blood still taints your heart.*

Standing above the bed, Kalafi drew her dagger.

Meliora stirred in her sleep, mumbling something about fires that burn, about pain and song.

"I must do this, daughter," Kalafi whispered. "If the slave blood spreads through you, one day you will discover their magic. The magic to become a dragon. To rise against me. To burn us all."

Meliora kicked in her sleep, brow furrowed. "Run, Kira! Run, Talana! I saved you . . . I saved you . . ."

With a deep breath, Kalafi raised her dagger above her sleeping daughter.

"Mother," Meliora whispered, eyes still closed. "You saved me, Mother. You saved me from the fire. I love you. I love you so much. Forgive me, Mother."

Tears fled Kalafi's eyes. She dropped the knife. It thumped onto the bed.

I love you too, my daughter.

The tears streamed, and Kalafi could not stop the memories—her slave knowing her, her husband dying at her hands, her daughter born, sweetest Meliora, smaller than the other babes yet just as beautiful.

"I will keep you pure," Kalafi whispered. "I will cleanse the weakness from you."

She turned away. She left her daughter's chamber. As she walked down the corridor, Kalafi's hands balled into fists, and rage simmered in her belly.

Meliora would have to see that slaves were unworthy of sympathy, that they had no hearts, no feelings, that they were barely better than beasts. At dawn, Kalafi would make the creatures work harder, doubling their workload. She would insist that the weak be culled. That the old and frail were burned in pits of fire.

"You wanted to save them, my child," Kalafi whispered. "But you will see them ground into the dust like the worms that they are."

ELORY

She tiptoed through the shadowy ziggurat, unchained for the first time in her life, holding her scroll before her like a shield.

As a child, Elory would hop at night between the huts where the slaves lived, as fast as she could move in her hobbles. She'd stretch out her arms, pretending to be a dragon, a magnificent beast flying through canyons. The thousands of huts had spread out, forming a great labyrinth, yet Elory had never gotten lost, not even navigating the darkness for hours.

Here, the innards of the ziggurat formed a maze far more convoluted.

She walked up a staircase—it was still strange to walk on stairs, which she had never seen in Tofet. Lanterns glowed on the walls, illuminating murals depicting seraphim battling sea serpents. With every flicker of the lamps, Elory started, sure that the seraphim on the walls were real, that they were about to strike.

Finally the staircase emerged from the underground, and Elory found herself walking along a colonnade. A wall rose to her right, built of sandstone bricks cobbled together with the bitumen she had spent her life hauling. More murals appeared here, showing scenes of tigers, hippos, and birds of every kind among rushes and palm trees. To her left stretched a portico of columns, exposing the open night. Between the limestone pillars, she saw a dark stream, lush gardens, and the lights of the city.

Elory paused and stared.

Several seraphim guards stood in the dark gardens, still, silent, facing the city. They did not see her, all their attention focused outward.

I can escape, she thought. *I can sneak between them, disappear into the city, find my family again.*

Her hand trembled, crinkling her scroll so loudly she thought the guards would hear. Her heart thudded even louder, pounding in her ears. And why should she not escape? She was small and fast. She could vanish into shadows in the night, leave this place. She perhaps could not escape Saraph itself; a great wall rose in the north, blocking her passage to the distant ruins of Requiem, and only one slave—the legendary Lumen—had ever scaled that wall and lived. But Elory could still flee the ziggurat at least, still find her family in Tofet.

And leave my sister? Elory thought.

She closed her eyes.

She had never seen Meliora before, the fabled Princess of Saraph, daughter of Queen Kalafi. Daughter of Elory's own father, the humble slave. But she had heard tales of Meliora a thousand times. Her father would whisper of her at night, making Elory vow not to tell, not to repeat the story, telling her that even Meliora herself did not know that she was half Vir Requis. The seraphim soldiers in Tofet would speak of Meliora too, singing her praises, worshipping her name, calling her a deity of beauty and endless piety.

"She doesn't know that I'm her father," Jaren would whisper to Elory at night, telling her tales of her famous half sister. "Meliora thinks that her father was the late King Harash. She doesn't know that she's half Vir Requis, and she doesn't have the magic to become a dragon. But someday, Elory . . . someday a child of Requiem will sit upon the throne of Saraph. Someday your sister will rule the world."

And now I must find that sister, Elory thought. *I must tell her who she is. I must beg her for aid. Not just for me. For my father. For my brother. For everyone suffering in chains.* She turned away from the gardens, from the path to freedom. *I will not escape while my people suffer, while I can find them a savior.*

She kept walking, found another staircase, and climbed.

She found herself walking down a dark corridor, leaving the hot night air behind her. Lanterns glowed on the walls, illuminating polished tiles. Engravings covered the walls, depicting scenes of seraphim slaying dragons, felling the halls of Requiem, and bearing collared slaves back into Saraph. In the land of Tofet, it was a tragic tale—the fall of Requiem, the breaking of a proud nation. Here, in the palace of Saraph, the story appeared heroic, the engraved seraphim handsome and proud, the dragons rabid and cruel, the slaves hook-nosed and hunched over, ugly demons thrashing in their collars like beasts.

At the sight of the engravings, Elory's heart wrenched.

Requiem is real, she thought. *It has to be real, if even the seraphim engraved it. We will fly there again, free, no collars on our necks. We will find our sky.*

As she kept walking down the corridor, the scenes continued to roll across the walls, showing piles of dead dragons and triumphant flights of flaming chariots. After walking for a hundred yards, near the end of the scene, Elory saw an engraving of a towering column. It soared all the way to the ceiling, dead dragons lying at its base. If engraved to scale, it must have soared hundreds of feet tall in real life.

Elory paused and stared.

"King's Column," she whispered.

This was only an engraving, of course, paling in comparison to the true King's Column from the tales. In the stories her father told her, King's Column rose in the heart of Requiem, the pillar around which the kingdom had been built. They said that King Aeternum himself, founding father of Requiem, had raised this column in a birch forest five thousand years ago, that since that time the kingdom of Requiem had worshiped it. They said that the Draco constellation itself, the stars Elory could not see from this land, blessed the column, that it would stand so long as Vir Requis lived in the world. Indeed, even in this engraving in the halls of Saraph, seraphim were attacking the column with lances and arrows, unable to topple it, even as lesser columns lay shattered at its feet.

"So long as a single Vir Requis lives, the column will stand," Elory whispered. She hesitated, then gingerly placed a hand against the engraved column. The limestone was cold and rough, not polished marble like the true column, but she imagined that she was touching the real King's Column, that she felt its magic flow through her.

You are blessed, child, a voice seemed to whisper within her. *You are a child of starlight. We watch over you from the stars. Always, Elory. Always.*

Elory bit her lip, eyes damp, hand against the column. She felt the ancient magic, a warm, soothing feeling that flowed through her. Her collar kept that magic at bay, not letting her summon it, but it filled her nonetheless like bitumen lying under the surface, waiting to be drawn. Even here, centuries after the fall of Requiem, captive and collared, the old magic filled Elory.

A magic of dragons.

"Requiem!" she whispered. "May our wings forever find your sky."

"Slave!" The voice boomed down the corridor. "What are you doing there? Where is your night pass?"

Elory spun away from the wall, heart leaping into her throat. She gasped to see two seraphim guards marching toward her. Their sandals clattered against the floor's polished tiles, and their halos' light reflected against their burnished breastplates and helmets. Their shields displayed the Eye of Saraph, and their spears dipped to point toward her.

Struggling not to faint from fear, Elory raised her scroll. She held it before her, her own weapon, the only weapon that could save her in the bowels of the ziggurat.

She knelt before the seraphim, lowered her head, and held out the scroll.

"Here is my pass, my lords! It bears the seal of Prince Ishtafel himself. He commanded me to bear this scroll to his sister—unopened."

She pulled back the scroll, afraid the guards would grab it. If they demanded to read it, they would read Ishtafel's orders that she report to the pleasure pit.

Thank goodness you don't know how to read, Tash, Elory thought. Unable to read the contents, the pleasurer had seen no point in breaking the seal. Perhaps, with this seal intact, the scroll still rolled up, Elory might just make her way through.

The soldiers stared at the seal, and their eyes darkened. Their wings stiffened.

"Prince Ishtafel's seal," whispered one.

Elory nodded. "I must deliver this scroll to Princess Meliora. Will you allow me to continue on my way, my lords?"

The seraphim glanced at each other, fear in their eyes. They nodded. "Go!"

They continued walking, passed by her, and quickly vanished into shadows.

Elory breathed out a shaky sigh of relief. She trembled, and cold sweat dripped down her spine. She had almost lost her life. She had almost lost the hope of Requiem.

We need a savior. We need one who can remove our collars like Tash removed my shackles—who can save me, who can save a nation. We need you, Meliora, the sister I've never met.

Standing here in darkness, alone, afraid, lost in the heart of her enemy, Elory raised her eyes and stared up at the dark ceiling. And there she saw it. Tears flooded her eyes.

"The stars of Requiem," she whispered.

It was only an engraving, an image of the northern sky. The Draco constellation was small, barely visible, a few stars worked into the stone, filled with silver, their shine dull. One constellation among a hundred. Her stars.

Our stars.

Our sky.

Elory raised her chin and kept walking, new strength in her heart, and as she walked she made a vow to herself. A vow she would cherish like the dream of Requiem.

"I will not just save myself, sparing my body from the cruelty of Ishtafel." The stars seemed to shine in her eyes, perhaps only her tears. "I will save all of you. I will save Requiem. We will see that sky again, and we will fly under those stars as dragons."

She kept walking through the palace until she found another slave, an old woman moving through the halls with a basket of laundry. The elder gave Elory directions, and she walked on, asking again a few stories up, this time from a boy slave who was sweeping the floor. In the shadows of night, as the seraphim slept, the slaves were everywhere—washing, dusting, polishing.

"Remember Requiem," she whispered to them.

They nodded, afraid, glanced around for their masters, then answered the prayer. "Remember Requiem."

As she passed by a window, Elory saw that she was so high up now that she could see Tofet, just a hint on the horizon. A shadow. A darkness where only the odd candle lit the night.

Remember Requiem, my people, she thought, staring at them, at the hundreds of thousands crying out in chains.

Already she saw trails of lights, clay lanterns held in trembling hands—the slaves leaving their huts, heading to their work. Dawn was only two hours away, and then the seraphim too would wake, filling the ziggurat's halls.

She turned away from the window. She kept walking until she reached a golden door where stood two seraphim guards.

Meliora's chamber.

Elory raised her scroll toward the sentries, showing them the seal, her amulet of power.

You gave me this seal, Ishtafel, so that I could enter the pleasure pit, so that I could train to pleasure you, Elory thought. *But you gave me the key to every chamber in this palace.*

The guards stepped back and Elory entered the chamber of her princess, her mistress, her sister.

JAREN

In the darkness of night, no moon in the sky, Jaren walked through the tortured land of Tofet.

The towering limestone walls, topped with seraphim guards. The huts of slaves. The bitumen pits where his wife had died, where his daughter had labored. The quarries where his son toiled every day, back almost breaking. The refineries and fields where bricks were made, the fields where slaves struggled to raise crops from the dry land—crops they would never eat. A land of misery, the Abyss risen onto the earth, a prison surrounded by hosts of seraphim, an enemy they could not slay.

A land of tears, Jaren thought. *The land where I lost my wife, where I saw my daughter kidnapped by the demon.*

He grimaced to think of Ishtafel. In the lore of Requiem, he was a tyrant, the seraph who had destroyed Requiem, who had slain a million of their kind, who had taken myriads here to slavery. In the lore of Saraph, he was a hero, the noble and handsome warrior who had conquered the world.

"And to you, my beloved Kalafi . . . he is a son."

As he walked through the darkness, Jaren lowered his head. All his life, he had tried to give hope to the children of Requiem, to cling to that hope, to cling to morality, to decency, to joy—even here, even in chains. Yet that day . . . that day long ago, he had shamed his people. That shame still lived inside him, even now.

I loved you, Kalafi, and I will always hate myself for it.

Jaren kept walking, and finally he saw the bridge ahead, spanning the Te'ephim River. The edge of Tofet. Beyond that arching stone bridge it lay—Shayeen, the City of Kings. The place where their bricks, bitumen, all their labor went. The great wonder of the world. The place that was now forbidden to him. The place where he had first met her—the first woman he had loved.

He glanced toward the sky. By the position of the stars, it was midnight, a week before the summer solstice. Just another night, not a festival to any god or hero. A forgotten night in the calendar. The same night he came here every year.

It was time.

Chains clanking, he stepped onto the bridge and walked, the water flowing below him. The bridge was wide enough to let twenty men walk abreast, built of sturdy stone. At its far side stood walls and towers and seraphim upon them, but Jaren would not walk that far, perhaps never again. When he reached the center of the bridge, he paused.

A figure was walking across the bridge from the opposite bank, approaching him.

The figure was tall and slender, clad in a dark robe and hood. It held no lamp but walked in darkness, barely visible, head lowered. A shadow among shadows, appearing only when it blocked a distant city light. Finally the figure reached him at the center of the stone bridge, raised its hooded head, and revealed two gleaming eyes, the pupils shaped as sunbursts.

Jaren bowed his head. "Another year, my lady. Another night of whispers."

The figure pulled back the hood, unveiling a fair, ageless face, the skin a golden hue, the hair long and flowing and the color of spring dawn. Her halo shone like fireflies, and her eyes seemed ancient—eyes that had gazed upon distant realms beyond the stars—but her face was smooth, eternal, the face of a statue, pure but cold and timeless.

"I've come to you again," Queen Kalafi said, voice cold and smooth as a dagger slipping between shoulder blades. "All year, I keep you chained across the river. This night you pull my own chain, dragging me here."

"I hold no chain, only truth," Jaren said.

"Truth can be a stronger chain than links of iron. The truth of our daughter has chained my hands for twenty-seven of these nights." Fire gleamed in her eyes. "I felt a flicker of affection for you once—a few moments ago for me, half a lifetime ago for you—but now I feel only hatred. I should slay you now. I should slay you and your children, Elory and Vale— yes, I know their names—and bury this truth in the sand."

Your son already murdered my wife, Jaren thought, the grief twisting inside him. *Your son already kidnapped my daughter. What would be death to me now?*

Jaren nodded. "You could kill me, my lady. You could have slain me countless times, as your son slays those women he beds. Many times, I've seen Ishtafel pluck a maiden from Tofet, plant his seed inside her for his pleasure, then discard her body—sometimes a body gravid with child—back in our land. Yet you, my queen, still meet me here every year, the man you took into your bed. Your son is cruel but yours is a gentle heart."

She sneered and drew a wavy dagger from her robes. "And your heart will lie at my feet if you anger me. I suggest you do not."

Jaren smiled thinly. "Now that the pleasantries are out of the way, how is she? Give me news of my daughter."

"Meliora is the same as always." Kalafi snorted. "Weak. Addle-headed. No more sensible than a pup. And yet . . . different this year. I showed her a glimpse of the truth. A burning in the bronze bull, though I had to abort the ceremony when she stepped into the flames herself. Rebellion brews in her heart where once only softness dwelled. Perhaps this dagger should carve out Meliora's heart as well. That heart is tainted with your blood."

She needs no dagger, Jaren thought. The Queen of Saraph needed only her words to cut his heart. Whenever she spoke of Meliora, Jaren grieved.

My daughter.

In the darkness of night, the memories of a different night flooded him, a night almost three decades ago. His back had not been crooked, his shoulders not stopped from years in the quarries. His face had not been lined, and no beard had adorned his face. He had been young, strong, perhaps even handsome, a house servant in the palace of the queen. In chambers of endless wealth, the walls and floors themselves made of precious metals and gems, he had tended to the queen. Gently washing her in her warm pool, treating the wound on her side, rubbing her feet, feeding her grapes, a servant to see to all her needs.

And those needs grew.

Her husband's heart was still beating when Kalafi had taken Jaren into her arms, into the hot pool where she soaked. She had stripped off his clothes, leaving him in but his collar. In the salty water, they had made love, her head tossed back, her fingernails digging into him, her wound sticky against him. She had cried out in her pleasure, a beastly sound, like the roar of a dragon. Jaren had closed his eyes, imagining that he himself was a dragon, flying home, flying far to Requiem, to old pillars among ancient trees.

But she had taken everything from him. She had taken the daughter he had planted in her belly. She had taken all his hope, all his dreams, all comforts he might have had in her palace. She had slapped him in chains, discarded him, tossed him into Tofet, letting him keep only his life—perhaps a curse, perhaps her cruelest act of all.

He looked back at the queen who now stood before him, robed on the bridge. She had not changed, still fair and cold as always, while he was a wreck of a man now, haggard, stooped, only in his fifties but feeling twice as old.

"Every year, I come here to ask about my daughter," he said to his queen. "I ask the same this night, but this year, I ask about a different daughter. I ask about Elory."

Elory. A light in his life. The girl who gave Jaren new hope.

I married a woman in Tofet, and she is gone now, slain by Ishtafel. Elory is new life, new light. Elory is a great star in my sky.

Kalafi tilted her head. "Elory is stuck where she belongs, laboring in the bitumen pits, and—"

"My lady, Ishtafel has plucked her from the pit. Elory now serves in the palace . . . serves him. The prince. The man who slew her mother before her eyes. My queen, I beg you." Jaren fell to his knees before her. "I bow before you, and I plead. Give Elory back to me. You have Meliora; let me have my other daughter."

Kalafi narrowed her eyes, considering, calculating. Finally she barked a laugh. "The hypocrisy of weredragons! You thrusted your manhood between my thighs, yet when your daughter craves the manhood of my son, you would refuse her?"

"My daughter craves nothing of him!" Jaren said, unable to curb the rage from entering his voice. He forced himself to breathe deeply, to calm himself. "My queen, please. Elory is a tender child, not yet twenty. She watched Ishtafel slay her friend, then slay her mother before her eyes, and now Ishtafel would . . . would do to her as he would, then discard her body too. Please, my queen. If not for Elory's sake, for mine."

She raised an eyebrow. "And what of my son? Should I ignore his wishes over yours? Should I deprive him of a play thing?" She tilted her head. "Or would you rather Ishtafel take another from among the slaves? That your precious child would be safe, but another's daughter endure him? I thought you nobler than that."

Jaren lowered his head. "All nobility flees before the bonds of family. You know this, my queen. That is why Meliora now lives in splendor. That is why you stand here before me."

"I stand here before you because Meliora is my daughter, because you are her father." Kalafi's lips peeled back into a lurid, carnivorous grin. "But Elory is nothing to me, born from a different woman's womb, and Ishtafel is my son."

Jaren did not want to use threats. Threatening a queen was a dangerous thing. But Elory needed him.

"And you will let me live?" he said. "You will let me, who knows the truth about Meliora, who could speak of her heritage, roam free among the slaves?"

She sneered at him, eyes narrowed. "You try to blackmail me while I hold a blade before you?"

"You could have thrust that blade countless times, my lady. But there is goodness to your heart. I've always seen it. Your heart is encased in iron and steel, and the yoke of your crown is as heavy as the yoke of a slave, but deep within you, the girl from Edinnu still sings. A seraph of righteousness. A seraph whom I once loved . . . who perhaps once loved me. Who perhaps still feels some lingering warmth toward this old, haggard slave."

"I feel nothing but disgust toward you. You are a filthy worm, a dirty creature, and I am ashamed of that night. Ashamed!" Her fists balled up, and she lowered her head. "But yes, Jaren. I loved the man you were. Thus is the curse of immortality—that I linger on, forever fair, watching you here every year . . . fading away, withering, dying before my eyes." She looked back up at him, eyes damp now, her fury gone, replaced with sadness. "Perhaps you're right, and my heart is still full of Edinnu's light and mercy. I would return Elory to you . . . but I cannot. I can no longer resist my son. Even I am frightful around him; he's become more powerful than I had ever imagined. He does as he would; I cannot control him, cannot take his toys from him, and Elory is his new toy. Beware, Jaren . . . he is becoming strong." Now fear filled Kalafi's eyes. "Ishtafel is a fire I cannot contain, and someday he will be stronger than I am. And he will grant you no mercy."

With that, the Queen of Saraph spun on her heel and walked away, leaving the bridge and returning to Shayeen.

Jaren remained standing on the bridge long after Kalafi vanished into the night.

All I have left is Vale, my son. Meliora—a daughter I've never met. Elory—a daughter I might never see again. He raised his eyes to the sky, imagining that he could see the Draco constellation there, the stars that did not shine here in the south, that ancient tales from the north spoke of in awe. *Please, stars of Requiem, if you can hear my prayers from here, grant Elory safety and grant her strength. Grant us all strength.*

Slowly Jaren turned, and slowly he walked away, leaving the bridge behind, returning to his hut. In only two or three hours, his labor would continue—a day of the whip, of the pickaxe, of sweat and tearing muscles under the cruel sun. For now, this night, he lay in darkness, thinking of starlight.

ELORY

When Elory stepped into the chamber, Meliora was already awake, sitting by the window, staring outside at the first light of dawn.

Surely the princess had heard the door open, had heard the guards announce Elory's entrance, had heard those guards leave and the door close again, and yet Meliora did not turn around, did not stir. She faced the light, staring between the columns of her balcony, her back to Elory.

The princess of Saraph was perhaps half Vir Requis, but she had the swan wings of a seraph. Those wings now draped across her back, dipping so that the tips rested on the floor. Meliora's hair flowed down between them, a waterfall of molten gold, topped with a thin halo. Elory could not see her sister's face, but she could see ugly burns stretching across her arm.

"My lady?" Elory whispered.

For a long time Meliora did not reply, only sat with her back to Elory, gazing out between the columns. The dawn's light rose, glowing around her like a second halo. Elory's heart quickened; soon the rest of the palace would awaken. What if Tash noticed her absence and reported it? What if Ishtafel heard? Elory stood still, pondering what to do. Should she speak again? Should she flee this chamber? Should she step forward, walk around Meliora, and face her?

She was still debating when finally Meliora spoke, her back still to Elory.

"You are a slave." Her voice was barely a whisper. "You are a weredragon."

Elory winced. She hated that word—weredragon. It was what the seraphim called her kind, what the enemies of Requiem had called her kind for thousands of years. She was Vir Requis, a proud child of Requiem, not a monster to kill or enslave. And yet how could she explain this to Meliora, to a woman who thought herself the purebred daughter of seraphim royalty?

"Yes," she simply replied. "I've come to—"

"You should leave. You're in danger here. No slave is safe around me."

Slowly, Meliora turned around, and for the first time in her life Elory gazed upon her sister's face.

Elory couldn't help it. She took a step back, heart thumping.

He lied. Her eyes watered. *My father lied. He lied to me. All my life, he lied to me, trying to comfort me, telling me I have a sister in the palace. Lying. Lying.*

Meliora of the Thirteenth Dynasty, Daughter of Queen Kalafi, Lady of Grace, Great of Praises, looked like the purest seraph, not a drop of Vir Requis in her.

Her cheekbones were high, her forehead tall, her skin pale gold. A noble face, the face of a goddess, immortal, impossibly fair, ringed with soft light. No slave had such flawless skin, such full lips, such ageless grace. And yet more than anything, Meliora's eyes scared Elory.

Seraph eyes.

The irises gleamed golden, shining with inner light, and her pupils were shaped as sunbursts. The eyes of immortality, the eyes of a fallen angel. Eyes that had never gazed up at the sky, seeking stars, had never stared down at the dust, seeking the shackles and blood.

"I . . ." Elory hesitated. "I've come to . . ."

To tell you that I'm your sister, she wanted to say. *To tell you that you're half Vir Requis, half "weredragon" as you call us. That the blood of a slave courses through you. That only you can break our shackles, raise Requiem, and lead us to our homeland.*

Yet she could say none of these things. She felt no more hope, only betrayal.

Lies. Lies.

"Why are you here?" Meliora rose to her feet and approached her, and an edge of despair entered her voice. "Didn't you hear what happened to my last slaves? How they nearly burned in the bull?"

Meliora towered above Elory, a foot taller. Standing before her, her head stubbly, her frame so small, Elory felt like nothing but a slave again, just a slave before a seraph mistress.

Yet here Elory stood, and she would not flee. Perhaps this woman was not her sister. But she was still sister to Ishtafel, to the man who would bed Elory, break her, strangle her if she displeased him. Meliora was, perhaps, still a soul who could help.

I still need her help. I need to learn the truth. I need to learn who she is.

"I've come because I'm scared, my lady." Elory raised her head and met Meliora's gaze, staring into those sunburst eyes. "I've come because Ishtafel, your brother, slew my friend. Because he will slay me if I cannot pleasure him. I've come because all the palace speaks of how you saved two slaves from burning in the bull." Elory knelt and bowed her head. "I've come to pray to you, my lady, that you save me too."

Meliora stared down at her, eyes narrowed, the tension slowly leaving her eyes. Her face softened, and the seraph knelt. She placed a finger under Elory's chin and raised her face toward hers.

"Did he hurt you, child?" Meliora whispered.

Suddenly Elory couldn't stop her tears from falling.

He killed my friend! she wanted to say. *He murdered my mother! He threatened to rape me! He destroyed my entire kingdom, and he placed my people in chains! He hurt me in ways that you cannot imagine, Meliora, in ways that you've never been hurt.*

But Elory only shook her head, tears streaming, silent, unable to speak.

The door opened behind them.

A seraph stepped into the room, his light falling upon them.

"I did not hurt her," Ishtafel said, smiling thinly. "But I will. Oh, sweet sister . . . I will."

Daniel Arenson

MELIORA

Her brother entered the room, and Meliora froze, kneeling by the slave.

For an instant, as Ishtafel loomed above her, she did not see the brother she had grown up with, laughed with, sung with, the brother who had taught her to play dice, to dance, to fly. She did not see her beloved Ish, the man she had always seen as a hero.

She saw the conqueror.

She saw the warlord who had smitten kingdoms, destroying Requiem and the giants and a hundred nations between them.

She saw the man they said kidnapped slaves from Tofet, strangled them in his bed, and tossed the corpses down for their comrades to see and fear.

Fire burned in his eyes, white and gold, and in them Meliora saw the fall of Requiem, the burning lands of Hakan Teer, the crumbling realms of Fe'an, the cries of millions. A breaking world, shattering under his wrath.

I was lied to, Meliora thought. All her life—deceived. Wrapped in silk. Hidden from what they did—from the cruelty of her mother, from the death that flowed from her brother's hands. All her life—sheltered. All her life—lies. Nothing but lies.

Slowly, she rose to her feet. She was five hundred years younger than him, countless times weaker, a mere girl in the presence of a god of light. Yet she met his gaze, and she spoke clearly.

"You will not touch her."

Ishtafel stared at her a moment longer, eyes narrowed, flaming, seething with his wrath. And then his face softened, and he laughed. His laughter claimed him. He tossed back his head, surrendering to it. It was a horrible sound. Somehow worse even than his anger. The young, bald slave scurried behind Meliora like a pup hiding from a larger dog behind its mistress's legs.

"Sweetest sister." Ishtafel shook his head and wiped a tear from his eyes. "Do you think I'm like Mother? That you can stop me from burning a slave in the bronze bull? Mother loves you, Meliora, and she has always pampered you, has always surrendered to your whims. But Mother fought one war—a war against the gods, a war she lost." Ishtafel took a step closer. "I've slain millions. I ground nations to the dust under my heel, and I showed them no pity. What makes you think I would pity this slave who defied me? I sent the wench to the pleasure pits, thinking she cared to learn how to service me, yet I find her here hiding behind your skirt. She will pay for this crime."

"Crime?" Meliora refused to look away, though her innards trembled. She was young, but she would show him that she was no mere girl, that she too was a ruler, strong enough to resist him. She had defied her mother; she could defy him. "What crime did the girl commit? Trying to stop you from claiming her body, from bedding her, from . . . from defiling her? Trying to stop you from strangling her and tossing her body back to Tofet?"

"She's a slave!" Ishtafel shouted, voice ringing across the room. Birds fled outside. "A weredragon! You speak as if they feel, as if they deserve mercy. They're animals." He reached out, fast as a striking asp, and gripped her arm, digging his fingers into the burns. "Look at you. Look at these wounds! You burned yourself to save a pair of the vermin. You've gone mad."

"I learned the truth!" Meliora shouted back. The pain flared across her. She felt like her brother could rip off her arm. "I learned the truth of what Mother does, what you do. That Tofet is not a land of singing, happy servants, that . . . that it's a land of bloodshed, chains, whips, disease. That . . . that they are human. That they can feel pain."

Ishtafel released her arm. He stepped back. His face softened, and his eyes became almost sad. "Sweetest sister." He sighed and turned toward the balcony, watching the birds in the distance. "The weredragons are like birds. Yes, perhaps they feel pain if you crush one in your fist. And yes, like birds, they can be pleasant pets, pretty and joyous." He turned back toward her. "But like the birds whose meat fills our bellies, like the birds whose feathers fill our pillows, they are ours. They exist to serve us. You would cry if you saw how chickens are slaughtered, Meliora. All children cry when they learn the pain that beasts suffer to serve men and women. They learn to outgrow it, and you will outgrow this. Soon the pain of slaves will be no more meaningful to you than the pain of birds or beasts."

Birds and beasts don't come into my chamber, begging for aid, Meliora thought. *Birds and beasts do not speak, do not pray to lost kingdoms. No man boasts of slaying birds and beasts in battle, yet engravings of Ishtafel's conquest of Requiem cover the halls of this palace.*

She looked at the slave. The girl knelt behind her, thin, almost famished, her skin bronzed from a lifetime in the sun, her shoulders still bent from the yoke, her ankles still chafed and scabbed from the shackles, her neck still collared.

Meliora knew what those collars did. As a child, over and over, she had heard Mother's warnings. Never remove their collars! Never, not even for a second, not unless a hundred soldiers with bows and lances gather.

They're weredragons, Meliora thought. *A race of people with magic. The magic to become dragons. Only the collars keep them in human forms. Without her collar right now, this very slave girl could become a dragon . . . could burn both me and Ishtafel to ash.*

Meliora tried to imagine the Requiem that had been. All the slaves in Saraph—six hundred thousand of them—flying free as dragons, wings hiding the sun, dragonfire casting its red light. A proud nation. Strong. A nation that could burn this city to the ground.

Suddenly Meliora felt something inside her, a tickling warmth, an urge to become a dragon. To spread not her feathered wings but creaking, leathern wings, to wear not muslin but a coat of scales, to roar out fire, to fly with her kin over forest and river, seeking marble columns. Again she thought of her recurring dreams, those dreams that emerged only on darkest nights—herself as a dragon, flying under strange stars, flying with the dragons of Requiem.

"They're not birds or beasts," she whispered. "They are dragons."

"They are slaves!" Ishtafel shouted. "Dragons? I slew the dragons! With an army of fire, I felled them from the sky. I made them what they are, miserable, wretches, worms—"

"Do not pride yourself on cruelty." Meliora stared into his eyes, speaking slowly. "There is no pride in conquest or bloodshed, only in kindness, only in decency. You enslave six hundred thousand. I saved two from the bull, and now I will save a third from you. That makes me worth more than all your wars could ever make you."

He raised his hand to strike her.

He had never raised his hand upon her before. All their lives, he had been her protector, her friend, her hero. As a child, when she would steal his armor and wear the oversized breastplate as a joke, he would laugh and muss her hair. When she had once placed a frog on his plate, horrifying their mother, he had roared with laughter.

Yet now he swung his hand toward her.

Meliora raised her own hand, blocking the blow.

Their arms slammed together, and the pain flared through her, but she wouldn't look away. She stared into his eyes.

"You've crossed a line, sister," he said.

"No." She shook her head slowly, hair swaying. "I did not cross a line but drew one in the sand. This woman is mine. You will not touch her. No more slaves will die at your hands. No more will they burn in the bull. I will burn down this palace, dying in the flames, to save only one."

Ishtafel's eyes narrowed the slightest. "There are other ways to die. Not only deaths in great pyres, but quiet deaths . . . as Father died."

"Father choked on a fig," she said.

Ishtafel snorted out a laugh. "Yes, child. A fig. You'll find that those who get in the dynasty's way . . . tend to find the bad figs."

Meliora's eyes stung. Her head spun. Her entire life was crashing around her, as surely as if the ziggurat itself could crumble.

My father . . . murdered?

Lies.

My entire life—lies.

She took a deep breath. *So I will fight this fire with fire.*

"Then let us play a game." She raised her chin. "You are fond of games, aren't you, brother? You are proud of your strength, your speed, your chariot of fire that charges into battle. I have a chariot too. Let us fly. Let us race our chariots across the city, from this ziggurat to the gates of the desert, to the land of Tofet. The wager will be this slave."

Ishtafel raised his eyebrow. "A chariot race?" He barked a laugh. "Sister, what makes you think I will play with you?"

She allowed a crooked smile to touch her lips, struggling to stop it from trembling. "Because you believe you are strong, fast, a hero. You believe that you can beat me. Race me, brother. Today. If I win, this girl is mine." She glanced at the girl who still hid behind her, then back at her brother. "She'll be my new slave, replacing those Mother stole from me."

Ishtafel took a step back, and amusement seemed to overshadow his rage. He smiled thinly, stared at the slave, and licked his lips. Then he returned his eyes to Meliora.

"And if I win," he said, "you will join me in a new feast in our grand hall. And before the lords and ladies of Saraph, you will kneel before me, and you will kiss my hand, and you will agree—with all to hear!—to be my wife, to bear me a son."

Meliora bared her teeth at him, sucking in air.

"Very well." She hissed. "We race. When the sun hits its zenith."

Ishtafel caressed her, running his fingers down her side to her hip, finally placing them on her belly. "This womb will bear a great prince of Saraph."

Meliora shoved his hand away. He nodded, winked at the slave behind Meliora, then left the chamber. His voice echoed from the hallway. "We ride at high noon!"

Meliora turned toward the slave. She knelt before her.

"What's your name?" she asked, voice soft.

The girl's trembling had ceased, and her eyes shone. "Elory. Daughter of Jaren."

Meliora took Elory's hands in hers and squeezed them. "You will be safe, Elory. I promise you. You will be safe with me."

The girl hesitated for a moment, then embraced Meliora. It shocked Meliora at first—slaves were never this brazen!—but perhaps . . . perhaps Meliora had to stop thinking of her as a slave. Perhaps she was a new friend.

"You're safe, child," she whispered, holding Elory in her arms. "You're safe."

Yet as she held the girl, Meliora wondered. Ishtafel was the greatest rider in Saraph, a man who had led hosts of chariots to war. Was Elory truly safe, or would the girl sing in the bull on Meliora's wedding day?

VALE

For the first time in his life, Vale was going to turn into a dragon.

Dawn rose around him across Shayeen, glinting off the platinum crests of obelisks, the gilded capitals of temples' columns, and the ziggurat that rose in the distance, soaring above the city. Though he had toiled all his life in the quarries, carving the bricks to build this glory, Vale had never seen the City of Kings. It was a place of wonder, of might, of magic.

Yet it paled in comparison to the magic inside him.

Since before he could remember, Vale had worn a collar infused with a seraph curse, holding his magic at bay. He now stood in a construction site, columns rising around him. Scaffoldings clung to the pillars, and slaves toiled across the site, digging, chipping, mortaring, climbing. Seraph slave drivers surrounded Vale, armed with whips, arrows, and spears. He was still trapped, still a slave in a foreign land.

But for the first time, he wore no collar, and no chains hobbled his feet.

For the first time, he felt his magic well up inside him.

He closed his eyes, savoring it. He didn't want anything to interfere with this, with the ancient magic of his people, the power he had always felt itching, had never been able to draw. Vale had come to this city to fly to battle, to save his sister, perhaps to die in war, but right now he didn't want to think of blood or flame.

He thought of starlight.

They said that a constellation shaped as a dragon shone in the northern skies of Requiem. Vale had never believed those stories, yet now he saw stars behind his eyelids. Now he felt silver light fill him. It was a feeling like mulled wine on a cold night, like gliding on the wind, like everything good and right in the world.

Vale inhaled deeply, suddenly wanting to weep. For twenty-one years, he had suffered under the cruel sunlight, under the whip, under the heel of his masters, but now . . . this moment . . . this moment was wonder.

He was changing. Even with his eyes closed, he knew that. Growing taller. His fingers lengthening. His body widening. He heard the chinking of scales, and in his mind, he was flying over Requiem, and that ancient kingdom was real. The halls of his forebears rose toward the stars, carved of purest white marble. The birch trees rustled. His family flew at his side, and a thousand other dragons flew around them. The Draco constellation shone above, and they were blessed. They were free. They were Vir Requis.

"Requiem," he whispered, tasting fire in his mouth, smelling smoke. "May our wings forever find your sky."

He heard a chinking, a creaking, a scraping against the cobblestones. Vale opened his eyes.

He looked down upon small slaves and seraphim, no taller than his belly. When he tilted his head farther down, he saw claws and legs coated with gleaming blues scales—not the faded, azure of the sky but a rich cobalt, shining like sapphires, like the sea in the tales of his father.

He took a deep, shuddering breath and exhaled. Smoke blasted down onto the cobblestones.

By the stars of Requiem.

Eyes damp, he looked over his shoulder and saw his body—the body of a dragon. Powerful. Covered in the same blue scales, each a jewel. A tail flicked behind him, tipped with spikes, and he spread his wings—leathern wings, indigo colored, tipped with brilliant white claws covered with azure mottles. He smiled, then laughed, a deep laughter, tears in his eyes, and sparks of fire left his maw. When he turned his head forward again, he saw himself reflected in a seraph's shield: a blue dragon, his jaws lined with sharp teeth like daggers, his head tipped with alabaster horns.

For that moment, all his pain, all his rage, the fall and captivity of Requiem—all was forgotten for the length of a few breaths. All was as it should be.

This . . . this is how we were meant to live.

The seraphim cracked their whips and aimed their lances and arrows.

"Chain him!" barked one seraph, and others raced forth with heavy shackles. "Chain the left leg!"

The feeling of peace vanished, and rage flared in Vale. Rage had always been a sickening feeling to him, a helpless fury, a wild animal in a cage. Yet now . . . now rage was fire, a fire that rose in his belly and filled his gullet. Now rage was a wonderful thing, no longer the warmth of starlight but the searing heat of dragonfire.

For the first time in his life, Vale was mighty.

For the first time in his life, he could fight back.

As the seraphim raced forward with chains, Vale bristled. His wings creaked. Why should he let them chain him? He wore no collar. He was a dragon. He was a warrior of Requiem. He could blow his dragonfire; he felt it in his throat, ready to expel. He could lash his claws, snap his jaws, whip his spiked tail. He could slay these seraphim; they were larger than his human form but so small by a dragon.

A growl rose in his throat, and sparks left his maw, reflecting in the seraphim's armor. The overseers carrying the chain paused, hesitating.

"Easy, beast." One of the seraphim—Shani, the same woman who had beaten Elory so many times—cracked her flaming whip. "Be a good little reptile, or we'll rip off every one of your scales. We slew a million of your kind in Requiem. I think we can handle you. Men! Slap the chain onto his ankle. Now!"

Vale growled again. He stretched out his wings, their leathern membranes creaking, and raised his tail with a clatter of scales. His claws scratched the dirt. Smoke puffed out from his nostrils. The overseers tugged back their bowstrings and raised their lances.

"Now, now, little reptile." Shani smiled thinly, standing before him. "Are you going to haul stones like a nice beast of burden, or are we going to have to shatter those pretty blue scales with our arrows?"

Vale lowered his wings and tail.

I must live for now. I must fly with the stones to the temple's crest. I must save Elory, not die here in a construction site.

A single glance at the ziggurat in the distance quelled his anger. The Eye of Saraph upon its crest stared back at him across the miles. It was there that Elory was trapped, serving Ishtafel. It was to reach that palace that Vale had to live.

The seraphim approached, and the manacle snapped around his ankle.

"Good . . ." Shani cooed. She approached and stroked his snout. "Now, you might get an idea into your mind that, once airborne, you could release your magic. That you could fall out of the chain, then shift into a dragon again and fly free." Her smile widened into a grin. "I urge you to try it. The shackle around your leg—do you feel how it squeezes? If you try to shift back into a human, and your leg shrinks, this manacle will tighten at once. Before your human leg can slip out, it will grab you, and you will crash down—unable to become a dragon again without ripping off your leg. I will enjoy seeing you smash onto the cobblestones. Many slaves have." She tugged the chain taut. "You're on my leash now."

Vale grunted. He had indeed contemplated that very plan. In his dreams all night, he had soared as a dragon in chains, released his magic in the air, and slipped from the manacles as a man . . . falling, falling . . . then soaring again, free, unchained. Now that dream crashed around him.

"Do you understand?" Shani cracked her whip. "Answer me!"

Vale grumbled his reply, speaking for the first time with his dragon throat, his voice deeper, rumbling, a sound of boulders rolling. "Yes, my lady."

"Now lift the stone. Fly!"

He moved toward the stone, a heavy disk, the segment of a column. It was so wide that, were he still in human form, his arms would not wrap around it. He gripped the stone in his claws, grunted, and flapped his wings.

Air blew across the yard, raising dust and pebbles and billowing the seraphim's hair. Vale rose a foot into the air. He gave his wings a mighty flap, rose another foot. The stone still lay on the ground, his claws around it. A few more flaps of his wings, a tug, and he was flying.

For the first time in his life, he flew as a dragon.

He laughed.

He was still a slave. A chain ran from his ankle to Shani's hand. He carried a great stone that threatened to dislocate his front legs. But by the stars of Requiem—he was a dragon, and he was flying.

He kept beating his wings, scattering dust below, rising higher. The shell of the Conqueror's Temple—Ishtafel's new monument of victory—rose before him. Its columns were still growing, built of round stones placed one atop the other. Scaffolding grew around the columns like scabs of leprosy, and slaves stood there in human forms, holding buckets of mortar.

Vale flew until he reached the top of a half-completed column. The chain tightened, and when he glanced down, he saw Shani a hundred feet below, holding the other end of the chain.

"That's high enough, reptile!" she shouted. "Lower the stone."

A sudden, searing need filled Vale to toss that stone down, to crush Shani under its weight. Yet dozens of other seraphim spread around him. He could crush one, maybe two with his burden. The rest would shoot him down.

I must live. I must survive for you, Elory.

Beating his wings and hovering, Vale lowered the limestone segment onto the top of the column. The workers on the scaffolding hurried to adjust the stone and apply more mortar, while other slaves drove metal spikes through holes in the top, further securing the segment. The column now rose two feet taller, with another two hundred feet to go.

Panting, Vale hovered in the air and looked around him. From up here, he could see a better view of the city. Several other structures were under construction: a massive archway, a hundred feet tall; a statue of the god Bee'al, a warrior with the head of a cobra, as lofty as a palace; and a new port along the river, its piers bustling with builders. When Vale glanced north, he could just make out the edge of Tofet.

Sudden guilt filled Vale. His father still languished there, alone—his wife dead, his children all missing.

I parted from you in anger, Father. But I will see you again. He ground his teeth. *When I escape from the palace with Elory, I will grab you too.*

He looked south toward the ziggurat. It rose across the city, the tallest building here, as large as a city itself. Somewhere in there, Elory was chained. Somewhere in there, Meliora—also his sister—ruled as a princess. Vale had to find them, had to—

"Down, reptile!" Shani tugged the chain. "Down to fetch another stone."

With a grunt and puff of smoke, Vale flew lower. He lifted another stone. He flew up again.

He labored on.

As he worked, he kept thinking. He had to escape. He had to fly across the city, reach the ziggurat, find his sister. Yet whenever he so much as glanced that way, Shani tugged the chain, and the other overseers cracked their whips.

Even if I break free from this chain, how will I ever reach the ziggurat? The seraphim would shoot him down. A million more lived across the city, each with wings that could fly—faster than dragons, if the stories were to be believed. Many of them were armed with arrows and lances. And even should Vale reach the ziggurat, how would he make it inside? How would he survive navigating the labyrinth of corridors within?

Is Elory lost to me?

"Faster, lizard!" Shani shouted. The seraph beat her wings, flew up toward him, and lashed her whip. The flaming thong slammed against Vale's back, cracking several scales, and he yowled with pain. "Keep working, worm."

Her whip lashed again, and Vale snarled. Shani smirked, hovering before him, so small he could have snapped her between his jaws.

Burn her, sounded a voice within him. *Crush her.*

"That's right." Shani nodded. "Hate me. Try to burn me." She hefted her shield, and below on the ground, her comrades tugged back their bowstrings. "I want to see you try."

Vale growled, hovering before her between the columns. He could do it. He could blow his fire. He would take a few arrows, but his rage would drive him on, and he'd fly across the city. He'd charge against the ziggurat himself. He'd slay all those in his path.

As Shani smiled wickedly, Vale noticed something for the first time. Each segment of the column contained the piece of an engraving. As the segments piled up, they formed a sprawling work of art, a scene coiling up the column. It depicted Ishtafel and his many battles, his chariots slaying the giants, crushing the demons, and finally felling dragons from the sky.

Millions of dragons fought the chariots of fire, and we died. Vale lowered his head. *What chance do I have, a single dragon?*

"Move!"

Shani whipped him again, cracking another scale. Grimacing, Vale flew down to lift another stone—this segment showed an engraving of Ishtafel lancing a beastly dragon. Vale's claws, wings, and legs all ached, just as much as he had ached as a man toiling in the quarry. Another bite of the whip had him flying higher, carrying the stone.

But as Ishtafel is hero to Saraph, so does Requiem have a hero, he thought, placing the stone down atop the column.

One among them had escaped.

Ten years ago, he had risen—a hero named Lucem, a young Vir Requis, a maker of mortar. He had scaled the wall surrounding Tofet. He had fled to freedom. He had given hope to a nation in chains.

Only one in five hundred years . . . one that proved it could be done.

Vale took a deep breath, staring at the ziggurat in the distance.

If Lucem fled, so can I. So can Elory. I will do this. I will fly to her. He looked back at Shani. *I will burn this seraph, burn them all, and fly. Fly as fast as I can. And if I die above the city, I will die in fire. I will die free.*

"Faster!" Shani cried, hovering before him, her swan wings spread wide. "Down, worm. More stones. Go!"

Her whip lashed, slamming against his cheek, cracking the small scales that grew there. His blood dripped.

Burn her.

Vale took a deep breath, prepared to blow his dragonfire.

Horns.

Horns blared across the city, a magnificent fanfare.

Hovering above the columns, Vale turned toward the sound, and saw the ziggurat bathed in light. Fire blazed as two chariots emerged from archways on its crest like bees leaving a hive.

Dragon eyes were sharp, and even from this distance, Vale saw the banner fluttering from the chariots. An eye within a sunburst. The Eye of Saraph. Sigil of the Thirteenth Dynasty.

Ishtafel's chariot.

Vale swallowed his fire, forgetting about Shani, saving his flames for another foe.

There is my true enemy.

MELIORA

At high noon, the lords and ladies of Saraph emerged from the ziggurat to drink wine, watch the chariots race, and see a life destroyed.

On a balcony high upon the ziggurat, Meliora stood in her chariot of fire, forcing herself to take deep, shuddering breaths. She clutched the reins so hard they dug into her palms. Her gilded breastplate felt too tight—she had never worn one before—and her shield was too heavy. A spear stood at her side, ready to grip, a weapon she had never wielded.

A life ends today, she thought, gazing at the city below. *If I lose this race, my brother will claim Elory, fulfill his desires, then when he's grown weary of her, crush and discard her corpse.* Meliora shuddered. *And then he will do the same to me.*

She glanced over at Ishtafel. He stood in his own chariot of fire upon the ziggurat, lance and shield in hand, breastplate so polished its light blinded her. His four firehorses nickered and kicked the air, scattering sparks. Most firehorses, those used for daily flights, spread wide wings of flame. Not the steeds of the races. These ones, woven of fire like their comrades, sported no wings; these ones would gallop on hooves of brimstone, tugging the chariots over every cobblestone, crack, and pebble between here and Tofet.

"Race well, sister!" Ishtafel called out to her. "Like the javelin flies!"

Ishtafel seemed more alive than Meliora had ever seen him. His teeth shone in his grin, blindingly white. His hair streamed like a banner. He wore no helm, but a gilded breastplate enclosed his torso, leaving his arms bare. He was a study in beauty, an epitome of youthful vigor, the warrior from the legends, the hero countless women across the empire desired.

Once I too thought him a hero, Meliora thought. *Once I thought him the greatest, handsomest, noblest warrior in Saraph.*

Now, looking at him, Meliora saw not a deity of light but a cruel god.

If she lost this race, she would grow to envy Elory, perhaps. The girl would last a week, maybe a month in Ishtafel's chamber, her corpse then discarded.

But I . . . Meliora winced. She herself would linger for centuries in his service, have to birth his son, have to see that son grow into a tyrant, have to watch that son grind the weredragons under his heel. And should Meliora so much as speak a word of resistance, she too would find a bad fig on her plate—or a dagger in the night.

She forced herself to take a deep breath, to raise her chin, to square her shoulders.

So I must win this race.

She looked around her. Her chariot stood on a balcony that thrust out from the ziggurat, a thousand feet above the city, tethered to four wingless, crackling firehorses, beasts of living flame. It was a small chariot, large enough for only a single rider, fire over coals, crackling and casting out light and sparks. The limestone facades of the ziggurat sloped below her toward the city, and above her soared the palace crest, a platinum triangle, large enough to be a palace in its own right, brilliant in the sunlight, engraved with a massive Eye of Saraph, the sunburst pupil larger than a man.

Many seraphim flew around the palace, dressed in white and gold. Soldiers hovered in breastplates, helms, and sandals, holding lances and shields. Lords and ladies flew in flowing muslin, wheeling in the sky, wings spread wide, drinking from horns of wine. A million more seraphim—people of the city—stood below, spreading into the distance, watching from the roofs of temples and forts, from the decks of ships, from the balconies of homes, from the cobbled streets. Even the slaves below—collared workers and a handful of chained dragons—turned to stare toward the ziggurat.

In the distance, so far she could barely see it, the city gates led to the desert, and there—just beyond the horizon—lay the land of Tofet. There stood the bronze bull, the god Malok. There rose the golden idol Meliora must reach before her brother . . . or see Elory burn, and see her own life shatter.

At Meliora's sides, two young seraphim, cherubs with soft wings, raised silver trumpets and blew a fanfare. As the sound rolled across the sky, Queen Kalafi herself emerged onto the balcony. The queen wore a resplendent kalasiri, the white muslin inlaid with ten thousand diamonds that caught the sun and shone. Upon her brow she wore her serpent tiara, forged of platinum and inlaid with jewels taken from the fallen halls of Requiem. The queen spread out her wings, displaying the jewels that shone there, woven into her feathers, and she raised her arms with them.

"Children of Saraph!" the queen cried. "We bask in glory. Here in the center of an empire that sprawls across the world. Ishtafel has returned, and a new Edinnu rises!"

Across the city, the people cheered.

"The Eight Gods cast us out from the heavens," Kalafi continued. "But we have risen again! To celebrate our triumph, to worship the Eight Gods with our new light, we mark our victory with a great race—a race of nobility. Ishtafel and Meliora, children of the glorious, eternal dynasty, will ride with fire through Shayeen—to the god Malok, to eternal joy and victory."

As the people cheered, Meliora stared across the distance. There was no glory to Malok, the cruel bronze idol who sang as he digested his victims. There was no eternal joy in an empire built upon the blood and broken backs of slaves. But there was hope, just a sliver—hope to save a life.

Every life is a world, Meliora thought. *Whatever gods might hear my prayers, give me strength, give me speed, help me save Elory . . . and help me save myself.*

She stared toward the horizon again. She couldn't see Malok from here, her destination, only a glint in the distance. The bronze bull rose ten leagues away, a full thirty miles. Last time Meliora had ridden there in a chariot of fire, she had flown leisurely above the city, and it had taken her three hours to reach the land of Tofet.

Now, by the laws of the race, she would ride on the ground. Now she would race her firehorses as fast as they'd go.

Ishtafel leaned toward her from his chariot. He gripped the reins with one hand, his whip with the other. "Ready, sister?"

She stared at him, holding her own whip and reins. "Let's ride."

The cherubim raised their horns again. Silence fell across the land.

Even the wind stilled, and the only movement came from a flock of sparrows flitting ahead.

With a blast that made Meliora start, the cherubim's trumpets blared.

The firehorses bucked.

The race began.

With showering flame, with thundering hooves, with a roaring crowd, the firehorses galloped down the ziggurat's slope.

Meliora grimaced, clenching her jaw so tightly she thought her teeth would shatter. The chariot rattled madly down the brick facade of the palace, like a sled down a rocky mountainside. Her neck felt ready to snap, her head to fly off into the distance, her arms to dislocate. Every segment in her spine knocked together, and the sound was deafening, a horrible storm of her firehorses' hooves, of brimstone thundering against the ziggurat, of her chariot bouncing, of her body slamming back and forth. All around her, the crowd roared, and Meliora felt ready to pass out. She could see nothing—only fire, only sparks, smoke, streaks of color.

"Ishtafel!" the crowd roared, muffled beyond the thundering. "Ishtafel!"

Meliora could not see her brother. It was all she could do to cling to the reins, to remain in her chariot. The speed was terrifying. Meliora had flown in chariots of fire before—leisurely flights, the breeze stroking her cheeks. Now a shrieking wind, hot as the flames of the Abyss, stinging with sparks of fire, slammed against her face, whipped her hair, screamed in her ears. Still she rattled down the ziggurat, a boulder down a mountain.

"Ishtafel! Ishtafel!" the crowd chanted.

Meliora's firehorses galloped down a staircase built into the ziggurat's slope, and her chariot leaped into the air, slammed back down onto the rock, leaped again. Fire showered in a great fountain, and Meliora was tossed from her seat. She flew through the air, clinging to the reins, nearly falling out.

I can't do this. I can't. I can't.

Terror flooded her, and still they roared down the ziggurat, the horses screaming, the fire washing across her. The chariot tilted and Meliora screamed.

Her chariot slammed onto its side, nearly spilling her from her seat. Still they clattered, stormed, flamed down the ziggurat's facade.

"Ishtafel! Ishtafel!"

The firehorses kept galloping. They reached the bottom of the ziggurat and kept racing, pulling her across a cobbled boulevard. Meliora cried out in pain. The road scraped across her shoulder, tearing the skin. He chariot still lay on its side. Sparks showered. Fire and smoke engulfed her. She could see nothing but the inferno, hear nothing but the roar of hooves and her own screams.

She wanted to let go. To fall from the overturned chariot, to roll across the road, to die.

I can't do this.

"Ishtafel!" they chanted. "Ishtafel!" And among them, a single voice, high, distant. "Meliora! Meliora!"

She fell from the chariot.

She dragged across the cobblestones, screaming as the road tore into her, as the horses kept galloping. She clung to the reins with all her strength, the chariot bouncing across the road with her, still scraping along its side, showering flame, scattering coals.

"Meliora! Meliora!"

Dragging behind the galloping firehorses, she saw them. The slaves.

They stood on roofs, in gardens, in construction sites. They stood among their masters, and they were chanting. Chanting her name.

"Meliora the Merciful! Ride, Meliora!"

She gasped in pain. Her blood dripped. Her skin tore. Their faces streamed before her, blurred into smudges, but she still saw their eyes. Their collars. Their hope.

"Meliora the Merciful! Ride, ride!"

Meliora screamed, shoved down her wing, tugged the reins, and dragged herself back into the fallen chariot. The firehorses kept racing down the boulevard, and Meliora thrust her hand against the cobblestones, ripping her skin, shoving the chariot back up.

She cried out in pain. Blood spurted from her hand, but she kept clinging to the reins. She had lost her whip, but the firehorses kept charging forth, and Meliora stood in the chariot again—bloody, cut, still in the race.

"Meliora, Meliora!" the slaves chanted, even as their masters shouted and whipped them. "Ride, Meliora, Savior of Slaves!"

She rode.

Sparks of flame roaring around her, smoke engulfing her, her blood dripping, her hair streaming, she rode.

She was heading down the Boulevard of the Victorious, one of the city's eight main arteries. Statues of the god Bee'al, a man with the head of a cobra, rose at her sides, hundreds of feet tall. Slaves and seraphim stood on the roofs of homes and temples, chanting and cheering.

Ishtafel rode in the distance ahead of her. He must have been a mile away.

Even in the heat of her flaming chariot, cold fear flooded Meliora.

She gritted her teeth. She clutched the reins. She had no whip, but she cried out to her firehorses, "Ride! Ride!"

The four beasts of flame galloped.

Meliora streamed across the boulevard like a comet, trailing fire—a creature of light, of heat, the wind in her hair, the sparks searing her skin. Her muslin kalasiri was torn, burnt, her skin red. She pulled her wings closer to her body, leaned forward, and charged forth. An immortal. A warrior.

I'm no longer the sheltered, pampered girl that I was. I am the wind. I am fire.

In her eyes, she saw starlight.

She saw birch forests below her, a dragon constellation above, marble columns in the distance.

The vision was so real, a vision of darkness and cold air and starlight, that she gasped.

I will fly like a dragon.

She thundered onward down the boulevard. Ishtafel still burned in the distance like a sun, charging across the miles toward the city gates.

Meliora narrowed her eyes.

No. I will not let you win. I will not let you claim Elory and break her body. I will not let you claim my womb for your son. I will win. I will fly like a dragon.

She reached toward the straps of her breastplate. She tore the armor off. She cast it aside, and it clanged onto the boulevard behind her.

She tossed off her shield.

She cast her lance aside.

She was not strong like her brother. He was nearly eight feet of muscle, clad all in steel, his shield and weapons heavy. She was weak in comparison. A thin girl, barely six feet tall, short among the seraphim.

And lightweight.

Clad only in scraps of muslin.

A spirit of fire. *I am fire.*

She punched the walls of her chariot, cracking them, tearing them off, remaining with only a floor and wheels.

I am fire on the wind.

The firehorses raced onward . . . and they were gaining on Ishtafel.

I am fire.

The firehorses charged.

I am the wind.

The chariot leaped over a crack on the road, flew through the air, slammed down and kept charging forth.

I am dragonfire.

With exploding flames and a wordless cry, she reached her brother. The two chariots charged side by side down the boulevard.

The statues of the gods streamed at their sides. The city homes and temples blurred. They were halfway through the city now, charging toward the gates.

"You're looking rather ragged lately, sister!" Ishtafel called from his chariot.

Meliora snarled at him. "And you're looking as pretty as always."

Not a scrape covered Ishtafel. His hair still streamed like a perfect banner of silken gold, and his armor still shone. His whip of fire still flew, slamming into the four firehorses pulling his chariot onward. That chariot still crackled with pure flame.

Meliora's chariot, meanwhile, looked like a guttering campfire, its walls gone, its wheels scattering black smoke and sparks. She herself looked no better; scrapes and burns covered her flesh, peering between the tatters of her kalasiri. And yet her firehorses still charged, faster than his now, less weight for them to carry.

She inched ahead.

"You are falling behind, brother!" she cried and laughed.

Ahead of her, beyond the flaming manes of her steeds, she could see it. Still distant but looming. The city gates. Beyond them lay a bridge over the water, a desert, and finally the bronze bull, her destination, her triumph. The hooves still roared, a deafening sound. The chariot rattled beneath her, knocking her teeth together, clattering her spine, whipping her head up and down. But hope soared in Meliora.

I'm going to win.

"You're forgetting something, sister!" Ishtafel called to her. "I never lose a battle."

His chariot charged forward, then swerved and slammed against her wheel.

Flames exploded.

Meliora screamed.

Her chariot scraped across the road, showering sparks, nearly tilting over. Chips of coal and brimstone scattered, and fire roared.

Grinning through the fire like a demon risen from the Abyss, Ishtafel swerved again, slamming his heavier chariot against her.

Black smoke burst out.

Blades thrust from his chariot's wheels, she saw. Black. Spinning. Shrieking. The scythes slammed into her chariot, tearing through the floor, shattering a wheel.

Meliora screamed as one corner of her chariot hit the ground. As her firehorses kept charging, her chariot scraped across the cobblestones, gushing smoke.

"Ishtafel, stop this!" Meliora shouted. "Sto—"

His chariot slammed into hers again, ripping chunks off, spurting fire that flowed across her. She screamed.

"Firehorses, ride!" she cried. "Faster, faster!"

Her chariot charged forth with a new burst of speed. Scraping across the stones. Tearing apart but still storming forward at maddening speed, the world blurring around her. She was slowly moving forward, leaving Ishtafel behind, escaping his scythes.

I have to escape him. To keep going. To—

Ishtafel's whip cracked.

The lash of fire flew from behind and slammed into her shoulder. She yowled as her flesh tore, as her blood sizzled.

The whip flew again, wrapped around her wrist, and yanked.

She cried out. The whip pulled her from her crumbling chariot, and she slammed onto the cobblestones.

The world shattered.

She bellowed—a hoarse, animal sound.

Her chariot raced onward, leaving her behind on the road. *No.*

Meliora snarled, yanked her arm free from the whip, beat her wings, and flew through the air.

The whip lashed again, biting her side, ripping her skin. She kept flying, dived down, and landed back onto what remained of her chariot. She grabbed the reins. The crowd roared at her sides.

The whip kept beating her, but she refused to fall again. She gripped the reins with both hands. She kept charging forth, her firehorses galloping. The gates rose ahead of her now. Only moments away. Massive gates, their archway tall as a temple, opened to reveal the desert.

Only a bit of floor remained on her chariot. One of its wheels was crooked, swaying madly, screeching, casting out sparks. But she was still fast. She leaned forward, eyes narrowed, staring at the city gates.

I am fast. I am dragonfire. I will win.

A wordless cry pierced the air, rising even louder than the roar of hooves.

A shadow fell upon her, and Meliora looked up to see Ishtafel flying above, wings spread out, blocking the sun. Beams of sunlight flared around him, and he plunged down, a swooping god, his lance tipped with light.

Meliora stared, and for an instant life froze. She stared upon her brother. Upon her death.

His lance thrust toward her.

With a cry, Meliora swerved.

The lance slammed down, scraping across her hip, shedding her blood, then driving into her chariot's wheel.

The wheel exploded with a shower of coal and brimstone.

Ishtafel soared, and finally the last remains of her chariot collapsed. The second wheel detached and slammed down. The floor crumbled.

The firehorses ran free.

Meliora's lips peeled back in a savage snarl. She still gripped the reins. Her wings spread out. Her feet scraped the cobblestones, then rose to stream behind her through the air.

She rode onward, no chariot left, her body bleeding and broken. Still racing.

I am the wind. I am fire. I am a dragon. I will win.

His whip flew again, slamming into her wing, tearing out feathers, biting the bone.

Meliora cried out hoarsely. Pain, white and searing, blinded her.

The wind whipped her wings like more lashes. She slammed down against the cobblestones. Her knees tore, and she howled in agony. Through narrowed eyes, she saw Ishtafel charging onward. Leaving her behind.

The city gates loomed ahead.

Meliora tried to spread out her wings, to fly behind her firehorses again. She could not. She dragged along the cobblestones, clinging to the reins, refusing to release her horses, refusing to surrender, knowing she had lost. Every stone on the road tore through her skin. Her brother charged forth in his flaming chariot, leaving her in his wake. He streamed toward the gates, toward victory.

I've lost. Tears burned as she dragged behind her horses. *I've lost Elory's life. My own life. I've lost everything. I—*

Fire.

White hot, screaming, streaming across the sky, fire greater than the flames of any chariot.

A roar shattered the sky.

Fire.

A great pillar of heat.

Dragonfire.

From the inferno it soared—a blue dragon, wreathed in flame, jaws open, wings wide. A dragon of Requiem.

Meliora gasped.

Suddenly, it seemed to her that she saw Requiem—the Requiem of old, the Requiem that had existed centuries before her birth, the Requiem that Ishtafel had shattered. The beast before her did not look like a slave; he was a noble warrior, proud, strong . . . and charging toward her brother.

Ishtafel cried out and raised his lance and shield.

The blue dragon stormed forth. A chain stretched from the beast's leg, dragging a seraph overseer. Arrows rose from the dragon's back, and its blood seeped, but still it roared, and it blasted more dragonfire.

The inferno crashed into Ishtafel, showering around his shield, and the prince screamed.

Ignoring the pain, Meliora stretched out both wings, even the wounded one. She rose above the ground. With both hands, she still gripped the reins, flying behind her four galloping horses.

The dragon slammed into Ishtafel's chariot, lashing claws, snapping its jaws. The seraph overseer on the chain, dragging behind the beast, flew through the air. Meliora ducked as the overseer flew above her, only inches away; the two nearly slammed together.

Shani, Meliora realized. *I know this overseer.*

From the corner of her eye, she saw the blue dragon and Ishtafel's chariot of fire entangled together, blasting out light, a battle of heat and sound and fury.

144

And then Meliora was charging onward, leaving them behind.

She stormed out the city gates.

Her firehorses pulled her across the bridge spanning the Te'ephim River, and there—there in the desert, upon the hill, rising from the land of Tofet, he shone. The bronze bull. Malok.

Her triumph.

Her firehorses raced uphill, and in the shadow of the bull, Meliora released the reins.

She slammed onto the dirt.

She glanced up, eyelids fluttering, and saw the sun reflecting in Malok's bronze hide, blinding her, searing, overflowing her vision, a field of endless white.

You are safe, Elory. Blood filled her mouth and the light filled her eyes. *You are safe.*

VALE

We flew in the darkness, in the cold wind, the dragons of darkness.

In his mind, Vale flew with them, with the old heroes of Requiem.

We hunted in the sky, tearing them down, burning their wings.

He could almost see those shadows and lights around him. He was fighting in the great war, the last war, the war of Requiem against the seraphim. With his comrades, with a million dragons roaring flame, he slew the enemy. He fought them hard—in stormy skies, in skies of fire, under the sun and in the shadows, in the tunnels underground. Killing the deities. Slaying the immortals. Watching his comrades die, his columns fall, willing to give his life in a great final stand.

We were their greatest enemy. We fell with glory.

Vale had been born in chains. He had never seen the great days of glory, the war of heroes.

But Ishtafel, this shining demon before him, had fought in that war. It was Ishtafel himself who had led the chariots into Requiem. Ishtafel whom Vale's ancestors had battled.

And now I fight with you, my forebears. Now I fight for your honor. To join you in the halls of afterlife, to sing forever in your mighty company. One last battle in our war.

With a roar, he blasted forth his flames, showering the Destroyer in his chariot. His claws scratched at the seraph's armor, and his jaws slammed against his shield. Arrows pierced his back, and seraphim swooped from above, but still Vale roared, still he fought.

To kill Ishtafel.

To redeem Requiem.

To die in fire.

And that fire roared—his own fire and the fire of the chariot. It burned him. The arrows cut him. Thousands of seraphim descended from the sky—as they had in the days of

old, falling from their cursed realm above the stars, falling upon
Requiem.

Their lances cut him.

Ishtafel rose in his chariot, charred, laughing, thrusting his
own lance.

The blade cut Vale.

And he roared.

As the arrows and spears shattered his scales, he roared for
old Requiem, for his sisters, for his slain mother, for his enslaved
father, for a nation chained. For Requiem.

"For Requiem!" he howled, wings spread wide, blood
falling, fire streaming. "Remember Requiem!"

And across the City of Kings, they answered his call.

They wore no armor. They bore no weapons. Their collars
kept their magic at bay, but their souls still shone with starlight.
They stood on the roofs, on the roads, on mountains, in deserts,
across an empire, and they raised their hands to the sky, and they
called out with him, their voices rising as one.

"Remember Requiem! Remember Requiem!"

The voices of slaves in chains. The voices of a proud
nation, an ancient magic.

For Requiem.

His fire roared in a pyre, and Ishtafel's lance drove into his
wing, and Vale fell.

He fell from the skies of the Requiem that had been.

He fell through skies of dragons.

He fell under the light of his stars, the Draco constellation,
under the gaze of the dragon's eye. Issari's star. The lodestar of
his people. Of his soul.

He slammed against the cobblestones, and the pain was
too great. The pain drove his magic out of him, like a punch to
the chest drives the air from the lungs.

The visions vanished.

His magic faded.

He lay on the ground, a human again.

Firelight blinded him, and the seraphim swooped down,
cutting, kicking, shouting, laughing. Their chains swung around
him. Their manacles snapped around his limbs. Shani herself
snapped his collar around his neck again.

"Fight me!" Vale cried. "Kill me! Let me die in battle."

They hoisted him onto his feet, and Vale roared, tried to summon his magic, to become a dragon again, but he was collared once more, his magic lost.

"Hold him up," Ishtafel said, stepping off his chariot. "Bring him before me."

Vale's eyelids fluttered. Blood covered him. He struggled to remain conscious. Shani gripped his arm, digging her fingers into an open wound, manhandling him forward. Other seraphim goaded him with spears. They dragged him across the cobblestones, wrapped in chains, bringing him before the prince.

Ishtafel stared at him—more than a foot taller, twice as heavy, but no longer fair. His armor was charred, and welts rose across his bare arms—the burns of dragonfire. Blood seeped down his cheek from a claw's strike.

They are deities of light, immortals, godly creatures, Vale thought. *But I hurt one. They can be hurt. They can be killed.*

"Do you cower from battle?" Vale spat blood. "Will you not fight me, chariot to dragon, man to man?"

"Kneel before your master!" Shani shouted. She twisted Vale's arm and kicked the back of his knee, forcing him to kneel.

Ishtafel stared down at him, ignoring his wound. "Dragon? Man?" He shook his head. "I see only a slave . . . and slaves are not worthy of death in battle. No. Yours will be a far more amusing death." A grin spread across the prince's face. "Load him onto the chariot! We will nail him onto the ziggurat's crest, and we will drink wine as the vultures drink his blood."

The seraphim roared with joy. They tugged Vale up. They shoved him into the chariot, kicking his back, and all he felt was the pain, and all he saw was the fire.

ELORY

Elory huddled in the shadows of the pleasure pit, fear coiling inside her like an icy serpent.

"You're not paying attention!" Tash glared at her. "I'm trying to teach you how to seduce a man, yet you're just staring at the ceiling. Eyes to me!"

Yet how could Elory focus on her lessons? As always, the pleasure pit was a den of shadows, candlelight, and the purple smoke that swirled from the hookahs of bubbling hintan. The other pleasure slaves lounged on rugs and piles of pillows, eyes glazed, some giggling, others barely able to do more than drool.

"Focus!" Tash said. Anger filled her brown eyes, but fear too. The slave—ruler of the pleasure pit—knew that if Elory failed to learn, failed to please Ishtafel, it would be both of them burned in the bull. "Now, show me what you've learned. Seduce me with your eyes alone. Flirt with those lashes!"

Elory tried, demurely lowering her gaze as Tash had taught her, then glancing up, blushing, and looking away with a shy smile. But her movements felt forced, fake, clumsy. How could she possibly focus on seducing Tash now when above her, upon the surface of the city, the chariots raced, and her fate was being decided?

Meliora could help but only if she won. If Ishtafel beat her . . .

Elory had the feeling that all the batting eyelashes, sweet caresses, and gentle kisses Tash had taught her would not save her from Ishtafel's wrath for long.

"You look like an alley cat who stumbled across a bulldog." Tash flicked Elory's forehead. "Think! Focus! We've only a few days left of training, and I'm not sending you up to the prince like this. I—"

The door slammed open across the pit.

Tash and Elory spun around. The other slaves raised their heads, blinked feebly, then flumped back onto their beds.

Two seraphim stepped into the smoky den—palace guards in breastplates, helmets hiding their faces, only their glowing eyes visible. They wore the Eye of Saraph upon their shields—the personal guards of the dynasty.

Elory felt the blood drain from her face.

She knew at once: the race was over.

"We seek the slave named Elory," one seraph said. "Who among you is Elory of Tofet?"

Elory stared, frozen in terror, unable to even breathe.

Tash, however, leaped to her feet, placed her hands on her hips, and glared at the seraphim. "It hasn't been a week yet!" She stomped forward, stepping over smoking slaves, and came to stand before the seraphim—two feet shorter, half their width, but raising her chin high. "I was given a week to train her. We're not ready. We—"

The seraph struck her with the shaft of his spear.

Tash cried out, lip bloody, and stumbled to the ground. She lay, staring up in horror and rage, blood dripping.

"If you don't shut your mouth, we bash it." The seraph spat. "Don't think because you were given dominion over this den of hintan that you're anything but a slave." The seraphim marched over the fallen Tash. "Elory! We seek Elory. Step forward, slave."

Elory rose to her feet. Her heart thumped in her chest, and her legs felt weak.

It's time. One of them won. One of them will claim me.

"Is the race over?" she whispered, stepping toward the seraphim. "I'm Elory. Who won?"

"Silence!" The seraph who had struck Tash reached toward her. "To me."

Sweat on her brow, Elory stepped closer, knelt, and tried to help the fallen Tash. Both guards, however, grabbed Elory's arms and yanked her forward. "Come with us."

She gave Tash a last look. The bloodied slave stared back, eyes huge with fear, and then the guards dragged Elory out of the pit.

As they climbed the stairs, Elory's mind raced as surely as the chariots. Who did these guards serve—Meliora or Ishtafel? Would she find haven with her half sister, a Princess of Saraph with the blood and kindness of Requiem within her, or was Elory doomed to suffer Ishtafel's cruelty—cruelty she might be unable to hold at bay even with her charms and seduction?

They emerged from the belly of the earth. They walked along a promenade, its northern side lined with columns, revealing the city. This was the place Elory had once walked at night, contemplating escape. Now sunlight fell through the portico, and the city roared.

Elory couldn't see far past the gardens, but she glimpsed people standing on roofs, and she heard a great cry from thousands. Chariots of fire flew above, and seraphim circled in the sky.

"Slay the beast!" people cried. "Slay the dragon!"

Before Elory could see or hear more, the guards dragged her away from the corridor and onto another staircase. They kept climbing through the ziggurat, floor after floor, the guards silent, and still the chants rose outside the window.

"Slay the dragon, slay the dragon!"

The thousands of voices cried as one.

They're killing one of us. Elory shuddered. Someone who rebelled. A dragon who stood against the masters. She stared out into the sky as they passed a window, staring north—north toward the land of Tofet, toward Requiem, a land of pain and a land of memory.

Ease his pain, stars of my forebears, she silently prayed. *If a dragon is to die, let him die easy, and let his soul rise to your light.*

Finally, when Elory was winded and her legs ached, they reached a golden doorway near the ziggurat's crest.

Over the past few days, Elory had been to both Ishtafel's and Meliora's chambers. She could not remember whose door this was, and her heart galloped, and sweat trickled down her back.

"Go kneel before your new owner!" the guards said.

The door opened.

Elory stepped into the chamber . . . and fell to her knees. She lowered her head. Her breath shook, and her tears flowed.

Thank the stars. A sob escaped her. *Thank the stars of Requiem.*

Before her in the chamber of gold and jewels stood Princess Meliora.

"You won," Elory whispered. "You won, my lady. You won the race."

Welts, blisters, and cuts covered Meliora. A bruise stretched across her cheek, and the tips of her hair were burnt. Her kalasiri was tattered and charred. Perhaps worst of all, one of her wings was cloven, bleeding, missing many of its feathers. But despite her sordid condition, the princess stepped toward Elory and pulled her into her arms.

For a long moment, they stood together in silence, holding each other. Elory pressed her cheek against Meliora's chest, closed her eyes, and for the first time in her life, she felt safe.

Finally Meliora spoke. "You're in danger here, Elory."

Still held in Meliora's arms, Elory raised her head and looked up into Meliora's eyes. "My lady? Will Ishtafel try to—"

"I will protect you from Ishtafel." Meliora's face hardened. "It's my mother whom I fear. She tried to have my last two slaves burned in the bronze bull. She forbade me from bringing more slaves here. If she finds you . . ." Meliora shook her head. "I'll have to find you work in the ziggurat. Far from Ishtafel and my mother. Somewhere where they won't see you, but where I can visit, help you, find you a good life. I'll do everything I can to protect you, Elory. I don't know how, but I will."

Elory pulled back from the embrace and looked toward the balcony. She took a few steps forward, moving between a giltwood table, a silver statue of a crane, and a vase full of dried rushes. She stood between porphyry columns and gazed out at the sunlit city.

Shayeen. The City of Kings. A glorious city of light and beauty, of temples that soared to the sky, lush gardens, obelisks tipped with platinum, soaring statues of the gods that rose as tall as the fallen columns of Requiem.

A city of chains.

A city of blood.

And on the horizon, across the river—Tofet. Six hundred thousand of her kind labored there in chains, digging the bitumen and forming bricks that had built this city.

"Slay the dragon!" the crowd of seraphim still chanted below.

They're going to kill one of us. Elory lowered her head, the hot wind billowing her cotton shift. *They're slowly killing all of us.*

"Elory?" Meliora asked.

Elory spun around to face the princess again. The sunlight shone upon the seraph's pale hair and the tips of her wings. And for the first time, Elory saw it. Meliora had the golden eyes of a seraph, the pupils shaped as sunbursts. She had the wings, the tall frame, the beauty, the golden-toned skin of a seraph. She looked so much like one of those cruel deities that at first Elory had doubted her father's story, had doubted that this immortal princess could share her blood.

But now, finally, Elory saw it.

It was the softness to Meliora's face—not the iciness in the faces of other seraphim. It was the kindness in her voice. It was the light in her eyes—not the searing light of the sun but a soft, good light. Starlight.

It's true, Elory thought, and fresh tears budded in her eyes. *She's half Vir Requis. She's my father's daughter. My older sister. She's the Princess of Saraph, yet she's one of us.*

"My lady." Elory's voice was barely a whisper. "I'm saved, but six hundred thousand Vir Requis cry out in pain, in chains. Across your empire, the people of Requiem cry for aid." Elory stepped closer, trembling now. "Our people, Meliora. They need you. They need their daughter."

Meliora's eyes narrowed. Pain, fear, and confusion seemed to battle within them. "I cannot save all weredragons." She lowered her head, the charred tips of her hair brushing her chest. "I'm not as powerful as you think, Elory. I've never even been to Tofet until a few days ago, and I cannot save the weredragons there, I—"

"Vir Requis." Elory stepped closer, hesitated, then dared to reach out and hold Meliora's hands. "The word *weredragon* is cruel to our ears. A slur. The name our enemies have used for millennia to demean us, to portray us as monsters. We are Vir Requis, Meliora. Children of Requiem. Our nation." Elory blinked, her eyes damp. "*Our* nation, Meliora. Yours and mine."

Meliora pulled her hands free from Elory's grasp and stepped back.

"I did not create the land of Tofet." Meliora's eyes narrowed further. "That is the work of Ishtafel and my mother. Not mine."

"Yet it is your land!" Elory stepped closer again, heart hammering, knees swaying. "Your people! Meliora . . ." Elory took a shuddering breath. This truth had to be told. This was a secret she could no longer bear. "My father told me, and when I first saw you, I didn't believe him. But I see it now. I see it in your eyes. You're one of us. Meliora . . ." She trembled. "We share the same father. You're half Vir Requis. You're my sister."

MELIORA

She stared down at her slave, tilted her head, and couldn't help it.

Meliora guffawed.

"What did you say?" she whispered.

Sunlight flowed between her columns, glittering on a room of splendor: silver vases, statues of gold and ivory, giltwood tables, platinum candelabra, priceless mosaics, jeweled incense holders, and all the comforts of an empire. Among this wealth stood Elory: a thin slave, shorter than Meliora's shoulders, collared and scarred.

A weredragon. A mere child.

"You're my sister," Elory repeated, reaching out to again grasp Meliora's hands. "Your father is Jaren, a slave from Tofet. He's my father too. He knew your mother when he worked in the palace thirty years ago, and—"

"Stop it!" Meliora shouted, surprised at herself. She should be laughing at this, shaking her head in wonder, not shouting. And yet the shock coursed through her, and she couldn't curb her anger. She hissed and balled her hands into fists. "You've gone too far, Elory. I've saved you from my brother, but you cannot say such things."

The tears flowed down Elory's cheeks, and the girl was shaking so wildly she looked ready to fall. "But it's true! I can see it in you. I can see the stars of Requiem in your eyes. Your father is not King Harash, Meliora. He's Jaren of Requiem, a man who once loved your mother, Queen Kalafi. You can help us! You can join us!" Elory sobbed, reaching out to her. "You can save us."

"I am not one of you!" Meliora shoved Elory's hands away, and now she too was trembling. "My father died. He died when I was a girl." The old pain, the fury rose inside her. "My mother killed my father. She poisoned him, murdered him! How dare you mock his memory?"

Elory blinked, shaking her head. "I . . . Meliora! You—"

"You will not call me that!" Meliora glared down at the girl. "You forget yourself. You will call me 'my lady' or 'Your Grace,' not my name. I saved you from Ishtafel, but I am not your friend, and I am certainly not your sister." Through her tears, Meliora laughed bitterly. "And I am not a weredragon."

Elory stared at her, eyes wide, cheeks pale. "A weredragon?" she whispered. "Is that what you still think of us? Of the blood that runs through your veins? You can become a dragon too. I know it. I know it must be true. You wear no collar, and the magic fills you." Elory stepped forward yet again, reaching out to hold Meliora's arms. "Reach for it! Reach for the magic, summon it, become a dragon. You'll know then that I speak truth, Meliora, that—"

Meliora struck her.

She had not meant it. She shocked herself. She had never struck anyone before, not in all her life. She gasped with the surprise, and her hand stung, and Elory fell to the floor, her cheek white and red. The slave gazed up at her, eyes wide, mouth open.

I'm sorry, Meliora thought. *I'm sorry, I'm sorry.*

She did not understand. She could not! None of this made sense. Why was Elory saying these things? Why did fear grow in Meliora, fear that . . . that this was true?

No. No!

She closed her eyes, shaking.

My father was King Harash! My mother murdered him!

She dug her fingernails into her palm, eyes screwed shut.

I flew in shadows, flew over birch forests, flew toward marble columns, a great dragon, my comrades at my sides.

"No." Her breath shuddered in her lungs. "No. No! You're lying. You're lying!" Her eyes snapped open, and she stared at Elory. The slave still lay on the floor, staring up at her, blood beading on her lip. "You have to leave."

Elory rose to her feet, clutching her hurt cheek. "My lady." Her voice was soft, hurt, frightened. "You don't have to believe me. You only have to believe your own magic. You only have to try. Our people cry out to you. They cry out for a savior."

"I am not one of you." Meliora's rage seared her tears dry. "I cannot be your savior. I have no magic within me, no blood of dragons in my veins. I'm only a sheltered, innocent princess who learned that the world is falling around her, that she has no power over an empire her family rules. Now leave. Leave this place! Return to the land whence my brother grabbed you. Return to Tofet. My chariot will take you there."

When Elory reached toward her again, Meliora grabbed the slave's arms. She pulled her out onto the balcony. She all but shoved Elory into the chariot that waited there, and Meliora could barely see, barely stand straight. All the world was the light of stars, the flames of war, the light of the bronze bull, the darkness of her fear.

"You have to believe me!" Elory cried from the chariot.

"Go!" Meliora shouted. "Firehorses, take her to Tofet! Take her from here. Take her away. Never come back. Never."

The firehorses reared and took flight, wings of fire hiding the sun, and the chariot left the balcony. Elory cried out from within, reaching down to Meliora, calling her name. But the firehorses were swift, carrying the slave off the balcony and across the city.

"Remember Requiem!" Elory cried, reaching out to her as the chariot flew into the distance. "Use your magic, become a dragon. Requiem! May our wings forever find your sky."

"Slay the dragon!" chanted the seraphim below. "Slay the dragon!"

Meliora stood on the balcony, tears on her cheeks, shaking so badly she had to clutch the railing, staring at it all—the vanishing slave, the city of hatred, the land of chains beyond, and it was too much, too much. Lies. All her life—lies. All her life—crumbling around her.

Meliora turned away from the view. She tried to stumble back into her room, but she was shaking too badly. She fell to her knees, banging them on the floor, and her wings draped around her, feathers missing and charred. She lowered her head. She wept.

Lies. All her life—lies.

Remember Requiem!

Slay the dragon!

Requiem! May our wings forever find your sky.

She knew those words. That prayer. That holiest of prayers. It had filled her dreams since her childhood—her dreams of dragons. Her dreams of stars.

Meliora knelt on the balcony, burnt, broken, and so afraid, lost in a city of blood and gold and tar. And all around, the chants still rose, pounding against her ears, shaking the balcony, shaking her life.

"Slay the dragon! Slay the dragon!"

ELORY

"Meliora!" she shouted from the chariot of fire. "Remember Requiem! Use your magic!"

But the princess no longer stood on the balcony, and Elory could barely see from within the chariot. She stood here alone, the firehorses spreading wings, galloping across the sky, carrying her back to the chains, to the yoke, to the pit of bitumen, to the death of hope.

How had this happened? The fire burned her tears. Meliora was supposed to save her. To save all of them. Now her sister had banished her—back to a slow death in chains, for her, for myriads of her kind.

"Meliora," Elory whispered, reaching toward the ziggurat, not knowing if any light could still shine upon her life.

Thousands of seraphim flew across the city, gliding on the wind, still chanting for death. Elory saw that a great chariot of fire, larger than hers, was flying toward the ziggurat's crest, moving close to Meliora's balcony and then soaring higher. Hundreds of seraphim flew around this chariot, chanting, singing, blowing horns. Thousands more stood in the city below or soared to behold the flaming carriage. The banners of the Thirteenth Dynasty unfurled and caught the wind.

When the distant chariot reached the ziggurat's crest, two figures emerged.

Elory had not thought her life could shatter further, but as she stared, whatever remained of this world collapsed around her.

Wreathed in light, his armor and hair woven of purest gold, Ishtafel emerged from the chariot, carrying a beaten, chained slave.

Vale.

My brother.

Elory screamed.

"Stop!" she cried to the firehorses dragging her chariot. "Take us back. Turn around! Take us back! Please!"

Yet the firehorses kept flying away from the ziggurat, and Elory screamed again. Something tore in her throat. She tasted blood. Her eyes burned. She reached out to the ziggurat, crying his name.

"Vale! Vale!"

She watched, her soul ripping apart, as Ishtafel slammed Vale against the platinum facade of the ziggurat, pinning him against the engraved eye within a sunburst.

She watched, barely hearing her own scream, hearing only the blood in her ears, as Ishtafel drew a hammer and nails, as the seraph laughed, as he swung the hammer, nailing Vale's hands into the ziggurat.

She watched, weeping, screaming, as Ishtafel swung his hammer again, nailing Vale's feet into the platinum.

The Prince of Saraph flew backward, his swan wings spread wide, laughing, a gilded god, triumphant. Before him, upon the ziggurat's crest, Vale hung, nailed into the platinum, arms spread wide, bleeding, still alive.

"Requiem!" Vale managed to cry. "Remember Requiem!"

And then his voice faded . . . drowning under the roar of the city, the chanting of seraphim, the horns of victory, and Elory's own screams.

"Vale! Vale!"

The firehorses kept dragging her chariot away, and she could only stare, weeping, reaching out to him, as the ziggurat grew more distant behind her.

Elory tried to shift into a dragon. She summoned all her magic, and her skin began to harden into scales, her fingernails to grow into claws. But the collar—the damn collar—shoved her back into human form. She tried again. For the first time in her life, actual scales appeared on her body—they were lavender, she saw, lavender scales like the ancient Vir Requis heroine Piri, the Healer who had fought the nephilim—but the collar again dug into her neck, cutting her skin, constricting her. She became a human again, a mere slave trapped in a chariot.

She wanted to jump off. To fall to the city below. To die. To never see it again. To never hear her brother's tortured cry. To forget. To die. To die. She wept.

The chariot kept racing across the sky, taking her away from her brother, away from her sister, away from the city, away from hope, away from light, away from the blood and screams, away into despair.

Meliora will not help me, Elory thought, turning northward. She saw it ahead: the huts, quarries, and tar pits of Tofet. *But one man still can. Our father.*

ISHTAFEL

"Behold the blood of Requiem!" His voice rang across the sky. "Behold the wretchedness of the reptile!"

Ishtafel hovered in the sky, a god of light, wings wide. Arms spread out, Vale hung upon the ziggurat's crest, a dying wretch.

Master and slave. Ishtafel grinned, sucking in air between his teeth. God and worm.

"So shall happen to any who strike a seraph!" Ishtafel cried to the city. "Any slave who defies a master will hang upon the Eye of Saraph, and the vultures will eat his flesh."

The crowd of seraphim roared across the city, cheering, worshiping him, praising his name. Ishtafel rose higher, a god among gods, and in his mind he was flying in Requiem again, slaying the beasts, shattering their halls, burning their forests. He had wanted to find a new enemy, and here he found one—the slaves, the miserable descendants of those warriors he had once crushed.

I will make you suffer, weredragons. Ishtafel licked his lips and gazed at Tofet on the horizon. *The empire will run red with your blood. The cries of your anguished souls, breaking under the yoke, will rise to Edinnu itself.*

As he looked down at the city, he saw them staring. Thousands of them. Slaves. The house slaves of the seraphim— cooks, gardeners, tutors, pleasurers. Thousands of reptiles in human forms, collared, staring at him. Silent. Among them rose the towering statue of Reehan, gilded and beautiful in the sunlight—his precious beloved whom the reptiles had slain. They would pay for that sin, now and every generation.

"Kneel!" Ishtafel shouted to the city. "Kneel before your god. Kneel, slaves!"

Yet across the city, they still stood. Still stared.

One among them raised his hand, and his voice rang across the city. "Requiem! May our wings forever find your sky."

The man stood on a roof, legs chained, hoarse voice rolling across the city. "Remember Requiem!"

Ishtafel's grin stretched his cheeks. "Yes." His voice was too soft for any to hear. "Remember Requiem. I want you to remember, slaves. To remember how I broke your kingdom."

He raised his lance. He tossed it. The spear shot through the sky, a beam of light, streaming down toward the city, and pierced the slave below. The creature fell, silenced.

"Make them kneel!" he cried. "Seraphim, make them all kneel."

He held his arms out wide, and the seraphim charged. Once more, they flew to battle. Once more, fire and light filled the sky.

"Remember Requiem!" a slave called, even as the wrath of Saraph descended upon them.

"Requiem!" cried another. "May our wings forever find your sky."

Their voices rose together across the city. "Requiem! Requiem!"

With flailing whips, with thrusting spears, the seraphim descended upon them. Blades drove into flesh. Whips tore into skin. The blood of the vermin splattered the city.

"Kneel!" Ishtafel cried. "Kneel before your gods!"

They bled. They cried out in anguish. And across the city, they knelt before him, the living among the dead. Once more, vanquished. Once more, worshiping him.

Good, he thought. *That is what they are. Nothing but worshippers. Nothing but his slaves.*

A voice spoke behind him, hoarse, cracking.

"A fire has been kindled. Starlight shines. Requiem will rise."

Ishtafel turned in the sky. His smile grew. "Still alive, are we?"

Vale hung upon the ziggurat's crest, a thousand feet above the city, his hands and legs nailed into the platinum. His blood dripped from many wounds, but he fixed his eyes on Ishtafel.

"Something has started here which you cannot stop," Vale said, the words bringing blood to his mouth.

"Good." Ishtafel nodded. "The city was getting a little dull."

He drew a dagger from his belt. He flew closer to Vale and scraped the blade across the slave's side. Vale screamed.

"Call out louder!" Ishtafel said. "Call so the vultures will hear. Ah! There they are. Look! They've come to dine."

Gazing into the sky, Ishtafel laughed and opened his arms, welcoming them down. The vultures circled above once more, then swooped to feast.

MELIORA

The chanting and screaming rose from outside, and Meliora covered her ears, wanting to silence the city, the screams, the songs, the endless din that would not cease its roar.

Lies. Lies.

Elory's words thrummed through her. Meliora stumbled across her chamber, fell onto her bed, covered her head with a pillow. She wanted to silence it all. The shouts and songs of seraphim outside, the screaming, the endless voices in her mind, the endless memories.

Memories not her own.

Memories of ancient lives.

Memories of dragons.

"No. No!"

She covered her ears, shoved her face against the bed, but even if she could silence the sounds, she could not silence her thoughts.

You are one of us, Meliora! You can become a dragon.

"I am a seraph!" she shouted into her bed. "I am a Princess of Saraph!"

You are a dragon.

Her fists shook.

I am the wind. I am fire. I am dragonfire.

"Remember Requiem!" the voices chanted outside . . . then fell silent.

Meliora rose from her bed.

She walked back onto her balcony.

She stared outside at the city and cried out in horror.

Seraphim were storming across the sky, swooping to the city, killing slaves. Blood dripped onto the balcony, and Meliora looked up to see a slave nailed to the ziggurat above her, moaning, barely alive. The city screamed in anguish, and the seraphim cheered, and above the carnage flew Ishtafel, laughing, his arms spread wide.

No.

Meliora's head spun.

Gods, no.

She let out a roar, wings spread out.

"No!"

She had not thought herself capable of more fear, more shock. She had not thought the world could tear any wider. Yet this seemed a storm, a shattering, a tragedy worse than anything Meliora had experienced. She howled with her fury, howled for the blood of Requiem, for the cruel light of Saraph, for a nation tearing apart, and Meliora flew.

She soared through the sky, a seraph of light, crying out her fury.

She soared toward the sun, a dragon roaring in rage, a dragon blowing fire.

Seraphim turned toward her, gasping, crying out in fear.

Meliora roared and blasted her flames.

Dragonfire.

Dragonfire screamed, spinning, crackling, gushing forth, slamming into seraphim, burning them down, and Meliora roared, and she wept, and her heart thrashed.

I am the wind.

I am fire.

I am dragonfire.

She spread her wings wide, wider than they had ever spread. She reached out her claws. Her tail lashed and her scales clattered, and she was dreaming, had to be dreaming, this couldn't be real, this was a dream, a dream, a lie, a dream . . .

"Requiem rises!" the slaves cried below. "Meliora the Merciful! Meliora of Requiem flies!"

Her tears fell, and Meliora wheeled in the sky, back toward the ziggurat, and she saw herself reflected in the platinum facade.

I am dragonfire.

She flew as a dragon, long and slender, a dragon with colors of starlight and sunlight, silver tipped with gold. Her scales were small and round like pearls, and long white feathers grew from her wings, from her tail, along her back like a mane. A halo still shone above her head. A great creature of light, half reptile, half bird, a dragon like a swan, white and long, eyes golden, roaring white fire.

I am a dragon of Requiem.

Her tears fell as jewels, and her fire stormed forth.

It was true. She beat her wings, a dragon in the wind. Elory was speaking truth.

"For Requiem!" Meliora cried out, her voice deep, roaring across the sky.

And above she saw him, swooping down, a god of light in a chariot of fire.

Her brother.

"You too will be vulture food, dragon!" Ishtafel cried. "You too will feed the birds!"

She growled, flying up toward him. "You will not kill him, brother. And you will not kill me."

In his chariot of fire, he hesitated. His eyes widened. "Meliora?"

She blew her white fire.

He raised his shield, and the flames engulfed it, screaming, showering around him, exploding like a sun.

With a roar, with showering flame, with smoke, with blood, with flaring light, dragon and chariot slammed together.

I am dragonfire.

Meliora did not know if this was real or a dream. She did not know how this could be, how she could be flying as a dragon, how she could have carried the blood of Requiem within her for so long. But she knew that she had to fight him. Had to kill him. Had to stop her beloved, horrible brother. And so she roared, and she fought him—fought him like the dragons of old—lashing her claws, snapping her jaws, calling out.

"Requiem! Requiem!" She roared out in her rage. "I won't let you hurt them, Ishtafel. I won't let you hurt another soul. It ends now."

Her claws grabbed his shield, trying to yank it free. Her tail lashed, slamming into his chariot. Her wings spread out, burning, and she felt like a phoenix, like a creature woven of living flame, of starlight and firelight.

He rose in his chariot, burnt, his armor dented, and stared at her. Their eyes met. She saw her face reflected in his golden eyes: the head of a white dragon, a creature risen from myth. And she saw the shock in his eyes, the understanding, the realization.

"It *is* you, Meliora." He shook his head in disbelief, then narrowed his eyes and raised his lance. "Of course. *Of course.* Mother poisoning Father, the secrets in her eyes, the weakness in your heart . . ." He sucked in air and snarled. "Of course."

With a roar, he thrust his lance.

The blade crashed into Meliora's shoulder, cracked her scales, and bit into her flesh.

Ishtafel loomed above her, leaning from his chariot of fire, driving the blade deeper.

"So you will die with them, sweet Meliora." He grinned—a maniacal grin, showing nearly all his teeth. "Instead of marrying you, I will smite you upon the city you profane."

He tugged the lance free and prepared to thrust again. Meliora screamed and blasted her fire.

Ishtafel's chariot rose higher, its firehorses rearing, screaming like storms. Meliora flew higher, dragonfire showering forth, claws lashing.

His chariot swooped, and his lance slammed into her again, digging into the same wound.

Meliora roared with pain.

Something shattered inside her.

Her magic spilled out like her blood, a mist of starlight.

She fell through the sky, a seraph again, swan wings beating uselessly. She spun. She tumbled. The chariot dived after her, Ishtafel sneering within, aiming his lance.

I am dragonfire.

She summoned the magic again—the ancient magic of Requiem, forever a part of her, hidden but now hers to wield. She soared, a dragon again, and slammed into him.

Her claws lashed in a fury. Her jaws snapped. Her fire sputtered.

I have to stop him. I have to destroy him, to . . . to kill him. Her tears and blood mingled as she fought. *For Elory, for poor Elory whom I banished, my sister. For the slave nailed into the ziggurat behind me. For all the slaves across this land. For a free people. For the Vir Requis.*

She lashed her claws, tearing into Ishtafel's breastplate, scattering the gilt, shattering the steel, cutting his skin, shedding his blood, the ichor of Saraph, burning her paw.

He's an immortal god, but I am a dragon of Requiem.

He shouted, rose in his chariot, and drew a sword—a long, curved blade, a shard of sunlight.

He thrust the blade, driving it into her chest.

Meliora screamed silently.

Her white fire rose, becoming a pillar of light. Her head rolled back. Her breath died.

She fell.

She fell as a dragon, pierced with his light.

She fell as a woman, her wings shedding feathers.

She fell as Meliora, as a princess of seraphim, as a daughter of Requiem, as a sister. A sister.

Forgive me, Elory. Forgive me.

Fire shone above her, and the sun blinded her, and the roar of the crowd flowed across her. She crashed through stone and wood and light and darkness.

JAREN

He walked through the city of Shayeen, chains around his feet, a collar around his neck, his head held high.

Coated in tar and dust, his back whipped, his frame frail, he walked with squared shoulders. He carried a staff of twisting wood, but his back was straight. He stared ahead, walking unafraid even through the land of the masters, for even in the searing sunlight of Saraph, he walked upon a path of starlight.

"The stars of Requiem will guide our way, daughter," he said to Elory. "Fear not and stray not from my side. Issari's Star shines upon us."

Elory walked at his side, trembling, afraid, but still walking with her head held high. No chains hobbled her feet. Several days' growth of hair covered her head, and her eyes shone with tears. Together, side by side, father and daughter walked along the boulevard between the statues of old gods.

"They will stop us." Elory glanced around nervously, fists clenching and unclenching. "They will slay us."

Jaren kept walking, chin raised, staff tapping, chains jangling. "We walk upon starlight. They will not stop us."

Indeed, it seemed that barely any of the seraphim noticed them. The golden masters flew above, heading toward the ziggurat in the distance. Other slaves bustled all around, some chanting for Requiem upon roofs, others kneeling in the dust, others dead, seraph arrows in their chests. Shayeen spun around them, flaring with fire, with blood, with starlight.

Ahead, before the ziggurat, a great, beautiful creature fell from the sky. Her scales gleamed like pearls and gold, and her wings spread out, white as swan feathers, a being halfway between dragon and swan. As she fell, she became a woman, a seraph with broken wings, tumbling down and vanishing in light.

"Meliora!" Elory said, gasping. "Meliora fell!"

Jaren kept walking, never faltering, never removing his gaze from the ziggurat ahead. "And Vale still lives upon the Eye."

Ahead he saw his son. Nailed to the great engraving of the Eye of Saraph, an eye within a sunburst, a thousand feet above the city. Barely visible from here. A speck of life. Flickering. Dying.

My son.

Seraphim streamed above them. Slaves roared on the streets and roofs, crying out to Meliora, to the "Princess-Slave!" The city bustled, flooded with death and hope, and soon others joined Jaren. A young boy, an arrow in his shoulder. A girl carrying her sister. A mother with her babe. An old man and woman. Collared. Beaten. Cut. Slaves.

A dozen slaves marched behind him. Then a hundred. Then a thousand marching together—ankles hobbled, backs whipped, heads shaved. The people of Requiem.

"Kneel, slaves!" cried a seraph, swooping toward him. He thrust his lance, spearing a slave child.

"Turn back, worms!" shouted another seraph and fired an arrow. The missile slammed into a woman. She clutched her chest and fell.

Jaren kept walking. Elory walked at his side. The thousands walked behind them.

"Kneel, slaves! Turn back."

More arrows flew. More spears thrust. More slaves fell.

Jaren kept walking, staff held before him, and more slaves joined them, emerging from homes and alleyways, forming a great throng. They wore only rags, but they carried shields of starlight.

"Remember Requiem!" cried one man.

"Remember Requiem!" rose the voices across the crowd.

They walked until they reached the base of the ziggurat, and there Jaren stopped and raised his staff. He stared up to the building's crest. To Vale. He could barely see his son from the distance. He did not know if Vale still lived. But he believed. He thought he heard his son call out, his voice flowing on the wind. Calling him. Calling his father.

Jaren held his staff high. "Kalafi! Queen Kalafi, hear me!"

The seraphim flowed down toward him in flaming chariots, arrows firing. Ishtafel led the charge, roaring like a wild, rabid demon of sunfire.

Be with me, stars of Requiem.

Jaren inhaled deeply, raised his staff, and thought of the Draco constellation, the great dragon in the sky, the protector of Requiem. The gods of a cruel world flew toward him, but he worshipped an older god. A god of distant lands. A god of dragons.

Light.

Starlight flared out from his staff, the Shield of Requiem. The fire of the seraphim blasted against it, scattering. Their arrows flew aside. The chariots tumbled backward, and the starlight spread out in a great dome, protecting the children of Requiem within its glow.

"Kalafi!" Jaren shouted, voice booming now. "Queen Kalafi, come speak to me, to Jaren Aeternum of Requiem. Come speak or the truth of Saraph and Requiem will spill forth like my light!"

The city seemed to freeze. Jaren stood on the road, staring up at the ziggurat, at his dying son, at the center of Saraph's power, at the palace where he had loved a queen, where his daughter had been born, where a son would live or where the truth of a daughter would roll across an empire. Everyone stared now—seraphim, slaves, all listening, all waiting to hear his words.

"The empire will hear me speak!" Jaren cried. "Seraphim and slaves will hear of Meliora, will hear of you, Kalafi! Free my son. Free Vale of Requiem! Free him or all will hear of a night long ago."

Of a young slave, Jaren added silently. A young man who had served a queen. A queen who had slain her husband, who had loved the young man, who had betrayed her dynasty, who held a secret . . . a secret that could save a life.

And onto the balcony she came, clad in muslin and diamonds, a crown on her head, fear in her eyes. Queen Kalafi, Great in Graces. Mother of his child.

She stood in the distance, so far he could barely see her, but he gazed upon her with the light of his stars. He stared into her eyes.

"Enough!" Jaren said. "Free him. Free my son!"

Free him or the empire will know who fathered your daughter, Jaren added silently. And he knew she could hear those words too. She stood in a great palace, a queen of gold and plenty, beautiful and immortal. He stood below on bloody earth, a slave in chains, ragged and aging. Across the distance, they stared into each other's eyes.

Thirty years ago, when I was young and fair, a servant in your palace, you took me into your bed. I gave you a daughter. Give me back my son.

Kalafi nodded.

She spoke two words—words for her servants, words he could hear even down here.

"Free him."

As the city watched, seraphim flew toward Vale. He screamed as they tugged the nails from his hands and feet . . . then fell silent. On the wings of seraphim, he glided down toward the ground, and the cruel masters of light laid Jaren's son at his feet.

"Oh, Vale," Elory whispered. She knelt by her brother and placed her hand on his cheek.

The other slaves gathered around, crying out in dismay, and seraphim laughed and shouted. Jaren knelt too before his son—the poor, ravaged thing they had turned his son into.

Vale lay shuddering, struggling for breath, his lifeblood leaking away, cut a thousand times. Dying. Ashen. Barely any life still in him.

"Vale!" Elory cried, trying to staunch his wounds. "Oh sweet Vale."

Beaten, broken, bleeding, Vale opened his mouth. He tried to speak, but only hoarse words left him. His teeth had been bashed in, his eye socket cracked, and a cut on his side exposed his organs. Vultures had pecked at his flesh, ripping bits off, tugging bits out. Elory wept, closed her eyes, and held Vale's ravaged hands.

Jaren looked up at the sky. The sun of this cruel southern empire beat down, white and blinding. But that sunlight was only a curtain, only a cage. Beyond it, far beyond the distance, shone the stars. The stars of Requiem were not visible from this land, but Jaren knew they were up there, knew they could hear him, blessed him.

"Stars of Requiem," Jaren prayed, staring up into the light, past the light, into darkness, to the gods of his forebears. "Shine upon him, Draco constellation. Shine your light. Heal your son."

Jaren thought that he could see them above, even past the sky of seraphim: the halls of Requiem, woven of starlight, twins to the fallen marble halls in a burnt forest. And they were waiting there: the heroes of Requiem, great kings and queens, warriors and poets, his own wife. Waiting for Vale, waiting to welcome him into their embrace.

"Now is not his time," Jaren whispered to them. "Let him live, stars of Requiem, souls of the Vir Requis. Heal his body. Let him live longer under the sun."

It seemed to Jaren as he stared skyward, as Elory wept, that he heard the song of harps from above, that he heard the souls of the fallen.

Let him rest, they said. *Let him no longer suffer in chains.*

Jaren shook his head. "He still has work upon this world. He still must walk at my side. He will not rest while his people languish. Let my son live. Let him fight."

The Draco constellation shone above, stars forming a great dragon with a gleaming eye.

Strands of starlight fell like rain.

The tears of Requiem shone upon the world.

The light of those who had come before. The light of stars. The light of dragons. It fell in curtains, gleaming, healing in the cruel sunlight.

"Breathe, Vale!" Elory shouted, the light cascading across her. She looked toward Jaren, eyes wet, holding her brother in her arms. "He's not breathing!"

The light kept falling, a silver rain, breaking apart, scattering, lifting Vale like a mother lifting a lifeless child. He hovered before them, limp, broken, wrapped in strands of starlight. The song of harps played in the wind, the song of Requiem.

You will always find our sky.

"Heal him, stars," Jaren whispered. "Heal my son so that he might walk your path upon the world."

As he stared at the hovering body of his son, it seemed to Jaren that he saw a figure all in white, woven of starlight. A young woman, angelic, clad in flowing robes, her braid hanging across her shoulder. Her eyes shone like the stars, gazing down upon Vale, and she laid her hands upon him. When Jaren looked up, back to the stars, he saw that the dragon's eye—Issari's Star—had gone dark, had descended to this world.

Jaren fell to his knees before the woman of light.

"Issari," he whispered. "Princess Issari, Priestess of Starlight, Eye of the Dragon. Blessed be your name, Issari Seran of Requiem."

Her hands rested upon Vale, rivulets of light spreading from them, wrapping around the broken body, mending, healing. Issari—among the greatest heroines of Requiem's first days, a founder of the nation, a great healer and priestess—raised her eyes from her task and stared at Jaren.

And then she was gone.

The light faded.

The song died.

Once more, the cruel sunlight of Saraph slammed down against the cobblestones.

Vale lay on the ground, wrapped in Elory's arms. Blood still coated him. A collar still encircled his neck. His clothes were still torn.

"He's alive," Elory whispered, sobbing, pulling him close against her. "Vale, Vale. Sweet brother."

His chest rose and fell with breath, and Jaren knelt and wiped the blood away, revealing healed flesh. Only scars remained upon his side, his hands, his legs, old white wounds, washed away.

Thank you, Issari, healer of Requiem.

Then Jaren could retain his composure no more. His body shook with sobs, and he pulled his son close, squeezing him, never wanting to let go. Vale's eyes fluttered open, and he smiled softly and held his father and sister.

The other slaves gathered around, gazing with wide eyes. Men, women, and children who had defied the seraphim, who had endured whip and spear, refusing to kneel before Ishtafel—now they knelt before Jaren and his family. Now they bowed their heads.

"A miracle," one old man whispered, back scarred from decades of servitude.

"The stars shine again!" said a young man, raising chained arms.

Elory nodded, staring skyward, the Draco constellation reflected in her eyes. "We are not forgotten."

MELIORA

"She fell from the sky."

"Fell like a star of Requiem."

"She fell like a dragon! A dragon all in silver and gold, of feathers and scales, of sunlight and starlight."

Meliora blinked. The world was fuzzy, the light like feathers, scattering around her, mottled with dust. She coughed, and pain raced across her. Everything hurt—her belly, her chest, her spine, her eyes, her head. She blinked again, struggling to bring the world into focus.

She lay in an alleyway between weedy brick walls. Laundry hung on strings above, and an alley cat hissed. Graffito sprawled across one wall, showing a crowned seraph—presumably Ishtafel—with a baby dragon chomping on his backside. Two hundred yards away, the alley opened up onto the main boulevard; a crowd marched there, crying out in many voices.

"She's awake!" rose one of the voices, one near Meliora. A shadow fell across her.

"I know she's awake. Step back, give her some room."

Meliora pushed herself onto her elbows and her eyes widened. She gasped.

"Kira!" she said. "Talana!"

Her two old slaves, saved from the bull and banished into Tofet, smiled at her.

No, not slaves, never again, Meliora thought. *Vir Requis. My people.*

The memories flooded her, as powerful as a storm. Elory telling her the truth. Leaping off her balcony. Flying as a dragon—a real dragon of Requiem.

My father is Vir Requis. Meliora trembled wildly. *The blood of dragons flows through me. I'm not the king's daughter.*

The shock flowed through her, spinning her head, and yet . . . and yet somehow Meliora had always known. Her short stature—only six feet tall, shorter than almost all other seraphim of the courts. Her childhood dreams of dragons. Her longing gazes at the stars at night. Her kinship with her slaves. Her people.

"You are my people," she whispered.

She winced. Every word shot pain through her. She looked down at her body, and she saw bandaged wounds, scratches, burn marks.

"We caught you when you fell," Kira said, dark eyes shining. "You almost *died*. You flew as a dragon, Meliora! How did you do that? A real dragon like the Vir Requis of old."

Talana—pale of skin, her stubbly hair red—shook her head. "Not like a Vir Requis. We have wings like leather. She had feathery wings and feathers on her back instead of spikes. And she still had a halo, even as a dragon."

Kira—darker than her companion, her skin olive and her stubbly hair black—groaned. "You've never even seen a real dragon."

"I have!" Talana stamped her feet. "They fly all the time over construction sites, and I watch them." She sighed wistfully and tugged at her collar. "I wish I could become a dragon someday. I can feel the magic inside me, itching."

"That's the cricket you ate yesterday." Kira glowered at her friend. "I told you not to eat it."

"Crickets are good!" Talana pouted. "If you stick 'em on a stick and fry 'em, they—"

Meliora rose to feet, wobbly. "Your collars," she whispered. "Your collars! You can become dragons without them."

The two young women, collared and hobbled, stared at their former mistress, lost for words. Meliora sucked in a breath and clutched her spinning head.

I have to remove their collars. I have to find the Keeper's Key.

Meliora had to lean against the alley's wall. She had seen the key before—a long, crimson key engraved with golden runes. It was imbued with ancient magic, tying it to the curse of the collars. It fit into no padlock. At a mere touch, its old, dark power let it break the curse upon the collars, then cast it again. For five hundred years, her family had safeguarded this key—the key to their power.

"The Keeper's Key," Meliora whispered. "A way to remove the collars. I have to find it."

Kira and Talana glanced at each other, then back at Meliora.

"But . . . my lady." Kira shuddered. "They say that only the highest ranking seraphim ever carry the key."

Talana nodded. "They say only one Keeper's Key even exists! That it's only carried by—"

"—the royal family," Meliora whispered.

She spread her seraph wings.

She flew.

Leaving her slaves—no, not her slaves, her fellow Vir Requis—Meliora soared into the sky and flew above the City of Kings. Many slaves were gathered around the ziggurat, and many seraphim flew above. Blood stained the steeple of the ziggurat, a red pupil in the great Eye of Saraph, but the slave who had been nailed there was gone.

And there, on the balcony beneath the bloodstain, she stood—Queen Kalafi.

Meliora flew toward her.

Her lips peeled back, her eyes narrowed, and her hands balled into fists.

The woman who lied to me. Meliora snarled. *The woman who blindfolded me, who kept me in a darkness of gilt and gemstones. The woman who raised me to spit upon the people whose blood flows through me, whose blood she spills upon our fair city.*

Kalafi stood in fineries, resplendent—her golden hair flowing and lustrous, her tiara gleaming, her kalasiri strewn with thousands of diamonds. Wings spread wide, feathers charred, blood staining her bandages, Meliora landed before the queen. They stood facing each other—an ancient seraph of immortal beauty, and a young daughter with dragon blood in her veins, only just awakened to the world.

"Daughter," Kalafi said, reaching out to her.

Meliora took a step back. "Mother."

"Meliora," Kalafi whispered, reaching to her again.

Again Meliora stepped away. The city spun below her, and the chanting pounded against her skull. She stepped into her mother's chamber, leaving the balcony. The heated pool steamed before her, and the splendor of the chamber glittered: columns of silver and gold, jeweled vases, statues of precious metals, artifacts from distant lands, priceless rugs, murals, mosaics. Everywhere Meliora looked: the luxury of an empire.

Meliora thought back to the land of Tofet, just across the river. A nightmare. A hellish landscape of cracked earth, pits of steaming tar, of slaves crawling, limping, suffering under the yoke and the whips of their masters, crying out. Slaves laboring to carve bricks for palaces such as this one. To dig up the bitumen that held those bricks together, that glued jewels to gold and stones onto mosaics, that waterproofed the ships that brought these treasures from distant lands. Black tar and the red blood of slaves—the fuel of the empire, of the dynasty Meliora had been born into, the dynasty that was a lie.

"They're my people," she whispered to her mother. "The slaves. The slaves in chains. The slaves whipped. The slaves burned in the bronze bull. My people. My blood. My father."

Kalafi stepped toward her, wincing, still reaching out to her. "My daughter—"

"Don't touch me!" Meliora shoved the queen's hands away. "Don't call me that."

Pain twisted Kalafi's face. "Meliora, all that I did, I did to protect you. To shelter you from the cruelty of the world, from—"

"From the truth!" Meliora shouted, and now she could not curb her tears. "You lied to me!"

"To protect you!" Kalafi swept her hand across the chamber. "To raise you like this—in comfort, in wealth. Not . . . not out there!" The queen barked a bitter laugh. "Would you have preferred to grow up in chains, collared, whipped, suffering in the dust like a slave?"

"I *am* a slave!" Meliora shouted, tears flowing. "All my life I've been a slave, kept in a gilded cage, collared with necklaces of gold, hobbled by ignorance. All while my family suffered. While my sister carried a yoke until her shoulders twisted. While my father—my true father—screamed under the lash. While hundreds of thousands of my people cried out in anguish, begging for mercy that would never come. While your son—your own son!—slew them for his sport. Would I have chosen chains? I would have abolished the chains! I would have smashed the cruel god Malok, and I would have sent the Vir Requis to their homeland, far from this accursed city, this accursed empire, this accursed family—"

Her voice died with a strangled cough as Kalafi gripped her throat. The queen sneered, tightening the grip, crushing Meliora's windpipe.

"You will not speak disparagingly of this family—this family that raised you." Kalafi's eyes burned. "I've given you everything, Meliora. The life of a princess."

"I would rather have the life of a slave." Meliora wrenched off Kalafi's hands and lifted a jug off a table, its porcelain painted with hunters and pheasants. "I would choose chains over wealth." She slammed the jug down; it shattered. She lifted an ostrich egg inlaid with jewels and golden wires. "I would choose the whip over jewels." She shattered the artifact and grabbed a jewelry box. "I would choose the collar over necklaces of gems." She tossed the jewelry box to the balcony; it shattered against the floor, its jewels spilling toward the city below. She fell to her knees, and she howled with her pain. "You lied to me!"

Kalafi stared down at her, calm now.

"Are you done having a tantrum?" the queen said. "Do you see why I withheld the truth from you, Meliora? Because you're still a child. Still only a pampered child."

"Yes." Meliora nodded and rose to her feet. She stared into her mother's eyes—a mother taller, fairer, endlessly older, a pure seraph, a pure being like Meliora would never be. "I'm a child. Nothing but a child. You made me this way. Ishtafel was my age when he conquered Requiem. Yet you kept me in a state of infancy, Mother. Deceived. Pampered. Crippled by fineries. But it ends now; that life is over. Elory came into my life—my sister!—and she started something, Mother. Something you cannot stop." She took a deep, shuddering breath and raised her chin. "The slaves will be freed. You will give me the key to their collars. My brother stole them from Requiem, but I will lead them home."

Her mother stared at her silently for long moments, face blank.

Finally the queen spoke in a whisper, "I should have killed you." She gave her head the slightest of shakes. "So many times I wanted to, was going to. When you were in my belly, a mixed child, I was going to see the women in the temples, to drink their poison and flush you from my body. When you were a little girl, when I could see your weakness, your short stature, your eyes that gazed upon your slaves as pets rather than livestock, I wanted to drown you in my pool, to hold your little body—so small, so weak!—under the water until you stopped flailing. When you stepped into the bronze bull, I wanted to let you burn, to hear you scream; if not for the embarrassment it would have caused me, perhaps I would have. Just last night, I stood above your bed as you slept, a dagger in my hand . . . and oh, sweetest daughter." She reached out to caress Meliora's cheek. "I wanted it so badly. More than I wanted anything, I wanted you dead."

Meliora stared at her mother in horror, seeing a different person, not the queen she had known, not the mother she had loved . . . but the bane of Requiem. A tyrant. A monster.

"Who are you?" Meliora whispered.

Kalafi smiled thinly. "Something you will never be. Pure." *Lies. All my life—lies.*

Meliora closed her eyes, and she thought of the years idled away, twenty-seven years blind. Almost three decades wrapped in silk and gold, a princess in a tower. And she thought of her dreams. Of wings in the night, of marble columns rising from a birch forest, of the stars—a million stars in a different sky, brilliant in the night, and among them a great celestial dragon. She flew with her kind. With Elory. And Kira and Talana. With millions of other dragons. Free in Requiem.

"Requiem," Meliora whispered, tears on her lips. "May our wings forever find your sky." She opened her eyes and stared at her mother through the veil of her grief and her joy. "Yours is the purity of poison, the purity of the finest steel blade thrust into an enemy's back. But I am a child of starlight. I am a child of Requiem. I am a dragon."

And in this chamber of wealth, this heart of an empire, Meliora summoned her ancient magic.

Starlight spun around her, glowing, spreading out, finally gathering into scales as small and bright as pearls, in claws like alabaster, in great wings of white feathers, larger than her seraph wings. She stood before her mother, a dragon—not a dragon like the others, a creature of spikes and wide scales, but a dragon nonetheless. A dragon of Requiem.

"This is not purity," Meliora said to the queen, her voice flowing through her long neck and jaws. "But this is truth. This is righteousness. You will open the slaves' collars, Mother . . . or all the empire will see that your daughter stands among them."

Kalafi screamed—a wordless, beastly cry of pain. She drew a secret dagger from her dress and thrust the blade.

Meliora beat her wings and rose in the chamber. The dagger scraped across her scales, chipping them. With a thrust of her claws, Meliora knocked her mother down.

The queen fell with a scream, her dress tearing to reveal the ugly, never-healing wound beneath.

Meliora stared down at the fallen seraph. Smoke blasted from her nostrils. Kalafi stared up, fear in her eyes, blood on her dress.

"Where is the Keeper's Key?" Meliora growled, white fire crackling in her maw. "Give me the key, Mother. The key to the slaves' collars. Where is the key?"

Kalafi began to laugh. Lying on the floor, pinned down beneath Meliora's claws, her wound exposed and dripping, the queen laughed as if watching jesters fight for sport. "You will have to kill me, daughter. So long as I breathe, the key will never be yours. Do what I did! I slew a husband. Slay a mother. Show me that you're a killer too."

Meliora's claws rested on her mother. How easy it would be, she thought, to simply lean forward, apply just the slightest more pressure, to pierce Kalafi's flesh. To make the queen suffer. To pay for all she had done.

With a deep breath, Meliora removed her claws off her mother.

"I stand above you now," Meliora whispered. "And I could kill you as easily as a child crushes a bug. But I grant you life, Mother. I grant you shame. A shame all the empire will know. Next time you see me, I will wear rags, my head shaved, my back whipped, for I am a child of Saraph no more. I am a child of Requiem, and we are a nation in chains . . . but we will be free."

As Kalafi lay on the mosaic floor, staring up in silent fear, Meliora beat her wings. She knocked over vases and statues, her claws clattered across the floor, and she burst out onto the balcony. She leaped into the air, and Meliora soared, flying high above the city, high toward the sun and across the wind . . . flying to the land of Tofet. Flying home.

ISHTAFEL

My sister. My sweet Meliora. The future mother of my children. Ishtafel trembled with rage. *A weredragon.*

He marched through the palace, fingernails digging into his palms. A crack split his breastplate, and his chest dripped ichor. The golden blood, the pure blood of the gods, sizzled as it dripped, forming a trail. In one fist, he clutched a feather, long as a sword, white as leprosy—Meliora's feather, the feather from her dragon form.

A creature half seraph, half dragon. Ishtafel sneered, bile rising in his throat. *A disgusting freak. A monster I almost impregnated.*

He stormed down a portico. To his right rose a wall, its murals depicting his ancient victories. To his left rose columns, and between them sprawled a view of the city. The crowds were dispersing, and an eerie calmness fell across Shayeen, but inside of Ishtafel the battle still raged—the battle against his sister, his battle against Requiem five hundred years ago . . . a battle he still fought today.

The weredragons rebel. He squeezed the feather in his hand, his blood staining it. *I will crush them. I will crush every one. I will grind them into the dust. Their sickening blood stains my family. That blood will spill across the empire.*

A slave appeared in the corridor before him, rushing forth with a jug of water. The man froze and knelt. Ishtafel stomped toward him.

Their blood will spill.

Ishtafel grabbed the man's skull. He shoved his thumbs forward, gouging out the creature's eyes, squeezing, crushing the skull, sneering as the man's screams died, as the brains dripped. He lifted the body and slammed it against a column, shattering its bones, then lifted it again and threw it again, tossing the dripping remains to the city beyond.

They will pay.

He left the columns, and he roamed the corridors of his palace, and he was roaming the tunnels again, the labyrinth beneath Requiem, the hives of the creatures, the greatest battle of his life, the war that still raged within him, that he would never stop fighting. He grinned and licked his lips.

My war will never die.

He found another slave sweeping a corridor, and Ishtafel laughed as he tore out the woman's organs, held them overhead, bit into the sweet meat. He roamed onward, a hunter, a conqueror. A weredragon lurked in the shadows ahead, a vile creature with shining eyes, and Ishtafel shattered its spine, tossed it down, crushed its skull under his heel. He roamed onward, covered in blood, finding the weredragons in their burrows, slaying them one by one, a god of light, a god of vengeance.

You dirtied my sister. Your poison infected my legacy. Your blood will forever spill.

He roamed the halls of the ziggurat, roamed the tunnels of Requiem, covered in the blood of weredragons. He lifted a heart in each hand, still beating, crushing them, his trophies of flesh and victory.

MELIORA

She walked into the land of Tofet, her dress tattered and burnt, her wings bleeding and missing half their feathers, her eyes dry, her shoulders squared, an emptiness in her heart. She walked into ruin, into a land of agony, into her home, into the place that had always been her home.

For twenty-seven years, this land hid just beyond the horizon, Meliora thought. For twenty-seven years, she had gazed upon the edge of Tofet from her balcony, seeing nothing but a haze. She had imagined a land of happy miners, whistling as they shoved trolleys on tracks. A land where slaves sang in lush fields and vineyards, laughed as they danced upon grapes, picked fruits from rustling trees, retired in lazy afternoons to fish in streams and lounge in meadows. Often Meliora had wanted to flee her palace, to come to this wondrous land she had envisioned.

Now she walked into Tofet, into the shame of Saraph, the agony of Requiem.

She walked through a rocky field where slaves, chained and beaten, labored under the cruel sunlight. They mixed clay with straw and bitumen, forming bricks in molds, crying out as their masters whipped them with lashes of fire. She walked along a quarry where, deep in the earth, slaves labored with pickaxes, chipping stones for the columns of temples and palaces, coughing in the dust, falling in exhaustion only to suffer the kicking boots of their masters. She walked along a pit of tar where slaves shuffled, heavy yokes chained to their shoulders, bearing baskets of bitumen. The fumes spun Meliora's head, and every moment, another slave fell, burning his or her knees in the bubbling tar, crying out as the whips tore into their flesh.

I lived in wealth, a palace grown from the toil of these people, a throne upon their broken shoulders.

All around her, for miles, they cried out in pain, in memory, begging for mercy, praying for a lost home. As Meliora walked between them, charred and bruised, her tears fell onto the dry earth.

"I'm sorry, children of Requiem," she whispered. "I'm sorry. I'm sorry for my brother. For my mother. Forever, I'm sorry."

Finally, past the miles of pain, Meliora reached a city of clay huts. A great limestone wall surrounded the place, topped with seraphim guards. There were as many Vir Requis in the empire as seraphim, and yet their city was so much smaller, over half a million souls condensed into an area barely larger than the palace grounds south of the river. Each hut was small, smaller than the carriages Meliora used to ride in with her mother, molded of crude, flaking mud. Gutters ran between them, overflowing with filth.

No children played here as they did in Shayeen; here children hobbled in chains, scrawny, their ribs pushing against their skin, digging for beetles, worms, scraps of food in the dry earth. No happy mothers idled in gardens here, playing with plump babies; here mothers sat in what shade was available, heads shaved, too weak to even brush aside flies, their breasts ravaged as their babes suckled for whatever drops of milk they could drink. No flowers grew in Tofet, filling the air with sweet perfumes; Meliora smelled only disease, filth, death. No birds sang; she heard only the clanking chains, crying babes, distant whips lashing, and screams.

She kept walking through the nightmare, the guilt and horror battling for dominance within her. She was deep in the labyrinth of huts when she heard a nearby scream, stepped around a bend in the dirt road, and gasped.

A seraph overseer stood ahead, his back to her, clad in a fine breastplate and flowing white robes. No dust or blood marred his wings of purest white feathers. His whip of fire flailed, the blows landing on a slave in the mud. The slave raised her arms, begging for mercy, gravid with child.

"Silence, you guttering rat!" the overseer shouted, landing his whip again, the thong tearing into the pregnant slave's arms.

"Stop!" Meliora marched forward. Her chest shook and she could barely breathe. She had never seen such cruelty. "Seraph, stop!"

The overseer spun toward her, snarling, not recognizing her in her filthy rags. "Stand back, girl. This slave only produced nine hundred bricks today. Quota's a thousand." He spun back toward the slave, raising his whip again.

"I told you to stop, son of Saraph!" Meliora leaped toward him and grabbed his arm, tugging him back.

The overseer spun toward her again, face flushed, teeth bared. "And I told you to stand back, you whore. You ain't no overseer. Go fly back to your momma." He raised his whip, then brought it down hard against Meliora.

She yowled in pain. She had always known whips were painful, had always known that people screamed beneath them. Yet Meliora had never imagined such pain—searing, all-consuming pain, almost too much to bear, pain that flooded her, impossible pain. She fell.

The overseer brought the whip down again, hitting her shoulder and back, and Meliora screamed.

"I ain't afraid to teach a seraph pup a lesson either." The overseer smirked and raised his whip again. "I'm going to stripe you just as good as any slave, girl."

His whip lashed.

Meliora grabbed a rock from the ground.

The whip tore into her shoulder, and she hurled the stone.

The projectile streamed through the air and slammed into the overseer's brow.

Blood spurted and the seraph fell. He hit the ground and did not rise.

Everything suddenly seemed so silent. Her wounds aching, Meliora rose to her feet and limped forward. She stared down at the seraph. He lay on his back, his forehead shattered and bleeding, his eyes staring lifelessly.

Dead.

Meliora stared down, feeling nothing.

I killed. I took a life.

And still she felt nothing. No horror. No guilt. She was a killer. A murderer. A slayer of her own kind.

No. Not my kind.

She stepped over the fallen overseer and knelt by the wounded weredragon.

No. Not a weredragon. A Vir Requis.

Meliora lowered her hand. "Rise, friend."

But the slave did not rise. She knelt and bowed her head. "Meliora the Merciful. Praised be your name, child of starlight. May the stars bless you, daughter of Requiem." The woman looked up, eyes shining and damp. "Our savior. A savior from the palace of gods, from the stars of our home."

Meliora shook her head. "I'm not a savior. I was sent by none."

A new voice spoke, coming from behind her, a soft, high voice, trembling with awe. "You are *my* savior, sister. The stars sent you here."

Elory.

Meliora turned around and saw a family.

Elory stood there, wearing cotton rags, her legs hobbled again, her head stubbly. With her stood a young man—the same young man who had, only hours ago, been nailed into the ziggurat, now healed. Behind them stood an older man, his head shaved but his beard long, brown streaked with white, and he held a staff in his knobby hand.

A family.

My family.

Meliora blinked at them, and now—now all those feelings she could not feel when killing a man flooded her. Grief. Fear. But also love, also joy.

She stepped toward them, hesitant, breath trembling in her throat.

"You . . . you are my brother," she whispered to the young man. She turned toward the older man. "You . . . are my father. You are my family."

Elory smiled tremulously and nodded.

"This is Vale . . . your brother," the girl whispered, gesturing toward the young man. "And this is Jaren . . . your father. We're your family, Meliora. We're the people who love you."

Tears flowed down Meliora's cheeks, and for once they were not tears of pain or grief; they were tears of joy. She stepped closer and pulled her family into an embrace. They wept too, holding her in their arms.

"Welcome home, Meliora," her father whispered. "Welcome home."

LUCEM

He stood on the hill, singing.

He curled up in his cave, watching the rain.

He talked to stones. He laughed with trees. He laughed. He laughed and laughed. He wept.

He watched the sun rise and set thousands of times.

"Good morning. Good morning." The sunlight streamed into the cave, and Lucem gazed at the drawings on the walls. His friends. Animals. Men and women. Funny creatures he had invented. "Good morning."

They could not speak, but he could hear them in his mind. They greeted him.

He took one of his friends with him today—a lump of wood with two knots, two eyes, and a little smile he had carved. A beautiful woman. His dearest companion, a wife, a confidant. Together they walked across the hill, chewing mint leaves. Together they speared fish in the river, and they even caught a wild goat, and that night they feasted.

He sang around the campfire.

"Old Requiem Woods, where do thy harpists play, in Old Requiem Woods, where do thy dragons fly . . ."

He spread out his arms, and he danced around the fire, clad in his tattered tunic. A dragon. In his mind he was always a dragon. He blew out his breath, and the campfire flared—his dragonfire.

He fell to his knees, and he howled.

He grabbed his collar, tugged it, smashed it with rocks again and again. He fell to the ground, crawled into his cave, and shivered.

It's all right, his friends whispered—the drawings on the wall, the little wooden blocks with eyes. *You're safe here. You're far from pain. You're far from Tofet.*

"I'm far from Requiem," he whispered.

Requiem. The home of his ancestors, the place he had heard of so many times as a child. His parents had told him—his parents whom the seraphim overseers had murdered. His parents who lay buried in Tofet in a mass grave. His parents whose bodies he had left behind—along with so many living, with so many suffering souls, crying out under the whip, begging for mercy that would never come, pleading for freedom . . . which he had found.

Lying in the cave, Lucem balled his hands into fists, digging his fingernails into his palms. He screwed his eyes shut.

"I'm sorry," he whispered. "I'm so sorry. I left you. I climbed the wall. I escaped Tofet. I left you. I'm sorry. I'm sorry."

His tears stung. He had been only eleven years old—only a child, yet broken, too thin, covered in cuts and bruises, the marks of whips on his back. He had been small enough to climb in the dark, to escape the guards, to come here, to leave them, to betray them . . .

"I miss you, Mother," he whispered. "I miss you, Father. I'm sorry. I'm sorry."

He dreamed of Requiem—dreamed of flying in the night, flying with his parents, with countless dragons, no collars around their necks. Flying in their sky, their columns rising below from the birch forest.

Dawn rose—as it had risen so many times. He crawled out of his cave again. He fished in the river. He chewed his mint leaves. He chewed carobs and wild figs. And he walked.

The wilderness rolled by around him. Hills speckled with mint bushes, white boulders, and carob trees. A few goats ambled on a hill, and the river streamed at his side. The sun beat down, and grasshoppers bustled in the rushes.

He slept in the tall grass. He caught another fish with his spear. He walked on.

When he finally saw it, he paused and stared. His guilt rose inside him like a demon, struggling to crash through his ribs, to consume his flesh.

"Tofet," Lucem whispered.

The wall of that cursed place rose in the distance, hundreds of feet tall. Atop it stood the seraphim, guards and overseers, mere glints of sunlight on metal from here. Behind that wall, they still languished—six hundred thousand souls, children of Requiem. All those he had grown up with, worked with, suffered with. Crying out to him.

You left us, Lucem!

"I'm sorry," he whispered.

You betrayed us!

"I had to leave, I had to." He trembled. "They hurt me so badly."

Now they hurt us! Now we suffer while you dance and sing around your fires.

Lucem took a step closer. Then another. His fists shook at his sides.

"I'm coming home," he whispered. "I'm coming back. They'll let me back in. They have to! They have to."

He kept walking, moving closer to the wall. Soon the guards would see him. Soon they'd cry out, fly to him, lift him up, take him home—back into Tofet. To his people. To the grave of his parents. To an end to this guilt, to this torture, an end to this madness in the wilderness.

Back to the whips, his friend said. *Back to the mines, to the stench, to the death all around you.*

The block of wood stared at him. Lucem stared back.

"You know nothing," he said.

You are a fool! she said, staring with her knot eyes. *You will die in there. Die! Die and leave me. Tofet is not your home.*

"It's my only home," he said. "And you're only a block of wood, and you know nothing, so be quiet."

She glared at him. *Requiem is your home!*

He hurled the wood as far as he could, then winced, ran after her, lifted her, cradled her.

"I'm sorry, I'm sorry."

Go away from this place, she said. *Go! Go! Never come back.*

"Stop talking, you block of wood."

Then stop acting like a fool.

He turned around, and he walked away, leaving the wall behind—leaving them all behind. And that guilt screamed, tearing at his insides.

He walked along the river. He walked past his cave. He hunted. He fished. He ate fruit. He chewed leaves. For many days and nights he traveled, singing, laughing, telling old stories again and again. He kept talking—always talking. It was important not to forget how to talk. It was important to remember his name. "Lucem, Lucem," he said, over and over. He found a small rock shaped like a woman, a new friend, and he slept holding her.

He crossed hills, mountains. He hid in caves. He roamed through forests. He kept singing. He kept talking. You had to keep *talking*. You had to remember. He made new friends on the way.

Finally Lucem reached the coast, and he stood on the beach, and he stared out at the sea.

The waves were cobalt, almost gray, crested with foam. Clouds covered the sky. Lucem stood for a long time, staring.

"Requiem," he said. "Requiem. Requiem." You had to keep talking.

His homeland lay beyond the water. The land of dragons, the land his people had lost. In ruins. Devastated! But . . . maybe some had survived. Maybe some still hid there—hid in the ruins, waiting for him, waiting to welcome him home.

Lucem inhaled deeply, spread out his arms, and reached for his magic.

His skin began to harden, forming the first hints of scales. His fingernails began to lengthen into claws. The nubs of wings rose from his shoulder blades. His neck thickened . . . and the iron collar tightened around it.

He choked.

He grinded his teeth and kept tugging on his magic.

Pain. Pain flared through him, squeezing his neck, creaking his bones, blazing through his head.

Keep shifting. Become a dragon! Break the collar! Fly, fly home, fly—

Stars spread out before him, endless, the stars of his people, hovering over blackness. He fell into the sand, and he floated among them, gasping.

He slept.

When he finally awoke, it was night, and clouds hid the true stars. He shivered, feverish, and when he reached to his neck, he felt blood.

As always, he was a human.

Lucem howled.

He clawed at his collar until his fingers bled. He grabbed a sharp stone. He stabbed the collar again and again until he cut his neck, and the stone fell, and Lucem fell after it into the sand. He shivered.

"Lucem, Lucem," he whispered. "I have to remember, I have to keep talking."

A crab walked up and examined him, then scurried away. Lucem reached for it desperately. He needed to talk to it. He needed to hear its voice. And yet it scuttled away and vanished in the darkness.

Dawn rose, and Lucem rose, and his guilt rose, and he walked along the beach. Thirst clawed at his throat and hunger rumbled in his belly.

At noon he saw a city ahead. No walls rose around it, and he saw obelisks capped with gold, great cathedrals soaring to the sky, grand palaces and humbler homes. Above the roofs rose banners, showing an eye within a sunburst—symbol of Saraph. The city spread along the coast, sending ships into the waters. A city of seraphim.

Lucem stared, eyes damp. "People," he whispered. "People."

No! his wooden friend said. *Not people. Seraphim! Seraphim aren't people.*

"You're not people, you're just a block of wood," Lucem said. "Be quiet or I'm going to toss you into the sea."

I'll float, said the block of wood. *But you'll just drown trying to save me.*

"Hush!" he said. "*I* need to keep talking. *You* need to be quiet."

The block of wood glared at him. Lucem tucked her under his sleeve and kept walking, approaching the city. He could see more details now. Seraphim flew above upon swan wings. Bells rang in a steeple. Two towering statues rose ahead, shaped as serpopards—felines with necks longer than their bodies. Those necks curved and coiled around each other, forming a gateway that led into the city.

People, Lucem thought, staring at the seraphim on the walls ahead.

You better hide, Lucem, his friend spoke from under his arm. *At least until darkness.*

"If you're so afraid."

I am.

"All right then."

He stepped aside and he hid in a grove of pines, watching the waves and the city until darkness fell. Then he walked again, trying to ignore the thirst and hunger. In the shadows, he slinked through the archway, and he entered the coastal city.

Hide, Lucem!

He scurried sideways, sticking to the shadows. Seraphim still flew above, even in the night. Two walked down the road, wings held against their bodies. Fair beings, tall, beautiful, their hair cascading and golden. Clad in armor. Gods. People. People.

Hiding in the shadows, Lucem heard them talk. They remembered how to talk.

"—fine wine there tonight, and Leishan is singing," one said.

"Your night to buy the wine," said the other.

"It's always my turn when the fine wine is poured, isn't it? Very well, though, we . . ."

The two seraphim walked by, and their voices faded. Lucem emerged from the shadows, and he slinked after them, rushing from shadow to shadow. Lanterns shone along the cobbled street, and the walls of homes rose all around. More seraphim walked ahead, moving toward a large, brick building with bright windows. The sound of laughter and song rose from within, and Lucem smelled fine food and wine.

A tavern, Lucem thought. A place of food, of drink, of joy, of companionship. Of talking.

More seraphim approached, and Lucem retreated into an alleyway between the tavern and a workshop. He crept through the shadows to the back of the tavern. Warm light, the smells of wine and roast duck, and the song of harps and conversation all leaked through the windows. Lucem sat down, pulled his knees to his chest, and closed his eyes.

"Play for us, Leishan!" a seraph inside cried out.

"Play for us, Leishan," Lucem whispered.

"Pass me more duck, my dear!" rose another voice inside the tavern.

Lucem smacked his lips. "It's delicious. Splendid."

Inside the merriment and feast continued, and huddling outside in the alley, eyes closed, Lucem was there with them. Talking. Laughing. Eating and drinking. Feeling the horrible demon of loneliness fade—if only for one evening. He stole food from the trash bin. He drank from puddles. He feasted and drank with them—with other living souls.

Lucem lowered his head. If he had looked like a seraph—tall, fair, with swan wings, with golden eyes—he could perhaps try to find work, save money, book passage on a boat. If he had no collar, he could shift into a dragon, fly overseas, find what remained of Requiem.

But I'm only an escaped slave. A collared Vir Requis, my magic imprisoned inside me.

In the darkness, he left the city.

Once more he walked across the wilderness.

For days he travelled, and he sang those songs, and he tasted that wine and that roasted duck, and he relived that night over and over—the hints of life, pouring out, washing across him, soothing his loneliness yet making it greater than ever before.

Finally, weary and famished, he crawled back into his cave. He huddled on his bed of leaves, and he stared up at his friends on the walls—the animals and people he had painted there. They feasted that night, and sang songs, a little tavern of stone here by the river. A little place of light, of comfort, of tears among the rising shadows of madness.

MELIORA

For twenty-seven years, Meliora had lived in a palace, sleeping in a canopy bed as soft as gosling wings, eating from golden plates, lounging in chambers where walls were coated with precious metals and gemstones. Tonight, for the first time, she stepped into a true home.

The clay hut, her family's dwelling, was small. The entire place was no larger than her bed back in the palace. A few candles burned in alcoves in the walls, and a round window afforded a view of several other huts. The floor was bare rock, the ceiling rounded and shadowed. A table stood in the center of the room, topped with bowls of gruel, and piles of straw lay on the floor—the only beds here.

Ishtafel will send all his wrath to slay me, Meliora thought. *Soon the might of his chariots and soldiers will sweep through this city of huts, and he will hunt me like a wolf hunts its prey. But right now, this night, I am at peace. Right now I am at home.*

Her family entered the hut with her: her sister, her brother, her father.

"It's not much," Jaren said, looking around at the bare walls. "But it's—"

"Home," Meliora said.

Elory smiled at Meliora and took her hand. "Sit with us, sister. Let us eat together, and let us pray."

They sat together on stools around the table. Their elbows touched. Elory closed her eyes, lowered her head, and whispered.

"As the leaves fall upon our marble tiles, as the breeze rustles the birches beyond our column, as the sun gilds the mountains above our halls—know, young child of the woods, you are home, you are home." Elory opened her eyes, smiled, and looked up at the shadowy ceiling. "Requiem! May our wings forever find your sky."

The others repeated the words, voices soft. "Requiem! May our wings forever find your sky."

As Meliora spoke the ancient prayer with her family, she remembered her dreams of Requiem, her dreams of flying with her kind, with a family of dragons, and now—here in Tofet—those dreams seemed so real, memories passed down through the generations. Even now, after so long, the memory was alive, the dream was real—her dream, the dream of her family, the dream of countless in chains. And it was too much, too real. Her body trembled, and her eyes dampened, and it seemed like the weight of five hundred years of servitude pressed down on her shoulders like a yoke.

"Meliora!" Elory said. She leaped from her seat and embraced her. "Are you all right? I'm so sorry. I know that this must be a bit much."

"It's beautiful," Meliora whispered. "Thank you so much for inviting me into your home, for sharing this prayer with me. Thank you, Elory." She looked at the others. "Thank you, Vale. Thank you . . . Father."

The two men reached across the tabletop and held her hands, smiling at her, their eyes kind. Queen Kalafi and Prince Ishtafel had never gazed upon Meliora with kindness, not true kindness; they had seen her as a pampered girl, later a womb to produce their heir. But here, in this humble hut, was a place of more warmth, love, and comfort than any palace.

The candles flickered in a hot breeze through the window, and Meliora noticed, for the first time, that stars were engraved into the clay ceiling. They formed the shape of a dragon.

"We will see those stars again," Meliora said. "We will see Requiem in our lifetime, and we will rebuild her halls. I promise this to you, my family. I promise."

VALE

Night had fallen, and the land of Tofet slept, a short few hours of rest before their labor began anew. Soon the overseers would move between the dark huts, shouting, kicking doors open, breaking the bones of those who did not wake, slaying those who resisted. Soon the labor of Requiem would resume, eighteen hours of toiling under yoke and whip. Soon the cruel sunlight would blaze upon them, burning their shaved heads, blinding their eyes that still gazed toward the lost homeland in the north. Soon another day of agony, bloodshed, and pain would begin—another day, another year, another generation.

But that is tomorrow, Vale thought, standing in the shadows between clay huts. Tonight . . . tonight things were different. For the first time in five hundred years, tonight hope shone.

All others slept in their huts, but Vale would not sleep this night. Darkness and silence spread around him, but starlight still filled his eyes, and harps still sang in his ears, and the visions of Requiem still floated through his memories.

"I saw you," he whispered to the sky. "I saw you, Issari Seran, Princess of Requiem. I saw you, King Aeternum, our greatest father. I saw you, Queen Laira, our mother of life. I saw you, stars of Requiem, dragon of the sky."

Requiem was real.

Vale closed his eyes.

"For so long, I doubted," he whispered. "For so long, I did not believe. I thought that Requiem was a story, a fairy tale, a fantasy told to soothe the weary souls of slaves. To keep us alive in this cruel land. For so long, I thought that nothing existed in the north but more sand, not a land of fallen columns, of birches under a good sky." He opened his eyes and looked up at the sky. "I cannot see you from here, stars of Requiem. But I saw you. I saw you."

In his mind, he saw them even now—the Draco stars, shaped as a great dragon. Upon him, he still felt her hands—the hands of Issari, one of Requiem's founders, the great healer of light who had defeated the Demon King, who had risen to the sky and formed the dragon's eye.

"Requiem was real," he whispered.

A voice behind him answered. "Requiem *is* real."

He turned around and saw Meliora there. His half sister walked toward him through the shadows, her halo casting its soft glow. Staring at her, it was hard to believe that Meliora was half Vir Requis; she looked like any other seraph. Her hair was long and golden. Her eyes were the same color, gleaming, the pupils shaped as sunbursts. Even in human form, she sprouted wings, feathery and white. But as she approached, Vale saw that she was unlike any other seraph he had ever seen. Other seraphim stared with flaming, cruel eyes. Other seraphim had faces like stone statues, heartless. Meliora's eyes were warm, her face soft, her lips smiling a bittersweet smile.

I saw her fly as a great dragon. And I see the dragon magic in her, even now.

"But Requiem is fallen," he said. "Ishtafel toppled her halls five hundred years ago."

Meliora reached him and halted. She looked around the city of huts. "I don't know much about Requiem. All I know is what I've read in books, seen in murals, heard in songs—all of them created by seraphim. But I know this much, Vale." She laid her hands on his shoulders and stared into his eyes. "Requiem is not a *place*. Requiem is not a column of marble, not a forest, not even the sky above us. Requiem is in our souls. Requiem is in our dreams, our hopes, our prayers. Requiem is alive, Vale. She has always been alive—here in Tofet, wherever our hearts beat. Requiem is not forgotten. Requiem was never gone."

Light and hope shone in Meliora's eyes, but Vale felt something different. The starlight lifted from his eyes, replaced by dragonfire.

Standing here, collared and hobbled again by his masters, Vale felt as if dragonfire once more filled his belly. Searing. Blinding. A hot fury that burned his innards.

"If Requiem still lives," Vale said, "let us fight. We fought them together, Meliora. We both fought Ishtafel, and we both tasted his blood. Let the sons and daughters of Requiem march to war. We will cast off our chains. We will overthrow our masters. With you at the head of our column, Meliora, a daughter of Requiem and a daughter of Saraph." Vale clenched his fists. "We will do what our forebears could not. Defeat the seraphim."

Meliora looked up at the dark sky. Her voice was soft, lost in memory. "Painted across the walls and ceilings of the palace, I saw murals of countless dragons falling before Ishtafel's chariots of fire." She placed a hand against her neck. "I wear no collar, but you do, Vale. So do all other Vir Requis in the empire. If we could not defeat Ishtafel with our magic, what chance do we have without it?" She shook her head. "None. We cannot defeat Ishtafel with strength of arms, and we have no dragonfire to blow."

Vale looked around him at the land of Tofet. Huts of clay. Huts of misery. Gutters overflowing with night soil. Seraphim masters patrolling the shadowy walls that surrounded this great, outdoor prison. A land of slavery, despair.

"We cannot remain here," Vale said. "We cannot continue this life. Better to die in fire than live in chains."

"We need no fire." Meliora held his hands and stared into his eyes. "We need one voice. A people united. Our father marched through the streets of Shayeen, and he faced my mother, and he freed you. He spoke for Requiem, and the stars shone, and you're here now. Healed. Saved." Meliora's eyes shone. "Let all the slaves now march. Let every man, woman, and child of Requiem march together—in chains, whipped, collared—toward the palace of Saraph. And let us speak together, a great voice that the empire will hear: We will be free."

MELIORA

In the darkness of night, two hours before the cruel sun would emerge, the slaves of Tofet rose.

In the shadows of a foreign land, countless miles away from their fallen home, the children of Requiem lit their lights.

For thousands of nights like this, they had arisen in the dark, chained and collared, lifting pickaxes, yokes, buckets, shovels. For thousands of nights like this, they would toil in the shadows until the cruel sun rose, crying out to stars they could not see.

This night they left their tools behind.

This night they raised candles.

This night they did not hobble forth as slaves. This night they marched as Vir Requis.

Through the darkness, the lights streamed forth, a river of stars upon the barren land. Through the darkness, six hundred thousand souls flowed. Through the darkness they brought light.

They flowed out from the huts of Tofet, but they did not move toward the bitumen pits, the quarries, the refineries, the fields of shattered bones where bricks baked in kilns. They did not kneel before their masters. They walked toward the city, a single column. They walked following a new leader, a beacon of their own.

At the head of the column, she walked. A tall woman, her body bruised and cut. A woman with ragged wings, half their feathers burnt and gone. A woman with the golden eyes of a seraph that shone with the light of Requiem. She no longer wore priceless gowns inlaid with jewels; only a burlap shift covered her body. No longer did blond hair flow from her head; she had shaved it down to stubble. No longer did she wear anklets of platinum and diamonds; iron shackles now bound her legs.

Only days ago, I was a seraph—a princess of seraphim. Meliora walked, chin raised, leading her people. *Now I am a slave. Now I am stronger than I ever was.*

The Te'ephim River flowed before her. For so many years, this river had divided the fair city of Shayeen from Tofet. For so many years, this river had been as a curtain, shielding Meliora from the truth in the north, the horror and shame of her empire. Across the bridge they rose: the walls, temples, obelisks, statues, and palace of Shayeen.

Today I cross the river again. Today I return to my old home with my new people.

She looked behind, away from the city of platinum, and she saw those people.

They were not tall or fair as seraphim. They did not wear gold and muslin and jewels. Their wings could not grow, and their backs were striped, their legs hobbled. But looking at them, Meliora saw true nobility. Her sister walked a few paces behind her, her frame frail but her head held high, her eyes bright. Beside Elory walked her brother, Vale, scarred, his chains clattering, yet nobler than any golden warrior from the fortresses of Saraph. With them walked Jaren, healer, priest of Requiem, his cheeks gaunt and his beard long—a father to them, a father to all Vir Requis.

And behind Meliora's family walked the multitude: a nation that flowed across the miles. An ancient people. An ancient song. People who had fought endless wars, endless tyrants, who had risen from ruin time and again, who had survived as all other nations fell, who still shone bright, even now, even in chains.

"Requiem," Meliora whispered.

She turned back toward the city, and she raised her candle high. She walked ahead of the column, leading her people, until they reached the bridge that spanned the river.

And here, upon the bridge between slaves and sovereigns, their enemy waited.

The seraphim flew down from above, an angelic host, wings tipped with dawn. Their spears shone like their haloes, and their shields were disks like many suns. Hundreds or more descended toward the people of Requiem, golden gods, so mighty and fair that even in a host of so many souls, even led in rebellion, some of the Vir Requis knelt and prayed to their masters.

But Meliora did not kneel. Nor did her family. She stood facing the seraphim who landed on the bridge. She bore no scepter of royalty, but she held an old wooden staff, the roots on its tip shaped as a dragon's head, and she raised it before her.

"Halt, children of Saraph!" she called, and her voice—which she had always thought too high, too fair, the voice of a child—boomed across the land. "Lay down your spears, and let me pass! I am Meliora of the Thirteenth Dynasty, daughter of Queen Kalafi. I am Meliora Aeternum, daughter of Requiem. Lay down your blades and let us pass, or the light of Requiem will sear you."

The seraphim jeered. Their voices rose together, mocking, shouting of weredragons to crush, of miserable slaves to be grinded into the dust. They covered the bridge, a shield of gold and light, spears raised, faces twisted in disdain. On the northern bank, the edge of Tofet, the children of Requiem stood still, staring, silent.

"Stand aside!" Meliora called. "Stand back from me, seraphim, for I am still your mistress. My hair is gone, as are my gowns, as is my innocence, as is my softness, as is my mercy to any who stand in Requiem's way. The stars of Requiem rise in the north! Stand back or their light will burn you."

The seraphim's jeers rose louder, and one among them stepped forth. She was a tall seraph, her eyes cruel, her grin twisted, and her golden hair fluttered in the wind. She carried a flaming whip in one hand, a chain in the other. A cut ran across her face, still fresh—the cut of a dragon's claw.

Shani, Meliora knew. The cruel overseer who had whipped Elory so many times, who had held Vale's chain.

"I know you, Shani of House Caraf!" Meliora said. "I order you to kneel before me. Kneel for I am your mistress, and I will allow you to live."

Yet Shani did not kneel. The seraph beat her wings, soared into the air, they plunged down to land before Meliora. The overseer snickered, her crooked smile twisting her scar, and spat on Meliora.

"I do not kneel before reptiles." Shani hefted the chain she bore. "I know who you are, Meliora the weredragon. This chain bound your brother. Now it will shatter your bones."

Slowly, staring at the seraph, Meliora wiped the spit off her face. "I will give you one more chance, Shani the Overseer. Kneel now before your mistress, or—"

Shani snorted. "I serve only Ishtafel, not his half-breed, reptilian whore of a sister." She beat her wings, rose into the air, and swung her chain. "You will kneel on shattered legs before I let you die."

Behind Meliora, her family cried out wordlessly. The chain swung down, each link the size of a fist. Meliora did not step back. She raised her staff before her.

The chain slammed into the wood, wrapped around the shaft, and locked into place.

Meliora swung her staff like a sword, yanking Shani sideways, and slammed the seraph down onto the earth.

"I told you that you will kneel," Meliora said softly.

Shani leaped up, sneering, and beat her wings. She soared toward the sky, the rising sun at her back. With a howl, the overseer plunged down, a goddess of vengeance, swinging her chain in one hand, her firewhip in the other.

"Die now, reptile!"

"Meliora!" Elory cried.

Let the light of the stars flow through me. Meliora looked to the sky, calling upon the light of Requiem. *Let me rise.*

As flame and chain came down, Meliora rose.

Her wings grew longer, feathers gilded in the sunrise. Her claws reached out, and her pearly scales chinked, and she soared, a feathered dragon of sunlight and starlight.

Shani's chain slammed into her shoulder, cracking scales. The seraph's firewhip drove into Meliora's wing, cutting through feathers and burning the flesh beneath. But still the silver-and-gold dragon soared, and her jaws opened, and she blew out her fire—a white jet, spinning and humming, a great harp string, a column like the one Aeternum had raised in a forest five thousand years ago.

Shani screamed.

The white flames slammed into the seraph.

Meliora flew higher, blasting out her flames, bathing Shani. The seraph cried out, wings beating, burning, her feathers turning black and falling. Shani tried to emerge from the inferno, tried to reach Meliora, to swing her weapons. But the flames kept washing over her, stripping off her hair, melting her armor, melting her flesh.

Finally Meliora let her flames die.

Shani fell and landed on the riverbank, a blackened corpse, ashes fluttering off bones.

Meliora rose even higher in the sky and spread her feathered dragon wings. The sun rose in the east, bathing her with golden light. Her tail flailed, tipped with feathers, and she could see the city ahead, drenched in light.

"So shall happen to all who stand before the children of Requiem!" Meliora cried, her voice booming across the land. "I am Meliora. I was one of you, Saraph! I served as your princess! But now I serve a greater light. Stand aside and lay down your blades! I come here not in war, not to conquer, not to burn. I come to show Shayeen the plight of Requiem, to show them the chains, the scars, the horror they had never seen. I bring Requiem into the city it built, and we will stand before the palace whose mortar is mixed with the blood of dragons. I come with only light, but if you do not stand aside, my fire will burn you."

She spun in the sky, blasting fire skyward, a great column of white light, King's Column risen in the south. Below her, the multitudes of slaves—descendants of the great warriors of the north—raised their candles, many smaller lights adding together to a constellation, a sky, a beacon of hope, of rededication.

"Remember Requiem!" they chanted. "Remember Requiem!"

As the slaves sang, as the lights burned, and as Meliora blew her flaming pillar, the seraphim took flight off the bridge.

At first Meliora thought they would attack, thought that she would have to fight them all, that that they would swoop with whips and blades and slay thousands . . . but as she watched, the light in her eyes, the overseers flew down to the riverbank, lowered their heads, and lowered their weapons.

"Follow, children of Requiem!" Meliora cried down to them, still hovering above as a dragon. "We enter Shayeen. We march to Queen Kalafi. We demand our collars removed. We demand freedom."

She flew before the camp, blowing her fire, and the children of Requiem walked below her. They crossed the bridge, holding their candles high, singing the old songs of Requiem. One by one, thousand by thousand, the slaves entered the City of Kings, and Meliora flew above them, and across the city seraphim stared but dared not attack, for they saw a goddess of scales and white fire.

But I am no goddess, Meliora thought as the people of Requiem walked down the boulevard between statues of the Eight. *I'm only a girl, exiled, torn, afraid . . . but I found new strength. In a world crumbling under lies, I found new truth. I found a new people. I found a new family.*

They marched toward the palace, six hundred thousand strong, and their voices rose together in an old song.

"Requiem! May our wings forever find your sky."

KALAFI

The wound blazed.

Always it blazed. Always the hands of the gods flared on her side, an eternal curse of their cruelty, a holy leprosy that would never heal. Yet now, this dawn, it flared with a new intensity Kalafi had not felt since falling from the sky three thousand years ago.

Morning's light streamed between the balcony's columns, red as blood. Kalafi lay in her salted pool, wincing in pain. She had spent all night in the water—the first time she had done so in years—and the water was cold now, too damn cold, yellowish with her wound's discharge. She needed more heated water, more salt, she needed her slaves here, yet her beast of a son had slain half the slaves in the palace in his overnight rampage. And so she lingered here, shivering now, afraid.

Kalafi had not been afraid in years.

I should have killed her, Kalafi thought. *I should have killed my daughter a thousand times.*

What madness had driven her to birth an impure creature, a half-breed, tainting the blood of seraphim with the reptilian curse? Kalafi could have mated with another—with her own son, if she were so concerned with purity of blood. Yet she had fallen to her temptation, had allowed that reptile to place his seed inside her. Jaren had been young only days ago, it seemed, yet now he was old, withered, a priest who had called upon ancient gods, who had summoned down the wrath of starlight.

And I should have killed you too, Ishtafel, she thought. Once she had been so proud of her son—a mighty warrior who had conquered this world, had built them a new paradise in a land of old pain. A beautiful being, untainted with memories of Edinnu, with old wounds that would never heal. How she had loved him! Yet the warrior had become a beast, an animal unable to curb his instinct, a mindless god who raped, tortured, butchered for sport, no end to his cravings, no boundary to his appetites.

"I birthed two monsters," Kalafi whispered.

"No, Mother. One monster. One son stronger than you've ever been."

Kalafi spun in the water and saw Ishtafel enter the room. She hissed.

"Leave this place!" She covered her nakedness with her arms. "I told you to never enter this chamber."

Yet he stepped closer across the mosaic of fish that sprawled across the floor. His armor was cracked, and blood and gore dripped off his hands and face. Bits of flesh dangled between his teeth, as if he were a wolf raising his head from a carcass.

"I've flown across the world, Mother." He licked his lips and sucked up a hanging strand of meat. "I killed the ice beasts in the northern pole, and I slew the griffins of the east, and I defeated so many enemies, Mother. Demons that would haunt your nightmares if you only saw a vision of them—and I fought them in their underground pits. Gods upon mountains, carved of ice, with pulsing hearts in their frozen breasts, creatures whose gazes would freeze and shatter your bones—I shone my light upon them, and I shattered them." He stepped closer, leaving a trail of blood. "And I slew dragons, Mother. I faced an army of a million dragons, the greatest army in this world, and I watched thousands of seraphim die around me, but I slew them. I defeated the enemy. And yet . . . and yet those dragons still live. Beyond the river. Here in our palace. And . . . in my sister."

Kalafi rose from the pool, wincing in pain. Her wound dripped pus. She grabbed a robe and covered herself, stood on the edge of the pool, and stared at her son. "You sicken me, Ishtafel. Your wars are over. You won them! Yet you prowl through this palace as if it were a battlefield—this palace that your father built—slaying my own slaves. Shedding blood upon priceless jewels. Acting like a beast among civilized souls and—"

"My father?" Ishtafel frowned and nodded. He looked around him. "Yes. My father built this palace. The king. A noble man, far nobler than me or you, Mother. A man who cared for the purity of our race, of our dynasty, of our legacy." Ishtafel contemplated the blood on his fingers, rubbing them together.

"And yet you betrayed that purity. You took a slave into your bed."

Kalafi snorted. "Do you think I don't know—that anyone doesn't know—how many slaves you've bedded?"

"Bedded, yes." Ishtafel nodded. "But I was always careful. Whenever their bellies swelled with my children, I took care of the problem. Do you see, Mother? My . . . what did you call it? Beastliness? That quality preserved our blood. That quality had our greatest enemies fleeing before my hosts. That quality built us an empire. You and father fell from paradise." Ishtafel clenched his fist, letting the blood drip between the fingers. "I built us a new paradise."

Kalafi snickered. "I don't recall blood staining the floor in Edinnu."

Ishtafel continued as if he hadn't heard her. "Do you know, Mother, that you almost ruined us?" He emitted a short burst of laughter, a sound like a snapping bone. "I almost married Meliora. I almost placed an heir in her belly. In the belly of a half-breed." He stepped closer, and suddenly his face changed, becoming a demonic mask, and his voice rose to a howl. "I almost fathered a monster!"

Kalafi nodded, stepping toward him until she stood only inches away from her son. "You did," she whispered. She placed a finger against his lips, covering it with blood, then brought her finger to her own mouth and sucked up the coppery liquid. "You almost fathered a monster, Ishtafel . . . a child like you. A child vicious. A child with no respect for the gods. For Edinnu's memory. For the light of Saraph." She spat out the blood. "All you are is a warrior. You will never be a king."

He stared at her in silence, face frozen, a mask of stone. His eyes were dead.

There is no humanity to his eyes, Kalafi thought. *There is no soul.*

Slowly that face changed, twisting into something resembling a hideous smile.

"But you're wrong, Mother." When his grin widened, she saw broken teeth in his mouth—not his own. "I will be king. Dawn rises upon a new ruler of Saraph. Farewell, Mother."

She hissed and tried to leap toward her side table, toward the blade that lay there.

She was too slow.

His hands pressed against her chest, shoving her, and she fell.

Time was too slow.

She fell for hours, she thought. She fell for years. Perhaps she had been falling since that day, since that war she and her husband had never stood a chance to win. She had fallen from the sky that day, hurt, bleeding, cast out from Edinnu, and still she fell . . . through blue skies. Through golden rain. Through ending and rising eras, through betrayal, through grief, through a lost daughter.

I'm sorry, Meliora. I love you.

The skies of Edinnu shone above her, the gilded clouds in dawn, the meadows with those flowers whose names she no longer knew, those trees of forbidden fruit, the land she had never forgotten, had never stopped trying to raise again here upon this cruel world, this place of so much hatred, so much endless pain.

She fell.

She fell from paradise.

She fell and she hit the floor, and her head hit the edge of the pool, and as she slid into the water she knew that her head had broken. That her skull had cracked. That she would not rise again, that this wound too would not heal, but that soon the pain, the guilt, the never-ending sadness would end.

I fought the gods. Her eyelids fluttered. *I fought in a great war such as my son would never know. I die at that son's hands. Queen of an empire, the woman who stood up to the Eight and resisted them, I die cracking my head on a wet poolside.*

She laughed.

She sank into the water, and blood rose from her, coiling, dancing, dancing with her, dancing the eternal dance, and she danced with them, with the spirits of demons and the ghosts of long gone years.

MELIORA

As she had a thousand times, coming home from strolls in the gardens or prayers at the temples, Meliora stood before the ziggurat of Saraph.

A thousand times, she had come here clad in fineries, her hair perfumed and brushed by her slaves, her body shining with jewels. Now she wore rags. Now her head was shaved. If not for the tattered, burnt wings that grew from her back, she would have appeared as any other slave.

For now I am a slave, she thought. *Now I am a child of starlight. Now I am mightier than I've ever been.*

Behind her they stood, flowing down the Boulevard of the Victorious from ziggurat to the city gates, hundreds of thousands of slaves.

No—not slaves, she thought. *Comrades. Vir Requis.*

Silence cloaked the city. Even with a nation behind her, with countless seraphim watching from the roofs of homes, Shayeen was silent. Not a breeze blew and not a bird sang. The sun beat down upon a still city.

Meliora raised her chin.

"Queen Kalafi!" she called out, staring up at the balcony. "Queen Kalafi, do you hear? Come speak to me!"

Her voice sounded almost too loud, echoing across the silent city. She thought that all her people, spreading across the miles, could hear.

Not a seraph or slave stirred. Not a soul emerged onto the balcony. The ziggurat loomed above her, its stairs stretching up its limestone facades, the massive bricks hauled here by slaves hundreds of years ago. Two colossal statues framed the staircase, carved as women with the heads of cats, ancient protectors of royalty. Its platinum crest shone, and the eye upon it—the Eye of Saraph within the sunburst—gazed down at her from a thousand feet above, reflecting the sunlight, nearly blinding Meliora.

"Queen Kalafi!" Meliora called again. "Come speak to those whom you enslave. Come hear those who demand their freedom. Mother! Come speak to your daughter."

Still—only silence. The world seemed frozen around Meliora.

A few chains rattled around her. She glanced to her side to see slaves shifting their weight, clenching and unclenching their fists. Only her family kept staring ahead at the ziggurat, still, faces blank.

Meliora looked back toward the palace and raised her staff.

"Hear me, Kalafi of the Thirteenth Dynasty, Great of Graces, Queen of Saraph! I am Meliora. I am a daughter of Requiem, and I am a daughter of Saraph. I grant these people freedom from chains! I will lead them north to their stolen homeland as I've led them here to your palace. Grant me the key to their collars! Grant me the key, for we are a free people, and we will no longer serve as slaves, no longer—"

She gasped and bit down on her words.

A chariot of fire emerged from a tunnel on the ziggurat, hundreds of feet above, and rose to shine in the sky like a second sun. Its four firehorses reared, wings casting off sparks.

From this distance, it was hard to see. Meliora made out barely more than fire and light beams. A figure stood within the hovering chariot, wreathed in gold, halo crackling and wings spread wide. And—

Meliora hissed.

The figure threw something down from the chariot.

A ball flew through the sunbeams, leaving a trail of gold, tumbling down and down, and finally slammed by Meliora's feet where it shattered, spilling its innards.

Meliora took a step back and couldn't help it. She screamed.

On the ground before her, shattered into several pieces on impact, was a woman's head. Half the face remained, enough for Meliora to recognize her.

"Mother," she whispered.

Elory screamed too and stepped back, covering her mouth. Vale cursed and Jaren whispered a prayer. Across the crowd of slaves, men and women whispered and mumbled and a child wept.

Meliora could barely hear them, barely see them.

Mother . . .

Perhaps her life had been a lie. Perhaps the old king had never been her father. Perhaps Ishtafel had never been a true friend, only one who craved her flesh. But here—here before her, these remains . . . this was her mother. Her true mother. The woman who had grown Meliora in the womb, birthed her in blood, raised her.

Memories flooded her again, as they had in Tofet, but these were not memories of dragons. She remembered a beautiful, angelic mother, rocking her, singing to her softly songs of old Edinnu. She remembered carefree days in the gardens, chasing her mother between the fountains, catching her, laughing with her, always laughing. She remembered a proud queen, teaching Meliora how to walk with pride, how to be beautiful, how to be royal, how to be proud.

In the past few days, Meliora had learned to hate her mother, learned to see a tyrant, but she could not erase years of love. Not before this horror.

My mother is gone.

Slowly, Meliora balled her hands into fists.

She raised her head from the remains on the ground, and she stared up at the flaming chariot that hovered far above, and she saw him there.

"Ishtafel!" she shouted, voice torn with rage, rolling across the city.

He raised his hand. "It is I!"

The sun rose to its zenith, casting its beams down upon him. Standing in his chariot, he spread his wings wide, a golden god. A killer. A king.

Meliora growled and shifted into a dragon. She soared, the air whistling, rising in a straight line until she hovered before the chariot. Not a hundred yards away, blood stained the ziggurat's platinum facade where Vale had hung.

"What have you done, Ishtafel!" she cried, beating her wings.

He stood before her, hands stained with blood. "I did what you could not! I did what I've been doing for centuries." A grin split his face, revealing red teeth. "Conquering. I conquered the world, Meliora. Did you really think I would let another rule it?"

Meliora hovered before him, scales chinking as she beat her wings. She stared at him, shaking her head, not recognizing him. Who was he? Who was this creature? Not her brother. Not the man who would bounce her on his knee, who would play ball with her in the gardens, who would listen to her prattle on endlessly about her dolls and puppies.

This has always been him, she realized, flying before the chariot. *The other him, the one who danced with me, who laughed with me—that was a mask. Here is the Ishtafel that Requiem saw five hundred years ago, that countless other enemies saw before they fell. Here is my true brother. Here is the true gilded, rotted heart of Saraph.*

"You're right," she said. "I could not kill Mother. But I killed a man in Tofet. And I killed Shani the overseer. And I will kill you."

She sucked in air and let flames rise in her belly, prepared to blast her fire.

Standing before her in his hovering chariot, he smiled thinly and pulled a key out from his pocket. A long, crimson key engraved with golden runes. He held it before her.

"Did you know, Meliora," he said, "that dragonfire is hot enough to melt metal? Even an ancient, magical key to open ancient, magical collars."

Meliora sneered and swallowed her flames. She sucked in air. The key! The Keeper's Key! The key that could open the collars of her people, that could give them freedom, that could take them back home, that—

"You want this, don't you?" Ishtafel smiled thinly. "It's the only one of its kind in the world, do you know? Yes, the power this key has—to let dragons dig for bitumen, to haul stones, and . . ." Ishtafel frowned. "Do you know, sister? I do believe that's all this key is good for. Doesn't seem like very much, does it?" He shrugged. "More trouble than it's worth, it would seem to me. Oh well."

With that, he closed his fist around the key, crumpling the metal in his hand.

"No!" Meliora shouted and flew forth, reaching out her claws.

Ishtafel grinned, lifted a shield and lance from his chariot, and thrust the blade toward her.

She roared out her flames, and her dragonfire blasted against his shield. His lance drove into her shoulder, and Meliora howled in pain.

"Meliora!" somebody cried below, but she could barely see them, barely hear them; the other Vir Requis stood a thousand feet below, unable to shift into dragons, their hope gone, the key crushed.

"Yes, scream for me, whore!" Ishtafel shouted from his flaming chariot. He laughed. "You will scream in my bed. You will scream as you give birth to my child."

"I will never—"

He thrust his spear again.

The lance drove into her wing, and she roared. Her blood rained. She blew her fire again, but his chariot rose, and her white flames passed beneath it.

He swooped, his firehorses kicking, and hooves of brimstone slammed into Meliora, cracking her scales, burning her skin. His lance thrust again, scraping across her back, tearing off small white scales like pearls. She screamed.

"Already you scream, Meliora!" He laughed, driving his chariot around her in the sky. "You are nothing but a slave now. My slave. My blood. My bearer of children. Your son will be king, Meliora! He will rise to crush your precious weredragons!"

Her lifeblood dripped to the city below. She spun in the sky. The city, the river, the desert beyond, the cruel sun—they all swirled around her. The souls below, calling her name. Her family—crying for her. Requiem—a dream, just a dream, slipping away.

No.

She growled.

I do not abandon hope. I will be brave.

She roared and charged toward her brother. She blasted fire, and the flames cascaded across his shield. She soared skyward, then spun, the sun at her back, and plunged down toward him, claws outstretched.

He raised his shield, and her claws slammed against it, denting the steel. She grabbed the disk with both front claws, tugging at it. She roared down fire, and the flames exploded, crashing against the shield, showering back up against her, igniting her feathers. She burned. She kept clawing, biting, and she tore the shield away, exposing her brother in his flaming chariot.

She opened her jaws wide and lashed down, prepared to bite.

He raised a sword, thrusting it into her mouth.

The blade scraped against her palate and sank into the flesh.

The pain blinded her.

White.

White fire.

Her own flames, burning her.

She fell. She fell through the sky, a human again, tumbling down, her seraph wings losing their feathers, blood in her mouth, blood raining, falling, falling toward her family, falling to death, to the death of hope. Above her, she saw him in the sky, laughing, his chariot a sun, his lance and sword raised, coated with her blood. He came swooping toward her, refusing to even give her death, refusing to ever release her from pain.

Requiem.

Shadows in the night.

Dragons in the wind.

A marble column rising from ruin to starlight.

Meliora tightened her fists as she fell. *I will not forget you, Requiem. I will not die. Not so long as I can fight.*

"Requiem!" she cried. "May our wings forever find your sky."

She found her magic, and she found her sky. She shifted, growing into a dragon again, her scales chipped, her body pierced, but still a dragon of Requiem, still fighting, still soaring through that sky.

His lance thrust.

She slammed against him, his weapon in her chest.

She cried out in agony, the chariot's fire washing across her, the hooves slamming into her. He leaned across his chariot, grabbed her wing, and tugged her up, and his sword drove into her shoulder.

She couldn't even scream. She couldn't even breathe.

She fell into his chariot, a human again, and lay at his feet.

"Sweetest Meliora." He leaned down, tugged her head up from the floor, and snapped a collar around her neck. "Don't die on me yet. I still have use for you."

She tried to breathe. She tried to live. Blood dripped into her eyes. She heard them cry her name below, heard them call for Requiem, heard them pray, but above it all roared the flames of the chariot. They flew down. Down. Spiraling. The sun spinning. The city spreading into hazy horizons, places she could never fly to, hope burnt.

I flew as a dragon.

She tried to raise her head. He placed a boot against her cheek, shoving her head back down.

I have to fly. I am the wind. I am fire.

She reached for her magic, trying to shift. She felt it. The starlight. The magic of Requiem. She saw them—the celestial halls, the great kings and queens of old, and she was shifting, growing, ready to fly, to—

She gasped in pain.

The collar squeezed her neck.

Her eyes rolled back. She sucked in air, trying to cling to life, her magic gone. The key crushed. She saw it lying beside her, crumpled, broken. She grabbed it in her fist.

Fire crackled, and every bone in her body seemed to shatter, as the chariot landed. Hands grabbed her—his hands, tipped with bloody fingernails like claws. Hands that had slain millions. They tugged her, lifting her, dragging her out of the chariot. He gripped her against him, his arm across her chest, pinning her body to his. Blood dripped around their feet.

"See your champion, slaves!" Ishtafel shouted, voice thrumming against her ear, impossibly loud, tearing at her eardrum. "See Meliora, the Reptile Whore!"

She blinked in the sunlight. She stood on the balcony, she realized. Her mother's balcony. The king's balcony. Below they spread across the miles, the children of Requiem, a proud nation, a nation of slaves. Lives she couldn't save.

The Keeper's Key. It's crushed. It's gone. She felt it in her fist, broken, crumpled into a ball. She trembled. She tried to shift again. She could not. She would have fallen to her knees were he not holding her up.

"Requiem," she whispered, hoarse, tasting hot copper. "May our wings forever find your sky."

"Wings, sister?" Ishtafel leaned forward, lips against her ear, his breath foul, smelling of rank meat. "Slaves do not have wings."

He kicked the back of her knees, forcing her to kneel, and wrapped an arm around her throat, constricting her.

"See how she kneels, weredragons!" Ishtafel called off the balcony. "Meliora calls herself a slave now. Then let her be a slave as you are! Kneeling, collared, and wingless."

He raised his sword.

He thrust the blade down.

Meliora screamed.

The pain shattered her. It claimed her. She wept with it. She tried to shift again but could not. She tried to fight him. She tried to rise to her feet, but he shoved her down. His sword lashed again, and she howled, a torn cry, and the crowd below screamed. Above her head, her halo crackled, shattered, blazed with red light.

"Take her wings, Requiem!" Ishtafel said, laughing, holding them up, severed, bleeding. "See if they fly."

He tossed Meliora's seraph wings from the balcony, and they glided down, mere feathers, feathers on the wind, mere dreams, mere clouds like the clouds of lost Edinnu. The blood flowed down her back and pooled on the balcony floor. The agony was a living thing, two demons digging through her, phantom wings that screamed, burning, flapping madly, every missing fiber crackling with the agony. Flames burned around her head, blasting her with heat.

"You defied me, sister." Ishtafel lifted her in his arms. "Now you learn the price of all who dare fight me." He raised her above his head, and he roared to the crowd. "Behold your leader, Requiem! Behold Meliora, collared, wingless, my slave."

Chariots of fire streamed across the sky. Hundreds of them, rising from behind the ziggurat, storming forth, leaving hundreds of trails like jets of dragonfire.

The slaves below screamed.

Meliora's blood dripped.

She clutched the crumpled key in her hand. She had to think. To focus. To feel her magic. To feel nothing else. To . . .

Her thought faded, and she fell into shadow, falling like her mother had fallen from Edinnu, falling like the columns of Requiem, falling until nothing was left.

ISHTAFEL

He tossed her into the prison cell—a beaten, pathetic slave, her wings cut off, cast out from his empire of light. No more golden glow haloed her, only a ring of red fire, the eternal flame of her curse. He slammed the cell door shut, sealing her in shadows. He grinned and licked her blood off his fingers, savoring the taste.

"Sleep awhile, Meliora." He stared at the closed, heavy door, grinning. "Rest. Regain your strength. You're going to need it."

Her blood was sweet in his mouth. Yes, tainted with the weredragon curse, but half of it was his own blood. What choice did he have? His mother was dead. So was his father. There were no others to pass on the pure blood of the Thirteenth Dynasty; the only other with that ichor was Meliora, impure as it was. She would have to serve, would have to bear him a child. And if that child too showed the weredragon curse, could shift into a beast? Well, such children could be culled, and her womb would bear him another child—again and again, until a pure child was born, one clean of the reptilian curse. That child's womb too could carry his seed, as could the womb after it, every generation purer, slowly filtering out the dragon, as one sifts golden flecks out of soil.

I can wait, Ishtafel thought. *I can breed out the disease from you, Meliora. But you will have to live for a long while.*

Leaving Meliora in her dungeon cell, Ishtafel walked down the corridor, hungry, famished, desperate for meat. Deep underground he prowled, seeking prey. Through the labyrinth he moved, deep beneath the ziggurat, the belly of his empire, until he found the pit.

He entered the candlelit chamber. Aromatic purple smoke wafted here, and green hintan bubbled in glass hookahs. The slaves lounged here upon tasseled cushions and rugs, clad in silks, eyes glassy. The place where Elory had gone to study; the place Meliora had snatched her from. Ishtafel moved through the chamber, hunger growing.

"My lord!" said one slave, rushing forward. She was a young woman with long brown hair, large brown eyes, and slender bones he could imagine shattering. "Welcome to the pleasure pit! I am Tash, and I would be glad to—"

He grabbed her, snarling, unable to resist any longer. He shoved her down.

"My lord, I would be happy to please you—" she began.

"Silence." He ripped at her clothes, tearing the silk, and he claimed her, clutching her body, staining her pale skin with Meliora's blood, laughing, drooling onto her, conquering her, soothing his hunger. For now. For now.

He shoved the slave away.

"I'll be back for more later." He snorted. "Clean up."

He left the pleasure pit. He climbed staircases. Still hungry. Still needing to feed.

He stepped onto the northern portico, stood between the columns, and stared out at the city. They were still there across the mote and gardens, clogging the streets. Myriads of them. Slaves. Weredragons. Their fists were raised, and they were chanting together in one voice.

"Free Meliora! Free Meliora! Blessed be Meliora the Merciful!"

Sandals thumped and armor clanked at his side. Ishtafel turned his head to see one of his generals approaching, a seraph named Kerael. Among the most ancient of seraphim, Kerael had lived during the fall of Edinnu, had fought the Eight Gods himself with lance and shield. He still bore that same old lance and shield, the steel three thousand years old. His breastplate was gilded, and his swan wings spread out, blinding in the sunlight.

"My king." He knelt before Ishtafel. "I swear my allegiance to you, my lord. The hosts of Saraph are ready, glorious Ishtafel. How may they serve you?"

Ishtafel motioned for the general to rise. "How many soldiers are currently garrisoned in the City of Kings?" he asked, already knowing the answer.

"Two full divisions, my lord, of proud sons and daughters of Saraph, each armed with a lance."

"Good." Ishtafel nodded. "And there are, I'm told, six hundred thousand slaves outside our doors. Have you ever heard of decimation, Kerael? The slaying of one in ten?"

Kerael had followed him through countless wars, from the conquest of Requiem to the slaying of the last dragons. Yet now, perhaps for the first time, Kerael seemed taken aback. His face paled, and it was a fraction of a second before he replied—an eternity.

"I shall spare the women and children, of course." Kerael nodded. "But—"

"No, Kerael." Ishtafel placed a hand on the general's shoulder. "It is the men we need for labor. You will *especially* slay women and children. I want sixty thousand corpses, skewered on sixty thousand spears. And I want those spears raised in the land of Tofet, a forest of flesh. I want them to remain there, rotting in the sun, festering, fluttering with vultures. And I want the survivors to see them as they toil. And oh . . . how they will toil. Their quotas will double as they work in the shadow of their dead. Now fly out! Take the chariots. Summon all your men." Ishtafel clenched his fists, grinning. "I will fly with you. We will make them pay."

ELORY

Elory stood outside with her people, fist raised, chanting for freedom.

"Free Meliora!" the slaves cried. "Blessed be Meliora the Merciful!"

Standing here with her brother, her father, and all her nation, Elory felt stronger than she ever had. They were no longer cowering in Tofet. They were standing united. Heads held high. Fists raised. Chanting in one voice.

"Free Meliora! Free Meliora!"

Their cries rolled across the city, flowing over the ziggurat, the statues of the gods, the obelisks, the temples, the boulevards and roads—this wonder their sweat and tears and blood had built, this city of their masters, this city they would topple with their voice.

"Remember Requiem!" Elory cried.

"Remember Requiem!" called her father and brother.

The crowd chanted together, spreading across Shayeen. "Requiem! Requiem!"

Elory knew that Requiem was not merely a place. It was not merely a kingdom. It was a nation. An idea. A prayer. It was a home for the lost, a haven for a cursed people, a light in the darkness. Requiem was hope.

She left her brother and father, and she climbed onto a statue of a seraph, a towering deity of limestone and gold. She was on the idol's shoulder, chanting for Requiem, when the fire rained from the sky.

Elory stared up, frozen, her voice dying on her lips.

Light.

Flames.

Death.

Death fell from the sky.

The chariots of fire flew out from the ziggurat, from fortresses, from temples. Their flaming wakes covered the sky like dragonfire. Thousands of them flew above, their firehorses rearing in the air, burning wings spread wide. In the chariots they rode—the seraphim, soldiers of the empire, lances rising, shields blazing like suns. The hosts of war. Hosts of heaven.

It's what Requiem saw, Elory thought, staring above, frozen in fear. *It's what our people saw that day five hundred years ago. Death. They saw death in fire.*

The chanting below died.

The chariots swooped.

And the screaming began.

Elory knew that in Requiem's tales, great events were remembered forever—King Aeternum defeating the demons of the Abyss, Issari Seran rising into the sky to form a star in Draco's eye, the fall of Requiem to Dies Irae's griffins, the heroine Queen Gloriae raising Requiem from ruin, the rebirth of Requiem under King Elethor, and the great Queen Fidelity who had saved the lost magic of dragons. Some stories of great heroism, of strength, of holiness. Others stories of destruction, memories to mourn. All great suns of light or holes of darkness, chapters that would forever fill Requiem's song.

This day, here in this distant land, was another day to shatter Requiem, another note in her undying song, another chapter in her endless tale. Another stain of blood upon a broken nation.

"Requiem falls," Elory whispered.

The blood of Requiem spilled across the City of Kings that day. Under the simmering sun, they died. The chariots flew everywhere, plowing into their ranks, and the seraphim thrust their spears, every soldier commanded to slay a soul. The firehorses, demons of sunfire, plowed through the ranks of slaves, hooves of brimstone shattering bones. The chariots rolled over fleeing children, and everywhere the spears lashed. Everywhere the seraphim swung their swords, cutting men, women, children, elders. Everywhere the bodies fell.

Elory ran.

They all ran.

They fled down the streets, hobbled, falling, slamming into one another. Too many of them. Too many. The chains between their legs too short. They fell. They rose, pushed forward, stumbling into alleyways, desperately seeking the city gates. They were too slow. Too many. Too many.

And still the fire rained.

And still the spears lashed.

Blood painted the city, and bodies piled up around temples and statues of silver.

Requiem dies today, Elory thought.

"Elory!" Vale cried, reaching out to her. "Elory!"

"Vale!" she shouted, trying to reach him, but countless slaves separated them, a great maelstrom, flowing through the streets, crashing down.

"Father!" she cried, trying to reach him, but the priest vanished into the crowd. "Vale!"

They ran, stumbling, dying. A spear flew from the sky, impaling a girl before her. Elory ran over the corpse. A chariot swooped down before her, and more Vir Requis fell, and a seraph's lance thrust into an old man.

Elory growled.

If Requiem dies today, then we die fighting.

The old man fell before her, pierced. Elory leaped forth, grabbed the lance's shaft, and tugged back with all her might. The seraph, leaning from his chariot, lost his grip.

With strength gained in the bitumen mines, Elory spun the lance around, thrust, and pierced the seraph's neck.

The soldier couldn't even scream.

Elory yanked back, tearing out his throat, and snarled, a wild animal, lance in hand.

I slew a man. She growled. *I will slay more for Requiem.*

"Elory!" Vale cried ahead. "Elory, run!"

She ran onward, spear in hand. More chariots charged through the crowd, trampling more slaves. Three seraphim flew above, laughing, children skewered upon their spears. The living ran over the dead. Vale managed to grab a spear too, managed to slay a seraph, but the enemies were too many, their chariots too fast, their lances too swift.

If we could remove our collars, we could rise as dragons, Elory thought, thrusting her spear, running onward. *We could hope to live, to defeat them.*

But they wore their collars, and they died.

With a handful of spears, crying out to their stars, they died.

And above the carnage, laughing, covered in blood, he flew. The god of light. The god of wrath. The tyrant. The destroyer of Requiem, the bane of slaves. Ishtafel.

"Flee to your holes!" the King of Saraph cried. "Flee to Tofet, slaves! Flee and cower. Any who sets foot in this city again shall die in agony. Flee! Flee and remember my gift of life, and remember my punishment of blood."

It was hours before the people of Requiem managed to flee the city. Myriads died before they limped, bloody and weeping, into the land of Tofet.

That night, the spears rose across Tofet, sixty thousand strong, and upon each spear the seraphim placed the corpse of a slave. The forest of the dead rose across Tofet, a decaying army, a memory of Requiem's blood and Saraph's eternal shame.

MELIORA

She lay in darkness.

She lay in blood.

She lay alone.

Her wings kept beating. Missing. Flaring with pain every movement. Every feather was a dagger. Every flap a sword into her back. Her wings—gone. Still there, phantoms, demons, tugging at her innards. A thousand cuts covered her, the wounds of Ishtafel's spears, but all that pain was as a caress, drowning under the agony that spread out from her back. Two wings woven of pain itself.

"Requiem," she whispered, cheek pressed to the stone floor. "Req . . ."

She tasted ash, rock, copper. She couldn't speak. She couldn't weep. All there was—shadow. All that remained—nothing.

Shadows, dancing.

Fire crackling around her head.

Demons in the dark.

Dragons.

Dragons under constellations, and stars exploding, and skies falling.

Fire. Fire haloing her brow, hallowing her body, coursing through her veins, tiny creatures, burning, rivers of dragonfire inside her. Her sweat dripped from her spine, into her eyes, into her mouth, onto the floor.

She melted. She melted into sweat and blood and tears.

I must live.

She was dead already.

I must live!

Nothing of her remained.

I must . . . I must . . . Requiem. For Requiem. For Elory. For my family. I must . . . live . . .

She flew upon clouds, and her wings beat, and she screamed, she screamed in pain, she screamed and screamed, but her wings were no longer the wings of seraphim. She flew on dragon wings. Leathern. Silver with golden claws, curtains of starlight and dawn.

She flew toward them—the halls of Requiem, woven of the stars themselves, celestial and rising from an astral forest.

The song of harps played on the wind, and her pain melted like the rain, and here was a place of goodness. Of peace. Here was Requiem reborn, the Requiem that had always been, the Requiem that awaited her. That awaited them all.

The halls of eternal rest, she knew. The halls of afterlife, the halls of the endless song of dragons. The song of harps welcomed her home.

Requiem! I found your sky.

She flew between marble columns, a silver dragon so small by their majesty. Beams of light fell between the pillars, illuminating the white trees and marble tiles, and in the distance, silver mountains soared. Meliora kept flying, feeling so light, free of all the weariness of the world, all the pain, all the worry, all the weight. A feather gliding on the wind, at home.

She kept flying between the columns and beams of light, and ahead of her she saw a throne rise in a pale hall. It was not a throne of gold, silver, or ivory like the thrones of Saraph. Here was a chair of twisting branches and roots, carved from an oak, polished and very old. A figure sat on the throne, cloaked in light.

Meliora flew down and landed on the marble tiles, and she shifted back into human form. As she approached the throne, no pain filled her. No more wings grew from her back, but her shoulder blades were healed, and she was whole—a woman like any other of Requiem, her true wings hidden within her. She approached the throne slowly, birch leaves scuttling across the marble tiles beneath her feet.

The figure of light left the throne and stepped toward her. As it stepped closer, the beams of light dispersed, and Meliora saw a king with a grizzled beard and warm brown eyes. No crown rested on his head, and he bore no sword and wore no armor, only green and silver robes, but she knew that he was a great warrior, the greatest in Requiem, the first king of her people.

"Aeternum," she whispered and knelt before him.

He smiled and held out wide callused hands, the hands of a woodsman. She rose, and he took her hands in his.

"I sinned, Aeternum, my king." Tears rolled down her cheeks. "I served Saraph. The blood of that cruel empire flows through my veins."

King Aeternum's smile was warm, his eyes soft. Kind eyes. The kindest, wisest eyes she had ever seen.

"Many of Requiem's greatest lights were not kindled in our land, my child. Queen Laira, my wife, Mother of Requiem, was born to a king in the cruel land of Eteer. Issari Seran, our greatest light, the eye of the Draco constellation, was once a princess of an empire that sought our fall. Queen Gloriae, the great heroine who rebuilt Requiem from ruin, was a child of Osanna, a dark land that toppled our halls. You too are a great heroine of Requiem, child. You are a pure daughter of starlight. The magic is yours, and the light of Requiem's stars will forever shine upon you, no less than it shines upon any other son or daughter of dragons. You will never be torn. In Requiem's halls, you are one. You are whole."

Meliora couldn't stop the tears. "But my family is torn. My sister. My brother. My father. The blood of Requiem calls out to me, a people in chains. I could not live in wealth while Requiem suffered. I cannot stay in this light while they still call to me. I can hear them. Even here, I can hear them cry out—for a savior, for mercy, for freedom. For me, Aeternum."

The king's eyes softened, and she saw the pain in her own heart reflected in them. His hands were warm around hers. "There is rest here for the weary. Would you abandon it?"

"I would. I would doom my soul to the Abyss itself, to an eternity of pain, if I could save but a single soul of Requiem. For five hundred years our people have called out for mercy, chained, forgotten. I must save them, my king. I must lead them home. I would give up the light of Requiem itself to deliver my people from darkness."

Aeternum lowered his head, and suddenly the great king— the founder of Requiem, the builder of King's Column, the father of the Vir Requis—knelt before her, and he kissed her hand.

The light blinded her.

She cried out in pain.

The agony dug into her back, and her phantom wings beat, and again she lay in darkness, her face against the hard floor. She drew a ragged breath, and the air sawed at her lungs. Her eyelids fluttered open. She saw shadows, craggy bricks, rusty chains. Her halo no longer cast its golden glow but red, angry light. The light of dragonfire. Meliora reached above her head, expecting to feel the warm softness of her halo. She winced and pulled her fingers back; they were burnt with fire. She felt trapped again in the bronze bull, a sacrifice to Malok.

Once more she lived. Once more she was imprisoned in the ziggurat, this palace where she had once lived in innocence, where she was now entombed.

She thought back to those celestial halls. Had she died and returned to this world, no longer a seraph but a fallen being of fire? Had she merely dreamed? Had she seen a vision of Requiem in its past or the Requiem beyond the stars? Meliora did not know.

But I know this, Requiem. I will fight for you. Always. So long as I can cling to life, I fight for your marble halls, for your great heroes, for all who need your magic. Requiem is hope. Requiem will rise again.

ELORY

It was ten days before the overseers allowed the survivors to bury their dead.

All that night they labored, and the night after that, and a third night too, pulling their dead off the lances like plucking rotten fruit off trees. The vultures cawed angrily, bellies full but still ravenous. No more dragons labored in Tofet; all now wore collars, the Keeper's Key gone. They did not dig graves but burned the dead in great pyres. Sixty thousand stars gone from the sky. Sixty thousand songs silenced.

The living no longer chanted as they worked, no longer sang, no longer looked toward the stars. Something inside them died too. Every Vir Requis lost a soul—brothers, sisters, parents, children. Every Vir Requis knew—a shadow fell that would never be lifted, a sadness that no light could ever cast aside.

So many fallen, Elory thought as the sun rose and set. *Each life—a world. Forever gone.*

She had lived through years under the yoke, in the bowels of the ziggurat, hungry and afraid and weak, but now for the first time in her life, it seemed that hope faded from Elory, that she could no longer dream of a savior, of a return to a lost home.

Could there ever be hope in a land of such pain, ever be light again in such darkness?

In the pit of bubbling tar, Elory gazed southward, and she could see the Eye of Saraph—the crest of the ziggurat—staring at her, always watching. Somewhere in there, buried deep, she lay—Meliora, her wings severed, perhaps as lost to Elory as all those who lay buried underground.

That night, after the last of their dead burned in the pyres, the people of Requiem lit candles.

They did not light their candles outside for the overseers to see. They did not rally and raise their fires high. They did not march upon the city, shining their lights, singing for freedom. In the land of Tofet, the slaves sat in their clay huts, and they lit their candles on stones tables, and they prayed.

Elory sat in her hut with her father and brother. They sat in silence. Four candles burned on their table: a candle for those who fell in the massacre, a candle for Elory's mother, a candle for the hero Lucem, and a candle for lost Meliora. Four lights, flickering in the breeze, soft and dying, soon to go dark.

She looked at the lights, then up at her father and brother. Haggard faces. Eyes dark.

"We failed," Elory whispered. "We marched for freedom and we lost our fight. Is all hope lost?"

Jaren stared at the candles, then raised his eyes to look at the stars engraved onto the ceiling—the Draco constellation, scratched with fingernails. In the candlelight, they seemed almost to shine. "Not so long as the stars shine," said the old priest, "though we cannot see their light."

Vale, meanwhile—young, angry Vale, lips thinned into a line, fists clenched—stared toward the floor. There, hidden under their straw beds, lay the lances he and Elory had snatched in the battle. The young quarryman kicked more straw over them, hiding the shafts.

"Not so long as we can fight," Vale said. "I don't know if there is hope to escape, to see Requiem again. But there is hope to slay more of our enemies, to shine our own light."

The candles melted, the flames guttering. Outside, across the land, a million candles or more shone their lights in huts. Perhaps that was hope, Elory thought—small, hidden lights even in the shadows.

"We will keep praying," she whispered. "We will keep fighting. And we will keep hope alive." She reached across the table and took her brother's and father's hands. "We will not abandon the dream of our people, and we will not abandon Meliora who languishes in darkness. So long as we can keep candles burning, we will remember Meliora, and we will remember Requiem."

"Remember Requiem," Vale said, face hard, eyes shining with fire.

"Remember Requiem," Jaren whispered.

Holding their hands, Elory prayed, and they whispered the words with her, the most ancient prayer of their people, a prayer for a land lost, for a dream that would always shine.

"As the leaves fall upon our marble tiles, as the breeze rustles the birches beyond our columns, as the sun gilds the mountains above our halls—know, young child of the woods, you are home, you are home."

BOOK TWO:
CROWN OF DRAGONFIRE

TASH

Tash lay in the palace gardens, pleasuring the lords of the court, when the sky burned and the severed wings fell at her feet.

"More wine, my lord?"

"Grapes, my sweetness?

"Smoke some *hintan* with me, master?"

The day had begun like many others. All morning, Tash had been working in the gardens, moving between the seraphim, offering all the pleasures of the empire—pleasures of fine food, drink, and hookah . . . and the pleasures of her lips, her stroking fingers, her warm flesh. The seraphim were tall, beautiful beings, demigods fallen from the sky, their swan wings purest white, their halos golden, and she was but a mere mortal, a slave . . . yet a slave who knew all the secrets of what they desired.

A slave Tash was, but one unlike the multitudes who toiled across the empire. Her head was not shaved; she sported long brown hair that flowed down to her hips. Instead of manacles, golden links surrounded her ankles and wrists. Instead of ash, perfume clung to her soft skin. Instead of rough burlap, she wore fine silken trousers, the fabric soft as summer sunset, and a top that revealed more than it hid. She was a pleasure slave, chosen from the pits of despair for her beauty, her coquettish lips, her knowing eyes, her tongue that could whisper sweet nothings and raise flesh to heights of unbearable pleasure. In a land of pain, she used her gifts of pleasure. Among a chained, broken people, she found her servitude in a gilded cage.

She looked around her. While most slaves labored in Tofet, a desert of sand and rock and whips, she served in wealth. The garden rustled with irises and lilies and jasmines, with fig trees, pomegranate trees, and date palms. Behind them soared the palace of Saraph, a towering ziggurat, framed by idols of gold, topped with a great platinum eye. Before them rose a portico of marble columns, and beyond sprawled the city of Shayeen, a realm of temples, bathhouses, theaters—a city of leisure and splendor for the fallen gods of lost Edinnu. The land of Tofet, where most of the slaves toiled, lay hidden beyond the horizon.

"Tash, darling!" cried a drunken seraph, waving an empty goblet. "More wine, my dear."

Tash giggled at the pink-cheeked man, a young lordling from the city garrisons. He lay on a blanket between the flower beds, his wings spread out around him. He had doffed his breastplate, and droplets of wine ran down his bare chest. His halo was pale in the sunlight, barely visible; it had been fading with every cup.

"Tash!" he cried to her. "Wine!"

She swayed toward him, deftly making her way between the other seraphim in the garden, dodging their reaching hands. Harps played, the peonies and jasmines rustled, and marble statues of cherubim pissed water into koi ponds. When Tash reached the drunken seraph, she poured him more wine from her jug. As the crimson liquid flowed, he reached out and pinched her soft flesh. She squealed as she had been taught, feigning delight.

"There's wine spilled on my chest!" said the lordling.

Tash stroked the seraph's long golden hair. "Let me drink it, my lord."

She leaned down, stared up into his eyes, and licked the wine from his chest. Across the gardens, the other seraphim saw and hooted. The young lord pulled her head up, and he kissed her roughly, his tongue seeking, and she kissed him back.

When I serve them here, I do not bear a yoke across my shoulders, she thought. *I do not cry in agony as flaming whips tear into my skin. I do not suffer in the desert, breaking my back under baskets of bricks. So let me service these lords and ladies, for the day I can no longer bring pleasure . . . there will be nothing for me but pain.*

As she left the lordling to his cup, making her way toward another seraph, Tash fingered the iron collar around her neck. Perhaps she wore no yoke, no chains, no burlap. But like all Vir Requis slaves, six hundred thousand of them here in this cruel southern empire, she wore the collar.

Tash winced. The curse of Requiem.

Ancient runes were engraved into the collar, keeping her magic at bay—the magic of starlight. Once, Tash knew, hundreds of years ago when the Vir Requis had lived free, they could summon the magic of the Draco constellation. In their land of Requiem, they could grow wings and scales, breathe fire, and take to the sky as dragons. They had been a mighty nation, a kingdom of magic, starlight, and dragonfire.

But those days had ended.

The cruel Ishtafel had crushed Requiem, felled the marble halls, slaughtered a million souls, and brought the rest here to captivity. Tash could feel the magic inside her; she had been feeling it all her life. Yet it tingled just beyond her reach, the collar's dark magic forever imprisoning the dragon inside her. And so she remained a human—a young, slender woman with quick hands, a quick tongue, a quick mind. A woman who would forever serve her masters, who would never find her sky.

"Sweetness!" called another seraph, a soldier with flowing blond hair and gleaming eyes, the pupils shaped as starbursts. He patted his lap. "Come, little one. Sit! Feed me grapes."

As she made her way toward him, Tash raised her eyes and gazed at the sky. They said that in Requiem far in the north, the sky had been a thing of many colors—sometimes golden, sometimes deep blue and purple, sometimes strewn with clouds in all the colors of fire. But here in the south, in the empire of Saraph, the sky was always a cruel pale blue, almost white, the sun large and viscious. A sky she would never reach. The seraphim had wings of feathers, and Tash had wings too—the leathern wings of a dragon, hidden inside her, forever bound deep within. Wings that could never spread wide, never glide upon the wind.

I still dream of you, Requiem, she thought, looking up toward that sky. *I still pray to find your sky.*

She had reached the seraph, and she had just settled down on his lap when the chanting rose from the city and the sky burned.

"Remember Requiem! Remember Requiem!"

Six hundred thousand voices crying out as one.

"Requiem!" they cried. "May our wings forever find your sky!"

Across the garden, the seraphim froze.

Tash leaped off the soldier's lap. Her entire body trembled.

"Remember Requiem!" rose the chant from beyond the palace gardens. "Remember Requiem!"

The seraphim leaped to their feet. Drunkenly, they spread their wings and soared into the sky, their cups—and Tash—forgotten. The gardens shook as the chant kept rolling.

"Remember Requiem!"

Tash could barely breathe.

She ran, leaping across the grass and over fallen mugs and puddles of wine. She raced up a staircase and onto the marble wall that framed the gardens. Heart thrashing, she gazed upon Shayeen, the City of Kings, the capital of Saraph.

Stars above . . .

Thousands of slaves—*hundreds* of thousands—were marching through the city, raising candles, chanting for Requiem. The slaves of Tofet—heads shaven, ankles hobbled, backs striped, necks collared. They marched together, calling out for freedom, and at their lead walked a tall slave, a woman in burlap, her head shaved.

The woman had a halo and swan wings.

Tash narrowed her eyes.

A seraph slave?

"Meliora!" the marching slaves cried. "Meliora the Merciful!"

Tash gasped and covered her mouth.

Meliora?

Tash narrowed her eyes. As the procession of slaves marched closer to the palace, Tash got a closer look. She had seen the Princess of Saraph before, daughter of Queen Kalafi. Many times, walking through the palace to a lord or lady's chamber, Tash had paused to kneel before the princess. Gone was Meliora's long golden hair. Gone was her muslin kalasiri dress strewn with gemstones. Gone were her cosmetics, her jewels, her aura of youth and health. But even marching along the city boulevard, barefoot, ankles shackled, head shaved—Meliora had the same noble face, the same halo, the same sunburst eyes.

"Meliora the Merciful!" cried the slaves.

Tash stood on the garden wall, the wind billowing her harem pants, watching as her people—myriads of Vir Requis in chains—chanted for freedom. She watched as a leader rose among them, Princess Meliora, daughter of the queen of Saraph, daughter of a common slave—a leader who shouted for Requiem.

Hope rises.

And Tash watched, eyes damp, as the wrath of Saraph descended from the sky.

The firehorses galloped across the sky, their brimstone hooves like thunder, their flaming wings spreading wide. Behind them streamed the chariots of fire, and within them the seraphim shone. Thousands of the deities, cast out from Edinnu, covered the sky.

And above them all he rose—King Ishtafel. The lord of Saraph, the blood of his slain mother still on his lips. The destroyer of Requiem. The cruel god of light. He flew in a chariot of fire, his wings spread wide, and from the city she ascended—Meliora, transfigured into a dragon of silver and gold, her scales gleaming like pearls, feathers ruffling upon her wings and tail. She blasted white flames, a dragon of light, a savior of Requiem, and Ishtafel plunged toward her, wreathed in fire and brimstone.

Tash watched, tears on her cheeks, as Ishtafel drove his spear into the feathered dragon, as Meliora lost her magic, as she fell in human form. She watched, weeping, as Ishtafel pulled the bleeding Meliora onto the palace balcony far above the gardens, as his sword lashed, as the blade cut through Meliora's swan wings.

Requiem fell. Hope fell.

And with hope fell the wings—gliding, almost peaceful, their white feathers stained red. The severed wings of a seraph, of Meliora's lost divinity. The wings glided down and landed at Tash's feet. Above her, on the balcony, Ishtafel roared to the crowd and Meliora screamed no more.

Tash's heart seemed to shatter within her.

Trembling, the screams washing across her, Tash lifted a fallen feather—a long white feather from Meliora's wing. A piece of the savior.

Flame of Requiem

As the sky burned, Tash fled the gardens. Feather clutched to her chest, she ran into the ziggurat. She raced along gleaming corridors, jeweled columns at her sides. She bounded down stairways, plunging deeper and deeper underground, entering the bowels of the city, the shadowy underworld where few seraphim ventured. Yet the screams still echoed above—echoed in her ears, over and over. The screams of the dying, of thousands of her people falling to the spears of the seraphim, those seraphim Tash served.

Tears blinded her.

My people die yet I flee into shadow. They march for freedom yet I burrow underground.

The grief, the terror, the guilt tore at her, and her heart thrashed, and her head spun.

Finally, dizzy, Tash stumbled into her home—the glittering cavern beneath the ziggurat. The pleasure pit.

Here was a place of smoke, shadows, flickering lights. Her little kingdom to rule. Curtains of beads and silk hung from the ceiling. The walls were roughly carved, no finer than the walls of a cave, peppered with alcoves full of candles, incense sticks, and gleaming crystals. The other pleasure slaves—Tash's girls—lounged upon tasseled pillows and rugs, smoking from hookahs. The *hintan*—a pleasurer's favorite spice—bubbled in the glass containers, gleaming green, while purple smoke rose from the slaves' lips. Two male seraphim were here today, lying on a rug, moaning as perfumed slaves pleasured them with spice, wine, and flesh.

Tash was a young woman, among the youngest in the pit, yet she ruled over the others, for she refused to surrender to the spice. Her mind was clear, her instincts sharp. With her wits, she had risen to rule her domain of shadows.

Let there be some safety here, she thought, gazing upon her girls. *Let this be a haven even as the world shatters above.*

She walked through the chamber, navigating between the curtains of beads, the bubbling hookahs, and the pleasure slaves who lay everywhere. The candlelight shone, the beads jangled, and the giggles of the slaves rose like music. But still those screams echoed in Tash's ears, and she could not forget the raining blood.

She thought of Elory, the young girl who had come here from the bitumen craters, who had vanished from the pleasure pit days ago. Tash had thought the girl insufferable at first, naive and dulled by the sun of Tofet, yet as she had taught Elory the ways of lovemaking, Tash had come to like the girl.

Are you still alive, Elory? Did you find safety up in the cruel world, or did—

The door to the pleasure pit banged open.

Tash spun around and felt the blood drain from her face.

Her heart seemed to stop.

There he stood—the new King of Saraph, the blood of his mother and sister still on his hands.

Ishtafel.

Tash hid the long white feather behind her back. Her heart, which only an instant ago had seemed frozen, burst into a gallop. Cold sweat washed her. She had just watched this seraph, the man who had destroyed Requiem, cut the wings off Meliora, and now he was here, bloodlust in his eyes.

Tash raised her chin. *I cannot let him hurt any others. I cannot let him hurt my girls.*

"My lord!" She rushed toward him, placing herself between him and her fellow pleasure slaves. "Welcome to the pleasure pit! I am Tash, and I would be glad to—"

He grabbed her, snarling, lust in his eyes—no longer bloodlust but lust for her. Not the playful, sometimes even wild lust of the other seraphim who called upon her services. His was a violent, cruel thing, the lust of a predator, of a conqueror.

"My lord, I would be happy to please you—" she began, heart thumping.

"Silence."

He ripped her clothes, and he did not let her do her work. She would not be pleasuring him today, would not pour him wine, giggle at his jokes, kiss every part of his body until he went mad with desire. No. He wanted her to give him nothing; he wanted only to take. And he took from her. He took all of her, clutching her with bloody fingers, laughing, drooling onto her, a rabid beast, a demon above her. She shut her eyes, shuddering beneath him as his fingers bruised her, smearing others' blood across her pale skin. Tash had made love to countless men, yet she had never had a man take her like this; he was not a man, she thought, not a sentient being but a charging bull of fire.

Finally he pulled out from her, and he shoved her aside.

He left her there on the rug. He left her as he had left Meliora—wingless, a broken thing. He left her as he had left Requiem—shattered.

She lay there in another person's blood, clutching her feather.

Remember Requiem, Tash thought. *Remember Requiem.*

Slowly, as a flame in old embers, a rage kindled in Tash. She had seen a nation march. She had seen a leader rise among them—Meliora the Merciful—only for Ishtafel to cut off her wings.

When Elory had spoken to her of her dreams—dreams of old Requiem, of Requiem rising again—Tash had scoffed. But something had happened this day. Something Tash knew she would never forget. She held her feather so tightly she crushed it.

Remember Requiem.

"Tash, are you all right?" whispered one of her girls, a slave with long red hair.

Tash rose to her feet, a deep ache between her legs, searing up her belly. She clutched the feather as if drowning at sea, clinging to a rope.

"No," she whispered. "I'm not all right. None of this is all right."

And then she heard it.

The chanting—not just in her memory but true voices, calling out, again and again.

"Free Meliora! Free Meliora!"

The voices of her people. The cry of Requiem.

We rise up.

Tash balled her fists.

And I will rise with my people. With Requiem.

Tash tightened her lips and left the pleasure pit. She made her way along the dark corridors, up the stairs, and back to the surface of the world. She walked along a portico, a wall of frescos to one side, columns to the other, affording a view of the city beyond.

"Free Meliora!" the slaves cried. "Free Meliora!"

Requiem cried out . . . and Saraph answered.

Fire streamed above, and there he flew—Ishtafel, rising in a chariot of fire, laughing, slick with blood, and the pain in Tash flared. A hundred thousand seraphim or more flew with him, their chariots covering the sky.

Tash stared from between the columns, feeling the world collapse around her.

Blood flowed across the city of Shayeen that day.

Fire rained.

Shrieking, laughing, praying to their gods, the seraphim descended upon the children of Requiem with spear and arrow, decimating the slaves, and a forest of the dead rose, corpses upon pikes.

Requiem shattered.

The screams rose, then tore, then fell silent.

Tash knew that all her life, she would remember the slaughter she saw here. She knew that if Requiem survived, her people would forever remember this day, the decimation of the slaves, the massacre of sixty thousand souls, their voices forever silenced, their light forever darkened. And she knew that she herself could never return to that glittering pit, to the smoke of hintan and incense, to the kingdom she had carved beneath the mountain.

Once Tash had thought herself merely a pleasurer, a queen of the glittering goddesses of the underworld. That life had ended. This day she was a daughter of Requiem.

The fire seared her tears dry, and Tash forced herself to stare at the slaughter. At the blood on the streets of Shayeen. At the piles of dead. At the seraphim who still dipped from the sky, thrusting spears, slaughtering the fleeing children of Requiem. She forced herself to see this, as King Benedictus in days of old had seen the slaughter at Lanburg Fields in Requiem's ancient war against the griffins, as Queen Lyana had seen the phoenixes descending upon the marble halls of Nova Vita, Requiem's lost capital.

I'm not a warrior like they were. Tash touched the collar around her neck. *I have no legendary sword to wield, nor can I become a dragon and blow my fire.* She reached down between her legs, feeling the pain Ishtafel had left. *But I still have this weapon, this weapon I've always fought with. And I will fight for Requiem. For our savior.*

She looked at the white feather in her hand. It was nearly as long as Tash's forearm. Meliora's feather. The feather of the great Princess of Saraph . . . and the great leader of Requiem.

Tash turned away from the city.

She faced the towering wall across from the portico. A fresco appeared there, several times her height, showing the fall of Requiem. Painted dragons fell while seraphim fired their arrows, and above them all flew the tyrant.

"You cut off her wings," Tash whispered. "You hurt me. You slaughtered thousands. You did not think slaves could fight you, Ishtafel, but I will fight. I remember Requiem."

MELIORA

She lay in darkness, alone, her phantom wings aflame.

How long had she languished here in this prison cell? Meliora didn't know. There was no night or day here, no way to tell the passage of time. A guard arrived sometimes, slid open a small metal square on the doorway, and shoved in a bowl of gruel and a cup of water. Whether she had three meals a day or one, Meliora could not tell. She could have been in here for days, perhaps weeks.

And still her wings burned.

Their fire lit the cell with a hot, red light, crackling, illuminating brick walls, a craggy floor, and a ceiling coated with spiderwebs. A chamber so small Meliora had no room to lie down, only curl up in the corner. She kept reaching over her back, trying to extinguish those flames on her wings, but felt nothing. Her hands passed through them.

Missing. Gone. She shuddered. *Ishtafel cut them off.*

Meliora could still *feel* them there as they said soldiers sometimes felt missing limbs. Yet the wings had fallen from the balcony, and the firelight did not come from burning feathers. It came from the halo on her head.

Wincing, Meliora reached over her head again, then pulled her seared fingers back. The fire crackled with new vigor. She ached for a mirror, ached to see what burned above her head. Her old halo, a thin ring of soft light, was gone. Instead flames now seemed to wreath her brow, a crown of dragonfire.

"Who am I now?" she whispered in the shadows. "What am I?"

Her mother was Queen Kalafi, a seraph fallen from Edinnu, but did the holy ichor still flow through Meliora's veins? She had thought herself a noble seraph princess, pure and fair, yet her long golden hair was gone; only stubble now covered her head. Her wings, once curtains of white, were gone too. Her halo was a thing of flame that burned her own fingers. Who was she now?

"A child of Requiem," she whispered.

She closed her eyes, and she thought of Requiem. She had grown up seeing that ancient kingdom of dragons. All her life, she had gazed upon Requiem in frescos, mosaics, paintings, engravings on great palace walls and temple columns. All her life, she had heard of a kingdom of reptiles, of ruthless enemies that Ishtafel had conquered.

And all her life, Meliora had dreamed of that distant, fallen land—and in her dreams, Requiem still stood, and she flew among the dragons, one of their number, not beastly but noble and proud, and the stars of the dragon shone above her.

Perhaps I've always known that I'm a child of starlight.

That land of marble halls and birch woods had fallen, but Requiem still lived. It lived here in Saraph—in the land of Tofet beyond the City of Kings. It lived in the thousands of huts. It lived in the small home of her father, the priest Jaren, and her siblings, Vale and Elory. It lived in the hearts of the slaves who had marched behind Meliora into the city, stood before the palace, and cried out for freedom. And it still lived within Meliora—a memory of starlight, a torch of dragonfire she vowed to keep carrying.

She could feel the magic deep inside her, warm, tingly. She tried to summon it again, to become the dragon. As a dragon, she could shatter the prison door, storm through the halls, burn all in her path. Breathing deeply, Meliora let the magic flow through her, rising, filling her like healing energy. Scales began to rise across her body, pearly white, and her fingernails lengthened, and—

The collar tightened around her neck.

Meliora gasped in pain, and her magic petered away.

Her scales vanished, and she fell to the floor, trembling, bile in her throat. She clawed at her collar, but it was forged of solid iron, engraved with runes of power. No saw or blade in the empire could cut through this collar, no fire could melt it— certainly not her fingernails.

But there is a key that can open it.

Coughing, weak from her wounds and hunger, Meliora reached into the pocket of her burlap shift. She pulled out the ancient relic she had snatched in the battle—the Keeper's Key.

Or at least what was left of it. For hundreds of years, the Keeper's Key had hung around Queen Kalafi's neck, allowing the royal family of Saraph to remove the collars from choice slaves. Only a few Vir Requis were ever allowed to become dragons—to dig in the tar pits, to haul heavy stones, and sometimes to entertain the people in the arena in mock battles from the old war.

But Ishtafel had crushed that key in his palm, forever sealing the Vir Requis—and her among them—in their human forms. Meliora examined the remains of the key. It lay in her palm, crumpled into a ball of crimson metal. The old runes upon it, written in gold, were barely visible, only a few squiggly lines.

Once again, Meliora tried to unbend the key, to tug the metal back into its long slender form. But she could not; she didn't have Ishtafel's strength, and even if she did, would she simply snap the key when trying to straighten it? As she had countless times, she brought the twisted ball of metal to her collar, hoping against hope that this time—finally!—it would work. The few crumpled runes on the key—whatever was still visible—gave but a soft glow, then fizzled away. The collar remained locked.

Meliora sighed and returned the crushed key to her pocket. If only she had grabbed the key from Ishtafel in time! She had flown so close. She could have burned him, stolen the key, freed the slaves, led a nation of dragons home to Requiem. Yet now she lingered here in a prison cell. Now the slaves cried out in agony, suffering under an even crueler tyrant.

"Perhaps I should have married him," Meliora whispered, eyes stinging. "Perhaps I should never have raced Ishtafel in the chariots, tried to save Elory from his clutches, led the slaves in revolt. Perhaps I should have birthed his heir, been a mother to our child of pure blood. My own mother would still be alive, and I would still be a princess, still have my wings."

But no. That would have been only an illusion. That would have been just as much a prison cell. Meliora knew the truth now—knew that her father was Jaren the slave. Knew that she was half Vir Requis.

"I will not forget you, stars of my fathers," she whispered in the shadows. "Not for all the palaces and gold in the empire. Requiem! May our wings forever find your—"

The lock on the cell door clattered.

Meliora froze, then scuttled backward, leaped to her feet, and hissed.

The heavy stone door creaked open. Torchlight flooded the chamber, brighter than her halo, crackling and casting out sparks. Meliora winced, staring at the dark, towering figure who stood in the doorway, wings spread out, head haloed with golden light.

"Hello, sweet sister," the figure whispered, voice smooth and deadly like a steel blade, and stepped into the chamber.

Meliora sneered. "Ishtafel."

He smiled thinly and stepped closer, the heat of his torch singeing her body. While she was covered in scratches, bruises, and dried blood, clad in rags, Ishtafel looked more resplendent than ever. Rubies shone upon his gilded breastplate, the metal forged to mimic the shape of his bare torso. His hair hung down his back, lush and golden. A crown rested on his head, mimicking his halo, and a lush cape of samite hung across his shoulders.

"My, my, but aren't you a wretched sight." He tsked his tongue. "Filth does not become you, sister. You were fair once."

"And I thought you noble once," she said. "Yet I saw the filth within you. I saw the blood of Mother, the blood of Requiem upon your hands. The blood of my own wings. You stand before me in gold, but you are covered with more filth than I ever will be."

He raised an eyebrow. "And so sweet little Meliora, the princess who once could speak of nothing but puppies and cupcakes, now waxes poetic about righteousness and evil. This cell has made you a philosopher."

She shook her head. "Not this cell but truth. I am no longer that innocent princess, it is true, not because I languish in the underground but because I know who I am. I know that dragon blood flows through me."

Sudden anger twisted his face. His eyes narrowed, the golden irises blazing around his sunburst pupils. His lips peeled back, baring his teeth like a rabid wolf over meat. He lashed his hand, slashing his fingernails across her cheek. She yelped. Ishtafel pulled his hand back, examining her blood on his fingertips. He licked a drop.

"True." He smacked his lips. "I do taste the dragon filth. But I also taste the ichor of the Thirteenth Dynasty, the pure, golden blood of my own lineage. Mother is dead. No other women of our family live. And that blood must be preserved." He grinned and licked his lips, smearing her blood across them. "Now that you've had time to languish in darkness, and now that your slave friends are broken, you will come to my chamber. You will clean up. You will wear gowns again. You will feed upon the fine fare your slaves grow. You will wed me, as planned, and you will bear me an heir."

She snorted. "So you would have an heir tainted with slave blood?"

"I will not." His grin grew wider. "You will bear me a daughter, Meliora. And she will bear me a daughter too, on and on, until the dragon blood is bred out of our line. We are immortal, my dear, and we can wait. We have time. In a few generations, the dragon blood will be gone from our family, and the Thirteenth Dynasty will be pure again. I spent five hundred years battling our enemies, burning out the impurity from the world. I can spend five hundred more breeding out the impurity from my family."

"You are insane," Meliora whispered.

He shook his head. "I am a god, sister. And gods strike down their enemies." He reached out his hand to her. "But you need not suffer. I have punished you, sister. I have punished you justly, and you have suffered for your sins. But you will find me a merciful god. Return with me to the palace, wed me, grow my daughters in your womb, and you will return to your puppies, your cupcakes, your days of careless wonder. Once more, you will sleep on a bed of silk, giggle in the gardens, and enjoy a life in the splendor I have built."

She stared at him, eyes narrowed, and shook her head slightly. "I don't know who you are." Her voice was barely more than a whisper. "I don't know where my brother is. Where is the brother who would run with me through the gardens, teach me to fish, teach me the names of birds? Where is the brother who pretended to drink tea from my toy cups, who taught me to spit off the balcony, who always laughed at the stupid jokes I read in my books?" She took a step back from him, and her back pressed against the wall. Her phantom wings flared—the wings he had cut off. "He is dead now."

"He is very much alive, I assure you." He reached out and took her hand. "Perhaps we both have changed. Yet one thing remains: our duty to Saraph."

She tugged her hand free. "My duty is only to Requiem. I will not become your wife, and I will not bear your heirs, and I will not return to who I was. That princess too is dead, as dead as the man you once were. I would rather choose a life of chains, true to myself, than a life of lies in a palace."

Once more rage flared across his face. His halo crackled, and his eyes blazed. "You will have no chains, sister, only a cell. Only darkness." He laughed. "We are immortals, Meliora. Enjoy the next hundred years in darkness. I will see you next century . . . and maybe then you will change your mind."

He stepped outside the chamber.

Meliora leaped toward him, shouting.

He slammed the door shut, knocking her down. She fell onto the stone floor, banging her elbows, and the door's lock clanked shut, leaving her in darkness.

She pounded at the door, screaming. "Ishtafel! Ishtafel! Wait!" She fell to her knees, and tears burned in her eyes. "I changed my mind! Let me out! Let me out . . ."

Yet he would not answer.

He would not return.

She had been in this chamber for only a few days, and it felt like an eternity. A hundred years of solitude awaited her.

Will he really leave me here for a century? When I emerge, Elory, Jaren, Vale . . . my family . . . they will be gone. And who will I be? A creature driven mad, a sniveling wreck.

"Ishtafel!" she cried, scratching again at the door until her fingernails bled. "Ishtafel!"

Nothing but silence answered her, and Meliora pressed her head against the door. Her halo of dragonfire crackled above her head, searing the stone.

I am dragonfire.

I am a daughter of Requiem.

I am free.

Meliora curled up on the floor, hugged her knees, and closed her eyes. She imagined herself as a dragon of gold and silver, feathers ruffling in the wind, gliding in the sky of her home.

TASH

She walked through the labyrinth beneath the ziggurat, holding her hookah of bubbling spice, a warrior of Requiem armed with smoke and gemstones.

Her anklets jangled with every step, the gold embedded with topaz. A ring shone on her finger, a gift from a sailor on a hot night last summer. Her only armor was her silken trousers and top, and she held her hookah before her like a sword. The green liquid inside bubbled, heated by embers in a hidden chamber, and purple smoke rose from the nozzle, dancing around Tash like demons of forgetfulness. It had been three years since Tash had danced with that demon; she had tamed it, used it as her familiar, her secret assassin.

I will fight for you, Requiem, the way I can. Fate made me a pleasurer. I will fight with pleasure instead of steel or dragonfire.

The dungeons beneath the ziggurat were deep, a place of many hidden kingdoms. Not only the pleasure pit hid here underground, but many other domains—the cisterns that stored water for the city of Shayeen, armories full of lances and shields, stores of grain and salted meats, glittering halls full of treasures . . . and the city dungeons. Here in the darkness languished the prisoners of the Thirteenth Dynasty. Here in the darkness waited hope.

"I will find you, Meliora," Tash whispered. "You don't know me, but I fight for you."

She thought back to that day in the gardens, seeing the march through the city. She had sat upon the lap of a seraph, giggling at his jokes, feeding him grapes, serving the masters, and she had seen six hundred thousand slaves marching for freedom, unafraid. She had seen a leader walk before them, rise as a feathered dragon—Meliora the Merciful. The shame of that day still burned through Tash. Her people had fought, bled, many died, fighting for freedom, fighting for Meliora.

And I just watched. I just fled.

And she remembered Ishtafel clutching her, fingers still bloody, thrusting into her, mounting her, taking her like a rabid dog takes a bitch.

Someday I will kill you, Ishtafel, Tash silently swore. *Perhaps you are a god of light, but I serve the stars of Requiem, and their light is soft, cold, impossible to see in the sunlight, yet stronger than you know.*

She reached into her pocket with her free hand, and she felt the feather there—the feather from Meliora's wing. A token of hope.

She walked down a staircase, hookah bubbling, heading deeper underground than she'd ever gone—deeper even than the pleasure pit. She reached a craggy corridor lined with torches. Muffled screams rose from ahead, and footsteps thumped. A deep voice laughed, a whip lashed, and a scream rose again.

Tash paused and gulped. Cold sweat trickled down her back.

The dungeons.

She forced herself to take a deep breath, inhaling just a little of the lavender smoke. She would be brave. She would be brave like the great heroes of Requiem. Like Issari, the Priestess in White, who shone in the sky. Like King Benedictus who had fought the griffins. Like Queen Fidelity the Wise who had fought the cruel Templers and rededicated the halls of Requiem.

Tash was no noble heroine like them. She was not tall, not proud, not a warrior in armor, not noble. She was only a pleasurer, no better than a whore, clad in the garments of her shame. But Meliora was pure. Meliora was noble. And Meliora needed her.

Tash raised her chin and walked on.

She reached an iron door set into a stone archway—the entrance to the dungeons. Two seraph guards stood here, wearing steel armor, holding spears and shields. Their eyes cast their own light, gleaming through the holes in their helmets.

"What are you doing here, slave?" one guard said, spitting out the words. She recognized this one—a fool named Erish.

Tash raised an eyebrow. "Slave? You called me nicer names last summer, when you guarded the hunting expedition the nobles took me on. Something about . . . sweet teats?"

She could not see through the man's helmet, but she swore that he was blushing. "Damn pleasure slaves got dirty tongues."

She thrust her tongue out at him. "That's how you like my tongue. I know." She reached into her pocket, struggling to hide her shaking fingers and the thrashing of her heart. She pulled out the rolled up scroll and held it forward. "I carry Ishtafel's seal. He's given me a pass to enter this dungeon. I bring . . . a special surprise, a gift for the man who guards Ishtafel's sister."

The guard grunted and grabbed the scroll. "Let me see that."

Tash's heart hammered as the guard examined the wax seal.

Please, stars of Requiem, let him believe me. Let him open the door.

A few weeks ago, Elory—a slave from the bitumen pits—had entered the pleasure pits, had come under Tash's tutelage. For long hours, Tash had taught the girl the ways of lovemaking—how to drive a man wild with a nibble to the earlobe, a kiss on the neck, a stroke at just the right places. And while Elory slept, exhausted from her lessons, Tash had spent long hours studying the scroll Elory had brought into the pleasure pit—the scroll bearing Ishtafel's seal. Slowly, whittling away in the shadows, Tash had copied that seal, engraving its shape—an eye within a sunburst, surrounded by runes—into one of her rings. She had melted a hundred candles, made hundreds of wax seals of her own, always tweaking, adjusting the marks on her ring . . . finally coming up with her own imperial seal.

Elory was gone now, but that seal remained, engraved into the ring in her pocket . . . its mark upon the scroll the guard now held.

The guard stared at the seal, eyes narrowing. At his side, his fellow guard tightened his hands around his lance. A vision flashed through Tash's mind—the seraphim flying in their chariots, descending upon the city, thrusting those lances into thousands of slaves.

Please, stars of Requiem. Please, Issari, the Dragon's Eye. If you can hear me from underground, far in a foreign land . . . grant me aid. Let me fool them. Let me fight with trickery if I cannot fight with dragonfire.

Finally the guard broke the seal, tugged the scroll open, and read—the words one of Tash's girls had written, the only one among them who could write.

Please, stars of Requiem, let Erish be somewhat literate . . . or illiterate and ashamed to admit it.

Finally Erish the guard grunted and rolled up the scroll. He snorted and glanced at his comrade. "Checks out. That gift to Gron?" He thrust his chin toward Tash. "Her sweet teats."

The other guard's eyes widened. "Why don't we get a gift?"

Erish groaned. "Because we're only gate guards, that's why. Lowest on the totem, as always. Cell guards always get all the perks."

"Sorry, boys." Tash reached up to pat their helmets, one guard at a time. "Maybe you'll get lucky next hunting trip you guard."

They grumbled, but they pulled the iron door open, revealing a corridor lined with prison cells. Tash sauntered through, carrying her hookah. The door shut behind her, sealing her in the palace dungeons.

Most prisoners in the empire were executed—sometimes inside the bronze bull, sometimes by a simple beheading, sometimes crucified on the hills or nailed to the ziggurat's crest. Here, underground, languished the greatest enemies of the Thirteenth Dynasty, those not allowed the mercy of death. Rebels. Traitors. Immortal seraphim doomed to languish in the darkness, lingering for eternity in their cells, driven mad—some had been mad for centuries. The doors were heavy stone; they looked less like the doors of a prison, more like the doors of tombs. Screams rolled through the hall, muffled, a sound like ghosts. Here rotted the living dead.

"Where are you, Meliora?" Tash whispered.

A third guard stood here, keys jangling from his belt. The brute spun toward her. Most seraphim were noble, beautiful beings, their bodies chiseled, their faces fair. This man was an exception; years of servitude underground had left him pale, and his hair was such a fine blond it was nearly white. His back was stooped, his gut large. Seraphim were children of the sun; in darkness they withered.

"What—" the guard began, then bit his tongue. His eyes traveled down and up again, taking in Tash's body like a thirsty lion laps up water.

She smiled and curtsied. "Good day, sir! I am Tash of the pleasure pit. My lord, King Ishtafel the Glorious, Great in Graces, has sent me here as a gift to you. He knows that you guard Meliora, his sister . . ." She made sure to note which cell the guard's eyes flicked toward. ". . . and he has commanded me to come here bearing gifts."

The guard frowned, his shelf of a brow pushing low over small, far-set eyes. "What gifts?"

Tash placed down her hookah between them. Heated by the embers, the spice bubbled, filling the corridor with its intoxicating, spicy-sweet scent. "This gift." Maintaining eye contact, she doffed her top and trousers, letting them fall to the floor, exposing her nakedness. "And this."

The guard's eyes widened. Saliva dribbled down his chin. He reached out to her breast.

Tash slapped his hand away with a gasp, all coy indignation. "Not yet, sir!" She smiled coquettishly. "Enjoy some spice with me first."

"But—"

"Listen to your pleasurer!" She stepped closer, stood on her tiptoes, and whispered into his ear. "Let me do my work. Just follow my every command, sir, and I promise you a night you will never forget. You will soon scream with pleasure louder than these prisoners scream in pain."

His sunburst pupils dilated, and his breathing grew heavy. "I . . . spice?"

Tash nodded, letting her lips touch his ear. "Hintan. The Treasure of the Desert. The Green Spirit. Have you never tried the spice, my lord?" She held up the hookah's nozzle. "Try it, my lord! Breathe deeply. Let its magic fill you."

He hesitated, then took the nozzle and gently puffed. At once he coughed, scattering purple smoke. "It's . . . sweet. And burning."

Tash took the nozzle from him. "Let me show you."

Smiling at him, never removing her eyes from his, she placed her lips around the nozzle. She breathed in but did not inhale. This spice inside the hookah was no ordinary hintan, not the kind even the most decadent of pleasurers smoked. Here was the distilled essence of the spice, purified again and again, powerful enough to knock out dragons. Tash breathed out, not letting any of the smoke fill her lungs. Even so, her head spun, and her fear faded under waves of joy—perhaps a good thing now.

The guard took the nozzle, and this time he breathed deeply.

"Inhale," Tash said. "Fill your lungs. It'll make the pleasure even greater."

He inhaled and his pupils dilated further. A thin smile spread across his lips, and his eyes rolled back. "It's . . . sweet. It's . . ."

Tash placed a hand on his chest. The guard collapsed and hit the ground with a clatter of keys.

She cringed. *Shh!*

Tash glanced behind her at the iron door that led into the dungeon, but it remained shut. The guards outside had not heard their friend collapse, it seemed, but Tash's heart beat so madly she thought they must hear it pounding. Trying to steady her trembling fingers, she pulled her clothes back on, then grabbed the guard's belt and tugged it off.

"I bet you wish I were doing this under different circumstances," she whispered.

She unslung the keys off his belt. The guard lay on his back, drooling, chest rising and falling in his stupor.

"Gimosh!" cried a voice outside the iron door.

Tash froze and grabbed the fallen guard's spear.

"Gimosh!" the voice repeated. "You remember where to stick it, don't you?" The guards outside laughed.

Tash grumbled. She prayed the brutes outside didn't enter for a glimpse of the show—a show now cancelled. She rushed toward one of the stone cell doors—the door the fallen guard had glanced at when Tash had said "Meliora."

Clutching the spear in one hand, she placed a key into the lock . . . and turned it.

The lock clacked, spilling rust.

Tash inhaled deeply, pressed her shoulder against the stone door, and pushed. The door creaked open, maddeningly loud. Tash cursed and let out a moan, feigning mad pleasure, hiding the sound of the creaking door; the hoots from outside the dungeon further masked the sound.

Finally the door had opened, revealing nothing but shadows.

"Meliora?" Tash whispered. She tiptoed into the cell. "Lady Meliora? I'm here to rescue you. I—"

A scream blasted her.

A wretched, pale creature leaped forth, lashing curling fingernails that must have grown two feet long.

Tash yelped and jumped back.

The creature hissed, its teeth gone. Only thin strands of hair grew from its scalp, and its skin clung to bones, nearly no fat or muscle on its body. Wretched wings grew from the beast's back, a few scattered feathers still clinging to them. Its one eye was gone, and the other blazed with hatred, the pupil shaped like a sun.

Tash thrust her spear, goading it back. She cried out, "Gimosh! Yes, Gimosh!"

Please don't let the guards outside hear.

The creature inside squealed, and Tash's spear lashed against its arm. With a wail, it retreated back into the cell. Tash grabbed the door and began to pull it shut.

She paused.

Her eyes dampened.

She thrust her spear through the doorway with all her strength, digging her heels into the floor, impaling the poor creature's heart. The seraph—or at least, the creature that had once been a seraph—let out a gasp . . . a sound almost thankful. It collapsed to the floor.

Tash spun away from the cell, spear in one hand, keys in the other. She gazed across the hall.

"Gimosh!" rose the voice of a guard outside the dungeon. "Gimosh, care to share her?"

Tash cursed. "Let him have his fun first!" she shouted at the door. "You can be next."

She moved across the craggy corridor, gazing at the cells. Twenty or more lined the walls, and each could contain another wretched, rotting creature. Which one did Meliora languish behind? Tash dared not call out the princess's name.

Orange light caught her eye.

Tash spun toward a cell. The light rose around the doorframe.

The light of dragonfire.

The light of Requiem, Tash thought.

More than anyone in the palace—more even than the mightiest lords and ladies—the pleasurers were the mistresses of information. Every man who visited her den spoke his secrets, and Tash knew that upon Meliora's head no longer shone a halo of golden light. Meliora the Merciful was now crowned with dragonfire.

Tash stepped toward the cell, placed her key into the lock, and pushed open the door.

Meliora stared back at her.

Many times in her life, walking through the palace to visit this or that lord, Tash had seen Meliora from a distance—a tall, beautiful seraph, her wings pure white, her halo golden, her skin fair and her eyes shining, her body shimmering with jewels. Ahead of her now stood a woman Tash barely recognized. Meliora's hair, wings, and jewels were gone, and dried blood and dirt stained her body. She wore only burnt rags. Yet her eyes were still strong, fiery with life—seraph eyes. Upon her head crackled a new halo, woven of red and orange flame.

"Tash," she whispered.

Tash's eyes widened. "You know my name, my lady?"

Meliora nodded. "I've seen you wander the palace. I know about the . . . pleasure pit. I've often—"

The lock on the iron door—the one leading into the corridor of cells—rattled.

"Gimosh! Gimosh, you done in there?" rose the voice of the guards.

Tash hissed. "We're about to have company." She shoved her spear into Meliora's hands. "Know how to use this?"

"Stick it into people?" Meliora gave her a wan smile.

"That's the gist of it." Tash knelt and lifted her hookah; the liquid spice still bubbled within over its embers.

The iron door creaked open, and the two guards stepped into the dungeon.

Tash ran toward them and lobbed her hookah across the corridor. The glass vessel shattered against one guard, spilling boiling liquid. The seraph screamed, his wings caught flame, and he fell.

Meliora raced forward and tossed her spear. The projectile flew across the hall and its blade slammed into a guard's thigh. The man cried out and fell. Eyes narrowed, lips tight, Meliora ran closer, knelt, and lifted the fallen spear.

The guard raised his own lance.

Meliora knocked it aside and thrust her spear with a cry. The blade crashed into the guard's neck and emerged from the other side.

The burnt guard on the floor began to rise. Meliora spun toward him and drove her spear down, impaling the seraph. He gave a last gasp, then fell limp.

"Bloody stars," Tash whispered, staring at Meliora. Where was the innocent, soft-cheeked princess she had known? Before her she saw a killer, the blood of her enemies staining her arms.

"Come," Meliora said. "We must hurry."

"Wait." Tears filled Tash's eyes to remember the poor creature she had seen in the cell. "One more minute."

Tash raced along the corridor, opening cell by cell, revealing the poor wretches within. Some cowered in the corner, blinded by the torchlight. Others squealed, hissed, screamed. A few wept and begged. Only one began to crawl out of the cell, a pathetic being, thinned down to bones.

"We need to help them," Meliora whispered, staring at the miserable creatures. She shuddered. "I . . . I almost became one of them."

Tash lowered her head. "We'll never make it out alive dragging them with us. We opened a door to their freedom. That's all we can do now, unless we choose to kill them. Their fate is in the hands of the gods now. Perhaps they still remember what they once were, and they will make their own way to freedom through the dark labyrinth that awaits us and them."

She knelt, took a dagger from a dead guard, placed it into her belt, then took Meliora's hand. "Come, my lady. Now we will flee. Quickly now."

They ran out of the dungeon, entering the long, coiling burrows that snaked beneath the ziggurat. As they passed by a shadowy corner, Tash reached down, pulled loose a brick near the floor, and retrieved a cloak from within. The underground was full of such hidden alcoves and passages, the secrets known only to the pleasurers, those who made it their trade to please men . . . and to know everything that transpired in the palace. Tash handed the garment to Meliora.

"Here, my lady. A cloak and hood."

Meliora donned the garment and pulled the hood low over her head. The wool seemed to douse her crackling halo; smoke draped across Meliora's brow as the fires extinguished. To the world, she now appeared as nothing but another slave. She snapped the spear in two across her knee, discarded the bottom half, and hid the business end under her cloak.

The two kept walking together—a tall woman hidden in a cloak, and a slender young pleasurer all in silk and jewels. They made their way through the darkness, seeking the light.

MELIORA

They climbed the stairs, leaving the underground, and stepped back into the light of the world.

They stood in a small, cobbled courtyard in the shadow of the ziggurat. A path led to a narrow road into the city. In the distance, Meliora could see the obelisks, temples, and palm trees of Shayeen. She paused for just a few heartbeats, breathing deeply, savoring the touch of air on her skin, the sunlight upon her face. She had not thought she would ever feel fresh air and sunlight again.

She turned toward Tash. The young slave stood nearly a foot shorter, her jewels gleaming in the sunlight. She looked like the kind of slave Meliora would have once wrinkled her nose at—a piece of meat for the pleasures of men. Yet now Tash seemed to her a woman wiser and braver than all the soldiers in Saraph's army.

"Thank you, Tash," she whispered. "Will you return to the pleasure pits now? If you want, I'll take you with me."

"Where do you go?" Tash asked.

"To the land of Tofet. To the house of my father." She squared her shoulders. "To rebellion. Perhaps to death. To a fight I perhaps cannot win but one I will fight nonetheless."

Tash raised an eyebrow. "A life of pampered languor, surrounded by jewels, spice, endless love and friends . . . or a life of blood that will end too soon. Perhaps we both have the same choice. And we choose the same path." Tash nodded. "I go with you, to whatever end. For Requiem."

Meliora's eyes dampened, and for an instant, she envied Tash, envied that the girl was pure Vir Requis, a whole daughter of Requiem. She herself was still half a daughter of Saraph, half a shameful thing.

She nodded. "For Requiem."

They had taken just a step forward when he swooped from the sky, wings wide, and landed in the courtyard before them.

Ishtafel.

Stars of Requiem.

Meliora's heart burst into a gallop, and she hissed and reached into her cloak for her spear.

"My dearest Meliora!" He held his lance in one hand, his shield in the other. "And if it isn't the little pack rat with her collection of jewels. Such lovely ladies shouldn't stray far from the beauty of the palace."

Meliora froze for an instant, staring at him. The man who had slaughtered countless souls. Who had lied to her, cut off her wings, locked her to rot in the dungeon. Rage. Rage filled her, and her halo of dragonfire crackled to life around her head, and she tossed back her hood before the flames could burn it.

"Stand aside, Ishtafel." Meliora lifted her halved spear. "Stand aside or I will—"

He laughed. "Or you will what? Cut me, my dear sister? Perhaps I underestimated you; you have, after all, found your way out here rather quickly. But you don't truly think that you can defeat me in battle, do you? A pampered little princess against an ancient warrior who has conquered the world?"

"I am no longer a princess." Meliora stared into his eyes. "I am a warrior of Requiem."

Ishtafel hefted his spear. "I slew a million warriors of Requiem. Only days ago, sweet sister, we danced in the grand hall of our palace. Come to me now. We will dance again."

Tash drew her dagger, claimed from the prison guard, and held the blade before her.

Before her courage could abandon her, Meliora raced forward, spear lashing.

Ishtafel swung his lance in an arc. Meliora had snapped her spear in half to hide it in her cloak, abandoning the lower half in the dungeon. With his longer range, Ishtafel easily parried her thrust. Almost lazily, he drove his lance forward, nicking her left arm.

Her blood sprayed across the courtyard, pattering against Tash, and Meliora cried out.

Tash screamed, blood on her face, and tossed her dagger. Yawning, Ishtafel raised his shield, and the dagger slammed against it and fell to the ground. Ishtafel kicked it aside.

Fear flooded Meliora, but she refused to surrender to it.

I am starlight.

I am the wind.

I am dragonfire.

She could not become a dragon with her collar, but Meliora roared with her rage.

"You murdered thousands!" she screamed, lashing her spear again.

He snorted and parried. "Millions."

"You are a monster!" She leaped forward, trying to spear him, but he parried again.

He yawned. "All the best kings are, my dear."

"You—"

He drove his lance forward, and this time he cut her right arm, spraying more blood. She had barely registered the blow when he swung his lance again, hitting the side of her knee with the flat of the blade.

Meliora yowled and fell to her knees before him.

"Good." He nodded. "That is how I like you. Kneeling before me."

With another thrust of his lance, he cut her fingers. She cried out, losing her grip on her spear. It clattered to the ground, and he kicked it aside.

Meliora began to leap up. Ishtafel swung his shield, knocking the rim against her face.

Pain.

Light.

Searing fire.

Meliora fell to the ground, slamming her cheek against the cobblestones, blinded with agony. Blinking feebly, she thought she saw Tash run forth, grab the fallen spear, thought she saw the shield fly again, knocking Tash down. All was white, blinding pain . . . and beyond it a red light, crackling, hot. The light of dragonfire.

Ishtafel knelt above her, reached down, and stroked her stubbly head.

"So frail," he whispered. "Still such a weak, innocent thing, a trampled baby bird, her wings clipped. I will nurse you back to health, my sweetest sister. You will be mine. You will watch your sons become great kings—kings to crush Requiem as I have crushed her."

Her eyes burned. Blood dripped down her face, pattering against the cobblestone.

I flew as a dragon, she remembered. *I soared as a great dragon all in silver and gold, coated with scales and feathers.* Her breath shuddered. *In my dreams, I flew with great herds of my kind, the hosts of Requiem of past and future.*

Ishtafel leaned down and kissed her brow. "Soon you will be beautiful again, fed all the fineries of the empire—strong enough to grow my child in your womb."

No. No, I will never more be a prisoner. Not in a dungeon of stone, not in a palace of plenty.

Her halo crackled with the flame of Requiem.

I will find the sky. I am dragonfire.

Her flames roared, blasting outward, and Meliora let out a howl, a cry of all her pain, her rage, her memory, and she leaped up, soaring like a dragon, seeking her sky.

Ishtafel faltered, eyes widening, the flames painting him red.

Meliora had once burned in a bronze bull, and today she charged like a bull herself, ramming into him, driving her halo of fire against his face.

Her crown of dragonfire burned him, and Ishtafel screamed.

The halo of fire flowed across his face, kindling his hair, melting his skin. He burned. He screamed like a wounded animal, a primordial sound, and the flames showered back onto Meliora, scattering across her scalp.

She knelt. She grabbed her spear from the ground. She shoved it forth.

The blade crashed into Ishtafel's armor, denting the metal, cutting through, driving into his skin. Still he burned.

"Meliora!" Tash cried.

Whistles filled the air, and Meliora glanced up to see arrows falling. Tash grabbed her, pulled her back, and the arrows clattered against the cobblestones. More whistled above, and Meliora glimpsed a hundred seraphim or more diving down from the sky.

"Meliora, run!" Tash grabbed her hand and dragged her onward. "With me!"

She held her bloody spear. Ishtafel burned before her, but still his lance thrust. She cried out as it hit her. More arrows fell, and one scraped across her thigh.

"Meliora, run!"

She ran.

Arrows clattered around them, and one drove alongside Tash's hip, tearing the skin. They raced onward, holding hands, leaving the courtyard and entering a cobbled alleyway. The walls of silos, armories, and temples rose around them.

"Hurry, with me!" Tash said, pulling her through a gateway into a covered walkway between brick walls.

"Where are we going?" Meliora ran with a limp, blood leaving a trail behind her.

"The underground of Shayeen. The secret passageways of the slaves." As seraphim dived down behind them, firing arrows, Tash tugged open a wooden doorway and pulled Meliora into a shadowy tunnel.

They ran through darkness, finally entering a wine cellar, and here Tash pulled her into a second tunnel, and they emerged into a narrow alleyway in the shadow of the ziggurat. A grove of palm trees rustled ahead, and they moved under the fronds, hidden from the sky, as above the seraphim cried out and the chariots of fire rained ash.

"We go into the city," Tash said. "We take the shadow path."

Meliora ran close behind, and they circled a well and stepped onto a narrow street, the sky hidden above the awnings of shops.

"The shadow path?"

Tash nodded and flashed a weary grin. "There are eight boulevards in the City of Kings and eight thousand secret roads. Ours is the shadow path, the way of slaves between the ziggurat and the land of Tofet."

Meliora glanced around her, seeking the palace soldiers, but the street was packed with a thousand others—shopkeepers hawking spices and dried fruits, young seraphim of common birth, and many collared slaves on errands from their masters. The chariots of fire still streamed above, but the shadow path was hidden from the sky, no less a labyrinth than the one beneath the ziggurat.

Is he still alive? Meliora thought as they raced into an alleyway of metalworkers. The clanging of hammers on anvils rose from smiths at their sides. *Is Ishtafel—*

His scream rose in the distance, answering her.

"Find her! Find the escaped prisoner. Bring her to me alive and bring the pack rat too!"

Meliora and Tash glanced at each other silently, then looked forward and kept running along the shadow path, vanishing into the City of Kings as screams of seraphim and the fire of their chariots filled the sky above.

VALE

"Faster!"

The whips flew.

"Move, slaves! Toil!"

Burning leather slashed through flesh.

"Faster! Toil or die!"

Sweat dripped across Vale, stinging his eyes, drenching his burlap loincloth, burning the whip's welts across his bare back. Those welts ached like scorpion stingers forever digging into him. His muscles were cramping, begging for relief, and the sunlight burned his shoulders and shaved head, leaving him dizzy, gasping for breath.

"Toil!"

The flaming whips cracked. The overseers smirked as they flew above upon swan wings, whipping any slave who dallied—a handful of masters ruling over thousands of slaves.

For a day, hope rose, Vale thought, back bent. *All hope has burned away.*

He spilled the basket of straw into the pit of clay. Joints aching, he lifted the barrel of bitumen and spilled the tar into the mix. He climbed into the sticky pool, sloshing through it, mixing the ingredients with his hobbled legs. His feet burned, and the manacles chafed his ankles; he bled into the mix. Across the field, thousands of other slaves waded through their own pits of clay, straw, and bitumen.

"Faster!" cried an overseer, and a whip cracked over Vale's head. "Shape the bricks. Move!"

Vale nodded, back striped too many times. Another blow, he thought, would kill him. Perhaps that would be a mercy. Perhaps he should resist, let them whip him to death, join the poor souls around the pits. He raised his head, blinked out sweat, squinted in the sunlight, and saw them. A hundred slaves or more rose around the field, impaled on spikes, their flesh food for crows. Most were rotten. Some still twitched and moaned.

Poor souls? Vale thought. *The dead are the lucky ones.*

"Go!" cried the overseer. "Mix! Two thousand bricks a slave."

The whip lashed again, and this time it slammed into Vale, tearing his back, knocking him into the hot clay. The seraph was still shouting above him, but Vale could barely hear. He lay facedown in the hot mixture of clay, straw, and tar, and he felt like he was back there—back upon the crest of the ziggurat, a thousand feet above the city, nailed into the platinum.

I almost rose to the stars of Requiem, he thought. *I was almost free from the pain.*

He wanted to lie here in the mud until the pain fled again.

He still remembered the shock of Ishtafel swinging his hammer, driving the nails into Vale's hands and feet, nailing him to the ziggurat. He still remembered his body convulsing, his soul beginning to rise . . . and he had seen them. The celestial halls of afterlife. A Requiem that still stood, woven of starlight, and the spirits of the fallen awaiting him. His mother. His grandparents. The ancient kings and queens of his fallen nation.

And I saw you, Issari. The Priestess in White.

The ancient princess of Requiem, among the founders of the nation, had descended from the stars, a great healer. Forever shining in the sky, the eye of the Draco constellation, she had descended to the world for him. She had gazed at him with sad green eyes, and she had placed her hands upon him, passing her starlight into him, healing his wounds, returning his broken body to life. In his mind, she had whispered soft words.

You will live, son of Requiem.

"Let me rest," he had whispered to her.

She had wept, her tears warm, healing his soul. *Your path of thorns has not ended, son of Aeternum, for you are descended from the great family of Requiem, a child of King Aeternum and all the kings and queens who followed in his dynasty. Your battle still looms ahead, Vale. We will watch you. Our light will forever fall upon you. You must find our sky.*

Vale had awoken then, his lungs filling once more with air, the holes in his hands and feet only faded scars.

And so I must live. With shaking arms, he pushed himself up from the mud. *My battle still awaits me, and I will fight for my priestess. For Requiem.*

He rose to his shaky feet. He did not know what that battle was, what his task would be, but Issari Seran, the Eye of the Dragon, had commanded him to live. And so he would live. Whatever it took, however much pain he would endure, he would survive.

His overseer stood outside the pit of mud, smirking. "Pity. Thought you were crow food. Would have liked to see them peck out your eyes. Now form the bricks! Two thousand a man. Go!"

Vale labored in the sunlight among the thousands of slaves. In the old days, under Queen Kalafi's reign, each slave had needed to mix a thousand bricks a day—backbreaking labor that had them working from dawn to dusk. The cruel Ishtafel, new king of Saraph, had doubled that quota. With thousands of others, Vale filled baskets with the sticky mixture of mud, straw, and bitumen. He hauled basket after basket into the field, where he poured the mixture into wooden molds, mold after mold, like filling a great honeycomb. After the sun had dried the clay, he pulled out the brittle rectangles, and he placed them into stone kilns where they baked, hardening into bricks that would build homes, schools, armories, and monuments to Ishtafel across the empire.

He worked in a daze, repeating the process over and over, suffering the whip whenever he faltered, moving as fast as he could, falling, crying out in pain, rising again.

Two thousand bricks a slave.

Countless lashes.

Each slave who fell short—more flesh upon the pikes. More food for crows.

In the fields of Tofet, they labored in chains, screaming, falling, dying, some surviving. Decimated. One in ten fallen to Ishtafel's spears, more falling every day. The nation of Requiem—crying out in greater anguish than ever before, withering under a cruel sun.

When finally that sun had set, and his two thousand bricks were loaded into carts, Vale shuffled back toward his home.

In the darkness, he walked between the huts where the slaves lived. His chains clanked between his legs, and his breath rattled in his lungs, full of dust from his labor. He could not stop coughing, a raw cough that tore at his throat like his shackles tore at his ankles.

He raised his eyes to the sky, hoping against hope to see it again—the Draco constellation, the holy stars of Requiem, which he had seen only once, that night Issari had healed him. Yet those stars were gone now, if ever they had truly shone.

The wind gusted, and three gibbets swung at his side from posts. Within the rusted cages languished three slaves, close to death—their only sin having failed to meet the new, doubled quotas. Vale had only a small waterskin, barely enough water to keep himself alive, yet he approached the cages, prepared to let the dying slaves drink. They stared at him with glazed eyes, reached out from the bars, bleeding lips smacking, desperate for a drink.

Vale turned away. Their agony was almost over. He would not prolong it. He shuffled onward, their screams echoing in his ears.

He tugged at his collar. If only he could remove this collar, could shift into a dragon again, could break the bars on the gibbets. He could free them. He could fly to the ziggurat, challenge Ishtafel again.

Vale raised his head, closed his eyes, and remembered how wonderful it had felt. To become a dragon. To see his scales gleam in the sun, deep blue like the evening sky. To let the fire fill his mouth. To spread his wings and rise in the sky. Freedom. It had been freedom.

He looked back down, saw the gibbets, the huts, the agony of Tofet, and balled up his fists.

I will fly again. Someday I will fight as a dragon once more. I fought Ishtafel over the streets of Shayeen, but my greatest battle awaits.

He kept shuffling forward until he reached his hut, a simple clay dwelling, barely larger than a cage itself. A birch leaf was engraved onto the door, an old symbol of Requiem. Vale opened that door and stepped into his shadowy home.

His sister, Elory, lay facedown on a pile of straw, biting a piece of wood. Ugly lashes crisscrossed her back, and she bled where the shackles chafed her ankles. Above her knelt Vale's father, wise old Jaren. The bearded priest was dripping ointment into the wounds on Elory's back. She grimaced with every drop that fell, and sweat beaded on her shaved head.

Rage flared in Vale.

"Who?" he demanded, speaking between gritting teeth. "Which overseer? Was it Karah? The new one, Eldor?"

Jaren raised his hands, silently urging calm. Elory pushed herself onto her elbows, staring at Vale with damp eyes.

"It was my fault!" she said. "I almost failed to meet my quota of bitumen."

The rage was blinding. Vale sneered and took a step back toward the door. "That's because Ishtafel doubled the quotas. I'm going to find who did this. I'm going to kill them. I don't care if they arrest me again, if—"

"Son!" Jaren reached out, trying to grab him, to pull him back into the hut. "You cannot help your sister by dying. Please, son. We must bide our time. We must—"

"Must what?" Vale said, voice hoarse, eyes damp. He shook himself free. "Bide our time for what? Our people have been waiting for five hundred years, Father. Waiting for a savior. Waiting for some hope. I thought that some hope rose. When we marched behind Meliora, I thought that finally the stars have heard our cry, that they sent us a savior. I thought that Meliora—your daughter, my sister—is the hope we've been waiting for all these years." He laughed bitterly. "But I was there. I saw Ishtafel cut off Meliora's wings, saw him drag her into his palace, saw our hope shatter. So yes. Let me go out and fight. Let me die avenging my sisters."

A voice, melodious and soft, rose behind him, piercing through his rage like a ray of light through storm clouds.

"Do not die for me, my brother. Together we will live."

Slowly, Vale unclenched his fists and turned around. He saw her outside, stepping toward the doorway, cloaked in wool. Within the shadows of her hood, her eyes shone, golden, the pupils shaped as sunbursts with many rays. She smiled at him tremulously.

"Meliora," he whispered.

JAREN

He sat with his family at the table, knowing that this brief moment of peace would soon shatter and burn.

We are together again, united in the shadow of a great, burning hatred that will soon spew its flames upon us. Jaren looked up at the ceiling where he had engraved the Draco constellation. *May we savor this moment, for it might be long years of blood, sweat, and tears before it returns . . . if ever we sit like this, together again.*

He looked at them all, one by one. They stared back from around the table, silent, all waiting for his words. Vale, his son, gaunt and scarred, his eyes blazing with fire. Elory, his sweet daughter, her brown eyes kind and soft, even after so much pain. Meliora, his eldest, her head now shaved like a slave's, crowned with a halo of dragonfire. And with them, too, sat Tash of the pleasure pits, a young woman with long brown hair, perfumed skin, and many jewels, and though Jaren had just met her, she too was like a daughter to him. She too was family. Perhaps all in Requiem were a family under the heel of Saraph. They all sat here in this small hut, surrounding the small table, sitting before clay bowls of gruel—a warm meal, perhaps a last meal.

Their chains, which had once hobbled their ankles, lay in a pile on the floor. Tash had come here with an iron key, which she had used to unchain new girls arriving into the pleasure pit. Now she had freed the chains that had bound Jaren and his family's legs. And yet their collars remained, preventing them from using their magic, for no simple key could unlock that cursed iron. So long as they wore those collars, slaves they would remain.

I am old, and I am frail, Jaren thought. He was not yet sixty, yet he felt over a hundred, wearied by years of toil. He could not fight this battle as the younger ones could, yet they looked to him for guidance, for wisdom . . . for leadership. For gifts he didn't know that he had to give. Perhaps that was the folly of youth—that the young, when faced with hardship, looked to their elders for aid, not knowing that even the very old wished for a teacher.

Yet Jaren was the only teacher they had now, and the young ones needed him. He would give them whatever guidance he could, would shepherd them through a storm he was not sure any of them could survive.

He spoke softly. "This is a precious moment. This is a moment of sweetness, of family, of peace. Our family sits together, bound by love and light, though darkness surrounds us. Before we face that darkness, let us pray."

He sang in a deep, rumbling voice as he lit candles on the table. He sang the old prayers of Requiem—songs of distant hills in dawn, rustling birch forests, blue mountains kissed with mist and sunlight, marble tiles and white columns. A song of dragons. A song of home. A song of their lost sky. The others sang with him as the candles burned, little lights shaped as the Draco constellation. The brightest candle he arranged to shine as the dragon's eye—Issari's Star.

"Many small lights can banish even the greatest shadow." Jaren looked across the candles at his family. "And now a great shadow surrounds us. The cruel tyrant seeks Meliora in every corner of Shayeen and Tofet, and he will not rest until he finds her. He will seek our dear Tash too, a new daughter in our family. And he will continue to enslave the rest of us, to grind us down, to break us, to slay us. And now we must decide: how can we keep our lights shining in this darkness?"

"We fight." Vale rose to his feet, nearly knocking back his stool. "We've collected and hidden two spears in this very hut. Other slaves have hidden weapons too. We rise! We march to the palace again, this time armed. And—"

"No." Jaren shook his head. "We marched once. We lost too many." He lowered his head, overcome by the grief, the memory of the decimation. "We cannot face the enemy, not in human forms, not while collared."

Vale slammed his fist against the tabletop. "Then we storm the ziggurat. We find the Keeper's Key. We—"

"I already found it," Meliora said, voice barely more than a whisper. She reached into her pocket, pulled out a crumpled ball of crimson metal, and placed it on the tabletop. The edges of golden runes were still visible; most of the ancient symbols were hidden within the crushed, metallic embrace.

Elory spoke for the first time, eyes widening. "The Keeper's Key! It's . . ."

"Useless." Meliora sighed. "Many times I tried to use it on my collar, to no avail. With the key crushed, its runes won't work. Ishtafel crushed it in his palm." She nudged the crumpled ball across the table. "Try it on your collars. Perhaps you'll have more luck than I did."

They all stared at one another, silent. Jaren reached across the tabletop first and lifted the broken key. The crimson metal was cold. Jaren had never touched ice before, but he imagined that it felt like this. Yet whenever his fingertips passed across what remained of the runes, he felt warmth. He had seen this key from a distance before—the overseers would use it when unlocking his wife's collar, allowing her to become a dragon and dig through the bitumen—though he had never come so close. Slowly he raised the ancient relic to his throat, bringing it near his collar.

Elory gasped. "Father, the runes on your collar! They're glowing! They're . . . fading."

Warmth surrounded Jaren's neck. The runes on the key too glowed, but then their light fizzled and dimmed. The collar remained around his neck.

He passed the key to Elory, and she tried it on her collar, then Tash and Vale both tried on theirs. In each case, the runes only flickered, glowed softly for an instant, then faded to darkness.

"There must be another key," Elory whispered. "Surely in the palace, there is another."

"There is only one." Meliora returned the crumpled key into her pocket. "There was only ever one."

"Then we fix this one." Elory nodded. "We'll heat the metal just enough, unfold it, return the key to its former shape."

Meliora shook her head again. "We would only melt the golden runes, perhaps beyond restoration. No. I dare not try to fix it myself, for fear that I would damage it further. But . . . there is one who can fix this key."

They all turned to stare at her. Meliora seemed to stare into nothingness, perhaps lost in memory.

"Who, daughter?" Jaren said, reaching out to touch her hand. "Who can fix it?"

She looked at him, eyes haunted. "He who made this key five hundred years ago. He who still lingers in a mockery of life, banished from our realm. He of whom the seraphim rarely speak." She shuddered. "The Keymaker."

ISHTAFEL

He lay on his bed, face aflame, grinding his teeth so hard they nearly chipped. He dug his fingernails into his palms, drawing blood. Every breath burned. All was fire. All was rage.

You burned me.

His fists shook.

You escaped me.

His hand rose, shaking. His fingers uncurled, dripping his own blood, and reached to the bandage on his cheek.

"My lord!" said the healer, a young woman in white robes, her halo glowing. "You need to leave the bandage on, my lord, you—"

He roared, swung his hand, and knocked her down. The effort tore through him like a demon, leaving him gasping for breath, coughing. His face blazed as if covered in embers. As the healer mewled on the floor, Ishtafel grabbed the bandage on his face.

He tore it off with one swift movement.

For an instant, silence.

For an instant, nothing but cold, white shock.

Then he screamed.

He rose to his feet, stumbled across the chamber of healing, and stared into the bronze mirror on the wall.

Slowly he began to laugh.

A dripping, red welt ran across his face, rising from the left side of his jaw, crossing his cheek and forehead, and finally running across half his scalp. The mark of Meliora's flaming halo. As he laughed, the wound twisted, lined with blisters. A second wound glared from his chest, the stitched cut from her spear.

"Yes, sweet sister," he said. "We are both changed."

Meliora lurked somewhere within these walls—in Shayeen, the City of Kings, or in Tofet, the land of slaves. There were no gates that broke these walls; winged seraphim needed no gates.

"Yet you have no wings, Meliora," he said, speaking to his reflection, to the halo of fire across his face. "You are trapped. And I will find you here. I will find you if I have to kill every slave in my empire, one by one, until you are mine."

He stepped out of the chamber of healing. He walked through the halls of the palace, stepped onto a dark balcony, and mounted his chariot of fire. His wounds roared across him, and he grinned and grabbed the reins. Bare-chested, he soared. His firehorses stormed across the sky, and the city sprawled below him in the night. Somewhere in those shadows she lurked—the sister whose skin he would burn until nothing was left.

MELIORA

"The . . . Keymaker?" Elory whispered, eyes wide, leaning across the tabletop.

Meliora nodded. "We do not like speaking his name in the ziggurat. He is a powerful wizard, ancient, a mystic being. His magic is so great they say it drove him to madness. With that dark magic, he made the key and the collars." She shuddered. "My family exiled him, fearing his power, fearing his madness. He lives far in the mountains, claiming dominion over a ruined fort."

"A mystic being?" Vale said, frowning. "Is he not a seraph?"

Meliora swallowed a lump in her throat. "I don't know what he is. He is never painted, never sculpted, never described in our ancient books. I never saw him. He was exiled centuries ago. But . . . I heard tales. Tales I dare not repeat. But though I fear him, I must find him. If there's any hope left to us, it's in his hands."

It was Jaren's turn to speak. The old priest looked at her with his sad brown eyes, his voice soft. "Yet how will we find him, daughter? The walls surrounding Tofet are high, and in five hundred years, only the hero Lucem has ever scaled them. Thousands have tried. Those are not good odds."

Meliora nodded. Lucem. The hero of Requiem. A legend among the slaves. Meliora remembered that day ten years ago. She had been only a youth, seventeen, naive and scared. The entire city garrison had risen into the sky, seeking the escaped slave in the hills, deserts, and mountains around the city. Since then, Lucem had been an embarrassment to her family—the slave who had found a blind spot in the walls of Tofet, who had climbed, who had killed a seraph archer, who had escaped into the wilderness. Her family had never spoken of him again . . . yet in Tofet, he was still a hero, forever remembered.

"No," Meliora said. "We will not try to scale the wall as Lucem did. It rises too high. All its blind spots have been found since Lucem escaped, and many guards patrol its battlements. There are no city gates in Tofet nor in Shayeen, it's true; seraphim need none, able to fly above the walls as easily as any dragon." She smiled thinly. "But there is a river. The Te'ephim River flows between Shayeen and Tofet, forever separating our two realms. And only where the river leaves the city is the wall broken—two exits. Two ways we can escape."

Vale grunted. The tall, dour slave gripped a spoon as if it were a sword. "Swimming won't work. Many slaves tried. I knew some of them. Good men." He groaned. "There are beasts in the water, reptiles with great teeth, smaller than dragons but hungry and vicious. Hundreds of them. Trained to feed upon the flesh of any slave mad enough to swim for freedom. And even if you made it past the reptiles, there are walls along the river too. Not as tall as the walls around the city, but guards top them too, armed with bows and arrows. Just waiting for a chance to shoot whoever the reptiles miss." He shook his head. "No, the river is death. I would sooner try to scale the wall as Lucem did than swim. At least we know one man who fled over the wall. No slave ever made it through the water."

"Yet I am no simple slave." Meliora placed her hands around Vale's fist that still clutched the spoon, and she stared into his eyes. "I have the eyes of a seraph. I have no more wings, no more long golden hair, and my halo burns with red fire. But cloaked and hooded, nothing but my eyes visible?" She smiled thinly. "Yes. I think I could still pass for a seraph. I will walk to the city port—there are no walls there—and book passage in a boat. I will sail out of the city." She nodded and tightened her grip around his hand. "I will find the Keymaker."

Silence fell across the hut.

They all stared at her, eyes wide . . . all but Tash.

Throughout the night, the slender pleasurer had said little, merely sat and listened. Now her eyes narrowed, and she rose to her feet. The candlelight reflected in her bracelets, earrings, and ring.

"Wait a minute!" Tash said. "This won't work. This won't work at all."

"It's our only hope," Meliora said.

Tash shook her head wildly, her long brown hair swaying. "It's a useless hope! Look. Do the numbers. There are . . . what, half a million slaves in Tofet? Maybe more?" She nodded. "And even if you fix the key, that's just one key. Imagine you could get every slave to line up, one by one, and you started opening their collars. Imagine it took you . . . say, thirty seconds to open a collar. It would still take six months to open everyone's collars. Half a year! And that's assuming you could even do it that fast. Meanwhile Ishtafel would kill us all. The seraphim wouldn't give us six minutes to work, let alone six months."

Vale grumbled. "At least it's some hope. At least we could get a *few* dragons flying before Ishtafel attacks."

Tash groaned. "A few dragons who'd die right away! Think, everyone. Ishtafel killed thousands of dragons in Requiem. Maybe even hundreds of thousands. He's good at killing them. Just opening a few collars won't work. We'd all need to fly as dragons, together—all of us, the entire nation of Requiem, roaring fire at once, surprising the enemy. That's the only way we'd stand even a tiny chance. To do that . . . we'd need over half a million keys. A key for every slave, kept hidden, secret . . . then all used at once." Her eyes shone.

Meliora winced. "According to legend, it took the Keymaker six days and nights to forge this key and embed it with dark magic." She sighed. "I don't think we'd have time waiting for half a million keys."

"We don't need to wait." A sly grin spread across Tash's face. "I know some magical secrets too. There is a way . . . and there is a map."

Tash took a round obsidian box from her pocket, the kind pleasurers kept spice in, and opened it. Inside, instead of hintan, was a folded piece of parchment. She unfolded it carefully, as if handling an ancient relic, revealing a crudely drawn map, showing mountains, rivers, and a coastline.

"It's the world outside the walls," Elory whispered, staring in awe. "How did you find this map?"

"The pleasure pits are the empire's hub of knowledge." Tash nodded. "Every man who comes into our den, who smokes our pipes, who drinks our wine, who moans under our kisses, his words are ours to collect. And we hoard that information like a miser hoards gold. This is a map to the most important, most magical, most sought-after treasure in the world." She pointed at a drawing of a ship upon an eastern coast, and her voice dropped to an awed whisper. "The Chest of Plenty."

They all stared silently, and Meliora struggled not to laugh. The Chest of Plenty? She had outgrown believing in that artifact years ago.

"Tash." Meliora spoke gently. "The Chest of Plenty is just a myth. Just a tale they tell children in the palace."

"Not a tale!" Tash's eyes flashed angrily. "It's real. One man who came into the pleasure pit, he'd even seen the ghost ship from a distance, beached upon the shore. He swears he heard the ghosts who guard the ship, who guard the chest within. Imagine it, Meliora! A chest that can duplicate whatever you place inside it—food, coins, jewels." Tash's eyes gleamed like jewels themselves. "For years, I dreamed of finding the Chest of Plenty. Of placing my own humble jewels inside it, only to see them multiplied a thousand times. I would have enough money to live as a queen. To build a castle somewhere, to have servants, to . . ." Tash's cheeks flushed. "Well, I suppose that dream is rather childish. An impossible dream. But the Chest of Plenty is real. Thousands of men have sought it, dreaming of growing rich off a single gold coin, but I'm the only one who has a real map."

Meliora sighed. Tash seemed earnest, excited, and she had saved Meliora's life. But how could Meliora believe this tale?

"Tash—" she began.

"Hush!" Tash glared at her. "I don't want to hear your doubt. The Chest of Plenty is real. It has to be real. It's real or . . . or all my dreams are meaningless. And I won't believe that." Her eyes dampened. "I won't! I'm going to escape with you on your boat. I helped you escape from your prison cell; you will help me escape from the city walls. You owe this to me. I will travel alone if I must, following this map, until I find the Chest of Plenty. Until I bring it back here and place your Keeper's Key within it."

"No." It was Vale who spoke this time. The gaunt young man rose to his feet, staring with hard eyes.

Tash glared right back at him. "And who are you to tell me what not to do? You're nothing but a—"

"No," Vale repeated, voice hard. "You will not follow this map alone. I'll go with you."

Everyone stared at him, silent. Tash gaped and rubbed her eyes. "You . . . want to come with me? You believe the Chest of Plenty is real?" She glanced down at her cleavage. "Or do you just believe *this* chest might be yours?"

"I don't know if the chest is real," Vale said, ignoring the jab. "I don't know if the Keymaker is real. I don't even know if our hope is real or just folly. But I know that here, in Tofet, there is no hope. So I will seek it beyond the walls." He turned toward Meliora. "We're joining you in your boat, Meliora. You'll smuggle us out of the city. You will go seek the Keymaker, and you will fix the key. Meanwhile Tash and I will find the Chest of Plenty to duplicate that key half a million times." He clenched his fists. "Soon a nation of dragons will rise."

ELORY

For the first time since the slaughter, the decimation that had left one in ten slaves dead, Elory dared to feel hope, dared to let the veil of grief lift.

Meliora will fix the key. Elory touched her collar, remembering the time she had begun to shift, had seen the buds of lavender scales before the collar had slammed her back into human form. *Vale and Tash will multiply it, one for every dragon. Requiem will fly again.*

"So what are we waiting for?" Tash was saying, leaping to her feet. "Let's go. Now! Before Ishtafel burns down every hut to find us. Before the sun rises."

When Elory glanced over at Tash, she felt her cheeks heat up. Memories of her brief time in the pit, of Tash's lessons, filled her with a strange, intoxicating feeling much like the spice's smoke. Here in the hut, Tash was all wildfire, but back in the pleasure pit, she had been like honey, her kisses and caresses awakening deep senses in Elory she could not forget. Elory had never loved another soul, not a romantic sort of love, but she had heard tales of romance, and she wondered if those feelings were akin to the ones Tash had instilled within her. Strangely, Elory missed the pleasure pit, missed the comforting shadows, the incense, the gentle touch of Tash's lips.

She shook her head wildly. She had no room for such thoughts anymore. Those days were over, and a new path lay before her, a path of war.

She rose to her feet too, and she approached the others, one by one.

"Goodbye, Vale," she whispered, hugging her brother, then turned toward Meliora. "Goodbye, sister. I will pray for you. I—"

"You will go with them," Jaren said, also rising to his feet.

Elory turned toward her father and gasped. "But . . . Father!"

Jaren's gaunt, bearded face was grim. "If Meliora can smuggle two slaves out of the city, she can smuggle a third. Tash and Vale have each other on their quest for the Chest of Plenty. I will not have Meliora walk her path alone. Join her, Elory. Help her find the Keymaker."

Elory's eyes dampened. She stepped toward her father and embraced him, placing her cheek against his thin chest. "Come with us, Father."

He shook his head and kissed the top of her head. "I am a shepherd of Requiem. I cannot leave my flock."

She looked up at him, tears in her eyes. "And I can? How can I leave the others to suffer? How can I leave you?"

He caressed her cheek. "Sweetest daughter. You are like your mother, a being of pure light and kindness. And here in Tofet, the masters will crush your light, grind away your kindness until only bitterness remains. Ishtafel will seek you again, seek to drag you into his palace, to take you away from me. If we must part, I would see you travel a road of hope with Meliora, not enter a prison of gold with Ishtafel. You are in danger here, Elory. We all are. Go with your sister. Bring back hope."

She held her father close. "I will return to you, Father. I promise. I love you. Always."

As he held her, Elory thought of her mother. Not that last memory, that horrible memory of Mother dying in Ishtafel's fire. She thought of the kindly mother she had known, the mother who would hold her like this, sing to her old songs of Requiem. She would not forget Mother either, not forget all those who had fallen, all those who still lived, desperate for salvation.

They stepped out of the hut in the darkness of night. Above, high in the sky, the chariots of fire were streaming across the river, and the distant cries of the seraphim rose. Around them spread the thousands of huts of Tofet, and Elory did not know if she'd ever see this place—the only home she had ever known—again.

"Come, quickly now," Meliora urged.

Elory nodded. Standing outside on the dirt path, she gave her father a last embrace, and her tears would not stop falling.

Vale joined the embrace, his arms stiff at first, but then his grip softened, and his eyes too shone with tears.

"Go," Jaren whispered. "Quickly, my children. May Requiem's stars forever shine upon you."

"Come on!" Tash said, hopping in the dirt. "Those chariots are getting closer."

Elory nodded, wiped her eyes, and released her father. Tash grabbed her hand, yanking her down the path. Meliora and Vale walked ahead. As they hurried between the dark huts, Elory looked back only once. She saw her father standing in the doorway, the candlelight limning his form. He raised his hand in farewell, and then Tash pulled Elory around a corner, and she did not see him again.

MELIORA

They hurried along the bridge, the dark waters gushing beneath them, four figures hidden in robes and hoods. Behind them spread the land of Tofet, cloaked in shadows. Across the bridge rose the city of Shayeen, lit with many lanterns. In the sky the chariots of fire soared, scanning the land below.

We'll never make it across the river. Meliora's heart thudded, and she felt her phantom wings again, aching to flap them, to fly from here, fly over the walls and vanish into the wilderness. How weak were those doomed to forever walk upon two legs! What hope did she have of reaching the port with Ishtafel's guards swarming?

Ten of those guards stood at the southern edge of the bridge, and several more stood in watchtowers, arrows nocked.

"Halt!" they cried.

Meliora halted before them on the bridge. The dark waters of the Te'ephim gushed below, and the cries of soldiers rose in the city ahead, seeking her and Tash, tearing down the city to find them. The light of chariots streamed above, and cold sweat washed Meliora. Truly a fool's quest! She wouldn't even make it across the river, let alone out of the city and across the wilderness to find the Keymaker.

"I told you I'd return with two more slaves," Meliora said, glaring at the guards from the confines of her hood, hoping she looked more angry than terrified. "They are my family's slaves, escaped from our house into Tofet. I've reclaimed them."

The seraphim guards raised their lances, and their torches reflected against their armor and helmets. "Let's take a look at them. And at you. Hoods off! Word is two criminals are out somewhere in this city. We got to be careful."

Meliora's heart beat even faster. Behind her, the others—Vale, Elory, and Tash—shifted their weight from foot to foot, still hidden in their hoods. Meliora had used this ruse—

pretending to be a mistress, with Tash as her slave—to cross the river into Tofet. Could she truly fool them twice?

Tash stepped forward, a slender figure hidden in burlap, and placed a small, hard object in Meliora's hand. Meliora held it out to the guards—a golden bracelet embedded with rubies.

"I don't want to report my house slaves escaping," Meliora said. "If the City Guard hears, they'll stick the poor bastards on pikes. Take this and let us through—no questions asked."

The guards' eyes gleamed like rubies themselves. One seraph snatched the bracelet, and another made a grab for it. Soon they were quibbling over how to dislodge the rubies and which guard got which stone. It had cost them Tash's silver ring to enter Tofet, but the girl had many jewels, given to her by a host of adoring seraphim lords.

Leaving the bridge keepers behind to fight over the rubies—they were already prying the gems out from the bracelet—the hooded companions made their way into Shayeen.

When rushing into Tofet, only a handful of chariots had flown above, and Meliora and Tash had soon lost the guards' pursuit in the shadow path. Now it seemed that the entire city garrison was out in the night—they marched down the streets, knocked on doors, and flew above in their chariots of fire. Their cries rolled across the city, and in the distance, Meliora could hear her brother shout in the night.

"Find them! Find the prisoners."

Ishtafel did not mention her by name. Good. Meliora smiled thinly in the shadows of her hood. Perhaps he was too embarrassed to have lost his own sister.

I hope your wound burns, brother, she thought. *I hope it screams with the same agony as my phantom wings.*

"Quickly, this way!" Tash said, directing the companions into an alleyway that ran between brick silos and refineries, the way so narrow they had to walk single file. At the end of the alley, they went down a flight of stairs, took a dark path between two hills, and finally tiptoed along an aqueduct. The shadow path of the slaves was a way of rooftops, tunnels, sometimes even sewers, a network connecting all of the city, as hidden as the passageways of rats.

The port wasn't far, less than a mile from the bridge, but the path seemed to wind on for endless leagues. They hurried through a brick house where fishermen cleaned their catches and fish entrails stank in buckets. They made their way across a barren backyard where fishing nets hung from ropes. Always the chariots flew overhead, and the sounds of guards breaking down doorways rose from the city streets.

Finally, standing between a few palm trees, Meliora could see the port ahead. A boardwalk spread alongside the Te'ephim River, and lanterns bobbed on the masts of sailing ships. There lay her road to freedom.

"Find the prisoners!" rose Ishtafel's cry above, and Meliora looked up to see a stream of fire. It was him. His chariot. She grimaced and clenched her fist, but he shot overhead, moving too fast to see her, and charged across the river into Tofet. A thousand chariots flew behind him, and his voice boomed in the sky like thunder. "Make the slaves pay! Break them until they bring out the prisoners."

Meliora hissed, and Elory gasped at her side.

Elory shuddered. "He's going to kill them. He'll decimate them again." She grabbed Meliora's arm. "We have to go back. We have to get Father! To fight. To—"

Meliora lowered her head. "We cannot."

Vale stepped closer, and anger kindled in his eyes. "You did not see the decimation, Meliora. You did not see the bodies on the pikes. If he's planning another attack, we—"

"We must bring hope," Meliora said, staring at him. She was tall for a Vir Requis, six feet from her toes to her shaved head, but Vale stood just as tall; he stared back, eye level with her. "More than ever, the people of Requiem need the Keeper's Key," she said. "We cannot fight Ishtafel while wearing our collars. We must leave this city."

They all stared at her. From across the river, screams already rose—the screams of slaves.

"They're dying," Elory whispered.

Meliora nodded. "Then we must hurry. We must fetch the key as quickly as we can. Come now. To the port."

Reluctantly the others followed. They made their way past the palm trees and stepped between a portico's columns. A cobbled boardwalk spread ahead along the riverbank. Lanterns swung from poles, casting orange light upon the river. Piers stretched into the water, lined with the small reed boats of fishermen. Several larger boats—the sailing ships of merchants—docked farther away.

"Tash, the jewels," Meliora whispered.

Tash nodded, stepped forward, and furtively passed more jewels into Meliora's hands: three anklets strewn with gemstones and a silver necklace.

"That's all I've got left," Tash whispered. "It better be enough. I—"

"Watch it!" barked a burly seraph, trundling between them. His girth knocked into Meliora and Tash, shoving them back, and his breath stank of spirits. Behind him, he dragged a collared and bruised slave.

Meliora winced and kept walking along the boardwalk. She had never been to the port before; her mother had always forbidden it. Meliora had always imagined a delightful, magical place, akin to the little stream that ran through the palace gardens. In her imagination, men and women sat dangling their feet in the water, singing songs while pups scampered between flower beds, and in the water sailed ships carved like swans, adorned with crystals, bringing with them the treasures from distant lands: sweet cakes, the softest silk, and exotic birds in cages.

Now Meliora understood why her mother had forbidden her to visit. Here was no place for a pampered, innocent princess. A drunk seraph lay on the cobblestones by an emptied bottle, drooling. A few pleasure slaves lurked in the shadows—not adorned in silk and jewels like Tash but coated in bruises and scrapes. As chariots shrieked overhead, raining sparks, gamblers were quickly packing up their games of dice and retreating behind the trees. The firehorses galloped above, and soldiers stood a hundred yards away, holding torches.

We must hurry, Meliora thought.

"Now, let's see who we can buy a boat from," she said. "Everyone seems to be fleeing the boardwalk."

She looked around, frowning. The last few fishermen were scurrying off the boardwalk, between the columns, and hiding in the grove of palm trees. The light of chariots reflected on the water, and more soldiers came marching onto the boardwalk, torches crackling.

"Forget buying a boat!" Tash said. "That one. Quickly!"

Meliora nodded and gestured for Vale and Elory to follow. The four cloaked and hooded figures made their way across the boardwalk and onto a pier. A reed boat swayed in the water, tied to a peg.

"Quickly, everyone in!" Meliora whispered. "We'll—"

"Halt!" rose a voice behind them.

Meliora's heart sank. She spun around to see a seraph, armed with spear and shield, march toward her along the pier. His eyes burned within his helmet like candles in a lantern.

Meliora's heart now threatened to leap out of her mouth. She held out her palm, letting the jewels shine. "I'm here to buy this boat. This boat is yours, yes? Of course it is. Take these jewels and—"

The soldier reached her and grabbed her wrist. "Are you trying to bribe a guard of the city?" He growled and reached for her hood. "Show your face, seraph! Who are you? I—"

Tash leaped forward and opened her palm, spraying out green, sparkly dust. The smell of purified hintan filled the air, and the spice covered the soldier's face. The seraph blinked, inhaled sharply, and coughed.

"I . . .," he whispered. "I . . . who . . .?"

Tash gave the man just the gentlest of shoves. He fell from the pier, vanishing into the water.

"A pleasurer's weapon." Tash flashed Meliora a grin, then leaped into the boat.

Vale and Elory followed, and finally Meliora stepped into the boat. She drew her halved spear from her cloak and lashed the blade across the rope several times, finally severing it. The current began pulling them downstream. It was a small reed boat, barely large enough for the four of them, and dipped deeply into the water.

Elory grabbed the oars and rowed, adding speed. They kept flowing down the river, moving farther from the bank. The water rippled around them, and Meliora thought she glimpsed gleaming, reptilian eyes that soon vanished.

"We've got company," Vale muttered and gestured to the boardwalk. Two seraphim guards had noticed them.

"You, fishermen!" one cried from the boardwalk. "There's a curfew, damn it. Get back here."

Meliora tugged her hood lower, clutching her spear. Tash drew her dagger, and Vale reached into his cloak and drew his own halved spear. Elory kept rowing, glancing around nervously.

"Damn it, I said get back here!" shouted the guard. The two seraphim spread their wings, took flight, and stormed toward the boat. "Are you deaf, damn it?"

"Wait," Meliora whispered, clutching her spear under her cloak. "Wait . . ."

The two seraphim descended to hover before the boat. "Turn around now and—"

Meliora leaped to her feet and thrust her spear. The blade tore through one seraph's wing. He wobbled in the sky, cursing, and Meliora reached out, grabbed his wounded wing, and pulled down hard.

The seraph slammed into the water with a splash. Those reptilian eyes shone again, and a crocodile's maw rose from the water, closing around the seraph.

At Meliora's side, Vale drove his spear into the second seraph's face. The soldier stumbled, and Vale reached out from the boat, tugging him down. The water splashed and the boat rocked. Elory hissed and swung her oar, shoving one wounded seraph deeper into the water. The crocodiles feasted. The seraphim sank. The boat sailed onward.

"Over there!" Elory said.

Meliora spun her head to see five or six seraphim race along the boardwalk. She cursed, lifted the jewels Tash had given her, and tossed them. "Catch!"

The jewels hit the boardwalk, and the seraphim knelt. Elory kept rowing, and the sound of seraphim arguing over a diamond necklace rose from behind.

"Take us farther from the bank," Meliora said. "Far from the boardwalk. We'll vanish in shadows."

Elory complied, guiding the boat until it sailed in the middle of the Te'ephim. The river was so wide that, from the riverbanks, the boat would appear as nothing but a speck, perhaps just another crocodile in the night. Chariots of fire still streamed above, and distant screams rose from Tofet, but the water seemed almost peaceful. They left the port behind, and soon they were sailing between two walls.

"Stay low," Meliora whispered, crouching in the boat. The others followed her lead. "Cover anything metallic so it doesn't glint."

They flowed onward, a lump of black on black. The riverbanks were now each a hundred yards away or more; if the guards along them saw the boat, they gave no sign of it.

We're nothing but a hippopotamus, Meliora thought. *Just a big hippo floating in the water.*

Ahead she saw it: the western walls of the city. One wall flowed northward, topped with battlements, curving to surround Tofet, trapping the slaves within. The other wall flowed southward, cradling the city of Shayeen, home of the seraphim. Each wall ended with a stone idol, three hundred feet tall, of a god with a hippopotamus head. The two guardians stood with hands raised, shadows in the night, torches lit within their eyes. The river flowed between them, leading out into the wilderness.

"Behold Ur and Talan," Meliora whispered, raising her eyes to stare at them. "Ancient twin gods of the water. Legends say that they set the first stones in this city, that—"

"Mythology later," Vale muttered and pointed. "Fire in the sky."

Meliora looked up and cursed.

Two chariots were descending through the sky toward them, diving to fly between the statues. She could see the seraphim within, raising their lances and shields. Four firehorses pulled each chariot, scattering brimstone and ashes, flaming wings opened wide.

"Bloody stars," Tash whispered, gripping her dagger.

Meliora rose in the boat. "Halt!" she cried out. "I lead lepers out from the city. I—"

But the chariots kept charging down, swooping to skim along the water, showering sparks, heading toward the boat.

"Escaping slaves!" cried a seraph in one of the chariots. "Burn them. Burn them down!"

Meliora readied her lance.

The chariots stormed forth, and she stared up into the eyes of the seraphim—of her people. Of the people she had once led. The people she would now kill.

"Meliora!" Elory shouted in fear.

She narrowed her eyes.

I am the wind.

The chariots charged toward the boat.

Meliora leaped into the air, vaulted skyward toward them, and beat her phantom wings.

"Meliora!" Elory shouted again below, but this time Meliora could barely hear. She heard nothing but the fire above, the wind in her ears, the beat of a million dragon wings.

I am the sky.

She had no more seraph wings, but in her mind she flapped the great wings of a dragon, and she soared, spear thrusting upward, and grabbed one of the flaming chariots.

Her fingers burned. She screamed. The fire raced across her arm.

I am fire. I am dragonfire.

The seraph in the chariot grunted and lashed his lance. Meliora thrust her own spear, parrying the blow. She swung her legs, and she leaped into the flaming chariot beside the seraph.

The man snarled and shoved against her. The wind whipped her hood off her head, revealing her halo of dragonfire. The flames crackled in a great expanding ring like the whips of fire the overseers used. The flames lashed the seraph's face, and he screamed, and Meliora shoved his lance aside and thrust her spear.

For Requiem.

Elory screamed below in the boat. The second chariot was circling above it, and the seraph fired down arrows. One arrow slammed into Vale's shoulder, and the young slave shouted.

Meliora thrust her spear again, driving it deep into the seraph's torso, and shoved him off the chariot. She grabbed the reins. She snarled.

Just like the chariot race down the boulevard.

She grinned savagely and drove the firehorses forward. She slammed into the second chariot of fire, and she leaped through the air.

The chariots blasted out flame.

Meliora soared skyward, then plunged down, spear lashing, and drove the blade into the second seraph.

His lance scraped across her thigh.

Fire seared her blood.

The firehorses tangled together, the chariots shattered against each other, and the great ball of fire plunged from the sky.

They crashed into the river.

Black water flowed above her head, dousing the fire on her arm, extinguishing her halo. She sank. Around her in the water, she saw the firehorses still kicking, sinking, their flames dying, leaving them as pale, withered things that faded into nothing. Her blood danced around them.

Meliora kicked underwater.

The water beckoned to her, demons of the deep tugging at her feet. The pain flared through her, and the river whispered, *Sink, join us . . . let us soothe the pain . . . there is no pain down there, only warm darkness.*

She sneered and kicked with all her might.

I do not die this night.

She rose in the water, shoving her way through the last, crackling pieces of the chariots. She saw nothing. She barely knew up from down. She kept kicking. She could not find the surface. She sank again.

"Meliora!" The voice rolled through the water, and she swam toward it. "Meliora!"

She bumped into him, and she cried out wordlessly, and arms wrapped around her. His legs kicked, and they rose together, and their heads burst over the surface.

Meliora gulped down air, coughed, inhaled again. The air was hot, full of ash, and beautiful.

Vale swam in the water, his arms still around her, breathing deeply.

"You saved my life," she said, love for this man—the brother she had never known—filling her with warmth.

He smiled thinly. "Just returning the favor, sister."

Hands reached down toward them—Elory and Tash leaning over the boat—and they climbed in, coughing. Scraps of fire still burned on the river, fading one by one like extinguishing stars. They sailed onward, passing between the towering idols . . . and out into the open darkness.

The boat flowed onward, leaving the walls of the city behind. Soon the darkness was complete, cloaking them like a blanket.

Meliora lay in the boat, letting Vale bandage her wounds with strips from his cloak, and she stared back at the city, at the lights fading in the distance, at the chariots of fire that still streamed overhead. The lights of Shayeen shone, and from dark Tofet still rose the screams of the dying.

"We will return to you, my people," Meliora whispered, guilt and pain in her heart. "We will return with the key, with the chest, with hope to see Requiem again."

The river pulled them onward. For only the second time since Requiem's captivity began five hundred years ago, slaves escaped into the wilderness.

VALE

The world.

Sitting in the boat, Vale stared around him as dawn rose, unable to speak, overcome with awe.

The world beyond.

Rushes and reeds swayed along the riverbanks, and farther back grew palms and fig trees. Ibises and herons waded through the shallow water, and hippopotamuses rose like boulders between lilies. Hundreds of sparrows and finches flew overhead. Looking westward along the river, Vale saw no signs of civilization. Gone were the huts of agony, the quarries of breaking backs, the fields of desolation and despair. Gone were the obelisks, temples, and palaces capped with platinum and gold.

The world. The true world beyond. It's real. It truly does exist.

Vale's eyes dampened. In five hundred years, only one Vir Requis—the hero Lucem—had ever made it past the walls. Often Vale had thought the world only a myth, and yet here it was—legend become reality.

Elory sat at his side. She smiled at him, wriggled closer, and leaned her head against his shoulder.

"It's real," she whispered. "We made it. There is an outside." Her eyes shone. "And Requiem is real too. It lies thousands of miles away, but it too exists. We will see the birch forests again."

Meliora and Tash sat before them in the boat, also looking around with wide eyes; neither one of them had ever seen the world beyond, for both had spent their lives in the ziggurat, one in the glittering pits underground, the other in the glittering halls of its crest.

Vale turned around and looked behind him. A few miles away, he could still see the great walled heart of the empire, divided in two—the city of Shayeen and the land of Tofet. As they sailed onward, he thought of those he had left behind. His father. His fellow workers in the quarries and bricklaying fields. Hundreds of thousands of other slaves. All of them were his family too.

I found the world, but not for my own freedom. To find the Keymaker and the Chest of Plenty. To find our magic.

Meliora pointed and her sunburst eyes narrowed. "Chariots."

Vale saw them. A hundred chariots of fire, maybe more, rising from the city, spreading across the land.

"They know we escaped." He grabbed an oar. "We must leave the river. Elory, help me oar. We make to the northern bank."

As the chariots streamed nearer, they rowed toward the riverbank and stepped out into the shallow water, scaring away several herons. Their boat was made of reeds, and when they pulled it between the reeds that lined the water, it seemed to vanish.

"Down," Vale whispered, kneeling in the shallow water between the rushes. "Hide anything reflective."

The others crouched around him, lowering their weapons into the water. Algae floated around them, and the rushes swayed, rising over their heads. Frogs trilled, dragonflies buzzed, and a snake coiled across the water.

Fire roared.

The air screamed.

A dozen chariots charged overhead, raining fire.

"Burn the rushes!" cried a voice above—Ishtafel's voice. "Burn them all down. They're hiding here. Burn the riverbanks! Burn every tree and every reed."

Vale looked up between the rushes and saw the tyrant there. Ishtafel flew in a great chariot, a shining god of gold. His lieutenants spread around him, nocking flaming arrows. Vale's hands balled into fists.

You murdered my mother. You cut the wings off my sister. You slaughtered millions. He grabbed his collar, wishing he could tear it off, rise as a dragon, fight Ishtafel again as he had over Shayeen. *Someday I will face you again, Ishtafel. I swear this. I will fly as a dragon again, and when I do, you will burn in my fire.*

But for now he wore a collar. For now the only fire was raining from the sky, the fire of Saraph.

The flaming arrows slammed into the reeds. Despite growing from water, the reeds—at least the part of them above the river—were dry and brittle. They caught flame at once, and the fire began to spread around Vale and his companions. Smoke unfurled, and more fire kept raining from the sky. Elory gasped at his side and clutched his hand.

Vale grabbed a reed at his side which hadn't yet burned. He snapped it off.

"Quick, take these." He snapped three more reeds and handed them to his companions. "Now swim. Go!"

He placed the reed in his mouth and sank underwater.

The water was murky, full of algae, leaves, and scurrying fish. He could barely see, and his eyes stung, but he made out the others sinking with him. Meliora's halo extinguished underwater, and Tash's harem pants fluttered like spirits. Elory still gripped his hand. They all closed their mouths around reeds, breathing through the tubes.

Vale led the way, swimming away from the burning riverbank, and the others followed. Only the tips of their reeds emerged from the water. The seraphim flew above; Vale prayed that the tips of the reeds would look like nothing but bits of leaf or wood on the water.

They remained underwater until they could no longer hear the chariots, then waited longer. Finally Vale dared raise his head from the water for a look. The riverbanks were burning, and the chariots flew in the distance, almost too far to see now.

Tash's head popped out from the water beside his, and she spat out her reed. Algae filled her hair. "I think we just lost a boat."

Meliora rose from the water next, her halo crackling back into life, and Elory followed. The reeds on the riverbank burned down quickly, and soon the companions found a patch of barren, charred land. They climbed over the hot earth and cinders, wincing with pain, and made their way onto a hilly, rocky land. Patches of fire burned ahead, and a tree blazed on a hilltop. Most of the landscape was dry soil strewn with limestone and chalk boulders, and Vale spotted a cave on a hillside.

"There." He pointed. "We'll seek shelter in the cave before more chariots arrive."

The others nodded, dripping wet. Vale couldn't help but notice that Tash's silken trousers and top became translucent when wet. Her breasts pressed against the thin material, and a jewel shone in her navel. She looked at him and smiled thinly, and he quickly looked away, feeling his cheeks flush.

What was it about Tash? He had been looking at the young woman too often since meeting her. Vale had no use for such thoughts. He was only a slave, doomed to toil, to suffer the whip, not to desire women, not to—

We're not slaves out here, he thought, still seeing Tash from the corner of his eye. *And why shouldn't I desire a woman? Am I not a man?*

But no. Out here in the wilderness, he was a warrior of Requiem. The only love of his life was the memory of that fallen land. He would allow no other desires to fill his heart, only the desire to see Requiem again.

They walked across the rocky land between burning bushes, climbed the hill, and made their way to the cave. It was smaller than their hut back in Tofet, no larger than their burnt reed boat. They crowded inside, covered with scrapes, bruises, and burns.

Again, Vale couldn't help but notice Tash at his side, pressing against him, slender yet curved, her hair against his shoulder. Yet again, he forced the thought of her away.

More chariots streamed outside, fire raining. More seraphim cried out.

Inside the cave, the companions huddled in silence. Meliora leaned against the back of the cave, pale, her wounds still bandaged. Elory prayed, lips moving silently.

"We wait until darkness," Vale said. "When night falls again, we move out. Meliora and Elory to find the Keymaker. Tash and I to find the Chest of Plenty."

If they truly exist, he thought. Perhaps both were merely old legends. But Vale had to believe, for if those were mere legends, then what hope was there for Requiem to be real? And Requiem was real, had to be real, even after five hundred years of servitude. That land had to exist, far in the north beyond desert, sea, and forest, or there was no hope at all, and he might as well burn in the fires.

"We will find them," Meliora whispered, sweat on her brow, her cheeks gaunt. "We will bring back hope."

Vale nodded, reached out, and took her hand in his. "We will see Requiem again. We will find her sky."

"But not before we sleep." Meliora closed her eyes.

They were wounded and weak, but most of all weary. They lay down together in the cave; it was just large enough if they lay pressed together. As soon as Vale closed his eyes, he fell into a deep slumber, and he dreamed of whips, bricks, and endless fire.

ISHTAFEL

He stood on the boardwalk, facing the three trembling soldiers—three traitors to the realm.

"Now then," Ishtafel said, pacing before them. "I heard you found some lovely jewels last night, didn't you? Oh, I am rather fond of the art of jewelry making. I possess many fine jewels myself. I own the Horn of Fidelium, did you know? Encrusted with the finest sapphires from the Arctic."

The guards hung before him from wooden levers, chained and dripping blood, their breath sawing at their lungs. These cedar beams were normally used to haul crates from the boats; they could quite easily bear the weight of three seraphim . . . three who would soon be much lighter.

"Forgive us, my lord," said one soldier. Blood dripped from his mouth, and his voice lisped between his shattered teeth. "We didn't know it was her, my lord. We—"

"Please!" Ishtafel raised his hand. "I understand! No need to beg. A stranger flowed by on the river. On a night when the city was searching for escaped prisoners, and the skies were lit with flaming chariots, it could have been anyone! And after all, the sailors tossed you such beautiful pieces of art."

Ishtafel examined the jewels in his hand, seized from these soldiers. Two anklets of silver, worked with topaz. A bracelet of impure gold inlaid with tiger's eyes. The jewels of a pleasurer, given to her by her seraphim lovers. *Her* jewels, the brown-haired little harlot he had claimed underground. The one who had fled with Meliora.

"My lord," rasped another soldier, hanging from the beam on chains. "Forgive us, my lord. Send us out to hunt them! We will scour the land, we—"

"You will scour the land?" Ishtafel *tsk*ed his tongue. "But my friend! You saw the escaped prisoners here on this very river. They sailed right by you! And you accepted their bribe. You let them sail on." Ishtafel tilted his head. "Perhaps you too are traitors to my crown?"

The soldiers began to beg, to pray, to praise him. They jangled on their chains, blood dripping. Ishtafel walked across the boardwalk, turning winches, moving the beams to dangle the prisoners over the water—just a foot away from the boardwalk. As their blood splashed into the river, the crocodiles within— massive, black-skinned beasts, twice the size of the crocodiles of the northern swamps—reared from the water. The beasts splashed, snapping their jaws, desperate for a meal.

"Please, my lord!" one soldier begged. "Forgive us!"

Ishtafel smiled thinly. "I am the King of Saraph. I am strong. I am proud. I am wise. They call my sister 'Meliora the Merciful.' That is not a quality to boast of."

He drew his sword and approached one soldier.

The man begged, screaming before Ishtafel even touched him.

The blade lashed. Blood sprayed. Half the man's foot splashed down into the water.

As the dangling soldier screamed, blood gushing, the crocodiles below thrashed in the water. One caught the morsel and swallowed, and the others snapped their jaws at the dripping blood.

"Oh, they are getting hungry!" Ishtafel said. "Look at my lovely pets." He sighed. "Poetic justice, isn't it? That the river where you suffered your shame should now feed upon your blood?"

He approached a second dangling soldier. The man pleaded, tears on his cheeks.

"Please, my lord! Please. My wife is pregnant, my lord. I only wanted a bauble for her, I only—"

Ishtafel swung his blade again. The man's toes fell into the water, and the crocodiles grabbed them.

Ishtafel kept moving between the soldiers. Slowly. Savoring the hot day, the scent of blood, the fervor of his river pets. He sliced the meal bit by bit—easier for the digestion— until the men no longer screamed. He slashed up what remained, letting the last morsels fall into the river, then spread his wings and took flight.

He soared higher and higher, the wind shrieking around him, rising until the air chilled and his head felt light. He could see for miles from here. South of the river spread Shayeen, glorious in the sunlight, its temples and palaces forming a tapestry, the ziggurat a jewel in its center. North of the water sprawled that wretched, filthy land of Tofet. Even from so far away, he could see the miserable slaves toiling, mere ants from up here.

"You escaped me, Meliora," Ishtafel whispered. "You and three other vermin slaves. Your people will pay for your sin. The river will run red with the blood of Requiem." A smile stretched across his lips. "I've only whetted your appetite, my dearest river pets. You will feed more. The elderly, the weak, the useless slaves who cannot meet their quotas . . . they shall fill your bellies, my lovelies."

He stared beyond the walls. The river spread into the distance between smoldering lands. She was out there somewhere—burnt in a field, drowned in the water, or still running. Thousands of chariots were streaming over the landscape, flying across the horizons, covering the sky with fire.

"Wherever you are, sweet sister, I will find you." Ishtafel licked his lips, remembering the taste of Meliora's blood. "I will bring you home."

MELIORA

As the sun set, the four escaped slaves stepped out of the cave into a ravaged landscape.

When first entering the wilderness, this mythical world beyond the walls, Meliora had thought it beautiful—a land full of animals, plants, clear skies, and wonderful landscapes. For once, her fairy-tale dreams from childhood had seemed true—the world was truly full of wonder and magic.

Yet now, after a night of fire, the landscape lay in desolation.

Scattered fires still burned in the darkness, the last bushes and trees crackling. In their light, Meliora could make out lumps along the riverbanks—dead crocodiles, hippopotamuses, and other animals of the Te'ephim River. The flowers were gone. No more birds sang, and no more wonder filled the world. Ishtafel's chariots had come, burned, and flown on, seeking her. She knew that they would never stop—not until they found her . . . or until she found the Keymaker and freed the dragons of Requiem.

I will free them, Meliora vowed, fists shaking at her sides. *And then the empire will truly burn.*

Elory came to stand at her side, and the scattered fires reflected in her brown eyes. "Are you ready, Meliora?" Elory gently touched her fingertips. "You're still wounded."

Meliora winced, just the touch of Elory's fingers stabbing her with pain. Her wings had been gone for perhaps a fortnight now but still ached; she could still feel them on her back, twitching, apparitions that perhaps would always haunt her. The new wound on her thigh, the lash of a seraph's spear over the river, blazed with more immediate pain. She felt lightheaded, her brow hot. Perhaps she was feverish. She could not remember the last time she'd had a proper meal, only a little gruel yesterday. She craved nothing more than to lie down in the cave and sleep some more.

"I'm ready," Meliora said. "My wounds are but a trifle compared to the pain inflicted upon those in Tofet. We march on. We have no boat but we have our feet." She smiled thinly at Elory. "We'll find the Keymaker. He'll fix the key."

Elory looked up at Meliora, no taller than her shoulder, weakened by years under the yoke, but her eyes shone with strength. "We'll find him together."

Vale and Tash emerged from the cave and joined them, both wrapped in their burlap cloaks. A tall man, young yet already haggard, his head shaved, his cheeks gaunt and his eyes simmering with endless rage. A young woman, her body softer, her hair long and brown, the fineries of the palace washing off her, as surely as they had washed off Meliora. Tash's hair no longer shone with scented oils, and perfume no longer sweetened her skin, and her only remaining jewels were her ring—its top engraved with a forged sigil—and the diamond in her navel.

"The time has come to say farewell," Vale said, and for once, his voice was soft, a voice like a flowing river more than a jagged stone. "Tash and I travel east to find the Chest of Plenty."

Meliora nodded. "And Elory and I travel west to find the Keymaker on the mountain. Let us meet back here in this cave, though I don't know how long our quests will take."

And I don't know how long the Vir Requis can still survive under Ishtafel's whip, she added silently.

She stepped closer to Vale, hesitated, then embraced him. At first he stood stiffly, but then he wrapped his arms around Meliora and held her in the darkness.

"I only just found you, my brother, and now I must leave you." She touched his cheek. "Sometimes I almost doubt that it's real. That you're real. That I have a brother who's kind and noble. A brother who saved my life in the river. Who fights with me for Requiem. I love you, Vale."

His embrace was warm. "And I love you, Meliora. I always have. All my life, my father told Elory and me stories of you, of our princess sister the seraph. Finally meeting you has been the best thing in my life. I know we'll see each other again soon. We will fly together as dragons, sister."

Meliora embraced Tash next, holding her close, and Elory hugged her brother and shed a tear. And then they were parted. Then they were torn apart in the darkness. Then Meliora was walking into the shadows, leaving Tash and Vale—the two souls who had saved her life, one after the other—in a world of darkness and fire.

She looked up at the sky, and though Meliora could not see the stars of Requiem from so far south, she prayed to them.

Please, stars of my father. Grant them safety. Grant safety to all of your children. Let me see Vale and Tash again. Let me fly with them and with all our people in the sky of Requiem.

VALE

"Are you sure you know where we're going?" Vale squinted, staring around him, struggling to see in the darkness. "I can barely see a thing, and your map is barely more than scribbles."

Tash placed her hands on her hips and glowered at him. "It's more than scribbles. It's a fine work of cartography. I do not draw scribbles, Vale. We just have to keep the Te'ephim River to our right, and it'll lead us to the sea. All rivers lead to the sea, you know."

Vale had not known that. He knew how to mix clay, bitumen, and straw, forming bricks for homes and granaries. He knew how to swing a pickaxe, carving out large stones for statues, columns, and temples. He knew how to endure hours of thirst and hunger, how to suffer the whip without falling, how to heal the wounds of whips across his family's backs. What did he know of geography, cartography, of anything in this world beyond the walls of Tofet—a world he had once thought a mere myth?

"I can't see the river," he said.

"I can." Tash pointed. "Do you see those glimmers in the distance? That's the moon reflecting on the water. And look, up there." She pointed skyward. "See that bright star? That's Kloriana's Star, holy among the seraphim, and it always shines in the east. We're going the right way."

Vale stared at her. In the darkness, Tash was merely a shadow, black on black. Aside from the moonlight on her hair, he might not have seen her. And yet he could smell her. Even after a night and day of flight, Tash did not smell like most slaves, the smell of sweat, blood, burnt flesh. She had a faint scent of jasmine, hintan, a touch of lavender, perhaps lingering remnants of the perfumes she had worn in the pleasure pits.

It would have been dark in the pleasure pits too, Vale thought. And Tash would be naked, perfumed, delighting men with her talents.

In the darkness, he felt his cheeks heat up again. He did not like these feelings. The old tales of Requiem were full of stories of lovers: the great King Aeternum and Queen Laira, founders of Requiem; the tragic story of Benedictus and Lacrimosa, torn apart by Requiem's great wars against the griffins, whose love lit the world; the tales of King Elethor and Queen Lyana who had fought the phoenixes and rebuilt Requiem from ruin; and poems of Tilla and Rune, lovers on opposite sides of Requiem's civil war. Those old stories were full of romance, but this had always seemed a mythical concept to Vale. In his twenty-one years, he had never spared a thought for love. What would he know of such things? No more than he knew about maps.

My only love is Requiem, he thought, hating the strange feelings Tash's scent stirred inside him, but proud that he could finally push thoughts of her away.

"So . . .," Tash said as they walked. "Ever poked a woman?"

Vale groaned. "What are you on about?"

He could just make out her turning toward him, and the moonlight shone on her teeth as she grinned. "You know, ever dropped your trousers, pulled out your spear—and I don't mean the one you're holding in your cloak—and poked a nice maiden twixt her nethers?"

He groaned louder. "I never knew pleasurers would use so many euphemisms."

Her eyes widened. "That means no! You're not even denying it." Tash nodded. "I wondered how much lovemaking you lot down in Tofet got to. When Elory came into the pleasure pit, she knew nothing. Nothing! I don't think she even knew she *had* nethers, or that boys have spears to stab them with. But I taught her." She leaned toward him, and her eyes turned sly. "I could teach you if you like."

Oh stars above, Vale thought. Tash—naked against him, kissing, caressing—

No.

He gritted his teeth.

He had no use for such things. They would distract him from his quest. He cared only for Requiem.

"Focus on finding the way to the shore." He turned to stare ahead as if there were anything to see in the darkness.

She nodded and touched his arm. "I understand. You're a little embarrassed. Not sure you could perform. Not sure you'd know what to do. You're all strong and tough and tall, a real man, and you're worried I'll think you're a boy, or maybe you're worried your reed will wilt. But I don't mind if it takes you a while to learn. We all have to learn sometime! Did you know—at my first time I was absolutely hopeless. The woman who taught me was a pleasurer too. I learned quickly. So will you."

Vale definitely did not want to think of any of those things—not himself "wilting" and certainly not the vision of Tash learning the ways of love.

"Why don't we walk silently?" he said.

She moaned. "Because it's boring! I'll grow bored to death on the way unless we can have sex. Vale, don't make me beg you! If you don't let me seduce you, I'm going to have to beg, and I'm really a horrible beggar."

He pointed ahead into the sky. "I suggest you focus your attention up at the sky, not down at your nether regions. Those aren't stars."

Three orange lights shone in the distance, moving closer, swooping down from the sky like comets. Distant cries rose from them.

Vale cursed and grabbed Tash's arm. "Down!"

She waggled her eyebrows at him. "Ooh, darling."

He groaned. "Be quiet and lie still. Under our cloaks. By that boulder."

He lay down and pulled Tash down beside him. They lay on their stomachs, pressing against a boulder, and pulled their hoods low.

Vale could hear the chariots fly closer, smell the brimstone and fire. Lying facedown, he could only hope that he appeared like nothing more than part of the boulder. Tash lay beside him, her body pressed against his, and a strand of her hair tickled his lips.

The chariots streamed directly above, the firehorses' hooves thundering through the air, the flames crackling. Sparks rained and singed his cloak.

Tash's hand trailed down his leg. "Vale," she whispered, "let's do it now. While they're flying above."

He raised his head just an inch, saw her smiling at him, and glared. "Hush!"

She pouted.

Ash rained and finally the sound of the chariots faded. Vale rose back to his feet to see them in the distance.

"Maybe you like boys?" Tash said. "That's all right; I don't judge. We had a few boys in the pleasure pit, you know. Some of the seraphim favored them."

"Enough." Vale continued marching. "We keep going. Quickly now." He turned around. "Tash! Come on."

She placed her hands on her hips. "You go that way, Vale, right back to Tofet. I'm going to walk the right way." She pointed. "Follow the star, remember?"

He grumbled but he changed course. They walked onward through the darkness.

Thankfully, Tash stopped talking soon, though the young woman still hummed, clucked her tongue, and sometimes mumbled to herself as they walked. Vale began to regret agreeing to accompany her on this quest. He should have accompanied Meliora instead to find the Keymaker—it seemed that was where hope shone brighter—not gone on this wild-goose chase, stuck here with the insufferable Tash.

The woman had seemed sympathetic enough back in Tofet. After all, she had helped Meliora escape from prison, and for that Vale was grateful. But stars above, once alone with her, Tash had regressed back to, perhaps, her true self—a loquacious, flirty little minx who boiled both his blood and temper. She confused him. She infuriated him. He had agreed to accompany her out of some sense of nobility, wanting to protect the helpless maiden perhaps, like the heroes in the old tales. Now he wondered if Tash would lead him to nothing but madness.

They walked for hours, and when dawn began to rise, Vale approached the river.

"Going for a morning swim?" Tash asked. "Naked?"

"Going fishing." He hefted his spear. "We need to eat."

The light was still dim. Hints of pink and blue appeared in the eastern sky, and the world began to appear around him, all in gray, black, and indigo. He could make out the river flowing at his side, a few trees with curling branches, rocky hills, and Tash's slender form. Soon the sun would rise and its light would drench the land, and they would need to find shelter and hide—perhaps another cave, perhaps between boulders or trees. But for now, Vale needed food. He had not eaten in a night, a day, and another night, and his limbs already felt weak from hunger, and his stomach knotted. He had never eaten fish before, but he had seen the overseers consuming them. He stepped onto the riverbank and hefted his spear.

Beads of light glimmered on the water, and the fires had not spread this far yet. Reeds and grass swayed around him, and Vale waded between them, the water rising above his ankles. As the light kept brightening, he caught sight of his reflection in the river. The vision was smudged and dark, and he stared down at it. Vale had never stared into a mirror before—at most, he had seen his reflection at the bottom of wet mugs or upon the surfaces of polished stones. Looking at his watery reflection now, he seemed thinner than he'd ever been. A gaunt wretch, cheeks sunken, eyes too large. A figure close to death.

The old stories of Requiem, the ones his father would tell, would often speak of the beauty and vigor of youth, of young heroes scampering across fields and soaring, laughing, rolling through the sky in abandon, not yet burdened by the worries of age. Vale was only twenty-one—in Old Requiem, he'd be considered at the prime of his youth, barely older than a boy. Yet he felt old. He looked old. He felt ready for death, having suffered too many years of whips, chains, hunger, exhaustion, as if all those five hundred years of slavery—stretching back to the fall of Requiem—weighed upon his shoulders.

And yet I'm still here. Still moving onward. Still alive. Still fighting. He closed his eyes. *I still remember you, Issari. I will never forget your starlit hands upon me, the love in your eyes. You told me that a great battle awaits me. I will live and fight on, my lady of starlight.*

Splashing sounded in the water beside him, and Vale's eyes snapped open. He started and his heart thrashed. He found himself wincing, expecting the lash of a whip, a habit he didn't know if he'd ever shake. But it was only Tash wading into the water beside him, naked as the day she'd been born, aside from the jewel in her navel.

"Tash!" he whispered, looking away.

She splashed him. "Join me, Vale! Off with your clothes. It's time for a morning bath."

He glanced at her, then quickly looked away, the sight of her naked body seared onto his memory. He was about to reproach her, even grab her cloak and cover her up, when another splash—this one softer—sounded below him.

He looked down and his eyes widened.

A fish.

Vale lifted his spear.

The fish lazily swam between the reeds and rushes, fat and sluggish.

Vale thrust down the spear, piercing it.

"Got you!" He lifted his prize from the water, already salivating. "Tash! Hurry up and wash yourself. We've got breakfast. I'll see if I can catch another."

She stuck out her tongue, the water now blessedly up to her shoulders. "See if there are any pears baked in honey and wine down there, will you? Maybe some almond and butter cakes too."

He scoffed. "It's fish and some algae if you can stomach it. Better than what we ate in Tofet. You house slaves went soft."

He expected her to roll her eyes, to splash him again, maybe to make a joke, but instead anger filled Tash's eyes. She waded toward him in the water.

"Don't you tell me that I'm soft." She glared, her eyes red. "You don't know what I've had to endure."

"What?" He matched her glare. "Did you endure firewhips against your back? Yokes that crushed your shoulders? Eighteen hours of labor a day, carving bricks and hauling tar in the blinding sun? Or did you just have to suffer baked apples sometimes instead of honeyed pears?"

Her eyes dampened, but then her rage seared the tears dry. "I had to live through things you cannot even imagine. I was thirteen when I was tossed into the pleasure pits. You suffered the whip; I suffered the lust of the seraphim. I would have chosen the whip a thousand times over what they did to me, to a mere child." Her voice shook. "For years, I sank into a deep hole. For years, I smoked the hintan, lost in a stupor, barely alive, a giggling, drooling, vapid thing, mere meat, semiconscious, as the seraphim masters had their ways with me. But I crawled out of that pit. I shoved the comfort of hintan aside, and I learned to accept pain, because pain gives me clarity, pain gives me strength. So yes, Vale of Tofet. I ate honeyed pears instead of gruel, and I wore anklets of gold instead of shackles of iron. And I suffered more pain than I can remember without dying inside."

The fish flapped on his spear, and Vale felt his anger wan. Why was he so mad at the woman? Tash had been kind to Elory, protecting her in the pleasure pit. She had saved Meliora from the dungeon. She had fought bravely against the seraphim during their escape from Tofet, and she sought the Chest of Plenty not for personal gain but to duplicate the Keeper's Key and bring Requiem hope. Why had he spent the past night and day mad at her? Was it because of her body—and by the stars, she was naked now in the water, only inches away—that intoxicated him? Was it because she awakened something deep inside him, something frightening, something that was all soft warmth and joy, unlike anything he had ever felt, anything he thought he deserved?

He nodded. "Let's eat breakfast. I'll catch you a fish too. I promise it'll be tasty."

She nodded, her face calming. She stepped out from the river and pulled on her cloak, then paused.

She stared down, frozen.

"Tash?" Vale said. "Are you all right?"

She spun back toward him, eyes wide. "I found something. Oh stars above, Vale. I found something."

ISHTAFEL

In his dreams he was still there. In darkness. Five hundred years ago. Young. Scared. Fighting with her.

"The cowards flee, my love!" Reehan cried, laughing as she swung her twin *xiphos* swords. "Like worms digging deeper into their holes. Let us hook them!"

Ishtafel fought at her side, swinging his own twin blades. Blood covered his steel breastplate, his long blond hair, his face—every part of him, sticky, hot, red, coppery, sweet. Some the blood of his enemies. Some the blood of his friends. Some his own blood.

And in the tunnels ahead, they scurried.

The weredragons.

Ishtafel swung one of his short, wide blades, blocking a blow from a massive weredragon longsword. The beast roared before him, bearded, eyes wild, clad all in steel plates. The brute's armor was thicker than his own, his sword longer and sharper, and fear flooded Ishtafel—cold, all-consuming terror.

He thrust his blade again, trying to reach past the weredragon's defenses. The tunnel walls seemed to close in around Ishtafel. He couldn't breathe in here, couldn't see. Behind the barbarian ahead, thousands more—filthy weredragons—lurked in the darkness, just waiting to strike, to cut him down.

I can't do this, Ishtafel thought, tears budding in his eyes as he swung his blade. *I can't survive on this world. We should never have rebelled, never have fallen from Edinnu. I'm going to die here in darkness.*

The weredragon lashed at Ishtafel again, and his longsword slammed into his armor. Ishtafel cried out and fell to his knees in the tunnel, these holes far beneath the realm they called Requiem. The weredragon grinned and raised his longsword, prepared to land the killing blow.

Reehan let out a battle cry. Her golden hair streamed, and
her bloody face twisted with rage. She leaped forward, twin
blades flashing. With one swing of the blade, she knocked aside
the weredragon's longsword. With the other, she cut the
creature's neck, sending him crashing down. Blood spurted onto
her, and she licked it off her face and smacked her lips.

"All right, my love?" she said, reaching down to help him
up.

Ishtafel rose without her help. His heart thudded against
his ribs. Sweat dripped down his face, mingling with the blood.

I can't do this, he thought. Only thirty years old—a babe
among the immortal seraphim—he had thought himself brave, a
great conqueror. He had vowed to his Mother: I will show you
my strength! I will build an empire for you. I will crush Requiem!

He had slain the dragons in their sky. With thousands of
flaming chariots, he had burned them down. Yet now, here in
these tunnels, he fought the creatures face to face. Here was no
realm of fire; here was blood, guts, bones, torn bodies and
organs across the walls, and fear, and screams. Here he would
die, no conqueror, just a soldier, screaming as the shapeshifters
tore him apart.

The weredragons charged. Side by side with Reehan,
Ishtafel fought.

They moved through the tunnels, thousands of seraphim
behind them, thousands of weredragons ahead. They climbed
rough staircases, ran through craggy tombs and libraries, fought
in cisterns, in granaries, in burrows barely wide enough to walk
through. And everywhere the dead fell, seraphim, weredragons,
piles of corpses underground.

As he kept marching through the tunnels, cutting
weredragons down, some of Ishtafel's fear eased. Bloodlust rose
to replace it. He was surviving. He was killing. He would win
this.

"I slay them for you, Reehan!" he cried, driving his sword
into a weredragon child, sending the girl crashing down. "I
conquer this land in your honor, my love. When we return
home, victorious, we shall wed in glory."

She laughed at his side, lashing her blades at an axe-
wielding weredragon. "Let us wed here, my love! Let us wed in

darkness and blood, for this is a domain of more glory than the gold of Saraph."

Her eyes shone as she gazed at him. Bloodied, her blades held before her, Reehan seemed more beautiful than ever. Here was no pampered lady like so many in Saraph. Here was a tigress, a huntress hungry for prey. Her wings dripped the blood of her enemies, and her smile was hot, deadly, lusting for him.

She is my love, Ishtafel thought, *the only seraph worthy to be my bride. She will bear me great heirs.*

"Very well!" Ishtafel said, laughing. He swung his sword at another weredragon, cutting the child down. "Let us wed here upon a pile of corpses, and you will wear their blood as your gown."

She saluted with her blade, laughing. "We will always hunt together, my love! We—"

A hoarse cry rolled over her words.

A young weredragon woman charged down the tunnel, screaming, thrusting a longsword.

"Murderers!" the weredragon howled. Her blade plunged down, crashed through Reehan's armor, and drove through her chest and out of her back.

The weredragon might as well have stabbed Ishtafel's chest. His heart seemed to shatter inside him.

Reehan fell, the blade piercing her, and gazed at him, reaching out to him.

"My love . . .," she whispered, and then her head rolled back, and she said no more.

Ishtafel screamed.

Something tore in his throat and filled his mouth with blood.

He leaped forward, blade swinging, and cut down the weredragon woman, nearly severing her entire torso with a single blow. He roared. He fought in a fury, lashing his blade into another weredragon, another, tears in his eyes.

"Reehan!" he cried. "Reehan!"

He knelt beside her, shivering, coated with the weredragons, and held her hands.

"Please, Reehan, please, my love. Wake up. Wake up, great huntress."

But she only lay limply, eyes gazing at nothing.

Slowly, Ishtafel rose to his feet. He took one of her swords. He stared forward, hissing out his breath. Around him, his soldiers gathered, warrior seraphim in steel.

"Enough!" Ishtafel shouted. "Enough killing."

"My lord?" asked one soldier. "Let us avenge her death. Let us slay them all, let—"

"No." Ishtafel's fists trembled around his hilts. "No, we will not grant them the mercy of death. The living weredragons will return with us to Saraph . . . and they will hurt. They will scream like she screamed." His voice trembled with rage. "For eternity they will suffer."

His eyes opened.

The echoes of battle faded.

Once more he lay in his chamber—five hundred years later—on a soft bed, surrounded by wealth.

Just a dream. Just a memory.

"I never forgot you, Reehan," Ishtafel whispered.

He would have given the world—all this world he had conquered—to have Reehan lie here in his bed. To hold her. Kiss her. Love her. Even after all these centuries, Ishtafel could remember every detail of her: the curve of her hips, her crooked smile, the light in her green eyes, the flash of her blade.

"I conquered this world for Saraph, but what is it without you, Reehan? There will never be another like you. You were a huntress of light and blood. Never more will another shine with your light."

He rose from bed. He walked across the mosaic on his floor, the tiles forming the shape of slain dragons. He pulled open his curtains, and he stared out upon the City of Kings.

The roads of Shayeen flared out like a great wagon wheel, lined with obelisks, temples, forts, and countless stone homes. Palm trees swayed, lush gardens flowered, and many ships sailed on the river. Beyond the horizon, Ishtafel could just make it out—the edge of Tofet.

"You will suffer, weredragons, for as long as I like," he whispered. "Eventually I will grant you the mercy of death, but not yet . . . not until I'm done hurting you."

He clenched his fists, lowered his head, and saw it again—
the weredragons, his lover dying in his arms, and the endless
tunnels coiling deeper, deeper into endless darkness.

MELIORA

They were walking across barren, rocky hills when the soil rose to wrathful life.

Dawn was spilling across the hills, but still Meliora and Elory trudged on. They had been walking all night, they were weary, and they kept scanning the sky for Ishtafel's chariots. But Meliora wanted to keep walking for as long as she could.

Every hour that we dally is another hour my people suffer, she thought. *Every hour before I return with the key is another hour Ishtafel is tormenting the slaves.*

"Are you all right to keep going?" she asked Elory. "Just for a little longer until we reach those taller hills." She pointed ahead. "There might be caves there or canyons, places to hide and sleep."

Even though dawn had just risen, it was already hot, the air thick as soup. Sweat beaded on Elory's brow and clung to the brown stubble on her head. Her eyes were glazed, and dust coated her burlap cloak and bare feet. She nodded.

"We'll keep walking." She smiled thinly. "I used to haul bitumen in the pits of Tofet. I can handle a little hike."

But Meliora was not so sure. It was true that Elory had lived a life of labor—but also a life of malnutrition and beatings, leaving her far shorter and frailer than Meliora. Though her wings were gone, Meliora still had the body of a seraph—tall, perfectly proportioned, a work of art. Elory was small and fragile and already wheezing as they climbed the hills.

"Elory." Meliora's voice was soft. "I never told you this, but . . . I'm sorry." She lowered her head. "For what you had to endure in Tofet. For what you all had to endure. I was living in luxury in the world's greatest palace, just a silly little girl. I chased butterflies, I laughed at puppet shows, I danced at banquets, forever a child, forever wrapped in silk and light. All that while, I should have known." Her eyes stung and her fists clenched. "I should have traveled across the river—just a couple hours away!—and seen how the slaves lived. I should have . . . done something. Somehow saved you. Somehow convinced my Mother to release the Vir Requis, or somehow fought against her, or . . . something. Bring you food and water. Visit you and heal you. Pray for you. But I simply lived like a pampered fool while my sister, my family, my people cried out for help." A tear streamed down her cheek. "I'm ashamed, and I'm sorry, Elory."

Elory stopped walking. She approached Meliora and held her hands. Elory's hands were small, dark, and callused, barely larger than the hands of a child. Meliora's hands were long and slender, pale, and soft, the hands of one who had spent her life in idleness.

"You did help us, my sister." Elory's eyes shone damply. "For so many years, I prayed to the stars. We all did. We prayed for a savior. And the stars sent you to us. My sister." Elory smiled through her tears. "You came to us in our hour of greatest need, and you led us into the City of Kings, marching at the lead of a nation. You rose before us as a dragon, blowing white fire, a pillar we will always follow. You fought for us. You gave us hope."

"I gave you nothing but death." Meliora's heart clenched, and she pulled her hands back. "I fought Ishtafel but I lost our battle, and he slew thousands to retaliate. Their blood is on my hands."

Elory squared her shoulders. "You are not responsible for those deaths, only Ishtafel. You did not lose your battle, sister. It was your gauntlet of fire. Perhaps you had to lose your seraph wings before you could find the wings of a dragon. We will find this Keymaker, and we will find our sky. And then, Meliora . . . then all of Requiem will follow your fire again, but that day, we will follow you as dragons."

Meliora lowered her head. "I cannot be that heroine, that leader you need. I'm no great warrior like Ishtafel. I'm not wise like our father. I'm not clever and quick like Tash, not strong like Vale. I'm not brave like you, Elory. I'm just . . . just a pampered princess. Innocent. As new to this world as a babe."

"Maybe." Elory nodded. "But you have us to help you."

Meliora laughed and wiped her eyes. "That's a little better. But you're right, Elory. You know what they say, don't you?

About losing a battle but winning the war? Well, I don't want any war." She pulled the broken key from her pocket. "I just want us to fix this damn key and get everyone to fly away—fly all the way across desert, sea, and forest—to Requiem."

"To Requiem," Elory whispered.

They turned back westward, and they continued walking across the hills. The sun had risen over the horizon now, casting its light over a rocky landscape. The Te'ephim River gushed to their left, tumbling over boulders and through canyons. Along the previous miles of their journey, the river had fed rushes, grass, and trees along its bank, a source of fruits and nuts. Here, however, the land was barren. Nothing but boulders rose along the river, and even moss did not grow on them. The hills ahead were lifeless, sprouting not a blade of grass, a dead, tan color like bones draped with mummified skin. The hills grew taller ahead, jagged and cruel and difficult to climb.

This is a cursed land, Meliora thought.

As they kept walking, the sense of dread grew in Meliora. It was too quiet here. No birds flew, and even no insects scurried underfoot. The place smelled wrong too—a muddy, wormy scent, faintly tainted with ash.

Meliora and Elory had crested a hilltop when the earth began to shake.

Pebbles cascaded down the hillside, and cracks raced along the earth, thin as strands of hair. The earth in the valley below churned like a pit of tar.

"Earthquake," Elory whispered.

Meliora frowned. "No. Something trapped in the mud." She gasped and pointed. "Look!"

Shapes were flapping in the mud in the valley, perhaps large fish, rising and falling. Stones cascaded around them, and bubbles rose in the mud and popped. A long form, similar to a human arm, rose from the earth, coated in the mud, then fell.

"They're people!" Elory said. "People trapped in the mud!" She began to run downhill into the valley. "Hurry, Meliora. We can still save them. They're still alive!"

"Wait!" Meliora said, reaching out to grab her sister, but Elory was running too quickly into the valley.

The things in the mud were rising taller, dragging themselves out of the earth. Slowly they took form, rising as tall as men, dripping soil. Rocks were embedded into their torsos, and worms crawled across them. They were vaguely humanoid, their arms handless, their heads misshapen lumps. At first Meliora thought them creatures formed of the soil, but when she hurried after Elory, she saw that ribs protruded from the beings' muddy chests, and red hearts pulsed within them, coated with soil and riddled with maggots.

Elory skidded to a halt and gasped, and Meliora came to stand beside her. Sucking, wet sounds rose behind them, and Meliora spun around to see more of the creatures rising on the hills behind her, blocking her retreat.

"What are they?" Elory whispered.

Meliora thought she knew, and her belly curdled. She was about to reply when the creatures screamed.

They were screams of rage, of pain, of hatred. Horrible sounds, wet, gurgling, anguished, the screams of drowning animals. Bubbles rose and burst across the creatures, seeping black tar like blood.

"A creator!" one of the creatures cried, opening a mouth full of broken stone teeth. It was taller than the others. Unlike its comrades, it had a soft skull like wet papyrus, full of mud. In two dark sockets, eyes moved on stalks, like worms inside burrows. A crown topped its head, formed of two jawbones strung together with tendons, as if this golem were king of its kind. It raised a dripping arm and pointed at Meliora. It had no hand, only the hints of finger bones sticking out from the mud like twigs. "A cursed creator! Make her pay. Strip off her flesh! Make her one of us."

"One of us," chanted the creatures.

The creatures began to advance toward her and Elory, raising their dripping hands.

"Golems," Meliora whispered. She had heard whispers of such creatures, but she had thought them only myths.

"Meliora, they're angry!" Elory cried.

Meliora's eyes stung. "They're in pain."

It had happened before her birth, if the tales were to be believed. They said that Queen Kalafi, banished from Edinnu, outcast from her gods' graces, had tried to become a goddess herself. To create life. In the tales whispered in the ziggurat, Kalafi had stepped out into the wilderness, and there she had labored—here in this valley! Here she had summoned all her power, molding beings from the clay.

They were meant to be beautiful, Meliora remembered, staring at these dripping, bubbling creatures. They were meant to be as noble as seraphim.

But Kalafi had failed.

The queen had begun her creation, forming from the clay bones, blood, hearts . . . but the creation of life was beyond her. Here still languished the culmination of her efforts, only half completed, still clinging to a mockery of life. Still in pain after all these years. Instead of angelic beings, the seraphim, cast out from their heavenly realm, had created monsters. The golems of the valley. Forever the shame of Saraph.

My siblings, Meliora thought.

And now the twisting beings swarmed toward her from all sides, crying for her blood.

Elory hissed and raised her spear. "Stand back!"

Meliora, however, placed down the spear she carried and held out open palms. "Wait, friends!" she said. "Golems, wait and hear me."

Yet the creatures would not slow down. One of them swiped a dripping arm at Elory, and the young woman cried out and thrust her spear. The blade sank into muddy flesh, not stopping the golem. The creature grabbed Elory, spraying her with mud. She thrashed in its grasp, unable to flee.

"Rip out their bones!" rumbled the Golem King, its wormy eyes moving within the sockets of its soft, fleshy skull. "Coat them with mud. Bring me their jawbones for my crown."

Two golems approached Meliora, reaching out toward her. One grabbed her arm, twisting many-jointed finger bones around her. Another rose from the mud beneath her, coiled around her legs, and bit down with stony teeth.

"Stop this!" Meliora cried. "Golems, I command you stop. I am your sister. I am the daughter of Queen Kalafi, your creator. Stop this madness!"

They screamed around her, hundreds of them, more still rising from the mud. Some fell and shattered, only to reform. They limped down the hills and across the valley, seeping blood, organs dangling out from muddy torsos, falling, breaking, rising again. Unable to live. Unable to die. Forever caught between creation and curse.

"She is the Creator's spawn!" cried a golem, worms dripping from its head.

"I will suck on her ribs," said another, limping forward, its one leg half the length of the other, mushrooms growing from its shoulders.

Others were tugging at Elory, stretching out her limbs. "Quarter her!" the golems said. "We will suck on her marrow. Tug her! Tug her until we hear the sockets pop."

Meliora snarled and kicked. "Stop this." As more golems grabbed her, she turned toward the king of the creatures, the golem with the soft skull and jawbone crown. "King Golem, hear me. I am Queen Kalafi's daughter. I can help you."

"Cursed creator, cursed creator!" the golems chanted. "Make her one of us, one of us."

One golem yanked at Elory's arm, a tug so mighty that Elory's bone popped out of its socket. Elory screamed. More golems began tugging at Meliora's limbs, and she fell into the mud, thrashing, unable to free herself.

"I can give you life!" Meliora shouted. "Stop this, golems. I can heal you!"

They knocked her down, and mud entered her eyes, and in the distance Elory still screamed. Their fingers wrapped around her, yanking, pulling her, quartering her, and Meliora shouted. Mud entered her mouth, and all she could see was the lumpy, dripping heads of the creatures and their dark, soulless eyes.

"Wait." The voice rumbled over the creatures' screeches. "Bring the creator's daughter before me."

The golems tossed back their heads, howling in protest, but they obeyed their king. They tugged Meliora to her feet, gripping her with their muddy digits, and limped forth, dragging her through the mud.

"Release Elory!" Meliora cried, spitting out mud. "Release my sister, or I won't give you aid."

The golems obeyed, tossing Elory down. The young woman lay in the mud, pale and shivering. Her arm popped back into her socket, and Elory screamed again, and then her eyes rolled back, and she lay limply in the mud. Meliora wanted to rush to her, but the golems kept dragging her, finally taking her to stand before the king.

The golem stood before her, eight feet tall, dripping moss and mud. Its heart thumped outside its chest, riddled with worms, surrounded by crooked ribs that thrust out like snapped branches. Its eyes moved down on their stalks, gaping from their shadowy pits. The jawbones forming its crown, Meliora realized, were the jaws of seraphim or perhaps Vir Requis—previous travelers to these hills.

"It was seven hundred years ago that your mother came to these hills," the king rumbled. "I was her first creation. She raised me from the mud, and she named me Eresh, and I was to her as a deformed child. She cast me aside and I watched, writhing in pain, lying malformed in the mud as she created my brothers. As she raised life, again and again from the mud—life doomed to suffering, life failed. I cried out to her. I begged her to spare the others, to stop bringing tortured souls into the world, but she did not see us as souls—only as her own failures. And still she raised more, even as we all cried out together, pleading for this mockery of creation to end. We begged her for death. We begged her for life. Yet she left us in this state of wretchedness, for she was no goddess. Kalafi, our creator, is forever accursed. Bring her before us. Summon your mother! Bring her here so that we may claim our vengeance, or we will exact our vengeance upon your sister who lies in the mud."

Meliora struggled to free herself from the golems grabbing her but could not. Instead she raised her chin, trying to muster what pride she still could. "Queen Kalafi is dead. Her own son, the tyrant Ishtafel, slew her. Your vengeance is fulfilled."

But rather than soothing the golems, this seemed to enrage them further. They tossed back their heads, and they howled to the sky. The hills shook.

"She was ours to slay!" King Eresh cried. Centipedes and beetles fled from his body, and his heart thrashed, heating up, melting mud around it. "The tyrant Ishtafel stole our vengeance, but we will take it out on you, daughter of the creator."

The golems began tugging at her again, and more advanced, dripping, hissing, gnashing their teeth.

"No," Meliora said. "You will not, for as the creator's daughter, I can help you. I can . . . I can try." She gulped. "I heard tales of how Kalafi created you. They were stories passed through the palace in shadows, in whispers, forbidden stories. My brother told me. They frightened me but I kept asking him to tell them again and again, and I would reenact the stories with my dolls. I know why you are half-formed. I know why Kalafi could not grant you true life." The golems leaned in, silent, and Meliora spoke softly. "She did not give you her blood."

"Blood flows through us!" rumbled King Eresh. "This blood we spill with every step, with every breath. This blood flows from our hearts which we wish would stop pumping. This blood is forever our curse."

Meliora looked at the oily black substance dripping from the golem's infested heart. "That's not blood," she whispered, "but bitumen mined from the pits of Tofet. To create life—true life, true children—Kalafi had to grant you her own blood. The stories whisper that she was too proud. Too protective of her noble blood, that she would not share it, and instead completed her spells with tar. That is why her creations failed—not for lack of power but for pride."

Eresh's eyes burned white, and his heart rustled with maggots. He gripped her with dripping, muddy hands, and the rocks and soil that formed his body creaked and scattered dirt. "Then we will take your blood, Meliora, daughter of Kalafi, for our creator's blood flows through your veins."

"If you take it you will get nothing." She stared into his eyes. "It would seep into the mud and vanish, leaving you forever without life, without death, and without vengeance. But if I were to give you my blood, my gift of life . . . you will finally be healed."

At least, that was what the old stories said—more old stories Meliora had thought mere myths, now risen before her.

"Will you let me try?" Meliora said.

The golems did not speak, those with eyes staring at the others, those with noses snorting, their breathing ragged, scented of worms and deep soil and rot. Still they said nothing.

"Let me heal you," Meliora said softly. "At least let me try. Let me end what my mother began, and let me bring you some relief from this tortured existence. I've learned, in only this moon, of horrors I never knew could exist—horrors committed by my mother, my brother, by those I thought my family and my people. I've left the city of Shayeen to fix the evil my family wrought. Let me fix this evil too."

Their grip on her arms relaxed, and Meliora raced toward Elory. Her younger sister lay in the mud, blinking feebly. Meliora knelt above her and touched her cheek.

"I'm all right," Elory whispered. "I've suffered worse in Tofet. Give them life, Meliora. Save them. They need you like we do."

Meliora raised Elory's fallen spear, and at first the golems rumbled and made to grab her again, but Meliora lowered the spear's blade to her own hand. She hesitated, then grimaced and cut a line across her palm.

What is a cut on the hand compared to losing my wings? she thought as her blood beaded.

She approached one golem, the weakest among them, a dripping creature that lay in the mud, gasping, reaching up and unable to rise. Its heart beat outside its chest, draped in mud, like a discarded organ in a battlefield. Its mouth smacked, toothless, bubbling, a slit in the soil, and mushrooms grew where eyes should peer. Meliora held her hand above the wretched soul.

"I am a daughter of Requiem," Meliora whispered. "A child of starlight. The blood of Requiem courses through me, red blood that has spilled too often over the centuries of our suffering. But I'm also a child of Saraph, and ichor flows through my veins—the golden blood of the deities, outcast from Edinnu. Blood that is godly, blood that I now grant to you. Let the ichor of Edinnu, blessed with the first light of creation, ignite true life inside you."

She tightened her fist, and a single drop of her blood—the red blood of Requiem mixed with the golden ichor of Saraph—dripped down.

Daniel Arenson

The golem's bubbling mouth opened, and the blood vanished into the muddy hole.

Silence fell across the hills.

The golem in the mud lay still, its last bubbles popping, its moans fading.

Meliora stared down, breath catching. *Did I kill it?*

She knelt in the mud. She placed her hands on the melted being in the soil.

"Rise," she whispered. "Take my gift of life and rise. Become life."

And slowly it rose.

No sunbeams fell upon it, gleaming with gold. No angelic choir sang. No cherubim flew above, blowing silver trumpets and playing joyous harps. Here was not a moment from ancient tales and frescoes, a holy miracle for poets to sing of and artists to paint across the walls of temples. And yet life still rose. Clumsy. Falling into the mud, breaking apart, rising again. A thing of filth, worms, dripping soil, awkward and limping, the struggle of primordial life bubbling up from the earth.

And yet it rose. And yet it fought.

The golem of mud took form, sprouting an arm that dripped off, another arm that replaced it, becoming solid, stones forming its bones and encasing its heart, its dripping flesh drying like bricks in a kiln. The insects and worms fled from it or dried up in its innards, and its eyes opened, deep sockets, shining with inner light.

"Become flesh," Meliora whispered.

The golem suddenly cried out, bent over, wrapped its arms around its belly, and Meliora was sure that she too had failed, that this being would die—or worse, fall into a pit of everlasting pain and agony. Its clay skin raised bumps which hardened, forming white scales, and feathers rose upon its head, bristly and sticky with mud. It raised its eyes and stared at her—golden eyes, feline, and its nostrils flared, inhaling the air.

"Breathe," Meliora whispered.

And life rose before her. A man. A man coated with silver scales, feathers on his head, feathers flowing down his back. Wings slowly sprouted from his shoulder blades. He blinked his golden eyes and stared at her, a being blended of Vir Requis blood, Saraph's ichor, and the soil of the earth. Life. He was life, true life sprung from her mother—and from her.

"Is he . . . Vir Requis?" Elory asked, coming to stand beside Meliora.

"He's like me," Meliora said. "Of different bloods. He's touched with starlight, with sunlight, and with the soil of the earth." She turned toward the life she had made. "I name you *erev*, from our ancient word for joining together, for you are made of many."

The other golems approached her, dragging themselves through the mud, creatures of dirt and suffering. One by one, they knelt before her, and she gave them her blood—a drop each—and they took solid forms, grew scales and feathers, and stood straight before her. The last drop she gave to King Eresh, and he transformed into the tallest among his brethren, his wings wide and golden, his scales gleaming like seashells, and his eyes shone a deep burnished gold. His crown of bones fell from his head and vanished into the mud whence he had risen. A hundred and twelve *erevim* stood before Meliora—her siblings, her children.

"You are healed," she told them. "You are life. Let this no longer be the Valley of Golem but the Valley of Erev, a blessed homeland to you."

They knelt before her in the mud, the wind ruffling their feathered wings.

"Blessed be Meliora!" cried King Eresh. "Blessed be Meliora the Merciful, our Holy Mother. We are now a nation. Like other nations we will build halls, and we will paint, sculpt, sing, and tell many tales. And in them we will remember our mother. Blessed be Meliora! Forever will the erevim fly to your aid should you walk in darkness."

And much darkness still lies ahead, Meliora thought. *I have saved one nation, but another still languishes in the dirt. Requiem still needs me.* She reached into her pocket and felt the crumpled key. *The path still winds through many shadows.*

"I thank you, King Eresh." Meliora bowed her head. "May your nation grow and become as plentiful as the stars."

The king of erevim stepped toward a hill, knelt, and raised a bundle from the mud. He brought it forward, laid it at Meliora and Elory's feet, and unrolled the leather encasing. Inside lay two longswords of ancient making, the blades thick and double-sided, the hilts wrapped in leather and large enough for two hands, the pommels shaped as dragon claws clutching crystals. Stars were engraved onto the blades, shaped as the Draco constellation.

Meliora gasped. "Swords of Ancient Requiem!"

Eresh nodded. "We claimed them from travelers centuries ago—they are treasures the seraphim stole from the northern realms. I grant them to you, Meliora and Elory of Requiem, for these are things of your homeland."

Elory knelt and gasped. She pointed at names engraved onto the hilts. "These are famous blades! Here lies Lemuria, the blade of Queen Kaelyn, a heroine of Requiem who fought the Cadigus Regime, the traitors to the crown. And by it lies Amerath, sword of Prince Relesar, an ancient hero who fought in Requiem's great civil war. These are royal blades of legend." Tears gleamed in Elory's eyes. "They belonged to the Aeternum dynasty, our ancestors, for we're descended of Rune through Lyana and many other heroes of Requiem."

Eyes wide, Elory lifted Lemuria, the thinner of the blades. Despite being smaller than Amerath, it looked so large in Elory's small hands, dwarfing the young woman, but when Elory swung it, it whistled through the air.

"It's so light," Elory said. "Queen Kaelyn slew many enemies of Requiem with this blade. It's an honor to hold it."

Meliora lifted Amerath, the second blade, the larger of the two. The pommel, shaped as a dragon claw, clutched an amber stone. While large and wide, it felt light in her hands, no heavier than a dagger.

"We will return these blades to their proper land," Meliora vowed. "They will never more lie buried in the mud. They will shine again in the halls of rebuilt Requiem."

Under the noon sun, Meliora and Elory left the Valley of Erev, the ancient swords upon their sides. As they walked across the hills, they saw that new life spread across the hills: grass rose from the dirt, flowers bloomed, and rushes began to grow along the riverbanks.

May we bring life wherever we go, Meliora prayed silently as they walked westward. *May life bloom again from the ruin Saraph has inflicted upon this world. May I live to see the birches grow again, halls of marble rising among them.*

ISHTAFEL

He flew over mountains of pines, rivulets, and flowering meadows, heading toward a place of darkness and screams.

He had always thought this land beautiful. Here rolled the low, rounded mountains of Relen, a wilderness Ishtafel had wandered often in his youth. He had not been young for five hundred years, yet the land below had not changed. Pine, olive, and carob trees grew upon chalky slopes, and wild goats and deer herded between them, feeding on wild grass and drinking from streams that flowed through verdant ravines.

I learned to hunt here, Ishtafel thought. *I learned to kill. I learned to fire arrows into the hearts of beasts, to skin them, gut them, smell the blood, hear their echoing screams.*

When later Ishtafel had gone to kill men, he would always remember the animals he had slain here, looking back fondly upon his first taste of death. That was something he could never get back, he knew—the thrill of it. The power. The drunken realization that with his own hands he could snuff out life—as easily as snuffing out a candle's flame. He had felt like a god. He had since become a true god, ruler of a reborn Edinnu, but that thrill now escaped him. Perhaps he had lost it in the tunnels of Requiem.

He flew here without a chariot, using his own wings, and when he shut his eyes, Ishtafel could imagine himself flying over Requiem again. He could still remember his first kill—a burly blue dragon with white horns and amber eyes. Ishtafel had dodged the beast's fire, thrust his lance, and pierced its neck. In its death, the blue dragon had returned to human form, tumbling down as a man with a red beard and a wooden leg. Ishtafel had tried to find the corpse after the battle, had offered a reward for any soldier who could bring him the body, but the red-bearded man was never found.

And the dead had piled up.

Ishtafel never knew how many Vir Requis his forces had killed that year; some said a hundred thousand, others said a million. To Ishtafel it had stopped mattering. All that mattered to him was to seek that thrill again. To be a boy, hunting in the woods. To experience the magic, the true power of taking life. His mother had once tried to create life. The Eight Gods of Edinnu had created many living things. But those were tricks for the weak. He, Ishtafel, was a god of death. There were only two true powers: to birth life and to take it.

He opened his eyes and stared back down at the forested mountains. He glided toward them, deciding that he wanted to walk the rest of the way. A ravine spread ahead between two piney mountainsides, and Ishtafel had to kick and thrust his spear, clearing an opening in the canopy. He glided between the pines' trunks and landed on the banks of a dried streambed, its water gone for the summer. Mossy stones rose here like cobblestones along a road, and Ishtafel walked alongside, stepping around boulders and over logs. Ivy grew upon the pines around him, and cyclamens dotted the forest floor, their leaves veined and their lavender blossoms swaying in the breeze.

He did not walk for long when he saw the wild boars ahead—a mother protecting a litter of cubs. He slew the sow first with a thrust of his spear, then spent a while collecting the young ones, lifting them one by one, and snapping their necks in his hands. Each gave a squeal and *crack* before falling silent. He tossed the little bodies aside, food for the crows and coyotes. He walked onward.

After an hour or two of walking, the landscape began to wilt around him. The canopy thinned out. The cyclamens were thinner, paler, then gone completely. A sticky film clung to the boulders, and the soil was gray. Soon no more leaves grew on the trees, and the air had a sickly, ashen smell. He was close now. The presence of the cursed ones flowed on the wind here, seeped into the soil, stained the landscape. Even locked behind stone walls, they exuded their rot into the world.

As he hiked through the ravine, Ishtafel grimaced. Nausea rose in his belly. The creatures he was about to visit sickened him. He had fought many creatures in his long wars—beasts of the sea, terrors of the mountains, creatures of deserts and caves.

He had fought demons that haunted the nightmares of lesser men, that had driven some of his soldiers insane. Yet now Ishtafel was approaching what were, perhaps, the foulest creatures in this world—for they had once been fair. They had once been like him.

The mountain slopes turned to cliffs at his sides, the ravine sinking into a deep canyon. As he kept walking, the walls grew taller at his sides, soaring taller than any temple. No more trees grew here, and the only sign of life was a few crows far above. The cliffs were craggy and gray, and Ishtafel imagined twisted faces on their facades.

After walking for another mile, he reached a towering gatehouse built into the canyon, three hundred feet tall. Each of its towers was shaped as Shafat, the god of justice—a bird of prey with the head of a bearded man. Between the two glowering idols stretched a massive stone archway, breaking a wall engraved with scenes of men cowering beneath swooping ravens with human heads. Seraphim guards topped the battlements, their armor bright in the sun. The gatehouse was so large, the guards seemed like nothing more than flecks from here.

Closer to the gatehouse, Ishtafel reached a staircase that rose toward a stone doorway worked into the brick wall between the cliffs. Ten seraphim stood before the doors on a platform, holding the leashes of serpopards—felines with curling necks longer than their bodies. The beasts drooled and sneered, but the seraphim bowed before their king.

"My lord Ishtafel, Great of Graces!" cried their captain. "It's an honor to kneel before you, oh glorious son of Edinnu."

Ishtafel was about to reply when a deep, guttural scream rose from beyond the wall, shaking the canyon. He cringed. The sound was almost too twisted to belong to a living, sentient being; it was demonic, a scream from the Abyss.

"Do they always make that sound?" he asked, grimacing.

The guards nodded. "Yes, my lord. Many guards have gone mad, my lord."

If their bite is as bad as their bark, Ishtafel thought, *you're in for a delightful little treat, my dear sister.*

"Open the doors," he said.

The guards obeyed, and Ishtafel stepped through the doorways and into the shadows.

A great hall awaited him, large enough for an army of dragons to fly in. The cliffs soared at his sides, and above, the seraphim had raised a vaulted roof of stone. An oculus, small and barred, let in a beam of light, leaving most of the hall shadowed. The scream rose again, guttural, tortured, echoing through this craggy nave. A second scream answered it, high pitched, shrill as ripping skin. Soon more voices joined the din—laughing, screeching, moaning, howling. The cacophony rose louder than charging armies.

Ishtafel beat his wings, rose to hover a hundred feet above the ground, and flew along the chasm. Cells had been carved into the canyon walls, rugged and barred. Within those holes he saw them.

"The dark seraphim," he whispered.

They tugged at the bars of their prison cells, hissing, leering, wagging their tongues at him. Too dangerous to be kept in Shayeen, they had been languishing here for centuries.

Traitors, Ishtafel thought. *Corrupted souls.*

They had been seraphim once, he knew. Among the mightiest seraphim, the greatest warriors, bodyguards to Queen Kalafi herself. Seraphim who had spat upon their rulers, who had rebelled against the Thirteenth Dynasty, who had suffered the horrible curse of Kalafi.

Banished from the light of Saraph, the feathers had fallen from their wings. Those wings had darkened, hardened, become the wings of bats, tipped with claws. Their eyes were no longer golden but blazing white, the irises colorless, the pupils slit—the eyes of snakes. Indeed, aside from their dark wings, they seemed bleached of all color. Their long and tangled hair, their skin, the fangs in their mouths, the claws that grew from their fingertips, all were a sickly white. Like seraphim, they were immortals, and no lines of age marked their faces, and their bodies were still young, well formed, beautiful, forever youthful, but their souls were rotted black, and no more halos shone above their heads.

Sixteen had rebelled against Saraph. Sixteen had been cursed. Sixteen had been imprisoned here, among the most powerful beings Saraph had ever known. Some called them the dark seraphim. Some merely called them the Sixteen. They called themselves the Rancid Angels—sinners of rotten holiness.

"A golden one enters!" screeched one of the dark seraphim.

The creatures hopped in their cages like rabid animals. "A king, a king! King Ishtafel enters our realm, murderer of Queen Kalafi!"

Hovering in the chasm, his swan wings spread wide, Ishtafel ground his teeth. So the news of his ascension had spread here too. He either had chatty guards or these cursed creatures possessed a sight their uncorrupted brethren did not.

"I have a deal for you, friends!" Ishtafel spread his arms open, spinning around to face cell by cell. "For too long have you lingered here in the shadows, blood of my blood. For too long did your wings wither, cramped in your cells. For too long did the corrupted sons and daughters of Saraph languish between stone and iron."

"Too long!" they cried. "Too long!"

Ishtafel nodded. "Yet who better than I, the son of Kalafi, knows of failed rebellions? My mother rebelled against the Eight Gods in Edinnu! And even the Eight Gods did not imprison her in stone but banished her here to build a new life, a new paradise. And yet you, who rebelled against the new Edinnu, which we call Saraph—you wither in cells."

"We wither!" they cried. "We wither!"

He flapped his wings, rising within the beam that fell from the skylight. His voice dropped to a whisper. "But I can free you."

Silence fell, perhaps awed, perhaps scornful. They all stared, their snake eyes shining white. Their bat wings creaked, and their claws wrapped around the bars of their cells.

Finally one among them spoke.

"You want us to hunt."

Ishtafel turned toward the voice, and he smiled thinly. "And hunting is what you crave."

He flew closer to her cell.

"Leyleet," he whispered.

Flame of Requiem

She smiled at him between her bars—a sly, hungry smile. "Little Ishtafel. The boy I once spanked over my knee now wishes me to spank his sister, am I right?"

Leyleet. Leader of the Sixteen. Once chief bodyguard to the Thirteenth Dynasty. Her hair had once been golden. The curse had left it white as milk, smooth and so long it hung down to her hips. Her eyes had once been golden, the pupils shaped as sunbursts. They now peered at him, pale like bowls of milk, the pupils a black slit. Her wings had once been soft and feathered. They were now black, veined with red, tipped with cruel claws like daggers. Yet she was still beautiful—still alluring with the curves of her body, the crookedness of her smile, the mocking intelligence in her eyes.

The memory returned to him—himself as a youth, only thirteen, peering through the lock of her chamber, savoring her nakedness. And her—already a century old, already so strong—knowing he was there, peering right at the lock, then grabbing him, striking him as if he were a child. He had never forgotten that humiliation. And he had never forgotten his lust for her.

"If I recall correctly, you knew me as a man as well." He refused to look away from those mocking eyes. "You used to scream so loudly in my bed the whole ziggurat heard."

She snorted a laugh. "You speak of me as if I were one of your paramours, a mere pleasure slave from the pits. And yet you loved me, Ishtafel. How you used to confess your love to me! How you begged your mother to let me be your wife! Oh, my poor Ishtafel . . . we would have made such a king and queen of Saraph. And now you are king . . . and now you are alone. The one who would be your queen fled from you. And so you come to me again, as you came to my chamber as a youth to gaze upon my nakedness." Her crooked smile grew. "Perhaps I need to spank you a second time."

He flew closer toward her cell. She leaned forward, gripping the bars, and he wrapped his hands around hers. He brought his face so close to hers that their noses almost touched. Gods, she still smelled the same, even here in her prison—the scent of sweet sweat and sex, more intoxicating than wine.

"What you need to do," he said softly, "is to fly out there, find Meliora, and bring her back to me alive." He pulled out a silken bundle and tossed it between the bars. It hit the floor of her cell and unfolded. "Meliora's nightgown. Smell it. Memorize that smell. And track her down like a hound tracks a hare."

Leyleet raised the nightgown to her nose, inhaled deeply, and smiled. "Your sister smells like honey and milk and the crotch of a whore."

"You will bring her to me," Ishtafel said. "Unsullied. Do this and I will release you from this prison."

She snorted. "And you will return my halo, my swan wings, let me play harps and sing pretty little songs with Meliora in your pretty little palace?" She scoffed. "I'd rather stay in this cell."

He growled. "Your curse I will not undo. You betrayed my family, Leyleet. You might have struck me as a child, but that was negligible compared to how you struck my family. My mother rebelled against the gods, woman. Did you really think you could rise up against the mistress of rebellion?"

Her eyes narrowed the slightest, her first sign of anger. "Your mother lost her rebellion."

"As did you."

She screamed. She thrust herself forward, pressing her face between the bars, snapping her teeth, nearly biting off his nose. He pulled back just an inch, laughing, and she spat on his face.

"Maybe I will bring Meliora back to your corpse, boy!" She tossed back her head and howled. "Maybe I will rule over that decadent cage of gold you call a palace, and maybe I will sleep in that soft, silken bed where you knew me so many times. I could not dethrone Kalafi, it's true; the whore was too clever. But I can easily kill you."

He tilted his head, amused. "And yet . . . and yet, Leyleet, I quite easily killed Kalafi. And I will quite easily snap that pretty little neck of yours. You bruised me once when I displeased you. If you displease me now, your punishment will be far more severe."

She stared at him, and for an instant her eyes blazed with unadulterated hatred. Then she laughed. Her leathern wings spread out, banging against the walls of her cell, and her chest heaved with her mirth.

"Do you remember what I told you when you were a boy, Ishtafel? When you gazed upon my naked breasts, coveting them, an awkward youth kneeling before a keyhole?"

He nodded. "You struck a deal with me. You told me that I could have your treasures if only I waited, if only I did not touch another woman for five years—then you would be mine. All I had to do was wait."

She nodded. "I have been waiting here for very long. And now we will make another deal. You will free me and my fifteen, and yes, Ishtafel . . . we will hunt your escaped sister. But I ask for one more thing."

"In addition to your freedom?" He frowned. "I should think that a gift great enough."

"Not enough. That would not be vengeance. I will bring you Meliora, and in return, you will bring me the bones of Kalafi, so that I will bury them here. Here in this cavern. Here I will toss them into the pit, and I will piss on them, and I will leave them to rot, while I return to the ziggurat and sleep in her bed, eat at her table, fill her pool with milk." Her eyes simmered, and her hands shook around the bars. "Kalafi's soul will be trapped here where she trapped us, while I and my fifteen live in her splendor. That is what I demand for Meliora's life." The dark seraph winked at him. "Maybe, as you sleep next door, I'll even let you peek through the lock now and then."

Oh, I won't need to peek, Leyleet, Ishtafel thought. *I will walk in and claim you in my mother's bed whenever I like.*

He pulled out a key and he unlocked her cell. He pulled the bars open.

After centuries in prison, he expected her to leap out, to charge to freedom, to fly into the sky and scream and laugh.

But instead she grabbed him. She pulled him into her cell. She bared her clenched teeth, gripping his shoulders.

"You do not crave the sky?" he asked her.

She sneered into his ear, her body pressed against him. "There is something I've craved more all these years."

Her claws tore through his gilded steel armor, as effortlessly as a child tearing paper. Those claws nicked his skin, and her teeth bit his shoulder, and he ripped off her clothes, again seeing that forbidden flesh.

He pressed her against the wall. She shoved him back, roaring, and knocked him down, cracking the stone. Their bodies joined, skin against skin, sweat mingling. They screamed in their passion, and around them across the canyon, the other dark seraphim screamed too.

Finally she screamed with a sound that nearly shattered his eardrums, and her claws ripped his skin. She panted, spat, and pushed him away.

"Now," she whispered and licked him, "we fly."

Ishtafel had walked to this canyon alone, lost in his thoughts. He flew out, soaring high, leading sixteen hunters with dark wings.

VALE

"Tash, wait!" Vale hurried after her. "It's not safe."

She spun toward him, holding up the golden coin. "Gold, Vale!" Her eyes shone just as brightly, and she bit the coin. "Real gold! And there's more."

The young woman spun around, her silken trousers and long brown hair fluttering. She raced forward a few steps across the grass, knelt, and lifted another coin.

Vale grumbled as he followed. The morning sun was already high in the sky, and the chariots of fire could return any moment. Yet instead of seeking shelter—a burrow between boulders, a hideaway under tree roots, maybe a cave if they could find one—the damn girl was running away from the river, seeking her treasures in the grasslands.

"You're going to get lost!" he called after her. "What good is gold to us anyway? We're escaped slaves, Tash. Are you going to walk back into Shayeen—where every seraph is waiting to slay you—and go shopping?"

But she seemed too excited to listen. She ran a few steps farther, then knelt again. She lifted another golden coin, turned around, and showed it to him. "That's seventeen so far. Every few steps I find one. Must be a wealthy man walked here, a hole in his purse. I'm going to collect them all."

Vale groaned, trudging after her. "Why, Tash? For pity's sake, just one coin's enough, if we're going to find the Chest of Plenty. You can duplicate it along with the Keeper's Key."

"But it might be a while until we find the chest." Tash knelt, lifted another coin, and whooped in triumph. "Oh, look, this one is platinum. Platinum is even more valuable than gold, did you know?" She bit this coin too. "I had to give up all my jewels as bribes, but I'm going to be rich again soon, Vale." She nodded. "I'm going to be the richest woman who ever lived, more than a queen."

"And yet still wear an iron collar," Vale muttered, "unless we get back to our quest."

As she raced ahead and he followed, Vale thought back to Tofet. Back in that hellish land, he would pray for an extra bowl of gruel, an extra few moments to catch his breath between forming bricks. Gold? What use was that? They had come here on a quest for freedom, not wealth. Unless . . .

Vale thought back to his last night at home. When Tash had spoken of the Chest of Plenty, her eyes had lit up. She had been safeguarding her map for years, she had claimed, dreaming of finding the chest, of duplicating her jewels, of growing wealthy enough to buy her freedom. Could it be that . . . that Tash had come here not for Requiem's freedom but to fulfill that old dream?

He looked up and saw that she had raced far ahead, entering a grove of olive trees on a hilltop. He ran in pursuit. If she wouldn't listen to reason, he would grab her. He would drag her back to their path. They must keep traveling east to the sea, not on this chase for useless coins.

"Tash," he began, "now listen, this is enough. We turn back now and—"

Movement ahead made him bite down on his words.

Tash froze. Vale reached her. They both stared, eyes wide.

A long creature walked ahead on many legs, the length and width of a lemon tree's trunk. Its segmented body was black but shimmered with hints of green and purple in the sunlight. A humanlike head grew from it, sprouting thick black hair and a long, shaggy beard. As it ambled forward, it paused, crouched, and expelled a golden coin from its backside.

Tash gasped. "A goldshitter!" She began spitting and scraping her tongue. "And I bit those coins!"

Vale would have laughed had the creature not spun around, hissed, and charged toward them. More hisses rose from behind, and Vale turned to see three more creatures drop from the olive trees. They too looked like long, segmented centipedes with dark armor, and they too sprouted humanoid heads with bushy beards. They bared sharp teeth and raised claws. For the first time, Vale noticed that several human skeletons lay between the trees, coated with ivy.

"You led us right into a trap!" Vale said.

Tash was busy spitting and scrubbing her tongue against her sleeve. "I bit it! I bit its poop!"

"Draw your dagger, damn it." Vale hefted his spear. All around, the centipedes approached.

Tash spat and drew her blade just as the creatures pounced.

With a cry, Vale thrust his spear.

One of the monsters leaped at him, mouth opening wide, dripping saliva. Its bulging eyes blazed under bushy black eyebrows. Its front feet reached out, tipped with claws, and Vale crouched and leaped sideways. His spear's blade scraped across the creature's scales, scattering sparks but doing the beast no harm.

Tash stood beside him, lashing her dagger. "Goldshitters everywhere!"

"Stop calling them that!" Vale said, thrusting his spear again.

He aimed at a creature's fleshy head, but it jerked aside, and the blade once more scraped against its armored body, showering more sparks. The demonic centipede leaped forth, slammed into Vale, and locked its jaws around his shoulder. The teeth bit down hard, and Vale screamed.

He swung his spear, scraping the blade against the creature's fleshy face. Blood sprayed, and the beast released him to howl. Lice rustled through its bushy black beard, and veins looked ready to pop on its nose. It reared before him, raising many legs tipped with claws.

Vale thrust his weapon.

The spear slammed into the creature's underbelly, pierced the yellow skin, drove through flesh, and slammed against the armor at the back.

Vale tugged the weapon free with a gush of blood. The creature gave a last mewl and collapsed. As it hit the dirt, its bowels loosened, spilling their contents. Coins chinked into the grass.

He spun around to see Tash facing two of the creatures, holding her dagger before her. One of the beasts leaped at her, and she tossed her handful of coins onto its face.

"Eat shit!" she cried.

The coins clattered against the monster, hitting its eyes, entering its mouth. Blinded, it reared, and Tash tossed her dagger. The blade sank into the creature, and it fell over, twitching madly, kicking its many legs.

Vale ran, shoulder bleeding. He leaped over the thrashing creature, vaulted off its back, and soared through the air. Another one of the creatures was leaping onto Tash, lashing its claws, scratching her arms. Vale dived and drove his spear down hard. The blade crashed into the beast's back, shattering the hardened plates, and pinned the centipede to the ground.

The creatures all lay across the hill, legs twitching, then falling still.

Tash scampered back, panting. The creature's claws had torn her silks and left bloody gashes. She fell onto her backside and stared at the coins that lay strewn around her. When she picked one up, it disintegrated between her fingers.

Vale knelt beside her. She stared at him, shivering, her eyes damp.

"I'm sorry," she whispered.

He examined the cuts on her arms. Most of the wounds weren't deep, but one looked like it needed stitching. "Let's get back to the river to wash those wounds."

She looked at the wound on his shoulder—an ugly ring of teeth marks—and winced. She lowered her head. "I'm sorry, Vale. It's my fault. I almost got us killed." Sniffing, she moved closer and embraced him. "I'm sorry. It's just . . . the sight of gold. For so many years, it was what the seraphim gave me for my services, what I thought I was worth—precious metals and gems. I'm sorry."

They rose to their feet, and Vale looked around them. He counted seven humanoid skeletons that lay beneath the trees, half-hidden beneath ivy and branches and ferns. Two seemed to be seraphim—Vale could see the bones of their wings. The others were humans. He wondered how ancient the latter were. Were here the original inhabitants of these lands, killed before the seraphim had fallen from Edinnu? Or were here other Vir Requis, perhaps survivors of the ancient war, perhaps even escaped slaves?

He knelt by one of the skeletons. Its leather pack had
opened, spilling out its contents. Most of what had been inside
had rotted away, but a glass bottle still lay here, half-buried in the
soil. When Vale pried it loose, he found amber liquid inside. He
pulled off the cork and smelled something stinging and vaguely
sweet.

"Whiskey!" Tash said, eyes widening. "As good as gold."
She froze. "Maybe there's real gold here too. Real gold the
skeletons had!"

Vale rolled his eyes. "Tash, we're not grave robbers."

"They're not in graves, so it's fine." She darted between
the skeletons but found nothing. "Damn, they're not even
wearing any clothes or armor. Not a belt buckle to be found.
What happened to their stuff?"

She kept exploring the area until she found a burrow, its
entrance draped with vines and lichen. When Tash pulled the
curtains aside, she revealed a cavern dug into a hillside, and she
gasped. At once she crawled inside.

"Tash!" Vale groaned and followed her. He knelt before
the burrow, lay down on his stomach, and crawled in after her.

They found themselves in a rounded den, not much larger
than the cave outside of Tofet. It was so small they had to
remain on their bellies, and their bodies pressed together.

"It's where the creatures lived," Tash said. "Stinks in here.
But look—back there."

She burrowed deeper, pushed aside dry leaves, and
uncovered a cache of rusted old metal. A few pieces were nearly
disintegrating but others looked newer. Vale helped her excavate
the treasure, and they laid out their findings on the grass outside
the burrow. They found a coat of chain mail, two steel helmets
coated with silver leaf, a bronze shield inlaid with silver stars,
and a battle axe engraved with old runes in the language of
ancient men. The artifacts were rusty but still usable. In addition
to these tools of war, they found a decorative lantern, shaped as
a dragon's head, complete with a tinderbox for lighting its fuel.

"I'm taking the axe," Tash said. She darted forward, tried
to lift it, and groaned. Its steel head thumped back down onto
the ground. "I think I'll just take a helmet and shield instead.

And the whiskey. And the lantern. And the skeleton's fancy leather pack for my fancy things."

Leaving the centipede creatures to rot, they traveled downhill—him in armor, both wearing helmets. The axe felt good in Vale's hands. For so many years, he had swung a pickaxe at stone. Next time he saw his masters, he silently vowed, he would swing this axe into their flesh.

LEYLEET

They flew through the night, creatures of darkness, sons and daughters of sin. They laughed. They hissed. They drooled. They rutted in the sky, groaning, screaming, bat wings beating. They flew onward on the hunt, nostrils flared, inhaling the scent of the world they had not seen in so long.

"We are free!" Leyleet shrieked, voice rolling across the landscape. "Free to hunt! Free to breed! Free to taste blood and suck marrow from bones."

The moon vanished behind the clouds as if it too feared the Rancid Angels. No stars shone. But the eyes of the fallen were sharp, piercing the night. Their ears picked up the stir of every mouse in the fields below, the scent of every living thing that cowered. And as the Sixteen flew over the fields, their dark wings spread wide, and all the land below cowered. Insects burrowed deeper underground. Birds awoke in their nests, frozen in fear. Those seraphim who lived outside the city of Shayeen, dwelling in villages and villas upon the hills, woke from their slumber, drenched in cold sweat, not knowing the danger but sensing it in every bone. Babes screamed. Children hid under their beds, preferring to face the ghosts in those shadows than the nameless terror that flew above. Even the farmlands wilted, the trees cracked, and dead fish washed onto the banks of the Te'ephim.

The Sixteen were out tonight, flying again after centuries in their prison of stone. The dark seraphim. The traitors to the crown. The cursed. Their screams shattered the sky and rotted the land like tar spilling across fields.

"I smell her, comrades!" Leyleet screamed. She laughed, dipped in the sky, beat her wings, and soared higher. "The girl traveled here. The girl is ahead! Meliora is near."

Leyleet raised the girl's nightgown, brought the silk to her nose, and inhaled deeply. Pleasure tingled through her, making Leyleet shudder. The half-breed whore smelled like innocence and sex, like purity and corruption, like a princess and a queen of rebels. The aroma was intoxicating, almost too powerful to bear.

When I catch you, Meliora, I will bring you back alive to your brother . . . but not before I hurt you. Not before I smell your blood, your insides.

She stuffed the nightgown back into her breastplate. No longer did Leyleet wear the stinking rags her captors had clad her in, but neither did she wear the gilded armor of seraphim. An iron breastplate, black as the night, covered her torso, and her white hair streamed out from the back of a dark helm. In one hand she gripped a sickle of jagged steel. Around her, her comrades were similarly armored. Their bat wings spread wide, their white hair streamed as banners, and their eyes blazed in the night like cruel stars. As they screeched, the sound cracked trees below and seemed to shatter the air itself, louder than thunder, and the light of their eyes blazed brighter than lightning. They were the Sixteen. They were the cursed ones. They were a storm unleashed upon the land that would never be imprisoned again.

"Smell her, comrades!" Leyleet cackled. "I smell her in the water, on the wind, the sweet stench of her skin, her blood, her beating heart. Follow, friends! Follow to Meliora."

They flew around her, laughter like snapping bones, drool falling like rain, wilting the trees below.

Leyleet was licking her lips, imagining Meliora's taste, when she saw the fire ahead.

Twenty flames burned in the sky ahead, leaving trails of smoke. When Leyleet inhaled, she smelled their stench—brimstone, metal, holiness. She spat.

"Chariots of fire," she hissed.

Around her, her comrades howled. Their wings beat in a storm. Their faces twisted, fangs bared.

"Seraphim!" they cried. "Cruel seraphim! Seeking our prize, seeking our prey!"

The distant chariots of fire were moving fast, heading in the same direction as the Sixteen, but they were not fast enough. Leyleet and her comrades kept gaining, and soon she could make out the firehorses, four of the flaming spirits pulling each chariot. Inside the vessels she saw them: the seraphim.

"Cruel masters," she hissed. "They imprisoned us, my brothers and sisters!" Her voice rose to a roar. "Halos shine upon their heads, while ours were stripped and we were locked in stone. Now they fly to claim our sweet Meliora, the virgin whose blood was promised to us. Fly, my Rancid Angels! Show them the darkness of our shadow."

Crying out in fury and joy, they flew.

Their screams tore the land below, ripping canyons into the earth. A tree burst into dark flames, and the fires spread. The clouds churned above, raining ash. With black wings and leering smiles, the dark ones swarmed.

The chariots of fire wheeled in the sky, turning to charge toward them.

"The dark seraphim!" their riders cried. "The fallen ones have escaped!"

Leyleet cackled, her laughter so loud it slammed against the chariots ahead, scattering their flames. "Kneel before us, holy ones! Kneel and beg for mercy as you made us kneel. Beg us for your lives!"

Yet the seraphim—noble fools!—kept charging to battle, sure they could be heroes, holy warriors facing evil, as if the Cursed Ones were beasts like weredragons or griffins.

We are not beasts, Leyleet thought, laughing. *We are not monsters to vanquish with holy light. We are the greatest sons and daughters of Saraph, the cursed among the cursed, those who shed their feathers and halos to reveal the purity within.*

With battle cries, with shattering shrieks, the seraphim of light and the seraphim of shadow slammed together.

Leyleet laughed as the firehorses charged across her, as she flew between them, lashing her sickle. Her blade sliced through the flames, cutting into the stony flesh within, scattering embers and burning blood. The lances of seraphim thrust toward her, and Leyleet soared, rising so fast the air slammed behind her in thunder. She plunged downward, sickle swinging, knocking back the lances, slicing through necks, faces, bowels, spraying red curtains. Her comrades fought around her, laughing as they lashed their sickles.

"You have halos, holy ones!" she screeched, voice as high as shattering glass, so loud it tore into their eardrums. "Your halos still glow!"

She swooped toward a chariot. Its rider charged toward her, and Leyleet parried its lance, streamed overhead, and lashed her sickle. The blade sliced through the seraph's halo, scattering light, and the man screamed. She swung her sickle lower, slicing through the top of his skull, exposing the brain within, then driving down to tear the firehorses apart. The chariot and the corpse within plunged toward the earth like a comet.

"You still have wings!" she cried. "The wings of angels!"

A few of the seraphim still flew, their chariots fallen. Leyleet laughed, charged toward one, and grabbed his thrusting spear. She snapped the shaft between her jaws, then swooped and rose behind the seraph. She grabbed the man's wings, swung her sickle, sliced them off, then kept digging.

"You will have cursed wings like ours!" she cried, laughing, tugging out the screaming man's ribs through his back, pulling out the lungs, forming dripping wings of flesh and bones. "Now fly! Fly, cursed one!"

She tossed the man free, letting him fall to the distant ground.

Five seraphim flew toward her from all sides, enclosing her in a ring of light. Leyleet licked her lips, her heart soaring.

They reached her. They thrust their lances.

She spun in a circle, sickle shattering their blades. They kept charging, and she spun faster, her blade scattering blood, tearing into their torsos, tugging out the entrails. She grabbed the slick serpents, tugging, pulling them closer, weaving them together, sending the corpses falling down. One seraph still made an attempt to fly toward her. She drove her fist into his chest, tugged out the still-beating heart, and feasted.

The seraphim had dared to challenge her. They fell, a rain of blood. In the sky, the Sixteen still flew, laughing as they fed upon hearts, livers, bones that crunched. They ate greedily, staining their chests, licking their fingers, then mating in the sky, slick with the blood of their enemies, singing for their victory.

"Fly on!" Leyleet cried. "Fly on with full bellies, with bloodlust kindled. Fly on and we will feast upon the blood of a princess."

They chanted all around her. "To Meliora! To Meliora!"

Leyleet grinned as she flew onward. Ishtafel had commanded her to bring his sister back alive, but alive could mean many things, and the Sixteen would have their fun before dragging what remained back to Ishtafel. Meliora's heart would still beat, but Ishtafel had said nothing about feasting upon her limbs.

Leyleet licked her lips, her wings ruffling over the wind.

I will drink you, Meliora. I will gnaw on your living bones as I drag you back to your brother. You might have escaped him, but you will not escape me.

ELORY

She walked through the forest, her sword drawn, waiting for enemies to emerge from behind every tree, boulder, and hilltop.

The land here is beautiful, Elory thought. Pines, carob trees, and cypresses grew upon the rolling landscape. Boulders of chalk and granite dotted the land, and anemones and cyclamens grew between them. Sparrows and finches bustled among mint bushes, ants scurried in their hives, and gopher holes rose from wild grass. The Te'ephim River gurgled to her left, lined with rushes, and ibises and herons drank from its water.

And yet, despite the beauty of this place, Elory still felt like she were back in Tofet.

Every bird that fluttered out from a bush, Elory started and winced, expecting a lash's blow. Every tree branch that creaked in the wind, she raised her arm protectively, expecting a blow from a master's fist. Even walking through patches of grass, no movement or sound around her, her heart kept racing, her eyes darting nervously, her muscles tense and ready to bolt. At her side, Meliora walked with her sword sheathed, but Elory kept her blade drawn, forever ready for more violence; she could not imagine a day without violence.

Meliora walked closer to her. "Elory, it's all right. You can sheathe your sword."

"I'll keep it drawn." Elory nodded. "Just in case."

Meliora raised her eyebrows. "Isn't your arm tired?"

"I'm used to hauling baskets of bitumen that weigh many times more." She smiled thinly. "I can carry a sword."

Meliora looked at her, eyes soft in concern. Her hair was slowly growing back; golden stubble covered her head, almost long enough for fingers to grasp. Her wounds were healing too, the scrapes and cuts on her body closed and scabbed. Even the wounds on her shoulder blades looked less swollen and inflamed; Elory had helped clean them just an hour ago in the river.

Flame of Requiem

My wounds too are healing, Elory thought. *The whip's cuts on my back are scabbed over, the pain in my arm is fading, and my bruises are fading, but the wounds inside me remain.*

"Are you sure you're all right?" Meliora whispered.

"You have to understand." Elory stared steadily into her sister's eyes. "All my life, I was beaten. Brutalized. Unable to resist as they cut me, kicked me, tortured me. For the first time in my life, I hold a weapon. A real weapon. An ancient sword of Requiem—Lemuria, blade of Queen Kaelyn herself. For the first time, I fight back against our enemies."

Meliora lowered her head. "And all my life, I was pampered, spoiled, fed sweets, perfumed, sheltered, and lied to. Unable to resist as they fed me the fairy tales. I never held anything more dangerous than a dessert spoon. Yet now I too hold a sword of ancient Requiem. And I too will fight our enemies." She drew Amerath, touched the blade to Lemuria, and smiled thinly. "I will always fight by your side, sister. Whenever you rest, whenever you sleep, whenever you're afraid or hurt, I'm here for you. I will never leave you. I will always walk the winding path with you, watching over you, and I will always love you."

Elory rolled her eyes. "You're going to make me sheathe my sword so I can hug you, aren't you?"

Meliora yawned. "Forget hugs. I want some sleep. I don't like walking in daylight, and I'm exhausted." She pointed. "I see a cave there on the hilltop, and I see some olive and fig trees too. Let's go eat and then sleep. We'll walk more at night."

They walked uphill together, moving between bushes along a natural path strewn with goat droppings. As they approached the cave, Elory's fear did not ease; if anything it grew. What if Ishtafel was hiding inside this cave? Ridiculous, she told herself. Ridiculous! Ishtafel was probably back in Shayeen, only his underlings still scanning the wilderness.

I must learn to put aside my fear, she told herself, walking onward, and inhaled deeply. *Tofet is far away. Ishtafel is far away. It's been a full day since we saw chariots of fire. We're safe here, many miles from danger. We're safe.*

Yet her heart would not slow down, and her hand sweated around her hilt.

"I'll go check those trees for fruit." Meliora pointed. "Will you check the cave, Elory? Make sure there are no warthogs living in this one like the last one."

Elory's breath shook in her lungs. Her head spun, and cold sweat trickled down her back. Why could she not stop this fear? It grew more than ever, and she could feel those whips again. Once more, she was stepping through the agony of Tofet, trying to work fast enough, cowering from the overseers. Meliora was gone. She had vanished between the trees, and Elory was all alone here. Alone in the open. Exposed. In danger.

Don't hurt me, she thought, eyes stinging. *Please. I'll be a good slave. I'll work hard. Don't hurt me, Master.*

She forced in air.

Breathe.

She exhaled.

Calm yourself. Be strong.

She looked at her blade.

This is a sword of Requiem. Be as brave as those who bore it before you, for you too are a daughter of dragons.

She took another step uphill toward the cave, her heart rate finally slowing, when the beast emerged from within, howling and charging toward her.

Elory screamed.

The creature leaping toward her was ragged, wild, some kind of ape covered in yellow fur and rags. Inhuman blue eyes stared with bloodlust. In one hand, the animal swung a heavy bone like a mace.

Elory nearly cringed, nearly begged.

I am a daughter of dragons.

She charged forward and swung her sword.

Her blade sliced through the bone club, sending its top half flying.

The wild ape before her hopped back, crouched, and hissed. It grabbed a heavy rock in its paw.

"Back!" the beast cried. "Back, thief. Back! Who are you? Are you a seraph? Back!" The creature tossed its stone.

Elory leaped aside, and the stone sailed by and clattered down the hillside. She looked back up, narrowing her eyes.

No, not an ape, she thought. *A man.*

"I'm not a seraph!" she said. "I'm not an enemy."

The man above still crouched, reaching out for another stone. He was a young man, she saw. Probably in his early twenties, maybe even younger. But his blond hair and beard were so long, dusty, and tangled, that he looked like an animal. His rags were threadbare, falling apart, revealing tanned skin. His blue eyes regained some humanity as they stared at her, and he tilted his head.

"Are you—" he began.

With a shout, Meliora came racing across the hilltop, swinging her sword.

"Meliora, wait!" Elory cried.

But it was too late. Meliora leaped toward the disheveled man, blade arcing. The hermit cried out in fear and tossed his stone toward Meliora. The rock sailed through the air and slammed into Meliora's chest.

Meliora cried out, slipped, and fell. The young man grabbed another stone and leaped forward, raising it, prepared to slam the rock down onto Meliora's skull.

Elory ran. "Stop this!" She bounded across the hilltop, kicked off a boulder, and jumped onto the young man's back.

The hermit cursed, and his stone thumped onto the ground. Meliora rose to her feet, wheezing and clutching her wounded chest. Elory clung to the man's back as he struggled, swinging his arms, trying to shake her off. He howled.

"A seraph!" He pointed at Meliora. "Seraph! She has seraph eyes. Kill her, kill her!"

"She's not a seraph!" Elory cried into his ear, still clinging to his back. "Do you see wings?"

"Seraph!" he cried, kneeling for another stone, even as Elory still grabbed him. "A mistress! Kill her! Kill her!"

Elory shouted louder into his ear. "She has no wings! Look."

The young man grimaced and covered his ears. "You shout. You shout too loudly. Too many voices. Too many old voices! Too much memory. Too much pain! You speak like a slave. Like a slave. Like a Vir Requis." He fell to his knees, shaking. "No wings, no wings." His voice sank to mere mumbles. "See no wings. No wings. Only eyes."

His arms fell limply to his sides, his head hung low, and his shoulders stooped. Elory released him and hurried toward Meliora, keeping one eye on the bearded hermit.

"Are you all right?"

Meliora nodded weakly, then winced. "It hurts. My ribs. But I'm all right."

The sisters stared at the young man. He knelt before them, head still lowered, still mumbling to himself. "No wings, no wings . . . slaves." He looked up at them, squinting, and his cheeks—at least what was visible beyond the dirt and yellow hair—paled. His voice was a mere whisper. "Slaves?"

Elory tugged at her iron collar. "Slaves."

The young man rose to his feet and pulled back his beard and hair. For the first time, Elory saw that he wore an iron collar like her own.

"Oh gods," Meliora whispered, eyes widening.

Elory stared and felt tears fill her eyes. She had always imagined a noble hero, a wise kinglike warrior, a tall and handsome leader of men. But here he stood. Not much older than her. Not much braver. A shivering young man, covered in filth, clad in rags.

She stepped closer to him, to the hero of Requiem, her tears falling.

"Lucem," she whispered.

MELIORA

"How?" Meliora whispered. "How is this possible?"

They hunkered together in the cave. The stony roof was so low they hunched over. A bed of dry leaves covered the floor, and chalk drawings covered the walls—drawings of falling dragons, of anguished faces, of a white column rising from a forest of fallen trees. Upon the walls of the ziggurat, the seraphim had immortalized scenes of fallen Requiem in towering frescos and engravings. Here in this cave, Lucem had remembered the horror with crude scribbles, drawn with stone on stone.

Lucem now sat before her, shoulders bunched inward. He was tall and barely fit in this cave, all knobby limbs. Smaller, Elory sat beside him, working at cutting his hair and trimming his beard with the spear's blade she had stolen from Tofet. With every blond lock that fell, Lucem began looking more and more human, and younger and younger. Soon he no longer looked like a wild hermit but like a lanky young man, eyes blue and peering.

"How is this possible?" Lucem repeated. He laughed mirthlessly. "I've asked myself that question many times. How is it possible—that I am here while so many others remained behind. That Requiem lies fallen. That cruel gods have conquered the world. None of these things should have happened, and yet here we are."

Meliora squinted, scrutinizing him. As Elory kept shearing him, Meliora realized that Lucem wasn't much older than the young woman; he couldn't have been much older than twenty.

"You must have been just a child when you escaped," Meliora said in wonder. "In Shayeen, the seraphim told of a vicious killer who slew many guards, a beast who stood nine feet tall, the deadliest Vir Requis to have lived since the days of old."

"And in Tofet," Elory added, "slaves told of a noble, kingly hero, a warrior both wise and brave, a crown upon his head, descended from the old kings."

As Elory worked at shearing the back of his head, Lucem snorted. "A vicious killer? A noble warrior? I was eleven years old and I looked six. I was hungry. I was small and quick and desperate. The cruel overseers murdered my parents—they died in the refineries, choking on the fumes." He clenched his teeth, balled up his fists, and lowered his head. "And so I escaped. I scaled the wall, hiding in its blind spot at night, too small to be seen. The seraphim starved me, made me no larger than a bundle of twigs. Their cruelty made me small enough to flee. But I never stopped feeling their whips, their fists, their . . ."

Lucem hunched over, overcome with emotion, unable to speak anymore. Elory placed down her blade, wrapped her arms around him, and stroked his hair.

"It's all right, Lucem," she whispered. "You're safe now. It's all right."

"It's not!" He raised his head so suddenly Elory fell back. "None of this is all right. That we're here and the others are still there. Still in chains. I . . . I wanted to go back so many times. To lead others up the wall, to bring them here. But whenever I tried to get close, so many seraphim flew in the sky, and twice as many patrolled the walls, and . . . I couldn't. I couldn't go back. I couldn't."

Elory embraced him again, whispering into his ear until Lucem calmed.

Meliora stared at them, and her fingers coiled around Amerath's hilt. The amber sword felt comforting in her grip, a relic of old Requiem. Holding the leather grip, she felt connected to those ancient kings and queens.

I am the daughter of Jaren, descended from Relesar Aeternum who held this sword, descended of Benedictus the Black, of King Aeternum who raised a marble column in a northern forest and founded a nation for Vir Requis.

She took a deep breath.

"Lucem," she said, "you've been free for ten years. Have you been hiding here the whole time? Or did you . . ." Meliora gulped, and her voice dropped to a whisper. "Did you try to find it? To find Requiem?"

He raised his eyes, staring at her. Haunted eyes. Eyes that, despite their youth, had seen too much.

"I tried," he whispered.

Elory inhaled sharply, and Meliora leaned forward.

Requiem. The kingdom of countless myths. The kingdom whispered of in Tofet, the kingdom whose destruction was portrayed in a thousand statues and murals, the kingdom some said was just a myth, as lost as Edinnu.

"What did you find?" Meliora's words were so soft they were almost silent.

"For a year or more, I walked north. I walked through storms that nearly drowned me. I walked through heat that nearly burned me. I walked across deserts and forests until I reached the coast, and I beheld a great blue sea—the northern border of the Terran continent. I walked along the coast for months, almost starving, moving from port to port, but I dared not enter any city I passed. I found no more cities of men. The Terran people who had once lived upon the coast—the remnants of Eteer, Goshar, and other ancient civilizations—all were gone. The seraphim did not enslave those people but slaughtered them all, down to the last child." Lucem stared at the cave wall, eyes dead. "Every port contained seraphim, and I dared not approach to seek passage on their ships. And so I could not cross the sea. I could not see the land of Requiem."

Meliora reached out and touched Lucem's iron collar, then her own collar. "But without this cursed iron around our necks, we wouldn't need a ship. We could fly. Fly across the sea to Requiem as dragons."

Lucem barked out a bitter laugh. "Look at my collar. Do you see any scratches? Dents? Any marring at all?"

Meliora shook her head.

Lucem nodded. "With as much effort as my labors in Tofet, I labored here to remove my collar. I spent hours bashing it with rocks. On my travels, I stole blades, plyers, hammers. I cut and bruised my neck so many times, trying to shatter this iron. I even snuck into a smithy once, took hot metal, tried to melt the collar off but only burned my skin." He pulled the collar downward, showing an ugly scar. "The runes upon it were forged in dark magic, and it cannot be removed. Our dragon forms are forever lost, and so is Requiem."

Meliora pulled out the crumpled key from her pocket. "Not if we can fix this."

For a long time, Meliora spoke, and Lucem listened. She told him of her life in the ziggurat, of the Keeper's Key that can open the collars. She spoke of losing her wings, of discovering Requiem, and of her quest for the Keymaker. She told him of the Chest of Plenty, of duplicating the key half a million times, of the dragons of Requiem rising together to flee captivity and seek Requiem. And as she spoke, Lucem was silent, asking no questions, simply listening.

When finally Meliora completed her story, Lucem crawled out of the cave, leaving her and Elory inside.

The sisters glanced at each other.

"Did we say something wrong?" Elory asked, frowning.

Meliora peered out the cave. Lucem was walking downhill toward the river, not turning back to look at them. Across his shoulders, he held his only belongings—a tattered old pack, a waterskin, and a makeshift spear with a rusted head.

With another glance at each other, the sisters burst out of the cave and followed.

"Lucem!" Meliora said. "Lucem, where are you going?"

He took a few more steps downhill, then looked over his shoulder at her.

"Where do you think? We're going to find that Keymaker. Are you going to just wait up there, or are you coming too?"

He resumed walking downhill. Meliora and Elory looked at each other, both with wide eyes, and Meliora couldn't help it. She grinned.

"Think we should let him tag along?" Meliora asked.

Elory glanced at Lucem; he had reached a valley and was now racing through the grass toward the riverbank.

"I think," Elory said, "that we'd be tagging along with him."

The sisters ran downhill, swords hanging at their sides, following a legend in chase of a myth.

JAREN

Under the burning sun they labored. In the heat and light of Saraph they screamed. In pits of tar and clay, their bones shattered, their backs broke, their skin tore, their souls cried out for mercy the masters would not grant. In darkness they hid, weeping, begging, praying to stars that would not answer.

Ishtafel, King of Saraph, rose above all, laughing above, a second sun, and under his flames the slaves burned.

Is this how Requiem perishes? Jaren wondered, toiling as another day began, mixing the clay and straw, forming the bricks to bake in the kilns. Not in battle, not with song, not with pride, but fading away in the dirt?

"Faster!" An overseer swung a wooden club, slamming it against Jaren's back with a crack. "Toil!"

Jaren couldn't help it. He cried out in pain. He fell. The seraph spat, clubbed him again, kicked his side.

"Up, old man!" The overseer laughed—a deep, throaty chuckle. "Up and toil. I won't let you die yet."

He screamed. Something tore inside him.

It is over. I fade now. I go to the stars of my forebears.

All around him, they screamed—the children of Requiem, whipped, beaten, broken.

No. I am their father, descended of their ancient king. I am their healer, their priest. Jaren pushed himself up, arms wobbling. *I cannot die here. Not as hope still flickers.*

He rose to his bleeding feet. He labored on.

As night fell again, they gathered before his home. The weak carrying the weaker. The wounded carrying the dying. Men, women, children with broken bones, open wounds across their bodies. Swollen, bleeding, coughing, shivering, convulsing, festering. The slaves of Tofet, broken, shattered, yet still clinging to life. Still clinging to a dream—a dream of Meliora returning. A dream of seeing Requiem again. Still clinging to life—so frail, so precious! A life even of pain, even of fear, of this endless agony, of centuries of torment—still to live! Still to draw one more breath, to see another dawn in the fields of dust and sweat, to utter one more prayer. To hope. To dream. To pray to see dragons again.

Outside his hut they gathered, dozens, then a hundred, and Jaren stood before them. He too was wounded. He too needed healing, needed water, needed rest. But his children needed him more.

"Come to me, my children." Jaren opened his arms. "Come and pray with me."

One by one, they approached. The first was a young girl, raped and beaten by her masters, bleeding inside. Her mother placed her down. She could barely breathe, merely lay gasping, raspy, gurgling. Jaren's eyes swam with tears as he knelt above her, as he stared up at the stars, as he prayed. He was not a great healer like Issari—the first priestess of Requiem—but he called upon her spirit, the spirit that had healed his son. And in the shadows and light, he thought he saw her form—a pious woman in robes, a braid hanging across her shoulders, her tears falling onto the child who lay in the dirt.

The young girl's eyes fluttered open, and she began to weep. Her mother stepped forth, lifted the child, and wept too.

"Bless you, Jaren Aeternum, shepherd of Requiem," she whispered.

The next slave approached, a father carrying his son; the boy's back was crooked, his clothes soaked with sweat and blood, his face torn in anguish. Again Jaren prayed, holding his hands over the boy, as starlight shone, as the spirit of the priestess wept, until the boy calmed.

Throughout the night they came, and Jaren prayed, healing them as best he could, soothing those he could not heal, guiding some into death. And even as dawn rose, and he returned to his labor, the wounded spread across Tofet, and the dead kept falling.

As he worked in the fields of clay, shivering with weakness and hunger, Jaren prayed a different prayer.

"Return to us, my children." His back burned in the sun. "Return to us, Meliora, Elory, Vale. Return with hope. We need you. Hurry, my children. All the eyes of Requiem are raised to you in hope."

LUCEM

People.

As they walked through the wilderness, Lucem could barely believe it.

Real people. Flesh and blood. Talking to me. Alive.

He looked at them. He had only met them, yet Lucem already loved them both, never wanted to part from them again.

Meliora was tall and fair, her cheekbones high, and her eyes shone gold, the pupils shaped as sunbursts—the eyes of a seraph. Yet kindness filled those eyes, and no wings grew from her back, for her father was Vir Requis, and she carried with her the pride and nobility of Requiem. Though clad in rough burlap, her body scratched and caked with dirt, her grace gave her a godly presence, a holiness greater than jewels and silk could ever bestow.

At her side walked Elory. While Meliora was a striking figure—a goddess of ancient legend come to life—Elory was fully of this world, a figure of warmth, of companionship, of goodness. Her eyes were large and brown, too large in her small face. She was short and slender—too slender—and scars peeked from under her tunic. Her head was shaven, her neck collared, her body bruised, yet she was beautiful to Lucem. A frail, warm, little thing, more precious than the greatest treasure.

Right away Lucem knew: he would come to admire Meliora, to respect her, to worship her divinity . . . and he would come to deeply love Elory, to connect with her soul, to see her as his dearest friend. One woman of holiness, golden yet perhaps searing to the touch. One woman of love, warm and soft and nothing but goodness.

Real people, he thought. *Real friends.*

Lucem remembered his long years in the wilderness—the friends he had carved from wood, painted onto stone, dreamed of, invented in his madness. They began to fade from his mind.

And he talked.

He talked to Meliora and Elory of old tales—of Requiem, sometimes myths of other lands. They talked back. They shared stories. They told jokes. Walking along the river, they even sang a song together.

And slowly it faded—that pain, that loneliness . . . easing under the healing presence of them.

I had to remember how to talk, he thought. *Now I talk again. Now I'm real. Now I'm here. I remember.*

VALE

The sun was setting, spilling red across the sky, when Vale and
Tash reached the sea.

"It's beautiful," Tash whispered.

Vale grumbled. "The marble columns of Requiem are
beautiful. The birch forests of the north are beautiful. This is . .
." He sighed. "Fine. It's beautiful."

The delta spread around them, lush with life. The
Te'ephim River broke into many rivulets here, each crawling
along a different path. Lotuses covered the water in a blanket,
pads deep green and blossoms red fading to pink. Many fingers
of land coiled between the rivulets, and upon them grew wild
grass, papyrus trees, date palms, flowering tamarisks, and carob
trees heavy with fruit. Birds flew above or waded in the water.
Vale saw terns, herons, plovers, egrets, ibises, and many other
species he could not name. Frogs trilled between rushes, and
crocodiles and hippopotamuses lay submerged in the water, only
their nostrils rising above the surface. A few miles away, the
delta spilled into the sea, swirls of azure and green water
mingling with deep blue.

Yet along with the birds and plants, other life lurked here
too, not as appealing. Vale pointed. "Beautiful aside from that."

Tash nodded and nervously tugged her hair. "Does ruin
the view, doesn't it?"

A city rose a mile or two away from the greenery. Even
from this distance, Vale spotted obelisks tipped with gold, the
columns of temples, and statues of gods that soared hundreds of
feet tall. What he first mistook for eagles circling the city he soon
recognized as seraphim.

"The city of Geshin," Tash said. She fingered the jewel in
her navel. "This jewel came from there. As did many of the gifts

the seraphim gave me—pearls, incense, hintan, and even little sweets. Do you see the ships out in the sea? They travel all along the eastern coast of Terra and to the islands beyond, bringing back treasures from distant lands."

Vale grunted. "I don't care about what lies beyond the eastern sea. All I care about is the sea in the north—beyond whose waters Requiem awaits us."

"Well, Sir Sour-boots, we need to find the beached ship on this coast, and the Chest of Plenty in its belly, if we're to ever reach the northern sea." Tash unfurled her scroll. "And according to this map, the ship's wreck lies two days' journey north along the beach. So come on. Let's get walking—and not stray too close to that city."

The sun dipped lower in the sky behind them, casting their long shadows across the tussocks of grass. Vale nodded. "We'll walk in darkness, and we'll keep a wide berth away from that city." He stared up at the sky where the first stars were emerging. "Kloriana shines in the east. We'll navigate by it."

"He can be taught!" Tash patted his chest, making his chain mail—the rusty armor found in the centipedes' cave— clink. "Just be careful not to stumble into the water in the darkness. Oh, and try to walk hunched over. You're too tall and the moon's full."

He grumbled and hefted his axe. "Try hiding that jewel in your belly button. Damn thing reflects more light than a knight's shield."

She stuck her tongue out at him, grabbed a scoop of mud, and slapped it onto her belly. She thought for a moment, smiled slyly, then scooped more mud and tossed it at Vale. He rolled his eyes, wiped off the mud, and began to walk through the growing darkness.

Tash darted after him, hopping around. "Go on, toss mud back at me!" She tugged his arm. "Grab me and wrestle me and get pretend angry. Why are you always so serious?"

He ignored her and kept walking, stepping through grass that rose past his knees. Why did the damn girl keep annoying him? She never seemed to shut her mouth. She was always teasing him, singing some song, even mumbling in her sleep. When awake, she bounced, hopped, swung her arms, and skipped, and when sleeping she kicked and tossed and turned. When she wasn't stripping naked to jump into the river, she still haunted his thoughts with those mocking lips, knowing eyes, and teasing hands that loved to brush against him.

"Answer me!" she said. They walked through a grove of acacia and date palms. "You never sing. You never laugh, not even at my wondrously funny jokes. You never tell jokes of your own. You're always like . . . like you're at a funeral."

He knelt to lift a bunch of fallen dates. "This fruit is still good." He kept walking. "We should move faster. We can eat while we walk."

Tash groaned, crossed her arms, and thumped down onto her backside. "No." She shook her head. "I'm not going anywhere until you answer me."

"Very well." He kept walking.

Tash let out a groan so loud finches fled from the trees. "Vale!"

He reeled toward her. "Hush! You're too loud."

"And you're too quiet!" She stood up and placed her fists on her hips. "Why don't you ever talk to me? Why are you so . . . so stiff? And not in a good way." She reached for his crotch, and he swatted her hand away.

"You're insufferable." Vale's hands curled into fists. "I'm not one of your seraphim to seduce."

"Oh, I can tell. You're not nearly as much fun as they are."

"Fun?" His rage exploded inside him. "You think that the people who destroyed our homeland, who enslaved us, who murdered countless are fun?"

She nodded. "I do! More fun than you'll ever be. You don't know what it's like to have fun, do you?"

He stepped close to her, bringing himself so close that their bodies almost touched. He towered above her—the top of her head just reached his shoulders—and glared down at her. She stared right back at him, chin raised, chest thrust out.

"No, Tash," he hissed. "When I was being whipped in the fields, I never learned much about fun. When I watched my sister brutalized, I did not learn about fun. When Ishtafel murdered my mother, when he murdered a hundred thousand souls before my eyes—a hundred thousand whose screams I still hear in the night—I did not learn about fun."

Her eyes softened. She dropped her hands to her sides, then hesitantly raised them and placed them against his chest, her touch gentle. "Those days are behind you, Vale. Ishtafel isn't here. But I am. A person who cares for you. Who wants to see you happy. Who . . . who loves you."

And right there, in that instant, all his anger against Tash melted, all his earlier rage—about her hopping, her singing, her flirting—it all vanished, seeming ridiculous to him now. His fists uncurled.

"When you suffered too much, perhaps you can never laugh," he said. "When you spent too many years in pain, perhaps you can never feel joy."

Tash shook her head wildly, hair swaying. "No. I refuse to believe that. Maybe your pain will never go away, Vale. Maybe old wounds never heal. But you can still find joy. You can still find a life with a little laughter, a little peace." She caressed his cheek. "Let me help you find that."

She stood on her tiptoes, wrapped her arms around him, and kissed him. Her lips were soft, full. Vale had never kissed a woman before, but he had dreamed—shameful, secret dreams—of kissing Tash many times. For a long moment, he stood, arms wrapped around her, kissing her.

Finally she playfully bit his bottom lip, pulled back an inch, and grinned. "Now that was fun, wasn't it?"

He nodded.

Her grin widened. "See? I told you." She hopped up and down, then grew somber and held his hands. "I'm sorry that I annoy you so much. I'm sorry that I'm like a bird, fluttering all around, never quiet. But I meant what I said. I love you. You are a Vir Requis, one of my people, worth more than all the seraphim I loved. Wherever your path leads, Vale Aeternum, no matter how dark the shadows on the way, I will walk that path with you. You came on this quest to fight for me, to protect me. Let me fight for you."

The sun was gone now, and the stars shone brilliantly above. They walked onward, and again Tash sang, her voice soft and fair. She sang Old Requiem Woods—one of the songs they sang in Tofet—and for the first time, Vale joined her.

The way was treacherous. Every mile, a rivulet crossed the land, forcing them to swim in the darkness. Mostly the moonlight lit their way, but every hour, chariots of fire flew above, casting down their light. When this happened, Vale and Tash leaped for cover, hiding between reeds, in the tall grass, or under the water. The fire streamed above, moving toward the city, casting light upon the distant walls. Even here, so many miles from Shayeen, the seraphim sought them.

As they traveled, Vale could judge the passage of time by the location of Kloriana's star. In the sunset, it always shone to the east, but it climbed the sky through the night, heading toward the zenith before dawn.

"Travelers would tell stories of Kloriana's star in the ziggurat," Tash said, wading through the dark water beside Vale. "Men said that most stars are like the sun, great balls of fire in the distance. But they said that Kloriana's star was not made of fire, but that it was solid, a great round world full of life. They said that half the world always lay in daylight, and half always in night, that some of its people dwelled in eternal sunshine, others in never-ending shadow. If you lived there, which would you prefer, Vale? To live in day or night?"

"Night," he said. "It's safer and the sunlight burns."

"Not me." Tash sighed wistfully. "I'd live in endless daylight. I'd never be in the dark again."

Vale thought about how, while he had labored in the searing sunlight of Tofet, she had languished in the shadows beneath the ziggurat. He said nothing more.

When Kloriana's star approached the zenith, the port city of Geshin vanished behind the southern horizon. The first hints of dawn began to rise, smudges of orange and pink that reflected in the rivulets of the delta and the sea. The flora was lush here, and mangroves grew from the water, their roots spreading everywhere in a great wooden city.

"We should hide between these roots," Vale said. "Eat the dates and fish we collected, then sleep until night falls again." He scanned the sky. "Chariots likely to return soon."

Tash stretched out her limbs, and her mouth opened wide with a yawn, emitting a roar that shook the landscape.

Vale blinked. "Tash, did you just . . . roar?"

She slapped a hand across her mouth. "I don't think so!" she whispered between her fingers.

The roar sounded again.

Tash's eyes widened. "Definitely not me."

Vale cursed and hefted his axe. "Put on your helmet and grab your shield. Now."

He spun around, staring at the landscape, seeing nothing. No enemies. No beasts. Yet the birds were fleeing, and even the crocodiles sank into the water and vanished. The roar died, and silence fell across the land. Even the rivulets of water seemed to still. It was so silent Vale could hear every chink of his chain mail, of his joints.

And slowly the landscape began to creak too.

A few roots of mangroves twitched, raining chips of wood. Branches shuddered. A deep, wooden clicking rose across the delta, and the curtains of lichen swayed.

"Bloody stars," Tash whispered. "Look at them."

At first, it seemed to Vale that chunks of the mangroves detached, shuffling forward.

Living trees! he thought.

But no. These were not trees but men and women, cursed and twisted. Their limbs were bent, covered with warts and scabs that looked like wood. Their hands and feet were swollen to obscene size, each twice the size of a human head, coarse and twisting, sprouting many roots and twigs. Wooden bumps and knots covered their faces and twisted torsos, and moss grew upon them. Their scraggly hair and beards hung low, greenish gray as lichen. Insects bustled across them, living within the burrows of their plantlike bodies. Only their eyes distinguished them from trees; those eyes shone, small and cruel and amber.

"Zamzummim!" Tash said, eyes wide. "Ancient demons."

The creatures emerged from all around, surrounding them, ten or more, each taller than Vale. Their mouths opened, revealing burrows bustling with insects, and they let out horrible buzzing sounds, shrill and so loud Vale cried out. Screeching with countless voices, they charged.

Vale swung his axe.

A zamzum leaped toward him, jaws opened, eyes blazing, hair fluttering, a demonic creature of rotted wood and mold. Its massive palms lashed out, large as shields, sprouting jagged branches.

Vale's axe slammed into one of those twisted hands, shaving off slivers of wood. The second hand slammed into him, knocking him down.

The zamzum leaped down toward him. More charged from either side. Vale swung his blade wildly, scattering chips of wood. A warty, heavy foot—large as an anvil—slammed into his chest, snapping rings in his armor. Vale cried out and lashed his axe, chipping the leg, cutting the wood. He managed to shove off the creature, leap to his feet, and spin around, blade lashing.

Tash was fighting several feet away. She had leaped into a mangrove and fought from the branches, holding her dagger and shield before her. Three zamzummim stood below, reaching toward her, swatting at her shield. Tash's dagger barely seemed to harm them. Blood dripped down her leg, and she cried out.

The sight of Tash hurt shot rage through Vale. He roared and swung the axe with more fervor. The creatures surrounded him, lashing at him, snapping their wooden teeth, and green saliva flew from their mouths. But what was wood? Vale had spent his life swinging his pickaxe into limestone. These creatures were nothing compared to that unyielding wall of stone. Their rootlike fingers cut him, but what was that pain? Nothing compared to the lashes his overseers had given him.

I can no longer feel pain, he thought. *But Tash can. And I won't let it happen. I won't let her be hurt like I was hurt.*

His axe swung, chips of wood flew, and the zamzummim fell before him.

As he fought, he was there again—in the streets of Shayeen—fighting not delta demons but the seraphim, running from them, seeing so many die, and his fury blinded him. All he could see was that old blood, and he could not stop attacking, could not stop cutting into them, howling, weeping.

You killed her. You killed my mother. You killed thousands.

"You killed them!" Vale cried, driving his axe down, again and again.

"Vale!" cried a high voice. "Vale, stop!"

But he could not stop. How could he? Ishtafel still lived. His people still were dying. He could not lower his blade, not until this ended, until he cut them all down.

"Vale!" Hands grabbed him. "Vale, they're all dead. They're gone."

Tash.

He could not see her. He saw nothing but Shayeen again.

But it was her voice. Tash. The young woman with the long brown hair, the infuriating songs, the flirty eyes, the woman he found insufferable . . . the woman who had kissed him. Who loved him. Whom he loved.

The veil lifted, and he looked around him. Dead zamzummim lay around him like fallen logs, his axe marks in them. Tash stood before him, gripping his arm. Concern filled her eyes, and blood trickled down her leg.

Vale fell to his knees before her.

"I can't do this, Tash." He lowered his head. "I can't forget it. I can't stop fighting it. I can't stop being there, even here."

She pulled him close, wrapping her arms around him, holding his head to her belly.

"I know," she whispered. "I know, Vale. I can't fix this. I don't know how. But . . . I can be here with you." She brushed moss back from his brow. "I can hold you when you remember."

She knelt before him, and he held her tightly, eyes closed. Her damp hair pressed against his face, and her body was warm, and slowly his anxiety faded, and those memories left him, and he was here again, in the present, holding her. The whips, the searing sun, the quarries, the death—it was all gone, and only Tash remained.

"We walk the shadowy paths together," he whispered to her. "Always."

They left the corpses behind, walked until they found a burrow between the jutting roots of trees, and lay down in the dry, shadowy den upon a bed of leaves. Vale lay on his back, and Tash curled up against him, her head on his chest. He spent a long time stroking her hair, again and again as she slept, and finally he sank into slumber too, Tash in his arms. For the first time in many days, he did not dream.

ELORY

"You must have been so lonely." Elory reached out and touched Lucem's arm. "Out here, hiding, all alone."

He walked beside her across the hills. The halved spear Meliora had taken from Tofet hung across his back. Though Lucem still wore only tattered rags, his beard and hair were now trimmed down to stubble, his body cleaned of dirt. He was thin, but not as thin as Elory; life in the wilderness, though perhaps lonely, had given him more vigor than the struggles in Tofet. Even in the moonlight, Elory thought him handsome, and his strong hands, bright blue eyes, and square jaw made her feel tingly—a strange sort of feeling, not unlike when Tash had kissed her in the pleasure pit.

"I wasn't always alone." Lucem skipped over a boulder and kept climbing the hillside. "I traveled often, sometimes even entered the villages and farmlands of seraphim, disguised in a cloak and hood. And there were animals who came and went. But . . . yes, it's nice to talk to another Vir Requis."

They had left the river far behind, traveling in the darkness across the hills, heading toward the distant Khalish Mountain, which still lay over the horizon. The Keymaker was said to live upon that crest, but many miles of wilderness still lay between them and that distant mount. The night was dark, and clouds sporadically hid the moon, plunging them into near total blackness. Meliora's halo was their main source of light; it crackled, woven of dragonfire, casting its red light across the barren hills. There was no grass here, almost no trees, and no wildlife that Elory could see. She might as well have been walking upon the desolate plains of Lanburg Fields, the place where Requiem was said to have fallen many years ago.

"Are you sure you know your way?" Meliora asked, moving to walk closer to Lucem.

After all this time in the wilderness, Meliora too looked different, Elory thought. Back in the ziggurat, Meliora had been like a fairy of purest beauty—pale cheeks tinged pink, a halo of gold, flowing blond hair, her tall and delicate form clad in silks matched in softness only by her swan wings. Later, freed from her imprisonment, Meliora had been shivering, feverish, beaten, her shoulder blades bleeding from the loss of her wings, her head shaved, her cheeks gaunt.

And now, Elory thought, Meliora was something different. No longer a seraph princess, but nor was she a beaten slave. Even with an iron collar around her neck, with her hair barely longer than stubble, Meliora looked like a queen of Requiem. Her back was straight, her shoulders square, and her body— once soft—had hardened, her fat melting to reveal taut muscles. With her crackling halo and her royal sword at her side— Amerath itself, ancient sword of the Aeternum dynasty of Requiem—Meliora could just as easily be walking through the halls of a reborn Requiem.

It seemed that Lucem noticed her striking presence too. The young man turned toward Meliora, and it seemed to Elory that she saw appreciation in his eyes, maybe even admiration.

Suddenly Elory felt rather plain looking. She had never spared much thought to her looks. Why would she? Beauty did not matter in Tofet, only a back strong enough to lift the bitumen, lungs strong enough to survive their fumes. Ishtafel had obviously thought her fair enough, but perhaps he had only lusted for her fragility—a fragility he longed to shatter.

I'm not tall and noble like Meliora, she thought. *I don't have the curves or alluring beauty of Tash.* She glanced over at Lucem; he was still looking at Meliora. *Why would he look at me when he can look at my sister?*

"Of course I know my way!" The young man puffed out his chest. "I've spent countless days traveling all across these hills and mountains. In my first year of freedom, I hid in a network of caves that runs beneath these hills. Seraphim covered the sky, seeking me, but they could not find me underground. I'm going to look after you, Meliora. And you, Elory. I'm going to lead you to Khalish Mountain and we're going to find this Keymaker."

Elory stepped closer. "Meliora doesn't need anyone to protect her." She raised her chin. "She led a nation of slaves against Queen Kalafi. She slew seraphim. She gave life to golems, life from her own blood, and created a race of erevim. She's descended from the Aeternum dynasty—as I am."

Lucem turned toward her and raised an eyebrow, and at once Elory cursed herself. She had rushed to protect Meliora's honor, but had she only hurt Lucem's pride?

Surely he won't only think me plain now, Elory thought, *but also unpleasant.*

Lucem nodded. "Yet even the greatest queen of light needs a guide when walking in shadows." A grin split his face. "Meliora, Princess of Seraph—also a Princess of Requiem. Now there's something I never imagined when I escaped your family, Mel. Can I call you Mel?"

Meliora gave one of her rare smiles. Elory did not think she had ever seen her sister smile so widely.

"No," Meliora said, "you may not."

Lucem matched her grin. "Oh, I see how it is. I'm to call you My Queen or Your Majesty, is it? You are, after all . . ." He puffed out his chest and spoke in baritone. "Queen Meliora Aeternum the First, Sovereign of all Requiem, Slayer of Seraphim."

And I am nothing to him, Elory thought, hating that feeling that suddenly sprang inside her. Jealousy? Foolishness! How could she be jealous? What mattered now was survival, that was all. Finding the Keymaker. Bringing a repaired key back to Tofet. Raising the dragons and flying back to Requiem. Not a silly, handsome, young hero who had spent the past few hours looking at Meliora and away from Elory.

And yet her jealousy remained. In the old tales of Requiem, Elory had heard of many lovers—the timeless and doomed love of King Benedictus and Queen Lacrimosa, or the star-crossed lovers Rune and Tilla, forced to fight on different sides of Requiem's civil war. After entering the ziggurat, Elory had thought that perhaps Tash had stirred those feelings in her, with her gentle caresses and warm eyes. Yet now feelings ten times more powerful flared inside her, tingling, warm, intolerable, growing whenever she so much as glanced at Lucem's bare arms or ready grin.

"Just call me Meliora." The tall haloed woman smiled thinly. "Though I wouldn't object to an odd Your Highness now and then."

Lucem opened his mouth, ready to say more when a shrill cry sounded in the distance.

They all froze.

A chill seized Elory's spine like demonic fingers.

For a moment, all was silent. Then the screech sounded again, so loud that Elory dropped her sword and covered her ears. Meliora grimaced and her halo cracked, and even Lucem paled.

"What is it?" Elory whispered when the shriek died.

Lucem stared into the sky. "I don't know. Not seraphim. I can't see anything."

Meliora was pale, and she pulled her hood over her halo, extinguishing the flames. "Hurry. We must find shelter."

They began to run across the hills, hunched over. Shelter? There was no shelter here. Elory saw no trees, no caves. By the Abyss, she barely saw anything at all, now that Meliora's halo no longer cast its night. She stumbled as she ran in darkness, and Lucem grabbed her hand, his grip warm.

The screeches rose again behind them, closer now, so loud that Elory nearly cried out in pain, thought her eardrums would shatter. Her father had told her that sound was actually ripples through the air, like the ripples on a pond, something Elory had never believed, yet this sound slammed against her with a physical force. She felt it against her chest, in her bones. A demonic cry from another world, a scream of pure hatred, pure malice.

She stared over her shoulders as they ran. Still she saw nothing. No demons flying. Certainly no chariots of fire. Nothing at all in the night. Nothing—

Wait!

It was just an instant. A shadow blotting out the stars, a mere flicker. Again! Another star blinked away for an instant. Something dark flying in the sky. Several of them.

Then they passed across the moon, and such fear filled Elory that she could barely keep running.

"Bat wings," she whispered. "Evil with bat wings."

The shrieks above coalesced into words, the voice of shattering spines, of falling columns, of shards of glass driving into flesh.

"We smell her, comrades! We smell the half-breed. Find her! Break her!"

Each word shook Elory's ribs, twisted her heart, churned her belly. She kept running, holding Lucem's hand. Meliora ran alongside, a mere shadow in the night.

"Drink her blood!" rose a cry above.

"Snap her bones and suck the marrow!"

"Feast upon her organs!"

Elory's breath rattled in her lungs. She glanced up and she saw them now. Oh stars, she saw them. White eyes like stars. Fangs and sickle blades. Bat wings tipped with claws.

"We see them, comrades!" the creatures screeched. "We see three! Catch them! Break them!"

"Seraphim!" Elory cried, running across the rocky land.

"Dark seraphim," Meliora answered, voice shaking. "The cursed one, traitors to Saraph."

Elory drew her sword. Lemuria, her ancient blade—borne by Kaelyn Cadigus herself in Requiem's great civil war—gleamed with inner light. "Then we fight them. We kill them."

"No!" Meliora said. "You cannot fight these creatures. Nobody can."

Lucem stared upward and grimaced. "You might not have a choice, sweetheart." He hefted his spear. "Draw that pretty sword of yours!"

Meliora had no sooner drawn her blade than the creatures swooped.

The white eyes blazed around them, slit down the middle with narrow pupils. Serpent eyes. Fangs shone as the creatures laughed, and the wings beat. A sickle flew toward Elory, and she screamed and swung her blade, heart lashing.

The blades crashed together, sparking. Elory cried out. The sickle's blow was so powerful her arm nearly dislocated again. She kept running, and a creature swooped before her, grinning luridly, and lashed its claws. Elory thrust her blade, parrying the claws, but more claws thrashed from her left, tearing through her side. She screamed. Her blood spilled.

At her sides, Lucem and Meliora were fighting too, weapons stabbing at the creatures. Amerath, the Amber Sword, swung in arcs, holding them back. Lucem growled as he thrust his spear again and again.

The dark seraphim flew around them in a ring, a demonic dance, grinning, laughing, screeching, a macabre song. Blood stained their faces. One of the creatures lashed his claws, cut Elory's leg, then licked his fingers.

"Eat them, eat them, flesh and blood!" they sang. "Bone and marrow, brains and liver, hearts and stomachs, fleshy treats!"

They're toying with us, Elory realized, blood dripping. *They're playing with their food.*

"Keep the tall female alive!" shrieked one of the dark seraphim. "Eat her legs, eat her arms, but keep her alive. Her womb belongs to Ishtafel."

The dark seraph who had spoken was female, a woman all in black and white. Her breastplate was darker than the night, her sickle a shard of shadow, her wings shadowy curtains of the Abyss. Her skin was white as a frozen corpse, her hair like ice draped across a tombstone, and her eyes were like cold stars, the eyes of a snake, yet hot—searing hot like fire heated until it lost all color. For an instant, even as she bled, even as the creatures danced around her, Elory could only stare at this she-demon, frozen.

There is no hope, Elory thought. *Not before this goddess. We are but playthings to her as mice are to cats.*

"Leyleet!" Meliora cried, raising her sword. "I know you. I know your name! Be gone, Queen of Darkness. I am Meliora of the Thirteenth Dynasty, your mistress. Leave this place and return to your lair."

The Dark Queen laughed, wings spread wide, sickle raised, and the air seemed to bend around her, and the earth shook. Stones rolled across the hills, a chasm cracked open, and the stars themselves began to extinguish. All the world seemed to fall as the dark seraphim—sixteen in all, the sixteen who had rebelled against the throne of Saraph—laughed with voices like dying nations.

"I shall be the first to feed upon you, Meliora!" shrieked Leyleet. "Your blood will fill my mouth as wine."

With a flash of her sickle, Leyleet swooped.

Meliora pulled back her hood, and her halo crackled to life.

The flames lashed out, a shock wave of fire, showering sparks, illuminating the night as brightly as red lightning. The fire slammed into Leyleet, and the creature screamed—this time a scream of pain, of fear. Her comrades cried out, covering their eyes against the light.

"The light of Requiem!" they cried. "The fire of dragons! It burns our eyes."

Leyleet screamed louder than them all. "Tear off her fire!"

The dark seraphim swooped again.

Elory snapped out of her paralysis. She raised her sword and charged.

"For Requiem!" she cried, blade lashing.

"For Requiem!" cried Meliora, thrusting her own sword.

The fire blazed, and the weapons flashed, and the dark seraphim slammed against them. All amusement was gone from their eyes now. Their claws tore at Meliora, ripping open the old wounds on her back, and her blood showered. Another creature grabbed Elory, tugging at her arm, and she swung her blade, screaming as her blood spilled.

Her blade slammed into the dark seraph's armor, doing him no harm. The dark deity laughed and swung his sickle again.

Blood.

Searing pain.

Elory screamed.

The side of her head burned, melted, shrieked, cracked, died. She yowled. Her blood gushed. She raised her hand to her left ear and found it gone. Her hand touched nothing but a wound, burning, ringing, screaming, white, searing through her. And still the dark seraph laughed, and his sickle swung again.

"Elory!" Lucem shouted.

He leaped forth, spear lashing, and suddenly this young man was the hero again—the fabled Lucem, legend of Requiem.

Face twisted with rage, Lucem vaulted upward, and his spear slammed into the dark seraph, knocking the sickle aside, driving the creature back.

"Elory!" he cried again, turning toward her.

She could not even reply. She could barely stay standing. The fire spread from her missing ear, driving through her head, down her spine.

It ends here. We die here. Our quest failed.

"Elory, I think I know where we are!" Lucem shouted, still lashing his spear, holding more of the creatures back. "I saw it when Meliora's fire flared. Follow me to safety!"

The young man leaped onto a boulder, vaulted through the air, and swung his spear, knocking a dark seraph aside. He began to run. Swinging her blade, Meliora followed, her halo of dragonfire casting out flames, lighting the darkness.

"Elory, come on!" they cried.

She ran too. The hole on her head where her ear had been screamed in agony, and her head spun, and the pain was beyond anything she had thought possible, but she ran too. She lashed her blade, holding the creatures back. Claws slashed at the companions, bat wings beat above, the sickles flashed, but still they ran onward, bleeding, falling, running again.

"Down this way!" Lucem cried, leaping into a chasm that had appeared in the hillside—a narrow ravine, barely wide enough to enter. Elory leaped into the chasm too, twisting her ankle, and ran after Lucem with a limp. Walls of stone rose at her sides, and Meliora leaped down behind her. The dark seraphim still flew above, and the companions ran with blades raised, swinging their weapons, knocking sickles aside.

The canyon opened up into a valley, and there ahead Elory saw it—a cave in the hillside ahead.

"We'll never make it!" she cried over the ringing in her ear.

Lucem grabbed her hand. "Run with me. Run!"

They burst out into the valley. Without the protection of walls around them, the dark seraphim attacked with more vigor. A sickle flashed, cleaving Lucem's spear. Claws thrust at Meliora, tearing her cheek. One dark seraph swooped, landed before Elory, and she swung her blade, knocked him aside, and ran around him.

"Cut them down, cut them down!" Leyleet shrieked, soaring above. "They're heading for the cave, cut them down!"

Elory ran as fast as she could. Only twenty yards separated her from the cave, but Leyleet was swooping, her wings opened wide, her laughter rolling.

I will fight as the heroes of Requiem did, Elory thought, running with all her speed. *I will never stop fighting for my stars.*

She leaped into the air and tossed her blade.

Lemuria flew, a shard of silver, and slammed into Leyleet's leg, sinking into the flesh.

The scream tore across the land, shattered stones, sent boulders tumbling, a sound that was deafening, blinding, a living thing. But still Elory ran, and Meliora and Lucem ran with her, and as Leyleet soared in her agony, they leaped into the cave and plunged into darkness.

A tunnel stretched before them, leading to shadows. Meliora's halo lit rough stone walls. Elory spun toward the cave entrance. Dark seraphim flew outside, storming toward the cave, their cries echoing.

"We'll be trapped in here!" Elory said. "They'll fly in!"

"No, they won't." Lucem gritted his teeth. "Move deeper. Go!" He reached up, grabbed a stone that jutted from the cave ceiling, and yanked it loose.

Dust rained.

A dark seraph streamed through the entrance.

Lucem grabbed Elory and pulled her backward, knocking into Meliora, stumbling deeper into the cave.

The entrance collapsed.

Stones rained, then a great boulder fell, slamming against the ground, cracking the walls. More stones tumbled, burying the dark seraph who was entering the cave, crushing his body, then his head, leaving only his arms exposed. And still stones fell.

"The whole cave's collapsing!" Elory said.

Lucem shook his head. "No. Just the entrance." He wrapped his arms around Elory, who was now shivering madly. "Look. It's all right."

A few last stones fell, and the dust settled. Where the cave entrance had been, now a pile of rocks rose, solid, blocking the exit. Only Meliora's halo now lit the shadows.

Elory took a deep, shuddering breath, her head spinning. Her legs would not stop shaking. The screams of the dark seraphim still sounded outside, and the boulders shuddered as the creatures slammed at them. Dust flew but the barricade held. Elory had to lean against the wall, and blood dripped across her shoulder.

"It's all right." Lucem held her close and kissed her forehead. "We're safe, Elory. We're safe."

Meliora stepped forward, eyes grim. Two ugly scratches ran across her cheek, dripping. "We're trapped, that's what we are. Unless this cave has another exit somewhere. Does it, Lucem?"

He bit his lip. "Not sure. I built a few of these booby trap doors years ago, back when I was hiding from the seraphim. Never had to use one until now, but I built at least . . . four. Maybe five. Might be they're connected underground." He flashed a grin. "Guess we'll find out."

Elory pulled away from his embrace, stepped toward the crushed dark seraph—only his hands were still visible—and wrenched his sickle free.

I lost an ancient blade of Requiem, she thought. *So I will bear a blade of evil. I—*

Her head spun madly, and she fell to her knees. Lucem knelt beside her, looked at her missing ear, and winced.

"At least you'll save money on earrings, right?" Lucem winked. He opened his pack and pulled out some large, flat leaves. "I always carry these around. Silverweed leaves. Good for healing even the worst of wounds. Hold this against your wound. It'll soothe you."

Elory took one of the leaves, and she winced when she touched it to her wound, expecting a blast of pain. But Lucem was right; the pain dulled, and coolness spread across the flames. Meliora took another leaf and held it to her wounded face.

"Break it down!" rose a screech outside.

The boulders shook. One stone—the size of a fist—came free and tumbled from the barricade.

"We have to move." Meliora touched Elory's head, her fingers gentle. "Can you walk, sister? We have to go now. This barricade won't hold for long."

Elory nodded. Holding the leaf to her wound with one hand, her sickle in the other, she rose to her feet. "Let's go see if Lucem doomed us to a slow death in darkness."

He gasped. "Oh, my dear heart! Never thank the hero." He sighed. "Let's go explore. Meliora, the human torch, would you be so kind as to lead the way?"

Meliora sighed. "I liked him better when he was a hermit."

She began to walk, heading down the tunnel into the deep blackness. As the screams still rose outside, Elory and Lucem followed.

VALE

In the dawn, they crossed the last rivulet, reaching the end of the delta. Behind them spread lush lands of fresh water, fruit trees, and wildlife. Before them stretched the coast, snaking into the horizon, nothing but sand on the left, sea on the right.

"Well, dear boy." Tash nodded. "Not much water or food ahead, and according to my map, it'll be another two or three days of walking. We need some water for the road."

Vale stared ahead at the coast. As lush and green as the delta was behind him, the land ahead was barren, nothing but golden and blue sea, no freshwater or fruit trees to be seen.

"It might not be seraphim, zamzummim, or gold-laying centipedes that kill us then." He smiled wryly. "It might be thirst. We'll have nothing but seawater for the rest of the journey. Unless you want to sneak into town and steal a few canteens."

"No need, my boy!" Tash flashed him a grin. From her leather pack, she pulled out a second treasure—the glass bottle she had found in the centipede's lair. The deep golden whiskey swirled inside. "We've got a bottle."

"Good." Vale reached toward it. "Spill out the whiskey and fill up water from that stream. Last freshwater we'll see for a while."

Tash gasped, eyes wide. She pulled the bottle to her chest. "You did not just say that."

He groaned. "Tash!"

"Don't you Tash me!" She cradled the bottle against her chest as if it were a babe. "This is precious stuff. We can't just spill it away." She bit her lip, and a wry look came into her eyes.

"You're not suggesting we drink it." Vale sighed. "That's seraphim juice."

She snorted. "Oh, you think everything fine and luxurious is for seraphim. But back in the day, we Vir Requis knew how to enjoy life. I still do." She uncorked the bottle and sat down under a pomegranate tree. "Now there's a lot in here, so I'm going to need your help."

Vale glanced at the pomegranates that hung above her. "We can drill into the fruits' shells and fill them with water."

"Sit now and drink!" Tash reached up, grabbed his hand, and yanked him down.

He sat with a groan. The stream gurgled at their side, and the branches of the pomegranate tree swayed, and the sea whispered in the distance. Tash drank deeply from the bottle, then smacked her lips.

"I detect an elegant bouquet of apple flavors and brown sugar, a hint of vanilla and caramel, and an undertone of maple and oak."

Vale raised his eyebrow. "Are you drinking spirits or a perfume shop?"

She handed him the bottle. "Try it."

He took a sip, forced himself to swallow, and grimaced.

"Well, do you taste the oaky apple flavors?" Tash asked.

He shuddered. "I taste all the things you did, at least after they were burned in dragonfire."

"Now you're getting the hang of it!"

She took the bottle from him, drank again, then handed it back.

Vale took another sip and winced. "And you really call this *luxury*?"

She nodded. "This is living, my boy." She leaned against the tree and grinned. "Relaxing under a tree, a stream flowing by our side, a beach below, dawn rising around us . . . good drink and good company." Her smile faded, and she looked into his eyes. "These moments don't last long, Vale. Not for us Vir Requis. Let's savor this moment while we can. This memory might have to sustain us on dark paths ahead."

He drank again. This time it didn't taste quite as bad.

They passed the bottle back and forth as dawn rose, and every sip was easier, and soon Vale found himself lying on his back, looking up at the swaying branches, the pomegranates, the blue sky above, the whispering beach in the distance.

A memory to last, he thought. *A good moment to savor.*

Yet what did he know of such things? Tash had scolded him that he could not laugh, could not have fun, and she had been right. There was something broken inside him. Something that had broken in Tofet. Something that he didn't think all the rivers, seas, or bottles could wash away.

Why do I live? he thought. *Why do I fight on when there's no hope for my life? Even if I could remain here forever in beauty, the nightmares would remain inside me. I've left Tofet, but Tofet will never leave me. I died on the ziggurat, pinned above the city. No matter how long I draw breath, I died that day.*

Tash spoke softly at his side. "It's beautiful here, but more than anything, I want to see the beauty of Requiem. All those places from the stories. There are no pomegranate or fig or date trees there, but there are different trees. Birch trees that spread for miles in a great forest, the place where the first Vir Requis lived wild. There is no sea, but there's the great Ranin River, fabled in the tales for its icy fresh waters. I was born here in Saraph, and for five hundred years, we lived here, but this is not our home. Our home lies across the sea."

Vale touched his iron collar. In Requiem he would not lie under a tree. He would fly over forests, fields, and ancient halls of marble and light.

"In my dreams," he said, "I saw the sky so many times. The sky is always pale searing blue or endless black here in Saraph, the color of steel and death, and the sun is always white and cruel. But in Requiem the sky is of many colors, a painting in gold, blue, purple, and all the colors of fire. Some days there are clouds, and some days there are storms. Some days it rains and on others the sun shines. Some nights the stars are hidden, and in others, the Draco constellation shines brilliantly above. But it's always our sky, ours to touch, ours to find. Do you know the old prayer of Requiem, Tash?"

She nodded, eyes damp. Her voice was but a whisper. "Requiem! May our wings forever find your sky."

And that is why I live on, Vale thought. *That is why I fight. Issari gave me this life, not so I could live in pain, but so that I could find that sky again.*

Tash hefted the bottle. Only a few swigs inside swirled. "Only two little sippies left. For Requiem!"

She drank and passed him the bottle.

"For Requiem," he said softly and emptied the bottle.

Tash nestled up against him and stroked his hair. "You will find that sky, Prince Vale Aeternum, son of Requiem. You will fly there as your forebears did, our great kings of old. You will be a king to us, and I will fly with you. Always."

He lay on his back, and she curled up against him, her head resting on his shoulder, her leg tossed across his leg, her arm across his chest. He stroked her hair—long, soft brown hair. His hands had always held pickaxes, stones, bricks; he had never imagined anything could feel so good to the touch. She looked up at him, pushed herself onto her elbow, and her hair draped around them in curtains, and he kissed her.

The world is full of want and pain, he thought. *My homeland lies in ruin, my father cries out in chains, and my mother lies underground. But right here, right now, the world is good. Right here I am in beauty with a woman I love. Let this be a small fire that warms us for the road ahead.*

His hand trailed across her body, moving down to the valley of her waist, where her skin was bare and smooth, then up the hill of her hip, where her silk trousers did not shield the warmth and softness beneath. She reached under his tunic, stroking his chest, and he hesitated, stiffened, but she kissed him and whispered softly.

"For years I pleasured men in the gardens and beds of Shayeen. I know where to nibble, to lick, to stroke, to bite, to drive men wild until they scream. But I don't want to do this to you, Vale. Those are mere tricks for petty lords. Let me love you truly. As a woman loves a man. And I want you to love me back, for I'm yours. Not only my body but my heart, my soul, my love. I've never given them to another, but I give all these to you, son of Requiem."

And at that moment, Vale loved her—loved her more than he had ever thought he could love another, loved her with a passion as great as dragonfire, as wonderful and all-consuming as flying as a dragon. He kissed her again, and their hands moved across each other's bodies, seeking, stroking, then moving faster, tearing at their clothes with an urgency only matched by their kisses.

Her body was so slender, so soft, a thing of such frailty and beauty that it seemed impossible that it should exist in this world. His hand cupped her small breast, and her hand reached down to stroke him, and she closed her eyes, lay on her back, took him inside her. He moved atop her, and it was like flying, like gliding on the winds of Requiem. They flew together as dragons, forgetting their collars, coming together like sky and stars, like prayers and song.

They blazed together like dragonfire, and she cried out, and he closed his eyes, lay atop her. She wrapped her arms around him, kissing his tears.

"It's all right, my prince." She stroked his hair. "Why do you weep?"

"Because this is precious," he whispered. "Because this is good. Because I'm happy."

She kissed his cheeks again and again until his tears were gone, then grinned and bit her lip. "Let's do it again."

For the first time in his life, Vale laughed.

MELIORA

They walked through the caves, her halo lighting their way, seeking a way out from darkness.

The wounds on her cheek still stung, a throbbing pain that worked down her jaw and neck. Her belly ached with hunger, her throat begged for water, and she was so weary—she had not slept for two days and nights—that her limbs shook. But worse than all was the fear, a coiling beast inside her. A fear of the dark. A fear of losing her way in shadows, of a slow death underground.

She turned toward the others. The light of her halo painted them red and orange. Elory walked holding a fresh leaf to what remained of her ear, and she held her sickle in her other hand. Sweat beaded on her brow despite the cold, and her eyes were sunken. Blood still stained her ragged tunic. Lucem walked at her side, his hand placed against the small of her back, shepherding her onward, and he held his spear.

"Lucem, have you ever walked this far deep?" Meliora asked.

The young man shook his head. "Never. I've only ever taken a few steps into these caves." He grinned. "Exciting, isn't it? We're explorers!"

Meliora groaned. "Exciting is discovering an almond in a bowl of walnuts. We need to find a way out. We cannot die here in the darkness. Not only our lives are at stake but all of Requiem."

"Cheery one, you are." Lucem nodded. "No pressure or anything. Only an entire nation depending on us. Maybe a little whistling will ease the tension?"

He rounded his lips and began to whistle an old tune when the shrieks rose behind them.

They all grimaced. The screams sounded far away, almost inaudible, but chilled Meliora's spine.

"Dark seraphim," Elory whispered. "They're breaking in."

Meliora cursed. "We need to hurry. We need to see if these tunnels lead to another exit in the mountains."

"That or find a hidden army in here." Lucem nodded. "About a thousand troops hiding away could really come in handy around now." He yanked at his collar. "Especially if they had the keys to these things."

Meliora groaned and began walking quickly, and the others followed. No, they would not find a key here in the darkness. The Keymaker still lived many miles away, and Meliora's hope for ever finding him began to fade. Even should she escape these caves, how would she make it across the mountains with the dark seraphim in pursuit—the most dangerous criminals to have ever lived in Saraph?

I was a foolish girl, she thought. *Just a foolish princess with delusions of grandeur, sure that I could become a savior, a messiah to Requiem.* She lowered her head. *Just a silly girl. I won't even make it to the Keymaker, let alone return with salvation and lead my people home.*

Perhaps sensing her turmoil, Elory walked closer. The young woman hung her sickle from her belt, reached out, and took Meliora's hand in hers. The hand was so small, like the hand of a child, and Elory didn't stand taller than Meliora's shoulder, and yet there was comfort here, there was strength that Meliora knew she could lean on.

"We'll find a way out." Elory's eyes shone in the firelight. "I know this. You did not fly through fire to die in darkness. When I saw you fly above a nation, a great dragon all in silver and gold, I knew that someday you would lead us home. I believe in you, Meliora. You led us this far. You will lead us onward."

Who says I want to be a leader? Meliora thought. Her eyes stung and her chest constricted. *I'm just a princess, that's all. Just a pampered princess, innocent, naive. I'm no heroine like the great Priestess Issari or Queen Gloriae. I cannot become the leader you want.*

Yet when Meliora looked into her sister's brown eyes, she saw such hope there, such admiration, that Meliora could not bear to crush that light, even if that light should soon fade. She nodded and squeezed Elory's hand.

"We'll find a way out, Elory. I promise you."

The scream sounded again behind them. It seemed closer now. The dark seraphim had entered the caves. Meliora tightened her lips and walked on.

The tunnel soon forked, and Meliora hesitated for a moment. One tunnel seemed wider, sloping upward; the other was narrow, sinking deeper.

"Which way do we go?" Elory asked. "The wider tunnel is a more natural choice, but the dark seraphim will know this. They'll follow us there."

Meliora thought for a moment. "Wait here." She stepped into the narrow tunnel that delved downward, tore off a strip of her cloak, and placed it on the ground. Then she walked back to the fork. "We take the wider tunnel."

As they walked onward, Meliora frowned and stared at the tunnel wall. She paused, moved closer, and let her halo illuminate the stone. The surface was smooth, and engravings appeared upon it.

"We're not the first ones to enter here." She placed her hand against the wall. "Look."

Figures were engraved onto the wall, life-sized: a goat, a lion, an eagle, and a man. Runes appeared around them in a language Meliora did not recognize. In the crackling firelight, the figures seemed almost to move.

"Who would enter so deeply into these caves to engrave these?" Elory asked.

Meliora frowned. "I'm not sure these are caves." She shuddered. "They might be man-made tunnels."

Lucem examined the engravings. "Man-made? The lion might have helped a bit." He clawed the air. "Claws and all."

They kept walking, and the tunnel grew wider, the walls and floor smoothing out. The firelight revealed engravings on the ceiling, these ones of flaming wheels. An acidic smell filled the air, and distant shrieks echoed like ghosts.

"Look at that." Elory pointed.

A towering engraving appeared upon a wall, showing a mountain of corpses. Men, women, children—all lay dead, eyes closed, mouths open in anguish, and above them blazed a fiery wagon wheel. More runes appeared here, coiling around the mountain of the dead.

"I know this symbol," Meliora whispered. "The flaming wheel." She shuddered. "The wheel of the Living Creatures."

"The Living Creatures?" Lucem asked. "Doesn't sound so bad. Better than the Living Monsters or the Undead Creatures." A shriek rose from behind, and Lucem winced. "And better than the dark seraphim that follow."

Meliora wasn't so sure. "There's an old legend of them in Saraph, but few ever repeat it. It's said that after the fall from Edinnu, when the seraphim lost the rebellion against the gods, we wandered this world, hurt and afraid and alone. It's said that the Eight Gods—the ones we rebelled against—sought to slay us in our new world. A wheel of fire appeared in the sky that day, and creatures descended from it." Meliora shuddered. "It's said that the Living Creatures were four, but that their wings were connected, so that they had to always walk together. It's said they killed many seraphim."

Lucem sighed. "Nothing but trouble since you two showed up. I was enjoying my little hill and carob trees, and now it's dark seraphim, Living Creatures, and stars know what's next."

They continued walking, and the tunnel kept curving, branching off, a dark labyrinth. At every fork, Meliora placed a scrap of her cloak in one way, then took the other path, trying to remember the way, soon realizing she was lost. Yet no matter how winding the path, the screeches rose louder behind them. Soon Meliora could make out voices.

"They walk into darkness, comrades! Our meals scurry ahead."

Laughter rolled through the caves.

"They seek to trick us with cloth!"

"We smell them, comrades! Smell their fear. Follow the scent! Drink their blood."

Lucem grimaced. "They're getting closer."

Meliora glared at him. "We're in a tunnel. The sky is up. The sun is hot. Any more obvious facts you want to remind me of?"

He groaned. "Yes—we need to move faster. Come on!"

They began to run. The tunnels twisted madly, and Meliora no longer bothered leaving scraps of cloth; pointless, if the seraphim were tracking their scent. The tunnels widened,

soon the size of temple halls. Meliora's halo barely lit the
shadows here, but she thought she made out engravings of
battles across the walls and ceiling. She glimpsed an eagle's head,
a lion's, a goat's, engraved larger than men upon the walls, and
everywhere the stone corpses and flaming wheels. Here was a
great tomb for the memory of that ancient slaughter, the Eight
Gods' last vengeance against the seraphim.

"We smell them ahead, siblings!" rose a cry—the shrill
voice of Leyleet. "We smell them, those who slew one among us.
We will split them open! We will pull out their ribs! We will saw
them in half! We will keep them alive so they scream!"

Lucem cringed as he ran. "Wow, they can saw you in half
and keep you alive? That's talent!"

"I'd rather they picked up painting," Elory said, running at
his side. "Maybe flower arrangement?"

Lucem flashed her a grin. "You made a funny! That's
great."

"Shut it, you two, and run!" Meliora said, racing down the
shadowy nave.

As the laughter of the dark seraphim rolled behind, they
ran on down the chasm. In the darkness, Meliora could only see
a few steps ahead, and she skidded to a halt when she reached
the dead end. Elory and Lucem stopped with her, panting and
drenched with sweat.

A stone wall towered ahead, and upon it was engraved a
massive wagon wheel, taller than Meliora, stony flames rising
from it.

"Damn it," Meliora said. "A dead end."

Elory spun around and drew her sickle. Lucem hefted his
spear, and Meliora raised her sword. In the darkness the
screeches of the dark seraphim still sounded, coming closer with
every heartbeat.

"Blood!" they cried.

"Bones!"

"Organs!"

"Kill, crush, eat!"

Meliora took a deep breath. "We fight. Here is our final
stand." She raised her chin. "There are fifteen of them, only
three of us, but Requiem has always faced unsurmountable odds,

and we've always overcome. For Requiem! For a memory of dragons. For—"

"Will you be quiet and help me?" Lucem said.

She spun around to see him grabbing the stony wheel engraved onto the wall, tugging at its spokes. "What are you doing, Lucem?"

He groaned. "Thought I'd plant a flower bed. What do you think I'm doing? It's a door, Your Highness! Help me open it."

Meliora's eyes widened. Indeed, as Lucem tugged, the wagon wheel engraving shed dust, creaking on the wall. She grabbed another stone spoke, and Elory grabbed another, and they pulled together.

The wheel creaked, then turned an inch. Another inch.

The wall trembled. They kept tugging, and the wheel gave a great turn, a full foot, and then loosened with showering dust. A lock clicked somewhere deep in the wall, and the great stone wheel swung inward like a door.

A chamber awaited beyond, awash with golden light. Elory entered the chamber first, followed by Lucem. Meliora entered last, then shoved herself against the round door, pushing it shut with a thud.

The sound of the dark seraphim faded behind the stone.

For just an instant, Meliora felt a sense of relief, of safety . . . and then she heard the creaking.

"Oh stars," Elory whispered, reaching out to grasp Meliora's hand.

Slowly, Meliora turned around from the door. She felt the blood drain from her face.

The chamber was large and round, surrounded with decorative columns carved into the walls. Old bones and skulls lay strewn across the floor. In the chamber's center rose a stone dais, and a great wheel of fire surrounded it, spinning and casting out light. In the center of the fire stood four creatures, glittering like burnished bronze.

They had the bodies of men but cloven hooves, and each had four faces and four wings. One was the face of a man, the second of a goat, the third of a lion, and the fourth of an eagle. The creatures were joined to one another by the tips of their wings, forcing them to stand abreast. Eyes blinked all across those wings, gazing in all directions.

"The Living Creatures," Meliora whispered. "They still exist."

Lucem leaned toward her. "The sky is up, Mel. The sky is up."

The Living Creatures took a step forward across their stone dais. Their four bodies moved as one, connected at the wings. Their many heads stared, and the eyes upon their wings blinked. Not only the flaming wheel cast light, but the creatures' bronze bodies emitted a light of their own, searing and cruel.

"Living Creatures!" Meliora said, kneeling before them. "We are Vir Requis, children of the stars, natives of this world. We come to praise your name! We—"

"You are of Saraph."

The sixteen heads spoke together—lions, goats, eagles, and men all uttering the words as one. The voices were deep, echoing, metallic, voices from another world.

"I am Vir Requis—" Meliora began.

The heads creaked, turning toward her, the eyes glittering. The Living Creatures took another step forward, and their arms rose, tipped with crimson claws. "We smell the smell of Saraph. We see the halo burn. The foul seraphim, traitors of the gods— we fed upon them. Yet they imprisoned us in stone. For five thousand years we lingered here, buried alive, but we never forgot your scent. The stench of betrayal. The stench of traitors." The flaming wheels spun madly around the creatures. Their claws rose, pointing at her, and the creatures' eyes blazed, casting out white light. "You will burn in the wheel of fire!"

The flaming wheel spun madly, then rose to hover above the Living Creatures like a crown, like the halo above Meliora's own head. They stepped off the dais, advancing toward her.

"You will not touch her!" Elory shouted, racing forward and raising her sickle.

Lucem ran forth too, hefting his spear. "You stand before the Queen of Requiem, Living Creatures. She is not yours to touch."

The Living Creatures raised their claws higher, and blasts of light and heat rippled out, slamming into Elory and Lucem.

They cried out and fell, banging against the stone floor. The wheel crackled madly, and heat drenched the room. Meliora fell back against the closed stone door.

"Stop this!" she cried. "Living Creatures, I have no wings! Seraphim have wings, yet I have none." She spun around to show them her back, then faced them again. "Seraphim bear halos of soft light, yet mine is a halo of fire—much like the wheel that burns above you. I praise you, Living Creatures! I kneel before you. I—"

"Silence!" they cried. "We smell your stench. We smell the blood of seraphim. The air reeks with you. And so you will die, seraph child, for your kind betrayed the Eight Gods. You have entered your tomb."

Elory and Lucem leaped forward.

"Requiem!" they cried together, charging with their weapons.

The Living Creatures roared, a sound that pounded across the chamber, rippling the air. Energy blasted out from them, slamming into Elory and Lucem, lifting them into the air, slamming them against the walls. Elory screamed and fell, fresh blood gushing from the wound of her severed ear. Lucem's head slammed against the wall, and he moaned and slumped down. And still the Living Creatures advanced toward Meliora, the four bodies moving together, the eyes glaring, the crimson claws rising to strike.

"Die," they hissed. "Die . . . die . . ."

Meliora stared at them, her meager halo's light drowned beneath their eternal flame. In the distance, barely audible, she heard other screams, heard claws against stone, the cackles of the hungry.

"You speak of smelling seraphim," Meliora said. "And you are correct. But that stench is not from me." She reached behind her and grabbed the stone door. "Saraph invades your tomb! I reveal to you the traitors!"

She tugged the stone door open again.

Behind her, in the corridor, wailed the dark seraphim.

"Seraphim, seraphim!" cried the Living Creatures. "Traitors with dark wings!"

Meliora leaped aside, scurried toward Lucem and Elory, and knelt by them.

The Living Creatures blazed with rage, fire blasting from their wheel, their bronze bodies casting out lightning. They charged, claws lashing, crying out in rage. The dark seraphim screamed, covered their eyes, fell back.

"The Living Creatures!" they cried. "The vengeance of the gods!"

Meliora shielded Lucem and Elory with her body, watching the devastation unfold.

A few dark seraphim charged into the room, flying toward the Living Creatures with lashing claws and snapping teeth. The Living Creatures' wheel of fire spun madly, casting out flames, slamming them into the dark seraphim. Lightning bolts blasted from the bronze bodies of the creatures, and their many mouths opened to scream.

One dark seraph fell, clutching its chest. Another slammed against the wall, cracking its armor. And still the fire blazed and lightning struck. Meliora pushed herself deeper into the corner, covering her eyes against the terrible light.

"Traitors to the gods!" cried the Living Creatures. "Dark ones, foul ones, cursed ones! The betrayers of Edinnu shall perish."

Another dark seraph crashed down, armor split open. The Living Creatures grabbed the man, pulled him up, tore him open, and the animal heads ripped through the flesh.

The Living Creatures made for the doorway, and for the first time in five thousand years, they left the stone prison. With their wings connected, they had to turn sideways, walking like crabs through the round opening. Still their fire and lightning blasted out, knocking dark seraphim aside. The cursed ones screamed in pain, burning, falling before the wrath of the gods.

"Come on!" Meliora said, grabbing Elory and Lucem and hoisting them to their feet. "We're getting out of here."

The two swayed, bloodied and bruised, but managed to heft their weapons and nod. Swinging her sword before her, Meliora leaped out the round doorway after the Living Creatures. Elory and Lucem followed, holding hands and swinging their own weapons.

The nave spread before them, large as an imperial hall. The Living Creatures were moving forward, their four bodies abreast, the eyes upon their connected wings blinking and casting out streamers of light. The luminous strands slammed into dark seraphim, cracking their armor. Another one of the cursed deities fell, gushing out the golden ichor of Saraph. The surviving dark seraphim flew in the chamber, swinging their sickles, chopping at the Living Creatures, but the godly warriors' bodies were like bronze, and the sickles sparked against them but could not cut them.

Above all soared Leyleet, Queen of the Dark. Her wings were spread wide, and the fire blazed across her, but she only laughed, her eyes alight.

"The gods are fools!" She cackled. "I spit upon the Eight Gods. I will slay their champions like a child slays ants."

The dark queen swooped, face twisted with rage, swinging her sickle at the Living Creatures, blasting out dark fire from her eyes. The gods of vengeance turned toward her as one, raising their claws, casting out their light. The flames exploded and the nave shook. Cracks ran across the walls and stones fell from the ceiling.

"Run!" Meliora shouted, racing through the battle.

Elory and Lucem ran at her side. They raced around the Living Creatures, and Meliora ducked as a blast of lightning flew over her head. Elory yelped and leaped aside, dodging a roaring pillar of fire. The walls kept shaking and boulders fell from above. One stone landed before Meliora and shattered, and she leaped over the debris.

"The traitors will die!" cried the Living Creatures, sixteen heads speaking together. "The cursed shall be cleansed from the earth."

Meliora kept running. A dark seraph swooped, sickle flashing. Meliora swung the Amber Sword, diverting the blow with a shower of sparks. Another dark seraph flew toward Lucem, and he roared and thrust his spear, knocking it back. Still the fire and light of the Living Creatures filled the hall, their bronze bodies gleaming, their heads roaring and shrieking, and their hooves shattered the floor as they advanced.

As they kept running, Meliora saw the tunnel taper ahead, leading to a narrow corridor. If they could just enter there, make their way into the shadows . . .

A great shriek pierced the hall. Wreathed in black fire, eyes blazing white like stars, Leyleet swooped toward them. A wound still gushed on her thigh from Elory's sword.

"For Requiem!" Meliora cried. A boulder crashed down before her. She leaped onto it and vaulted through the air.

Leyleet flew toward her, sickle flashing.

With a scream, Meliora—still airborne—swung her blade. The Amber Sword arched. The sickle lashed. Meliora ducked her head, and the blade scraped across the top of her hair, shearing the stubble even shorter. The Amber Sword slammed into Leyleet's armor and knocked the dark queen back, cracking her breastplate. With a shout below, Lucem tossed his spear, and the weapon flew and slammed into Leyleet's chest, digging into her flesh.

Meliora landed on the ground.

Leyleet screeched.

Meliora ran, pulling Elory and Lucem with her, and they leaped into the tunnel ahead. Light flashed and fire blazed as the Living Creatures charged, and Leyleet screamed again, awash in their rage, her voice rising so loudly the walls crumbled and boulders rained.

Leaving the fire behind, Meliora, Lucem, and Elory raced through the narrow tunnel, breath ragged. When the way forked, Meliora looked for her pieces of cloth, though she hardly needed to; the acrid stench of the dark seraphim, the very stench that had saved her life, was a better path.

Finally they saw daylight ahead, and they burst outside onto hills and mountains awash with sunbeams. The landscape spread into the horizons, barren, lifeless, and beautiful.

We're alive. Oh stars, we're alive. There is still hope for Requiem.

Elory fell to her knees, breathing raggedly, blood staining her neck and shoulder. In the daylight, Meliora could see that at least half the ear was gone; only a shell remained around the canal. Lucem gasped for breath; a thousand cuts and bruises covered him. Meliora's own clothes were bloody, and the wounds on her cheek blazed like embers pressed against her face.

"Elory, up." Meliora reached down to her. "On your feet, Elory. Now."

Lucem glared. "She's hurt."

"She'll be more than hurt if we don't move. We don't yet know who'll win the battle in the caves. If Leyleet is still alive, if she triumphs, she'll never stop hunting us. Elory, up! Lucem, help her. Carry her if you must. We must move."

Shuddering, her breath sawing, Elory rose to her feet. Lucem wrapped an arm around her, and she slung her arms around his neck. Meliora led the way. They raced across the hills, heading down into a valley, then up another slope. The sunlight blazed down, drenching them with sweat. From the cave the echoes of battle still sounded.

As they ran, Meliora stared ahead into the northwest. Somewhere there, beyond the hazy white horizon, it lay. The mountain of Khalish. The Keymaker. Hope for a crumbling nation. They raced onward.

JAREN

It was past midnight when the door creaked open and evil, cloaked and hooded, entered Jaren's hut.

Jaren had been up most of the night, healing the wounded of Tofet, guiding the dying to their rest, and whispering words of comfort to the grieving. Every night now, more wounded visited his door, and more dead piled up, a slow genocide, the old, the weak, the young, all perishing under the whips and heels of Saraph. Under Queen Kalafi's rule, the slaves had labored to build great monuments, and while they suffered, the queen had cared to keep most of them alive, to keep her labor force at work.

But Ishtafel, it seemed, delighted in torture for its own sake, delighted in working more and more slaves to death every day. And every day it was Jaren who prayed over the pits of the dead.

Days of labor in the heat. Nights of healing and prayer. A slow agony, a slow dying, an endless waiting for hope that might never come, for children who might never return. The torturous wait for an ancient race to fall—not in battle, not in glory, but a death stretched out, twisted, with more hope for the relief of death than for a savior.

Jaren lay on the straw on the floor. Shivering even in the heat. Alone in darkness.

"Be safe, Meliora, Vale, Elory," he whispered. "Return to me. Return with the treasures or return with your lives. We all pray for you, my children. We—"

The creaking door interrupted him.

Jaren pushed himself onto his elbows as the wooden door opened. A cloaked shadow stood outside, holding a lamp.

"Kerish, is that you?" Jaren asked, rising to his feet. "Is the wound on your leg still aching, is—"

The figure stepped into the hut, and Jaren lost his breath. Golden eyes blazed within the figure's hood, the pupils shaped as sunbursts casting out their rays.

A seraph.

"My lord!" Jaren said. "How may I serve you? I—"

The seraph pulled back his hood, and Jaren lost his breath.

A cold, handsome face stared back at him, ageless yet ancient. The jaw was square, the hair golden. An ugly scar rifted the man's face, crawling from the corner of the jaw, across the nose, and onto the brow—the mark of a flaming halo pressed against the flesh. The seraph's eyes were like flames themselves, horrible to behold, yet cold, soulless, the eyes of a beast.

Ishtafel.

"My lord," Jaren whispered, kneeling before him.

Every fiber inside of Jaren screamed. He wanted to charge at Ishtafel, to pummel him. He still had some strength in him. He wanted to grab the seraph's neck, to squeeze, to crush.

You murdered my wife, Ishtafel thought, trembling. *You kidnapped my daughter and tried to rape her. You nailed my son to the ziggurat's crest. You murdered a hundred thousand of my people.* His breath shook. *You destroyed Requiem and put a nation in chains.*

"Yes," Ishtafel hissed, looking down at him. "I see the rage in you, the hatred. That's good. Hatred will keep you alive more than hope, more than prayer. And it makes this little game so much more fun. Rise, Jaren Aeternum. That is your name, is it not?"

Jaren rose to his feet, unable to douse the rage inside him, but knowing that this seraph could shatter his bones like a child snapping twigs, knowing that he had to live, that he had to survive this night. For his children. For all the wounded who still needed him.

"Yes, my lord," he whispered.

Ishtafel nodded, lips stretching into a thin smile. "Aeternum, Aeternum . . . the name of an old weredragon dynasty, is it not? Your family once ruled the throne of the reptilian kingdom."

"That was a long time ago, my lord."

Ishtafel frowned. "And yet . . . and yet you long for those days to return, do you not?" He glanced up at the ceiling, at the

Draco constellation that was engraved there. "You still dream of Requiem, I see."

Jaren lowered his head. "A man can still dream, my lord, even while serving."

Ishtafel's hand reached out, fast as a striking snake, and grabbed Jaren's throat. The fingers squeezed.

Jaren gasped for breath. Stars spread before his eyes. The tendons in his neck creaked. Bringing his face close, Ishtafel snarled, and now those eyes blazed with unadulterated hatred.

"You sent your children into the wild," he hissed. "Vale, the worm I pinned to my palace. Elory, the pathetic little wench who fled my bed. And Meliora . . . sweetest Meliora, my sister, your daughter." Ishtafel barked a laugh. "That makes us related, doesn't it, old man? You bedded my mother, didn't you? She was a fine woman. Beautiful. Lovely teats I loved to suck on myself as a baby. Of course, I enjoyed sucking her blood more."

"My—my lord!" Jaren managed. "If you would kill me, then kill me. I—"

Ishtafel released his grip, tossing Jaren down. He fell to his knees, clutched his throat, gasped for breath.

"Kill you?" Ishtafel laughed. "But then my fun would end! How would I torture you if you were dead? No, old man." Ishtafel drove down his heel, stomping Jaren's wrist, pinning his hand down, creaking the bones. "I want you to live, Jaren Aeternum. I want you to live to see your people die, your children suffer, your nation collapse."

"Why?" Jaren whispered, hoarse, his wrist twisted under Ishtafel's boot. "We build you monuments. We dig bitumen. Why—"

"I need no more monuments, old man. All my work in this world is completed, all my enemies conquered. But now I found a new task, a new game. To slowly destroy Requiem. Life by life. A slow death." Ishtafel licked his lips. "And you will be the last to die, heir of reptilian kings."

Ishtafel released his heel, and Jaren pulled his wounded arm to his chest, cradling the wrist. "Is that why you came here?" Jaren whispered, staring at Ishtafel. "To tell me that?"

Ishtafel raised his eyebrows. "Oh, but that would be so rude! To simply come unannounced to bandy words? No, Jaren.

I came here to bring you something. A gift." He reached into his cloak, pulled out a bundle of cloth, and tossed it at Jaren. "A memento from Elory. Enjoy what remains of her, for you won't see the rest of her again."

With that, Ishtafel turned and marched out of the hut.

Jaren didn't want to look, didn't want to know, but his fingers seemed to move on their own, unfolding the bundle.

His breath caught and he wrapped up the cloth again. He closed his eyes, but he still saw it there: a bloody ear. Elory's ear.

His breath burst into a pant now, his heart into a gallop, and the hut spun around him.

Elory . . . oh stars, Elory . . .

Sweat soaked Jaren, and his head wouldn't stop spinning. He had to do something, to bury it, to find Elory, to save her if she still lived. He had to lean against the wall, and blackness spread across him.

Shivering, he stepped out into the night.

The huts of Tofet spread around him in the blackness. The land was silent but for the scattered sounds of weeping and moaning. The air was hot, soupy, and his sweat wouldn't dry. Jaren forced himself to walk, each step a struggle, each breath a battle, until he reached a patch of dry earth. He buried the ear there, buried a piece of his daughter, and the memory of burying his wife filled him, a memory like a demon, clawing inside him. He fell to his knees in the dirt between the huts, and his tears fell.

I spend my nights healing others, but how can I heal my daughter? How can I stop this pain?

He lowered his head and closed his eyes.

Please, stars of Requiem, if you can hear my prayers from this place, show me mercy, show me your light.

And in the darkness, the light of stars shone.

Kneeling in the dust, Jaren raised his head, and above him he saw columns woven of starlight, pale birches coated in frost, a glittering hall all in light. The pain, the fear, the weariness, all seemed to fade in this place, and Jaren floated through the halls of ancient Requiem.

Figures were moving between the columns, appearing, vanishing, cloaked in white. Harp strings played, echoing, fading, notes from many songs. He glimpsed ancient kings and queens, heroes and heroines, warriors and priests, the ghosts of old Requiem, those who had fought the demons, the griffins, the phoenixes, the countless enemies who had tried to topple these halls. All now memories, myths, beams of starlight, and fragments of song.

Ahead Jaren could make out three figures, all cloaked in light. When he drew closer, they came into focus, the light parting to reveal their forms.

A woman sat on a throne, golden locks framing her pale face. Her eyes shone blue-green, and she wore pale armor. Here was Queen Gloriae Aeternum who had raised Requiem from ruin and restored her to glory. At her left side stood a young prince, his yellow hair falling across his brow, his brown eyes eager—Kyrie Eleison, guardian of the throne. At the queen's right side stood a young woman, tall and clad in leggings and a tan vest, her mane of black curls cascading across her shoulders—Agnus Dei, the queen's twin sister, a woman who had slain many enemies of Requiem.

My ancestors, Jaren thought, kneeling before them. *The great warriors of Requiem who rebuilt our nation from only seven survivors.*

Queen Gloriae rose from her throne and held up her hand. "Rise, Jaren Aeternum, son of Requiem."

At her side, Agnus Dei tilted her head and squinted. "He looks a bit like me. Same noble eyes."

Young Kyrie snorted. "There are warthogs who look nobler than you do, Agnus Dei. Don't insult the man."

Her eyes widened, and Agnus Dei let out a roar. "Be quiet, pup! Or I'm going to ram into you like a warthog."

"You're thinking of bulls," Kyrie said. "Bulls ram. Warthogs just rut in the dirt and mud."

"Oh, you enjoyed rutting in the mud last time we went out on a hike," Agnus Dei said, smiling crookedly, and Kyrie blushed a deep crimson.

"Hush, Agnus Dei!" the boy said.

Queen Gloriae glared at the two. "Hush the both of you!" She returned her eyes to Jaren, and her gaze softened. "Forgive their frivolity, my son, for here is a realm where all worries, all pain have ended."

Kyrie snorted. "Not when Agnus Dei slaps me. That still hurts."

Agnus Dei raised her fist. "I'm going to pound you to prove it, pup."

"Hush!" Gloriae said again. She stepped closer to Jaren, placed her hands on his shoulders, and smiled. The starlight clung to her, spreading out to warm him, to soothe him. "Your stars do not forget you, Jaren. Nor do the souls of your ancestors. We've heard your prayers, and we weep for the pain we see in the world. We weep that we cannot fight for Requiem anymore, for our wars have ended, and the torch has passed. To you, Jaren. To your children. They are alive, my son. They still quest for hope, though the road is full of many dangers, and much darkness must pass before the light shines upon them. Do not abandon your hope, for hope shines even in the greatest darkness. So long as you can draw another breath, take another step, live for another heartbeat—there is hope." She leaned forward and kissed his cheek. "Sometimes you cannot see the stars, but they always shine. Even when blinded, even in total darkness, there is always light."

That light now grew brighter, streaming all across Jaren, blinding him, healing him, and when he could see again, he was back in the dirt of Tofet.

Had he fainted, merely dreamed? Or had he seen a true vision of the celestial Requiem beyond the stars? He didn't know. A voice seemed to echo within him, perhaps his own, perhaps the voice of Queen Gloriae, fading like the last note in a harp's song.

There is always hope. There is always light.

"You're alive, Elory," Jaren whispered. "I know that you're alive. Stay strong, my sweet daughter. I love you. I will see you again."

Dawn broke. Jaren rose to his feet, and his work continued.

VALE

He woke up at sunset, lying on the sand, Tash nestled against him.

Soon their journey would continue, but Vale just wanted to lie here, to never get up. A blanket of fronds covered them, hiding them from the world; should any seraphim fly above, they'd see nothing but some scattered branches on the beach. The waves whispered, and between the palm branches, Vale could see the sky fade to deep blue and gold. He lay on his back, and Tash still slept, her cheek against his chest. Her leg was tossed across his, and his arms were wrapped around her, his hand resting on the small of her back. She slept naked, her skin soft and warm against him.

He looked at her in the dying light. When awake, Tash was always speaking, singing, mumbling to herself, and prancing around. Yet sleeping, she seemed so peaceful, so young, almost fragile. She knew so much more about the world, but Vale realized how young she was—barely more than a youth.

As am I, Vale thought. *Yet I feel so much older.*

On their journey, Tash had spoken of healing him, of bringing joy back into his life. But right now, lying here, Vale felt that it was his task to protect her, to heal her, to fight the world for her.

I love you, Tash, he thought and kissed the top of her head. *I've never loved another, and you light my life. You light my life of darkness. For you, I will fight armies, I will burn the world to protect you.*

She mumbled in her sleep, lips scrunching together, and opened her eyes. She smiled at him.

"Where's my morning tea?" she asked.

He ran his fingers up and down her back. "We have a few sips of water left. How's that?"

She pouted. "I demand that you fetch me tea and cupcakes, my handsome servant."

He gave her backside a playful pat. "Once you fetch me my slippers, my lovely maid."

She gasped. "You did not just do that! Not you!" She grinned and bit her lip. "I *am* teaching you to have fun, aren't I? I knew I could do it! Soon you'll be whistling and dancing."

"Not likely," he said.

"I'm going to *make* you dance. Make you!" She crawled atop him and chomped down on his nose. "A special kind of dance, at least."

As the sun set, she tossed back her head, straddling him, moving atop him. He held her slender waist, then ran his hands across her body, marveling at every curve of her, at the softness of her skin, and she grasped his chest so tightly it almost hurt. When he could not bear it any longer, he rolled her over, and she lay beneath him, wrapping her limbs around him, and he clutched her hands and squeezed them, and she cried out his name.

They lay together, breathing deeply.

"You *are* a good dancer," Tash said.

"I'm still not singing."

She nibbled his bottom lip. "Next time I'll make you burst into song. That's my new goal." She grew serious, then wrapped her arms around him and held him close, nuzzling his neck. "You're the best I've ever had, Vale. All the other men . . . that was work. Same as your work in the fields. You're the first man I ever made true love to." She rose to her feet. "So let's go find this Chest of Plenty, because I want to do this many, many more times."

He nodded and reached for her breasts. "How about Plenty of Chest?"

She groaned and slapped his hand away. "Now you're making jokes! Lovely." She looked down at her chest. "And sadly, these little pups aren't nearly plentiful enough." She tugged him to his feet. "So let's keep going."

As the sun vanished, they walked along the beach. Only the moon lit their way. The waves rolled across their bare feet, and sea shells gleamed in the moonlight. Tash reached out and held his hand, and Vale wondered what it would be like to be free—truly free, no collar around their necks, no people waiting for them to return with a magical chest. To just . . . go out some nights with Tash and walk. Walk as far as they wanted, for as long as they wanted. To make love whenever they pleased.

And to shift into dragons.

Vale thought back to that day—that most wonderful and horrible of days. For the first time in his life, he had been without a collar, tasked with carrying heavy stones to the top of columns. For the first time, he had used his magic, become a dragon, flown into the sky, battled his enemies. The day ended with his blood, with nails driving through him, with his death upon the wall and resurrection at the hands of Issari, the Priestess in White. That day he had learned that he still had a battle to fight.

Someday I will fly again, he thought. *Someday we all will, not in battle, not for glory or blood. We'll fly together in peace, Tash and I under the moonlight.*

As they walked, they talked of the Requiem that had been, the Requiem from the stories. He spoke of the first King Aeternum, his ancestor, who had founded a kingdom for those outcast, those hunted, those who could become dragons, and of that ancient king's war against an army of demons. Tash then spoke, telling him that she was descended from the great Kyrie Eleison, a prince of Requiem who had survived the griffins, who had fought with Queen Gloriae herself to rebuild Requiem from ancient ruin. They spoke too of the legendary King Elethor and Queen Lyana who had defeated the phoenixes, the wyverns, and the nephilim, and they told tales of Requiem's tragic civil war, and how Rune and Tilla, star-crossed lovers, had fought against each other in one of Requiem's darkest hours.

"Do you think that in hundreds of years, people will tell tales of us?" Tash asked.

Vale nodded. "They'll probably tell the story about how you ate centipede shit."

She gasped. "No!" She shoved him. "Never tell anyone that story. That tale will be buried in time. Damn goldshitters!"

Vale was about to say more when a shrill cry rose in the distance.

He froze.

Tash shivered. "Ghosts," she whispered.

"There's no such thing as ghosts," Vale said.

She rolled her eyes. "Giant centipedes with human faces who poop out golden coins are real, but you think ghosts aren't."

They continued walking along the dark beach. The banshee cry did not return. The only sounds were the waves and the wind. Perhaps that's all that they had heard; the wind, no more. No clouds glided above, and the moon hung low, full and bloated and white as bone. Its light spread across the sea like a spine, rising and falling, and it seemed to Vale no longer a soft, beautiful light but sickly.

They walked onward until they saw a pale glow ahead on the beach, strands of greenish light wreathed around shadows. As they walked closer, they saw fluttering movements, dark spikes like blades, a living organism of light and darkness beached on the sand. A cry rose again, shrill and inhuman, a sound like an echo in deep chambers, soon fading.

Tash squeezed Vale's hand, staring ahead. Her face was pale in the moonlight, her lips tight.

They walked closer until details emerged, and they stood before it: a shipwreck on the beach, large as a palace. When working in Shayeen, Vale had seen many ships sail along the Te'ephim River, but he had never seen a ship so large. When still seaworthy, it must have held a thousand men. The hull now tilted, many of its planks shattered, the stern missing. The bow jutted upward, and the ship's figurehead reared toward the moon, forged of iron, shaped as a nude woman with the head of a goat. Black masts still rose, tilted, coated in mold, dripping strands of rotted rope and scraps of sails. The tattered canvas billowed in the wind, rising and falling like pale ghosts in the night. The wind moaned through the ship's hull, rattling the shattered planks, emerging from portholes and rusty cannons in a frosty haze like breath. The wreck seemed alive, moving, moaning, breathing, creaking. The moonlight limned its form, but a different light—greenish and gray—seemed to lurk within its ancient hull, seeping between the planks and bristly deck.

"We found it," Tash whispered, staring up at the wreck with wide eyes. "The ship of ghosts."

Vale grunted. "No ghosts, Tash. Just wind moaning through the hull and billowing the sails."

"There are ghosts." Tash shuddered. "Ghosts who guard the Chest of Plenty. It's in there, Vale!" Her eyes shone. "It has to be! Just like the tales. The greatest treasure in the world, a chest that can duplicate any treasure you place inside it, turning but a single coin into a hoard. And the dead guard it."

"I fear the living, not the dead. I fear the searing sunlight, not the darkness." His voice darkened. "I died in Shayeen. I died upon the ziggurat. There is nothing to fear from the souls of the departed, no more than there's reason to fear the shadows."

"But I'm afraid." Tash gulped. "We can fight the living with blades, with tooth and nail. But how can we kill those who are already dead? Many have tried to claim the Chest of Plenty, and none have succeeded." She took a deep, shuddering breath. "But we will. We have to. Meliora might fix her key, but we'll need half a million keys—one for every Vir Requis—if we're to ever rise together. And so I will enter this ship, and I will fight whoever guards that old treasure, and I will bring it back."

"Hopefully we won't have to fight anything more than wind and maybe a few crabs." Vale hefted the axe he had found in the centipedes' lair. "Whatever's inside, I'm ready for it."

Tash did not draw her dagger. "I doubt steel can cut whatever's inside. It didn't help those warriors from the tales who came to this place." She winced. "I'd wait until sunrise, but the sun brings seraphim. So we enter in darkness, seeking light."

They stepped closer across the sand. Until now the night had been sweltering hot, but now the air was icy. Vale couldn't suppress a shudder; he had never felt cold before, only heard of "cold" from the northern stories, yet now an iciness ran up his feet, trailed along his bones, and filled his belly. The sand felt like ice. Tash too was shivering.

As they moved closer, Vale looked at iron cannons that thrust out from the broken hull. He had never seen cannons before—the armies of Saraph did not use them—but he'd heard of these weapons from ancient Requiem tales, great guns that could blast out metal and fire.

"This ship belonged to men," he whispered. "Perhaps to Vir Requis. It predates Saraph's conquest of the world."

Tash nodded. "And now it belongs to the dead."

They crossed the last few feet of sand, and they reached the back of the ship. The stern was gone, perhaps lost in the shipwreck centuries ago. In its place gaped open a cavern, cloaked in shadows, leading into the hull. The moonlight did not reach this place; Vale saw nothing but darkness inside. Creaking, a whisper, and moaning wind rose from within. The air grew even colder, and their breath frosted.

Vale lifted the tinderbox and dragon-head lantern he had found in the centipedes' lair. He sparked flint against firesteel, then lit the lantern's wick. Orange light flickered through the iron dragon's eyes and mouth.

He glanced at Tash. She looked back, the light reflecting in her brown eyes, and she raised her chin. Holding the lantern before them, they entered the ship.

A nave of rotten wood awaited them. Vale had thought the ship looked large from outside; from in here, it seemed twice the size, large enough for dragons to fly through. All around rose curved planks like the ribs of a wooden whale. Portholes rose high above, peering out to the night sky; the moonlight filtered in, beams like pale fingers. Moss and algae hung from a bannister high above, and the skulls of men lay strewn across the sandy floor.

Tash started and drew her dagger with a hiss. She pointed. Vale looked and saw shadows scurrying, and he hefted his axe and raised his lantern. But the orange light only revealed a crab scuttling away. He lowered the lantern, heart racing.

"See any chests?" Vale said. He only spoke softly, but his voice seemed loud as a shout in here, echoing between the beams.

Tash winced and put a finger against his lips. Her eyes darted.

A shriek sounded across the ship.

The cry rose louder and louder, impossibly high pitched, until it shattered and broke apart into a thousand little cries that faded. In the silence that followed, Vale's ears rang.

"Still think it's the wind?" Tash whispered.

This time Vale wasn't too sure. "Let's find the chest and get out of here."

They kept walking, moving deeper into the ship. Ahead rose an anchor, taller than a man, the iron covered in barnacles and moss. Water pooled by a smashed balustrade, and white eyes shone there, then vanished with a pattering. A face in the shadows, stern and pale, made Vale start and raise his axe, but it was only an old painting still hanging from a wall, half the canvas rotted away.

Tash knelt, brushed sand away, and lifted a dark object. Vale brought his lantern closer, revealing a skull, snails nesting in its eye sockets. Tash grimaced and tossed it away. It knocked into femurs and scattered them.

They froze as the bones clattered, waiting for another shriek.

Instead they heard a deep voice.

"Go . . . go . . ."

Vale spun around. The voice had spoken right behind him. He raised his lantern and the flame swayed, casting dancing shadows like demons. Nothing. Nobody there.

"Did you hear that too?" he asked Tash.

She nodded. "It sounded so mean. I thought . . ." She peered into the shadows. "But nothing. Whoever spoke is gone."

Or still here around us, Vale thought.

"It wants us to go," Vale said, smiling grimly. "I think not. I think we'll stay for a while."

Tash nodded, sweat on her brow. "Just a short while."

They kept walking until they reached a dilapidated wall. A doorway led into a dark chamber, smaller than the grand hall they had entered. An old table stood here, covered with scrolls, the parchment so rotted it crumbled when Vale touched it. Sand rose around the table's legs. A skeleton still sat in a giltwood chair, its clothes rotted down to the buttons and buckles, and a beard still clung to its skull. No wing bones; this one hadn't been a seraph.

"Old Captain Bony here has seen better days," Vale said. "Wonder what tales he'd have to tell."

Tash looked at the skeleton and grimaced. "He'd tell us where to find the chest, I wager. I—" She started. "Vale, did you do that?"

He tilted his head. "Do what?"

"Grab my arm."

He shook his head. "I'm only holding your hand."

"Something grabbed me." She spun around, dagger lashing. "Somebody is here with us."

Vale looked around the captain's chamber. Nothing but the table, the scrolls, the skeleton in the seat. He lifted his lantern, banishing the shadows from the corners, the ceiling, the floor. Nothing.

"Nobody is here," he whispered.

Tash cringed. "He's here. I can feel him. I can feel his breath against my neck. I can feel his presence here. He's behind me." Her voice was a trembling whisper. "He hates us, Vale. He hates us so much."

"Who, Tash?"

"The captain. All of them! They're all here." She closed her eyes, taking a shuddering breath. "So much hate."

Vale groaned and squeezed her hand. "Tash, listen to me. Don't be frightened. They can't hurt us anymore. If they're here, they're nothing but echoes, just whispers, just spirits still clinging to old bones. But the danger in Tofet is alive and real, and it's what we must fight."

She nodded. "Let's keep exploring."

They kept searching the chamber, and when Vale kicked aside sand, he found a wooden trapdoor. The wood was so old and damp the iron lock tore out when Vale tugged it, and the trapdoor swung open. A staircase plunged down into shadows.

Tash grimaced. "I don't suppose you think the Chest of Plenty might be up on the deck, resting in the moonlight."

"I've never heard of treasures kept up on deck, Tash."

She gulped and nodded. "You go first."

Holding his axe and lantern, Vale took a step down, testing the staircase with his weight. The wood creaked but held, and he took another step. Tash followed, and they descended down a narrow staircase. Sand covered the stairs, mold spread along the walls, and the waves whispered outside, flowing across the outer hull. In the murmur, Vale thought he heard other sounds: the clanging of swords, the dull thunder of cannons firing, wind hitting sails, and many voices rising together, then screaming, endless screams, the sound so muffled he wasn't sure he wasn't imagining it.

"They're still drowning," Tash whispered. "Again and again, they're crashing. Do you hear them, Vale? So many lives lost."

He winced. "All right, so maybe there are a few ghosts here. But they can't harm us, Tash. No more than reflections in a mirror can leap out at you. They're just reflections on the beach."

He kept descending the staircase, heading toward a dark doorway, when eyes flashed below.

A creature emerged from the shadows, bloated and gray, like a waterlogged corpse, only half in this world. It unfurled from the cavern below like a mollusk from a shell. Alabaster claws reached up, and a jaw unhooked, lined with teeth, revealing organs that gleamed and pulsed within its gullet. Its eyes shone white, then became black pools, expanding, sucking in the light, and the creature screamed.

Vale did not hesitate.

With a wordless cry, he charged downstairs and swung down his axe.

The blade passed through smoke. The creature vanished, leaving only a cackling echo. The walls creaked, and strands of frost spread across them. The sounds of the ancient battle faded.

"Rephaim live here," Tash whispered, face pale. "These are not usual ghosts, Vale. I've read about them in the old scrolls. Most ghosts are souls who don't realize they died, souls trapped in this world. But not rephaim. Rephaim made it into the afterlife . . . and were banished, too cruel and hateful to rest in peace." She winced and touched her temples. "They're so hateful, Vale."

"And easy to kill, apparently." Vale nodded at his axe. "If you like, you can wait outside."

She shook her head. "No. You need my help down there." She looked down at the dark passageway the creature had emerged from, and she shuddered. "Let's go."

The lantern flickering before them, they stepped into the lower chamber. No moonlight shone through portholes here, and the lantern's light seemed so weak, barely piercing this darkness. Vale could see only several feet ahead, and even then the vision was smudged. Shadows lurched with every step, leaping, swooping, dancing around him. The air was so cold he thought it could extinguish the flame.

"Whole lot of junk down here," he whispered.

As he stepped forward, shining the light from side to side, he revealed piles of objects. Sacks hung from hooks. Jagged swords hung on a wall. Cannonballs piled up in the corner, and the bones of both fish and men lay across the sandy floor. Rusted chains coiled like cobras. Countless chests and crates lay everywhere, coated in grime.

"More like plenty of chests than a Chest of Plenty," he muttered.

Tash groaned. "You've already told that joke." She knelt, lifted a seashell, and nodded. "We're going to have to test them, one by one. I'll put my seashell into the chests. Whichever one duplicates it is our winner. Keep that axe handy!"

She stepped toward a pile of crates. Their wood was so rotted Vale was surprised they didn't fall apart. He raised his axe, prepared to slice through any other apparition that approached. In his other hand, he held his lantern.

Gingerly, Tash tugged open the lid on one crate, then yelped and fell back a step. Vale's heart leaped into a gallop.

"What is it?" He prepared to swing his axe.

Tash pointed. Vale brought his lantern down to reveal a collection of crabs fleeing out of the chest.

"Maybe this is it," Tash said. "Maybe it duplicated one crab into many." She placed her seashell into the emptied crate, closed the lid, then opened it again. Another crab escaped.

Vale blew out his breath. "Wonderful. You found the amazing seashell-to-crab chest. Useful when you're hungry for crab legs. Not very useful for freeing a slave nation, unless you plan to defeat the seraphim with a plague of crabs."

She sighed, retrieved her seashell, and approached another wooden box. This one was large as a coffin, carved of wood that had once been ornate. A rusty lock held it shut but fell apart at a tug from Tash.

"I'll try this one," she said and tugged open the lid.

Clawed white hands reached out from the box, grabbed her, and yanked her inside.

Tash vanished into the shadows.

For an instant, Vale could only stare in shock.

He gave a strangled yelp, leaped forward, and reached into the chest. His hands sank into nothing. Heart hammering, he shone his light into the crate. It was empty.

"Tash!" he cried. His pulse pounded in his ears. "Tash!"

Laughter answered him, coming from all around, spinning in circles. Countless voices were laughing—some deep and guttural, others shrill. They surrounded him, dancing an invisible dance. Vale spun around, raising his lantern, trying to see them, but he saw only shadows.

"Where is she?" Vale shouted. "Bring her back or I'll burn this ship down!"

The laughter rose louder, and he could see them, just glimpses—shadows, streaks of light, faces appearing and vanishing. A host of the undead, mocking him. Vale swung his lantern around him.

"Return her to me!" he demanded. "Or this ship will burn."

"Then she will burn too!" rose a shriek.

Another voice cackled. "She will join us! She will spend eternity in our drowned hull. Burn her, living one. Burn her!"

The voices chanted together. "Burn her, burn her!"

"Show yourselves!" Vale demanded. "Or are you cowards who hide in shadows? Face me."

In a ring around him, they appeared.

Vale inhaled sharply between his teeth.

The creatures creaked forward, raining dust. Skeletons, draped in scraps of ragged leather and rusted iron, their jaws unhinged in lurid grins. Crabs bustled in their ribcages, and barnacles clung to their bones. Wisps of pale light wrapped around them, holding the bones aloft, forming the vague shape of flesh—diseased skin, leering eyes, bloated faces. Their bodies had rotted centuries ago. Banished from the afterlife, the souls had returned to find nothing but old bones to nest in.

"Where did you take her?" Vale said.

Their jaws opened and closed, and the rephaim cackled. They raised old blades and muskets, and upon their rusted shields and breastplates, Vale saw faded paint forming red spirals.

He inhaled sharply.

They're Vir Requis! he realized. *Minions of the Cadigus regime!*

He knew the tales of Cadigus. All Vir Requis did, even enslaved in Tofet. Not many liked telling those tales, but still the whispers had passed from parent to child. Stories of evil Vir Requis, murderous, foul, Vir Requis who had stained their kingdom, who had dethroned the Aeternum family and created a reign of terror before losing their power in Requiem's great civil war. And here they stood before him! The rotted bodies of those traitors, risen again.

"She dances now in our halls!" the rephaim said, speaking together in dozens of voices. "You see but a shell of our kingdom, living one. But our realm is vast. And she dances for us. She dances!"

Their light flared, blinding, green and white and blue, and Vale saw it. Just a glimpse. A vision that shook the ship, that made him fall to his knees. In the light, he saw the ship restored, once more sailing upon dark seas. Hundreds of men filled it, clad in black armor, the red spirals upon their chests. Hundreds of other ships sailed around them, and dark castles rose on tors. Beneath stormy clouds flew thousands of dragons, roaring out their fire. The empire of Cadigus, traitors to Requiem, lingering forever in this mirror world.

And Tash—Tash among them.

"Tash!" he cried, reaching out to her.

He saw her upon a deck, again wearing many jewels, dancing like a wick in a flame, spinning, leaping, swaying, clad in black silk, tears on her cheeks, the haze of booze and spice in her eyes.

"Tash!" he cried, leaped toward her, tried to grab her . . . but she faded away, and the light dimmed, and Vale was back in the belly of the ship.

Once more the rephaim surrounded him. Their luminous, ethereal faces twisted atop their skulls, some snarling, others grinning. They stepped closer, raising their chipped blades.

"She dances for us. But we have no use for you, living one. Your soul we banish, and your bones we'll watch fade to dust."

A rusted sword swung his way.

Vale parried with his axe.

The blades slammed together, raining rust.

"Hear me, sons of Requiem!" Vale shouted. "Stop this. I know who you are. I—"

With a hiss, another undead warrior lashed a sword his way. Vale leaped back, swinging his axe. Another sword swung and slammed into Vale's armor, chipping the steel rings, knocking the breath out of him. A bearded warrior, an octopus nesting in its rib cage, swung down a hammer, and the heavy iron hit Vale's shoulder. He roared in pain.

"She will dance and he will rot!" they cried. "We will watch the crabs feast."

"Vir Requis, stop this!" Vale said. "I know your name. You are warriors of Requiem, soldiers of Cadigus. I am one of your number!"

They laughed, moving closer, lashing their weapons. "We care not. We fought Vir Requis, we slew Vir Requis! We fight only for ourselves. You are no brother of ours. The living are our enemy."

One of the rephaim swung a chain. The iron links slammed into Vale, most hitting his armor, but one link rose to hit his cheek. He cried out and fell. When a sword lashed down, he raised his axe, barely parrying. His lantern fell and extinguished; only the light of the rephaim now lit the ship.

"But you still fought for Requiem!" Vale shouted. "I know your story. I've heard of your pride, your vengeance. You fought to make Requiem an empire, even if you needed to slay the old king, to betray the old dynasty, to kill all those who opposed you."

Rage flared in their eyes, blasting out with white light. Their faces twisted and their shrieks rose, creaking the ship, cracking slats of wood on the walls.

"The old Aeternum kings were cowards!" they cried. "Weak, sniveling, pathetic—worms who let Requiem fall to ruin. Betray them? They betrayed all of Requiem with their wretchedness. The Aeternum dynasty had us kneeling in the dirt

425

before griffins, phoenixes, demons, wyverns. We soldiers of Cadigus made Requiem strong!"

Vale shoved himself to his feet, axe swinging, knocking them back. "Yet Requiem has fallen! You could not save her. The children of Requiem now kneel in the dirt, enslaved to the seraphim. We wear the iron collars of slavery." Vale tugged at his iron collar. "Millions of Vir Requis are dead. Half a million of our kind, chained and beaten, now serve the enemy while Requiem lies in ruin."

Their cries rose to a deafening pitch. Crates shattered. The walls cracked. Slats of rotten wood rained from the ceiling.

"The living one lies! We built an empire to last an eternity. We hail Cadigus! Requiem will never fall."

"Requiem fell!" Vale shouted. "I came here to save her, to find a treasure to give her hope, to raise Requiem against the cruel seraphim who enslave her children. While you sing and dance in your ship, your descendants languish in chains. Help us, warriors of Requiem. Grant me the Chest of Plenty, so that we may create many weapons to fight the enemy." He raised his fist. "For Requiem!"

"You lie, you lie!" they cried. "Requiem will never fall."

Vale shook his head sadly. For over a thousand years, these poor rebels had hidden here, rotting away, unaware of all that had passed, forever guarding their vainglory.

Perhaps they are slaves just as much as we are.

"I speak truth," Vale said. "If you still have a doorway to the afterlife from which you were banished, if only a keyhole, gaze through it and hear the whispers of the fallen. A hundred thousand slaves were slain only days ago. Seek them. Speak to them. Hear the cry of dragons."

The rephaim stared at him, then vanished.

Darkness, complete and enveloping, filled the belly of the shipwreck.

Silence fell. Vale could hear nothing but his breath and the barely audible whisper of waves outside.

Were they gone? Had they fled in consternation at his words?

Tash . . .

His eyes stung.

"Tash!" he cried. "Rephaim, return her! Sons of Requiem, return now and—"

With blazing, white, blinding light, the rephaim reappeared.

Their spirits now shone so brightly they nearly drowned out the bones within. Their eyes blazed like smelters, white and searing gold, casting out steam. The fallen rebels of Requiem raised their heads and cried out in anguish, shrieks that snapped planks of wood, cracked the rotting crates, shattered bottles and jars within. The shipwreck rattled madly, and Vale fell onto his back, and it seemed that the entire beach shook. Holes opened above, water gushed into the chamber, and green light flared upward, crashing through the shipwreck like the horns of an underground predator rising through prey's flesh. Above he could see the sky alight.

"Requiem fell!" the rephaim cried, voices torn in agony. "Requiem fell!"

Vale nodded, head lowered. "I'm sorry, friends."

"Friends?" they shrieked. "We are no friends of pathetic slaves, collared, weak. We served General Cadigus! We are strong, proud, noble warriors who fought our enemies, not submitted to collars and chains." Their light blasted out, shattering more planks of wood, and their faces twisted into grotesque masks, the jaws opening impossibly wide, the eyes burning.

Vale pushed himself to his feet as the shipwreck shook. "I do not submit!" He tugged at his collar. "I fight. Even collared, I fight. Tash fights with me. We slew seraphim. We came here to find a weapon—to find the Chest of Plenty, to duplicate a key that would open half a million collars, that would let Requiem fly again. But you stole Tash! You hide the Chest of Plenty! If the last light of Requiem fades, her death will be upon you, sons of Cadigus."

"He lies, he lies!" they said. "We fought for Requiem. You let her fall. The blood of Requiem was pure! Lesser heirs weakened her, let Requiem fall to rot, to disease, to slavery."

"My blood is not weak!" Vale shouted into the storm. Winds raged around him. Waves pummeled him. The light seared him. "I slew seraphim. I died for Requiem, as you have died. I rose to the starlit halls. But I returned to life! The priestess Issari, our mother, gave me life again so that I may fight. I left the afterlife as you did. But I do not cower in a shipwreck, dreaming of old glory. I fight! Will you fight with us, sons of Requiem?"

They screamed. They stormed around him, and again Vale was there—in a sea full of ships, dancers on the decks, thousands of soldiers singing, chanting, banging drums, waving swords, and Tash dancing around them, her silks fluttering, jewels shining upon her, her eyes glazed with spice—the endless dance of afterlife on the dark seas. The dragons coiled above.

"We will fight!" they cried. "We fight always for Requiem. Requiem! May our wings forever find your sky."

The sea rose and fell, roared skyward, collapsed, and the ships sank, and cannons blasted, and everywhere shone that light, fading to darkness . . . shadows . . . silence . . . and the whisper of waves.

Vale lay on the sand.

He coughed, took a deep breath, raised his head, and looked around him.

The shipwreck had collapsed. Slats of wood, shattered balustrades, chipped masts, rotting sails, rusting cannons, chains, an anchor—all lay strewn across the beach. The eerie light had faded and the moon shone above.

A moan sounded at his side. "Vale?"

He flipped over, heart bursting into a gallop, and saw her there.

"Tash!"

She lay on her side on the sand, coughing. The jewels she had worn in the fever dream were gone. Once more, she wore her baggy harem pants, and only a single jewel shone in her navel. Sand and seaweed caked her hair.

For a moment, Vale couldn't even move. So much love for her filled him that it hurt.

I almost lost her. She is as precious to me as the halls of Requiem and all her heroes of the afterlife.

Vale pulled Tash into his arms, and he nearly crushed her against his chest, kissing her hair, her forehead, her lips.

"I . . . I was dreaming," she whispered, blinking in confusion. "I was dancing in a great fleet of Requiem ships. I saw dragons, Vale! Real dragons! Dragons of the past . . ."

Holding her against him, Vale looked over her shoulder. In the sand, hundreds of crates had shattered. A single chest stood among the wreckage, still whole. A faint light clung to it, then rose in wisps.

"Dragons will fly again." He kissed Tash's forehead. "Again we will soar."

ELORY

She sat in the dark valley, her shame burning like her wounded ear.

No, not a wounded ear, Elory thought. *I no longer have an ear at all. A missing ear.* She lowered her head. *A deformity.*

She glanced across the campsite. Meliora sat farther back in the valley, her hood dousing her fiery halo. But even in the pale moonlight, Elory could see her sister's beauty—the high cheekbones, pale skin, large glowing eyes, and short hair like softest golden fleece. Meliora's limbs were long, well-formed, the body of a goddess carved of marble.

At Meliora's side sat Lucem, conversing with her softly. While Lucem had none of Meliora's ethereal beauty, he was handsome in his own way. Rugged. Unshaven. Slender but strong. His eyes were bright, and he moved his hands animatedly as he talked, telling stories and jokes, making Meliora laugh.

Elory looked back at her lap. If before she had felt plain by Meliora—what with her scrawny limbs, short stature, and darker skin—now she felt downright monstrous. Meliora's wounded cheek was even healing nicely, only hours after the battle, her seraph ichor shrinking the cuts. Meanwhile, the left side of Elory's head was a nightmare. When she touched it, she winced. Only the shell of her ear remained around the canal. Most of the auricle was gone. With Elory's short hair—it had barely grown since leaving Tofet—the wound was exposed to all.

I'm ugly now, she thought. *A deformed creature. I'll never be beautiful like Meliora, like Tash . . . never be someone whom a man could love.*

She looked back at Lucem, cursing the feelings inside her. Why must those feelings surface? She had felt something for Tash, a low flame, perhaps a mere spark, something that could never grow, for Tash's kisses had been a thing of duty, not love.

And now . . . now, even here in dark danger, Elory felt new love kindle within her, this love burning bright. Yet why would Lucem look at her when he could gaze at Meliora?

She noticed that Lucem had stopped talking, that he was looking at her. Elory's cheeks burned and her fingers tingled. Hurriedly she looked away, shame and embarrassment now battling within her.

"Elory!" he said. "Elory, come sit near us. There are some lovely, comfortable limestone recliners here." He patted the boulder he sat on. "Mmm . . . limestone! It's what Queen Kalafi used to sleep on."

Elory merely looked at her lap where she clasped her fingers.

Through the ringing in her ears, Elory heard Meliora whisper something sharply, but she couldn't make out the words. Pebbles cascaded as Lucem rose, walked across the emptiness separating them, and sat down beside Elory.

"Hmmm, not bad!" he said, patting the rocky ground. "My backside detects some granite pebbles—nice and sharp!—some dust, just a tad of chalk . . . very comfortable." He leaned toward her. "Nada? Not even a little smile?"

She couldn't help it. She gave him that little smile, but it soon faded. She couldn't even bear to look at him, and she turned her head away so he couldn't see her wounded ear.

"Does it hurt terribly?" Lucem asked, and his voice softened.

Elory shook her head. "It hurts, but not as much as I thought it would. It's just that . . ." She twisted her fingers. "I feel ugly."

His eyes widened. "*You* feel ugly? I once had a vulture attack my face; it thought I was a dead carcass. When I was a kid and looked out my hut window, seraphim kept trying to arrest me for mooning. I once turned milk to yogurt just by looking at it." He touched her chin. "You're beautiful, little one."

He's just saying that, Elory thought. *He just wants me to feel better is all.*

"Thank you," she whispered.

He gasped. "You don't believe me! I can tell. But it's true. And no missing little ear can change that. It can't take away your large, brown eyes, your smiling lips, the kindness I see in your face." Gently, he pulled her face toward his. "You're absolutely the most adorable little thing I've seen."

Elory looked over his shoulder, and she saw that Meliora had stepped away, was now a mere shadow, too far away to hear them. She looked back at Lucem, and she saw the honesty in his eyes. His hand reached out to caress her fingers, and her heart quivered.

He likes me? Lucem—likes me?

"You're not ugly either." She smiled. "I wouldn't say you're the *most* adorable thing I've ever seen—those baby pigs we saw yesterday beat you—but you're up there."

She leaned against him, and he wrapped an arm around her and kissed her cheek. For the first time in many days—perhaps in her life—Elory felt safe.

LEYLEET

She screamed in the caves, coated in blood and flesh. She tossed back her head, opened her arms wide, laughed, licked the blood.

"We slew the gods!" She rose in the cave, wreathed in black fire, her laughter shattering against the walls. "We slew the champions of the Eight. We are gods! We are gods! We are gods!"

She stared down at the corpse—the Living Creatures, now the Dead Creatures. She laughed. A hysterical laugh. A laugh that tore at her wounds, ripped her thigh open, spurted out her blood, yet still she laughed, spinning around, her voice so shrill it shattered the organs in the corpses.

"The Dead Creatures, the Dead Creatures!" she cried, and around her they chanted, her warriors, her comrades, the eleven survivors. The dark seraphim danced around the corpses, the macabre dance of death, slick with blood. "The Dead Creatures!"

Leyleet stared at them. Four bodies linked at the wings. Four heads on each—goat, lion, eagle, man. Their bronze hides torn apart, exposing the organs within. Around them lay the corpses of four dark seraphim, their limbs torn off, their flesh burnt and melting across the skulls. The survivors too bore horrible wounds. One dark seraph flew around the cave, laughing and dancing, his legs ending with exposed bones. Another dark seraph's entrails hung loose, yet still he danced and sang for glory. A third had been burnt as badly as the corpses, but he cackled and spat upon the dead.

Leyleet herself was wounded. The weredragons had thrust their blades deep into her thigh, into her belly. Already the wounds festered, stinking, the ichor sweet. She thrust her fingers into the wound on her thigh, dug around in the hot moistness, pulled her fingers free and licked the juices. Just to whet the appetite.

"Feed," she said. "Feed, friends. Feed upon the dead gods and fill your souls with their strength!"

They dived through the cave. They landed on the corpses of the Living Creatures. And the dark seraphim fed. They tugged open the cracks on the bronze bodies, pulled out organ after organ, and ripped into the flesh. They tore off the wings and chewed. They yanked free the jaws and ripped at the meat. They cracked bones, sucked out the marrow, played the bones like flutes. They paraded, gobbets of meat in their hands. And they fed upon their own dead—hunched over the fallen seraphim, ripping them open, picking at strips of meat and savoring the sweet, glistening treasures within. They licked the blood off the floor and walls, and they licked the blood off themselves, and they rutted in the puddles, slick, red, screaming with their appetites.

As Leyleet feasted, she tried to imagine feasting upon Meliora. Ishtafel needed her womb, that was all.

Your limbs will be mine, Leyleet thought and licked her lips. *We will share your delicious legs. One for me, one for you. Your arms will follow, then your face. I will deliver to Ishtafel your womb as promised, wrapped in what remains of your body . . . and he will think of me as he spills his seed into it.*

"Meliora fled these caves!" Leyleet cried. "Meliora fled as a coward, but we defeated her champion, and we absorbed its strength. The flesh of the Living Creatures fills our belly, and soon—"

Leyleet screamed.

Around her, the dark seraphim howled.

They doubled over. Pain. Pain! Agony coursed through Leyleet. She clutched her belly, shivering, gagging. Rotten meat! Foul meat! The Living Creatures coiled inside her, clawing at her organs. She screamed. Blood filled her mouth.

"Poison, poison!" the dark seraphim cried.

Leyleet screeched, tore at her throat, clawed at her belly, desperate to tug out the meal. Poison, poison! Bad meat!

She fell to her side, convulsing. Around her, the others writhed. Boils sprouted on their necks, bloating, growing to obscene size. As Leyleet thrashed, she touched her own neck, felt the boils rise there too, swelling to the size of her fists, then growing still.

Across the hall, the boils twisted, ballooned, opened mouths and screamed, opened eyes and wept. When Leyleet reached to the growths on her neck, she felt their tears, their teeth biting her.

She laughed.

"We absorbed them!" She spoke with four mouths. "We absorbed their strength."

She rose to her feet, and the others rose around her. Every dark seraph now sprouted four heads, each head topped with flowing white hair, each staring with blazing serpentine eyes.

"We are the dark seraphim!" Leyleet's mouths cried out. "We are the Rancid Angels! We are the living darkness!"

They all spun around her, shouting wordlessly.

They beat their bat wings, the twelve that remained, and flew through the winding caves. They burst out into the night. The dark hills spread around them, and they soared toward the bloated moon.

"We are stronger than we've ever been!" Leyleet called to them. "We are mighty. We have the strength of gods now. Hunt! Sniff them out! Find Meliora and our mouths will feed upon her. Fly!"

Beating their dark wings, the multiple mouths shrieking, they flew into the darkness, hunting ichor and blood.

MELIORA

Sunset spilled across the land when they saw Khalish Mountain ahead.

"Home of the Keymaker," Meliora whispered.

The mountain soared, charcoal and black. A few scattered trees grew around its base, fading higher up the slopes. Many fires burned on the mountain, and at first Meliora thought them campfires, maybe torches, maybe chariots of fire, but she saw no movement of men. High on the mountaintop she could see it— the ruins of an ancient fortress.

She turned toward her companions. Elory and Lucem were staring up at the mountain.

"It's as if the stars fell and now burn upon it," Elory said.

Lucem sighed. "If only the Keymaker could unlock our collars down here so we could fly up." He cracked his neck. "It's a long climb."

They started that climb as the sun dipped below the horizon. The way was steep, and many rocks threatened to trip them, and many boulders blocked their way. The moon had thinned and barely gave off light, but the light of many fires lit their way. The flames emerged from holes in the mountainside, though Meliora could see no fuel.

"I smell something like tar." Elory sniffed. "A little like the bitumen I used to haul in Tofet. The mountain is leaking it. That's what's causing the fires."

"We just need some sausages to roast," Lucem said. "A nice bottle of wine and a mandolin. Maybe some taters to bake."

"What's taters?" Elory asked him.

"Oh, you're a precious little thing," Lucem said. "*Potatoes.* I forgot that they don't exist in Tofet. I used to sneak into seraph farms to steal them." He smacked his lips. "One of these days, I'm going to cook you one, Elory."

"Taters must be a delicacy worthy of kings!" Elory said, eyes wide.

436

As Meliora climbed beside them, guilt filled her. While Elory had been surviving on gruel, and while Lucem had been stealing his taters, she had been dining on delicacies: honeyed duck on beds of wild rice and leek, pears and figs stewed in honey and wine, fresh crustaceans and clams and all other treasures of the sea, and countless other fine comestibles.

"May we all dine together in a rebuilt Requiem this time next year," Meliora said. "A fine tater feast."

They continued climbing between the fires. They were low on water; only a few sips remained in Lucem's waterskin. They had eaten nearly all the fruit and fish they had collected on the journey here. Meliora's belly ached with hunger and her throat was parched, but she knew her pain paled in comparison to those still suffering in Tofet.

They climbed all night, and their limbs were shaking, their bodies drenched with sweat, when they finally reached the mountaintop. Dawn rose, casting its pale light upon ancient ruins that soared before the companions.

Meliora had expected to find a castle built atop the mountain, but it seemed like the mountaintop had been carved down to form a fortress. The stony peak had been chiseled away—the work must have taken years—forming the shape of columns, archways, turrets, parapets, and colossal statues shaped as lions, goats, and serpents. Engravings covered the columns and walls, depicting men and beasts many times the size of men.

The castle must have once been spectacular, a marvel of architecture. But time had worn it down. The stone reliefs were faded and chipped; it was hard to tell which beasts they portrayed. The statues were cracked, and some parapets and turrets had fallen and lay strewn across the mountainside. The archways were crumbling, the parapets and columns smoothed by centuries of rain and wind.

"Do we just walk up and knock on the door?" Lucem asked.

"I don't see a door," Elory said.

Meliora pointed. "But I see an entrance."

An archway loomed ahead, leading into shadows. Perhaps wooden doors had once stood within, rotted away years ago. Two statues flanked the entrance, shaped as lions with long, twisting necks that ended with women's heads. The statues were so large they would have dwarfed dragons. Meliora led the way toward the archway, and the others followed.

"Lower your weapons," Meliora said. "We don't want to appear threatening."

Lucem looked up and down their bodies. "Scrawny, bruised vagabonds in rags sure are intimidating. The smell is at least." He sniffed and grimaced.

As they walked between the towering statues, it seemed to Meliora that the stone heads turned—just the slightest!—that the statues' eyes moved, following the companions as they entered the shadows.

A massive hall greeted them—larger even than the great banquet halls in the ziggurat of Shayeen. Dust and dirt covered the floor, hiding any fine tiles or mosaics that might lurk below. Columns soared, so wide that they could have formed towers, their limestone facades engraved with cuneiform writing in a language Meliora could not read. Iron braziers, large enough to boil men, rose from the dust, their embers long gone dark. Statues still stared with crystal eyes, shaped as hideous beings formed from different species: women with heads of snakes and wings of birds, men with the heads of horses, serpents with the faces of babes and the wings of bats. The statues too were covered in dust, and cracks ran across them.

"This place was built by the ancient Terrans," Meliora whispered. "Thirteen city states of humans once lived in this continent. Look, see that statue? A woman with a snake's head? She is Shahazar, an ancient goddess of men. See that statue there, the one of a man with his palms open? That's Taal, the Father God."

Lucem cocked an eyebrow. "For a seraph princess, you know a lot about the lore of men."

Meliora smiled thinly. "My brother used to boast of slaying the gods of men. He claimed he was the only true god."

"Lovely fellow, he is," Lucem said. "Can't wait to roast his godly arse with dragonfire. Now come on, enough sightseeing, more exploring. We need to find this Keymaker fellow." He coned his hands around his mouth and cried, "Keymaker!"

The cry echoed through the hall and chambers beyond, growing louder and louder. Dust rained from the walls. The palace creaked. Meliora and Elory cringed.

It seemed to take ages before the echoing died down and the dust settled. Meliora realized that she was holding her breath, and she shakily exhaled.

"Lucem, hush!" Elory said. "We don't know who else might be living here."

He looked around. "I see nobody but statues. I—"

The palace creaked again.

Dust showered.

Stones moved.

Meliora spun around toward the sound in time to see a great stone door slide down from above the archway, slam onto the floor, and seal them in the grand hall.

Darkness fell.

"Look what you did, Lucem," Elory whispered.

Meliora cringed and pulled back her hood. Her halo crackled to life, casting its light across the hall. In the dancing shadows, the statues seemed to move.

A growl rose.

Meliora wrapped her fingers around her sword's hilt.

"I don't suppose that was your tater-craving stomach, Mel?" Lucem whispered.

She dared not answer, not even breathe. The growl rose again in the darkness, and a shadow stirred. Two bright eyes opened in the hall ahead, gleaming yellow in the blackness.

At her side, she heard Elory and Lucem gasp and reach for their weapons.

Meliora forced herself to release her hilt, to raise her open palms in a gesture of peace, mimicking the statue of Taal which rose at her side.

"We are friends!" she called out to those eyes in the distant shadows. "We come seeking aid. We come seeking the Keymaker. I am Meliora, daughter of Queen Kalafi of the Thirteenth Dynasty. I—"

The growl rose again, louder this time, drowning out her words.

Meliora narrowed her eyes and stepped closer. Her halo cast back the distant shadows. She inhaled sharply. At first she thought the beast ahead just another statue, but its eyes shone, and its chest rose and fell with breath. It had the body of a great lion, thrice the size of any lion Meliora had ever seen in Shayeen's menagerie. Its tawny fur was matted and dank. Its front paws were clawed, but its back feet ended with hooves, and a goat's head sprouted from the lion's back, the teeth bared, the horns curling. When the lion flicked its tail, Meliora saw that a snake's head hissed upon the tail's tip.

"A chimera," she whispered.

Lucem leaned close to her. "It's mixed of different things! Sort of like you, Mel."

"Hush!" Meliora glared at the boy, then looked back at the chimera. "Guardian of the mountain! Noble beast! I've come seeking the man known as the Keymaker. Does he live here? Does—"

"I am the Keymaker," said the chimera. All three heads spoke at once—the lion, the goat, and the snake, their voices metallic, otherworldly. "I forged the ancient collars to block the magic of dragons. I forged the Keeper's Key. I emblazoned the runes upon them. I am the keeper of magic, the dealer of secrets, the master of power. I make keys and locks and riddles. I do not guard this mountain, but I guard the magic of men."

Meliora glanced back at the shut doorway, then returned her eyes to the chimera. She reached into her pocket, pulled out the crumpled Keeper's Key, and held it out in her palm. Her halo's light fell upon the crushed ball of metal, its runes hidden.

"The Keeper's Key is broken, Keymaker. I've come to beseech you to fix it."

The chimera's lion head growled, the sound so loud the chamber shook. Upon his back, the goat's head screamed, sharp teeth shining, horns rising. The snake tail lashed, hissing, baring its fangs.

"Broken!" the beast cried. "An ancient work of mastery—crushed as one crushes the skull of an enemy. Shame, woe! Shame upon the seraphim that they should mock our magic!"

Lucem and Elory reached for their weapons, but Meliora shook her head.

"There is a seraph who mocks you, chimera," she said. "One who breaks all things. Ishtafel, son of Kalafi, broke this key. He crushed it in his palm, spitting upon the mastery that went into its magic. He slew Kalafi, your ally. He sees the collars you forged as mere iron, no more impressive than scrap metal."

The chimera reared, clawing the air. "Scrap metal! The iron collars are works of great mastery, of ancient magic, each one a greater triumph than this entire palace. Scrap metal!" The lion roared. The hall shook. Stones rained from the ceiling. "I should tear Saraph apart for spitting upon precious gifts they cannot comprehend."

"Scrap metal is all they are now," Meliora said. "All they are without the Keeper's Key. Ishtafel now sits upon the bloody throne of Saraph, no key in his hand, the iron collars left to rust. But I fight him! I am Meliora, daughter of Kalafi, and I will see Ishtafel cast off his ill-gained throne. And I beg you, Keymaker—grant me a new key. I will treat it as a precious gift, as the masterpiece of a wise deity."

Somehow, Meliora figured that a monster that had created hundreds of thousands of slave collars cared not for tales of uprising and freedom. No. This beast worked for the art; justice or cruelty were meaningless to him.

The chimera stared at her, eyes glimmering, saying nothing. The snake hissed. The goat glared with red eyes. The lion contemplated.

"Well?" Elory said, stepping forward.

Meliora's heart skipped a beat. Elory would surely speak of Requiem! She would tell a noble tale of an oppressed people struggling for freedom, of trapped dragons who had to rise, of collars to discard—simply infuriating the creature further.

But Elory was, apparently, wiser than Meliora had given her credit for.

"Well?" the girl repeated. "Will you let Ishtafel simply treat your collars as useless, magicless trifles?" Elory scoffed. "I hear he's even collaring new slaves with iron collars made by seraph smiths. He forges them on anvils in the heat and sweat of Shayeen, and he calls them equal to these." She tugged at her own iron collar. "Without a key, Ishtafel says, his collars are just as good as yours, chimera."

The chimera roared. The creature bucked, clawed the air, and slammed his paws down. The palace shook.

"To compare works of brilliance to crude iron! That is like comparing the Frescos of Felinar to a scribble drawn in mud. You've come here to mock me?"

Meliora shook her head. "We've come to worship your skill, O Master Keymaker!" She stepped closer and held out the broken key. "Please, Master. Fix this key or forge us a new one, and I vow to you: For eternity, the children of Saraph will admire your masterwork."

The chimera stared at her, a slyness in his eyes. The snake's tongue slipped out with a hiss.

"I do not forge runes for free," said the chimera, speaking from all three heads. "Not for Queen Kalafi. Not for you."

Meliora winced. "Master Keymaker, I have no money. But I promise that if you grant me this key, I will return with payment once I dethrone Ishtafel. I will bring you many jewels, golden coins, gemstones, and—"

"Do not mistake me for a vain son of Saraph!" The chimera clawed the floor. "I care not for your glittering baubles. I care for wisdom, for locks, for keys, for artistry. I am a keymaker, a keeper of knowledge, a master of riddles." Sly smiles spread across the chimera's three heads. "Each of my heads will ask you a riddle, daughter of Saraph. If you answer all three correctly, I will make you a new key. But if you fail . . . your bones will join the dust on the floor."

Meliora looked down at the dust, wondering how much of it was comprised of old bones. She looked back up at the chimera and nodded.

"Ask me your riddles," she said.

* * * * *

In his mountain hall of shadows, the chimera seemed almost to enter a trace. His body relaxed, and two of his heads—the goat and the snake—drooped and closed their eyes. Only the lion head remained alert. With narrowed, gleaming eyes, the lion

turned to gaze at those who had entered his chamber. He spoke
with a low voice, like a spirit from long ago.

"I inspire the poet
And the warrior's sword.
I send forth rivers of blood.
I raise wonders
And heal broken lands.
I destroy like wildfire and flood.
All crave my wonders.
Men seek me
In fields of enemies slain.
Yet finally claim me
And gain my love
You'll find only yoke and chain."

Meliora frowned. She glanced over at her companions.
Lucem too was frowning and tapping his chin, while Elory had
closed her eyes and was mumbling to herself, repeating the
words.

"What inspires poets?" she whispered. "Landscapes?
Sunrises?"

"Beautiful naked women!" Lucem said, eyes brightening.

Elory groaned. "Beautiful naked women don't destroy like
wildfire and floods."

"Oh don't they?" Lucem asked.

"Shush!" Meliora clenched and unclenched her fists,
thinking over the words. "The answer is . . . something obviously
powerful but dangerous too. Something men craved yet which
enslaves them."

Lucem nodded sagely. "I told you. Beautiful women. The
ol' yoke and chain."

"And I told you—shush!" Meliora glared at him.

And yet she wondered—was Lucem right? Surely men had
fought wars over beautiful women, and surely beautiful women
could be dangerous. But . . . no. Whatever the answer was, it
healed broken lands—lands, not hearts.

"Answer!" said the lion's head. He bared his fangs.
"Answer now, for I grow weary of waiting." He licked his lips.

"Answer or I will feed upon your flesh, for I have no use for fools who cannot answer my riddles."

The chimera took a step closer to them.

"Wait!" Meliora said, and her halo of dragonfire crackled with fear. "Wait, we need time to think. We—"

"Answer!" demanded the lion, rearing and roaring.

Meliora winced and sweat dripped down her brow. She couldn't die here. She had to answer. She had to fix the key if she were ever to lead her people home. They needed her. Her father. All her people in chains. They needed her—the daughter of King Aeternum—to lead them home, yet would she die here in the darkness, food to an ancient beast? She wiped her brow. Her damn crown of fire was too hot, and—

"The answer is beauti—" Lucem began.

"No!" Meliora shouted, leaping forward and shoving him aside. "The answer is: Crown!"

The chimera remained very silent, the lion head staring with narrowed eyes, the other heads still lowered. The companions stared, holding their breath.

Finally the lion nodded. "Truth." Its eyes closed, and it lowered its head.

Meliora breathed out a shaky breath of relief.

"I still think it was beautiful women," Lucem whispered. Elory gave him an angry elbow to the ribs.

Upon the chimera's back, the goat head rose, and its eyes opened. It stared at them, and its horns curled upward into the shadows. It too spoke.

"When the sun shines
I lurk in the shade.
When the moon glows
I stab like a blade.
Men create me yet cannot slay me.
Kill your enemies
And I'll soil your victory.
Escape a drowning ship
But you can't escape me."

The goat stared at them, waiting, and lowered its horns as if ready to thrust them.

The companions frowned again, thinking, mumbling to themselves.

This one seemed like it should have an easy answer, Meliora thought. It was something that was always there—even in the beautiful sunlight and moonlight. Something . . . man-made. Something you can't escape.

"Chains?" Meliora whispered to her companions. "Certainly chains would soil any victory, would ruin any beautiful day of sunlight or night of moonlight. Certainly they're something one could not escape."

"If not chains, maybe slavery?" Elory said. "Maybe even our iron collars? We can't escape those."

The goat let out a shrill scream, almost human-like, the scream of a tortured prisoner broken beyond any measure of pain. "Answer!" it cried. "Answer my riddle now, or my horns will gore your flesh."

Meliora grimaced and tugged her collar. "So what do we say?" she whispered to Elory. "Chain? Collar? Slavery? It has to be one of those."

"No," Lucem said. For the first time today, he appeared somber, no smile on his face, and his eyes were haunted. "One can break a chain, unlock a collar, but there is something one cannot escape." He lowered his head. "I know. I escaped Tofet but could not escape this."

"What?" Meliora whispered.

Lucem turned toward the chimera. "Guilt," he said.

The goat nodded, closed its eyes, and lowered its head.

Meliora exhaled in relief, not even realizing she had held her breath. Elory stepped closer to Lucem, held his hand, and leaned her head against his shoulder.

The chimera's tail—a slithering snake—rose next. It turned its head toward them, its tongue slid from its mouth, and it hissed out its riddle.

"I give the warrior his courage.
I'm medicine to the ill.
Men seek me through shadows

Upon mountain and under hill.
Struggling souls crave me
Like a hungry man craves bread.
Let me out of your door
And death steps in instead."

Silence fell. The companions pursed their lips, thinking.
"Answer!" hissed the snake.
"You haven't given us any time!" Meliora said.
The chimera approached, and the lion snarled, the goat
sneered, the snake hissed. "Answer! We grow weary. Answer or
we'll feed upon you."
Meliora stepped back, wracking her mind. "All right!" She
glanced at her companions. "It's . . . what is it?"
Already the riddle's words were slipping out of her mind.
The chimera advanced and raised its claws. Lucem raised his
spear, trying to hold it back.
"Wait!" Meliora said to the chimera. "Give us a moment."
"You've waited long enough!" The beast pounced.
Meliora grimaced and leaped aside. She drew her sword.
"You cheat, chimera! You must give us time to think."
Her heart thudded and her fingers tingled. It wasn't fair!
The chimera obviously didn't want them to win, didn't want to
forge them a new key. Yet without a key, Requiem would
languish in slavery, slowly dying. Without a key, there was no
hope, there—
She froze.
The chimera leaped at her, and Meliora cried out and fell
back, swinging her sword before it.
That's it! Meliora thought.
"Chimera, it's—"
But Elory cried out the word before Meliora could.
"Hope!"
The chimera stepped back. Its three heads rose and spoke
together: "You have answered our three riddles."
Meliora exhaled in relief, and sweat dripped into her eyes.
Lucem fell to his knees and just breathed. Elory stared up at the
chimera, eyes damp.

The chimera's heads rose high, and their eyes closed. Rings of light coiled around the creature, blue and white, spinning faster, soon forming a dome around it. The mountain hall shook. Dust and pebbles danced on the floor. Winds blasted out from the light, blowing the companion's cloaks.

The light faded, the winds died, and the chimera stood before them again. One of its paws was held out, and upon it rested a crimson key.

ELORY

They stood outside on the mountain, three collared slaves.

Three people hurt, beaten, brutalized, healing.

Three exiles from a fallen home, still clinging to hope after so many tears, so much blood.

Three Vir Requis.

The sun set around them, painting the ruins, the mountains, and the land beyond gold and bronze. Wind blew, ruffling their cloaks. They stood in a triangle, facing one another, staring, silent.

Meliora held the key in her hand. Waiting. Hesitating. Not sure how to approach a moment of such importance, a moment that would be branded upon the song of Requiem with dragonfire.

"Five thousand years ago," Meliora finally said, "new stars began to shine in the sky, shaped as a great dragon. They chose a few blessed souls. Hunters. Gatherers. Priests and healers. People scattered across a world just rising from darkness. And the stars blessed them, gave them a holy magic . . . the magic of dragons." Meliora's voice dropped to a whisper. "And they were hunted. Cruel warlords and kings raised armies of demons to slay those who could grow wings, breathe fire, and rise as dragons. Yet one man gathered these hunted souls together. In a forest of birch trees, King Aeternum founded the kingdom of Requiem—a kingdom to last for eternity."

Elory and Lucem moved closer together, reached out, and clasped each other's hands. Their eyes shone damply.

Meliora continued speaking. "Today, the Vir Requis believe that Jaren is descended of that ancient king, that I myself bear that old blood of royalty. Yet for five hundred years, we did not fly. We did not sing among the birches. We suffered in chains, our magic stolen from us." She reached up and touched her collar. "The time has come to fly again."

Elory and Lucem looked at each other, then back at her. Meliora looked at them. Lucem, the hero of Requiem, the first to escape Tofet—a young man who taunted her, told jokes, smiled readily, yet hid deep pain and guilt. Elory, her sweet sister whom Meliora had only just met, small and meek yet strong as the greatest heroines of the Requiem that had been.

I love them more than all the palaces in the world, more than my life. I love them like Requiem.

"Step forth, Lucem," Meliora whispered. "You were first to scale the walls of Tofet. You will be first to spread your wings."

His eyes widened. "Mel! I mean—Your Highness! I'm nothing but the son of a bitumen refiner. I'm not worthy of flying first."

Elory leaned toward him and whispered from the corner of her mouth, "She's testing it on you. You know, just in case the new key causes collars to constrict until they squeeze your head off."

"Ah." Lucem tugged at that collar. "Puts a damper on that whole holy moment for Requiem. But I accept!" He stepped forth. "Unlock me, Meliora Aeternum, Heiress to Requiem, and if my head pops off and rolls downhill, tell everyone that I died battling Leyleet in the caves."

He cleared his throat, closed his eyes, and raised his chin.

Meliora hesitated. What if it failed? What if hope died here upon the mountain? What if—

"Mel!" Lucem whispered. "It's itching. Hurry."

She nodded, took a deep breath, and pressed the key against his iron collar.

For a long moment, nothing happened. Meliora caught her breath, staring, waiting. Her hope began to fizzle. It wasn't working! It—Wait!

She gasped.

The key was warming up in her hand, soon almost intolerably hot. The runes upon it brightened, then glowed, then cast out bright light. The corresponding runes on Lucem's collar shone with their own light. The key thrummed madly in Meliora's hand, shaking so violently she almost dropped it. She gripped Lucem's shoulder with her free hand, keeping the key pressed against his collar, letting the light flow. Lucem sucked in breath, eyes closed, jaw clenched, fists tightened, and she was hurting him, oh stars, he was in pain, and—

With a *crack*, his collar opened.

Meliora gasped and stepped back.

Her key dimmed and cooled. The iron collar fell to the ground.

Meliora and Elory froze, staring. Lucem brought his fingers up to his neck. The skin was raw, scarred—the wounds of a thousand times he had tugged, hammered at, tried to melt the iron.

"Well," he said, "my neck's a bit cold already. Anyone got a scarf? At least now I can wear that ruffled collar I've always wanted. Though I'm not sure I'm quite as safe from axe blows to the neck, which I hear is a real problem these days in Tofet, and—"

Suddenly tears filled his eyes, and Lucem lowered his head and trembled.

Elory rushed forth and embraced him. Meliora smiled tremulously and touched his arm. They stood together for a long time, overwhelmed, tears on their cheeks.

"It's . . . I can't tell you how many times . . .," Lucem began, then rubbed his eyes. He took a shaky breath and embraced Meliora so tightly he nearly crushed her. "Thank you, Meliora. Thank you."

She laughed through her tears. "Are you going to keep standing here hugging me, or are you going to fly?"

He blinked. "Blimey, I forgot the most important part. Better step back." He took a few paces away from Meliora and Elory, inhaled deeply, and spread out his arms.

No light glowed across him. No angelic choirs sang. No beams of starlight fell in a crown of luminescence. And yet a miracle occurred upon the mountain that evening, a miracle that brought fresh tears to Meliora's eyes and song to her heart.

Scales flowed across Lucem, red as rubies and fire and the blood of dragons. His fingernails lengthened into claws, fangs sprouted from his mouth, and wings unfurled from his back, creaking and leathern and deep crimson like wine. His body lengthened, widened, and he fell onto his hands—only they were no longer hands but great dragon feet. Smoke blasted out from his nostrils, and a tail flailed behind him, tipped with black spikes.

He stood before them, a dragon.

Meliora fell to her knees before him. She lowered her head. "A dragon. A dragon of Requiem."

Elory too knelt. "Requiem rises."

The red dragon nodded. "Not bad, this. Little mortals kneeling before me." Lucem still had the same voice, albeit stronger, fuller, echoing in his elongated jaws. "Now let's see what these wings can do."

He spread his wings wide and beat them several times. Dust rose in clouds. Pebbles cascaded down the mountainside. Air blasted Meliora. The red dragon began to rise . . . then wobbled and crashed down onto the mountainside, cracking a boulder.

"Might take a bit more practice," Lucem said.

Elory patted the dragon's red scales, then stepped toward Meliora and raised her chin.

"I'm ready," she whispered.

Meliora placed a hand on Elory's shoulder, then raised the key in her other hand.

The light glowed. The collar fell.

Elory stood before her, her collar gone for the first time in her life. She sniffed and embraced Meliora, resting her cheek against Meliora's breast.

"I love you, sister," Elory whispered. "Always."

Meliora kissed the top of her head. Elory's hair was growing out, thick and brown and soft. "I love you too, sweet little sister. Forever."

Elory stepped back, closed her eyes, and she too became a dragon. Lavender scales gleamed across her, deep purple near her belly, lightening to violet on her back. White horns grew from her head, and white spikes ran down her tail in a palisade. She was a smaller dragon than Lucem, slender and short, but when she puffed out smoke and let fire fill her maw, she looked just as fierce.

"It's real," Elory whispered. "The magic inside me. It's always been real, waiting all these years." She lowered her head and shed a tear, then reared and clawed the air and roared. Her cry tore across the mountain, rolled across the land—a great wordless cry of freedom, of magic restored.

Finally Meliora brought the key to her own collar, the light shone, and the collar fell. As she stood in human form, Meliora felt the magic inside her, and she hesitated.

The one time I summoned Requiem's magic, I still had my seraph wings, she thought. *I became a dragon of both scales and feathers, great swan wings growing from my back. If I shift now, will I be wingless?*

"Come on, join the fun!" Lucem said, beating his wings and rising several feet into the air again. "Fly with us, Mel. Fly like—ah!"

Again the red dragon crashed down, cracking another boulder.

Meliora sucked in breath, closed her eyes, and reached deep inside her for that warm, tingling magic.

She felt her body growing. She heard scales clattering. Fire heated her belly. Her claws sank into the mountain.

When her transformation was complete, she kept her eyes closed, not daring to look. But she could hear the others gasp.

"Oh, Meliora . . .," Elory whispered.

"Blimey," Lucem said.

Meliora cringed. She had been right! Surely her wings were gone! She braced herself, opened one eye to a slit, and looked over her shoulder at her body.

Such shock filled her that she spurted out fire.

"Stars," she whispered. "Thank you, stars of Requiem."

Her body was long, slender, covered in small silvery scales like pearls. No more feathers grew from her tail; that tail was thin and quick as a whip, tipped with ivory spikes. Instead of swan wings, great leathern wings, white as drifts of snow, grew from her back, tipped with golden claws. Fire crackled above her head, its orange light falling upon her snout, and she realized that even in dragon form, she wore a crown of dragonfire.

I'm a dragon. A true dragon of Requiem.

She flapped her wings. She soared into the sky.

She spun as she flew, pointed upward in a straight line, rising and rising, and she blasted up her fire. The flames shot skyward, a white pillar. Her wings spread wide, and she laughed as she spun, sending forth her flame.

With a cry of joy, Elory flew too. The lavender dragon shot up beside her, laughing, and blasted her own fire—orange flames flaring out into yellow. She was a smaller dragon than Meliora, but when Elory roared again, the mountain shook.

Grumbling curses, Lucem finally managed to fly up with them. He wobbled, dipped, yelped, beat his wings madly, and finally steadied his flight.

"I think I'm getting the hang of this," the red dragon said. "I—whoa, careful, Elory!"

The purple dragon laughed and playfully slammed against him, tossing him into a tailspin. Lucem cursed, righted himself, and kept flying.

The three dragons spread their wings wide, found a wind current, and glided. The mountains and hills rolled below in an endless landscape, and in the distance, the Te'ephim River spread in a silver line.

"It's beautiful!" Elory cried over the wind. "All my life, I knelt in the dust, looking up at the sky, dreaming of it . . . and now I'm here, looking down. A dragon. No longer afraid."

"I'm afraid!" Lucem said, wobbling and dipping in the sky.

Meliora breathed deeply as she flew and smiled. She had never felt such peace, not in all her years in the ziggurat. She had never seen such beauty, not among all the artwork of Saraph. She had never felt so noble, not even as a princess in an empire's palace.

"Requiem!" she whispered. "May our wings forever find your sky."

Elory and Meliora repeated the ancient prayer—the same prayer the children of Requiem had been singing for five thousand years, the prayer of outcasts in forests, of warriors in battlefields, of survivors in ruins, of freed slaves seeking to return home.

"We fly now in the sky of Saraph," Meliora said. "But we will fly in Requiem's sky again."

She turned to look north. She could see far from up here, farther than she had ever seen. The horizon lay many miles away, yet that distance was but a fraction of the way to Requiem.

Vast deserts, plains, and seas lay between here and her lost home, but Meliora vowed that she would see that home, that she would fly in Requiem again.

But not yet, she thought, turning away from the northern view. *This day we fly south.* She let fire fill her jaws, and she growled. *This day we fly to Tofet.*

TASH

He slept beside her on the grass, covered in a blanket of palm fronds, and Tash's heart twisted at the pain she would cause him.

"Sweetest Vale," she whispered and kissed him.

The hint of a smile touched his lips, but he did not wake. Tash lay beside him, looking at him. His face was thin, still careworn, but handsome, she thought. She had let so many seraphim into her bed—men tall, fair, of purest form and beauty—yet she had loved no man until this one, until her sweet Vale, despite all his scars and the pain written across his face, even now.

I began to heal your pain, Tash thought. *To see you smile, to hear you laugh. To place love into your heart . . . only for me now to break that heart.*

Silently, she slipped out of their bed of grass and leaves. The landscape rolled around them: hills, valleys, and the river that flowed between them. Somewhere in the west lay Tofet—a hive of disease, chains, agony, death. Somewhere in the north or south lay other lands . . . new lands, unexplored, lands of freedom.

Tash stared at the Chest of Plenty.

It lay in the grass beside them, so small. She could have cradled it in her arms. And yet it was wealth. Freedom. Hope. Life—life away from war, from pain, from death. It was the treasure she had dreamed of all her life. So many times as some drunken lord had bedded her, Tash had closed her eyes, ground her teeth, and imagined finding the Chest of Plenty. So many times, Tash had lain awake at night as the other girls slept, working on her map, coming up with a thousand plans: how she'd escape Shayeen, find the chest, build a great treasure and sail away to freedom.

Tash fingered the jewel in her navel. As Vale still slept, Tash unpinned the jewel and pulled it free. She held it in her palm. A small diamond, impure and pinkish, inlaid in a ring of gold. Some seraph or another had gifted her that jewel in the garden. It wasn't worth much on its own; perhaps enough to trade for a sturdy cloak, boots, and a leather belt, with enough left over for a couple nights in a tavern and a bottle of wine. Hardly a fortune. But with this chest . . .

Tash closed her eyes. *It'll be like I always dreamed.* Enough diamonds to bribe seraphim guards at any port in the empire, enough to book passage on a ship—to *buy* a ship! Enough to sail far away, find an outpost in the distance, someplace far from Ishtafel. Maybe she would even reach the end of the empire, find a land beyond that still stood, where seraphim would not find her. She could buy a mansion, servants, all the fine wines and food in the world. The collar would remain around her neck, but she would gild it, encrust it in jewels, be a queen in a distant land.

Fingers trembling, Tash opened the chest and placed her jewel within. She closed the chest top.

Nothing happened. No glowing light. No angelic song. Not even a rattle to the chest. She opened the lid.

Diamonds spilled out. Thousands of tiny diamonds on golden rings. Tash bit her lip, dipped her hand into the chest, and ran her fingers between them. She was wealthy. Just like that—wealthy. She turned the chest upside down, spilling them all out into the grass, then placed a single diamond back inside. She closed the lid. She opened it. Thousands more diamonds shone inside.

"Endless wealth," she whispered. "Endless freedom."

She looked back west and winced.

And there lies endless pain.

Tash closed her eyes, shuddering. How could she go back to Tofet—after all she had seen there? After Ishtafel had murdered a hundred thousand souls, after all the pits of corpses, the dead upon spikes, so much pain, bloodshed . . . How could she walk that path when the other way lay freedom and wealth?

Tash opened her eyes. She lifted the chest, leaving all but one diamond in the grass. Vale would find them, at least. Have a treasure to carry with him wherever he wanted to go.

"I wish I could take you with me, Vale," she whispered. "But you'd never understand. You'd never go with me."

She looked away from him. She could not stare at his face for an instant longer; it stabbed her full of pain, as cruel as spears. Holding the chest under her arm, tears in her eyes, Tash began to walk north.

She took ten steps, then stopped, trembling. Her body shook. Her tears fell. She wanted to return to Tofet. She couldn't. She couldn't.

I can't go back there. I can't. I've dreamed of this for so long. I can't go back.

Weeping, she took another step away.

"Tash?" rose his voice behind her.

Her heart sank to her pelvis and shattered.

Stars, no. Stars, don't let this happen.

She turned around and saw Vale standing there, the diamonds around his feet. At first he seemed confused. He stared down at the treasure, then up at her, head tilted. Then his eyes narrowed, and he understood. Something terrible filled his eyes, something not angry, but more pained than a slave under a whip. The shattering, icy pain of betrayal.

"Tash," he whispered.

She wept. She trembled. "Come with me," she whispered.

"Where?" He spoke so softly she could barely hear.

"Anywhere." The chest under her arm rattled as she trembled. "Away from war. Away from pain and torture. Away from this empire. We can be rich, Vale! We can be free." She placed the chest down, walked toward him, and tried to embrace him. "We can find a new life, and—"

"You tried to leave me here." He stared at her with shock and agony in his eyes. "You tried to take it. To steal the chest away. To . . . to leave me and Requiem, and—"

"There's no hope for Requiem!" Tash shouted. "Don't you understand, Vale? Don't you see? Millions of dragons fought Ishtafel in the old days. Millions of dragon warriors, soldiers in a great army, trained for battle. And he killed them! He killed them all, and he took everyone else captive. And now you think slaves can kill him, even without our collars? He's going to kill us, Vale. Kill us all! There's nothing in Tofet but pain, blood, death—"

"Then I will die!" he shouted, face red, gripping her arms. "Then I will die again, as I died upon the ziggurat. I will die a thousand times for Requiem. Tash!" His tears fell. "How could you do this? How could you betray us? You're a daughter of Requiem, a Vir Requis, a—"

"A slave!" She shoved against his chest, trying to break free. "Just a pleasure slave! Not even a whore. Whores get paid. I'm nothing but a slave to them, Vale, and I won't do it anymore. Never again. Never! I won't let them touch me, bed me, toss jewels onto my naked body. I . . . I finally found someone I love, Vale. Someone I love truly. And now you just want to go there, to go back to what we fled. You remember what it was like. The whips, the spears, the fire. You want to go back and die. And I can't see that. I can't see that happen. I can't . . . I can't . . ."

She wanted him to embrace her, to comfort her, to stroke her hair, maybe even tell her that he'd go with her. But he only stared at her, the pain in his eyes. And a new emotion crossed his face.

Rage.

His lips peeled back, his eyes blazed, and his cheeks flushed. His hands balled into fists.

"Still you lie," he whispered. "Love?"

"I love you—" she began.

"You lie!" He raised his fist as if to hit her, and she cringed. "All you do is lie. Love me? You tried to leave me! To betray your people, to leave us to torture, to death. You tried to leave Requiem to ruin. Do you have any notion of what you've done?" He gripped her so tightly his fingers dug into her arms. "For thousands of years, we fought for Requiem, we died for Requiem, we—"

"Do you know who you sound like?" she shouted, struggling to free herself, her hair whipping around. "You sound like them! Like the ghosts in the shipwreck. Like the cruel Vir Requis of the Cadigus regime. They too boasted of fighting and dying for a cause. But I don't want to fight, Vale. I don't want to die. I don't want to suffer, to bleed, to kill for some ideal, for some nation that fell five hundred years ago. Requiem is gone, Vale. It's gone forever, but I'm still here. *We're* still here. You and I." She gave up on freeing herself and lowered her head, sobbing. "We can leave all this behind. We can find a better life—a life of wealth. We have all the money in the world now, enough to sail away, to buy palaces, or just buy a humble home if you prefer, somewhere beyond the empire. I only tried to leave without you because . . . because I knew you wouldn't want this, and it broke my heart. It broke my heart, Vale."

"The only heart you broke is mine." He shook his head, his whisper barely audible. "How could you? After all we suffered . . . knowing that Meliora and Elory are out there, fighting for Requiem, that my father is back in Tofet, that . . . that we finally had a chance. How could you?"

Tash fell to her knees in the grass. She wept. "I'm sorry, I'm sorry." She tried to hug his legs. "I'm sorry."

He lifted the fallen chest. He stared down at her, and she saw it inside those eyes—shattering, eternal pain of betrayal. He spun around and began walking.

"Wait," she whispered. "Vale, wait . . ."

But he would not turn back. He kept walking.

"Wait!" she shouted, still kneeling in the grass.

He only walked faster, heading west across the land, taking the Chest of Plenty. Tash shoved herself to her feet, shaking so wildly she almost fell again. She followed him, blinded by tears, leaving her jewels behind, and as she walked, it filled her—the crushing guilt.

"I'm sorry," she whispered. "I'm so sorry."

She kept following him, not knowing if he'd ever forgive her, and if she could ever forgive herself.

VALE

She kept trailing behind him, calling his name, but he would not look back. She kept begging him for forgiveness, voice rolling across the land, but he would not answer.

He traveled by night, hidden in shadows, carrying the Chest of Plenty under his arm. Traveling to Tofet, for a hope to reunite with Meliora, to duplicate her key and raise Requiem again. In those long nights, Tash calling behind him, the stars shone above in a great blanket, and Vale felt very alone, very small, carrying the hope of a nation . . . as the traitor of that nation followed.

"Vale!" she cried out. "Vale, wait. Vale, forgive me!"

And yet, whenever she called, he walked onward through the darkness.

In the days, he slept, hidden in caves, in burrows, in tall grass. Tash would creep up to him then, try to stroke his hair, to kiss him, to plead forgiveness. And each time he shoved her away, rose to his feet, and walked onward, leaving her behind.

"I'm sorry," she whispered. "Won't you forgive me?"

Yet how could he? He had loved Tash. After so many years of pain, he had allowed himself to feel love, to feel joy. And she had betrayed not only him but Meliora, Elory, Jaren, all of them.

Had she come on this quest not for Requiem, but only for herself? Had she seen him as only a bodyguard, protecting her until she found the chest, until she could stab him in the back?

He walked onward through the nights, ignoring her, forcing her out of his mind. He thought only of Requiem, only of meeting Meliora again, of raising the dragons.

It was a new moon, the land cloaked in blackness, when Vale finally saw the lights of Shayeen ahead.

Vale stopped, the sight stabbing him like nails driven into his palms.

The lights were still distant, a mere cluster on the horizon, but bright as the fallen moon. The capital of Saraph. The greatest light in the world. The City of Kings, home to Ishtafel, to those who had destroyed Vale's own home.

Ahead of that city spread a dark land, enclosed by walls. No lights shone within this prison. No towers or golden domes rose. No lanterns hung over bustling streets. There in the distance, in shadows, lay Tofet, the land of pain.

Vale grimaced. Pain flared in his hands and feet. Again he could feel it—Ishtafel swinging the hammer, driving the nails into Vale, pinning him to the platinum crest of the ziggurat. Again he felt his life ending, the agony of the soul tearing from the body . . . only to see stars, to feel Issari's hands upon him, to return to the pain. To fight. To face the battle ahead, the great battle for Requiem.

Will that battle begin now? Are you heading back too, Meliora, with the key?

He tugged at his collar, aching to get the Keeper's Key from Meliora, to fly again.

He looked around him, struggling to see the cave in the darkness, the place where he was supposed to meet his sisters. Yet it was still too dark. He could barely even see the river; only when squinting could he make out the dark surface of the water in the jagged blackness. The landscape still smelled of the old fire, and the earth was bare and burnt.

He walked slowly, and finally he came across it, almost by accident—the cave in the hillside. The meeting place.

"Meliora?" he whispered, standing outside the cave. "Elory?"

No answer came. Vale dared light his lantern, only for a moment. He cast its light inside the low, shallow cave. Empty.

A sudden pang stabbed him.

Here is where we spent our first hours of freedom, where Tash nestled against me.

He lowered his head. Suddenly he wanted to forgive her, to turn back, to find her in the darkness, to hold her again. To stroke her hair, kiss her lips, feel her warmth, protect her from the evil in the world. To love her again. Yet as soon as those feelings surfaced, so did the memory: Tash walking away, holding the Chest of Plenty.

Maybe she never truly meant to leave, he thought. *Maybe another step, and she would have regretted it at once, turned back, resisted temptation. Maybe—*

A shriek sounded in the sky, cutting off his thoughts.

Vale spun around and stared upward, clenching his fists.

He saw nothing. Only the blackness of night. Another shriek rose, closer this time, and others answered the call—creatures in the sky. Yet he didn't see the fire of chariots.

Standing on the burnt earth, he opened the Chest of Plenty. He placed the axe head inside and as much of the shaft as would fit, closed the lid until it banged against the handle, then opened it again. A second axe thrust out. As the screeches filled the night, Vale raised a weapon in each hand. He stared upward. He still saw nothing.

"We smell one, comrades!" rose a feminine voice, demonic, so shrill it raised Vale's hackles. "We smell a weredragon! Sweet meat! Sweet blood!"

Vale's heart pounded. Where were they? He could see nothing. Those were not the voices of seraphim above.

There!

He glimpsed them, just shadows blotting out the stars, and he could smell them—a smell of blood and rot. They spiraled down, eyes white and glowing, claws pale as bones. As they flew lower, Vale saw that they had the bodies of men and women, clad in black armor. They beat bat wings, and they held sickles. Each had four heads, cruel and pale and fanged. Only the light from their eyes lit them.

"We smell it, Rancid Angels!" cried one, a bloodied woman; her four heads cried out together. "Another weredragon, a reptile! Kill it, drink it, eat it!"

Vale cursed. He could not defeat so many; a dozen or more flew above. A part of him craved to swing his axes, to fight them, to die, but he had to live. He had to survive just a little longer, to deliver the chest to Meliora.

He hurried toward the cave, crawled inside, and hid in the shadows. Outside he heard the wings beat, the screeches, smelled the stench of them.

Another weredragon? Had these creatures seen his kind before, slain them? Had they . . . had they hurt Meliora and Elory?

Vale crouched lower in the cave, praying they hadn't seen him, that they'd miss the cave in the darkness of a moonless night. He readied his axes just in case, prepared to swing them, to cut them down before they could enter. The Chest of Plenty stood at his side, his treasure to protect—the hope of Requiem, here, only his humble blades to defend it.

"Down, Rancid Angels! There, in the shadows! We smell it, we see it, we will drink it!"

The wings beat in a fury, the creatures cackled, and Vale tightened his grip on his axes, teeth bared.

But the creatures were not flying toward him.

He hissed.

Outside the cave, he saw them—the light of their eyes glinting against their claws—flying away, past him, downward toward the valley.

They howled and a woman screamed.

For a second Vale froze.

"Tash," he whispered.

She screamed again, and Vale burst out from the cave. His body thought on its own. He ran, axes raised, and roared.

"Rancid Angels!" He leaped toward the valley. "Come, meet my blades!"

They were flying over the valley, swooping toward a shadow. Tash! Tash knelt there, her hair fluttering, raising her humble dagger. She met his gaze for just a second, and at that second, Vale felt nothing but that old love again.

Then the foul creatures flew toward him. Their sickles swung.

Vale flashed his axes.

He knocked aside one sickle. He slammed aside reaching claws. They flew all around and above, laughing, mocking him. Another claw thrust down, and he knocked it aside. He leaped up, swung his axe, hit armor. A sickle slammed into his back, chipping his chain mail. They flew faster around him, dancing in the air, eyes lurid.

"A meal, a meal! A weredragon meal! Chop him up, tug him out, pull him to pieces. Feed, drink!"

Tash leaped to her feet, ran forward, and stood beside him. She flashed up her dagger as the creatures flew all around.

"You came to save me!" she cried.

Vale growled and knocked aside a sickle. Another blade hit his armor, cracking the rings, cutting the skin beneath. Vale beat the creature back with the swipe of an axe. "I'm not sure I saved anyone."

"Then you've come to die with me!" Tash grinned. "I knew you still loved me. I knew it! It's very romantic, dying together."

"I'm not dying without a fight!" Vale leaped upward, axe swinging, and managed to cut a creature's leg. Sizzling golden blood rained down.

The beasts screeched, and their faces twisted, losing all amusement.

"He cuts us, he hurts us! End this game. Kill, kill! Eat, drink!"

The creatures swooped down together, no longer dancing. Pale hands grabbed Tash, yanking her skyward, and claws slashed at her. She screamed, blood spurting. Vale roared, swung his axes, knocked a creature aside, but hands grabbed him too, tugging him upward, and fangs bit into his shoulder, and he knew that hope was lost, that here—so close to the end of his journey, so close to raising the dragons again—here he died in darkness.

"Vale, I'm sorry!" Tash cried, dangling before him in the creatures' grasp, bleeding. She stared into his eyes. "I love you. I'm so sorry, and I love you."

The fangs dug deeper into Vale, and the claws yanked his axes free, and his feet no longer touched the ground. They were drinking his blood.

"I love you too, Tash," he said. "I love you always, in this life and the—"

Light blinded him.

Fire shrieked.

Air blasted against him, showering sparks.

Roars tore across the sky, and Vale looked up, and he saw them there, flying in from the west.

"Dragons," he whispered.

MELIORA

She roared out her fire.

Her wings churned smoke and sparks.

A white dragon, she charged forth, claws stretched out.

To her left flew Lucem, a red dragon, fire in his maw. To her right flew Elory, lavender scales reflecting her flames. Three streams of fire lit the night.

Ahead of them, the dark seraphim screamed. They dropped those they held—the bloodied Vale and Tash. Wings beating madly, the creatures stormed toward the dragons.

"Dragons fly, dragons burn!" they cried. "The curse is broken, kill them, eat them!"

Meliora counted eleven of them. She grinned, letting fresh fire fill her maw.

Now they will see the wrath of Requiem.

Her white fire streamed forth. A dark seraph screamed. The flames washed across him, heating his armor, melting his skin, tearing holes through his wings. At her sides, Elory and Lucem blasted their dragonfire, and the inferno blazed across two more dark seraphim.

The demonic angels stared with their white eyes. Each one now sprouted four heads—the curse of the Living Creatures—and each of those heads screamed.

Three of the survivors stormed toward Meliora. They were tall beings, seven feet of dark steel and claws, yet so small by her dragon form. A sickle swung her way, and she knocked it aside with her claws. She thrust forward, closed her jaws around a dark seraph, and bit deep, denting his armor. She tore out a chunk of flesh and metal, spat it out, and clawed the seraph down. Another flew from behind. She lashed her tail, knocking it aside, then bathed it with fire.

She glimpsed her fellow dragons. Lucem shredded a dark seraph's wings, then swiped his claws, knocking the creature down. Elory flew in rings, spurting fire, burning the enemies. Steel flashed.

A voice yowled.

Meliora glanced up in time to see Leyleet, Queen of the Dark, swooping toward her. Before Meliora could react, the dark seraph landed on her back, and twin sickles flashed.

Meliora screamed.

The blades cracked her scales, dug into her, and her blood dripped. She bucked madly, struggling to tear Leyleet off her back.

"I will ride you down to your grave!" Leyleet shrieked from all four mouths, lashing the sickles again. Silver scales flew through the night, and agony flared across Meliora.

"Sister!" Elory cried, but dark seraphim flew toward her and Lucem, shoving them back.

"I will bring you to Ishtafel!" Leyleet screeched, straddling Meliora's back, lashing her sickles again and again like a fisherman scaling a fish. "Your womb will be his, but when he's done with you, you will be mine to toy with, you—"

With a scream, Meliora released her magic.

She fell through the night.

Above her, Leyleet tore free from her back, roaring with rage.

As Meliora tumbled down, she glanced up, saw the dark queen swoop with her blades. The ground rushed up from below.

Meliora summoned her magic again.

She soared, blasting up a blaze of white fire, a great pillar like King's Column in the north. It lit the dark like a beam of starlight.

Leyleet screeched, tried to dodge the fire, but the flames washed across her. The dark seraph thrashed, caught in the blaze. Her four heads bloated, tore apart, dripped their innards. Her wings shredded, the skin curling back to reveal the bones. Her armor melted. And still the creature screamed, again and again, an endless cry, refusing to die. All other dark seraphim fell, crashed onto the earth, lay as shattered corpses, and still their queen howled, clinging to her mockery of life.

Meliora had no more fire within her. Her flames died.

She landed on the ground, a silvery white dragon, splashed with blood.

Leyleet landed before her.

The dark seraph was melted flesh over bones. No more skin remained. No more eyes. But those four heads turned toward her, red skulls, and the jaws opened, and they spoke together, voices impossibly deep and distorted.

"You will fail, daughter of Aeternum. Your dynasty will fall. You will never see Requiem, daughter of dragons. With my dying breath, I curse you: You will never see Requiem."

Meliora released her magic, returning to human form. Amerath, the Amber Sword of Requiem's monarchs, reappeared at her side. She drew the ancient blade. She stepped toward Leyleet. She thrust her weapon.

The blade drove into Leyleet's charred, exposed chest, slid between the ribs, and crashed into her heart.

Meliora tugged the blade free, and Leyleet crashed down upon the hill, spurting blackened ichor. Her body fell apart, gobbets of flesh turning into beetles, bones melting into worms, and the little creatures fled into the shadows and were gone.

The red and lavender dragons landed beside Meliora and returned to human forms—young, yellow-haired Lucem and thin, brown-eyed Elory.

Meliora turned around.

In the light of the burning corpses, she saw them.

"Tash," she whispered. "Vale."

They stared at her, hesitating for a moment. Blood dripped from cuts and scrapes across them.

"You're wounded!" Elory said, rushing toward her brother. "You're—"

Vale ran forward, scooped Elory into his embrace, and grabbed Meliora and pulled her close too. He squeezed them, eyes shut, holding them against him.

"My sisters," he whispered. "My sisters."

VALE

With heat and light, his collar opened and fell.

Instantly, before he could even rub his sore neck, Vale summoned his magic and shifted. Upon the dark hills several miles out of Tofet, he became a dragon.

Earlier that year, he had become a dragon in Shayeen, chained and whipped, forced to haul stones. But now he stood as a free dragon, head proudly raised in the night. Fire flickered in his maw, illuminating his blue scales.

Three other dragons stood before him on the hill: Meliora, a silvery white dragon with golden horns; Elory, a slender lavender dragon; and Lucem—the actual Lucem, hero of Requiem!—a long red dragon.

Only one among them still stood in human form.

Tash stood holding her collar in her hand; the Keeper's Key had opened it. Yet still she did not become a dragon. The wind ruffled her long brown hair and baggy pants, and her eyes kept moving back and forth between the dragons. The Chest of Plenty lay at her feet.

Vale stared at the young woman.

When the dark seraphim had attacked, why had he leaped out of his cave to fight for Tash—to die for her? Why, looking at her, did he still love her? She had betrayed him! She had nearly betrayed all of Requiem. He wanted to hate her. He wanted to hate her with the heat of dragonfire, to blast that dragonfire her way, to burn her, at least to exile her, at least to tell the others what she had done.

And yet still that love for her filled him.

She was afraid, a voice whispered inside him. *She lost her faith in Requiem, too weak to resist temptation, to follow her old dream, and she regretted it. She would have turned around after another two steps if I hadn't stopped her. She's good at heart. She wouldn't have truly left. She fought bravely against many enemies.*

That voice inside him begged Vale to forgive her, and yet he could not. The hatred and love battled within him.

"Aren't you going to shift?" Elory asked, bringing her scaly head down near Tash's.

Tash looked at her collar, then lowered her head. "I'd like to. I'm just . . ." She glanced up at Vale and met his gaze, pain in her eyes. "I'm not sure I'm worthy of becoming a dragon."

"Tash!" Elory said. The lavender dragon released her magic, once more becoming a slender, short-haired girl with brown eyes. She held Tash's shoulders. "Why would you say something like that?"

Tash looked down at her feet. "I'm not a warrior. I'm not brave or noble. I'm just . . . just a pleasure slave. And . . ." Another look at Vale, then back at her feet.

Vale looked away, ignoring her attempts to meet his eyes again.

She still seeks my forgiveness, still seeks absolution before joining us as dragons. I saved your life, Tash, and I love you, but I cannot give you what you want.

"All right," Tash whispered as if she had heard Vale's thoughts. She was looking at Elory, but Vale knew that she was speaking to him. "Let's try this magic thing."

The young woman closed her eyes, took a deep breath . . . and gasped. Golden scales flowed across her like coins. Horns sprouted from her head, and wings burst out from her back. She flapped those wings, rose into the sky, and gave a spin.

"You're beautiful!" Elory said, shifting back into a dragon and rising to fly beside her friend.

The golden dragon looked down at Vale, maybe hoping he'd call her beautiful too, but he looked away.

"Enough," Vale said. "Back to human forms, everyone. Into the cave. I see fire in the distance."

He pointed. On the dark horizon the balls of fire rose from Shayeen, heading their way. Chariots of fire. Vale grimaced. Had they been seen, or was this a routine patrol?

The dragons all returned to human form, raced toward the cave on the hillside, and entered. Complete darkness fell, and Vale dared not even light his lamp.

"Were we seen?" Meliora whispered, kneeling at his side.

"I don't know." Vale sneered. "If they saw us, we burn them. We fly out. We fight as dragons. We—"

"Wait." Meliora touched his arm. "Wait, brother."

Fire crackled and red light lit the land outside. The thunder of firehorse hooves filled the sky, and the smell of fire and brimstone wafted. Vale stiffened, prepared to burst out of the cave, to fight as a dragon. His muscles tensed, and he longed for the battle.

His fists unclenched as the chariots of fire flew over the cave, heading into the distance. At his sides, the others exhaled in relief.

"Lovely place, this," Lucem said, wiping sweat off his brow. "I forgot how much I missed Tofet. We're miles away and already dark seraphim and chariots of fire are trying to kill us." He shuddered. "Remind me—why didn't we decide to just fly to some nice little island, get rich and fat off duplicating coins and coconuts?"

Lucem laughed at his own joke, but Vale cringed. He couldn't help but glance at Tash. She crouched at his side, her cheeks red, and stared down at the floor.

When finally the firelight outside faded, they all stepped out of the cave and onto the dark hills. Meliora, a tall woman, her halo of dragonfire crackling above her head. Elory, dark and small and quick, her eyes shining. Tash, still staring down at her feet in shame, her hair hiding her face. Lucem, the legendary hero of Requiem, revealed to be only a young man with a ready smile and eyes that hid old pain.

And me, Vale thought. *With nothing but pain inside me. Pain for what the seraphim did to me. Pain for what I saw Tash do.*

Perhaps pain was all they knew, all Vir Requis could ever know. In the old tales, Requiem suffered tragedy after tragedy. Every generation brought war, genocide, slavery, nearly extinguishing that light. Every generation the columns of Requiem fell, only for heroes to build them anew.

Why do we keep fighting? Vale thought. *Why do we linger on, struggling to maintain our torch of dragonfire, when darkness so often falls? When we suffer so much?*

He looked at his sisters, at Lucem, at Tash . . . and he thought he knew.

Because between the dark nights the day still shines. Joy can still bloom through suffering like flowers between cobblestones. Perhaps Requiem will never know peace. Perhaps our kingdom will never enjoy an era of prosperity and grandeur. But with every death, new life shines. With every fall, we rise anew. We suffer, but we also love. We hurt, but we also feel joy. For those little flickers, like starlight in darkest night, I will always fight. If not for a Requiem of eternal peace, I will fight for a Requiem of blood and starlight. If that is our fate, that is better than endless darkness where no stars shine.

"What do we do now?" Elory whispered. "Our boat is gone. How will we sneak back into Tofet with the Keeper's Key and the Chest of Plenty? Do we swim? Do we scale the wall like Lucem once did?"

Vale smiled thinly at her. "We don't need to swim or climb, my sister." He stared up at the dark sky. "Dawn is still an hour away. We fly."

ELORY

The five dragons flew through the night, silent, their fire hidden inside closed jaws, shadows high above the landscape of ruin.

At first flying had felt strange to Elory; she had wobbled in the air, no more graceful than a toddler first learning to walk. Yet this night she would have to fly with the grace of the bellators, the legendary and ancient knights of Requiem.

The others flew at her side. Tash, a golden dragon. Lucem, red. Meliora, silvery, her feathers gone. Vale, blue and burly. She knew their colors, yet Elory could barely see them in the darkness, only the faintest hints of them. No moon shone in the sky, and the only light came from below.

A path of fire stretched across the land, semicircular, several miles long. The wall of Tofet. Upon its parapets the seraphim guards stood, halos bright, torches brighter. A wall of fire, of holy light, of death to any who dared approach it. Across the river, a few miles away, Elory could see the bright lights of Shayeen shining upon towers and temples. The City of Kings, home to seraphim masters, was bright as day, even now. Yet that was not her destination, and Elory hoped she would never enter that hive of light and gold and splendor again.

She looked down. Now her destination lay there below— in the vast stretch of darkness. From up here, higher than eagles, Tofet was but a black pool across the land. Barely any lights shone, only the moving flickers of seraphim patrolling the streets, holding torches. No towers rose here, no temples, no warm homes with firelight in the windows. A place of darkness, of chains, of death.

A place we will liberate, Elory swore. *I swear to you, my people, you will be free. You will fly with me in the sky of Saraph and in the sky of Requiem.*

Firelight flashed below.

Elory stared down and hissed.

"Chariots!" she whispered.

Three of them were rising from below, crossing the river, soaring skyward. Three perhaps the dragons could handle, but a battle would raise the others, and soon a thousand chariots would light the sky. No. This was not the time for war, but the time for silence, for shadows.

The other dragons saw and nodded. They flew higher, fanning out—so high the air grew thin and cold, barely letting Elory breathe. Her head spun. She glided, flapping her wings only when she began to dip.

The chariots streamed below them.

Please don't let them see us. Don't let the firelight illuminate our bellies.

She flew eastward, Meliora at her side. The other dragons flew westward.

The chariots below charged onward, flying across the walls of Tofet and into the wilderness.

Elory let out a shaky breath of relief, and the dragons glided downward, back to where the air was thicker. She took several deep breaths, calming the spinning of her head and the thrashing of her heart.

She glanced at her fellow dragons, then down below. A dark patch sprawled in the south—the fields of bricklaying. A darker patch spread beside it—the pit of bitumen. Near them, lit by only a few scattered torches, spread the city of huts, a small place—far smaller than Shayeen across the river—where over half a million slaves lived.

That is where we land, Elory thought. *In the heart of suffering. From darkness will rise fire.*

She began to spiral down, wings wide, jaws clenched shut to hide her fire. Only the faintest glow filled her nostrils; Elory still thought it strange to be able to see her nostrils, but she had a good view of them in dragon form. The other dragons spiraled down around her, their scales giving the slightest of chinks.

"Hush!" Elory whispered. "You're chinking, Lucem."

The red dragon grimaced at her side, stiffened his body, and wobbled down beside her.

They glided lower. Soon Elory could make out individual huts in the darkness. They seemed so small from up here, as if they were toys, as if she could reach down and pluck them up.

Firelight flared below.

Another chariot of fire—just one—rose from the walls and soared.

Elory cursed silently. The chariot was heading toward them, casting its light.

She swerved sideways, silent. Lucem flew with her. The other dragons scattered to other directions. They were too low already to soar and hide in darkness. Elory's heart beat madly against her ribs.

Did he see us?

She stared down and saw the chariot still rising. Four firehorses tugged it, wings casting out sparks. A single seraph stood in the chariot, lit by the firelight.

He saw her. Their eyes connected.

The seraph's eyes widened and he opened his mouth to shout.

Elory snarled and charged.

She streamed through the air. She reached the chariot in a second. The seraph began to cry out, and his voice died within her jaws. She snapped those jaws shut, severing his head. Hot, sticky blood spurted, filling her mouth with its coppery taste. Her heart beat madly. She spat the head out.

The firehorses reared in the sky, and Elory released her magic.

She landed in the chariot in human form, blood still in her mouth. The headless corpse lay at her feet. She grabbed the reins.

The firehorses calmed.

Elory gave the reins a gentle tug, nudging the beasts to glide through the sky, pulling the flaming chariot behind them.

Finally Elory could breathe, could think. She trembled, and sweat drenched her.

What have I done? Oh stars, I killed a man, I bit off his head.

She stared around, fearing that somebody had noticed. But no other chariots of fire flew. The other dragons glided around her, staring with wide eyes, and Elory directed her chariot down.

She landed on a patch of bare earth outside the hut city. The other dragons glided down farther away from the light, vanishing between the huts.

Her knees trembled. Her pulse pounded in her one ear, and sweat drenched her. Elory couldn't think. Her mind was a storm, her body felt on fire, she was going to faint, she—

Calm yourself, Elory, spoke a voice in her head. *Right now you must remain calm.*

Refusing to think, to fear, just operating on cold logic, she climbed out of the chariot. Glancing around, she resumed dragon form. She dug a hole with her claws, tugged the headless seraph out from the chariot, and buried the corpse. She sniffed, looked around, found the head a few meters away and buried it too.

She return to human form. Leaving the chariot and firehorses on the field, she headed between the huts, vanishing into the shadows.

Please, stars of Requiem, don't let any other seraphim see us, don't let them know, don't let them suspect—not until we're safe.

A shadow approached between the huts, and Elory's heart leaped into a gallop, and she nearly shifted and lashed her claws. But it was Lucem, slinking forward, back in human form. She rushed toward him, and he wrapped her in his arms and kissed the top of her head.

Other shadows approached. Meliora, a hood dousing her halo. Vale, tall and grim. Tash, tiptoeing forward, glancing around nervously.

"We made it," Meliora whispered.

Lucem rolled his eyes. "Once again, Mel, the sky is up."

Firelight fell onto the road. The Vir Requis hurried behind a hut. A seraph walked down the dirt road, holding a torch. Hiding behind the clay wall, Elory held her breath and squeezed Lucem's hand. When finally the light faded and the guard had walked by, the Vir Requis released their breath.

"Come," Elory whispered. "I know the way."

They walked between the huts, avoiding the larger dirt roads, slinking hut to hut. Vale carried the Chest of Plenty under his arm. Elory carried the Keeper's Key, while Tash carried a humbler iron key—the one she had used to unlock Elory's shackles back in the pleasure pit long ago.

Another chariot of fire streamed above. The Vir Requis froze and hid again, pressing themselves against a hut's wall. When the firelight passed them, they walked onward.

Finally Elory saw it ahead. It looked like any other hut, but she knew this was the place.

Home.

Her eyes dampened. After all Elory had seen in the world—the great ziggurat of gold and ivory, the open wilderness of forests and hills, underground caverns of ancient days, a mountaintop palace full of magic—this hut seemed so small, so sad. So many bad memories filled this place. So many times Elory had lain in this hut, shivering from the wounds of the whip, her father stitching and healing her. So many times her mother had embraced her in this hut, soothing her tears, applying balms to her wounds, and singing to her old songs of Requiem. For eighteen years Elory had lived here, and seeing it now nearly broke her heart.

Home. A home of pain, of death, of fear, of love. The only home I've ever known.

Meliora looked at her, smiled sadly, and placed a hand on her shoulder. Vale stood at her other side and placed an arm around her.

The three siblings—the three Aeternums, heirs to a dynasty, hurt, broken, fighting for their nation—walked forward together.

They entered the hut.

He knelt inside in prayer. Her father, tall and gaunt, bald and bearded. He looked up, and his eyes widened, and Elory's eyes flooded with tears, and her body shook with sobs. She raced forward, fell to her knees before him, and nearly crushed his thin frame in her embrace.

"Father," she whispered, sobbing against him. "Father."

He wept too, holding her close. "Elory, Elory. You're alive. I knew you were alive. You're alive. Oh stars, you're alive."

Vale joined them, and even the gruff young slave shed tears, squeezing them close, shaking. Meliora knelt too, wrapped her arms around them, and held them silently.

"I'm here, Father." Elory smiled and blinked away her tears. "I'll never leave you again. I promise."

Lucem and Tash stood at the doorway, glancing around nervously. Elory rose to her feet and approached them. She took their hands in hers, ushering them into the hut. Her heart trembled at their touch. Tash—her closest friend. Lucem—the first man she had ever loved. They were her family too, just as much as her father and siblings. All of Requiem was her family.

"Father, you remember Tash, and this is Lucem."

The young man bowed. "Yes, the famous Lucem himself! I heard I'm something of a legend around these parts. But not like you. I'm honored to meet you, King Aeternum. At least, the descendant of King Aeternum, hopefully to be our real king soon. Not here. Bit too crowded here. In Requiem, I mean. If we get there. Um . . ." He glanced at Meliora. "Mel said there would be taters."

Elory rolled her eyes.

Jaren looked down at the Chest of Plenty which Vale had placed on the floor, then up at his son, then at Meliora and Elory.

"Did you . . .," the old priest whispered. "Did you find them? The chest and key?"

Elory reached into her pocket and pulled out the Keeper's Key. She stepped forward and brought the key to her father's collar.

The collar opened.

Elory removed it from around Jaren's neck and tossed it to the floor.

"We found them, Father." She stared into his eyes, and her rage seared her tears dry. "We found them, and now, Father . . . now we fight."

TASH

She kept glancing at Vale, trying to meet his eyes, hoping he'd forgive her, but he hated her, he hated her still, and Tash hated herself.

I would have turned back, she thought, kneeling in the hut. *I just had to take another step toward my freedom, to hesitate, to feel the guilt, to turn back toward Vale and curse my stupidity.* She hung her head low. *But you had to see me, Vale. You had to call out, to try to stop me when I would have stopped on my own. I would have. I have to believe that I would have. And I'm so sorry.*

She raised her head, trying to meet his eyes again. But Vale stood across the hut, pointedly looking away from her, talking instead to Lucem.

Tash's shoulders stooped.

I'm going to show you, Vale. I'm going to make amends for what I've done. I'm going to show you that I love Requiem, that I'll fight for her, that I'm sorry for my betrayal.

Elory approached and sat beside her. "Are you all right, Tash?"

Tash looked at the girl, and fresh guilt filled her. Back in the pleasure pit, perhaps she had treated Elory too harshly, commanding her as if she, Tash, were a seraph herself rather than a slave. The girl was kind, meek, truly believed in Requiem's cause.

Another one I mistreated, Tash thought. *Another one I must prove my worth to.*

Suddenly Tash hated who she was. Hated herself. A pleasurer who, while the others toiled in the dust, had serviced seraphim with kisses and caresses. A slave who had looked down on other slaves as if she were superior. A traitor who had almost ruined Requiem, who had almost fled with the Chest of Plenty.

I don't belong here with these noble, kind people, she thought, looking at the others. *I'm not like them. I'm not good and brave and strong like they are.*

"Tash, are you all right?" Elory whispered.

Tash nodded. "Yes, and I'm ready. Let's try this."

She took a deep breath, opened the Chest of Plenty, and placed the Keeper's Key inside.

The others all gathered around her. Meliora, Lucem, Jaren, Vale; they all stared. Tash gulped and opened the chest.

Hundreds of crimson keys, engraved with golden runes, spilled out.

"It works!" Tash whispered.

Lucem whistled. "Now all we need is a mug of beer, and we're set for life."

Instead of beer, Tash grabbed her collar, which she had opened outside the city but kept with her. She placed the iron around her neck, took a deep breath, and snapped it shut. Next she lifted one of the duplicated keys. For a second she hesitated, worried that the duplicate would fail, that the chest had copied the key but not the magic inside it. Yet when she brought the replicated Keeper's Key to her collar, the runes glowed, and the collar opened anew.

Hurriedly, Tash reached into her pocket, and she pulled out her second key—a smaller, humbler key. A key she had used long ago on the shackles around Elory's ankles. She placed this key into the chest too, duplicating it a thousand times. Keys to open chains.

The pile of keys—some crimson and gold, others simple iron—piled up in the hut.

"Dragons," Tash whispered. "Thousands of dragons. Thousands of warriors of Requiem."

Elory grabbed Tash's hand and squeezed it. "Let's make more."

JAREN

He labored in the dirt under the blinding sun, but this day, hope filled Jaren.

The whips hit his back, but he thought of Requiem.

His joints ached, his skin burned, his head swam with weakness, and he thought of dragons rising.

His body was almost broken, his life almost spent, and thousands languished around him in chains, the overseers taking their lives day by day. But Jaren clung to his life.

Because his children were back. Because there was hope.

That night, as always, he limped back to the huts—breath rattling, back torn open, spine nearly cracked with the agony. That night, as always, instead of sleeping, Jaren stood outside his hut. As always, the children of Requiem came before him—the wounded, the dying. Mothers too thin to produce milk, their babes starving. Elders beaten, whipped, kicked, their limbs broken, begging for healing or a blessing before death. Young men and women in the prime of their youth, yet frail as the elders, coughing, shivering, bleeding. They all came before Jaren Aeternum as they did every night.

He was descended of kings, but here in Tofet, he was a priest, he was a healer.

The first of his people approached, limping—a young girl, no older than twelve or thirteen, her arm crushed. Her father walked with her, face pale, eyes damp.

"Please, Papa Jaren." Sweat glistened on the girl's brow. "It hurts so bad."

Jaren prayed, calling upon the stars to heal her wound, to ease her pain. She cried out as he set the bone, then shivered, whispering her thanks.

Before they stepped aside, Jaren held the father's arm. He passed a sack into his hand.

"Keys," Jaren whispered. "Keys to remove your collars. Keys to remove the chains around your ankles."

The slave's eyes widened. "Do you jest?"

Jaren shook his head. "A blessing, my son. A miracle. Keep them secret. Hand them out to every hut around yours; there are two hundred keys in this sack. Spread the word to wait. To wait until the Night of Seven."

Night of Seven. Among the holiest nights in Requiem's calendar. It was the night that Requiem remembered the great fall two thousand years ago—the genocide that had slaughtered all but seven Vir Requis, the Living Seven who fought the tyrant Dies Irae, who rebuilt Requiem from ruin. Queen Gloriae Aeternum had sat upon the Oak Throne that night two thousand years ago, and now—here, far from Requiem, chained in a distant land—the slaves of Requiem would rise in new defiance.

"Two nights from this one," whispered the slave, accepting the sack. "May the stars bless you, son of Aeternum."

Another slave approached, the whip lashes on his back infected. Jaren prayed, applied ointments, and stitched the wounds. To this man too, he gave a sack of keys. Inside were Keeper's Keys and simple, iron keys for the shackles around the slaves' feet.

He stood out in the night for hours, handing out the keys. He finally slept, allowing Elory to continue the work.

In the daylight, they toiled again.

In the darkness, they healed more slaves, handed out more keys.

"Keys for your collars," Jaren whispered to the ill and wounded approaching. "Keys for your shackles. Tomorrow night we rise. May our wings forever find Requiem's sky."

"Bless you, Papa Jaren!" they said. "The stars will forever shine upon you. Tomorrow night we rise."

Dawn rose.

"Toil!"

Whips lashed.

"Faster!"

Boots kicked.

"Die!"

Slaves fell into the dust, fading, flickering out.
Darkness fell.

They gathered in the hut. Slaves. Rebels. Children of starlight. An old priest and his children. A young hero. A young woman who'd fled from darkness. Those who had stood up against the shadows, who had shone a light, who had bled and prayed for their lost kingdom. Heroes of Requiem.

Jaren stood before them, and he spoke softly.

"Two thousand years ago, a tyrant named Dies Irae raised an army, and he toppled the halls of Requiem, and he slew all but seven of our people. Those seven Vir Requis—the great heroes of our nation—raised Requiem again from ruin. We've all heard their names in many tales: Benedictus, Lacrimosa, Gloriae, Agnus Dei, Kyrie Eleison, Terra, Memoria. Seven names we remember and praise even now, so many generations later."

Vale's eyes flashed. He had always imagined himself strong and noble like the great King Benedictus. Elory's eyes shone. She had always loved tales of Queen Lacrimosa, the great mother of Requiem.

"Tonight is the night we remember those old heroes," Jaren said. "And this night again, Requiem lies in ruin. Our people are dying. Our kingdom lies across the sea, its halls fallen. And this night again, heroes rise. This night we fight. And every night hence, for thousands of years, the Vir Requis will remember new names. Lucem. Tash. Elory. Vale. Meliora."

He looked at them, one by one, as he spoke their names. They stared back, eyes determined.

"And Jaren," Meliora whispered, reaching out to hold his hand. "My dear father, the kindest, bravest man I know."

Jaren squeezed her hand, looking at her—his eldest, his sweet Meliora.

You are Kalafi's daughter, and for so many years, I never knew you, but I love you, Meliora. I love you all. You are all my children.

"Let us pray," Jaren said.

They all held hands in a circle, and they spoke together. "As the leaves fall upon our marble tiles, as the breeze rustles the birches beyond our columns, as the sun gilds the mountains above our halls—know, young child of the woods, you are home, you are home." Their voices dropped to whispers, and tears shone in their eyes. "Requiem. May our wings forever find your sky."

They left the hut together.

They stood in the darkness in a land of pain, of fire, of blood . . . and they called upon the starlight.

Their collars clanked to the ground, and scales chinked across them.

For the first time in his long life, Jaren Aeternum summoned his magic and became a dragon. Green scales rose across his body, green like the birch leaves of home, like the old flags of Requiem. Silver spikes grew from his tail. He was a frail dragon, too thin, too hurt, too weary, but as he soared skyward, he was as a great king of old.

His children rose around him. Red. Gold. Lavender. Blue. And one silver dragon with golden horns, no more feathers upon her.

They rose into the sky, and they blew their fire upward, lighting a great beacon.

"Requiem!" they cried.

And from the land below, the voices rose in answer. Hundreds of voices, then thousands, then a nation crying out together. One word. The word that meant everything to them, the word that had meant everything for over five thousand years.

"Requiem!"

From below they rose. One after another. Soon a hundred, then a thousand, then too many to count—a kingdom of dragons, rising from the darkness, blowing their fire.

Collars and chains clattered down, and the light of Requiem shone.

BOOK THREE:
PILLARS OF DRAGONFIRE

Daniel Arenson

TIL

They crept through the ruins—a man, a woman, a child—
seeking life in fields of death.

Please, stars of Requiem, Til prayed silently, moving through
the snow. *Let there be others. Please.*

The snow kept falling and she couldn't stop shivering. Her
woolen cloak was too ragged, and the wind invaded its holes to
claw her skin. Her patches of rusted armor, cobbled together
over the years, felt like ice pressed against her. Holes filled her
boots, snow sloshed around her toes, and Til began to wonder if
the cold would kill her before the fire of the seraphim could.

The ruins of Requiem spread around her. Clouds veiled
the sun, allowing only dim light to fall upon the devastation.
Columns lay shattered around her like the bones of giants.
Icicles clung to statues of dragons and ancient kings. An archway
still stood on a hill, the entrance to some old temple, the walls
around it long fallen. Only crows now stood upon what
remained of the battlements, the priests and warriors long fallen.
Homes, schools, libraries, hospitals—all now lay as strewn
bricks, covered in snow. Forgotten. Dead like the denizens of
this place.

Nova Vita, fabled capital of Requiem, Til thought, shivering as
she walked among the snowy ruins. She lowered her head. *Like
every other place, you too are gone.*

"There's nothing but death here," she whispered.

At her left side, her father grunted. "Let's take a closer
look. We'll scan the city."

Til turned to look at him. Father was tall and haggard, his
eyes dark. Like her, he wore a tattered cloak, the gray wool
dusted with snow. Like her, he sported flaming red hair, most of
it hidden beneath his hood. Like her, he held a bow, and a sword
and quiver hung across his back. Yet he seemed more hopeful to
Til, stronger, braver.

486

Flame of Requiem

He still believes, she thought. *Still believes we can win this rebellion. Still believes other Vir Requis survived.*

Five hundred years ago, the seraphim had come here to Requiem. Five hundred years ago, they had carted off nearly all the Vir Requis in chains.

But a few Vir Requis had remained in their homeland. A few had avoided the chains, had hidden, had survived, had passed the torch of Requiem to a new generation. For five centuries, free Vir Requis had been fighting the seraphim here in Requiem, haggard but wearing no collars, hiding in forests and caves, keeping the old flame alive. As most of their people languished in slavery far in the south, these few had remained, had fought on. Til. Her father. Her brother. Perhaps they were the last.

"I want to leave," whispered Til's brother. "Please, Father. Please. I'm scared. They'll find us. I want to go back to the caves. *Please.*"

Til turned to her right. Her brother, Bim, walked there. He was only eleven years old—a full decade younger than Til—but his eyes were older. Dark eyes, too large in his gaunt face. Haunted eyes. The eyes of an old soldier who had seen too many killed, had killed too many. Bim too carried sword and bow, the weapons too large for him, and beneath his hood, a man's helmet wobbled on his head.

Forced to grow up too soon, Til thought. She placed a hand on his shoulder. *Like I was. Like we all were. But will he live to be my age?*

"Soon," Til said, trying to make her voice soothing, though fear coiled through her. "Soon, Bim. We just have to see if any others live in this city."

His eyes flooded with tears, and his breath shuddered. "We've been looking for others for so long. For years. For years, Til! It'll be the same here as everywhere else. Just bones."

He pointed.

Til looked and her spirits sank deeper. Three skeletons hung from the frosted branches of oaks, swinging in the wind. The crows had stripped them bare. These were not the skeletons of Requiem's ancient warriors, those who had fallen in the Great Calamity five hundred years ago when Prince Ishtafel had shattered this land. The ropes around their necks were too fresh.

No. Here were others like Til and her family. Others who had survived the war, who had been living in hiding, fighting from the shadows all these centuries. Still falling. One by one. Last lights going out after a great flame, last stars vanishing long after the sun had set.

Father approached, placed his arm around Bim, and turned the boy away from the grisly sight. "We keep going, son." Father's voice was but a whisper. "Just a little longer. We might yet find life here."

They walked onward, and with every step, Til's hope shrank. When she had been a youth, there had been others. Not many but enough to give Til a sense of camaraderie, of hope to see Requiem reborn. She had fought with them, the last free Vir Requis, the ancestors of those who had survived the war, who had hidden in tunnels and forests while the seraphim had carried their brethren to southern slavery. For centuries they had hidden in their ravaged homeland, scurrying from hole to hole, fighting in the forests and ruins.

Until five years ago.

Til lowered her head.

Until the disastrous rebellion.

The man had led them, the prophet, the one who had claimed to be king. He had gathered all free Vir Requis, all those who had cowered and hidden in Requiem. A thousand dragons had flown that day, flown against the Overlord, the cruel seraph who ruled over these ruins.

And the dragons had burned. They had fallen screaming.

Hundreds had perished in the flames that day, and the survivors—mere dozens—had fled. For five years now, the Overlord had been hunting them. Killing them one by one. Til's comrades. Her mother. Her older brother. Until this was all that remained: a haggard father; a frightened son; and her—a young woman with red hair, old patches of armor, and fading hope in her heart.

As they kept walking, fire crackled above.

At once Til, her brother, and her father leaped aside. Father crouched behind a toppled statue, and Til and Bim huddled under a fallen log. Red light fell upon the snow. Til's heart pounded, and she clutched her sword's hilt. Peering from under her snowy hood, she saw them above.

Chariots of fire.

She grimaced, cold sweat on her brow. She still remembered those chariots tearing through the rebels five years ago. She still remembered the seraphim, deities from the sky, slaying her mother and older brother. A thousand times in her dreams, she had seen these chariots fly into Requiem—the Old Requiem from five hundred years ago—and topple this city.

Only three now flew above, their firehorses shedding ash, and suddenly Til wanted to summon her magic. To become a dragon. To fly, to blow her fire like she had during the rebellion. To burn down the seraphim, even if she died in their fire.

And why shouldn't she? She was not like the Vir Requis slaves who languished in the south, captives of Saraph. Her ancestors had avoided the chains and collars, had remained in Requiem, had learned to survive in these ruins. Til was a warrior descended of warriors. She had been fighting in these ruins all her life. She reached down, felt her magic tingling there—the ancient magic of Requiem. The magic that would let her fly as a dragon. To fight instead of cower.

The chariots flew onward, and Til released her magic and lowered her head.

No, she thought. *The rebellion is over. There is no more hope to fight the seraphim, only hope to maybe find more Vir Requis. To maybe live another day.*

With the chariots gone, they emerged from their hiding spots. Bim was crying. The damn boy was always crying lately.

"You have to be strong." Til grabbed his shoulders, leaned down, and stared into her brother's eyes. "You hear? You're eleven years old, old enough to fight, to be a man. To be strong."

"I want to go home," he whispered.

Til's throat tightened. "This *is* our home." She swept her arm across the ruins. "See this place? This is Nova Vita, the ancient capital of Requiem. Where our ancestors are from. See the old walls, the archway, the bridge?"

He shook his head, shivering. "I see only burnt stones. Only bones. I want to go back to the cave. The place in the north where we hid. To hide. To hide from the fire. They're going to burn us." He covered his eyes, and his voice dropped to a whisper. "The seraphim."

Father approached and brushed snow off Bim's shoulders. "Come, son, just a little farther. There might be others here. Other survivors."

Til looked over Bim's head and met her father's gaze. He stared back, his green eyes so weary in his haggard face. She had the same eyes. Eyes that clung to hope though the mind knew there was none.

She nodded. "We keep going."

They kept walking through the ruins as the snow fell. As they stepped over frosted bricks, Til imagined a home standing here, a hearth crackling, a family gathered together in prayer and love. She walked alongside a staircase that rose only four steps, leading to a pile of rubble and smashed statues, and she imagined a temple standing here, soaring toward the sky, full of priests who sang the old songs. When she gazed up at the clouds, she imagined millions of dragons flying above in every color.

This was a great nation once, Til thought. *A nation now enslaved in the south. But I will never be a slave. I will never wear a collar. Better to live like a rat, scurrying from hole to hole, than live in a cage.*

The sun was low in the sky when she saw it ahead. Til froze and gasped. Her father and brother stood with her, staring with wide eyes.

"There it is," Till whispered. "It's real."

She had always known her father to be stern, laconic, but now the haggard man knelt in the snow, and his eyes dampened.

"King's Column," he whispered.

The ancient pillar was still distant, miles away, but easily visible. It soared above the treetops, three hundred feet tall. Til had never seen it before, but like all Vir Requis, she knew the tales. Thousands of years ago, the legendary Aeternum had raised that column in the forest, a beacon to summon the wild, hunted Vir Requis from across the world. It had become the backbone of Requiem, the kingdom of those who could grow wings and scales, breathe fire, and rise as dragons.

For thousands of years, Til knew, the enemies of Requiem had tried to topple this column. Yet so long as a single Vir Requis breathed, the column would stand. And so even now, in these ruins, with the seraphim burning the sky, King's Column still soared.

"Thousands of years ago, this was a beacon to our hunted, outcast people," Til said. "I pray that it acts as a beacon still. If any others survived the rebellion, I pray that we find them here."

Other survivors. Til did not know if any still lived in these ruins. She had not seen others for months now, not since her mother had died. Perhaps they were all that remained—her, her father, her brother . . . and the collared slaves in the south. Yet if others still lived free, they would be here, she knew. Here at this ancient heart of an ancient kingdom.

The ruins were thick here, with countless bricks, staircases, and columns buried under the snow. Walking was slow but they dared not fly. In human form, they would quickly leap and hide should more chariots burn above. As dragons they would be visible for leagues. As she walked, Til tried to imagine the great manors and temples that had risen here, the heart of the city. In her mind's eye, she could see Requiem standing again, beautiful in the winter, a safe home.

I pray that someday Requiem rises again, she thought. *If there is any holiness left in this place, and if you can hear me, stars of my forebears, let us survive long enough. For thousands of years, empires have risen to destroy us, only to fall. I pray that we live long enough to see Saraph fall too, to see Requiem reborn, but the darkness is great, and the wait is long, and I'm afraid.*

She stared ahead at King's Column, seeking solace from this ancient pillar, yet when she stepped closer, a strangled yelp left her mouth.

Her father grunted, and Bim covered his eyes.

Stars above, Til thought. She walked closer, dreading what she saw, unable to turn away. Sickness rose inside her, and she knelt over and gagged.

In the stories, King's Column shone like starlight, carved of purest marble, a pillar like white dragonfire. Yet now dried blood coated the stone, flaking and rancid. Hundreds of skeletons draped across the column, strung along chains, like a lurid maypole from the Abyss. They were human skeletons, wingless—the skeletons of Vir Requis.

Bim let out a strangled yelp. Til pulled him into her arms and pressed his face against her shoulder.

Ancient magic still protected the column, Til knew, and the seraphim could not topple it. But they could defile it. They had turned it from a beacon of hope into a monument of Requiem's fall.

"They're all dead." She stared at her father with dry eyes. "We leave. There's nobody here."

But she was wrong.

There was life here.

Cruel life. Life of sunfire and steel.

They rose from the ruins. They descended from the clouds. They burned the sky and melted the ice. Hundreds of them, casting out blinding light.

The seraphim.

Some flew in chariots of fire, pulled by winged horses of flame. Other seraphim spread their own wings, and the firelight shone against their armor, spears, and golden hair. At their lead flew a glittering deity, his armor gilded, a blinding halo around his head. He was a burly figure, beautiful to behold, his blond locks flowing, a figure who seemed woven of light. A sigil of a rampant lion glittered upon his breastplate.

Til knew this one. The Overlord. Commander of the north, this land that had once been Requiem.

"Run!" Til whispered.

She raced through the snow. Her brother and father ran with her. Til whipped her head from side to side, seeking shelter—a cave, a fallen log, a huddle between walls. Finally she spotted a fallen column ahead, a hollowed out space below.

But it was too late.

They saw her.

"Weredragons!" the seraphim cried. "Weredragons below. Seize the reptiles! String them up with the others."

For five years—five terrible years since the doomed uprising—Til had slunk through the ruins in human form, hiding in holes and caves, scurrying between trees and hills, her sword and arrows her only weapons.

The time to hide was over.

This day, in sight of her defiled column in the heart of her stolen kingdom, Til summoned her magic.

Scales flowed across her, rattling like a suit of armor, deep orange trimmed with yellow. Wings burst out from her back, tipped with black claws. Her tail lashed. She took to the sky, the color of fire, and blasted out her own flames. Her father and brother shifted too, both rising as black dragons, and their fire pierced the sky.

The light of Saraph flared. The sun was setting, but the light of a thousand suns now covered the sky and ruins, gold and white. A voice tore through the air, a voice so loud its waves pounded against Til and cracked trees below, a voice mellifluous yet terrible, a voice like a beautiful dirge. The voice of a god.

"Slay the reptiles!"

Til didn't have to look to know—this was the voice of the Overlord.

"Fly!" Til shouted to her family. "Don't look back, just fly!"

The three dragons shot forward, the fire and light blazing behind them. Flames rained, so hot even the frozen trees kindled and burned. More seraphim kept rising, emerging from the forest and ruins, plunging from the clouds, covering the world with their light. Their lances rose like a second forest, their eyes were cruel stars, and their wings shone like clouds in dawn. The hosts of heaven, wreathed in splendor, angels of wrath and retribution—they stormed from all sides.

"Slay the beasts of darkness! Slay the reptiles for the glory of Saraph."

And so this is how we die, Til thought. *Not hiding in shadows but roaring in light. We die in fire.*

The seraphim charged toward the dragons from all sides, a luminous noose. Til reared in the air, spread her wings wide, and blasted out her flames.

Her dragonfire roared outward, slamming into a chariot. The firehorses scattered, and a seraph screamed. More seraphim charged from her sides, thrusting their lances. The firehorse hooves thundered, and the tips of lances gleamed, and Til knew that she would join them—the skeletons on the pillar, the last free warriors of Requiem.

Two jets of flame blasted at her sides, framing her, crashing forward, slamming into seraphim. The immortals screamed, their armor melting, their skin peeling, their chariots falling like comets. Two black dragons stormed forth—her father, her brother—blasting out fire.

"For Requiem!" Til cried.

Her dragonfire stormed forth, shrieking, spinning, slamming into another seraph.

"Fly, children!" Father cried. The black dragon clawed the air, spraying dragonfire in all directions. "Don't fight. Fly! Fly!"

Roaring, Father charged forth, barreling between seraphim. Lances slammed against him, chipping his scales. Firehorses washed across him, burning his wings. Yet still the black dragon flew, blasting out his fire, burning them down.

"Father!" Til cried, flying toward him through the enemies. She swiped her tail, knocking down a chariot. A lance sliced her wing, and she screamed, roared her fire, burned the seraph down.

"Til, take your brother!" Father shouted. Flames blazed across him, and blood seeped from his cracked scales. "Take him south. Take him to the coast. Find others! Find them in the south. Go—"

His voice died   under a shriek and blaze of blinding light.

Til rolled in the sky, blinded, crying out.

The sun seemed to crash onto the world. Light blasted out. Wings buffeted her. She tumbled, reached out, managed to grab her brother. They beat their wings as a holocaust of fire and sunlight flared. In the center of effulgence he flew, wings wide, halo thrumming, lance bright as a falling star—the Overlord.

Father turned toward his children.

"Go," the black dragon whispered.

With a roar, Father soared.

"No!" Til cried, tears in her eyes.

She clung to her brother as Father soared into the light, as he reached toward the Overlord, as dragon and seraph slammed together.

Flame of Requiem

She cried out as the Overlord thrust his lance, as the blade crashed through Father's chest, as it burst out from his back.

"Father!" Bim cried.

Til howled. She wanted to fly up, to save him, to slay the Overlord, to slay them all, to die. To die. To burn in fire. Yet she couldn't release her brother. She could only watch, weeping, as Father lost his magic upon the lance.

The overlord—a massive seraph, eight feet tall—raised that lance. Father was skewered upon it, a man again. The life gone from his eyes.

"Sling him up with the others!" the Overlord cried, tossing the corpse toward a chariot. "Peel off the flesh and string his bones up across the column." Smiling thinly, the Overlord turned in the sky to stare at Til. "Now . . . come to me, children. Come join your father."

Time seemed to freeze.

All the world became just her and him. A dragon and a seraph. A grieving woman, her heart shattered, staring into the eyes of her father's killer.

Father—gone.

Everyone—gone.

My brother.

Her tears streamed.

My brother lives. He lives. He lives.

I have to fight, I have to kill him. I have to die with Father.

"Til," her brother whispered.

He lives. One other lives.

The Overlord stared into her eyes, and his smile grew. "Come to me, children." He reached out his palm. "Come home."

Til lashed her tail, slamming it against her brother, spinning him around in the sky.

"Fly, Bim!" she cried. "Fly!"

They flew, roaring out their dragonfire. The jets shrieked, slamming into seraphim, knocking them aside. The two dragons, orange and black, siblings, perhaps the last two free dragons in Requiem, charged into the hosts of heaven. Their tails lashed, tearing into chariots. Their claws ripped through armor. Lances slammed against them, tearing off scales, yet they kept flying.

Til soared, blasted fire, melted one seraph. Another flew from her left, and she snapped her jaws, ripping his torso apart. She shook her head madly, scattering blood and flesh. Her brother flew at her side, his dragonfire washing over the enemy, burning their wings, their faces.

They flew onward.

They rose higher.

They burst into the clouds, vanishing into swirls of snow.

Flames rose through the clouds. Arrows and javelins flew through the shadows and light, a forest in the sky. The flames of chariots filled the darkness.

Til and Bim flew onward. Silent. Their fire hidden in their jaws. The clouds coiled around them, and snowy wind buffeted them. The chariots flew everywhere, faded patches of light like the sun behind veils. The dragons swerved, rising higher, lower, dodging the enemy. An arrow pierced Bim's wing, but he ground his teeth and kept flying. Silent. Tears in their eyes. Two shadows in the night.

They flew for what seemed like hours, never leaving the clouds, pushing themselves onward until the firelight faded, until the sounds of pursuit were a mere rumble in the distance.

Finally they could fly no more. They were too weary, too hurt. They glided down from the cloud cover, emerging into a dark world. The forests of Requiem spread below, silent in the night. The two dragons spiraled down. They all but crashed through the forest canopy, scattering icicles and frozen branches, and thumped into the snow.

Their magic left them.

They knelt in the darkness, shivering, weeping, humans again.

"He killed him," Bim whispered, even as his teeth chattered. "The Overlord, he—he—"

Til pulled her brother into her arms. She hugged him, squeezing him, nearly crushing him, and her tears fell into his hair.

"He's with Mother now," she whispered. "His pain has ended."

She could not see her brother in the night, but she felt his shuddering breath against her, felt his hands around her back.

"What do we do?" he said.

Til stared upward. Through the hole in the canopy, she could see the night sky. The stars of Requiem shone above—the Draco constellation. The god of her people. The stars that had forever blessed Requiem. The stars that, she had to believe, still looked down upon her.

"We do what he commanded us." Til held her brother close, wrapping him in her cloak. "We travel south. We seek others. We seek life and hope even in this darkness."

"There is no hope," Bim said. "Not without him."

She gripped his shoulders and stared at his dark face, barely visible in the night. "Even in this night the stars shine. There is always hope, even in the darkest shadows. So long as we draw breath, we will fight for Requiem. If not with dragonfire then with every heartbeat, every breath in our lungs. We must stay alive. We must keep Requiem's memory within our hearts. We must believe, Bim."

He lowered his head, shivering. "Believe what?"

Til raised her eyes, though tears now marred her vision, and the stars blurred. "That Requiem can rise again."

Perhaps it's but a dream, she thought. *Perhaps Bim and I are the last. Perhaps all other resistors have fallen. Perhaps the slaves in Saraph will never return, and perhaps they too are gone. But I have to believe. I have to trust in my stars. For you, Father, I will go on. I promise you.*

The siblings held each other close, shivering until the dawn.

MELIORA

Around her they soared.

Hundreds of thousands rising into the sky.

Dragons.

Dragons in every color, rising in the night. Thin. Weary. Some mere children, others elders missing their fangs. The scars of whips still showed upon their bodies, and holes filled their wings. They had been beaten down in human forms, and they showed their wounds as dragons, but still they soared. Their fire blazed in countless pillars, rising like the columns of a flaming temple. The light shone upon their scales. Red, blue, brilliant green, gold, silver—a mosaic in the sky.

"Requiem rises," Meliora whispered, flying with them.

She beat her wings, spinning and soaring higher, and she blasted out a great pillar of white flame. Her flaming halo crackled above her head. They spread below her, flying higher— the great nation of Requiem, their firelight burning the sky.

"Hear me, O Requiem!" Meliora cried, her voice ringing across Tofet. "Arise, arise, sons and daughters of Draco! Fly for freedom. Fly for your stars. Fly for Requiem!"

They rose around her, streaming higher, dragonfire soaring skyward. Their voices rang together, torn with pain, with tears, with awe, with joy.

"Requiem rises!"

And from the south, rose new fire.

Meliora spun in the sky and snarled, smoke blasting from between her teeth.

"The seraphim," she hissed.

They rose from Shayeen across the river. A hundred thousand chariots of fire, leaving trails of flame and smoke. They painted the sky red. The night turned bright as day under their wrath. Their firehorses' wings spread out in a burning canopy, and the seraphim raised their spears. At their lead he rode, his armor bright, his halo a great ring of gold.

Ishtafel.

The seraphim cried out together, spears gleaming, chanting for war. Ishtafel's voice rose above them all, tearing across the sky.

"Slay the reptiles! Slay every last one. Saraph, Saraph, rise with fire! Slay every last dragon."

The dragons of Requiem bellowed in fear. Child dragons, no larger than ponies, wailed in the sky. Elders prayed. The stronger dragons stormed forth to protect the weak, fangs bared, fire crackling.

Vale, a great blue dragon, darted up beside Meliora. "We must fight."

The seraphim kept charging, howling for war, the firehorses' hooves deafening like countless blasts of thunder.

No, Meliora thought. *We're too hurt, too weak. We cannot defeat them.*

She soared higher and roared out her fire, a beacon for Requiem. "Fly north, Requiem! Fly north! Flee them! Flee the city!"

A few dragons began to fly north at once, but most bustled in a confused mass, and the chariots of fire flew closer.

"Elory!" Meliora shouted. "Elory, lead them out! Lead them north. Father, help her!"

The two—the green elder and the young lavender dragon—nodded and flew north, blasting twin jets of fire.

"Follow, Requiem!" Jaren roared, casting out firelight, green scales clattering. "Follow me, Jaren Aeternum. Follow me north!"

Elory flew at his side, raising her fire, crying out. "Follow, children of Requiem! Follow us north—to freedom, to home!"

The green dragon led the way, raising his pillar of fire, while Elory flew madly from side to side, shepherding the dragons onward.

Lucem flew up to hover at Meliora's side, facing the approaching seraphim. The red dragon growled. "Time to burn some seraphim."

Meliora slapped him with her tail. "The sky is up, Lucem."

499

Scales flashed, and Vale and Tash came to fly with them too. His scales shone deep blue, while hers glittered gold like coins.

"We fight with you, Meliora," Tash said, snarling.

Vale roared out a great cry. "For the light of Requiem, we fight!"

While most dragons were fleeing the city, flying after Jaren, hundreds rose to fly around Meliora, to join the defenders. Their roars rolled across the sky, and their wings churned smoke and fire.

"For Requiem! For Meliora!"

The chariots stormed across the river.

The warriors of Requiem charged forth to meet them.

Above the field of bricks and dust and agony, dragons and chariots slammed together.

The fire of chariots and the fire of dragons blasted across the sky. Meliora roared out her inferno, slashed her claws, whipped her tail. A chariot stormed toward her, and she soared, spun, lashed her tail, slammed the spikes into the firehorses. Another chariot flew from below, and Meliora swooped, reached out her claws, and tore the rider apart. Ichor rained.

Around her, her companions fought. Dragonfire washed across seraphim. Spears shattered scales. Fangs tore into armor and tails smashed chariots. Firehorses drove into dragons, tearing out their magic, casting them down as screaming, bleeding men and women.

"Welcome home, Meliora!" rose a voice across the battle—Ishtafel's voice. "You will watch your people burn before I drag you back to your cell."

She saw him ahead, and Meliora growled. She rose to fly toward him, but a dozen chariots stormed her way. She roared. She blasted her fire. Her tail whipped, her claws lashed, and she tore into the seraphim around her. A lance thrust and dug into her side, and Meliora screamed, her scales cracking. She spun, scuttled forward, and grabbed the seraph in her jaws. She bit deep, tearing into the armor, tearing the flesh beneath, and pulled back, cutting the man in half. She spat out his upper torso and roared, blasting fire skyward, holding the chariots back.

The other dragons fought around her in a fury, crying out for their kingdom. Every moment another dragon fell. Lances drove into them, picking them out from the sky. They lost their magic in death, falling as men, women, children, bleeding, slamming down onto the field where they had labored for so many years—falling finally as warriors, not slaves. And always the chariots stormed forth, thousands and thousands, covering the sky, and still more rising—an inferno in the heavens.

"Ishtafel!" Meliora roared, meat and metal in her mouth. "You will die too, coward. Requiem is free!"

"Requiem is free!" the other dragons cried.

Meliora glanced behind her, just for a second. Countless dragons were fleeing the battle, flying so close together their wings touched. The scaly mosaic covered the sky. At their lead flew Jaren, blowing his fire. But as Meliora watched, thousands of chariots were making their way past the dragon defenders. Their fire blazed across those who fled, and the lances of the seraphim drove into dragons, sending them falling down as humans.

We're not going to make it, Meliora thought, heart sinking. *We're—*

"Sweet sister!" The cry rose above, and fire crackled.

She looked up and saw him charging down toward her.

"Ishtafel!" she roared. Growling, she narrowed her eyes and stormed up to meet him.

Ishtafel laughed as he flew, wreathed in the fire, and his lance pointed down toward her. A white and gold dragon, Meliora blasted forth her fire.

Her white flames crackled and streamed over the charging firehorses. Ishtafel raised his shield, and the blaze exploded across the disk, scattering like a collapsing sun. The firehorses crashed against Meliora, their flames washing across her. Her scales expanded in the heat and cracked, and she bellowed with rage. She whipped her tail, beat her wings, soared higher and swooped toward the chariot.

Ishtafel grinned, protected within his armor, the gilt melting and peeling off the steel. He thrust his lance skyward.

The blade drove into Meliora's front foot, cutting through the scales and flesh, then bursting out the other side.

Pain blasted up her leg, along her back, into her head, and she screamed.

Ishtafel tugged the lance back with a shower of blood. She couldn't even breathe.

A hole in her hand, Meliora lost her magic. She fell. She landed in the chariot beside him, a woman again.

"You've come back to me, sister!" He reached toward her, grinning. "Now stand with me here and watch as—"

With her good hand, she drew her sword and thrust the blade into his chest.

He yowled, the blade denting the steel and cutting the skin inside.

Before she could push the blade deeper, he swung his fist into her cheek.

Meliora fell. She saw nothing but light and shadows.

Don't faint. Live. Live!

She summoned her magic and rose as a dragon.

Pain throbbed through her. The blazing agony of a shattering world filled her wounded hand. Her eyes began to roll back, but she sneered and blew her fire.

Chariots slammed into her.

Fire washed over her.

Meliora lost her magic again and fell.

She tumbled through the battle, a woman again, passing through fire. She slammed onto a dragon's back, rolled across its scaly flank, and fell again. The ground rushed up toward her, strewn with corpses.

You will never see Requiem! Leyleet shrieked in her mind. *With my dying breath I curse you.*

"No," Meliora whispered and clenched her shattered hand. "I will find your sky."

She shifted into a dragon, soared, blew her fire against a chariot. She tried to find Ishtafel again but did not see him. Dragons and chariots flew everywhere.

"Ishtafel!" she roared. "Ishtafel!"

She blasted fire, knocking back another chariot, and surveyed the battle. Hundreds of Vir Requis, maybe thousands, already lay dead below, their human bodies torn apart. Many dragons still flew, battling the seraphim, but they were falling fast.

When Meliora spun her head northward, she saw the bulk of the dragons still fleeing, following Jaren. But hundreds of seraphim had made their way around the dragon defenders. They were now falling upon the flanks of fleeing slaves, cutting into the dragons—the young, the old, the wounded, sending them crashing down. Thousands of other chariots kept streaming forth.

"Kill them all!" Ishtafel cried somewhere in the distance, laughing. "Kill all the dragons!"

Meliora's heart sank.

Does our dream end here? Did we rise as dragons only to fall in battle?

She sneered.

No. We must escape. We must make it back to Requiem. I will not see our dream end here.

"Meliora!" a red dragon roared, and Lucem came to fly beside her, tail knocking a chariot out of his way. "Meliora, the seraphim are tearing into us!"

"The sky is up, Lucem!" Meliora cried back. "Now fly with me."

She was bleeding, burnt, her scales cracked and her front foot ravaged, but still she flew. Lucem flew at her side. They stormed toward the nation of fleeing dragons—half a million strong—and charged into the ranks of attacking seraphim.

Dragonfire and blood filled the sky.

VALE

He saw Meliora fall.

He saw Ishtafel laugh above her in his chariot.

Vale roared and charged toward the tyrant.

Chariots flew toward them, and Vale lashed his tail and claws, knocking them back. Seraphim thrust their lances at him, and he shattered the spears and blasted his fire across the soldiers. He stormed through the battle, burning down the enemy, and howled with rage.

"Meliora!" Vale cried, seeking her in the blaze. "Sister!"

He could no longer see her, but he could see Ishtafel. The King of Saraph flew before him, his armor shining, chariot casting out flames, a god of light and wrath, a sun shining upon the battle.

Vale flew toward the tyrant. All around him, thousands of dragons battled thousands of chariots. The sky rained blood, scales, and ash.

Issari, the Priestess in White, told me that a great battle awaits me. Vale roared and blew his dragonfire. *This is my battle.*

"Vale Aeternum!" Ishtafel called in delight.

Vale growled. He had fought Ishtafel before over the city, had watched the deity slay sixty thousand slaves.

But today we are no longer slaves. Today we are dragons.

He blasted his dragonfire.

The inferno crackled and spun, driving toward Ishtafel, but the tyrant rose in his chariot, dodging the flames. He swooped, lance thrusting.

Vale swiped his claws, knocking the lance aside. He snapped his jaws, trying to bite Ishtafel, but he bit only fire and cried out in pain. He swung his tail toward Ishtafel but hit the seraph's shield.

"Last time I nailed you to my palace!" Ishtafel laughed and thrust his lance. "This time I'll skewer you in the sky."

Vale dipped in the sky, and the lance scraped across his back, tearing off scales. He yowled. He blew his fire again, but Ishtafel raised his shield, and the flames scattered and showered back onto Vale.

The chariot spun around and the firehorses charged, slamming into Vale.

He cried out as the fire washed over him, and the hooves slammed into his head.

He fell.

Burnt and cut, he lost his magic, tumbling down as a human.

He grabbed his magic again. He rose as a dragon, blowing his dragonfire, but only sparks now left his mouth. He was too weary, too hurt, his belly empty of flames.

Ishtafel charged, and his spear flashed and drove into Vale's wing. The leathern membrane tore.

Vale roared and snapped his jaws, tried to blow fire, but cast out only sparks.

The spear thrust again, scraping across his cheek, tearing it open and scattering scales.

Vale fell, tumbling, barely clinging to his dragon magic.

"Grab him!" Ishtafel shouted, all amusement now gone from his voice. "Hold him up!"

Chariots of fire streamed forth, twenty or more, surrounding Vale. He slammed down onto one. Others drove into his sides, their fire washing across him. Seraphim stood within, swinging chains. Grapples drove into Vale's flesh. Chains tightened around him. The chariots flew higher, trapping him in the chains, stretching him out, displaying him like a tortured prisoner upon a metal cross.

Vale thrashed, whipped his tail, knocked one seraph down. The chariots pulled farther apart, stretching his chained limbs, driving iron links into his soft underbelly. Vale roared, stretched so wide his joints nearly dislocated. He hung in the sky, helpless like the time he'd been nailed onto the ziggurat. As all around in the sky the dragons and seraphim battled, Vale hung in his chains, roaring and flailing and unable to free himself, knowing he was going to die.

I'm sorry, Tash, he thought, grimacing in pain. *I'm sorry.*

The memories flashed before him. Tash and him, traveling through the wilderness to find the Chest of Plenty. Kissing in the delta. Making love. Laughing together. The light in her brown eyes, the softness of her hair flowing between his fingers, the warmth of her smile, her love.

And then the tears. The anger. Tash betraying him, betraying Requiem, only to turn back after two steps—and Vale turning away from her. Leaving her love behind.

Now, as he faced death, tears filled his eyes.

I'm sorry, Tash. I love you.

Ishtafel hovered before him in his chariot.

"And now, son of Aeternum, I will kill you. Slowly. I will first carve out your entrails. Then your liver, then your stomach, then peel off your skin. And still you will live. I've done this many times, and I know how to keep you alive. Only when you beg and call me 'master' will I cut out your heart."

Vale thrashed in his chains, tossed back his head, and howled. His wings beat. Spurts of fire left his maw.

No. No! I was meant to fight for Requiem in a great battle, to save our nation, not this, not this!

Ishtafel hefted his lance, smiling. He spread out his swan wings, rose from his chariot, and hovered in the air. He aimed his lance at Vale's belly, eyes narrowed like a surgeon examining his patient.

"Issari!" Vale cried out. "Issari!"

"Your gods can't help you, reptile." Ishtafel grinned. "I am your only god now. We begin."

Baring his teeth, Ishtafel flew forth, lance flashing.

"Vale, no!" rose a voice from below.

Golden scales flashed. Fire blasted. Crying out, Tash soared, placing herself between Vale and the thrusting lance.

"Tash!" Vale cried.

Her fire roared out, slamming against Ishtafel, washing across him, an inferno, a storm, engulfing the seraph.

Emerging from the flames, Ishtafel's lance drove into her chest, cracking her scales, and burst out of her back.

"Tash!" Vale roared.

Ishtafel screamed, falling, wings ablaze.

Seraphim flew downward after their lord, and Vale thrashed, tearing off the chains.

"Tash!"

She stared at him in the sky, a golden dragon, a lance piercing her, then lost her magic.

The lance tore free and tumbled.

A young woman clad in silk, Tash fell from the sky.

Vale pulled his wings close to his body and plunged after her. Seraphim flew everywhere. Ishtafel was still screaming somewhere in the distance, and fire flared, and the battle of countless dragons and chariots stormed all around. Vale dived, reached out his claws, and grabbed Tash.

He spread his wings wide, and they caught the wind. Air whistled through the hole in his right wing, but he managed to steady his flight, to descend toward the earth. Tash hung in his claws, limp.

Gently he placed her on the ground. His heart seemed to clench, and his breath caught. The battle still raged above them, blood rained, and corpses lay strewn across the field. Vale released his magic, returned to human form, and knelt above Tash.

"Tash," he whispered and touched her cheek. She still lived, her breath shallow, her eyelids fluttering. A hole gaped through her chest, and blood poured down her belly and soaked her silken trousers.

"I . . . I burned him," she whispered. "I burned Ishtafel for you, Vale. I . . ."

Tears filled his eyes. He tore off his shirt and held the cloth to her wound. She winced. Her face was so pale, turning grey.

"Issari," Vale whispered, looking up at the night sky. "Heal her, please. Heal her, great priestess."

But he could not see the stars, only the raging dragons and chariots and flames.

"Vale." Tash's voice shook, so weak. "Hold me. Don't leave me. Don't look away."

Tears falling, he held her in his arms, cradling her shivering body. "I'm not leaving you, Tash. Never. I promise."

She coughed weakly, reached up, and touched his cheek. "I love you, Vale Aeternum. And I'm sorry for what I've done. I'm sorry."

"You are forgiven," he whispered. "I love you too. I always did. I always will."

"Fight for them, Vale. Lead them home. To Requiem."

She was growing so cold in his arms, and her blood would not stop pouring. "You will fight with me! I will heal you. The Priestess in White will heal you. I—"

"No." Tash shook her head. "I'm no daughter of a great dynasty. I'm no heroine. I'm just a woman who loves you, who loves our home across the sea. I will see Requiem again, Vale. I can see her already." Her eyes shone, and she stared skyward. "She's up there, Vale, a Requiem all in starlight, and her harps are calling me home." Her tears streamed. "I will find our sky. I fly to it now."

"No, Tash." His tears splashed her cheeks, and he kissed her lips. "Don't leave us. Don't leave me. I love you."

"This is a good way to die," she whispered. "In your arms. I will always be with you, Vale. Always. In your heart and in your stars."

Her eyes closed, and her breath died upon his kiss.

Vale held her close against him, rocking her, her head against his chest. A sob shook his body.

I love you, Tash. I love you. Goodbye, daughter of Requiem. Goodbye.

MELIORA

They're too many.

Meliora fought across the sky, her dragonfire down to mere spurts, her silvery scales cracked. Her front foot—a hand in her human form—was ravaged, dripping, blazing with an inferno.

Too many seraphim . . . we cannot beat them.

The dragons had crossed the wall and were flying over the wilderness now, but countless chariots of fire kept attacking, flying in from every direction, culling the dragons. Every heartbeat, another Vir Requis lost his or her magic and tumbled down through the night. Ishtafel had murdered sixty thousand Vir Requis last time Meliora had rebelled; now he would slaughter them all.

"Dragons, fly!" she called out. "Fly with me, faster! Fly north!"

Yet Requiem lay so many miles away; it would take weeks of flight to get there, and the seraphim would harry them every mile.

We'll all die long before we reach the coast, Meliora knew. *Even as dragons.* She snarled. *Then let me die giving the others hope. Let me kill as many seraphim as I can, even if only a handful of dragons escape. That handful will rebuild a nation.*

She charged into battle, flying across the rim of the camp, tearing into the ranks of attacking seraphim. Lucem roared at her side, a red dragon, his fire still flowing. Elory fought with them, scales chipped and bleeding, but still the lavender dragon swiped her claws and tail, sending seraphim down dead.

For every seraph killed, it seemed that a dozen Vir Requis fell, resuming human forms in death. Men. Women. Children. They fell like rain through the darkness.

The fall of Requiem, Meliora thought. *We rose in light and now we fall in shadow.*

Yet even in the darkness a new light shone.

The sun rose in the east, and from the light they flew.
"Meliora the Merciful!" they cried. "Meliora, our mother!"
She looked into the light, and her eyes dampened.
The erevim.
They flew in from the dawn, the life she had made. Beings
raised from the mud, given the blood of both Vir Requis and
seraphim. Men and women coated with scales, swan feathers
growing from their wings and heads. They flew toward the
battle, crying out her name. They had multiplied in the
wilderness, and a thousand or more now flew forth.

"We fight with you, Meliora!"
With battle cries, the erevim charged against the chariots
of fire, lashing their claws at seraphim, tearing at their flesh with
sharp teeth.

"For Requiem!" rose new voices in the west. "For
Requiem, slay the immortals!"
Meliora spun in the sky, saw them, and gasped.
"Hope," she whispered. "Hope rises."
They flew in from the lingering shadows, a hundred
ghostly ships sailing through the sky, translucent, firing their
cannons. Ships of Old Requiem. The rebels who had once risen
up against the Aeternum family; they now came to raise Requiem
from ruin. Upon their decks, thousands of skeletons danced,
rose, shifted into ghostly dragons of smoke. The creatures
stormed forth, blowing out white fire.

The seraphim shouted in fury, then in fear, and finally in
pain.

The astral dragons flowed across them, tearing them apart,
ripping limbs off torsos, severing wings, sending corpses falling.
Ships blasted their astral cannons, sending chariots crashing
down. The erevim flew between the apparitions, blood on their
claws, still calling out her name.

"Meliora, Meliora!"
The dragons of Requiem flew on.
Blasting out fire, clawing the enemies in their way, they
flowed across the sky.
They flew away from Tofet.
They flew away from the army of seraphim.

Flame of Requiem

They flew through blood and fire and rain. To freedom. To a dream of Requiem.

LUCEM

The dragons flew, and flying among them, Lucem thought of home.

For the first eleven years of his life, home had been in Tofet. A home of the whip, the shackles, the pain of carving and molding bricks. Then, for the second half of his life, home had been the wilderness—huddling in caves, wandering the darkness, singing to nobody, talking to invisible friends.

Lucem looked around him. He flew as a dragon on the wind, and thousands of other dragons flew with him. Their scales shone brilliantly in the sun like a field of jewels. Lucem's eyes stung. So many times he had dreamed of seeing this— seeing the people of Requiem rise in their dragon forms, no collars around their necks. Free. Leaving Tofet and the corpses of seraphim behind.

And leaving two other souls behind, Lucem thought, eyes dampening.

Elory flew up to him, a slender dragon, smaller than most. Her scales were deep purple near her belly, growing lighter along her flanks, turning pale lavender on her back. Her horns were small and white, her eyes kind. One of her ears thrust out from her head, violet and scaled. The other was missing.

"How are you, Lucem?" she asked softly.

He blinked the tears out of his eyes. "I just . . . I just wish they could have been here. My parents. I keep looking around, hoping to see them, even imagining that they fly with us. But then I remember. How the overseers killed them a decade ago." He lowered his head as he flew. "How they'll never see our freedom."

Elory flew a little closer and touched her wing to his. She reached out her tail, gently tapping his own tail.

"I'm sorry, Lucem. I miss my mother too—so badly that it physically hurts." Elory's eyes shone damply. "I don't know what'll happen next. I don't know how many enemies await between us and Requiem. But whatever happens, I'm here for you. Always. I love you, Lucem, and I'll always fly by your side."

They flew together, side by side, bodies touching.

Lucem stared forward as they flew. Across the thousands of dragons, the wilderness sprawled to the horizon. Thousands of miles still separated them from Requiem, and many enemies perhaps waited along the way. And yet beyond the horizon it lay. Their homeland.

Let Requiem be my third home, Lucem thought. *Let it be a home to all of us. A home of light, of safety, and of peace.*

MELIORA

The children of Requiem gathered in the wilderness under the heat of the blinding sun.

The land was burnt around them. The rushes along the river, the trees, the forests, all had burned in the fire of Saraph when the first slaves had escaped to find hope. Now half a million Vir Requis had fled their captivity, and they covered the land.

Most stood or lay as humans, nursing their wounds. Many flew as dragons above the camp, protecting those below. The Vir Requis carried their meager supplies with them—skins of water, sacks of oatmeal, a few pickaxes, some dried fruit, not much more.

Meliora walked up a hill until she stood above the camp. In dragon form, her front foot had been wounded in the battle, and now her hand was bandaged, blazing, screaming with movement. The hot wind billowed her tattered burlap robe, and her good hand rested on the hilt of Amerath, her ancient sword of kings and queens. The sun beat down upon her, browning her limbs, and her halo crackled above her head.

What a figure she must have struck, she thought. Only a few months ago, she had been a different person. Nobody from that time of her life would recognize her now. Once she had worn gowns of finest muslin, adorned with precious jewels. Swan wings had grown from her back, and golden hair had cascaded across her shoulders. Her skin had been pale, soft, powdered. Today that skin was tanned and covered in scabs and bruises. Her hair was but stubble on her head, and instead of a golden halo, she stood crowned with dragonfire. No more swan wings grew from her back, but two scars ran there along her shoulder blades, reminders of who she had been, who she could never be again.

Flame of Requiem

My seraph half died with my wings, she thought. *I am nothing but a daughter of Requiem now, pure.*

"Children of Requiem!" she cried, and below the hill, the people turned toward her. "Hear me, children of Requiem!"

They stared up at her. Thin, hungry, wounded. Wearing rags. Their ankles still chafed from the chains they had discarded. A brutalized people, heirs to a kingdom they had never forgotten.

Meliora summoned her magic and soared as a dragon.

She rose high and cried out, her voice rolling across the camp.

"I am Meliora Aeternum! I brought you the Keeper's Key, and I freed you from your collars, but the danger has not passed." She flew across the multitudes below, letting them all hear. "The cruel Ishtafel was dealt a blow, but if he still lives, he's licking his wounds, and he's building a new army. If he's dead, then whatever heir Saraph places upon the throne will hunt us. We will fly fast. We will continue fleeing."

She could see the fear in them. That was good. They needed to be afraid now. That fear twisted Meliora's own heart.

"You are free now, children of Requiem!" she said. "You are free warriors, no longer slaves. And you will fight to see Requiem again. Our kingdom lies across many miles. Even as the dragon flies, Requiem lies a moon away, and many dangers wait along that path: armies of seraphim and creatures even darker. And even should we reach Requiem, we will find nothing but ruins."

The crowd murmured below. Some cried out in anguish.

"But we will fly there nonetheless!" Meliora said. "Because Requiem is our home. It has been our home for five thousand years, since our ancestor, King Aeternum, raised a column in a birch forest. That column still stands! It awaits us. We will seek it across the miles, and we will be a proud nation again. This I promise to you, Vir Requis. I will lead you to our land. I will lead you home."

They cried out to her, hundreds of thousands, the last survivors of an ancient race. "Meliora the Merciful! Praise Meliora!"

She blew a pillar of white fire, a twin to King's Column in the north. "Follow, children of Requiem! Follow my light. Follow me home."

They all rose from below, dragon after dragon, ascending into the sky. They flew behind her. Freed slaves. Proud warriors. A nation.

"Not bad, Mel." Lucem flew up to her side, the sunlight bright against his red scales. "Could have used a few puns, maybe a couple dirty limericks, but overall not a bad speech."

Meliora rolled her eyes. "You and your dirty limericks."

The red dragon grinned. "Want to hear a few new ones?"

"No!" She spurted fire his way.

They flew onward, and behind them the children of Requiem followed, covering the sky.

VALE

As the nation of Requiem flew above, Vale and Elory stood below on the hill, both in human forms.

"I wish I could take her with us," Vale said.

Elory held his hand. "I do too. But the journey is too long, too perilous."

"She belongs in Requiem." Vale had to force the words out of his tight throat.

"Maybe she already is in Requiem," Elory whispered, looking up at the sky.

But Vale did not look up. He looked down at the ground, down at her. At Tash.

She lay there, wrapped in his cloak, her face so pale, so fair. Vale knelt and stroked her long brown hair.

"I love you, Tash," he whispered. "I know that I'll see you again someday."

Elory knelt at his side, and she placed her hand on Tash's. "And I love you too, Tash," she whispered. "Goodbye, sweet friend."

You saved my life, Tash, Vale thought, stroking her cold cheek. *You gave your life for mine. And . . . I never had a chance to love you enough. Our last few days, we fought, we hated, we hurt each other. But know that I forgive you, that I love you. Know that for all eternity, Requiem will know your name, know of your sacrifice.*

Finally Vale looked up at the sky.

You gave me new life, Issari, our holy priestess. You told me that a battle awaits me. Yet I would have lost my battle if not for Tash. Why do I linger on, hurt, so many scars upon me, and she lies here, so fair, so cold, no gift of life given to her?

Yet the Priestess in White was silent. Perhaps Vale had no power to summon her the way his father could. He was no priest, no wise man like Jaren. Perhaps Issari had never heard his prayers, had never seen his pain. Vale did not know. He did not know why he kept living as so many died—as thousands of Vir Requis remained here, buried in Saraph.

Maybe I've not yet faced my battle. It hurts. It hurts to go on. To live without you, Tash. I will fight on, but I don't know if I can bear this pain.

He shifted into a dragon, and he dug a grave, and he gently placed Tash inside. She was far from Requiem here, but Tofet was too far to see too. The land was burnt now, but in time grass would grow here, trees would rustle, and flowers would bloom again. The river would flow through life, and birds would sing. This place would be beautiful come next spring, a good place for her to rest.

As he placed dirt onto the grave, Vale swore that if he survived the journey, and if Requiem was rebuilt from ruin, he would return for her bones, and he would place them in a coffin carved from Requiem birch, bring them to rest in the land of her forebears, and someday he would rest at her side.

"Sleep well for now, sweet Tash," he whispered to the grave.

Still in human form, Elory leaned against his scaly neck, and she patted his long snout.

"I know that you hurt, Vale. I know that it hurts more than you can bear. But I'm with you." She kissed his cheek, her lips soft against his blue scales. "And so is Father, and so is Meliora, and so are all in Requiem. We all love you, prince of dragons."

She shifted too, and they rose into the sky together, a blue dragon and a lavender one. They flew with their people, taking some pain with them, leaving some pain behind, heading onward to hope and light and a dream of home.

ISHTAFEL

He lay in the bloody field, convulsing, screaming.

He rattled in their cart, crying out, begging them to kill him.

He thrashed in his bed as they placed ointments upon him, roaring that he'd kill them all, vowing to kill himself too.

Meliora's halo had burned him, leaving a scar across his face. Now dragonfire—roaring, all-consuming—had washed across him.

He screamed.

He wept.

He thrashed in pain.

He lay in his palace, Ishtafel thought. The walls spun around him. He fainted. He woke, fresh bandages across him. He stumbled out from his bed, seeking a blade, seeking a rope, seeking a way to end his life, but he ended up falling to the floor and trembling.

He slept. He dreamed.

In his fever, he was back in Requiem, flying through hosts of dragons, traveling through the tunnels, slaying the demons one by one in the darkness, watching his soldiers die.

"They fled," he whispered, tasting blood. "The weredragons fled me."

He stumbled through the halls of his dark palace, dripping, his bandages trailing behind him. He tore them off one by one, leaving a wake of puss and ichor. No more servants filled the palace; all had fled. Those seraphim who still wandered these halls saw him, gasped, and fled too. One woman fainted.

"A mirror!" he shouted. "A mirror!"

Yet they would bring him none. He limped onto a balcony into the searing sunlight, and he raised his arms before him, and he laughed. Dripping, melting arms, the skin gone. When he touched his face he found nothing, and he screamed.

He stared into the northern distance. They had flown there. They were gone.

"Twice you burned me, dragons," he spoke into the distance. "But I still live. I am a god of fire. You cannot kill me. You only strip the flesh away, leaving my soul stronger, tempering me like iron in a forge."

Iron.

Ishtafel sneered.

"Bring me iron and gold!" he shouted.

He summoned his chariot, and he rode in fire, a thing of flames, and his steeds took him to the city smelters. There he entered the darkness, and he stood before roaring fires that melted metal in a cauldron, and he laughed.

"Forge, men! Forge and hammer and temper."

The cauldrons boiled and hammers swung, and Ishtafel laughed.

On a dark night, he stepped out from the pit, and he walked through the city, clanking, thudding. All who saw him fled. Down cobbled roads he marched, between obelisks and colossal statues, making his way to his ziggurat.

"A mirror!" he shouted as he stepped into the palace.

Finally two soldiers approached, bearing a tall bronze mirror, and knelt, shivering. Ishtafel stared at his reflection.

He wore new skin—skin of metal. A mask covered his face, drilled into him, shaped as the face he had once worn, the face now gone. Gilt covered the iron. More metal covered his limbs and torso, sealing him inside. His wings spread out, the feathers burnt away—wings of raw leather, tipped with black claws. They almost looked like dragon wings. His halo still blazed above his head, brighter than ever.

"Now I am truly a god," he whispered.

He beat his wings. He soared off the balcony. The ziggurat's platinum crest streamed behind him, the place where he had nailed up the weredragon prince—the prince he would still catch and break.

"My army of light failed," he whispered, beating his naked wings. "The dark seraphim failed. It's time to summon . . . *them*."

He soared until he reached the Eye of Saraph, the engraved eye upon the ziggurat's triangular crest, the great watcher of the empire. It stared from within a sunburst, larger than him, ever guarding his domain.

"Hear me, Eye of Saraph!" Ishtafel cried, hovering before the engraving, his wings spread wide. "For long you watched over us, and now I call you to cast forth your light. Raise the beam! Shine your column to call your children home."

Slowly, the great stone eye began to open.

At first only a slit shone with terrible light, nearly blinding Ishtafel. Then the eye opened wider, exposing its innards, heat and light more terrible than the cauldrons of molten metal that had forged his new skin. A beam of searing, golden light slammed into Ishtafel, bounced off his armor, and blasted skyward.

Above, the storm clouds gathered. Clouds rarely gathered in the heart of Saraph, this dry southern land, but now a maelstrom brewed, the color of bruises. Lightning flashed. Thunder tore across the land. And still the light flared, passing from the eye, through Ishtafel, up into the sky, shattering the heavens.

A second great eye—this one dark and swirling—opened above.

"Descend, children!" Ishtafel cried, laughing, arms and wings spread wide. "Join us in this world, ones of Edinnu. Fall, fall from the heavens, fall and rise in new glory!"

Above him, they shrieked, his old pets, barely visible in the clouds, eyes like stars, collapsing, rising again, blaring out with terrible hatred. Their wings darkened the sky.

"Fall and slay dragons!" he shouted.

From the heavens they fell, covering the land, coating temples and palaces like tar, shrieking out in rage and hatred, a song for the blood of dragons.

TIL

They travelled through the snowy forest, shivering even in their thick cloaks, moving fast, daring not stop.

We must reach the southern coast, Til thought as she trudged onward. *We must live. We must find the sea.*

"I'm cold." Walking at her side, Bim hugged himself. His teeth chattered. "Can we build a fire?"

Til shook her head. "No fires. Not yet. Not until we're sure we've lost them."

She looked around her, seeking any sign of pursuit. The trees rose all around—maples, oaks, and many birches. Ice encased the branches, topped with snow. Fallen logs, branches, and roots lay everywhere, twisting like a city, white and brown. When Til looked up, she saw a blue sky between frosted branches.

No seraphim. No Overlord.

Yet the memory wouldn't leave her. Again and again, she saw it before her eyes. The Overlord, a god of light, his halo like the sun, his armor golden, a figure of splendor and holiness. Again and again, she saw the deity's lance driving into the black dragon, slaying her father, turning him from a dragon into a man again—a man skewered upon the shaft. Even in the cold, Til suddenly felt hot, as if the chariots of fire flew around her again.

She shook her head, banishing that memory, yet her father's words still echoed in her mind.

Take him to the coast. Find others.

"Til, can I remove my armor?" Bim said. "The metal is too cold. Can we build a fire soon?"

She looked at him, and pity filled her. The boy was too thin, too pale, his breath frosting. A decade ago, when Til had been that age, things had been better, she thought. A thousand Vir Requis had still lived in the ruins of Requiem, eking out a life in tunnels, caves, and forest camps. Yet now food was scarcer, shelter harder to find, and they were always moving, never spending two nights in the same place. Always seeking others, finding none. The past five years, since the tragic uprising against the Overlord, had thinned their family down to raw bones, leaving haunted eyes in gaunt faces, stiff fingers that never strayed far from the hilt, haggard legs that knew to always trudge on, always keep moving, keep seeking.

"Another league," Til said. "And we'll build a fire, and we'll tell old stories."

They moved on through the forest, shivering in their cloaks. Soon Til saw prints in the sand, raised her eyes, and descried the rabbit ahead between the birches. Silently, she nocked an arrow in her bow, and she pierced the rabbit with her first shot. They saw no other animals; this paltry meal would have to do.

"There will be more food on the southern coast," Til said to her brother. "It's warm there, Bim, and no snow falls, not even in winter. There are plenty of deer on the plains, and the rivers aren't frozen and many fish fill them. All other Vir Requis survivors will have traveled there."

Bim eyed the scrawny rabbit in Til's hands. "If there are others."

"There are," Til promised. "We have to believe."

Because what else is left to us? she thought. *If not for this hint of hope, we might as well doff our cloaks, lie down in the snow, and let the cold seize us. We have to believe there are others. We have to keep moving.*

They kept walking until they found a valley, the canopy a thick latticework above, perhaps thick enough to disperse the smoke of a fire. It was colder here in the shade, and Til could not stop shivering, but she set camp near a fallen log. She and her brother spent a few moments collecting firewood and arranging a small campfire. Ice coated the branches; no tinderbox or kindling would ignite them, Til knew. She glanced around, stood silently, and listened. She heard nothing. No seraphim. No sounds of pursuit.

Finally she nodded, inhaled deeply, and summoned her magic.

She rarely became a dragon anymore. Dragons were large and loud. Flying above, they puffed out smoke, visible for miles. Even walking through the forest, their scales clattered, their large bodies rustled the trees, and the smoke from their nostrils left a trail. Yet now she allowed the orange scales to flow across her, allowed fire to fill her jaws. She spent a few moments puffing out weak flames, melting the ice around the branches, until finally the campfire burned. Then she became human again.

They sat on the fallen log by the fire, warming their fingers, and cooked the rabbit. There was barely any meat on the bones. Even the wildlife of Requiem was gaunt, struggling to survive.

"On the southern coast, the meat is rich and fatty," Til said, gnawing on a bone. "There are plump bison and fish so large they can feed a family for a week."

Bim snapped a rabbit bone in two and sucked on it. "There will be seraphim there too."

"Not as many." Til waved her hands over the campfire, trying to disperse the smoke, to scatter a single plume that could rise and alert others to their presence. "The Overlord lives here in the north, and most of the battles were fought here. The south has always been the backwater of Requiem, even in the glory days before the seraphim arrived. A quiet place. A few others survive there; I'm sure of it. Warmth. Food. Safety."

"But not for Father." Bim lowered his head. "He won't ever see the south."

Til tossed her rabbit bone into the fire. She moved closer and sat beside Bim on the fallen log, wrapped her arm around him, and rested her cheek on the top of his head. She stroked his hair.

"Have you heard the tales of Kyrie Eleison?" she asked him.

Bim nodded. "You told them a million times."

"Then I'll tell them a million and one times. He's our ancestor; we're directly descended of his lineage. When he was a boy, he was lost here in this wilderness. He thought he was the last Vir Requis, the only survivor of the griffins who had crushed Requiem. Three thousand years ago, he traveled through these very forests, seeking others. His family dead. His belly empty. The enemy flying everywhere."

Bim sighed. "Your story isn't making me feel better."

"But Kyrie found others." Til squeezed her brother against her. "He found a new family, new hope. In the darkness, he lit a new light, and Requiem rose again. Now we are in darkness. Now we are alone. Now we struggle to find new life, new hope. And I believe, Bim, that Requiem will rise again. That King's Column will be cleansed and rededicated, that many other columns will rise around it, that dragons will fly in the open again. Father believed too. That's why he wanted us to go south. To seek others."

Bim lowered his head. "But those are just old stories. What if there are no others? What if . . . what if we're the last?"

"There are others." Til took his head in her hands, turned it toward her, and stared into his eyes. "Countless Vir Requis live across the southern sea, in the heartland of Saraph, though they are chained and collared and cannot become dragons. But they live too, and they pray. They pray to rebuild Requiem. Our nation still lives, all over the world, and our prayers still rise to the stars. We grieve. We hurt. We shiver in the cold. But we do not give up, Bim. Not so long as our legs can walk and our hearts can beat."

Bim frowned. "I hear something."

At first Til heard nothing. She stiffened, cocked her head, listening . . . but heard only the wind creaking the trees, the crackling fire, and—

There. She heard it.

The shuffling of snow. Padding feet. A snort and heavy breathing. The sounds came from all sides, and yet no light of halos or chariots filled the forest. The sun was dimming, shadows falling. The sniffing rose louder.

Wolves? she thought, reaching for her bow.

Bim stiffened at her side, drawing an arrow. Slowly, the siblings rose to their feet, weapons raised, staring from side to side.

From the shadowy forest they emerged, and Til cringed. "Serpopards," she said.

The creatures were vaguely feline, but larger than any cat Til had ever seen, larger even than horses. Their fur was black and bristly, their paws tipped with claws. Their necks coiled upward, longer than Til was tall, tipped with the heads of lionesses. The creatures growled, baring their fangs, and slinked forward from all sides. Til counted five of them, forming a ring around the camp.

"Seraph pets," Bim said, moving his arrow from side to side.

Til had seen such creatures before from a distance. Back during the uprising, the seraphim would lead them through the forest on leashes, sniffing out the trails of Vir Requis survivors. These ones wore no leashes, though collars still encircled their necks, and their nostrils flared. Their masters could not be far behind.

Til did not hesitate any longer.

She fired her arrow.

Before it could even meet its target, the serpopards pounced.

Bim's arrow fired too with a *twang*. Both arrows slammed into the creatures, digging through the furred flesh, only enraging the beasts. Long necks stretched out, and jaws opened wide to bite.

One creature slammed into Til, and she fell, shouting. The lioness head snapped at her, lashing fangs against her patches of rusted armor. At her side, Bim fell too, raising his arms before his head, trying to ward off another serpopard.

Til growled, writhed madly, and kicked hard. She managed to knock the creature off her, tossing it into the campfire. The flames raged and showered sparks.

At once she leaped up and grabbed her sword's hilt. Before she could draw the blade, another serpopard leaped onto her, knocking her back down. The claws lashed at her, reaching between her plates of armor, cutting her chest.

"Til!" her brother screamed.

Panic rose in her. Her blood spurted as her heart lashed. She tried to draw the sword, but the creature's paws pinned down her right wrist. The campfire blazed at her side, spraying sparks onto her clothes, drenching her with heat. The serpopard's neck rose skyward, six feet long, and then the head plunged down, jaws opening to rip out Til's throat.

With her left hand, Til reached into the campfire and grabbed a burning log.

She screamed as the flames burned her, but she wouldn't let go. She swung the torch into the serpopard's striking head, knocking it aside an instant before the fangs tore into her. Those fangs now scraped across her armor, and the head thumped into the snow at her side, its fur kindled.

When Til leaped to her feet, she saw Bim firing arrow after arrow, knocking back serpopards. Several lay dead around the campfire, but more kept emerging from between the trees. Their eyes gleamed in the shadows, and their growls rose all around. A hundred or more were advancing.

Another one leaped at Til's side. She swung her sword, knocking it back. At once she spun the other way, thrusting the blade into another pouncing creature. Claws tore at her leg, and she cried out and fell to one knee.

"Can we shift now?" Bim cried as more serpopards raced among the trees. Their eyes and growls filled the shadows, and the sun vanished behind the horizon, leaving only the campfire to light the darkness.

Til cursed. She hated shifting into a dragon. But any hope of remaining silent here was long gone, and with the serpopard corpses burning, the smoke and light would be filling the sky.

"Shift!" she cried and summoned her magic.

With a clatter like the armor of a racing army, their scales rose across them. Fangs and claws slammed into the hardened plates. Two dragons moved in circles around the campfire, blowing flames in a ring.

The dragonfire roared. Ice melted across the trees, and the serpopards burned. Their fur and flesh crackled, giving out a foul stench, but more kept racing forth. They leaped between the trees, and three serpopards slammed into Til, clawing at her orange scales. She spun around madly, struggling to shake them off. One managed to tear off a scale, and its teeth sank into her, and she bellowed. Several more of the creatures covered Bim—a black dragon, only half her size. Their claws drove under his dark scales like splinters under fingernails, and he swung his tail, struggling to knock them off. Their dragonfire kept spurting, but more creatures kept racing through the forest.

"Fly, Bim!" she cried.

"I can't!" He fell, overcome with more serpopards, their weight pinning him down. As a young dragon, he wasn't much larger than the bristly, long-necked felines.

Til roared, forsaking all promises to remain silent in this forest. She rolled onto her back, crushing a serpopard who clung to her. She spurted fire across the camp. The trees blazed. She whipped her tail, knocking more beasts aside, then leaped up toward her brother.

She grabbed one of the creatures attacking him. She dug her teeth past fur and flesh, ripping out a chunk of its back. She spat out its backbone and roared, then swiped her claws, knocking another creature off her brother. With a lash of her tail, she sliced through the necks of the last serpopards clinging to the black dragon.

"Now fly!"

They soared, blasting fire, an inferno that washed across the forest and spurted into the sky. More serpopards leaped at them from the treetops, clawing at their scales, falling to the blazing forest. With a few more flaps of their wings, the two dragons smashed through the canopy and rose into the night sky.

Smoke hid the sky, and only Issari's Star still shone, the eye of the dragon, and then it too vanished. The forest below swarmed with black felines leaping in the shadows, and the trees below still burned. Black smoke, both of charred trees and flesh, unfurled and washed across the dragons.

They flew through the inferno, holding their breath, until they emerged from the smoke.

We're safe up here, Til thought. *We're safe so long as no seraphim are near, and—*

And then she saw them.

Chariots of fire.

The flaming horses thundered across the sky, and seraphim raised bows in their chariots. The missiles flew through the sky, and Til cried out and soared higher. An arrow slammed into her horn and embedded there. Another grazed Bim's flank.

The enemy flew everywhere. Dozens of the chariots circled in from all sides, firing their arrows, deadlier by far than their pets.

Flame of Requiem

And so we die here, Til thought. *Here, two days away from King's Column. So far from the warmth of the southern coast. Here we die in snow and flame.*

She looked at Bim and saw the fear in his eyes. The chariots flew closer. He stared back, panting, blood on his flanks, his wings churning the smoke.

No, Til thought. *No, not yet. I promised him that there is always hope, that we will always fight on. So long as our wings can beat. So long as we can breathe fire.*

"Fly with me," she said, giving him the slightest of smiles, and dived.

She plunged toward the forest. Bim flew with her. They crashed through the canopy . . . then curved their flight and flew forward.

They raced between the trees, twenty feet aboveground. The canopy rose above. The snow melted below under their heat. Between the trunks, the long-necked felines still growled and pounced, leaping from below, desperate to catch the dragons flying above them. Others leaped from the treetops, knocked aside with flaps of the dragons' spiky tails.

Til tried to curve her flight, to whip between the trees, but she was moving too fast, and the trees were too close. She slammed into a birch, cried out in pain, and shattered the trunk. The tree fell and she kept flying. Bim slammed into an oak, cracking the bole. He fell to the snow, then rose and flew again, narrowly dodging the serpopards that leaped.

They kept flying, so fast the dark forest streaked around them. They blasted their fire, lighting their way, slamming into birch after birch, uprooting the trees. Icicles hailed down, stabbing their backs. Melted snow ran in rivulets.

And above the fire still burned.

The chariots of fire descended from above, casting down fire. Arrows rained, and Til yowled as one tore through her wing. She blasted dragonfire, and the blaze crashed into the canopy and spurted upward, washing across a chariot. More covered the sky.

The dragons kept racing across the forest. The landscape now sloped downward. As much as they could, they whipped between trees, but they couldn't avoid crashes. Splinters drove into their scales and cut the thick skin on their underbellies. Trees fell and burned. And still the fire streaked across the sky.

A chariot swooped ahead, plunging between the trees. Til and Bim flew sideways, dodging it, racing onward. When the chariot tried to follow, its flashing reins wrapped around an oak, sending the chariot flying in one direction, the firehorses in another. A second chariot plunged between two pines, and Til roared out her dragonfire, roasting the seraph who stood within. She rose higher, emerged above the canopy, and plunged back downward and flew between the trees again. The forests of Requiem burned.

A voice rose above, angelic, mellifluous, a voice so kind and beautiful that Til could almost weep. The voice of a god.

"You cannot escape us, Til Eleison. Come to me, my child."

Tears filled Til's eyes. The voice was so warm, so benevolent. She wanted to obey, to seek that voice, to hear it comfort her.

He knows my name. He knows who I am, how I hurt.

Ahead, she saw it. A golden glow in the sky, as bright as the sun. She could just make him out above the trees. A heavenly figure, swan wings spread wide, a halo around his head of flowing golden hair. A man in gilded armor, beautiful, noble, all knowing, merciful.

The Overlord.

"Come to me, child," his voice rolled across the land, the voice of harps and song. "Rest your weary head in my embrace. Let me claim your life, so that you might find comfort in death."

And now Til wept. She wanted to rise from the forest. To fly to him in the sky, this god in the heavens. To let him welcome her soul. To leave her hurting, hungry body here in the forest, to forever live in that radiance.

She began to rise toward the sweet song and light.

Bim reached out and grabbed her.

"He's lying." The black dragon stared at her, gripping her with his claws, still flying between the trees. "He wants to kill you, Til. To kill you. Live. Live! Don't die like Father."

That memory now flooded Til—the Overlord thrusting his lance, a god of wrath, slamming the blade through Father, raising the corpse.

Til howled, and now she wanted to fly skyward not to join him but to slay him, to cast down this cruel god upon the burnt forests of her homeland, even if she died in that searing light.

But I made a promise. I promised to take Bim south. To the coast. I promised to live.

Til snarled, dived low to the ground, and grabbed one of the leaping serpopards. She soared, crashing through the canopy, carrying the long-necked feline in her claws. She flew toward the godly light and tossed the dark creature. The serpopard tumbled toward the Overlord, neck flailing, and crashed into the light. The creature burst into flame and slammed against the Overlord, and white bursts of light blazed across the sky.

The Overlord shrieked, all his grace gone, now a being of white fury. Til blasted dragonfire his way, then dipped down and flew between the trees again. Bim flew at her side. The light still blazed above, lighting the night, melting snow and ice.

The land sloped downward, and Til knew this land, knew every curve and fold of the hills. She crashed through the last few birches, dodged charging chariots of fire that were braving the forest, and there below she saw it—a red strip in the night, halving the landscape.

The River Ranin.

"Follow me, Bim!" Til cried.

She flew downhill, whipping between the trees. She smashed into an alder, cracking the trunk, and plunged down into the dark river.

An instant later, Bim dived into the water with her.

She swam underwater, eyes open and stinging. The fire blazed above, casting orange light into the river, revealing stones and algae. Bim swam at her side, tail flailing.

"Keep swimming!" she said, bubbles rising from her mouth. "For as long as you can."

Arrows whistled into the water around them. One cracked a scale on her back, but she kept whipping her tail, driving herself onward. She plunged deeper until her belly skimmed the bottom. Bim kept swimming at her side, cheeks puffed out, his tail and wings propelling him onward.

Her lungs ached for air, but she kept moving. Finally, when she could stand it no longer, she raised her nostrils from the water and spurted up fire. Bim followed suit.

At once arrows rained.

The dragons sank back underwater.

"Come!" Til said to her brother, tapping him with her tail.

They spun around in the water and began swimming back from where they had come, diving deep, moving against the current. Above her, Til thought she could see the fire streaming in the opposite direction—the chariots following the current.

There was only one way to be sure.

Til released her magic, returning to human form underwater. Bim followed her lead, becoming again a scrawny boy, his cloak fluttering in the water.

They swam toward the riverbank and raised their heads from the water. They gulped air.

Til stared eastward down the current and saw the chariots flying there, firing arrows into the water. The Overlord flew above them, brighter than the others, wings as wide as a dragon's.

She forced herself to look away. She grabbed Bim, and they raced out of the water and back into the forest.

They ran through the shadows, silent, jaws clenched, trying to ignore the pain of their wounds. The fire still crackled in the east, and the yips of serpopards sounded in the west, but here the forest was empty, dark, a place to run and hide.

Because that is what we're best at, Til thought, smiling grimly. *That is what you trained us for, seraphim. That is what five hundred years of survival gave my race. We run. We hide.* She clenched her fists as she raced between the trees. *But one day, Overlord . . . one day we will rise again. And that day we will fight.*

They moved through the forest, crossing miles, until the sounds of pursuit faded in the distance. Finally, in a shadowy ravine, they crawled under an outcrop of stone, and they built a wall of snow to hide themselves from pursuit.

They huddled, holding each other for warmth, weak, wet, hurt, still bleeding.

"We're safe, Bim," she whispered, holding her brother, their cloaks wrapped around them. "We're safe now. We're safe."

They held each other until dawn, trembling with cold and weakness.

They kept walking south. To safety. To a dream of hope . . . a dream Til never wanted to wake from.

MELIORA

The dragons of Requiem were flying north across the plains, hundreds of thousands strong, when the rancid creatures rose like a storm cloud, shrieking for death.

They had been flying for three days now across the deserts of Saraph, moving fast, fleeing the inferno of captivity. Meliora had been driving her dragons hard, allowing no rest. They had not touched ground since her speech on the mountain outside the walls of Tofet. Thousands of dragons now flew across the sky, a shimmering veil of scales and fire. On each dragon's back rode two Vir Requis in human forms, sleeping, nursing their wounds, and feeding from their sparse supplies.

Flying at their lead, Meliora glanced at the sky. The sun had reached its zenith, casting down blinding light and heat that spun her head and baked her silver scales. She couldn't even imagine how hot the black-scaled dragons felt.

But soon we'll be in the north, she thought. *In the cool air of Requiem, flying in a gentler sky. Soon we'll fly over forests, not rocks and sand. Soon we'll be home.*

Her foot still throbbed, pierced by Ishtafel's spear. She tried to let the pain motivate her, keep her flying, keep her strong. Jaren had prayed over the wound, and it had closed and was healing fast, yet the pain still blazed up her leg with every flap of her wings.

She reared in the sky, raised her head, and blasted up a pillar of fire. Most dragons, born of two Vir Requis parents, blasted crackling red dragonfire. But Meliora, born to a seraph mother, blew white flames like a pillar of starlight. The column rose high, a beacon for her people.

She turned to face them—thousands of dragons bearing riders. They were children of Requiem, an ancient nation, but they were also her children. Hers to protect, to lead across the miles to their lost home.

Flame of Requiem

I was born of both Requiem and Saraph, she thought, *but I left the ichor of seraphim in Tofet. Here let me be woven of pure starlight, a mother of Requiem.*

The dragons were weary, Meliora knew. Puffs of smoke rose from their nostrils. Their eyes were glazed. They began to dip in the sky. But Meliora would not let her people camp. There was nothing below but sand and rock, and Ishtafel was following them. Meliora could not see her brother's hosts from here, but she knew that Ishtafel would never let them flee. He would be flying over the horizon, even now, determined to slay them. Meliora would not let him catch her.

"Children of Requiem!" Meliora cried. "A new shift begins. Rest now, dragons, and rise, riders!"

Across the cloud of dragons, the human riders rose. Wings burst out from their backs. Scales flowed across them. The number of dragons now doubled in the sky. The newer dragons flew with fresh vigor, their eyes brighter, fire in their jaws. They glided downward, flying below the wearier dragons, those who had been flying since dawn. Those weary dragons lowered themselves so their bellies skimmed the backs of the new flyers, then released their magic. The Vir Requis lay down on their comrades in human form, ready for rest.

Like this we can fly forever, Meliora thought. *At least until hunger kills us.*

They had taken their meager supplies from Tofet—some dry oatmeal, some bags of flour, a few gourds of water. Not enough. Constantly, the dragons were duplicating the food in the Chest of Plenty, but with only one chest, it was slow work—too slow to feed half a million souls. Soon they would have to find more food and lots of it, or they wouldn't have to worry about pursuit.

Lavender scales flashed in the sun, and a slim, one-eared dragon came flying toward Meliora. Elory was smaller than most dragons, but Meliora knew that her sister was just as fierce. She had seen the violet dragon slaying many enemies with her flames.

"Do you think that tonight we can sleep on solid ground?" Elory asked. "The people need time to build fires, to bake bread from our flour, to feel earth below us."

Meliora shook her head, her pearly scales chinking. "No. We will not rest. We will dip down only to drink from the river, only to hunt any wild animals we see across the riverbanks. But we will not place our feet on solid earth. Not until we reach Requiem."

She looked ahead toward the north. Requiem—if truly that fabled land existed—still lay across countless miles. Past deserts, plains, mountains, seas, and forests—impossibly distant. The ancient homeland. The prayer of her people, their beacon, their heart. The only place where they could be free, rebuild their kingdom.

A memory stabbed Meliora like a spear. Once more, she stood in darkness before Leyleet, queen of the Rancid Angels, a cursed seraph with bat wings and cruel white eyes. Once more, Leyleet's demonic voice echoed in her mind.

You will never see Requiem, daughter of dragons. With my dying breath I curse you.

Meliora grimaced, the horror of that night returning to her. She had slain Leyleet in the shadows, ridding the world of her malice. But did the dark queen's final words truly carry power?

Will I truly die on this journey? Meliora thought. *Am I truly cursed to lead my people to freedom, only to fall before entering our homeland myself? Or will Ishtafel and his hosts reach us in the wilderness of Saraph, slaying us all in these hot southern lands?*

She shook her head wildly. Foolishness. There were no such things as prophecies. Requiem had always forged its own future—from the first King Aeternum to the great Queen Kaelyn and finally to her, Meliora, a daughter of their dynasty. Those old monarchs had defeated their enemies.

"And I will defeat mine," Meliora whispered. "Requiem will not fall on my watch. She will rise again."

Even if I must give my life to her, she thought and shuddered.

She was about to lead the dragons down to the river, allowing them to dive and scoop up water before soaring again, when the shrieks sounded in the north.

Meliora caught her breath. She stared ahead, eyes narrowed.

She could still see nothing, but a stench filled the air, rancid, the smell of rotten meat and sulfur and mold. The distant cries rose again, reminding her of vultures fighting over corpses. When Meliora squinted, she could see a cloud rising from beyond the hazy horizon. Many dark specks flew there like flies over filth.

"What are they?" Elory asked. The lavender dragon wrinkled her snout. "I can smell them even from here."

Smoke washed across them, and with flashing red scales, Lucem darted up to fly between the sisters.

"Meliora, you really need a bath," the young red dragon said. "The whole damn nation can smell your stink."

Meliora glared at the dragon. "You're the one who's been living in the wilderness for ten years. But no, Lucem. This isn't dragon stench, as potent as yours is." She pointed her claws to the north. "Your eyes are sharp. What do you see?"

Mumbles rose across the crowd of dragons; more of them were now noticing the cloud ahead. The dark flecks were flying closer, moving at great speed across the sky. Their stench churned Meliora's stomach, and their cries made her wince. The sound was so high-pitched, so cruel, it seemed to twist her very bones.

"Whatever they are," Lucem said, "I wager they're not friendly. And sadly, not very edible, judging by the smell."

Meliora looked over her shoulder and cried out. "Warriors of Requiem! Forward! Fly with me!"

Dozens of dragons rose from the crowd, soon hundreds, then thousands. This nation of freed slaves—their freedom only days old—had no army. But they had already fought one battle, defeating the seraphim over Tofet, and already they knew who their warriors were. The stronger dragons now flew forth— those who had wielded pickaxes or hauled bitumen in the fields of their captivity. The elders, the children, the weak, the wounded—they moved back to fly behind the defenders.

When Meliora looked across the crowd of fighters, she saw her father flying there. Jaren, a green dragon, was a healer, a priest, not a warrior. In human form, he was tall and haggard, and as a dragon he was long, thin, older than the others.

She flew up to him. "Father, I need you to fly back, to protect the elders and children. I—"

"I fight." Jaren stared at her, eyes hard. "I'm a healer, yes. And I'm old. And I'm thin. But my fire is still hot, and my faith in Requiem strong. I fight with you."

The shrieks from the north rose louder now, morphing into twisted laughter. Meliora sneered. The distant beings were closer now, only several miles away. They had large, feathered wings, dark colored, indeed like vultures. They seemed the size of dragons, and she estimated their number at a thousand. Dark clouds gathered above them, as if the sun itself hated the sight of them, shielding its light from their wretchedness. With every mile they crossed, coming closer, disgust grew in Meliora.

"Ugly buggers," Lucem muttered.

Meliora swallowed the instinct to gag. She could finally see the creatures clearly. Indeed, they were as large as dragons, perhaps larger. Yet their bodies were humanoid, female and withered. Dented slabs of armor covered their chests. They had no arms, only wide wings with oily, rotting feathers, tipped with claws. The creatures' heads were massive, large as dragon heads, yet still human—the faces of crones, wrinkled, covered with moles, the noses long, the teeth sharp. Serpents grew from their heads instead of hair, hissing, tongues darting. Worst of all, however, were the creature's legs. While their bodies were those of giant women, the legs were those of vultures, ending with black talons the length of sabers.

"Harpies," Meliora said. She spat out fire.

She had heard of such creatures. Every son and daughter of the Thirteenth Dynasty of Saraph had. Thousands of years ago, they said, the ancient gods of Edinnu had tried to create life, to forge servants of beauty and holiness. Their first attempt had failed. Instead of beings of beauty and nobility, their creations had bloated, withered, rotted. The gods had envisioned pure immortals, their skin soft and unblemished, their hair golden and flowing. Yet boils covered that skin, and nests of snakes topped their heads instead of halos. Disgusted, the gods had caged their deformed daughters, deeming them harpies—cursed creatures. The gods had learned from their mistake. Their second creations flourished, the mighty seraphim. Yet the harpies lingered on, caged, growing mad over the millennia.

And now they're here, Meliora thought, staring at them. Creatures of purest hatred, creatures who lived for nothing but slaughter. There was only one soul who could have freed them, who could command them.

"The King of Saraph," she whispered. "Ishtafel. These are his servants now."

The thousand harpies screeched and raised their talons. Their wings beat, blasting their stench onto the dragons. Their jaws opened wide, dropping halfway down their chests, exposing rows of fangs and white tongues. Their talons reached out, tipped with dry blood, and the snakes on their heads writhed and added their shrill voices to the chorus.

"Weredragons, weredragons!" the harpies cried. "Creatures foul, creatures cruel. Slay them, slay them, sisters! Slay them for our master."

The harpies cackled, and their saliva fell like rain. Their eyes blazed, bugging out, veined and bloodshot. They stormed forth, crossing the last mile toward the dragons. The creatures were outnumbered but seemed to know no fear, only rage and hatred.

Meliora reared and blasted her fire skyward, her white pillar of light, a beacon of strength for her people.

"Requiem!" she called. "Hear me, Requiem! A new battle approaches. Fight! Fight for your nation, for your stars, for your lives!"

Meliora charged, roaring fire. Her fellow dragons flew around her, hundreds of warriors. Elory and Lucem flew to her left, fire blazing. Her father flew to her right. Above, bellowing with rage, flew Vale, her brother; the blue dragon blasted a great stream of fire that rained sparks.

As the flames raced across the sky, the harpies opened their jaws wide. Jets of ice blasted from their mouths, casting out frosted clouds. The frozen pillars thrust toward the dragons, icicles the size of oaks.

Fire and ice slammed together.

The dragonfire scattered, dispersed into fountains that rained down as sparks. Some of the icy shards melted, but many spears of ice made it through the inferno, dripping and still sharp.

Dragons screamed as the ice slammed against them. An icicle, large as a battering ram, drove into a dragon at Meliora's side; it pierced his chest and burst out from his back. The dragon screamed and lost his magic, returning to the form of a young man. The icy shard tore the smaller human body apart, and the man tumbled down, halved and gushing blood. Other icy shards flew all around, cutting into other dragons, ripping wings, tearing scales.

Meliora howled. Instinctively, she banked left, dodging a pillar of ice. Guilt and terror filled her as the ice slammed into a dragon behind her, sending a woman plunging down toward the desert. More bodies rained. Smoke, frost, and fire filled the sky.

"Burn them down!" Meliora shouted. "Burn them all!"

She inhaled deeply, prepared to blow more fire. Ahead of her, several harpies emerged from clouds of frost and fire, cackling and flying toward her. Massive talons—larger than her claws—reached toward Meliora.

She screamed and blasted fire, but her flames missed the harpies. She tried to bank but slammed into another dragon. Harpy talons scraped across her shoulder, ripping out scales. Blood spurted and Meliora yowled in pain. Another harpy swooped from above, landed on her back, and dug its fangs into her.

Meliora nearly lost her magic.

She growled, refusing to lose it.

She swiped her tail like a scorpion, driving it into the harpy on her back. She felt the tail's spikes pierce rotted flesh, and gray blood sprayed. With a roar, Meliora swiped her claws, knocking back a harpy ahead of her. She blasted more fire, her wings scattering sparks and smoke, trying to hold them back.

Yet the creatures were everywhere. Their faces, bloated to obscene size, leered all around Meliora. The eyes bugged out, bloodshot. The snakes on their heads thrust forward, snapping their mouths. Another harpy thrust its talons, slamming them into Meliora, cutting her again, ripping her chest. She yowled.

She blasted more dragonfire.

Flame of Requiem

Her white flames washed over the harpy assaulting her.
The creature's wings ignited. The snakes on its head burned. For
a moment the harpy seemed like a phoenix, woven of nothing
but fire. Then it fell. Another flew forth, and Meliora spun
around, lashed her tail, and drove the spikes into its head.

The harpy's head shattered, leaking its innards, but the
snakes upon it still lived. They coiled around Meliora's tail, biting
her. Pain pierced Meliora. Poison spread through her. She
bellowed in agony, twisted around, and blasted more fire.

Her own flames washed across her tail, burning the
snakes, cauterizing her wounds. The shattered harpy fell.

For a brief moment, Meliora could breathe, could spare
the battle a glance. It seemed barely any harpies had fallen, yet
the corpses of Vir Requis still rained. Hundreds already covered
the desert below. Whenever the dragons blasted fire, the harpies
responded with clouds of ice, blocking the flames. Whenever the
dragons charged, the harpies spat out their icicles, piercing
scales. Every instant, another dragon lost his or her magic, falling
down in human form, frozen, bleeding, dead or dying.

We're not an army, Meliora realized, heart sinking. *We're only
freed slaves. Too weary. Too famished. Too weak. They will slay us all.*

She tossed back her head and roared.

If we die, we die fighting.

"Light the sky with fire!" she cried. "Dragons, fight for
your stars! Fight for your lives! Fight or Requiem!"

She beat her wings with all her strength, driving forth
toward the enemy.

Her family fought with her. Her sister, a slim lavender
dragon. Her brother, a great blue dragon, his fire a mighty
stream. Her father, green and wise, now roaring with fury.
Hundreds of other dragons—they were all her family now.

A harpy flew toward Meliora, blasting not icicles but a
cloud of frost. The frozen miasma flowed across Meliora, and
her scales chipped, and her muscles stiffened. She could barely
breathe, but she managed to blow her dragonfire, piercing a way
through the frozen cloud. She stormed forth, snapped her jaws,
drove her teeth into the harpy's neck. She pulled back, tearing
out rotted flesh. The harpy fell. More flew around her, freezing
her scales with their breath. Meliora spun in circles, spreading

her fire, melting the ice. Her claws lashed, scattering the gray blood of the creatures.

Her blood spilled but her hope soared. Slowly, one by one, the harpies were falling. Elory roasted one with dragonfire. Vale cast another down, tearing the beast open with his claws. Lucem and Jaren fought back to back, flames forming a ring around them, burning the harpies. Thousands of other dragons fought with them, finally overwhelming the enemies. Meliora's flames were down to sparks, and her blood dripped, and with her final drop of strength she slew the last of the creatures.

She had vowed not to land until they reached Requiem, but Meliora could barely cling to her magic. She flew down and all but crashed onto a rocky plain. Corpses spread around her, some smashed beyond recognition; what the harpy claws hadn't done, the fall from the sky had. Meliora released her magic and lay among the dead, lacerations and frostbite covering her.

Other dragons landed around her and released their magic. They too were wounded. Gashes bled across them, left by talons and fangs. Frost covered some, and others nursed swelling serpent bites. Hundreds of wounded lay among the dead. Healers rushed among them, bearing what meager supplies they had—the bandages and ointments they had taken from their humble huts in Tofet.

So many dead, Meliora thought, staring into the eyes of the fallen around her. *Only three days out of Tofet, and so many fallen already.*

Jaren came walking toward her, back in human form. The tall priest still wore his burlap robes from Tofet, and he leaned on his wooden staff, limping from an old wound. Frost covered his beard, melting as the clouds parted and the sun emerged. He knelt above Meliora.

"I will pray for your healing, daughter." He placed his hands upon her.

"No." Meliora struggled to her feet, removing his hands. "Heal the others first. Heal those who followed me to war. I'll wait."

Those words hurt him; she saw that. She could see the thoughts in his eyes.

Flame of Requiem

*You are my precious daughter. I lost you before you were even born,
only to meet you twenty-seven years later. I can't lose you again.*

"I'm fine," she whispered, though every word hurt to utter.
"Pray for the warriors of Requiem. They need you more than I
do."

As he turned toward the others, praying to the stars to heal
their wounds, Meliora raised her eyes, seeking more harpies in
the sky.

Instead she saw two distant figures—dragons, their scales
bright—approaching from the south.

A red dragon and a black dragon. Meliora's breath caught.
She raised her hand, summoning them.

The two dragons flew closer and saw her signal. They
spiraled down and landed before her, winded, puffing out smoke
and spurts of flame. Both were young and slender, their scales
clanking as they breathed raggedly. When they had caught their
breath, they released their magic, becoming two young women
clad in white livery—one with dark hair and olive skin, the other
pale and sporting red stubble on her head.

Meliora stepped closer to them. "Kira! Talana! Tell me
what you saw."

A lifetime ago—stars, it had been only months!—the two
young women had served Meliora in the palace, her loyal
handmaidens. Meliora still felt shame at remembering who she
had been then—a pampered, ignorant princess who had treated
Kira and Talana as one might treat pups. She had saved them
from Malok, the bronze bull, and burn marks still covered their
arms, the scars perhaps permanent. That had been the day
Meliora had changed, the day her innocence had burned away in
the bronze bowels of Malok. Today Kira and Talana served her
not as handmaidens but as scouts, two of the fastest dragons in
Requiem, their eyes sharp, their wings swift, their loyalty
unquestionable. As the nation of Requiem flew across the
wilderness, Kira and Talana were its eyes in the distance. But the
two looked not to the north, their destination, but south—back
toward Tofet, the land they were fleeing, the land where Ishtafel
still lurked.

"My queen!" they said, kneeling before her. "You're
wounded!"

"I'm not queen of Requiem," she told them. "I am her beacon, her voice in the wilderness. Never mind my wounds. Tell me what you saw."

They rose, eyes darting.

"We saw an army," Kira whispered, her black eyes wide. "A great army that darkened the sky, with more warriors then grains of sand in the desert."

Talana shivered, even more pale than usual. "Ishtafel leads them, my que—I mean, my lady. But he's no longer fair. He's all clad in steel and gold—not just armor but new skin, even covering his face, and his wings are now featherless like the wings of a bat. But the creatures he leads are even fouler." She hugged herself. "They . . . They . . ."

"They look like this," Meliora finished for her, voice soft, and pointed at the steaming corpse of a harpy.

The two scouts turned to look and shuddered. The harpy lay only a few yards away, the size of a dragon. Gray blood and maggots seeped from its wounds, and its tongue hung from its mouth, long and white and bustling with ants. A few snakes still lived on its head, hissing and spitting venom.

Kira and Talana nodded.

"Harpies," they whispered together, for they too—once slaves in the palace of Saraph—had heard the tales of these creatures.

Meliora stepped closer to her scouts and placed her hands on their shoulders. She looked into their eyes, one after the other.

"How many were there?" she asked. "By your best estimate, how many?"

Kira gulped. "More than the seraphim who flew against us in Tofet. I'm good at counting. I always used to count seraphim from the window of the palace. But here is a greater army than I've ever seen, ten times the size of the greatest garrisons of Saraph. A million harpies fly toward us, moving fast. As fast as dragons."

Talana nodded, lips trembling. "A million."

Frost seemed to flow across Meliora again. She stared into the bulging, bloodshot eyes of the harpy corpse. Her wounds flared with pain, and the voices of the dead Vir Requis seemed to cry out to her.

You promised us freedom! You promised us a home. Now we die. Now we all die.

Meliora turned away and closed her eyes.

A thousand harpies ravaged our ranks, she thought. *A thousand nearly tore through our defenders, nearly reached our children, nearly crushed our hope. A million will kill every last dragon.*

"We must rise," she whispered, opening her eyes. "Jaren! Vale! Raise the dragons. Let the wounded ride on those dragons strong enough to fly. Rise, dragons of Requiem! Fly! Fly with all your speed. Leave the dead."

Meliora tried to shift into a dragon, tried to fly with them, but she was too weak. Her magic petered away. Elory rushed forth to grab Meliora as she wavered.

"Ride me, sister," Elory said, turning into a dragon. "Ride me until you're well enough to fly."

A few dragons began to rise. Others were digging quick graves—with dragon claws and sandy soil, the work didn't take long—and soon they too rose.

Perhaps Meliora would never know how many had died here—thousands, perhaps tens of thousands. But as the dragons of Requiem flew onward, she knew one thing: If Ishtafel caught them, none of them would survive.

Bleeding, grieving for their lost, the dragons of Requiem flew into the north. Just beyond the southern horizon, just out of the dragons' sight, the foul army followed.

VALE

We were a nation in the dust, Vale thought as he flew. *We've become a nation of the sky.*

He looked across his people. Hundreds of thousands flew around him, dragons in every color. On their backs rode others in human forms, living out their lives in the air. Mothers nursed their babes. Elders sang old songs. Healers changed bandages and chanted prayers. Every once in a while, dragons would spot a herd of animals below—wild deer or sheep sweeping across the land, sometimes merely a stray rabbit—and then dragons would swoop, capture the prey, rise with it again. On scaly backs, men and women lit braziers and cooked the meat. All life— eating, sleeping, praying, singing, dreaming—all in the sky.

Vale rose higher, ascending until the air thinned and he could barely breathe, until he flew above all other dragons. Then he turned to look behind him.

From up here, the horizon spread farther, and he could just see them. Just a hint. A dark stain across the miles, its details invisible. If he hadn't known better, he'd have called it a dark cloud.

But Vale knew what that distant, southern darkness was.

"Harpies," he muttered. "A million harpies following a twisted king."

He looked below at the dragons gliding northward, seeking their homeland—a home that still lay days, maybe weeks, maybe even months away. He might never know how many dragons the thousand harpies had slain. Some estimated— those good at counting great numbers—that ten thousand Vir Requis had fallen to the ice and talons.

If only a thousand harpies slew a myriad of dragons, Vale thought, *this southern army will kill us all.*

He dipped lower in the sky, beat his wings, and darted forward. He flew over the other dragons—this flying city spread for miles—until he reached the head of the camp.

Meliora flew there, her scales silvery-white, touched with gold when the sun hit them right. Every few miles, she raised a pillar of white fire that soared like the fabled King's Column in the north, a beacon for her people to follow.

Can Ishtafel see that beacon from the south? Vale wondered.

He descended until he flew by his sister.

"He's still following," Vale said. "I can now see him when I fly high enough. I flew as high as I could, higher than any bird, so high I could barely breathe and the air was cold even under the sun. The horizon must be a hundred leagues away from up there, and Ishtafel is just on its edge."

"Too close," Meliora said.

Vale nodded. "We must prepare for meeting him, Meliora."

She spun her head toward him, and her eyes narrowed. Smoke plumed from her nostrils. "No. We will not face him in battle. Not here. Not in Saraph. If we must face him, it will be in Requiem. In our homeland. If we must have a final stand, let it be in our holy sky, fighting beneath our sacred stars."

Vale closed his eyes for a moment, remembering that day—that day of more horror and awe than any other. The day he had beheld Issari Seran, the Priestess in White, the Eye of the Dragon. The day he had died.

Ishtafel had nailed him to the top of the ziggurat, driving the spikes deep into Vale's hands and feet, leaving him to die in the sun. As his last breath fled his lungs, as his heart stilled, Vale had seen her.

Issari.

A woman woven of starlight.

Thousands of years ago, Issari had fought alongside King Aeternum himself to found the kingdom of Requiem. She had risen then to the sky, forming the eye of the fabled Draco constellation, the stars they said shone upon Requiem—the stars one could not see here in the south. For millennia, they say that Issari gazed down upon Requiem, and she had descended to heal Vale, to return him to life.

As he flew here, Issari's words to him echoed in his mind.
A great battle awaits you, son of Requiem, she had said, placing
her luminous hands upon him, healing his wounds, returning his
soul into his body. *Live, child of Aeternum. Your war has not yet ended.*

Vale opened his eyes, looking again across the kingdom of
dragons in the sky. He had thought his life's battle had been in
Tofet. Yet now it seemed a greater war awaited. Had Issari
meant that his great battle—the reason for his rebirth—was his
battle with the army of harpies, a battle for Requiem's own
rebirth?

"Meliora, sooner or later, we'll have to face him again."
Vale looked into her eyes. "Either in our sky or here in his. This
is a battle we cannot escape, and a battle that, right now, we
would lose. Requiem can no longer rely on impromptu defense,
nor can we rely on ghosts or erevim to save us. We need an
army. Not just a horde but a true, trained military like Requiem's
Royal Army of old."

The white dragon shook her head sadly. "Armies require
months, even years of training. Armies require ranks. Structures.
Units within units—flights and battalions and commanders for
each. Ruthless discipline. Hardened souls."

Vale smiled grimly. "All things that we already have."

Meliora stared at him, frowning, and slowly her eyes
widened. "Of course."

He nodded. "The strongest among us, going back
centuries, have been organized into teams and sub-teams. All our
lives, we practiced ruthless discipline, hardened our souls and
bodies. Every dragon here who's strong enough to lift a pickaxe
or yoke already has a team. Let our old slave teams become our
new military units. Let that routine—working together, wielding
tools, every man and woman knowing their place—become the
foundation for our army."

"Yes." Meliora bared her teeth. "Yes, we will have an
army. And you, Vale, will lead it."

In dragon form, he had no eyebrows, but he gave his best
attempt at raising one. "Surely there's a better choice for general.
Somebody older, wiser, stronger."

Meliora herself raised a scaly brow. "Who? Father? He's a
priest and healer, not a warrior. Me? I am as a savior to these

548

people, not a general. You are of royal blood, Vale. You are an Aeternum, the descendant of our great warriors of olden days— the blood of King Benedictus, of King Elethor, of the hero Relesar flows through your veins. But there's a far more important reason, Vale, why you should lead." Her eyes darkened. "You faced Ishtafel before. You're the first dragon to have defied him, to burn him. You fought Ishtafel twice and lived."

Her words stabbed him like daggers. He grimaced and looked away. "Yes, I faced Ishtafel in battle twice. I died the first time, sister. I live now only because Father prayed to the Priestess in White to heal me. When I faced him again, I would have died if not for . . . if Tash hadn't . . ."

He could say no more, and tears stung his eyes, and his throat tightened.

Tash.

He lowered his head, the pain overwhelming.

I miss you, Tash. I love you. Always.

It had been several days since her death, and the grief only seemed to grow. Tash—the woman who had infuriated him, the woman he had come to love. Tash—the woman who had almost betrayed him, the woman who had given her life to save his. Tash—the woman who had freed Meliora from her prison, who had found the Chest of Plenty, who had assured Requiem's escape from captivity.

Yet you will never see Requiem, Tash, Vale thought. *I will never hold you again, never kiss you again, never laugh with you, perhaps never laugh again. I love you always, Tash. Your loss is forever a hole inside me.*

Meliora seemed to notice his pain. Her eyes softened, and she flew closer and nuzzled him, her snout hot against his neck.

"I'm sorry, Vale. Her loss pains me too. I cannot imagine how much worse it must be for you."

He raised his eyes, looking at the sky. The sun was setting and soon the stars would emerge. The Draco constellation did not shine this far south, but Vale knew that Tash's soul would rise to that place—those celestial halls he had glimpsed upon the ziggurat.

I know that someday, I will see you again, Tash.

He returned his eyes to Meliora. He nodded. "Requiem will have an army again. And I will lead it."

LUCEM

The dragons of Requiem flew over the wilderness of Saraph, hundreds of thousands strong, covering the sky—a great nation of fire, tears, and blood.

As they flew, leaving so many dead behind, many dragons shed tears. Many others still bled from their wounds. On their backs, children wept, their mothers trying to comfort them, crying too. Elders prayed. Men and women spoke in low voices, eyes darting with fear, seeking enemies on the horizon. Fear, grief, pain—they filled the exodus, spreading from the slowest dragons in the rear to Meliora's pillar of white fire which led the camp, miles in the north.

Yet as Lucem flew here on the wind, he could feel none of that grief or fear.

For the first time in his life, he felt joy.

A feeling pure. Wonderful. Greater than anything he had thought possible to feel.

He inhaled deeply, gave his wings a sturdy flap, and rose higher. At first, he had wobbled while flying, but now it felt as natural as walking. He looked across his nation, trying to count them, unable to. So many dragons—dragons that flowed from one horizon to the other, filling the sky, all flying together after that pillar of white dragonfire, that column in the north, seeking the true pillar of marble.

For so many years, Lucem had languished in his cave. Alone. Afraid. The hero of Requiem, the only one who had ever escaped Tofet—only to become an exile, nearly mad with loneliness. For so many years, hiding in the wilderness, he had dreamed of this. Dreamed of the rest of his nation escaping, rising together as dragons, flying as one.

"Enemies may fly in pursuit," Lucem said. "And many enemies may await us in our fallen homeland. But right now, here, in this sky—we are free. We are dragons."

A high voice spoke on his back. "Not me! And stop talking to yourself. You woke me up."

Lucem looked over his shoulder to see Elory stretching and yawning with all the glorious grace of her human form. She wore a cotton tunic, and her brown hair was growing longer—it was now almost long enough to cover her missing ear, the mark Leyleet had left on her. Several days of flight had been kind to Elory, he thought. She no longer seemed as gaunt as before, and a rosy hue tinted her cheeks.

"Good," he said. "It's my turn to ride you. Into a dragon with you."

She blinked and rubbed her eyes. "No. Not a chance. I didn't sleep nearly long enough."

Lucem snorted and released his magic.

He tumbled down in human form. Elory fell, squealed, and shifted. Soon she flew as a one-eared dragon, scales gleaming violent in the sunlight, the spikes on her tail white as milk.

"Lucem, you bloody pest!" she cried.

He shifted back into a dragon and rose to fly beside her. "Best way to wake up."

She groaned and slapped him with her tail. "Best way to get me to clobber you."

He winced as her tail kept thumping him. "All right, all right! I'm sorry." He reached his own tail around to his sides, rubbing the sore areas her spikes had left. "I suppose I deserved that."

Elory's eyes still flashed with rage. "I forget sometimes that you spent ten years in the wilderness. Probably raised by monkeys, you were. No idea how to behave among us dragons."

He grinned and puffed out smoke. "I'm a wild beast in need of taming."

The violet dragon obviously struggled to remain mad, to keep glaring at him, but when Lucem reared and gave out a squeaky little roar—something that sounded a lot more like a puppy yapping than a dragon bellowing—she relented and laughed.

"I don't know whether to hate you or laugh at you, Lucem."

"Definitely laugh at me." He winked. "Laughter is always better than hatred."

She sighed and moved to fly closer to him, so close their cheeks touched, and their wings flapped one atop the other. Lucem's smile then turned sad, and he closed his eyes, basking in her warmth and presence.

"I'm so happy here, Lucem," she said. "And yet I'm so scared. I'm so scared this dream will end."

"Dreams are never everlasting things. They always end. That does not diminish their beauty. That does not make them less important."

"I know, but I want ours to last for more than a few days! Stars, Lucem. We spent five hundred years in captivity. Will we die before we ever reach Requiem?"

He looked at her, their cheeks still pressed together, their eyes only inches apart.

"This *is* Requiem," Lucem said. "Even if we cannot reach our homeland in the north, even if we never see our stars—this here, right now, this nation in the wilderness, this is Requiem reborn. And I will savor every moment I have with this nation. Every moment that I have with you, Elory. Because I love Requiem, but even more, I love you."

She sighed. "Oh you silly thing. Such a silly, wild beast to tame." She slapped him again with her tail. "You make me love you, don't you? You make me hate you, you make me slap you, you make me laugh at you . . . and you make me love you. Wild beast indeed."

He grinned. "So now can I ride you?"

She rolled her eyes. "Fine! But be careful, or I'm likely to fly upside down as you sleep, sending your slumbering backside down to its death."

As Lucem released his magic above her, landing on her back in human form, he turned to look south. Beyond the horizon, he knew that they were still flying. Ishtafel. A million harpies, a force to slay every last dragon.

I won't die by falling off Elory, he thought. *But we might die before the sun sets and rises again. All of us. Here, far from our homeland.*

He lay on his stomach and draped his arms across Elory, caressing her lavender scales.

I will do whatever I can. I will fight. Kill. Fly to the end of the world and back. Only to spend another moment with you, Elory. Only to live this dream a while longer.

The white pillar of fire rose in the north, and the dragons of Requiem followed. Lucem closed his eyes and slept.

ISHTAFEL

The harpies shrieked, storming across the sky, their rot dripping across the plains, their eyes blazing white under the shadows of the clouds that forever shadowed their flight. A million strong, they had languished for millennia in their prisons—the gods' first, failed attempts at life, older siblings to the seraphim, deformed and cruel, nursing their hatred through the eras.

Yet now they were free from the prison cells of Edinnu. Now they flew here in Saraph, this new realm of godly light Ishtafel had forged. Their talons gleamed. Their feathers churned their stench. Their withered faces, covered in boils and hair, twisted in hatred—the faces of crones, bloated to obscene size, the mouths full of teeth, the throats thirsty for the blood of dragons. Onward they flew, foul life, beasts who knew nothing but hatred.

Yet they were beasts that would serve him, Ishtafel thought. For he had given them freedom. He had given them the chance to prove their strength. The dark seraphim failed him, as they had failed to topple his mother's reign. But the harpies knew no failure; all they knew was to hunt, to kill, to feast upon the flesh of their enemies.

"Soon you will eat dragons!" Ishtafel cried, standing in his chariot of fire high above the land. "Soon the blood of Requiem will fill your bellies and stain your lips."

His voice emerged strangely from his golden mask, metallic, almost like the sound of the bronze bull Malok. More metal covered his body now, a new skin, replacing the skin the dragons had burnt off. No more feathers grew on his wings; only thin membranes stretched across the bones, the feathers burnt off, leaving him almost like a dark seraph, cursed and foul. And yet his halo still shone, a beacon of his dominion and retribution.

The harpies cried out in joy, horrible sounds, the caws of vultures, the grunts of rotting beasts, the wails of slaughtered hogs. They were larger than him, as large as the largest dragons. A single harpy could, perhaps, crush even him, the King of Saraph, the mightiest of the seraphim.

They will devastate Requiem.

For too long, he had shown the dragons mercy. Slaying them only one by one. Allowing them to live in their miserable huts, to reek and rot in Tofet, staining his empire with their wretchedness. He would have to burn down and bury that entire land to cover the stench. For too long, he had let the weredragons languish in their pathetic excuse for life.

That mercy was over.

"You will die long before you reach your homeland, weredragons," he said. "All but you, Meliora. You will live. You will return to your true homeland . . . to Saraph. To the ziggurat. To your prison cell. And there, my sweetness, in darkness and chains, you will bear my heirs."

He grinned inside his mask, the movement stretching his wounds, leaking blood, shooting pain through him. Good. The pain kept him alive. The pain kept his hatred burning hot. He stared ahead, and he could just see them on the horizon—a wake of smoke. The trail of dragons . . . getting closer every day.

"No more slavery, dragons," he whispered. "Only death. Only mountains of your bones."

MELIORA

"No." She shook her head as she flew, crossing the mountains of Khalish toward the distant valleys. "We cannot stop. We cannot land, not even for an hour. Not with Ishtafel on our tails."

Her father flew at her side, scales green as the fabled forests of Requiem. Jaren looked at her with sad eyes.

"We're out of food, my daughter. The fish and animals we hunt below are not enough to feed a nation. The Chest of Plenty cannot duplicate food fast enough for half a million dragon mouths. We need more flour. Fruit and vegetables. Milk and cheese."

She narrowed her eyes, puffing out smoke. She looked behind her at the hundreds of thousands of dragons, then back at her father. "Then we'll tighten our belts. We can endure a few more days of hunger."

"But can we endure disease?" Jaren asked. "An illness runs through the camp, and fewer dragons can fly every hour. They ride the strong, shivering in their human forms, and the fever is spreading—even here in the sky. We need medicine. Medicine that can be found in the city ahead."

Meliora spat out smoke. She stared ahead. There, in the distance, she could see it on the horizon. A great mountain rose ahead, crowned with a city of limestone, sandstone, and bronze. Walls surrounded the mountain's base, and brick structures sprawled across the slopes. On the mountain's crest perched a great, round fortress, shaped as an egg.

The city of Keleshan. Home to Saraph's largest garrison of troops outside the capital. If Shayeen was the heart of the empire, here was its fist.

"We're not ready to fight another battle," Meliora said. "Not here, not in Keleshan. We veer west. We avoid this city and travel over the western deserts. I would not approach

Keleshan, not even for food and medicine. Not even our new army can face these foes."

Jaren gazed at her with sad eyes. "They never told you, did they?

She frowned. "Tell me what, Father?"

He turned to stare toward the distant city. "Why do you think there are walls around Keleshan? The seraphim have wings and can easily fly over them, and no enemies threaten them, not in this world they so easily conquered. Those walls are there to keep people in. More slaves. More Vir Requis." He lowered his head. "The people of Requiem were chained not just in Tofet. They serve in this city too, and in the cities along the northern coast."

Meliora inhaled sharply.

More slaves. More Vir Requis.

And she knew: She could not simply fly by. She would fight for Keleshan, this city on the mountain. She would test her new army. She would kill.

She would raise more dragons.

She spun in the sky and flew toward her brother. Vale flew among a hundred dragon warriors, the vanguard of the camp—all Vir Requis who had once labored in the mines. Thousands of other warriors now flew around the camp, organized into their old units. The brickmakers guarded the eastern flank. The bitumen diggers—Elory among them—flew in the west. Other units—once bitumen refiners, masons, farmers, shipwrights, and many other laborers—flew in their own formations. The new Royal Army, formed from the strongest slaves, surrounded the weaker Vir Requis—elders, nursing mothers, children, babes.

Now they will fly to war, Meliora thought.

"Vale," she said, "ready your troops. We're about to test their mettle."

She repeated Jaren's words to him, and while he listened, the blue dragon sneered and puffed out smoke, staring at the city ahead.

"So we fight for food," Vale said. "For medicine. And for freedom. The blood of Saraph will spill today . . . and new dragonfire will rise." With a roar, the blue dragon reared and blasted fire skyward. His voice rolled across the camp. "Royal Army, rise, rise! Fly with me at the vanguard. Fly to war!"

With thousands of roars, the new army of Requiem stormed to the head of the camp. Their cries shook the sky. The sun began to set, but their fire lit the darkness.

They stormed across the miles, and Meliora flew with them, roaring out her fury. Her family flew at her sides: Vale, a blue dragon, commander of the Royal Army; Elory, a lavender dragon, smaller but just as fast, her fire just as hot; Jaren, her father, his scales green, a healer who did not hesitate to fight to save lives. Behind them flew thousands of others. Their captivity had weakened their bodies but hardened their souls, instilling deep wrath within them. Now this fury would wash across their enemies of light.

From the walls and roofs of Keleshan they rose—hosts of seraphim, bearing lances and shields. From the oval fortress on the mountaintop rose many flaming chariots, their firehorses storming toward the dragons, and the seraphim riders raised bows and arrows. As the dragons flew closer across the mountains, more and more seraphim kept emerging, an erupting volcano, a host that covered the sky like clouds of red and orange and flaring white. Thousands soared, prepared for battle, flying in formations, spears glinting, halos burning, chariots thundering like a storm.

"Hear me, Requiem!" Meliora cried. "We fight to free our brothers and sisters. We fight for our freedom. To war! To war! For stars and column, fly!"

"For stars and column!" they answered her call. "For Requiem!"

Thousands of their roars sounded together. Thousands of flaming pillars rose in a blazing forest. The dragons stormed forth, howling with rage, no longer slaves, no longer broken and afraid. Here were no refugees, no broken souls.

Here was an army of dragons, an army like the great hosts of Old Requiem, charging for glory.

Ahead of them, the seraphim stormed across the sky. Their wings spread wide. The light of their halos flared out. The setting sun gleamed on their gilded breastplates, and their chariots rose above, forming a great canopy, a sky of fire. The distance shrank between the two hosts. The earth itself seemed to shake, the heavens to burn. Only a league separated the forces, then a mile.

"Blow your fire, Requiem!" Vale shouted, rearing at Meliora's side. "Burn them down!"

Arrows flew.

Lances thrust.

Dragonfire washed across the sky.

VALE

A great battle awaits you, son of Requiem.

As he stormed across the sky to the wall of fire, words of starlight echoed inside him.

Live, son of Aeternum. Your war has not yet ended.

As he flew to blood, pain, killing, maybe death upon the plains, Vale thought of Issari. A priestess of starlight. A mother of Requiem. A kind, guiding light, the woman who had given him life, who had birthed Requiem thousands of years ago.

I fight for my family, he thought. *I fight for my people. But I also fight for you, Lady in White.*

He stared at the enemy ahead—countless seraphim, some in chariots, others flying with their own wings—and blasted his dragonfire.

Thousands of flaming jets blasted from the dragons around him.

Arrows flew from the enemy host, darkening the sky. The projectiles—each was longer than a human arm, tipped with blades to dwarf daggers—slammed down into the charging dragons, some snapping against scales, others driving through and finding flesh. Dragons roared and lost their magic and fell, screaming, as men and women.

Vale kept flying, roaring his flames.

The dragonfire washed across the first ranks of seraphim. Feathered wings kindled. Gilt melted off steel armor. Skin peeled and seraphim screamed, flesh burning, but still the immortals charged. Their lances thrust, the blades like longswords.

Vale bellowed and swerved. A lance scraped across his side, shattering scales, and he kept flying. He swung his claws, tearing through armor, digging into a seraph's torso, tugging out the innards, and casting the man down.

"Fight, sons and daughters of Requiem!" he cried. "You are an army! You will slay the enemy!"

Lances drove forth all around him. The blades slammed into dragons. One lance scraped across a dragon's underbelly where no scales grew, ripping the beast open, spilling the organs. All around, men and women fell, screaming, many already dead, their magic lost. The corpses slammed against the hills below.

More seraphim stormed toward Vale. He bucked in the sky. He whipped his tail around, driving the spikes into a seraph's side, piercing his gut. He rose higher, dodging a lance, and propelled himself forward. He closed his jaws around a seraph's head and shoulders, bit down, tore the man in two, and spat out the arms and head. Another seraph shoved his lance forward, and the blade scraped across Vale's back. Scales flew like coins from a cut purse. Vale roared, grabbed the seraph's shield in his claws, and shoved it aside. He blasted his dragonfire, washing the seraph with the flames, sending him falling down to the ground like a comet.

Fire, godlight, smoke, scales, blood, fangs, steel—they swirled through the sky, a great dance of death. Though bodies fell, though lances thrust, though countless seraphim still swooped from above, the dragons never lost their composure, never broke formation. All their lives, these Vir Requis had danced this dance macabre. All their lives, they had toiled in the valley of death, allowing the seraphim to beat them, slay them, and still they had toiled.

Now, in the sky, no enemy would shatter their strength.

Still they worked together—worked not at cutting stone but cutting flesh, not at mining black bitumen but the golden ichor of immortals. They sang again—no longer their songs of slavery, songs of straw and clay and tar and sweat, but songs of Requiem, songs of pride, of marble, of starlight, of a home among the birches and in the northern sky. A song of dragons.

Before them they fell—a rain of seraphim, wings ablaze, and the corpses of the immortals littered the fields of Saraph, as plentiful as the crops that grew there. The crops the Vir Requis had planted; the crops they would claim.

The food in this city is ours, Vale thought as he lashed his claws, swung his tail, blew his fire. The medicine in the houses of healing. The bricks of the temples, fortresses, silos. The cobblestones on the roads. The wine in jugs, the water drawn from wells, the wealth and work of this city—all these were made by Vir Requis slaves. All would belong to free dragons.

They fought through the night.

In the darkness, the chariots of fire cast out their light. Their firehorses tore through the ranks of dragons, wings aflame, sending men and women plunging down. The seraphim riders fired their arrows, slaying warriors, breaking the lines, and storming through the ranks of elders and children, cutting them down. Nursing mothers. Babes. Elders who had survived decades of servitude. As the lines of Requiem's army crumbled, they fell to their deaths below.

Yet even as Vale's army regrouped and charged back into battle, those they protected joined the fight.

Young dragons, no larger than ponies, blasted out streams of fire. Old dragons, their teeth fallen and their scales cracked, slammed into the ranks of seraphim. Every dragon fought this day, and in the fires above the city of Keleshan, all of Requiem became an army. All fought for their nation, for a memory of their stars—a memory that had passed through the generations. None here had ever seen the stars of Requiem, and none had seen King's Column, but those lights still shone in their hearts.

Dawn was rising when the seraphim began to fall back.

Those chariots and seraphim that still flew retreated into the city, their light vanishing behind the walls. The dragons of Requiem cheered.

"The city is ours!" they cried. "Requiem rises! Requiem rises!"

A rumble rose ahead.

The city shook.

As the dragons cheered, Vale stared at the city with narrowed eyes, his belly churning.

Light grew within the massive, oval fortress that crowned the city, leaking through the windows and doors and between the bricks.

Vale sneered.

"Hold your ranks!" he cried. "Warriors of Requiem, rally here! Hold the lines!"

On the mountaintop, the egg-shaped fortress shook, then began to crumble. Bricks rained from its rounded facades. The arches collapsed around the base. The towers that rose upon its crest cracked and tumbled. Soon the entire structure was collapsing, casting out beams of light.

The great stone egg was hatching, and a creature unfurled from within.

Vale stared, hissing. His heart sank and fear thrummed through him.

A colossal beak, large as a dragon, thrust through the disintegrating stone shell. A wet, feathered body emerged, and wings spread out, large as fields. The massive bird rose upon the mountaintop, claws the size of houses, and raised its head to the rising sun. It let out a great cry, a sound that rolled across the city, scattering stones, bending trees, cracking the walls and flattening the farms below.

"He is Ziz!" Meliora said, darting up to fly by Vale. The silver dragon's scales were cracked and bleeding, burns spread across her wings, and blood stained her claws and mouth. "The ancient sunbird of Saraph, a great symbol of the nation. They say he sleeps for a thousand years, only to rise again. I thought it only a tale."

Vale grumbled. "Well, that tale is taking flight before us, and he doesn't look too happy that we woke him up."

As Ziz's wings flapped, they snapped palm trees, toppled roofs, cracked walls across the city. The wind buffeted the army of dragons, tossing them back in the sky. Ziz rose higher, and his wings spread wide like storm clouds, hiding the sun. Darkness fell across the land.

"Ziz, Ziz!" chanted the surviving seraphim upon the walls.

Vale sneered, puffing out smoke.

We have no time for this. Ishtafel gains on us every hour that we delay. He glanced behind him, and in the darkness he could see a sickly smoke on the horizon—Ishtafel's troops. Coming closer.

He looked around him. Many from his army had fallen. Hundreds of Vir Requis lay dead upon the fields and city roofs below, perhaps thousands. Those dragons that still flew hurried to form new lines in the sky, readying what flames they could muster. Most were too weary for full blasts of dragonfire; only weak puffs of smoke left their nostrils, and only sparks left their jaws.

The sunbird shrieked again, circling above. The cry was deafening. Vale couldn't help it; he screamed in the noise, his ears thundering, feeling ready to shatter. Several dragons lost their magic and fell, covering their ears, nearly hitting the ground before rising again as dragons. Flames burst from Ziz's eyes, and the sunbird turned in the sky . . . and came swooping toward the dragons.

"Ziz, Ziz!" the seraphim cried. "Feed upon the dragons!"

Fear—icy, overpowering—flowed across Vale.

The bird plunged down, covering the sky, its beak large enough to swallow dragons whole. The dragons of Requiem cried out and began to scatter. Vale stared skyward and saw his death.

Live, son of Aeternum. Your war does not end here.

He let starlight fill his mind.

Vale roared, his cry rising so loudly all the Royal Army could hear, even over the shriek of the mythological beast swooping from above.

"Fly, Requiem! Fly and burn him down!"

Vale soared.

Hundreds, soon thousands of dragons soared with him.

Their dragonfire rose, and Ziz's wrath fell upon them.

Pillars of dragonfire slammed into the bird's wings and rained, showering back onto the dragons. Claws tore at feathered flesh. Yet Ziz did not burn, and his blood did not spill. His talons swung, as large as dragons, plowing through the hosts of Requiem. Their blows knocked the magic out of Requiem's warriors; they fell as men and women. The wind stormed, slamming into dragons, sending them tumbling through the sky, crashing against one another. The sunbird screeched again, and more men and women fell, eardrums pierced and bleeding.

"We can't hurt it!" Meliora cried, flying by Vale as the wings beat above them, and the storm buffeted them. "None can slay Ziz."

Vale roared and flew higher.

A great battle awaits you, son of Requiem.

"We will slay him!" he cried.

He flew higher, rising among falling dragons, until he flew before the head of the beast. Above the span of its wings, the

565

sun shone brilliantly, nearly blinding him. Ziz cried out, beak opened wide, large as a temple's nave.

Head spinning, barely clinging to his magic, Vale blew his dragonfire.

He had been breathing fire all night, and he had to reach deep inside him, to summon all his pain, the pain of his captivity, his torture in Saraph, to reach for all his grief over the loss of Tash, the loss of thousands, to raise all his pride, his honor, his love of Requiem and her stars. With mourning, fear, nobility, and fury, he cast out a great jet of dragonfire, hotter and brighter than any he had blown.

The inferno shrieked across the sky and crashed into the great bird's eyes.

Ziz tossed back his head and cried out again, but this time it was a cry of pain.

Vale stormed forth and lashed his claws at the great bird's neck.

It felt like clawing a granite cliff. Vale roared, feeling like his claws would snap off. He barely dented the beast, and the beak plunged down. Vale flew backward, blasted fire again. The beak snapped shut, missing him by inches. The talons rose, lashing at Vale. He tried to fly backward again, but he was too slow.

The talons slammed against him.

Each of those sharp, yellow nails was as large as a dragon. Thankfully, the sharp end missed Vale, but the polished surface of the talons crashed against him like the columns of a crumbling temple.

The pain seemed to shatter every scale across him.

Vale lost his magic.

He fell as a man.

He tumbled between dozens of soaring dragons, their fire rising around him. Dozens of other Vir Requis fell with him, dead or dying.

"Vale!" With a flash of red scales, Lucem soared and caught Vale in his claws. "Vale, old boy! You all right?"

Vale groaned and shook his head, hanging in the red dragon's grip, still in human form. "Just stunned a bit."

Dipping to avoid another lash of the great talons, Lucem snorted. "That's what you get for trying to be a hero like me. There's only one legendary hero in Requiem, old boy, and that's Lucem the Red. But come, let's be heroes together." The red dragon grinned toothily. "I'm the only one who ever scaled the walls of Tofet. What's killing a giant bird the size of a mountain?"

Vale took a deep breath, clearing the pain, and shifted back into a dragon, tugging himself free from Lucem's grip. They were now flying below Ziz. The massive bird's wings hid the sun again, casting darkness across them. Hundreds of dragons were rising around them, blowing fire, trying to burn the beast, but Ziz kept flying. The talons kept lashing, and Vale grimaced to see the bird's beak close around a dragon and swallow.

"Fly with me," Lucem said and began diving, moving away from the great bird.

Vale growled. "Do you flee from battle?"

The red dragon snorted and looked over his shoulder at Vale. "Dive as a hero or soar and die as a martyr."

With a grunt, Vale followed. The two dragons plunged downward, weaving between their comrades. The other warriors of Requiem, all rising to attack the bird above, cried out in rage and fear.

"Vale the commander and Lucem the hero flee from battle!" one dragon cried.

"Our prince and hero are cowards!" said another dragon.

Across the battlefield, dragons looked around in dismay. Some began to flee the battle.

"Lucem—" Vale began.

"Trust me!" said the red dragon.

Eyes narrowed, smoke blasting between his teeth, Lucem kept swooping. The ground rushed up toward them, littered with corpses of both Vir Requis and seraphim, cloaked in shadows under the veil of wings. An instant before he could hit the ground, Lucem curved his flight, reached out his claws, and grabbed a lance from a fallen seraph.

"Grab one!" Lucem said, rising again.

Vale spread his wings wide, trapping air, and reached out to pluck a fallen lance like a raptor grabbing a fish.

Again they soared. Their fellow dragons parted before them. The two dragons, red and black, rose with spears in their claws, heading back toward the massive sunbird that hid the sky.

"Take the right!" Lucem cried.

Vale grumbled. He thought he knew what Lucem was thinking. "Meet you in the middle."

The red dragon grinned. "Not sure our lances are long enough, but I'll try."

The dragons parted ways, Vale curving his ascent toward the right, Lucem to the left. As hundreds of dragons blew fire all around, Vale rose above Ziz's wings again. Once more, he emerged into the blue sky.

The head of the bird shrieked above, the beak crushing more dragons. Several warriors of Requiem were flying around the head, blasting dragonfire, but none could burn the great sunbird.

Ziz is impenetrable to claws and fangs, fireproof, impossible for dragons to cut, Vale thought. When the bird screeched again, Vale grimaced, his eardrums thrumming so madly he thought they'd rip. *It hurts our ears. Time to hurt his.*

He flew closer, dodging the snapping beak. Other dragons flew all around, and streams of dragonfire crisscrossed the sky. The beak lashed again and again, fast as striking vipers, devouring dragons. In the distance, across the great feathered head, Vale could glimpse a soaring red dragon, clutching a lance.

There! Vale stared. He saw it. When Ziz's wings blasted air, raising the feathers on the head, the hole revealed itself—no larger than a man's head.

Its ear.

A few hundred yards away, Lucem was charging toward the head. Vale bared his fangs and charged too.

The great bird spun its head from side to side, finally settling on Vale. Its eyes narrowed balefully, and the bird thrust its head forward, beak snapping.

Vale cringed.

The beak opened wide, prepared to grab him.

Wincing, Vale released his magic.

He shrunk at once to human form and fell. The beak snapped shut inches away. The lance tumbled and spun through the sky.

Before the beak could snap again, Vale shifted back into a dragon. He grabbed the spear and soared. Lucem came flying forth.

"Now, Vale!" the red dragon cried.

Vale whipped around in the sky, dodging the snapping beak, rose higher, ascended above the head . . . then released his magic again.

As he fell in human form, he grabbed the lance.

There.

Wind gusted, raising the feathers on Ziz's head.

There!

Falling as a man, Vale thrust his lance.

The blade—long and sharp as a sword—drove into the massive bird's ear. Vale pushed with all his might, feeling the blade tear through the eardrum, driving deeper, and he kept pushing until the shaft sank deep into the head.

Across the great head, Lucem shoved forth his own lance, driving the blade and shaft into Ziz's opposite ear.

The sunbird screamed.

It was a sound so horrible, so loud, so anguished, that Vale covered his ears and fell, still in human form. He thumped down onto the creature's wing. Above, the massive head thrashed, the lances still embedded into it. Blood leaked. The wings trembled, struggling to beat.

Vale rose as a dragon. He flew higher. Lucem flew with him. Below them, the great bird cried out—a sound that seemed almost afraid, almost human.

Vale expected to feel triumph, pride in Requiem, maybe only relief—but instead he felt pity. He felt guilt.

We slew a mythological beast. We slew a frightened animal, newly hatched.

Below him, Ziz's head swayed, and the great bird the size of a city began to fall.

Vale had to look away, his eyes suddenly damp.

All across the sky, the surviving dragons cheered. Many fired down dragonfire, roasting the sunbird as it fell. The earth and sky shook as Ziz slammed against the land, its one wing draped across the city wall, the other across the fields. The animal gave one more cry, weaker, softer . . . and then fell silent.

"Damn yeah!" Lucem cried. "That's how it's done."

The red dragon flew in circles, hooting with joy. But Vale only lowered his head.

A great battle awaits you, son of Requiem.

"But it was not this battle," he whispered. "Not this slaughter far from our home."

As Lucem still yipped with joy, and as the dragons cheered all around, Vale turned to look south. The gray cloud in the distance was moving closer—Ishtafel's hosts. They had fought a bloody battle here, one that had tested Vale's new army and all his resolve. But the greatest battle still awaited—one that Vale hoped he would never have to fight.

MELIORA

We must move fast.

She glanced toward the south, where a shadow approached. Ishtafel and his host of harpies, a million strong. Only an hour or two away.

Meliora pulled her wings close to her body and dived. The city of Keleshan rose below upon the mountain, the egg-shaped fortress on its crest broken, the great bird itself dead upon the walls and roofs. The last few seraphim fled from the city, scattering in all directions.

But there was still life in Keleshan. Still many souls. Awaiting her. Awaiting salvation.

In the dawn's light, evil rising like a tidal wave behind her, Meliora Aeternum, Mother of Requiem, descended into the city of Keleshan with a pillar of white fire. From homes, huts, fields, and refineries they emerged—the slaves of the city. Hobbled. Collared. Beaten and broken down, but singing, calling out her name.

"Meliora the Merciful! The Queen of Requiem arrives!"

Meliora had not known her tales had spread this far, yet these people sang for her, weeping in the city streets and on the roofs. Her people. Her children. Children of Requiem.

Kira and Talana flew at her sides, her trusted handmaidens-turned-comrades. The two young dragons carried crates, which they shattered in their claws. Keys—thousands of keys—rained onto the city.

"Open your chains, children of Requiem!" Meliora cried, flying above the homes and temples and fields. "Unlock your collars, Vir Requis. Summon the magic of starlight, and fly with me! Fly with your nation."

Hundreds of thousands of dragons, freed from Tofet, flew above the city. Thousands more rose from Keleshan below— wobbling, afraid, flying for the first time in their lives. Their chains fell. Their collars lay smashed on the streets. And they rose, dragon after dragon, scales bright, fire hot, tears in their eyes and their songs filling the sky.

"Requiem!" they sang. "May our wings forever find your sky."

The ancient song of Requiem—the song their people had sung for thousands of years, since King Aeternum and Queen Laira had raised a column in a northern forest, since Priestess Issari had shone her light. Past the eras, the generations that had fought and fell and wept and prayed, the song of dragons remained. That song spread across the camp, filling their hearts—the prayer of a nation.

Yet in the south, a different song rose.

Meliora could hear it now, and she shivered.

A demonic buzz. Shrieks. Jeers. Cackles. The song of harpies, and above it a distant voice—almost impossible to hear—deep, calling out to her. Vowing eternal pain. The voice of Ishtafel.

Meliora sneered.

That is one battle I will not fight, not yet, not here. This day we slew a great enemy, but Ishtafel is an enemy we cannot defeat.

"Fly, dragons of Requiem!" she shouted, rising higher in the sky. "Fly north. Fly with me. To the coast. To the sea. To Requiem!"

She raised her pillar of white dragonfire, a twin to King's Column in the north. The camp gathered around her beacon.

She flew north, leaving the city of Keleshan behind, and they followed. They had lost many, and they had gained many more. Together they flew, moving as fast as they could, seeking a home, fleeing the darkness.

ELORY

As the dragon flew northward, leaving the sacked city behind, Elory kept glancing over her shoulder and seeing, hearing, remembering.

Ishtafel's host of harpies flew perhaps fifty leagues away—just close enough to cover the horizon. And they were closing the distance quickly. Every hour that Elory looked behind her, the enemy seemed a mile closer. Before fighting in Keleshan, only Requiem's scouts or highest flyers—those who dared rise until the air thinned to nearly nothing—had been able to see Ishtafel in the south. Yet now he was always there, seen even from normal altitude.

Even with one missing ear, Elory could hear them. Cackles. Chants. Shrieks. Their stench carried on the wind, assaulting her nostrils even from here. Even with so many dragons flying around her, Elory could not feel safe. Not with that host of killers on her trail.

Only a thousand harpies devastated us, slaying ten dragons for each one of them. Elory shuddered as she flew. *Now a million of those creatures fly in pursuit, gaining on us.*

She forced herself to look away, to gaze around at her fellow Vir Requis. The dragons flew in a great camp, a kingdom in the air. About a third of them flew as dragons; the others rode their comrades, resting in human forms. The new arrivals from Keleshan had swelled their numbers. The Royal Army surrounded the weaker dragons, and at the head of the column flew Meliora, raising her white flames into the sky, a beacon that even the southernmost dragons—several miles behind—could see and follow.

And Ishtafel can see it too, Elory thought.

Worse than the sight of that distant cloud, than the noise, the stench, the fear—were the memories.

The images kept flashing before Elory—when she stared into the distance, when she slept, sometimes surprising her, creeping up on her. Whether they pounced, lurked, cut, taunted her, the memories were always there.

Ishtafel tossing down the bruised, ravaged body of Mayana, the young laborer from Tofet, Elory's dearest friend. Ishtafel's lance thrusting into Mother, slaying the dragon who had only been trying to protect her daughter. And Ishtafel dragging Elory into the ziggurat, promising to invade her body once her training in the pleasure pits was complete.

I don't know how to forget, Elory thought. *I know how to fight an enemy who flies in this sky, but how do I fight an enemy inside me?*

She craned her neck around to look at her back. Upon her violet scales they slept: three young children, their parents slain in this war. The eldest was barely a youth, the youngest a babe.

There will be many more orphans before we reach our homeland, Elory thought. *I promise you, children, that I will fight, kill, even die to build you a home. A place where you can be free, safe, where you can grow up like the Vir Requis of old, proud and strong.*

She flapped her wings and flew faster, gliding over thousands of dragons below, until Elory reached the head of the camp. Meliora still flew there—she hadn't slept for days, it seemed. Farther back glided a long, green dragon—Jaren, Priest of Requiem.

"Father," Elory said, coming to glide at his side.

He seemed to hear the hurt in her voice. He turned toward her, eyes soft, and caressed her with the tip of his wing. "My daughter."

Elory had been strong through her battles. She had faced the lashes of the overseers and stayed standing. She had fought in the most cursed of days, the decimation in Shayeen. She had battled the seraphim over Tofet, she had faced the Rancid Angels in the darkness, and she had slain harpies and battled a bird the size of the sky. Throughout her wars, she had roared in fury and pride, and she had fought as a warrior. Yet now, with these children sleeping on her back, with her memories free to fill her in the clear sky, tears filled Elory's eyes.

"Father," she said, "can you tell me the story again? The one I always loved the most? About Queen Laira?"

The green dragon nuzzled her with his snout, smiled sadly, and nodded. "Of course."

Again, Jaren told her that tale—a tale over five thousand years old. The tale of Laira, the Mother of Requiem, the kingdom's founder and first queen.

"Laira grew up in a tribe of hunters who roamed the northern plains," Father said. "She was a frightened girl, blessed with the magic of starlight, magic she had to hide. The other tribesmen tormented her, starved her, beat her, slew her mother, slew all others with her magic—the magic to become a dragon. Laira escaped her tribe of nomads, and for many days, she wandered the wilderness. She was cold. She was hungry. She was wounded. The nights were dark and she thought that dawn could never shine."

Elory nodded, her tears falling. "But she found something."

"She found something." Jared smiled. "A hidden canyon in an escarpment. A waterfall. And a group of others—others hunted, exiled, others the world called 'weredragons.' People who could grow wings and scales, breathe fire, rise as dragons. They fought a great war, those early outcasts hiding in the canyon. King Aeternum led them to battles against the demons of the Abyss. Issari, the Priestess in White, healed their wounds, then rose into the sky, becoming the eye of the Draco constellation. And it was Laira, first queen and great mother to our family, who prayed to our column, who blessed that pillar that still calls us home."

Elory now repeated that prayer. Laira's Prayer. The prayer that now belonged to all of Requiem.

"As the leaves fall upon our marble tiles, as the breeze rustles the birches beyond our columns, as the sun gilds the mountains above our halls—know, young child of the woods, you are home, you are home. Requiem! May our wings forever find your sky."

Elory was descended of Laira and Aeternum, they said—the many generations running unbroken from those early founders to her. To Vale. To Meliora. And Elory whispered a prayer of her own.

"May we find that home again," she whispered. "May we see those birches, those golden mountains. May we pray again in the light of our column, and may our wings again find the sky of Requiem."

"We will find Requiem," Jaren said. "I promise you, Elory. Our road is long and strewn with thorns. Like Laira, we are in darkness, but we are not lost. Our homeland awaits us, and we will raise her halls again."

The sun was setting. The children on her back awoke, and Lucem flew up to carry them onward. Elory released her magic for the first time in a night and day. She lay on her father's scaly back, closed her eyes, and slept. For the first time in many nights, Elory did not dream of the horrors of Tofet; she dreamed of a lost girl, wandering a dark forest in the north, seeking a home, moving by the light of the stars.

BIM

Claws reached out from the darkness, grabbed him, shook him, cut him.

"No," he mumbled in the shadows. "No. Release me. Stop!"

But the creature kept shaking him, a beast in the darkness.

"Up, Bim!" the troll said. "Up. Run!"

Bim's eyes fluttered open. Shadows spread around him, and orange light crackled in the distance. The trees swayed, branches creaking and scattering snow. His sister knelt above him, gripping his shoulders and shaking him.

"Up, Bim! We have to run."

Bim moaned. He didn't want to run again. He wanted to return to sleep. He wanted to sink into the snow, to let them burn him. To finally die, finally rest.

But groggily he rose. He rose like he did every hour or two. And he ran through the darkness with his sister, fleeing the fire.

He didn't look over his shoulder. He never looked anymore. But Bim heard them. Thunderous hooves in the sky, beating wings of fire, and the voices of seraphim, calling to him, calling for his blood, vowing to bugger him and his sister with their spears, to snap their bones, to tug out their entrails. He smelled them too—the smell of burning wood, of brimstone, of sulfur, of dried blood. The light of their chariots painted the forest red, and still Bim and Til ran.

"Here!" Til whispered.

Her hair was red as the flames, and snow dusted her cloak. Her pieces of armor, collected from many corpses, lay strapped across patches of fur, silent as they ran. She pointed toward a fallen tree, its roots rising like a wooden fairy fort. Below the roots, under the trunk, gaped a black burrow. The firelight grew closer behind, the chariots closing the distance.

His sister all but shoved him into the burrow. He crouched in the den, the icy trunk above him, the roots rising like the bars of a cage. Til crawled in next and huddled beside him, pushing herself deeper.

The chariots stormed above.

Ash fell outside the burrow like gliding snow.

The wooden burrow creaked, and the seraphim laughed above. Bim cringed, hugging his sister. Her arms nearly crushed him. He screwed his eyes shut, the smell of them filling his nostrils.

"Find the weredragons!" cried a voice above.

"Skin them alive!"

"We'll make coats from their skin and flutes from their bones!"

Bim huddled deeper, pressing his back against the tree. Til squeezed him so tightly he could barely breathe.

"It's all right," she whispered into his ear. "They'll fly by. Count with me. One . . . two . . . three . . ."

Shuddering, he counted with her, forcing the words out in a hoarse whisper. He had to just think of the numbers. Just numbers and nothing else. Not the blades peeling off his skin. Not the hooks cutting into his belly, pulling out his insides. Just numbers, that was all. He pretended that he was counting dragons.

His heartbeat slowed. Til's grip relaxed and he forced himself to breathe.

"Twenty-three . . . twenty-four . . ."

Moments until life or death. The number of breaths before torture or another hour of dreams.

"Twenty-seven . . ."

And their sounds faded. The firelight died down. The seraphim flew onward, leaving only ash, shadows, and echoes in their wake.

Bim relaxed, closed his eyes, and slept in his sister's arms.

Again he dreamed, the troll lurking in the shadows, circling him, sniffing. Again its claws grabbed him, tugging him, the fangs biting.

"Up, Bim! Up. We have to move."

Flame of Requiem

The troll kept shaking him, burning him with torches, and his eyes snapped open. Firelight blazed all around, and heat drenched Bim. He still lay under the log, the roots rising before him. Beyond them, the forest was burning in the night.

"Burn them down! They hide here. Burn them!"

His sister pulled him out of the burrow, and again they ran. Through flames. In shadows. Down valleys and up hills, moving between the trees, fleeing the inferno. They ran until they found ruins—a village of Old Requiem, a mere well and silo and the shells of a few homes—and they hid between crumbling brick walls. They shivered in the darkness as the fire burned below the hill, and they slept again.

"We'll reach the coast," Til vowed, holding him close, smoothing his hair. Her voice rose in his dreams—the voice of the clawed beast, of a mother, of an ancient queen. "We'll find safety, Bim. I promise. We'll find a home."

LUCEM

As he flew with the camp, Lucem kept looking over his shoulder at Elory; she slept in human form, curled up on his scaly back. Again and again, every mile, he turned his head to check on her, to see that she still rode him, that she was *real.*

Every time he looked, he half expected her to vanish, half expected this all to be some fever dream. He kept waiting to find himself back in his cave, talking to his clump of wood, or to a pinecone, or to a rock he had painted a face on. He kept waiting for a brief moment of clarity, just enough to realize he had finally gone completely mad.

How can this be? Lucem kept thinking as he flew with the dragons. *How can she be?*

He didn't deserve this. This couldn't be real. He was a coward! He was the boy who had climbed the wall of Tofet, had escaped, had abandoned his people. He was the man cursed to linger in a cave, to go mad with loneliness, his punishment for his betrayal. What had he done to deserve this blessing? To fly with so many dragons, fly by Meliora the Merciful herself, Queen of Requiem? To bear on his back Elory Aeternum, princess of dragons—a woman he loved and who loved him?

He could not imagine a better life, a more precious moment. This couldn't be real. He had lost his mind. These dragons must be leaves in the wind, and Elory must be another block of wood with knots for eyes. He must be back in his cave. He was not a good enough man to deserve this.

Neck twisted around, he watched her as she slept. Elory lay across his back, her cheek resting on her palm. Her face was calm as she slept, and her brown hair was growing, no longer stubble but a messy mop that fell across her brow; soon it would be long enough to completely cover her missing ear. Her burlap tunic was tattered, revealing many scrapes, cuts, and bruises, and her frame was still too thin, her skin burnt. The marks of her collar and manacles still showed around her neck and ankles.

Gazing at her, both love and pity filled Lucem, and he knew: This was real. He truly was flying here, Elory on his back, and she was hurt, and she was scarred, and though her wounds would heal her soul might not.

While I was in my cave, all those years, safe from pain, she was suffering under the whip. For ten years as I lingered—just a few miles away—she was suffering.

The old guilt filled Lucem, worse than ever—guilt mingled with love.

He began to descend in the sky. He flew below the other dragons of Requiem, heading lower in the sky, leaving the others above. A forest sprawled across the land of Saraph, and he kept gliding down.

"Lucem!" Meliora cried above. "Lucem, you all right?"

He looked up at the white dragon who flew above. "Just a quick break to water the trees!" he called back to her.

She nodded and Lucem kept gliding down. Despite their haste, few dragons had agreed to act like birds, dropping their waste from above, and many commonly dipped down for some quick privacy before rising again.

Elory rose on his back, stretched, and blinked. "Lucem, why are we flying down?"

He spotted a clearing in the forest below, and he spiraled down toward it. "Because I wanted to tell you something."

She raised an eyebrow and scampered onto his neck. "You know, I can hear you in the sky too."

"And so can thousands of other dragons. This stuff's private."

He glided into the clearing. Cedars and pines rose around them, and dry needles and pinecones lay strewn across the earth. Cyclamens grew in the shade of chalk boulders. The sky was bright with thousands of streaming dragons in every color. Elory climbed off Lucem's back, and he released his magic, returning to human form too.

He took her hands in his. "Elory."

She stared at him with soft eyes, her hands warm. "Lucem?"

She's beautiful, he thought. *She's kind. She's strong and brave and wonderful. And I don't deserve this.*

"Elory, I want to say that I'm sorry." He gazed into those brown eyes, marveling at their beauty, still holding her hands. "I'm sorry for everything."

"For what?" she whispered.

"For running away. For leaving you in Tofet—leaving everyone. I knew the agony of Tofet for the first eleven years of my life, and I can't imagine suffering another decade in that fire. I'm so sorry, Elory, and I don't know if this is real. I don't know if the dragons above us, if you here, if your hands in mine . . . I don't know if this is real or just a dream. Because this is too good. Too wonderful. More than I deserve."

Her eyes softened, and she kissed his cheek. "It's real. And we all deserve this—a homeland. A nation. A family."

He kissed her lips. "I love you, Elory." He caressed her cheek, marveling at its softness, at how large her eyes were, how her soul shone through them. "I love you more than I thought it possible to love another. I love you always."

They kissed again, arms wrapped around each other, a long, deep kiss as dragons flew above. She felt so frail in his arms, half his size, small and thin from her years of servitude, but stronger than great queens and heroines.

"So that's why you brought me here." Elory bit her lip. "To ravage me."

Lucem couldn't help but grin. "If I tell you the world might end tomorrow, that this might be our last moment, would you allow the ravaging to continue?"

She tapped her cheek and tilted her head. "I might just be the one ravaging you."

He glanced up at the sky. Thousands of dragons were still flying above; it would be a while before the camp passed them by. Lucem took Elory by the hand, and he led her under the cover of a twisting pomegranate tree, its canopy rich and rustling. He had barely made it under the tree before Elory grabbed him, all but leaped onto him, and kissed him again.

They fell onto the grass, lips locked, and Lucem closed his eyes. He reached under her tunic, and her hands slipped under his, and he pulled his cloak over them. Their naked bodies pressed together under the burlap, and his hands explored her body. Her frame was slender, her bones delicate, and he winced when his fingers passed over the many scars on her back.

"Does it hurt?" he whispered.

She shook her head and nuzzled his neck, kissing him. "Keep stroking me."

Their hands explored each other and they closed their eyes. They had never made love before, but it felt natural, as if they had been made for this, had waited years for this. He moved atop her, her short brown hair tickling his nose, and she wrapped her limbs around him. It felt better than flying, better than blowing fire. It was joy—pure, distilled, perfect.

This is real, Lucem thought. *Thank you, stars. Thank you. I don't know what I did to deserve her. But right now, this moment is perfect. Right now is pure joy. Tomorrow the world might burn, but here, now, this instant in time—this is purest joy I never thought I would feel.*

"I love you," he whispered.

She nibbled his bottom lip. "Right back at you, O hero of Requiem."

They lay together under his cloak, holding each other, still naked, watching the dragons fly above beyond the branches.

"I never want to leave this place," Elory said, nestling against him.

He kissed the top of her head. "When we reach Requiem, I'm going to build us a little home. Not too large, not too fancy. Just a comfortable little house. And we'll have a garden, and we'll plant a pomegranate tree like this one." He frowned. I'm not sure if pomegranate trees can grow in the cold north—they say Requiem is very cold. But they have birch trees there, and they say birches are beautiful too. And in the summers, we'll lie like this under our tree, in our garden, outside the house. And we'll just lie all day, being lazy, and naked, and—" Suddenly he felt his cheeks flush. "I mean, I don't want to dream too far ahead. I don't want to pressure you. Maybe you'll want to live with Meliora, not with me, and . . . oh dear, I'm not scaring you away, am I? Because if I am, I—"

"Oh, hush." She kissed his lips. "Of course I want you to build me a home. And of course we'll live together and have a little garden."

"And . . . the being naked a lot part?" he asked hopefully.

She rolled her eyes. "Depends how much housework you do."

Finally, as the last few dragons flew above, they shifted back into dragons and flew again. Heading away from their pain, away from guilt, from fear. Flying to a promised homeland. To a dream of a house, a garden, and more moments of joy.

TIL

For the first time in a month, the sun emerged from behind the clouds, shining down upon the ruins of Requiem, but it brought no warmth, no joy, no beauty to this land.

Til and her brother walked across the scorched earth, their few belongings slung across their backs—fur pelts, an iron pot, some rope, an old canteen, and two scrawny rabbits on a rope. Their tattered cloaks billowed in the wind, and ash filled their hair and smeared their faces.

Around them, the landscape was in no better shape. In the old tales and songs, Requiem was a land of beauty—her forests pristine, her plains blooming with flowers, her skies full of birds and dragons and golden light. All that was gone. The fabled birches were burnt, shattered, fallen, and soot covered the hills and valleys. Only a few scattered ruins rose in the distance—the stubs of columns, the shells of walls, crumbling towers. Even the sky had lost its beauty; red smoke coiled there like clouds, and ash rained.

And every mile, they found them.

The dead.

"Don't look, Bim," Til whispered as they walked by the gallows on the hill. "Just look ahead. Just look and imagine the coast over the horizon."

Yet she knew that he looked. He always looked, sneaking glances. The cages hung from the wooden posts, rusty, creaking as they swung in the wind. The skeletons languished within, jaws still open in screams. Most of the skeletons were bare. One still had some thawing flesh, and the crows bustled, tugging skin off the bones. Wooden signs were nailed onto the gibbets, written in the tongue of Requiem: "Weredragons."

"You did tell me that we'd find others," Bim said.

Til frowned and looked at him. He kicked a stone, not looking at her.

"Don't joke about that." She kicked the stone into a rut before he could kick it again. "All right?"

Still he didn't look at her. He only shrugged. "Someday we'll join them. Just two more skeletons in two more cages."

Til stopped walking. She grabbed Bim's shoulders, spun him toward her, and glared at him. The boy was only eleven years old, shorter than her but not weaker. Perhaps in some ways stronger, for his hope was lost.

Hope drives us onward, Til thought, *but it hurts. Hope hurts so much. The hopeless feel less pain.*

"We will not end like that." Til grabbed his chin and raised his head, forcing him to stare at her. "Do you understand? We will not. Father did not die so we could too. He died to let us escape, to continue this quest. To find a safe place. To find other survivors."

Bim stared at her, his eyes sunken into his gaunt face. His hair was red like hers, but it now seemed white with ash and snow. No emotion showed on that face. No life filled those eyes. No fear, no hope, no anger—blank eyes.

I'm looking at the dead, Til thought. *He's dead already.*

"All right, Til," he said. "All right. We'll go south. We'll find others."

But he doesn't believe, Til knew. *I promised to take him south, to give him a better life, but he doesn't believe there's a reason to live.*

Still holding his shoulders, Til looked around her at the devastation of Requiem. The burnt forests. The ruins of old towns. The smoke and skeletons in cages. Countless more skeletons lay strewn across the valleys and hills, some buried, more beginning to show themselves as the snow melted. Spring was near, but would any flowers still bloom here, or would only death sprout from the earth?

She looked back at Bim.

What could this do to a child—to always run, hide, never sleep for more than an hour, face death with every breath? When Til had been his age, a full decade ago, she had lived among other Vir Requis, a thousand souls. Their life had been hard, but they had tunnels to hide in, they had warmth, they had company and dreams and songs. What kind of life could Bim still have, and would the scars inside him ever heal, even should they find safety from death, anan end to constant running and fighting?

Til sighed. "You're right, Bim. You're right. Sooner or later, we all end up as bones. We all die. Perhaps we'll die tomorrow. Perhaps we'll die in sixty years, and those years go by quickly. Death is final. Death is unforgiving. Death—whether now or in a few dozen more winters—is certain. But so long as we draw breath, as our hearts beat, as our legs can walk and our wings beat, we will fight. We will believe."

"Believe what?" Bim said, voice softer now, cracking.

"That we can still build a new world. That we can find joy. That life is beautiful." She embraced him. "It's hard to see here in this ruin, but there is so much that's beautiful and good in this world. So much that our ancestors fought for and won, so much that we can still find. Do not let your eyes see only ugliness. Let them weave new landscapes of what can be."

Yet as they walked onward through the desolation, Til wondered. Was the southern coast but a dream, a fool's hope, and would she find only ruin there too? If that was so, Til vowed that she would move on. She would travel to the east or west, or gather enough food and fly across the sea, or make her way north to the arctic and the cities of ice they said rose there.

We move onward, until we find a home—a hope of peace or a rusted cage.

She sang softly, the old songs of Requiem, and told her brother stories of the old heroes and heroines. The ash kept raining, the skeletons swayed in their cages, and the ruins spread out before them into the south.

ISHTAFEL

The boy cowered under the bed, panting, trembling, praying so hard to the Eight Gods to save him.

"I never rebelled against you," he whispered again and again. "I was born here—here in Saraph, never in your garden. Please, gods, please, don't let her find me, don't let her hurt me."

Yet of course she found him. She always found him. There were hundreds of rooms in the ziggurat, hundreds of beds to hide under, but she always found him. He heard her shriek in the hall, the cry of a dragon. He heard her footfalls patter through the palace. Seeking him. Sniffing him out. A wolf hunting her prey. The door swung violently on its hinges, slammed into the wall, and tore free from the doorframe. It crashed onto the floor with a shower of splinters, and the boy started. He scurried deeper under the bed, pressing himself against the wall.

Please, gods, please, gods, please, let her go away, please help me. Please. I'm sorry.

Yet the gods had banished his mother, and they would not save him from her.

"Ishtafel, you little piece of filth!" Queen Kalafi screamed. "You miserable little worm, you wretched scum!"

She knelt and reached under the bed, a rabid beast, her fingernails like claws, her golden eyes shining like two suns, her teeth bared. The boy wailed and tried to dodge those hands. He tried to escape from under the bed, to race to safety. But his mother had always been able to grab him, and she grabbed him now. She tugged him out from under the bed, lifted him into the air, and shoved him down onto the mattress.

"I'm sorry!" he cried. "I didn't mean to eat the cake. I'm sorry. I can bake another. I—"

She slapped him. "Shut your maggot hole. I'm sick of your lies. I should toss you into the bronze bull and hear you sing. But I want to hurt you myself. You who ruined my body, who ruined my life, who ruined this family, a weak, pathetic link in a great dynasty. Shameful, shameful! You should never have been born." She shook him wildly, and his head whipped from side to side. "You should never have lived."

She beat him then. She beat him as he screamed, until he could barely breathe, until he felt like every bone in his body was breaking. And even then, as a boy, he knew that a madness lurked inside Queen Kalafi. He knew that she was raging against herself, her life, her banishment, not against him. But he was small. He was weak. He was hers—her precious heir, hers to torment, to blame for all the pain of this exile, of this hot land so far from the locked gates of Edinnu.

And so she beat him. She beat him until he slumped onto the floor, blood dripping from his nostrils and mouth.

"Next time you disobey me, I'm going to send you into Requiem, and I'm going to let the dragons rip out your guts and feed them to you. You won't like that nearly as much as the cake you stole. You will not shame me again."

Kalafi, Queen of Saraph, stepped out of the room, leaving her son bleeding on the floor.

For a long time he lay, struggling to breathe, to wait until the bleeding stopped. But long after the pain faded, his mind stormed, and he trembled, the fear refusing to leave him.

I should escape, he thought. *Escape this palace. Escape this city. Fly across the wilderness.*

He had wings—the feathered wings of a seraph. He could fly away. He could cross the deserts and sea, find a safe place where Mother could not reach him, and—

No.

The boy shuddered.

There was danger out there. Across the sea, they waited—the weredragons. Bloodthirsty men and women from a land called Requiem. People who could turn into dragons, their wings so much larger than his, their claws and teeth even sharper than Mother's.

They would rip him open, Ishtafel knew. They would tear out his entrails and feed them to him. His mother had told him this, and his mother never lied. Whatever punishment she vowed, she carried out.

"I have to stay," the boy whispered to himself, tasting his blood. "I have to stay here. Mother will protect me from the dragons. I have to be *good.*"

He limped toward the window, and he stared north. There, across the city, across deserts and seas, it lay—the land of dragons. The creatures who would hurt him, from whom only his mother could protect him.

"But I will grow," the boy whispered. "I will grow stronger every day, until I can kill them all. Kill everyone who hurts me. Kill the dragons . . . and kill you, Mother."

His eyes snapped open.

He breathed out shakily.

Just a dream. Just a memory.

Once more Ishtafel was an adult, a great king, five hundred years old. His mother was dead—he had killed her himself. The boy was dead too. A man, a king, a god now lay under the sky.

Ishtafel rose from his blankets, his new metal skin creaking. He stretched out his dry wings, looked around him, and beheld a field of bones and blood.

The city of Keleshan, once home to a great garrison of seraphim, lay in ruins before him. The dragons had come here. The dragons had left death. The walls of the city had fallen, and the great egg-shaped fortress on its crest had hatched. The city's inhabitants were gone—the seraphim dead or fled, the slaves escaped.

But new denizens had come here.

The harpies swarmed across the city. Ishtafel stood on the mountainside, watching them. They bustled across the fields like vultures, gnawing on the corpses of seraphim, ripping off skin, dragging ribcages through the dirt, guzzling down innards. Thousands of other harpies scuttled across the walls, roofs, and streets of the city, seeking both the living and dead, ripping into the flesh. Blood stained the harpies' withered faces, and bits of flesh clung to their talons.

Ishtafel spread his burnt wings, the feathers lost to the dragonfire. On the mountaintop, where the stone egg had hatched, the harpies had built their own mountain of corpses. The dead seraphim rotted in the sun, limbs slung together, and the harpies bustled above, digging into the meal. As Ishtafel approached, they hissed, snapped their teeth, and squealed with bloodlust and hunger. The beasts were larger than him, larger even than most dragons, their talons like lances. Yet they knew him as their lord. Shrieking, they retreated, their bloated heads— the heads of crones, covered in warts—bowing.

He flew to the top of the rotting pile. The harpies returned, surrounding him, feeding. And Ishtafel fed with them, tearing into his meal, letting the meat fill him, the ichor stain him. Because it was not his blood. Because it was not his pain. He was strong now, and none would ever hurt him again.

You hurt me, Mother, and now you lie dead and rotting. He licked the ichor off his lips. *You burned me, dragons, and so you too will soon rot. Your mountain will rise into the sky, and we will feed upon it.*

He tore off flesh, swallowed, and grinned. He beat his wings and soared, and his host rose with him, a foul army that covered the sky. A new day rose and their hunt continued. They would not rest until their next meal was the flesh of weredragons.

MELIORA

Dawn rose, and she saw it in the north, gold and blue, a sight so beautiful her eyes dampened.

The edge of Terra, Meliora thought. *The edge of this cruel southern continent.*

Thousands of years ago, her mother's family had fallen from Edinnu, the blessed realm in the firmaments. The Eight Gods had cast out the seraphim, the immortals who had rebelled against their makers, banishing them to exile in Terra—a massive continent beneath the sky, a desolate land of rock and sand and heat. In the unforgiving land, they had forged a new kingdom, had raised a nation called Saraph, and they had spread across the world, crushing all other nations.

Terra, this southern continent, had always seemed like Saraph's true earthly home. The place where the seraphim had cowered, nursed their wounds, built, grown strong. It had always seemed to Meliora that lands across the sea, while now part of her family's domain, were somehow not truly parts of Saraph but mere colonies—foreign, conquered lands.

She did not reach the border of the empire here, for that empire now spread across the sea too. But in her mind, this coast, this edge of a continent—here the heartland ended, and there across the sea, Requiem began.

"Beyond the water it waits," she whispered. "Requiem."

Around Meliora, the other dragons cried out in joy and hope.

"The coast!" rose a voice.

"The edge of Saraph!"

"Requiem is near!"

They called out with joy. Old dragons wept. Young dragons spun in circles, whooping. On the dragons' backs, those who rode in human form played drums and timbrels, and their voices rose in song.

Yet as the camp celebrated, Meliora remained silent. Again Leyleet's words returned to her.

You will never see Requiem, daughter of dragons. With my dying breath I curse you: You will never see Requiem.

Meliora narrowed her eyes. She would ignore those words. There was no use for them now. So long as she could fly, she could fight, she could lead. That was all that mattered now.

"My lady!" The high voice rose from the south. "My lady Meliora!"

Meliora turned in the sky to see a slender black dragon flying over the camp.

Kira.

Meliora's former handmaiden, now her scout, wobbled as she flew over the thousands of other dragons. Smoke spurted from her nostrils in short blasts. The young dragon was exhausted, but Kira still flew fast, streaming over the other dragons, calling out to her.

"Lady Meliora!"

Kira shot across the last mile, then descended to hover by Meliora at the head of the camp. The young black dragon panted, puffing out great clouds of smoke, barely able to speak.

"Ride on my back, Kira." Meliora dipped to fly beneath her. "Rest and speak."

The dark dragon gratefully thumped down onto Meliora's back, releasing her magic, becoming a slender woman with black hair and dark eyes. Kira crawled onto Meliora's neck and lay on her belly, limbs dangling, probably looking to the world like a monkey slung across a branch.

"My lady, he grows closer!" Kira said, still breathing heavily. "Ishtafel and many harpies. They're flying faster than before, and a stench of blood rises from them, and blood stains their mouths and talons. I was barely able to fly back faster than they chased." Kira shuddered. "They'll be upon us within hours."

Meliora clenched her jaw. Harpies flew faster than most dragons. Kira perhaps was young and quick, but most in Requiem were larger, older, slower dragons. Since leaving Tofet, Meliora had relied not on speed but on uninterrupted flight. Ishtafel's harpies still needed rest every day, but Vir Requis could fly in shifts, the dragons bearing those in human forms, taking turns flying and sleeping. Hope had begun to rise in Meliora that, if they only kept flying, they would flee Terra and leave Ishtafel's forces behind.

Yet now, at the coast, would their short days of freedom end?

She turned to look toward that northern coast. It still lay thirty leagues away. Only moments ago it had seemed close to Meliora, but now every mile seemed the length of an empire. As she stared north, she saw another dragon flying toward her, this one red.

"Talana!" she cried.

The red dragon, Meliora's second handmaiden-turned-scout, came to fly before her. She too panted, spurting out smoke, and her eyes were wide with fear.

"My lady Meliora!" Talana said, hovering before her. "Great armies muster on the northern coast! Thousands of seraphim, my lady! And . . ." The dragon shuddered, scales rattling. "The Seven fly with them."

Meliora hissed. "Impossible. The Seven died thousands of years ago."

Talana would not stop shaking. She glanced back toward the coast, then looked back at Meliora. "I saw them!" she whispered. "Great figures of light. Towering. Burning. Hurting my eyes. Seven suns. Like in the stories. They are here."

Meliora's heart sank into her belly. Ice seemed to encase her bones and lungs.

No. It can't be. Not them. They died. They died millennia ago, back in the rebellion against the gods.

"Kira, Talana, go rest." Meliora had to force the words past her stiff lips. "Go to the center of the camp. Regain what strength you can before we reach the coast."

The pair nodded and flew off, leaving Meliora with her fear. She stared ahead toward the coast. It was closer now, close enough to see its cities, great settlements of stone that rose before the water. And there, even in the searing daylight, shone beacons of light, clustered together.

The Seven?

A large blue dragon came flying toward her, eyes hard, staring north.

"Who are these Seven?" Vale rumbled, fire flicking between his teeth.

Meliora gulped. "Thousands of years ago, when we rebelled against the gods in Edinnu, great champions fought among the seraphim. Some called them *Amesha Spenta.* Others called them archangels. Only seven fought with the seraphim; only seven ever lived. Great beings of liquid light, larger, stronger than seraphim; we were as toddlers by their glory. But nobody has seen the archangels since our rebellion. Most seraphim assumed them dead, while others claimed that the Eight Gods had forgiven them and welcomed them back into Edinnu. They became to us things of myth—mere paintings on frescos, sculptures in temples, not beings of this world." She stared ahead, teeth clenched, breath heavy. "Yet I see bright lights ahead. And I saw truth in Talana's eyes."

Vale grunted. "We slew Ziz. We will slay them."

She turned to look at her brother. Vale was staring ahead, eyes hard. Many scars and wounds covered the blue dragon— welts on his underbelly, holes in his wings, and raw patches where his scales had fallen. Yet still he flew with bared teeth, fire in his nostrils, the warrior of Requiem, head of her hosts, ready to spill more blood.

"Yet Ziz was still a beast of this world," Meliora whispered, her fear not allowing her to speak any louder. "Now we face unearthly terrors. Creatures woven not of flesh but of light itself." She turned to look behind her, staring across the thousands of dragons. "And in the south, they gain on us— creatures of darkness. We are trapped between light and shadow."

Vale sneered, jaws opening to release a short burst of fire. "We will shine our own light. We will roar our fire. Our homeland lies beyond the water. We will shatter any who come between us and Requiem."

The dragons of Requiem flew onward, crossing the last miles between harpies and sea, between Ishtafel and the light ahead, trapped between two hosts. When she looked behind her, Meliora could see the rotted host, closer than they had ever been, a cloud of dark specks in the distance—no more than an hour's flight away.

"Take all our forces and put them at the vanguard," Meliora said to her brother as the coast approached. She could now see walls and towers ahead, and she sneered.

Vale stared at her. "Ishtafel gains on us. We might be facing a war on two fronts."

"If we are trapped, we are dead. No, brother. We cannot fight on two fronts. We cannot. All forces ahead! We smash through the enemy and we make to the sea."

There was no hope to evade this enemy, Meliora knew. The entire coast of Terra was settled, and the enemy knew they were flying this way. They had been waiting.

Meliora growled and blasted her pillar of dragonfire skyward.

"Hear, O Requiem!" she cried. "We near the sea! We near our home! Fight the enemies of Requiem, fight for your stars, fight for your lives. To war!"

Around her, the Royal Army stormed forth, thousands of dragons with fire in their mouths. "To war, to war! Requiem rises!"

Ahead, they rose from the coastal walls and towers. A wall of fire and light. Thousands of seraphim ascended, some in chariots of fire, others flying fast upon their own wings. Meliora sought those beams of light, those Seven Suns, but she didn't see them. She prayed that Talana had been wrong, that she had just imagined the great lights.

They're dead. They died thousands of years ago.

"Requiem rises!" the army called.

With dragonfire, with flying arrows and lances, with blood and flames that filled the sky, the hosts of Requiem and Saraph slammed together.

The skies burned. Blood rained on the coast.

Meliora roared as she fought. She blasted her fire, lashed her claws, bit into the flesh of seraphim. She cried out for Requiem, and she cried out wordlessly—for death, for victory, for her stars, for rising from ruin. Yet even under this blinding sky before a blue sea, she was back there—in the darkness outside Tofet, fighting the Rancid Angels, hearing the demon's words.

You will never see Requiem.

Flame of Requiem

The wings of dragons darkened the sky. Their fire rose in great forests and columns—a rebuilt Requiem of flame. The seraphim circled everywhere, and the firehorses plowed through the hosts of dragons, and seraphim thrust their lances from blazing chariots. Corpses rained onto the coastal cities and sank into the sea.

"Cut through them!" Vale cried in the distance. "Requiem, cut through the enemy, to the sea! To our home!"

Meliora blasted out fire, melting a seraph who flew toward her. She soared, spinning, cutting other seraphim down with her whipping tail. She rose higher, higher than any eagle could fly, and stared south, and there she saw them—the harpies approaching, darkening the sky.

She stared back down, and the battle looked to her like a different coast—a sea of fiery waves slamming against a land of scales. The seraphim were a terror, thousands of them crashing into the lines of dragons, yet as Meliora stared down, the hint of hope rose in her.

Requiem was breaking through.

A handful of dragons tore between the seraphim and made it across the water, only to turn back and charge against the seraphim still attacking the hosts. Elsewhere, chariots crashed into the water, raising pillars of smoke and steam, and dragons roared and fought with more vigor. Below in the coastal cities, Vir Requis were racing between the buildings in human forms, finding slaves and opening collars, and soon a thousand new dragons rose—only just freed, already flying to battle, slaying their masters.

We can make it through, Meliora thought. *We can leave this cruel land. We can cut through them, we can cross the sea. I will see Requiem.*

"I will see Requiem!" she whispered, tears in her eyes. "I will see our stars."

And then she saw them—the lights rising.

White, searing lights, burning her eyes.

Seven suns rising.

Her hope burned in their radiance.

"The archangels," she whispered.

Daniel Arenson

LUCEM

He was flying beside Elory, crying out for victory, when the archangels rose from beyond the city.

Lucem cringed.

"Bloody bollocks," he muttered. "One sun's bright enough in Saraph. Damn seven of them just rose."

He beat his wings, hovering in place, and forced himself to stare into the light. He could barely see past the glare of the creatures. When he squinted, he could just make out their forms. They were humanoid and winged, slender and well-formed, but much larger than men or seraphim, larger even than dragons. They seemed woven of pure light, luminescence taken form. They were pure white like the noon sun in summer, but golden eyes blazed in their heads, barely visible past the glare of their bodies. In their right hands, each archangel held a mighty sword that seemed forged of molten metal that did not drip. The blades were as long as the spine of a dragon. In their left hands, they held great whips woven of fire, each lash thrice the length of even the longest dragon tail.

"Take them head on!" rose Vale's voice from above, and the blue dragon charged, roaring. "Burn them down!"

Across the sky, hundreds of dragons—the vanguard of Requiem—stormed to battle.

"For Requiem!" Elory shouted at Lucem's side, charging forward.

"Wait!" Lucem cried and tried to grab her tail, but she flew too quickly, racing across the sky toward the archangels.

This won't end well, damn it.

Lucem grunted, curbing the urge to flee. Every fiber in his body wanted to turn around, to escape this light, to fly to safety, to hide again in his cave.

No. I fled once. I abandoned my people before, and they called me a hero. This time I fight.

598

Lucem roared and flew after his comrades.

Ahead, the archangels plowed through the dragons as easily as trained soldiers cutting through toddlers.

One archangel swung his massive whip. The flaming white thong cracked the air and sliced through a dragon, cleanly cutting the beast in half. For an instant, both halves of the dragon tumbled through the sky; then they shrank into human form, the arms on one half, the legs on the other, falling toward the coast. Another archangel lashed his sword. The blade cleaved a dragon from back to belly. The dragon too lost his magic, falling as a lacerated woman.

The archangels' light intensified as they fought, spinning madly, coiling and blazing, emitting a hum. Lucem had thought them made of sunlight, but now they seemed almost like beings of living lightning, crackling the air, their humming inferno almost melodious, almost like the song of Malok. They stormed through the lines of Requiem, scattering dragons, cutting them down. Vir Requis tumbled through the air before them, falling as men and women.

Lucem stared in horror.

I have to flee. I have to fly away. I have to hide. Oh stars, I have to hide.

"Burn them down!" Vale was shouting in the distance. "Burn them down!"

"Burn them!" Elory roared, flying above, streaming down with a flash of lavender scales.

Hundreds of other dragons joined the charge, blasting their flames. The streams of dragonfire crackled through the air, slammed into the archangels, and showered in fountains.

The godly beings seemed unfazed. They kept lashing their massive whips. One thong tore through three dragons with a single swing, cutting them all down, scattering limbs. Another archangel rose high upon his mighty wings, then swooped, blade plunging, cutting through dragon after dragon. The corpses thumped onto the city below.

Lucem flew closer to one of the archangels. It loomed above him, larger than he had thought, dwarfing him. It turned its terrible golden eyes upon Lucem. Those eyes swirled like

599

smelters of molten metal, gold touched with white, seeing all, digging into him, burning him like shards of hot metal.

The whip crackled the air, casting out bolts of lightning, and swung toward him.

Lucem blasted his fire and dived.

The whip swung over his head with a shriek that nearly shattered Lucem's eardrums. The air boomed like thunder. The blade swung, and Lucem swerved, soared, blasted more flames. His dragonfire crashed into the archangel and showered back onto Lucem, burning his scales.

The whip lashed again, and Lucem ducked his head.

Pain.

White, searing light.

Lucem screamed.

The agony raced across his head, and he lost his magic.

Lucem fell, a man again.

He cut me. He cut open my skull. I'm dying. I'm dying. I'm sorry, Requiem.

The city rushed up below to meet him, walls and towers and courtyards, and everywhere the dragons flew. More corpses fell all around Lucem. Maybe he was dead already. He could barely see the battle above, just flashes of light and spurts of fire and the roar and hum.

"Lucem!" rose a voice.

Violet scales streaked. A dragon plunged down, wreathed in smoke. Claws reached out and grabbed Lucem mere feet above the city roofs.

They soared.

"Lucem, can you hear me?" Elory cried.

Clutched in her claws, he blinked and touched his head. He felt nothing. No pain. No blood. He was unhurt.

"I . . . I'm fine." Lucem pulled himself free from her claws, fell a few feet, then shifted back into a dragon.

At once the pain flared again, and he screamed. Flying before him, Elory gasped.

"Your horns . . ." she whispered.

Lucem reached up with his claws, seeking his horns.

He touched pure fire and agony.

He screamed and nearly lost his magic again.

And he knew—the whip had severed the tips of his horns. Just a few inches. Enough to sear him with pain.

"Your ear, my horns," he muttered. "What will they take next? Better not be anything . . . special. I need my special parts! And I haven't even shown them off to you yet, Elory."

She rolled her eyes. "Focus on killing those archangels, O great hero of Requiem."

Kill them? Lucem looked up at the battle raging in the sky. The dead were still falling. Lucem winced as a disemboweled corpse plunged down only a foot away; he had to swerve aside to dodge it. No. You could not kill these beasts. At least not with fire or claw. As he watched, several dragons slammed into an archangel, lashing claws, biting into the flesh of molten light, only to scream and burn.

"We might as well try to cut fire," he muttered.

Elory winced. "So it's impossible. We cannot win this."

Lucem grunted. Impossible. Impossible! Yet they had also said it was impossible to scale the walls of Tofet. They had said that nobody could escape that land of pain.

Yet Lucem had scaled the wall. He had escaped. He had done the impossible.

He would do it again.

"Not with dragonfire," he said. "Not with claws or fangs. Fly with me, Elory! Follow my lead."

The lavender dragon nodded.

Leaving the dragons and archangels to battle above, Lucem and Elory swooped.

Every heartbeat, Lucem knew, Ishtafel was drawing closer. They would do this quickly. He dived across the coastal city, traveling over the roofs of homes, workshops, manors, courtyards, seeking, eyes narrowed.

There!

A portico of columns rose along the coast, supporting a roof over a limestone veranda that faced the sea. Lucem dived low, skimming the ground. He roared, narrowed his eyes, and slammed himself against a column.

The pain bloomed inside him. He yowled. An instant later, Elory slammed into the column too.

The limestone cracked.

Ignoring the pain, Lucem backed up, then slammed himself into the column again.

The column shattered and fell.

Panting, Lucem grabbed one end of the heavy limestone pillar. "Elory, help!"

She nodded. She understood. She grabbed the second edge of the column.

They flapped their wings mightily, scattering sand across the beach. They grunted, jaws clenched, barely able to rise. Yet slowly, foot by foot, they flew higher, carrying the column in their claws.

They rose higher. The battle swirled around them, a symphony of sound and light. A corpse fell, slammed into Lucem's back, and rolled down toward the city. He grimaced but kept rising with Elory, carrying the column.

An archangel loomed above, its hum deafening, its light blinding. Its whip swung forward, ripping through five dragons. Its blade lashed, tearing through other dragons that charged toward it. Behind this giant of liquid light, its comrades were slaying other dragons, plowing through the lines. Several dragons were trying to escape but wailed in fear, for in the south, clearly visible now, the host of harpies was charging forth, their shrieks and stench carrying in the wind. Some dragons tried to fly north, to cross the sea, only for the whips and blades of light to cut them down. The bodies fell into the water and washed ashore.

"Ready?" Lucem shouted.

Elory nodded. "Together—now!"

The archangel ahead noticed them, turned its golden eyes toward them, and advanced through the sky, wings blasting out beams.

Lucem and Elory roared with effort, pulling the column backward . . . then drove it forth with all their might.

The limestone capital slammed into the archangel's head.

The giant being shrieked.

It was the sound of ten thousand bones shattering, of oceans boiling and steaming away, of the sky itself cracking. The column kept driving forward, plowing through the head, shattering it. The sun seemed to burst. Luminous chunks of skull scattered through the sky. The innards of the head leaked, molten metal, purest white rimmed with gold.

The archangel's colossal corpse fell through the sky, almost graceful, silent, like a great feather.

It hit the city and blasted out, exploding with fury, knocking down buildings for several blocks, casting shockwaves that roiled the dragons in the sky.

Those dragons cried out in victory.

At once, hundreds dipped in the sky, gathering columns that had fallen in the explosion. They rose, three or four dragons carrying each pillar.

The archangels shrieked, fighting back. A whip tore through one column, halving the stone. Another archangel swung its blade, shattering another column. But it was too late to stop the dragons of Requiem. Six archangels remained, and thousands of dragons were now dipping to grab stones—some lifted columns, and some dragons merely grabbed chunks of the buildings.

A pillar drove into another archangel, cleaving through the effulgent torso. The beast screamed and fell and blasted apart. A roaring red dragon swung an entire stone balcony, ripped off a manor below, cleaving through the wing of another archangel. A second dragon cast forth a stone statue of a goddess, driving it into the archangel's head, shattering the skull. All across the sky, the dragons were fighting, using the city as their weapons.

We do not defeat the hosts of Saraph with our dragonfire, Lucem thought wryly, *but with the monuments we built for them as slaves.*

"Requiem rises, Requiem rises!" the dragons chanted as the last archangel fell, shattering against the city, then going dark.

Yet the cheers died quickly.

In the south they flew, only several miles away now—a host of harpies, hiding the sky. Their voices cried out, shrill, thirsty, promising death.

Lucem's heart sank.

"Fly, dragons of Requiem!" cried Meliora, streaming above, and blew her white pillar skyward. "Fly with me—over the sea! Fly after my light."

Leaving the city, leaving their dead, leaving the continent of Terra, the dragons of Requiem flew across the water—a nation escaping their centuries of captivity, a nation heading home. Behind them, the hosts of darkness cried out and laughed and buzzed and hid the sun behind their wings.

ISHTAFEL

He stood on the coast, licked his lips, and watched them flee across the sea into the northern distance.

"Good, Meliora, good," Ishtafel whispered. "Let your hope build. Fly toward your home. Dream of Requiem. Very soon now, just as you think you've grasped your dream in your claws . . . I'll be there to snatch it away." He clenched his fists. "Just as you snatched her away from me."

He cringed in sudden pain, the memories of Reehan filling him. His strong, noble, vicious Reehan—a great light among the immortals. Ishtafel had been fighting for five hundred years, and he had never met a warrior as deadly and proud as his Reehan.

I would have married you, he thought. *I would have made you my queen, the mother of my children, and damn the royal blood of my line.* He shut his eyes. *But they murdered you. The weredragons. They took you from me, my most precious prize.*

Ishtafel looked around him at this city on the northern coast of Terra, the hot continent where Saraph had first risen. The city, once a jewel of the empire, lay in ruins around him. Palaces, silos, temples, manors—all lay shattered. Palm trees, vineyards, gardens—all had burned. The slaves of this city had escaped with the reptilian horde, leaving the corpses of seraphim—corpses the harpies were now consuming. The rancid creatures bustled about the ruins like carrion crows, guzzling the dead. Ishtafel had allowed them this meal, a feast before the slaughter. The ichor would strengthen them before the great war to end all wars, the extermination of Requiem.

"I've never loved another soul, Reehan, and I've never met any stronger woman . . . until my sister was born. Until Meliora."

Reehan had fought with him against the weredragons— and fallen. He had thought her strong. Perhaps he had been wrong. Bloodthirsty, rabid, and beautiful, yes—but ultimately not strong enough.

But Meliora . . . his sweet Meliora . . .

Once Ishtafel had thought his sister not even capable of strength—like expecting a kitten to hunt as a tigress. Meliora had always been like a pet to him, a sweet little princess to laugh with, play with in the gardens, to listen to her silly songs and chatterings about butterflies, cupcakes, and fairy tales. He had at first recoiled from Mother's request that he should marry his sister, had agreed only to preserve the royal blood of their dynasty.

"And then . . . then the kitten roared," he whispered.

When Meliora had first defied him, it had surprised Ishtafel, then enchanted him. Suddenly the naive girl had shown her bite, and he had begun to see her not as a mere womb but as a prize to conquer. And when she had revealed herself to be half weredragon, tainted with the very blood of the beasts who had slain Reehan . . .

"I can think of no sweeter prize than you, sweet sister. I can think of no greater joy than fighting you, breaking you, making you pay for all the sins of your people. The more you defy me, the more of my hosts that you slay, you prove your womb even worthier for my seed."

Finally, here on the coast, his archangels slain around him, Ishtafel saw Meliora for what she truly was—a conqueror, a killer, his sister.

You and I, Meliora—the two greatest killers this new Edinnu has ever known. How I will enjoy breaking you!

Creaks sounded behind him, and Ishtafel turned to see Kelaksha, Queen of the Harpies, approaching. The creature was massive, as big as the mightiest dragon, walking on talons that cracked the cobblestones. The harpy, oldest among them, lowered her withered head toward Ishtafel. That head was as large as a curled-up man, wrinkled and covered in boils and hairs. Cruel eyes, no larger than his, stared from folds of flesh. Serpents coiled on her head instead of hair, and she opened her mouth, revealing a white tongue and dagger-like fangs. The stench of her breath assailed Ishtafel—the stench of the rotten bodies Kelaksha had been consuming.

"The sea is wide, Master," the harpy hissed. Rot dripped from her mouth with every word. "It is too far to cross."

Ishtafel stood facing the massive beast. He was barely taller than her talons. He reached out a metal-encased hand and caressed the withered cheek of the harpy.

"You were the first, were you not?" Ishtafel asked. "The first creature the Eight Gods created, their failed attempt at life?"

Kelaksha stared at him with those small, pale eyes. Upon her head, the hair of serpents hissed and stared too.

"I was the first," she hissed, saliva dripping down to burn holes into the cobblestones of the city.

"How must it feel," Ishtafel said, "to be considered a shame, a failure, a deformity? To spend thousands of years imprisoned because you are ugly?" He stroked her bristly cheek. "To be without pride, without a home?"

The harpy bristled. Her dark wings spread out, dripping rot from their oily feathers. Her talons dug deep into the earth. Her hair of serpents shrieked.

"The gods are cruel. But you give us a home, Master. You see our strength."

Ishtafel had no more eyebrows within his face of metal, but he raised what remained of the burnt, swollen flesh above his eyes. "Do I, my dear? These ruins? This continent? No, my sweetness, for you and your kind are far too foul and rancid to live in Terra, the great continent of the south. Requiem will be your home. Across the sea, in the cold north, you will reign above the corpses of the weredragons. But only, Queen of Harpies, if you dare fly across the sea. If you prove yourself weak . . ." He hefted his lance. "I will make you miss your prison in Edinnu, and I will make you think the Eight Gods merciful."

The harpy hissed and beat her wings. Her talons shattered stones, and she rose toward the sun, crying out in fury. Across the coastal ruins, the other harpies rose like flies disturbed from a carcass, darkening the sky, raining their rot. Ishtafel rose with them, burnt wings churning smoke.

"To the sea!" he cried. "To the greatest flight of our lives, a flight the poets will sing of! To war! To victory! To Requiem!"

The sea was wide. Even flying with all their speed, it would take three days and nights to cross. There would be no food, no water, no rest along the way, and Ishtafel knew that many of his harpies—the weak ones to be culled—would fall along the way, and the sea would bury their shame.

But for those who survived awaited their greatest trophy.

"The extermination of a race," Ishtafel whispered as he flew. "The genocide of Requiem in their very homeland, and their flesh to feed our bellies.

They flew across the ruins and beach, and the sea spread below them. The harpies and their snakes screeched and clawed the air, and their wings beat in a storm. Ishtafel flew at their lead, a god of metal, wings spread wide.

Soon, Meliora. He smiled thinly. *Soon I will feed your limbs to the harpies . . . and the rest of you will be mine.*

The sea spread to the horizon, and beyond it . . . the land of weredragons.

JAREN

The nation of Requiem flew over the sea, and Jaren flew at their lead, Meliora sleeping on his back.

For days now, Meliora had flown at the head of the camp, daring not sleep for more than brief moments. For days, she had blown her pillar of white fire, leading her people in their exodus.

"Sleep now, my daughter," Jaren whispered, looking over his shoulder at her. "I will lead them onward as you rest."

Behind them spread their ancient nation—the Vir Requis flying between sky and water, spreading out for miles. Jaren had heard many tales of Old Requiem, had even read the old scrolls which Queen Kalafi had kept in her chambers. He knew the story of Requiem from its founder, King Aeternum, to its captivity in Saraph. Never in its history had so many dragons flown together, had this entire, ancient race risen in a single great flight.

My ancestor, King Aeternum, founded a small tribe of only several souls . . . and now we are as plentiful as grains of sand upon the beach, flying to our ancient homeland that Aeternum gave us.

It was a day of great history, of uprising, of danger, yet Meliora seemed suddenly like a child, almost peaceful as she slept on his back. Her body was cut and bruised, thinner than it had ever been. Her cheek rested on her hands, and her hair was growing back, still barely long enough to cover her ears, soft and gold. Even as she slept, her halo crackled, a low flame that warmed Jaren's scales. She wore humble burlap, and a string of beads adorned her neck, made from the clay and bitumen of Tofet. Some in Requiem had offered her fine gowns of muslin and silk, taken from the sacked city of Keleshan, but Meliora had refused the garb.

"I wore kalasiri gowns as a princess of Saraph," she had told her people. "Today let me wear rough burlap and clay beads, for I am a freed slave, a daughter of Requiem, and these garments have more nobility than any fine imperial raiment."

Meliora was descended of two noble houses—the Thirteenth Dynasty of Saraph and House Aeternum of Requiem—and she bore their nobility in her countenance, her conduct, and her courage.

"But now rest, Meliora," Jaren whispered. "Now sleep. For the road ahead is still long."

He knew that many in the camp wanted to crown Meliora, to name her Queen of Requiem, yet she had refused. Not until they arrived in Requiem, until they stood in the light of King's Column, would they choose another to rule them.

Let her just be my daughter until then, Jaren thought.

He returned his eyes forward, staring across the water. The sea now spread to all horizons, and Terra was no longer visible in the south. No Vir Requis had ever left that southern continent, not in five hundred years, but according to their stories, Requiem lay ahead. Still distant. Still several days of flight away—the weak riding on the strong. But awaiting them. Their ancient homeland.

"Requiem," Jaren whispered.

He wondered what they would find there. Hosts of seraphim and beasts they could not imagine? Piles of rubble? Perhaps even other Vir Requis, some who had survived the slaughter and captivity five centuries ago?

Sometimes Jaren wondered if Requiem existed at all. In his darkest moments, he began to worry that Requiem was but a myth, a legend told in Tofet to give workers hope. That they would find nothing here at all, only water and death.

He closed his eyes, summoning that memory. The night he had buried Elory's ear, the night he had nearly lost hope, lost his life. The night his soul had risen to the celestial halls, seen the fabled Queen Gloriae, the day she had told him to still fly, still fight for Requiem.

"Was that only a dream?" Jaren whispered. "Only the hallucination of a broken mind?"

The sun was setting, and as darkness fell across the sea and sky, so did shadows seem to engulf Jaren's soul. He had seen so many die—countless thousands perish in Tofet and the fields of

Saraph. He had lost his wife to Ishtafel's lance. Would now the last Vir Requis perish, chasing a mere dream, a land that was but a myth? And even should they reach land again, would they find only more enemies, trapped between a new host and the harpies that still gave chase?

"Why do you let so many perish?" Jaren whispered, staring up into the indigo sky. "If you're truly up there, spirits of Requiem, why do you let us die? Why do you let so many suffer? Why did you let the yokes and whips break our backs for five hundred years?"

No voices answered him. No celestial columns shone above. No ancient kings and queens appeared before him in the shadows. Perhaps they did not exist; perhaps they had always been only hallucinations, dreams, hopes. Foolishness.

The sun dipped below the sea, casting red light like blood, and Jaren's chest tightened, and his head spun to remember so many dying in his arms.

He raised his eyes, seeking to look away from the water below. The last sunlight faded, and there above he saw them.

At first they were dim. At first Jaren doubted his eyes, thought that surely his eyes were playing tricks on him. He kept flying, kept staring, and tears filled his eyes.

Voices rose across the camp, one by one.

"Bless Requiem!"

"Requiem, our wings find your sky!"

Old, grizzled warriors wept. Children prayed. Dragons danced in the sky, calling out in joy, and the tears of Requiem fell like rain. Those Vir Requis who rode in human forms, sleeping or nursing their wounds, rose as dragons too, their voices rising in song.

Jaren's tears fell.

"I'm sorry," he whispered. "I'm sorry to have ever doubted you, Requiem."

Above him it shone, brilliant in the night, and for the first time in five centuries, the children of Requiem gazed upon its light—the Draco constellation.

The stars were arranged as a great celestial dragon, rising in the northern sky, skimming the sea. Brightest among them shone the eye of the dragon, Issari's Star, a beacon said to be formed of Issari's soul itself.

Roused by the song of dragons, Meliora rose upon Jaren's back and shifted. She flew beside Jaren, her eyes damp, staring at the distant lights.

"Our stars," she whispered. "Our fabled stars. Their light guides us to Requiem. The celestial dragon calls us home."

Meliora rose higher in the sky, spinning as she soared, wings spread wide, a great silvery dragon the color of starlight. Jaren rose with her, his green scales bright in the night, the color of Requiem's forests that he now knew awaited them. With them rose Vale, dark blue, and Lucem, red as fire, and Elory, deep purple in the night. They flew together, leading the others onward—away from the blinding heat and sunlight of captivity, toward the gentle light of stars.

"Home," Jaren whispered. "Requiem is real."

VALE

The Draco constellation rose throughout the night, ascending toward the sky's zenith, shining bright. As the other dragons sang and prayed, Vale gazed upon those stars, and more than pride or joy, he felt grief.

In the night, the dragons of Requiem sang and danced in the sky. The sea spread below, the starlit sky above. The dragons raised no fire, letting the light of their constellation shine bright, guiding them home. They sang together in a one voice, the ancient prayers of their people, the prayers that had sustained them through centuries of toil. Yet Vale did not join them, could not feel that holiness.

"You should have been here with us, Tash," he whispered as he glided on the wind. "You should be seeing these stars with me."

He lowered his head, looking away from the light, missing her, aching for her.

She appeared in his memories, so real, as if he could reach out and touch her. Her long brown hair which he loved to stroke. Her mocking brown eyes that could see into his soul. Her coquettish smiles, her small pale hands. Her body pressed against his, clad in her silks, a jewel shining in her navel. And he thought of her kindness—the woman who had risked her life to save Meliora, who had found the Chest of Plenty, and who had fought just as hard to heal Vale's heart, to soothe the pain she had seen within him.

Yet how can I remain strong with you? Vale thought. *You healed the hurt inside me, but now you're gone, and now the pain seems too great to bear. I miss you so much, Tash. I love you so much.*

He imagined her here with him, gliding at his side, a slender golden dragon. She would grin at him, eyes alight, and they would gaze at those stars together, knowing that soon they would be home, that soon their wars would end, that soon they would be wed, grow old together, pray to their stars every night.

But you'll never grow old, Tash. You'll always stay young in my memories. I promise that I will never forget you, that I will think of you whenever I look at our stars.

Chinking scales sounded beside him, and Vale turned to see a white dragon flying at his side, her horns and scales shimmering with hints of gold and silver. The dragon smiled at him, her golden eyes sad, their pupils shaped as sunbursts.

"You don't sing with us." Meliora's eyes were sad, and she glided closer, nuzzling him with her snout. "Can I fly with you, brother?"

Vale looked at the white dragon, his older sister—the sister he had just met this year. He spoke softly.

"Throughout my life, toiling in the inferno of Tofet, I would sometimes gaze south toward the distant lights of Shayeen. As the chains chafed my ankles, as the whips tore into my back, as the thousands cried out around me, I would try to imagine the palace rising in Shayeen, the City of Kings. I would try to imagine my sister there—Meliora of the Thirteenth Dynasty, Great of Graces, Princess of Saraph."

Meliora lowered her head, and now tears streamed down her scaly cheeks. "I'm sorry, Vale. During those years, I would live in the palace, and I would stand on the balcony. And I would gaze north—north to Tofet. From my balcony, I couldn't see much that lay across the river, only a haze. I imagined that the slaves lived like my handmaidens. In comfort. Always with food, with drink, with shelter, with song. When I first entered Tofet and saw the bronze bull, saw your broken bodies, the despair in your eyes . . ." She shuddered. "I never forgot how much grief I felt then. How much guilt. To know that I had grown in comfort over the blood, sweat, and tears of the Vir Requis. I didn't know then that I'm one of you, but I knew that my life had been a lie. I knew that I was no beloved princess, but that I was a tyrant."

Vale nodded. "You didn't know. You couldn't have known. Father always told us that—told Elory and me. 'Meliora does not know who her father is,' Jaren would say. 'Nor do any others in Shayeen or Tofet. But she's one of us. A Vir Requis. A daughter. A sister. A great light that we pray will return to us someday.' Jaren repeated these words to us again and again in our little hut."

Gliding at his side between sea and stars, Meliora gazed at him through the veil of tears. "And did you believe him?"

He smiled grimly. "For many years, I wondered if those stories were true, if indeed you're my sister, or whether Father simply told a story to comfort me and Elory. I often prayed to whatever gods might listen to see you, Meliora, if only a glimpse from the distance. If only another seraph in the sky above Tofet. I thought that if I could gaze into your eyes, I'd know the truth."

Meliora nuzzled him again. "I'm real. And I fly here with you. And I love you, Vale, my sweet little brother."

He bristled. "Sweet little brother?" He smiled wryly. "I don't know if anyone would call me sweet."

The thought popped into his mind, unbidden: *Tash would.*

It seemed like Meliora could read his thoughts. She smiled at him sadly, raised her eyes, and gazed at the stars.

"She looks down upon us, Vale," she whispered. "The woman we love, the woman we miss, the woman we will never forget. Tash is up there, and we'll see her again, and we'll sing of her in the halls of Requiem." She paused. "No, wait. Those are the wrong words. Tash is not just some heroine for our people, a figure for legends." She looked at him. "She was a woman you loved, who you lost, and I have no words of proper comfort, and I cannot ease that pain. All I can say, Vale, is that I'm sorry for your loss, and that I love you dearly, and that I'm always here for you. Some shadows do not pass. Some hurts do not heal. All we can do is kindle new lights—together."

He gazed at those stars above. It seemed to him that Issari's Star, the eye of the dragon, gazed down upon him, that the silvery light was sad yet loving.

You too gaze down upon us, Issari, you who returned me to life, you who still blesses us.

"The stars never forgot us," Vale said softly. "I realize that now. They were with us always, through our long captivity, and the souls that dwell there wept for our pain. Those stars are real, and so are the spirits who dwell there. We will make them proud, Meliora. You and I. We will lead our people on, and we will rebuild our home, and we will raise new temples for those stars, and—"

"Enough!" She nudged him. "Forget talk of great nations and legends. What matters now is you. And me. Brother and sister. All right, little brother? Don't make me slap you."

He couldn't help it. He grinned, and his pain seemed to wash away with that grin, and he knew: Things would be all right. There was still joy and family and love in the world.

"If you slap me, I'm going to annoy you to death. We little brothers are good at that, you know."

She growled. "We have many years of bickering to catch up on, don't we?"

Vale laughed—one of the very few times in his life he had laughed, all of them this year. "We do and we will."

They flew onward, brother and sister, leading a nation of dragons. The sea spread below and the stars guided their way until morning.

TIL

Across ruin, desolation, and a wilderness of death they had traveled, sometimes flying, sometimes crawling, passing through fire and ice to finally come to this place. And there, past a veil of haze in the south, they saw it.

Til's tears fell like the rain.

"The southern coast," she whispered.

The rain fell before her in warm curtains, and mist floated across the forested hills and valleys. The sun glowed behind the veil of clouds. There was no snow here in the south, and the air was rich, warm, scented of trees and soil and the distant sea. A healthy smell. The smell of life. A distant city rose by the water, still leagues away, a day's walk. Only a few of its towers rose through the mist, overlooking the sea.

"We made it." She hugged her brother. "We reached the coast. We'll find safety here."

Bim stared south with her, the rain streaming down his hair and face, washing away the dirt of their journey. His makeshift patches of armor, strapped across his furs, gleamed wet, and he rested his palm on the pommel of his sword. For the first time in months, perhaps in years, hints of hope showed on his face. It was subtle; anyone else would have missed it. A slight widening of the eyes. A slight upward twist to the lips, soon gone. A slight flush to the cheeks. But Til was his sister, and she could read him like a priest reading the old scrolls.

Finally I see life in him. Her tears mingled with the raindrops. *His soul is not crushed. He's not a roaming dead. He still dreams. He still can feel hope. He still can be a boy.*

She squeezed him between her arms and mussed his hair. "You see that city in the distance? That's Lynport. An ancient, legendary city of heroes, Requiem's southern jewel. What say we go explore?"

He didn't move from the grassy hill they stood on, just kept staring south through the rain. "There'll be seraphim." His voice was soft, cracking. "There are always seraphim."

She nodded. "Maybe. Maybe a few. But maybe some other survivors too. Other Vir Requis."

Bim lowered his head. "Or maybe just more dead."

Til turned him toward her and stared into his eyes. "Listen to me, Bim. Yes, we might find more seraphim here, and we might find more dead. And maybe we won't find any other survivors, and maybe the city will be swarming with enemies. And if that happens, we'll move on. We'll travel along the coast, moving westward, until we find a place. A cave maybe, not just a temporary hideout, but a real home. A place where we can fish, forage for fruit and berries, and live here in the warm south. Far from the Overlord in the north. Far from danger. We can still find a life here. The rebellion might be over, but our lives are not."

Bim nodded. "I never wanted the rebellion," he whispered. "All I ever wanted was . . . to do what you said. Find a cave we didn't have to run from the next day. Find a life away from danger. Just a place to . . . to live. Day by day. Breath by breath. Without a war, without a quest, without even a hope. Maybe that sounds sad to you, having no hope. To me it means just living in a quiet place. In peace. You only feel hope when you're afraid. Hope is our cure to pain. I want our pain to end. And not in a cage or grave. Just in a quiet place where it's warm."

It was the most he had said in weeks, perhaps in years. Til held her little brother close, nearly crushing him against her, and kissed the top of his head.

"We'll find that quiet place," she said.

They kept walking through the wilderness as the rain fell. Unlike the north, a land of maples and oaks and birches, here in the south grew many twisting pines. On a grassy hill they found wild apple trees, and they filled their bellies. When several mourning doves took flight above, Til shifted into a dragon, rose for just an instant, and grabbed the birds. She roasted them with her dragonfire, and she and Bim enjoyed the meal in human form. They walked onward.

As they crossed the last few miles toward the sea, they encountered many remnants of old Requiem, the kingdom that had sprawled here five hundred years ago. An aqueduct snaked across the hills, taller than a dragon but only a few hundred feet long, ending with a pile of bricks. On a hilltop rested the capitals of columns, carved as dragons, but the pillars themselves were missing, perhaps stolen years ago. A massive statue lay fallen in the grass; once it must have stood as large as a palace. It was carved as an ancient, bearded king clad in a flowing robe—King Aeternum, founder of Requiem.

As they talked here, Til tried to imagine what life had been like before the seraphim. The splendor of Requiem would have covered these hills, but the true glory would be above— thousands of dragons in the sky, for the sky had always been the true domain of Requiem, even more than her forests and mountains and rivers. That sky was as lost as the land below. Even as she walked here, Til saw the distant light of halos— seraphim flying.

She and Bim crouched at once, hiding in the tall grass.

"Seraphim are here," he whispered.

"I count only five." She smiled. "Not too bad. And look, they're already flying away. And I see none over that city."

They both peeked from the grass, staring south. The distant ruins were closer now. Til had never seen ruins in such good condition before. From here, a few miles away, she could see buildings—real buildings, several stories high, and towers of stone that soared toward the sky. She was used to seeing the cities of seraphim, and she knew their slender, graceful architecture. But here ahead were the ancient structures of Vir Requis, carved of marble and many columns.

"A city of Requiem still stands," she whispered. "Lynport did not fall to the seraphim."

Hope kindled inside her. Could it be that . . . that Vir Requis still lived here? Many of them? That they had survived, defended this city through the ages, protected a small Requiem in the south?

The sun was setting by the time they reached the city gates, and no more seraphim had risen. Long shadows spread across the land, and crimson stained the sky. In the distance, still a league away, the sea whispered.

The city rose before the siblings. *No, not 'rose,'* Til thought. Lynport seemed to *loom.* The city gates were like the mouth of a stone beast large enough to swallow dragons. The portcullis had long ago rusted away, leaving only shards of metal like teeth. The walls were pockmarked and stained with old fire. Beyond them rose steeples, towers, and many roofs, but while from the distance they had seemed fair and gleaming in the rain, in the sunset Til now saw that they were decrepit, crumbling, full of crows. No doors filled the gatehouse, but Til could see only shadows beyond. Wind moaned, expelled from the city like icy breath, ruffling her hair.

"The city is alive," Bim said, and once more that dead look returned to his eyes. "The city is afraid." He turned toward her, eyes blank, staring at Til yet through her. "We must leave this place."

Til couldn't suppress a shudder. The wind moaned again, racing through the city and emerging from the gates, almost forming words.

Shoo . . . shoo . . .

"Maybe you're right," Til whispered.

She turned away from the gatehouse, facing north again, and cringed.

The sun vanished behind the horizon, but new light flared in the distance. Chariots of fire. A hundred or more, moving in from the north, patrolling the wilderness. Seeking her.

"On second thought . . . the city isn't looking that bad now." She cringed. "In fact, creepy place full of shadows to hide in? That sounds pretty good."

She grabbed Bim's hand and began pulling him toward the gateway.

"Til . . . are you sure?"

"No." She walked toward the shadowy gateway. "But I know that outside is fire, outside is light, outside is the wrath of the seraphim. We spent many days running, seeking the smallest of burrows—under logs or boulders or bushes. Here is a full city of burrows." She loosened her grip on him, realizing that she must have been hurting his palm. "And we might still find others, Bim. Let's go exploring. We are creatures of starlight and dragonfire. We need not fear the darkness."

The chariots of fire crackled behind them, moving closer. Clutching their swords, the siblings stepped through the old gateway, entering the city of shadows.

A dark cobbled road stretched ahead, lined with brick buildings. In the distance, the black towers rose toward the clouds. The rain stopped and mist floated through the city like ghosts. The moon was but a haze in the veiled sky, its faded light the only illumination. Til could barely see more than the outlines of the buildings.

"Should we turn into dragons?" Bim whispered. "We can light our fire."

Til stared ahead into the shadows. She couldn't see more than a block ahead. It seemed to her that the mist was a living creature, scurrying down alleyways, peering from behind every building. The wind moaned, so lifelike that for an instant Til was sure a figure was whispering ahead. Something thumped in the distance, just a soft sound, barely audible, soon gone.

"No." She shook her head. "We don't know who lives here. We move quietly, hidden in shadows. We find a place to sleep. Just until the daylight."

They stepped deeper into the city, moving between old brick buildings that rose several stories tall. Taller structures rose behind them, dark steeples cutting across the dark sky. It was hard to see in the shadows, but the buildings seemed dilapidated, no curtains or shutters in their windows, no doors in their frames. All wood and fabric had rotted away, leaving only craggy stone. No lanterns or hearths shone. If anyone lived here, they lived in darkness. When Til trailed her hand against a brick wall, it came back covered in soot.

"Fire burned here long ago," she whispered. "Dragonfire."

"Let's find a place to hide," Bim said. "The seraphim are coming."

The siblings glanced behind them. The city walls loomed there, blocking the view of the wilderness. The gates revealed nothing but darkness beyond. Til couldn't even hear the chariots of fire anymore.

"They're not coming," she whispered, daring not speak any louder. "They don't enter this city. They never enter. That's why it's still standing. They never destroyed Lynport."

She looked ahead again, staring down the shadowy road toward the dark skyline. All her life, Til knew ruins to be crumbling piles of rubble—perhaps a few standing columns, perhaps a section of aqueduct, maybe a single tower or two, but no more. In the north, that was all that remained of Requiem. While Lynport was certainly crumbling and old, the city still stood. Rotted, yes. Lifeless, perhaps. But still standing.

Why did the Overlord never destroy this place as he did all our other cities? she wondered.

"I don't like this place." Bim clutched her arm. "We need to leave. Now."

Til shook her head. "There are seraphim outside. This city is safe. We—"

The wind shrieked, ruffling their cloaks and hair, drowning Til's words. Mist swirled and shadows danced in alleyways and dark windows. Clattering sounded in the distance, echoed, and faded.

"The city screamed," Bim whispered.

"Just the wind." Til drew her sword. "Let's make our way toward the coast. I'll feel better by the sea."

They continued walking, leaving the gateway behind. The boulevard was wide and must have once been fine. Lantern poles still rose alongside, their lights long darkened. Alleyways branched off into shadows. The houses grew larger as they walked, and soon Til saw a towering structure, lined with columns and topped with steeples.

"A temple," she whispered. "A temple to the Draco constellation. This is a holy place to Requiem."

"Nobody but ghosts lives here now." Bim shuddered. "Let's keep walking. I don't want to stop until we reach the sea."

Til paused, staring at the temple. The columns soared before her, embracing shadows. What wonders lay within? Would Til find ancient jewels, books of Requiem lore? Perhaps only the skeletons of ancient priests? She longed to enter the temple, to become a dragon in its hall and light her fire, to explore those secret chambers. After all these years of traveling through ruins—to find an actual temple, a relic of the golden age!

She had taken a step toward the portico when shadows stirred between the columns.

Til froze.

She narrowed her eyes. Had she truly . . . ?

There! She saw it again. A pale figure, moving between the columns, peering with black eyes—then vanishing.

"Mist," she whispered. "Just mist."

Feet pattered behind her.

She spun around. "Bim?"

A scream, high pitched like steam, rose across the city of Lynport.

Til grimaced. She covered her ears, still holding her sword with one hand. The sound rose louder, louder, twisting, rising like a living thing, and Til doubled over and screamed. The sound seemed to *crack*, then vanish, perhaps just rising too high for her to hear.

She looked at Bim. He stared back, eyes wide, lips pale.

"To the sea," Til whispered.

They continued walking, faster now, almost jogging. And Til saw them. She saw them everywhere. Gray mist in windows and alleyways. White eyes staring and vanishing. Padding feet. Cackling. The laughter of children, a thousand demonic girls, a young boy singing an old nursery song, then screaming, vanishing into shadows.

Til and Bim ran.

From the buildings around them, they rose.

Shadows. Mist. Screams. Twisting faces. Pain.

Til cried out in agony.

Pain. They were pain.

"Stop!" she cried, but they kept rising, flowing from alleyways, from gutters, descending from the clouds. They had no forms but they had faces, and those faces screamed. They had no bodies but they felt pain. They danced around her, hand in hand. They laughed. They wept. They twisted on the ground.

"Bloodstained reptiles!" they screeched, voices demonic, impossibly high-pitched, the sounds of shattered glass coalesced into words. "Bloodstained reptiles, bloodstained reptiles! Run, run, run!"

Til screamed and swung her sword, trying to hold them back. She cut through mist, but the faces floated all around. They formed in the reflections on glass windows. They twisted in the clouds above. They leered from shadows. The ruins came alive around her, writhing, the buildings leaning in. Arms grew from the buildings. Arms reached out. Eyes opened on the ground.

"Bloodstained, bloodstained! Weredragons! Run, run, run!"

They ran. The creatures laughed. They tugged at Til and Bim's cloaks, they danced between their feet, they danced around, a great ring of them in the sky, surrounding a great face, and the buildings laughed and wept, and the sky wept, and the arms reached toward them, dripping black blood, and the arms wept. They were happy. They were sick. They were in agony. They raged. They lusted. They begged for death.

"What are they?" Bim cried.

Pain. Pain. Just pain.

"Just run!"

Her head spun. Her pain throbbed inside her, living demons inside, tearing her up. Souls. They were souls.

Just run.

Just run.

"Run, run, run!" the creatures cried.

She knew their name. She wept. She fell. She rose and ran again. She knew them. She knew them.

"Dybbuks," she said.

Bim screamed and doubled over, creatures tugging at him, pulling his skin, pulling his eyes.

"Stand back, dybbuks!" Til shouted, sword lashing.

The ring of them spun around her, and the city creaked, bricks rearranging themselves, steeples leaning forward, eyes blazing within them.

She had heard of these creatures—a disease of Edinnu, taken down into the world, infecting all they touched, ripping feelings from dead souls they consumed. Hungry demons, devouring the pain, the fear, the rage of those they slew. They had grown fat on the feelings in this city, had consumed the pain of Requiem, of countless slain Vir Requis. And still they hungered, an infection that ached to spread.

"Til!" her brother screamed. "Til, they're in me. It hurts. It hurts. Bloodstained. Bloodstained. Run, run, run!"

His voice rose higher, twisting, and his eyes bugged out, and he clawed at his face.

Til shifted into a dragon.

She beat her wings and blasted out fire in a ring.

The shadows parted, and the dybbuks laughed.

"Bow down! Bow down!" they chanted. "Bloodstained, bloodstained, bow, bow, bow!"

"Bow!" Bim cried below, twisting on the ground, writhing, smoking, screaming. "Bow down, bow bow!"

They laughed. They danced. Bim rose and danced. They danced around her. They danced inside her. They spun. The arms reached out to her, the buildings laughing, breaking, their eyes staring, and their arms wept.

I don't know.

Til screamed, wept.

I don't know what you mean.

She roared out her dragonfire. It was all she knew. Roar. Roar. Fire. Fire. Run, run, run.

The dance. They danced. They spun all around her, and she danced with them, and they were inside her, and they lied. They lied to her. They felt things. They were feelings. They were things. They were buildings with arms.

"Lie, lie!" she cried. "Not mine. Not mine! Not feeling. Not my feelings. Not my pain."

"Your pain! Pain of Requiem. Pain of dragons."

She fell to her knees, human again, dead again, a thousand dead again. A city dead again. A nation falling. Inside her. Inside her. She felt them, the disease spreading, the chunks torn off their deaths gushing through her, new blood inside her, pumping through her veins. Pumping through her belly.

Lie, lie, they lie! They lie!

"Lie!" they cried. "Run, run, run!"

She screamed. She clawed at her face. She reached into her mouth. She reached inside her.

Take them out. Take them out!

Bim smiled. He stared at her. White eyes. Toothless smile.
He reached his hand toward her. It bled. It healed. It was
nothing but bones. It bled. It healed. His skin vanished. His skin
appeared. He was in daylight. He was in darkness. He was a
living one. He was a dead one. He danced. He sang. He died and
screamed. He smiled and reached out to her.

"Tell a lie," he whispered and took her hand.

She lied. She danced. They all danced. They were dragons,
dead, broken. They were shadows. They were buildings with
arms. They were the sea.

The sea.

She saw the waves. Waves with faces. Screaming waves of
blood.

She stared into the water.

The screams rose around her, shattered . . . fading. Fading.
Floating. Fading.

She stared at the waves. The sea was breathing. The waves
were breath. There were bodies beneath them. The dead
breathed. The world breathed. Requiem breathed.

She stared.

"Tears," she whispered. "The sea is made of tears. The sea
is breathing. The waves are breath."

She remembered. She had been traveling to those waves,
to—

"Father."

The dragon died upon the lance. She screamed. "Fath—"
The sea breathed. The waves were its breath.

For so long, she had traveled, hiding, trying to reach that
sea. And now she floated here. Floated above the buildings,
dancing with the dybbuks. A dance of dybbuks. A dance in the
sky. But the waves did not dance. She—

"No!" the girl screamed. And her father lost his magic,
returning to a human, a human impaled, staring at her, coated in
blood. And she ran. She ran through the forests. She ran in the
wilderness. She ran cross ruins. Run, run, run.

Run, run, run. Run. Hide! Hide. Kill. Kill, kill, kill.

She shivered in tunnels among the bones of dead dragons,
and she prayed, and—

The sea breathed.

She stared.

The waves were its breath.

She floated among the feelings, and her brother danced with her, and he laughed, and he was alive, and finally he felt. Finally he felt so much.

She turned in the air, and she stared across the walls to the northern darkness, and she saw the fire. The fire of ten thousand chariots, filling the sky. Fearing this place. They dared not enter. Not this city. Not this darkness. Not these feelings. Not this place where seraphim feared to tread. But she had entered. She could hear the sea, calling to her. It had always called her. It still breathed.

She flew as a dragon.

"I'm sorry." She wept. "I'm sorry, Father. I'm sorry. I couldn't save you. I'm sorry. I couldn't. I had to run. I had to run, run, run."

Run, run, run.

Fly.

She tried to beat her wings, but she died.

She tried to blow her fire, but the seraphim burned her, shoved their lances inside her.

She tried to grab her brother, but she was born in pain, screaming. Her father beat her. She tried to fly, but she was afraid, trapped in an alleyway, a man holding her down. She died. She died a hundred thousand times. She died in the fire of seraphim, screaming, lingered on, fled, died at the walls, drowned in the sky.

The disease spread into her. The dybbuks laughed, carrying with them the devoured pain of Requiem, spewing it into her, grabbing her pain.

Bim screamed, laughed, danced with them. He was but a shadow. Only a face in the darkness, that was all. Only mist. And above him shone the stars.

"The stars of Requiem," Til whispered. "Issari's Eye. Staring. There's no pain there. No pain in starlight."

The sea breathed.

There was no pain in the sea.

There is pain in life. Life is pain. We are born in pain. We are drenched in pain from birth. We die in pain. We are but glimmers of starlight between pain and pain. There is no pain in starlight. There is no pain in the sea.

Til forced herself to stare at the star, to let it consume her. To rise above the buildings with arms. To rise above the clouds. To be—

Run, run, run!

Bow, bow, bow!

—to be nothing but starlight. Nothing but sea. Nothing but breath. Breath. Waves. The waves were its breath.

She flew.

She reached out and grabbed the shadow. She held her brother in her claws.

"Lies, lies, lies."

She flew through them, holding him.

They clawed inside her. They tore at her skin from the inside. They died a thousand times. They made her die a thousand times. She died a thousand times over every street, but still she flew. She stared up at the stars. She stared at the sea. She refused to fear them. She would not fear. There was no fear in starlight. There was no pain in the sea. The waves were its breath.

She flew over the city, holding Bim in her claws, and there on the edge of the water, she saw it. A towering fortress on a hill. A fortress with white arms that reached out in the black night. A fortress with eyes. A fortress where Vir Requis had been dying for thousands of years. A fortress that died. That made her die. That felt. Its arms wept.

Til roared out her fire.

Her flames slammed into the building, showering up, spraying onto dybbuks that still danced around her. The massive creature laughed, rising higher, built of bricks and mist and flesh, eyes blazing like furnaces.

Now you will die, Til of Requiem. Its voice spoke in her head. *Now we will feed upon your pain too.*

She flew.

There is no pain in starlight.

I am woven of starlight.

Flame of Requiem

There is no pain in the sea.
The waves are its breath.

She blasted her dragonfire and charged headfirst into the towering fortress of demonic shadow.

Bricks showered around her. One of her horns snapped. Her scales cracked. She screamed and kept flying, tearing through it, a great lance like the lance that had driven into her father.

The building collapsed around her. Turrets slammed down and shattered. Bricks rained. She flew through the dust, the screams, the fleeing demons within, casting back their shadows with her firelight, until she flew over sand and sea.

She dipped down. The wind whipped around her. Her scales bled. But there was no pain in the sea, and the waves were its breath, and she plunged into the water and lost her magic.

The water flowed over her, inky black, washing them away, and they fled her. The dybbuks. The shards of souls. The endless deaths and the endless pain. They rose around her, swirling shadows, vanishing in the cleansing waters of Requiem, until only the waves remained, only starlight above.

The waves breathed, and they bore Til and Bim and laid them upon the sand.

Til rose to her knees, shivering, her sword lost. Bim knelt in the sand, his back turned toward her, his shoulders stooped and head lowered.

Til reached out hesitantly. When he turned around, would his eyes be purest white, his face twisted and dead, still a dybbuk?

"Bim?"

With a shaking hand, she touched his shoulder.

He spun toward her.

He shed tears.

"Til," he whispered.

She cried too, and she pulled him into her arms and embraced him, and they shivered together.

"It's over," she whispered, rocking him gently. "It's over, it's over. We did it, Bim. We reached the coast. We'll be safe here. We're safe. The seraphim dare not enter the city."

"Stars, I wonder why," Bim said.

She laughed through her tears. "You were right to fear that place. But we're safe now. We—"

In the distance, the fires burned.

They did not rise above the city, but they flew along the coast, having skirted that hive of possession. Now they stormed along the beach, heading toward her and Bim.

Countless chariots of fire that lit the darkness. The most Til had ever seen since the failed rebellion five years ago. Countless seraphim flew between them, and above all rose the great light of the Overlord, a sun in the night.

"Hello, Til!" rose a voice from the effulgence. "Welcome, child, to your grave!"

Til and Bim shouted, shifted into dragons, and soared. The countless seraphim flew toward them from all sides, burning the world.

MELIORA

They had been flying over the sea for days now, no food, no water, growing weary, getting scared. And always behind them cried out the harpies, forever on the horizon. Growing closer.

The leagues of water spread ahead, and still no sight of land.

"Will it never end?" Elory whispered, flying at her side.

Meliora glided on the wind and licked her dry palate. Her voice was hoarse. "It will end."

"You should drink," said the purple dragon. "We still have some canteens with water in the camp. Shift with me into human form and—"

"No." Meliora shook her head. "There are those who need water more than I do. The elders and children will drink first. Not us, the young and strong."

Young Meliora might have been, but it was hard to feel strong. Not after this endless flight from Tofet. She had not touched ground since her speech on the hill outside the walls of their captivity, and with each day, her strength waned. Her throat and mouth were so dry that even when she tried to sleep, riding on another dragon, the pain woke her up. Some of her cuts were infected, she thought. The welts leaked pale ooze. She had barely slept since leaving Tofet, barely eaten, and the weariness made her head spin.

But worse than all was her fear.

She feared that Requiem lay too far, that they would perish and drown in the sea, a nation of six hundred thousand souls drowning only leagues away from their homeland. She feared that even should they reach Requiem, that a great enemy would await them there, one too powerful to vanquish. She feared that Ishtafel would catch them, would end their dream of rebuilding their nation.

And she feared Leyleet's words, that curse that would not stop echoing.

You will never see Requiem, daughter of dragons. With my dying breath I curse you.

She forced those words out of her mind. Requiem surely lay just ahead, just beyond the horizon. Soon they would be home.

"Soon it will be over," Meliora told her sister. "After all your pain, Elory—it will be over. For all the children of Requiem. I cannot imagine the pain you went through in Tofet, my sweet sister. I cannot imagine the agony so many endured for five hundred years, while I lived in comfort." She lowered her head. "Leyleet told me that I would never see Requiem, and perhaps I don't deserve to lead our people home. Not I, who dined in palaces and slept on beds of silk while you toiled in the mud. It should be Jaren, or you, or Vale who leads this camp, not I."

The lavender dragon flew closer to her. Her eyes shone damply. "And yet it was you who gave us hope. You who gave *me* hope. You who marched with us, a multitude of slaves, into the City of Kings to demand our freedom. You who first flew as a dragon, soaring above us, letting us see your majesty. And you who led us out of the land of Tofet. And you will lead us home, Meliora. You will lead us through the gates of Requiem, and you will rebuild our land. And you will be our queen in the rebuilt marble halls."

Meliora's eyes stung. "I don't deserve a crown. I would see Jaren sit upon a new throne in a rebuilt Requiem. Or if not him, then Vale. Or you. Or Lucem, for he is a great hero of Requiem, one who gave our people hope long before I led you in a march. I just . . . I just want to undo all this. Everything that my family—my other family—has done." She stared at Elory pleadingly. "Do you understand? I caused you so much pain. I lived in a palace your hands built, wore clothes you wove, ate food you farmed, lived as a princess of an empire that rested upon your yokes. I need to atone for all that. I must be the one who fights this war, who fights for our freedom. But I deserve no honor. I don't deserve a place in songs of epics, and I should not be the first to enter the gates of Requiem, nor the first to wear her new crown."

Elory smiled thinly. "Let's focus right now on finding Requiem, and then we can argue about who'll wear the crown."

"I volunteer!" A red dragon shot toward them, wagged his tail, and grinned. "Let me do both. I'll be the first to set foot in Requiem, and I'll be her first new king. King Lucem the Lovable. Has a nice ring to it."

Elory rolled her eyes. "You are nothing but a peasant. Perhaps when I'm princess, you can be my lovable servant."

Lucem's eyes widened. "Peasant? *Peasant?*" The red dragon clutched his chest with his claws. "She wounds me! Do you hear how she wounds me, Meliora? Yet I heard what you called me— a great hero of Requiem. At least somebody respects me."

The sisters sighed and kept flying.

Requiem flew onward across the sea.

The sun set and the stars emerged. High above them, no longer on the horizon but rearing across the zenith, shone the Draco constellation. Meliora was prepared to shift back into human form, to ride for a while on her father or another dragon, when cries rose across the camp.

"The stars!" dragons cried.

"Praise the stars of Requiem!"

The cries swept across the camp, and dragons stared upwards, calling out in joy and awe.

Meliora looked up and gasped. Her eyes dampened.

"It's true," she whispered. "The stars bless us."

Above in the sky, luminous strands were coiling out from the Draco stars, flowing across the darkness like milk spilled from jugs. Slowly the strands of starlight connected the stars of the constellation and flared out in filigree, forming the shape of a great celestial dragon. The Draco constellation was no longer just stars but a beast of the sky, its tail coiling, its head rearing, its claws gripping the firmaments, all woven of light. Draco's eye shone brightest, Issari's Star gazing upon her children.

"The stars guide us home," Jaren said, rising up to fly at her side. "Requiem is close. Look, Meliora. Look ahead."

She gazed northward, and there she saw it.

Tears streamed down her scaly cheeks.

"Thank you, my stars," she whispered, trembling, and she could not stop shedding tears.

You were wrong, Leyleet. You were wrong. I see her. I see her ahead. I see Requiem.

The coast lay on the horizon, still many miles away. But Meliora could see Requiem even in the darkness. Lights lined the coast, shining like the stars. Great cities rose there—perhaps the cities of seraphim, perhaps even settlements of Vir Requis said to have survived the war five hundred years ago.

Once more, Meliora raised her pillar of white dragonfire, a beacon for her people to follow.

"Hear me, children of Requiem!" she cried. "Our homeland awaits us. Requiem lies before us. We are home!"

"We are home!" her people cried. "We are home!"

They flew onward, crossing the last few miles of dark water, the Draco stars shining above. The coast grew brighter ahead, the many lights shining, and joy swelled in Meliora's heart, and—

She gasped.

She narrowed her eyes.

Those were no city lights along the coast, she saw.

The coast was burning.

"Chariots of fire," she whispered. "Thousands of them."

Across the flight of dragons, cries of fear replaced the cries of joy. The dragons all stared ahead, and the firelight blazed, washing out the light of the stars.

Even in the heat of dragonfire, cold fear flowed over Meliora as the dragons flew onward—toward Requiem, toward the seraphim, toward war.

TIL

She flew, an orange dragon, rising above the beach, blasting her fire. Bim flew at her side, a small black dragon, his fire rising with hers.

Around them, the sky burned with the holy light of seraphim.

The immortals rose everywhere, covering the beach, the sea, and more flowing in. They hid the night sky. Their light bathed the world. Flaming chariots flew in rings, their firehorses thundering across the firmaments. Their seraphim chanted from within, raising their lances and bows, their halos shining. Above them all, in the center of the luminous maelstrom, flew the Overlord—a great light, a sun, a god. All other seraphim nearly drowned in his light, and his glory blasted down in great beams, falling upon Til and Bim, searing them.

"Til!" Bim shouted. "Til, what do we do?"

Die, she knew.

Die.

They had fled from seraphim before, but never this many. Here was an army. An army larger than the one that had crushed their rebellion five years ago, slaying all but her family. An army like the one that had destroyed Requiem five hundred years ago, crushing this ancient kingdom.

We die.

The seraphim surrounded them. Til felt that she flew within the sun, light all around her, searing her scales, nearly blinding her. Her brother screamed at her side. The city vanished in the light. The sea no longer whispered, and flames hid the sky.

A melodious voice spoke above, so fair, so holy that Meliora wept to hear it. The voice of a comforting angel, of a kind god, of a father, of a mother. A voice that promised to soothe all pain.

"Come to me, Meliora," said the Overlord. "Come to me, Bim. Fly into my light, children of Requiem, and let me relieve your weary heads. Come rest in my brilliance. Your pain is over."

Til found herself flying higher, ascending toward the light. Her pain could end. She could rise into the Overlord's presence, bask in his light, let him claim her soul, discard her broken body. She could forever seek comfort in his light, burned away, becoming part of his light.

We can ascend, she thought. *We can rest. We can become illuminated.*

As she flew higher, his figure came into focus, the light surrounding him with a great sphere. The Overlord stood taller than most seraphim, nearly the size of her dragon form. His long platinum hair streamed as if floating in water, and his golden armor shone. His halo hummed with holiness, and he held a great lance longer than a man, tipped with sunlight.

Til recognized that lance.

The lance that had driven into her father, piercing the dragon. The lance Father's human body had hung on.

The lance the Overlord would drive into her and her brother.

"Yes, we die," she whispered. "But not ascending into light. We die as dragons. We die in dragonfire."

She roared and blasted up that dragonfire, a great fountain rising toward the Overlord.

Bim roared with her, blasting his flames.

"For Requiem!" the black dragon cried.

"For death!" Til answered the cry.

For Father. For all those you killed. For a last stand and death in glory.

The Overlord swooped, lance plunging downward, light flaring. The two dragons soared to meet him, breathing fire, rising toward death in flame.

And from the south, countless voices answered their cry.

"For Requiem!" rose a first cry, distant, barely audible.

"Requiem rises, Requiem rises!" rose a thousand other voices.

"To war! To victory! To our home!"

All around, the seraphim shrieked. Their wings beat madly. They spun in the sky, breaking the sphere they had formed around Til and Bim. Their lances thrust toward the sea.

"Requiem!" rose the voices, and countless whips beat, and roars rolled across the sky, and an inferno of fire blazed across the world.

Til spread her wings as wide as they'd go, halting her ascent, and spun toward the south.

Her eyes watered.

There above the sea she saw them.

"Dragons," she whispered, tasting her tears. "Dragons coming home."

VALE

All his life, Vale had been fighting.

In the pits of Tofet, he had fought against the sun that burned him, the thirst that bloodied his throat, the whips that lashed him, the exhaustion that threatened to slay him like so many of his comrades. In the great uprising against the overseers, he had fought his masters, had battled Ishtafel in the sky, had blown his fire against many enemies across the southern continent.

But now, he thought, *I fight a different battle. Now I fight for my homeland.*

The sky exploded around him.

Fire flared in great streams.

Shadows burst and shattered.

The columns of Requiem had fallen, but great pillars of dragonfire rose.

They stormed forth—six hundred thousand dragons, roaring, breathing fire, crashing into the enemy, coming home.

The royal army was only days old, but it had already fought great battles, and it fought here with its greatest fury.

The hosts of seraphim crashed into them. Flaming chariots drove through the dragons, casting corpses down to the beach. The arrows of seraphim filled the air, their tips as long and sharp as daggers. Lances cracked through scales. The seraphim flew from all sides, and the darkness of night vanished under their light.

Yet the dragons still stormed forth.

Warriors. Elders. Children. They all fought this night, flying over the beaches, burning down the seraphim before them. The immortals fell with blazing wings. The chariots crashed down, slamming into the water and onto the ruins of an ancient city. Towers, roofs, and walls shattered beneath them, and fires burned among the bricks.

Vale blew his fire, knocking the seraphim down, leading the charge into their ranks. He soared through fire that washed across his scales. He fought with his family. He fought with his people. He fought for Requiem and he fought for the women who forever lit his heart, who would forever shine down upon him. For his mother, fallen in the slave pit. For Issari, a priestess of legend. And for Tash.

For the first time in five hundred years, the Vir Requis fought in their sky.

TIL

The sky rained blood and fire, and Til flew, her dragonfire washing across the battle.

Requiem is real. Her tears steamed in the fire. *Requiem returns.*

Her heart soared and she trembled as she fought the enemy over the ruins. For so many years, she had sought others, hoping against hope to find a handful of survivors, perhaps just one, just another sign of life in ruin. For so many years, she had feared that she and her family were the last, that soon they too would die and all of Requiem's light would perish with them.

But we found others in the south. She flew with them, with dragons who covered the sky, burning down the seraphim. *We found a nation.*

Her tears kept burning in her eyes. It had been years since she had seen other dragons—true living dragons, actual Vir Requis. Her people. Thousands of them—really here, not just in her dreams. Even though war blazed around them and hundreds were dying, pure joy filled Til, for she was no longer alone. Countless others knew her pain, her hope, her love of Requiem. She would never more hide in shadows.

Til knew at once who these others were. Not survivors of the ruins. Not other vagabonds like her. Here were the ancient people of Requiem, the descendants of those first captives. Freed slaves. Free warriors. New hope and light for their land. They fought for their ancient, stolen homeland. They fought for their freedom. They fought to rekindle the light of Requiem in her sky.

And I fight a second war, Til thought.

She stared above her, and she saw him still there, his light nearly blinding her. The Overlord.

The tyrant of Requiem's ruins, the seraph who had slaughtered thousands, fought in a fury. His lance thrust again and again, piercing dragons, sending them falling to the ruins as men and women. His shield swung, cleaving through dragons, sending scales showering through the air. His light blasted out and his halo shone, brighter than dragonfire. The warriors of Requiem fell before him.

"Bim, stay with the others!" Til said. "Fly to the back line!"

Her brother fought at her side, covered in scrapes, his black scales dented. He roared and blasted his dragonfire against two swooping seraphim, kindling their wings. Two more dragons—a one-eared lavender dragon and a red dragon with sliced horns—flew up to fly around Bim. The three fought together, back to back, burning more enemies.

Til beat her wings, whipped her tail, and flew higher. She charged through the battle, moving toward the light, knocking down those seraphim in her way. An arrow slammed into her leg, and she bellowed but kept flying. A lance scraped her side, and she whipped her tail, slicing a seraph in half. A chariot charged toward her, and Til soared and rained down fire onto its rider. The seraph screamed, armor and flesh melting. She flew onward, heading into the glare.

Ahead of her, the Overlord thrust his lance, piercing a silver dragon. The dragon lost her magic, returning to a human—a young girl, younger than Til. The Overlord swung his lance, tossing the corpse onto another dragon. His shield swung, knocking the second assailant down. Blood stained the great seraph's armor, but his light still shone purely.

"Fight them, seraphim!" the Overlord cried in his deep, holy voice. "Fell the scaly beasts! Rid the world of the evil reptiles, and let the holiness of Saraph shine here again."

Til stared at him, growling.

He truly believes it, she realized. *He truly believes that he's good. That we are evil. That he's doing holy work.*

For the first time, Til realized that perhaps good and evil did not truly exist. All her life, she had imagined herself fighting a wicked enemy, imagined herself fighting for goodness. Yet in the Overlord's eyes, the seraphim were holy and righteous, while dragons were but monsters, creatures of fangs and fire.

For just that moment, Til doubted herself, doubted her battle.

Then the Overlord slew another dragon, and Til roared and charged, fire blazing.

Her inferno shrieked, spinning madly, and crashed into the mighty lord of light.

The Overlord spun toward her, the dragonfire washing across his breastplate. He screamed in the flames, a deafening sound. He rose higher, emerging from the inferno, and gazed down at her. Molten gold dripped off his armor, and he sneered toothily.

Til stared in horror. Her dragonfire had melted the flesh of many seraphim, yet it had washed over the Overlord like water around a boulder.

"There you are," he said, pointed his lance, and charged toward her.

The blade drove forth, coated with the blood of dragons. The blade that had killed her father.

Til roared out flame and released her magic.

The dragonfire washed across the Overlord again, and she plunged down through the sky, a human. The lance thrust over her head, slicing a lock of her red hair.

She shifted back into a dragon and soared, blasting out more flames. The fire crashed into the Overlord, washing over his legs, and he bellowed in pain.

Til snarled.

There. I hurt him. He can be hurt.

The Overlord swung his shield toward her. The metal disk, wider than a man's arm span, flashed with light, its sharp edge stained with blood.

Til screamed and swerved, trying to dodge the blow, but she was too slow. The shield scraped across her front leg, cutting a deep gash. She screamed. She nearly lost her magic. She forced herself to beat her wings, and her dragonfire burst forth, washing across the Overlord again, but seemingly not harming the seraph.

His shield swung again, slamming into her side, cracking her scales.

Til lost her magic.

She fell, blood spilling from her side, eyes rolling.

The battle spun around her. The sky and sea whirled. Above her the light shone, and he laughed.

No.

Still in human form, Til gripped the hilt of her sword.

"Goodbye, Til!" the Overlord called above her, laughing. "Goodbye, my darling."

No.

The dragons all flew around her and above her. The lost dragons of Requiem, come to rebuild their homeland.

No. No. I will not die now. Not so close to Requiem's rebirth.

She shifted. She soared, an orange dragon. Bleeding. Burnt. Haunted by countless deaths, countless days and nights of running and hiding. A broken woman, perhaps one too hurt to ever heal. But a woman who would still fight. A dragon who would still roar.

She rose toward him through the battle, washed him with flames, and soared higher.

He spun beneath her, raising his lance.

Til kept ascending, rising high above all other seraphim, high toward the stars of her people. The Draco constellation shone above her, strands of starlight connecting its stars, a great silvery dragon watching over her.

Below her he roared, a twisted creature, burning in his own sunlight, his halo flaring and sputtering. His lance rose toward her, prepared to cut out her heart.

Til swooped and released her magic.

She plunged down as a human.

His wings beat and his lance rose

Til drew her longsword.

The lance scraped across her side, cracking a plate of armor, and she thrust her sword downward.

The blade—a weapon of the bellators, Requiem's ancient order of knighthood—crashed into the Overlord's halo.

Light.

Sound.

Fury.

The halo shattered, exploded, cast out thousands of burning white shards. Til screamed as they burned her. She tried to summon her magic again, to lash into him with claws, but the light was too great, the sound washing across her.

As he fell, the Overlord reached out and grabbed her throat.

"So . . . there's some bite to the bitch," he hissed, his voice no longer melodious but ugly, raspy. Broken shards of his halo still sputtered over his head. Other shards, like broken metal forged of light, had lacerated his head, his face, his eye. The luminous blades thrust out from him, leaking golden ichor that flowed down his skin, burning rivulets into the flesh.

Til tried to shift again, but when scales began to rise across her, and when her body grew, his grip tightened around her throat, constricting her, and she lost her magic like a collared slave. The Overlord's wings still beat, holding them high above the ruined city and beach. He sneered, licking the ichor.

"You . . ." Til struggled for breath, rasping out each word. "You . . . lost. Requiem . . . rises."

"No, my little sweetling." He tightened his grip. "Requiem falls now between my host and the harpies flying from the south. And you will die now, at my moment of greatest glory, in the battle where we eradicate all weredragons. Die now, girl. Die. Die."

She couldn't breathe. Her neck creaked. Blackness closed in around her, until she saw only him, only his lacerated face, only his burning golden eyes, the pupils like sunbursts, his bloody teeth. Then stars flowed over her vision—stars like those of Requiem, floating everywhere, rising in columns. Caught in his grip, she floundered, trying to slap him, to kick him, until her limbs lost all strength and hung loosely.

The Overlord screamed.

Horns burst out from his chest, sizzling with ichor, then pulled back.

His shriek tore across Til, leaving only ringing in her ears. His grip loosened and she gulped down breath.

The Overlord thrashed in the sky, clutching at his wounds, beating his wings, wailing in agony and rage. Behind him flew a small black dragon, horns bloody.

"Bim," Til whispered hoarsely.

She shifted into a dragon.

She lashed her claws, ripping into the Overlord's chest, shattering his armor and lacerating the skin. She lashed her tail, driving the spikes deep into his side. She blasted out fire, burning one of his wings.

With a roar that tore across the sky, the Overlord fell.

He plunged down like a comet, a ball of light, tearing through dragons, burning them and still crashing downward, leaving a trail of smoke. When he slammed onto the beach, the world seemed to shake, and buildings collapsed in the city.

Til flew down, weaving her way between dragons and seraphim that still battled around her. She bled from multiple wounds. Her breath rasped. She all but crashed onto the sand and lost her magic on impact. Bim landed at her side and lost his magic too.

For a moment, sister and brother lay in the sand, too hurt and weary to move. Beside them he moaned, twitched, smoked—the Overlord.

Til rose to her feet. As dragons and seraphim battled in the sky, she limped toward him.

The Overlord lay on the beach, his last strands of light flickering. His lance lay at his side. His left wing was lacerated, and shards of his halo still pierced his head and face, their light fading. His armor had cracked and melted, revealing burnt flesh. He seemed smaller this way. Almost human. Just a dying man like the countless who had died in this land.

"Please," the Overlord whispered, voice hoarse, ichor in his mouth. "Please, Til. I only wanted to ease your pain. I'm sorry. I'm sorry, Til. I—"

With a sudden movement, the Overlord reached for his lance.

Til kicked his hand aside, crushing his fingers, and grabbed the weapon.

The Overlord bellowed, trying to rise from the sand. Til kicked him down and placed the tip of the lance against his neck.

They both froze. He stared up at her, eyes wide, face pale. She stared down into those heartless eyes. Golden eyes. Sunburst eyes. The eyes that had laughed as he slew her father. Her hands trembled around the shaft of the lance.

"Look away, Bim," she said, voice soft, never removing her eyes from the Overlord.

Her brother stepped closer. He stared down too. "I want to see this."

Til's legs shook, and she tightened her grip on the shaft.

"You murdered him." She stared at the Overlord, speaking through grinding teeth. "You murdered thousands. And you murdered my brother's soul. You are not a god, Overlord. You are a monster."

Lying in the sand beneath her, burnt and bleeding, the lance against his neck, the Overlord laughed.

"You are like I am," the seraph said, sputtering out saliva. "You call me a murderer, yet now you threaten to murder me. You call me a monster, yet you and your brother delight in death. Look at him, Til! Only a boy and already bloodthirsty. We are the same, whore of Requiem. Just killers. Just like your father was. Just like—"

She drove the lance into his neck.

He gave a last sputter, and his breath died. His body loosened, and his eyes saw no more.

"Maybe we are monsters," Til whispered. "But you made us so. We will find redemption in the halls of a rebuilt Requiem."

She turned away from the corpse and faced Bim.

He stared back at her, and she expected to see another blank gaze, a lifeless face, a haunted boy with a heart of stone.

But instead Bim wept.

"Til," he whispered.

She fell to her knees, pulled him into her embrace, and clung to him, smoothing his hair, nearly crushing him, weeping too.

"We did it, Bim," she whispered, shaking, her arms wrapped around him as he wept against her shoulder. "We did it. It's over now. It's over."

MELIORA

"Requiem," she whispered, staring around her. Her body trembled and her eyes stung. "I'm in Requiem."

Dawn rose across the land, illuminating ruin and death. The city on the coast—the fabled Lynport, the ancient jewel of Requiem's south—lay fallen, its halls collapsed under the rain of chariots. Thousands of corpses lay everywhere, both of seraphim and Vir Requis. The battle had ended, leaving the land bleeding and ravaged, blood and death upon the beach, in the water, and on the forests and hills beyond.

And here it was. Even in ruin. Even bloodied and burnt. Here was holy ground.

Requiem.

Meliora knelt on the beach. She lowered her hands. And she felt it. The sand of her homeland. Each grain a miracle.

They gathered around her on the beach. Her family. Her friends. The people Meliora had once oppressed, living as a princess in their tyrant's palace. The people she would now die for, the people who had chosen her to lead them, the people she would always love. Along the coast, the plains, the hills they gathered, the children of Requiem.

Meliora shifted into a dragon and soared.

She rose high, circling her people. They crowded below in human form, as plentiful as the grains of sand on the beach, spreading out for miles. They wore tattered burlap. They were thin, weary, wounded, but their eyes shone, and they prayed and wept and sang with joy.

"Hear me, children of Requiem!" Meliora said, flying above as a white dragon. "For five hundred years, we cried out to the stars. Chained. Beaten. Collared. For five hundred years, we dreamed of our homeland. Through fire and rain, through death and despair, we have traveled here, defeating many enemies. And we have reached holy ground. We have reached Requiem."

Their voices rose together, chanting for their land.

Meliora glided on the wind, staring south. She rose higher, so high the people below faded to but distant specks, then just a blur along the coast. She flew so high the air grew cold and thin, and she could barely breathe. She stared south, and there she saw them, a gray haze on the horizon, still a hundred leagues away.

A cloud of harpies.

Ishtafel.

She glided down until she flew close enough to call to her people again.

"We have traveled for many days, through much danger, and we found our homeland. But our fight is not over, Requiem! An enemy approaches from the south, an enemy greater than any we have yet faced. Ishtafel flies toward us, leading a host of harpies, and he seeks to steal our homeland from us, so soon after we've reclaimed it."

The people below cried out, some in dismay, others in rage.

"We will fight him!" Meliora cried. "Not because we crave war. Not because we crave victory or glory. We will fight him because we have no choice. Because he seeks to destroy us, to slay us all. No longer will he offer us the collar, only the lance. And so we will fight him, Requiem. But not here. Not upon this coast. We fly north! We fly to the heartland of our realm. To Old Requiem, the place where our nation was born. If we must make a final stand, it will be in the light of King's Column. Arise, children of Requiem! Arise and fill your hearts with song. We fly north! We fly to our column! There we will fight this war. Not as slaves. Not as exiles. We will fight andas proud Vir Requis defending our home."

They roared. They rose as dragons.

They flew over the ruins, over the corpses of seraphim, leaving the coast behind . . . flying north, flying over Requiem.

ISHTAFEL

They landed on the coast of Requiem under clouds of smoke, so weary they barely mustered the energy to feed upon the corpses of seraphim.

Ishtafel walked across the coast, grinning savagely. His body blazed with an inferno of agony. Every step, every twitch of his muscles, every breath bathed him with the fury of collapsing suns. His muscles ached from the long flight across the sea. His throat was parched and bleeding, his belly roiling with hunger, his limbs shaking with weakness. And yet those pains vanished under the all-consuming flood of pain from his burnt flesh—the burns of dragonfire, the fire of Tash, the reptilian whore.

But still Ishtafel walked across the coast. As around him myriads of harpies collapsed onto the sand, breathing raggedly, gasping for breath, crawling to find food, Ishtafel held his back straight. He crossed the sand onto the solid earth of Requiem. He stood in the shadow of a ruined city under a sky of raining ash.

"Here it was," he whispered, tasting his blood as his face tore within his mask of metal. "Here we landed so long ago."

Ahead, Ishtafel could see it again—Requiem five hundred years ago, on the first day of his invasion. In his mind, these ruins stood again as the great city the weredragons had called Lynport, their southernmost outpost. In his memories, those weredragons still filled the sky, thousands of them, clad in armor and roaring fire—not ragged refugees but soldiers in a reptilian army.

"And we slew them, Reehan," Ishtafel whispered. "We slew them together."

He remembered the glory of that day. He had flown with his lover in one great chariot, its flames red and gold, their eight firehorses pulling them into their first battle. Ishtafel and Reehan had fired their arrows together, felling the beasts. They had raised shields together, blocking the dragonfire, had thrust their lances as one, cracking scales. Together they had led the charge. Together they had conquered this land.

Yet we did not fall together.

He winced to remember her lifeless body in his arms. To remember the light, fury, and love in her eyes go dark. He had slain many weredragons then. He had captured the rest, tormenting them for centuries. And now, here in this land, his revenge could be complete. Here he would grind their bones to dust in the light of their column, and he would send that column crashing down.

He looked across the coast, the city, and the hills. Thousands of seraphim lay dead here, burnt with dragonfire. The harpies were gorging themselves on the dead, gaining strength from the flesh and ichor. Their claws tore into the corpses' torsos, and their mouths dug deep into the cavities, tugging out organs. The snakes upon the harpies' heads feasted too, growing fat on the meat.

Ishtafel beat his aching, featherless wings. He rose higher above the ruins, and he stared north across the land he had conquered, the land he would now crush. There in the distance, many leagues away, they flew.

"The weredragons," he whispered in the hot, smoky wind. "And you, Meliora, future mother of my children. You will live. And you will envy the dead."

He brought Meliora into his mind. Her tall, slender frame. Her terrified eyes. Her waiting womb. He would soon fill that womb, and her children would rule over this land of bones.

He flew toward the feasting harpies. He dined with them, staining his lips, and he slept. In darkness they would fly again. For now he dreamed of burning dragons, of twisting tunnels, and in his dreams it was Meliora traveling the underground with him, not Reehan, and it was Meliora who died in his arms, and it was her corpse that he seeded, and her lifeless flesh from which emerged the glory of his dynasty.

MELIORA

For seven days and nights, they flew over the wilderness of Requiem, cleansing the land.

Hundreds of thousands of dragons, they flew over the southern forests, burning the seraphim who flew toward them, casting their bodies down upon the land.

They dived toward Castellum Luna, the fabled fortress of the south, where Princess Mori Aeternum herself had faced the phoenixes many centuries ago. Here too seraphim lurked, but the new Royal Army of Requiem slew them and burned their corpses, scouring the land of their light.

They kept flying, traveling northward, until the great Amerath Mountains soared to their left, the ancient range where many great battles had been waged. Chariots of fire rose from those rocky crests, and many dragons fell here, but here too the seraphim crashed and burned upon the mountainsides. The host of Requiem flew onward, leaving a trail of death, of ichor, and of a purified home.

Jaren flew with her, leading the camp, a green dragon, a priest and healer, his prayers soothing the wounded. Vale stormed ahead at every enemy that rose, a vicious blue dragon stained with blood, leading the Royal Army in battle, slaying the enemies. Elory and Lucem flew here too, never far apart, the princess and the hero of Requiem, inspiring their people.

And I lead them all, Meliora thought. A woman torn in two. A woman in pain. A woman returning to a home she had never known was hers.

Countless times, Meliora had imagined this day, imagined flying over Requiem, scouring the land from the stain of Saraph, rebuilding a homeland for dragons. Yet now as she flew here, she did not feel the glow of holiness, and the stars had never felt more distant. Requiem was beautiful, a northern land of great forests, mountains, and rivers, and yet as they flew across their land, they stained it with blood.

With the blood of seraphim, Meliora thought. *The blood of my second half.*

"Daughter," Jaren said to her, gliding to fly at her side. "You do not sing with the others. You do not seem to rejoice in our victories, in our return to our land. Are you all right, daughter? There is sadness in your eyes"

Meliora looked at her father—her true father, the father she had only met this year. The green dragon was a great priest, a holy leader of Requiem, a healer. And yet blood stained his claws, and scratches, dents, and burns marred his body. Flecks of dried ichor still stained Meliora's own claws, and she could still taste the flesh of her enemies in her mouth.

"In my dreams," Meliora said, "I envisioned a pure Requiem. A Requiem like the celestial one beyond the stars, untouched by war, by death. Yet we found a bloodstained Requiem. Perhaps I was an innocent girl. As I had imagined Tofet to be a land of plenty, I imagined Requiem to be a land of beauty. Yet here too I found only agony, only destruction, only bloodshed."

Jaren looked at her with soft eyes. "Requiem has never been a land of peaceful beauty, daughter. For thousands of years, since our ancestor Aeternum raised his column, it has been a land of bloodshed. A land we had to constantly defend, constantly fight for. A land that burned over and over, fell again and again. We did not come to Requiem to find peace. We came to find our home of old."

"And we came as killers." Meliora lowered her head. "We—her sons and daughters—came here not as priests, not as holy pilgrims, but as warriors. We do not cleanse Requiem with light but with blood."

Jaren nodded, his eyes damp, and his voice was soft. "Thus has been our lot. In all our history, men of peace—from King Aeternum to King Benedictus to Queen Fidelity—were forced to blow dragonfire. To raise swords. To become warriors. Killers. Our enemies not only slew our children, but they forced us to slay theirs. That has ever been our greatest curse."

Meliora stared at her father, eyes burning with tears. "But they did not slay their own people!" Her voice rose louder, hoarse. "Vale slays the seraphim with pride, perhaps even with a sort of painful joy. But . . . . oh, Father. The seraphim are my people, just as much as the Vir Requis are. As our ancestors beheld the destruction of Requiem, here do I behold the destruction of Saraph. How are we different from Ishtafel who slew so many in Tofet? Here we too kill. How can we rebuild a holy, pure kingdom when so much blood stains our hands?"

Jaren stared ahead into the distance. The forests rolled for many leagues, fading into hazy mist, and the mountains soared to their left. Even as they flew here, the warriors of Requiem were battling several last seraphim who flew above the mountains.

"We will not be those who rebuild Requiem," Jaren finally said, speaking softly. "Not my generation, nor yours. We have bled too much. We have spilled too much blood. Our souls are forever scarred, our hands forever bloodstained. Our task will not be to rebuild Requiem, daughter. That has never been our task. We—the generation of the whip, of the desert, of the collar—are those tasked with staining our hands, our souls, our homeland. Only those born here, in a land we kill for, can rebuild the marble halls of our forebears with clean hands and clean souls."

Meliora closed her eyes as she flew, and Leyleet's words again echoed in her ears.

You will never see Requiem.

Perhaps Meliora finally understood that curse. She had seen the land of Requiem, but Requiem had always been more than soil and sky. Requiem had always been something beyond the physical. An idea. A dream. A home. Peace. These Meliora would never see, for even should she claim this land and defeat Ishtafel, her soul could no longer be mended. Her hands could no longer be cleansed of blood, even should she cleanse Requiem of the seraphim.

So no, I will never see the true Requiem, a Requiem rebuilt and pure. I will forever be the warrior, the column leading the camp, the one who slew.

"Then let us sin," Meliora whispered and looked at her father again, and tears streamed down her cheeks. "Let us kill. Let us bear this burden. We will sin so that our children do not. We will kill so our children can live in peace. We will destroy so they can build."

They flew onward until Meliora saw it ahead—a great forest of birches, their branches still coated with snow. Countless birches, the holy trees of Requiem, spreading for miles. They had reached the fabled King's Forest, the heart of their nation.

We are near King's Column.

Shrieks sounded behind her, and Meliora cringed. As she flew closer toward the pillar of Requiem, so did her brother.

With blood and fire, the Vir Requis had found Requiem. Soon the great battle to reclaim it would flare.

VALE

"We're near." Til, flying as an orange dragon, pointed with her claws. "We'll be there by sundown."

Gliding on a cold wind, Vale stared ahead but saw only leagues of snowy birches rolling into the horizon. It was so damn cold here in the north. Vale could not imagine how the ancient Vir Requis had ever tolerated this weather. For the first time in his life, he saw snow and ice, felt the chill of true winter, as cruel as the blazing sun of Saraph in the south. Yet he would endure a thousand blizzards for just a sight of it on the horizon—a marble pillar rising, the heart of his nation, the column of his first king.

He turned to look at the orange dragon again. "You saw it," he said. "You actually saw King's Column."

The orange dragon lowered her head. Til had joined their forces on the southern coast, along with her younger brother, a small black dragon named Bim. At first, Vale had not believed her story. Vir Requis who had survived the fall five hundred years ago, who had hidden here all this time, no collars around their necks, avoiding both death and slavery? It seemed impossible, yet for the past few days, Til had predicted every landmark—every old ruin, every mountain, every river and plain. All Vale knew of Requiem's landscape came from old maps; Til knew the kingdom like her own scales.

"I saw King's Column." Til lowered her head, and smoke trailed from her nostrils in two thin streams. "It still stands, but the seraphim have profaned it. They painted its white marble with the blood of dragons, and they hung the skeletons of Vir Requis from it on chains, turning it into a macabre maypole."

Vale grimaced, remembering the mountains of dead the seraphim had raised in Tofet. If some guilt at slaying the immortals had filled him over the past few days, it now burned away in his rage.

"We will cleanse the column," he said. "And we will build many more columns around it, raise the old palace again, and worship the stars. We—"

A yawn interrupted his words.

Til stared at him with wide eyes, then laughed. Vale felt the scales on his cheeks heat up.

"When's the last time you've slept?" Til asked.

Vale considered. "I can't remember. Over Castellum Luna?"

Her eyes widened further. "That was two days ago! And—" Now it was she who yawned. "I don't think I've slept since then either."

Vale looked over his shoulder at his back. Lucem and Elory lay there, cuddled and sleeping soundly. They had been sleeping there since before dawn. Vale curled up his tail and tapped them.

They rose, yawning and stretching and blinking.

"Hey!" Lucem said, shoving Vale's spiky tail away. "I was sleeping."

"You've been sleeping all day," Vale said. "Take a turn flying."

The young man grumbled but dutifully leaped off Vale's back, and Elory followed. Both turned into dragons. Quickly, several young dragons above—Vale recognized Meliora's former handmaidens, as well as the young Bim—landed on Elory's back, shifted into human form, and instantly fell asleep.

That left Lucem's red, scaly back. Vale flew higher, dipped down onto the red dragon's back, and released his magic. He lay down in human form, his muscles aching.

The orange dragon hovered above, released her magic, and landed on the dragon too. For the first time, Vale got to see Til's human form up close. She was a young woman with long hair the color of her scales. She wore pelts of fur, many leather belts and straps, and assorted plates of rusted armor, no one piece matching the other. A sword and quiver hung at her side, and she carried a bow.

Vale knew that he was gaunt, haggard, bruised, that he looked about as healthy as any man who had lived through slavery might look. Til looked just as haggard and weary. Ash stained her freckled skin, dry leaves filled her fiery hair, and haunting pain filled her eyes.

Her life here in Requiem was no easier than ours, Vale thought. *And yet she is beautiful. And noble. As fair as proud as Queen Gloriae of old.*

Sitting before him on the dragon, she reached out and touched his neck, her fingers slender and callused. The skin around his throat was still chafed from the cursed collar.

"I'm sorry, Vale," she whispered.

He tilted his head. "For what?"

She looked down at the forest. "For not being there with you. With all of you. For hiding here. While so many Vir Requis suffered in slavery." She looked back at him, eyes damp. "I should have been there with you, fighting the seraphim. My surname is Eleison; I am descended from the great knights of Ancient Requiem, who had fought forever at the side of your family, the Aeternums. Yet . . . I failed my duty. I failed to protect you." She lowered her eyes. "My family remained here and hid. We should have been there to overthrow the shackles with Meliora. With you."

Vale caressed a bruise on her cheek. "You too bear the marks of war, of Requiem's suffering. I do not think, my lady, that you fought any less nobly, nor that your task was any less important for our people. In years to come, if we survive this war, the books will speak proudly of the courage of Eleison— the family that stayed, that survived, that fought for Requiem for five hundred years in shadow."

She yawned again. "I fought in shadow. Now I will sleep in daylight." She lay down. "And you sleep too!"

He lay down beside her. Lucem's back wasn't particularly wide, forcing Vale and Til to press together, slinging their limbs across each other. Her red hair tickled his forehead, and their faces were but an inch apart.

"Sleep well, Vale Aeternum, my prince," Til whispered, smiled, and touched his cheek. "Dream of dragons."

"Sleep well, my lady," he replied. "Dream of something nicer than dragons. I suggest fluffy bunnies."

She laughed softly and slept, her arms around him.

Vale was weary yet sleep eluded him. He lay on his side on the red scales, holding Til close.

If I sleep, she'll fall off the dragon, he thought. *I have to protect her. To hold her close. Or she'll fall. She'll die. I'll lose her like I lost Tash, like I lost my Mother, and—*

He clenched his jaw. The pain flared through him.

Again Vale saw it, the sight he had never stopped seeing. Ishtafel thrusting his spear, impaling Tash, and the young woman dying in his arms, smiling softly, her soul departing.

Vale's chest began to tighten, his heart to beat faster, his mind to storm with grief. Remembering Tash's death seemed worse than all his battles, and in his mind, he saw the rest of them dying. Til slipping from his grasp and falling. Meliora burning. Elory perishing under the lance. Countless dragons dying before the harpy horde and—

He forced himself to breathe.

Breath after breath.

He looked at Til again. She still slept, smiling gently. The wind ruffled her hair, and she nestled closer to him, her leg tossed across him. As Vale gazed at her, slowly his anxiety faded, replaced with soothing warmth.

Til is still alive, he thought. *So are my sisters and father. So is our nation. There is still hope here, still life, still love.*

He closed his eyes, and he slept too, but he did not dream.

ELORY

Blood.

Searing sunlight.

The crack of whips on flesh.

With cries of agony, with sand and tar, with twisted shoulders and breaking backs, the children of Requiem toiled.

"Faster!"

The flaming whips flew, ripping through skin.

"Up!"

The chains rattled. Slaves fell. Masters roared.

"Toil!"

Elory cried out in pain. She struggled to walk across bubbling bitumen that burned her soles. Chained to her neck, the yoke nearly crushed her shoulders. The baskets of bitumen swayed from the yoke, their fumes burning her nostrils. The whips of fire lashed, again and again, tearing into her back. She screamed. She wept. And around her they died. Her dear friend Mayana. Her mother. A hundred thousand others.

"You will be mine," Ishtafel said in his chamber of gold and jewels. The tall, handsome prince reached out to caress her. "You will be my slave. Your body will belong to me."

Elory trembled, begging, but he showed her no mercy. He hurt her. He burned in fire, rising, covered in metal, shrieking for her blood, and all of Requiem burned around Elory.

"We see it!" cried a voice.

"They have defiled it."

"Curse them! Curse the seraphim!"

The voices danced around her, torn in mourning, and a cold wind moaned.

Elory opened her eyes, shuddering. She forced a deep breath.

A dream. Just a dream.

She was in her human form, lying on a dragon. When she looked up, she saw a night sky strewn with stars, brightest among them the Draco constellation. The moon shone there too, full and silvery. Many dragons flew all around, fire flaring in their mouths, crying out.

"Curse the seraphim!"

Elory blinked, turned around, and stared north.

She lost her breath.

Her hands curled into fists.

With a deep breath, she leaped off the dragon she rode, shifted into her own dragon form, and rose higher.

Curse them.

Ahead of her, it rose from the forest, hundreds of feet tall, the moonlight upon it. King's Column.

In the old tales they had told in Tofet, King's Column was a great monument, purest white, rising from the forest as a beacon for all Vir Requis. Elory's ancestors, King Aeternum and Queen Laira, had raised the column to summon all those hunted for their magic, and the stars had blessed the column with their magic. So long as a Vir Requis lived in the world, the column would stand. Through endless wars—against the demons, the griffins, the phoenixes, and many other enemies—this column had stood.

Like many others before them, the seraphim could not fell nor even scratch King's Column. Yet they could profane it. Even in the moonlight, Elory could see that old blood stained the marble, hiding its shine. Many chains were attached to the column's crest, draping downward toward the forest like ropes from a tent pole. Upon those chains they hung—hundreds of skeletons. The skeletons of Vir Requis.

Requiem's greatest artifact had become a monument to death.

Elory expected to feel rage. All around her, the dragons blasted their fire in fury, and voices cried out for revenge. Elory wanted to feel that anger. She wanted to feel hatred.

But more than anything, she felt grief.

She didn't know who those dead Vir Requis were. The original inhabitants of Requiem, their bones hanging here for five hundred years? More resistors like Til, those who had stayed and fought?

Each had dreams, hopes, people they loved, Elory thought, staring at the skeletons. *They did not deserve this.*

"We'll bury them," Elory said, flying toward the column. "We'll bury them with honor."

Lucem flew up to help her, and soon other dragons joined their task. Elory had spent years burying the dead in Tofet; she did not shy away from these bones. For long hours, the dragons labored, unchaining the skeletons and gently laying them down upon the holy ground of Requiem.

When the remains had been removed and the chains tugged off the column, they counted over a thousand skeletons. A thousand martyrs of Requiem. A thousand who would finally be at peace.

Requiem was cold, far colder than anything any of them— aside from Til and Bim—had ever felt. Snow still coated the birches, and the ground was frozen. Yet dragon claws were sharp, and Elory and her family labored, digging graves. Not mass graves like the seraphim had them dig in Tofet. Each of these slaves would rest alone upon a hill, a tombstone marking his or her grave.

Jaren moved between the graves in human form, holding his staff, praying over the dead.

"We come from starlight, and to starlight we go." The priest knelt before each grave, placing down a simple stone, for no flowers grew in the winter of Requiem. "May your soul rise to those stars and rest in their light."

A few skeletons still remained to bury. Elory moved farther east, down into a valley, seeking room for more graves without disturbing the holy birches. She walked in dragon form, and she walked alone, the moonlight and the fire in her mouth lighting her way. The sounds of prayer still rose behind her, but walking here apart from the group, she could hear other sounds: the creaking trees, the wind, her chinking scales, and the sounds that never left her memories. The sounds of screaming. Of dying. Of Ishtafel's decimation that had slain sixty thousand souls in the city of Shayeen.

Finally Elory found a moonlit clearing. Here was a good place to dig. She would have to uproot no birches here, and it would be a beautiful place for the fallen to rest, and in the spring many flowers would bloom here. Elory touched her claws to the frozen ground, prepared to dig, but suddenly the pain was too real. Suddenly she could barely even breathe.

She released her magic. She fell to her knees, shivering in the cold—it was so damn cold here in Requiem. Her tears streamed down her cheeks.

"I miss you, Mother," she whispered. "I miss you, Mayana, my friend. I miss you, sweet Tash. I miss you and I love you all, and I'm so scared. I'm so scared without you."

A soft voice sounded behind her.

"You have me."

Elory turned around, at first expecting to see Lucem. But she saw Meliora standing there.

"I know," Elory whispered, rising to her feet.

Meliora stepped closer and embraced Elory. Her sister was much taller—Elory barely even reached her shoulder—and the embrace felt so warm, so safe, that Elory almost felt as she had in her mother's embrace.

"You're safe, Elory, I promise you." Meliora kissed her forehead. "You are loved. You are in Requiem. I did not know your mother, but I know that she looks down upon you now from the stars, and that she's proud of you. As I'm proud of you."

Elory rubbed away her tears. "How can you be proud of me? I'm not a warrior like Vale. I'm not a healer like our father. I'm not a leader as you are. I'm not a hero like Lucem. I'm not brave, not strong, not wise like all of you."

Meliora frowned. "I prefer hugging you, little sister. So don't make me clobber you." She kissed Elory's forehead again. "I could tell you that you are strong, brave, noble, heroic. But I don't need to. Because you prove these things yourself, every day and night, Elory. The harpies will soon arrive, and if we survive them, for many generations the Vir Requis will speak of your courage, and they will love you. As I love you, my sister. Always."

Elory shuddered and laid her head against Meliora's chest. "My courage? So why am I so afraid? I know you want to make our final stand here, to fight the harpies by our column. But I just want to run. To hide. That doesn't sound very brave to me."

"Will you run?" Meliora asked. "Will you hide?"

Elory shook her head vehemently. "I will never run from a fight. I will always fight with you, Meliora. You are my heroine, my leader, my light in the darkness."

"You are your own light, Elory. And a very bright one. And you are braver than I am, and you survived far greater hardships than I can imagine." Meliora squared her shoulders and raised her chin. "We will survive this too. The time comes upon us, only hours away. Our greatest battle. Our final battle. Ishtafel draws near."

Elory stepped back. "Then let's dig the last graves. The old dead will rest before more join them."

She shifted back into a dragon, sank her claws into the frozen soil, and began to dig a grave. Even using dragon claws, it was slow work, for the icy ground was hard as rock, and Elory strained to pull out each chunk.

She had dug three feet deep when the grave collapsed.

Frozen soil tumbled downward.

Elory gasped and stared. She let fire fill her mouth, lighting the shadows.

Meliora shifted into a dragon and peered down, lighting her own fire. "What is it?"

Elory blasted down a short burst of flame. The fire shot into the grave . . . and into darkness beyond.

"A tunnel," Elory whispered.

She returned to human form and made to leap inside.

"Wait," Meliora said. "We don't know if it's safe."

Elory smiled at her sister, tilting over the edge. "As safe as a sky full of harpies?"

"Fair enough." Meliora sighed. "Go on."

Elory jumped into the tunnel. Dust rained around her, and for a moment she coughed. At first she saw nothing. But when Meliora leaped into the tunnel, the half-seraph's halo of fire lit the darkness.

The tunnel walls were paneled with gray bricks. It was too narrow for a dragon but the perfect size for Elory and Meliora to stand abreast.

"What is this place?" Meliora whispered, looking around, her halo crackling and casting its dancing light.

"The fabled tunnels of Requiem!" Elory looked around with wide eyes. "I've heard of them. They say that the Vir Requis built these tunnels thousands of years ago, back in the Griffin Wars. In our stories in Tofet, we tell of the last Vir Requis survivors fleeing here from the griffins, of King Elethor fighting the cruel Solina here, and many other tales."

Meliora nodded, and her face hardened. "Ishtafel would talk of tunnels. He lost somebody here, they whispered in the palace. A lover. Only the chatter of slaves and soldiers. I asked Ishtafel once about the tunnels of Requiem, about what happened to him here. He grew very pale and very quiet, and he refused to say more, and so I knew it was true. This is the place where his beloved was slain." She placed her hand upon the brick wall. "Well, perhaps not this spot exactly, but somewhere here in the underground. This is a sad place."

"But also a place of wonder," said Elory, "if the tales are to be believed. They say that many old artifacts and books of Requiem were stored here." She squinted. "I see something. Come on!"

"Wait—" Meliora began, but Elory was already racing down the tunnel.

The tunnel stretched ahead, roughly a hundred yards, before opening up into a wide chamber. When Meliora stepped in after Elory, her halo cast its light.

Both sisters gasped.

"It's beautiful," Elory whispered, tears in her eyes.

"It's a library." Meliora's eyes widened. "A library of Vir Requis books."

The chamber was large as a temple's nave and lined with bookshelves. Countless books stood here. All were wrapped in green leather, and silver words appeared on their spines. Elory stepped deeper into the room and examined some of the books.

"They're stories." She touched a spine reverently. "The stories of Requiem. Of her old days and heroes. Books of tales.

Of songs. Of family lines." She spun toward Meliora. "Here is the greatest treasure of Requiem—all her lore. All those stories we would tell in Tofet were always missing pieces, but here is the full wealth of our nation's heritage. Do you know what this means, Meliora?"

Her sister nodded. Her voice was barely a whisper. "That we can rebuild not only our halls but our lore. That we can restore the culture we lost."

Elory spotted an archway leading into a second tunnel, and she began to walk. Meliora stepped forward and placed a hand on her shoulder.

"We don't have much time, Elory. He'll be here soon."

Elory nodded, head lowered. She ached to explore these tunnels, to find their many treasures, the heritage of her nation. But Meliora was right. Ishtafel and his harpies perhaps were slower than dragons, since they needed rest along the way, unable to fly on one another's backs, but they were relentless in their pursuit. They would be here within hours. There would be a time for rebuilding Requiem after defending it.

Elory was about to walk back with Meliora, to step out into the world, when a glint in the far tunnel caught her eye. Elory frowned.

"Just one moment," she said and darted forth.

She left the library behind, ran along the second tunnel, and entered another towering chamber. Her eyes widened and she gasped.

"Bloody stars," Elory whispered.

Meliora gasped. "Almost as beautiful as books."

It was an armory. Thousands of suits of armor hung from the walls, their silvery breastplates engraved with birch leaf motifs. Thousands of green shields hung alongside them, emblazoned with the Draco constellation in silver. Finally, countless swords gleamed on racks, their pommels shaped as dragonclaws clutching hilts.

"We need to get everyone in here," Elory whispered. "Now." She turned toward Meliora, and she saw that tears dampened her sister's eyes.

"My brother flies here, thinking he'll meet a band of ragged exiles." Meliora bared her teeth and clenched her fists. "He will meet the great Royal Army of old."

VALE

Dawn rose over Requiem, shining on a cleansed King's Column, a forest of birch leaves, and thousands of soldiers in armor.

Vale stood at their lead, wearing a full plate suit. Upon the breastplate were engraved three birch leaves, and his shield displayed the silver Draco constellation on a green field. At his side hung his sword, a heavy two-handed weapon with a dragonclaw hilt. Vale had never worn armor before, but it already felt like a second skin.

Like the second skin Ishtafel now wears, he thought, a bad taste in his mouth.

The Royal Army stood behind him, organized into the same units they had worked with back in Tofet. The bricklayers formed one brigade, the bitumen haulers another, and so on— thousands of laborers trained in ruthless discipline and strength, now soldiers.

At Vale's right-hand side stood Elory. The girl was short and slim, barely larger than a child, but she too wore armor and bore a sword. At Vale's left stood Lucem, the legendary hero who had first defied the seraphim, and he too wore steel.

"We fight with you, Vale," Lucem said, voice somber.

"Always," said Elory.

With them too stood Til Eleison, her long red hair blowing in the wind. One of only two Vir Requis who had avoided captivity and survived, she no longer wore her old patches of fur and rusted armor. Instead, she wore full plate armor, and stars adorned her shield. If anyone here was truly a warrior of Old Requiem, it was Til—she who had remained, who had survived, who had never stopped fighting for her nation.

"I fight with you, Vale Aeternum," she said, gazing into his eyes, her cheeks pale and strewn with freckles. "Ever have the

Eleisons fought alongside the Aeternum Dynasty, knights to the crown. Today let our old families fight together again."

Ahead of them rolled the forest of birches, silent, still. Even the wind had died, and the snow glimmered under the sunlight like a field of stars.

But soon they will be here, Vale thought. *Soon these trees will burn.*

He turned to look behind him, and he saw King's Column soaring there, three hundred feet tall, the chains gone, the blood washed off its marble. It shone in the dawn, purest white, unblemished. The heroes Kyrie Eleison and Agnus Dei, survivors of the griffins, had found this column rising from ruin thousands of years ago, and even then it had been ancient. Its capital was shaped as rearing dragons, carved of marble, and upon it perched a true white dragon—Meliora.

The heiress of Aeternum, half seraph but a true daughter of Requiem, seemed carved of marble herself, her scales shining. She gazed toward the south, watching, waiting. Above the white dragon, Issari's Star still shone, soon fading under the rising sunlight.

But Vale knew that Issari still watched over him. He remembered his death upon the ziggurat, remembered the Priestess in White descending from the heavens to heal him.

A great battle awaits you, she had told him. *Live.*

And Vale knew that here—here in this forest, under Issari's light, was the great battle he had survived for. The battle to save their column. To restore their sky.

Vale lowered his eyes and looked at his troops. Row after row of soldiers, all in armor, all bearing swords. All staring ahead. Waiting. Knowing that here, after all their struggles, their pain, that here was the battle of their lives. Elders stood here. Young men and women, some barely more than youths. Freed slaves. Proud defenders of their ancient realm.

Vale spoke to them, voice ringing across the silent forest.

"Children of Requiem! We stand in the light of our column. We stand upon holy ground, a free nation. Requiem restored. Yet an enemy flies forth to slay us, to shatter our column! For hundreds of years, this enemy enslaved us. And now we tell Ishtafel: We stand strong! We grew strong in the heat of Tofet. We remain strong in the cold of Requiem. Requiem lives, and we will always find our sky!"

Vale drew and raised his sword. Thousands of warriors drew their own blades, a new forest of steel. Farther back, behind the column, stood the civilians of Requiem, hundreds of thousands of them, and while they had no weapons, they raised their fists in salute.

Upon the column's capital, three hundred feet above the forest, Meliora tossed back her head and raised a pillar of white fire.

From the south rose a foul stench and evil cry.

Vale spun southward. His chest tightened and he gripped the hilt of his sword.

They're here.

He could not see them yet, but they were moving fast, their cries louder every moment. Hideous shrieks. The stench of rotting meat. The thud of oily wings. A sound like a storm.

"We smell them, sisters!" rose a distant cry among them.

"We smell the weredragons!"

"They hide in the forest!"

"They hide by their column!"

"Break them, snap them, eat them, drink them!"

The harpies cackled, screeched, cried out for blood and meat. Above them all rose a deeper voice. The voice of a man. Of a seraph. Of a god.

"I see you, Meliora!" rose the voice of Ishtafel. "I've come to take you home."

She is *home,* Vale thought. *We all are.*

He summoned his magic and rose as a dragon.

"Arise, dragons of Requiem!" he cried, soaring higher, emerging from the forest. "Today we fight. Today we die. A day of dragon's blood. A day of harpies crashing down. A day of sacrifice and victory. Requiem rises!"

And from across the forest, they rose. Their armor, shields, and swords morphed with them, melting into their dragon bodies; they would reappear with their human forms should the battle move to the ground. But even as dragons, they wore armor—great spiked helmets, massive breastplates, and heavy greaves found underground—the armor ancient but still strong. The dragons rose. Soldiers. Elders. Even children. Today all of Requiem was an army. Today no man, woman, or child would remain hidden from war.

Today Requiem rose in all her wrath.

Dragons darkened the sky and hid the sun.

Before them they flew, covering the south, swarming forth, a great nation of rot. A million harpies, buzzing, shrieking, spreading back for miles, each a beast devoted to murder, to the ripping of flesh, to the death of dragons. And before them all he flew, his armor burning bright in the dawn, casting back beams of light—a god of gold and steel, a god of beauty, of hatred, of death.

Ishtafel.

Here it begins, Vale thought. *The greatest battle of our lives. Perhaps the greatest battle in Requiem's thousands of bloody years.*

And it began.

The dragons stormed forth across the sky, soldiers in front, civilians behind, all roaring, wings beating in a storm. The harpies howled, charging, dripping rot, beating rancid wings.

"Fire!" Vale roared and blasted his dragonfire.

Across the front line, thousands of armored dragons—the vanguard, the Royal Army, the strongest in the nation—blasted forth a great curtain of flames, more fire than had ever burned above these woods. The great cloud of flame covered the sky, racing forth, a sea, a storm, a burning holocaust of Requiem's rage.

The harpies changed form, arranging themselves in a massive wall, a hundred beasts high. Their maws opened, lined with fangs, and they spewed their ice. The icicles shot forth, longer and sharper than lances, wreathed in fog.

Fire and ice slammed together.

The sky seemed to crack.

Steam blasted outward. Fire roared and showered down. Thousands of icicles made it through the inferno, dripping, and shrieked across the sky.

One icicle drove into a dragon at Vale's side, piercing the beast's neck. Where a dragon had been, a woman fell, head nearly severed. More icicles flew all around him. Dragons roared, lost their magic, and rained toward the forest. A shard of ice,

larger than a sword, scraped across Vale's side, chipping his
scales. He barely felt the pain.

"Burn them!" he shouted. "More fire!"

Countless icicles stormed toward him. The frozen fog
charged like a living beast.

Thousands of flaming jets streamed forth in reply.

The sky itself burned.

Water bubbled.

Steam burned dragons and they fell, clutching at their
blazing armor. More icicles slammed into dragons, tearing
through necks, chests, heads, ripping bellies open. Frost coated
other dragons, freezing scales, eyes, hearts. The bodies rained,
losing their magic in death. Hundreds of men and women fell,
cracking the frozen trees below them.

"Fire!" Vale shouted and blasted his flames.

Across the front line, the soldiers of Requiem—men and
women who for years had wielded pickaxes and borne baskets of
bitumen—blasted forth their dragonfire with the fury of the
southern sun. Elory, Lucem, Til, thousands of others—their fire
roared with his.

"Rise!" Vale cried. "Form a wall! *Wall!*"

The fire and ice again slammed together.

The dragons kept charging, rising higher, dipping lower,
forming a wall of dragons from the treetops to the heavens. The
hosts flew through the inferno of steam, smoke, fire, and ice and
slammed together like worlds colliding.

The sky cracked.

Trees shattered below.

All of Requiem shook.

Within an instant, the front lines mashed together, each
force driving into the other. Harpies crashed through dragons.
Talons drove forth, longer than swords, ripping through scales,
cracking dragon ribs, digging out innards. Wrinkled, warty heads
spun around Vale, sprouting serpents. Rotted mouths opened,
and fangs dug into dragons. The harpies laughed as they fought,
tugged out organs, fed upon the wetness, fought again, coated in
blood.

Vale roared. He fought like he had never fought. Not over
the City of Kings, not in the inferno of Tofet, not in his many

battles journeying here had Vale fought with such fury, seen such bloodshed. He bellowed, crying out to his stars, blasting his fire. His flames washed over harpies. His tail swung into their wrinkly gray flesh. His claws tore open their breastplates and the skin beneath, and snakes fled their innards.

They hurt him. Their fog washed across him, freezing his scales. Their talons scraped across his dragon-armor, denting the steel. Their snakes bit into his belly, and their shards of ice pierced his armor. Yet though he bled, Vale kept roaring, kept fighting, kept burning them down.

All around him, the multitudes fought—a great song in the sky, a song of death, of shadow, of light, of rot, of fear, of ascension. Ice and fire danced together. Dragons and harpies rose to the heavens and fell like rain.

And all through the battle, he shone above, laughing, wings spread out—the god of gold and steel, the god of light, the lord of hosts, the King of Saraph and destroyer of Requiem. Ishtafel of the Thirteenth Dynasty. Burned. Rebuilt. His voice ringing across the sky, rising to a shriek, inhuman, the voice of crashing empires and drowning children, of shattering forests and shattering nations.

"Here I capture you, dragons!" he cried. "Here I slay you. Here I shatter your column. Here Requiem will fall, here she will fade from all memory. Slay them, harpies! Slay them all and feed upon them."

The world trembled and the sky wept. The forest burned. The nation of Requiem had fled here to find new life; here they would find a rededication of their kingdom or a death in battle. Here they all fought—from elders to children—and their fire rose together in crackling pillars, as bright as the marble column that rose behind them.

LUCEM

He wanted this to be a dream.

Just a fever dream in his cave.

He missed that cave now. He missed his wooden friends, his drawings on the wall, the river, the birds, the loneliness. This had to be just a nightmare. This could not be real.

And yet still they flew around him. Countless dragons and harpies, blowing fire and ice. The faces seemed to float around Lucem: the bloated, wrinkled faces of crones, covered in warts, snakes on their heads, hissing at him, leering at him, mocking him.

You will dance with us forever, Lucem. You will be as we are.

Fear—overwhelming, all-consuming, colder than the icy fog of the creatures—washed over Lucem. His red scales clattered as he shook. Dragons died around him. Men, women, children—they all fell, breaking upon the trees of King's Forest. A carpet of the dead.

Lucem tried to blow his fire, to kill the harpies, but he could barely even breathe.

I have to run, he thought. *I have to land in the forest, to run between the trees, to hide, to escape this place, to return to my cave.*

A harpy streamed above him, and Lucem ducked, cringed, blasted his fire. A dragon stormed forth, crashing into the beast. Thousands of others fought all around him, slamming together, blood and fire and ice surrounding them.

I'm not a hero, Lucem thought. *I've never been a hero. All I did was escape Tofet. All I did was flee.*

Now he just wanted to flee again.

Another harpy drove forward, grabbed a young dragon, and tore her apart. Scaly limbs fell, becoming human again before they hit the trees. The girl still lived, limbless and screaming, until the harpy ripped into the torso. Three more harpies stormed downward, and their talons thrust, piercing the chests of dragons that rose to meet them, emerging from their scaly backs.

Lucem dipped lower in the sky.

He flew down to hover over the treetops.

I can run between the trees. I can escape. I can hide.

He trembled. He had survived one tragedy before. He had been the only Vir Requis to have fled the seraphim, to have found safety, found life. Here was just more death, more disaster, and he could flee this time too, he could again be the one who made it out. He could find a new cave here, maybe make his way south and return to his old cave, or—

A cry above, high and pained, tore through his thoughts.

He stared above and saw her there, fighting above him, a slender lavender dragon blowing yellow fire.

Elory.

And she was hurt.

A harpy talon had scratched her leg, and her blood dripped. Several of the rancid beasts surrounded Elory now, reaching out more talons. The lavender dragon spurted her fire and swung her tail, struggling to hold them back.

Lucem's fear vanished under a wave of guilt.

I abandoned my people ten years ago. I will not do it again. I will never more leave those I love.

He howled and soared.

His fire blazed skyward.

Several harpies dived down to meet him. Their wings spread wide, dripping disease. They had no arms, but their talons stretched down, massive and gleaming. Their shrieks tore at his ears.

I fought dark seraphim. I slew archangels and a massive bird the size of a mountain. And I will slay these beasts.

His dragonfire slammed into one harpy, igniting the foul creature's feathers. Lucem curved his flight, dodging reaching talons. One harpy managed to slam into him, and her teeth dug into Lucem's shoulder. The snakes on her head bit too. Lucem roared and clawed at the wrinkled, feathered skin, tore the creature off, and blasted his fire.

The harpy fell, and Lucem kept rising. His tail whipped around him, knocking back other harpies; each of the creatures was larger than him.

"Elory!" he cried.

She still fought two harpies, and several of her scales were missing. Lucem roared out dragonfire, torching one of the creatures attacking her. The massive beast, half crone and half vulture, blazed and screeched, a great firebird. Elory blew her own flames, burning the second harpy. Their tails whipped side by side, knocking the creatures through the sky.

Harpies fell around them, and the two dragons roared, back to back. Around them, countless harpies and dragons still flew.

"Elory, are you all right?" he shouted, looking over his shoulder at her.

"You mean besides facing a million harpies? Yes, splendid!"

I love that dragon more than life, Lucem thought. *I will never leave her. I would die for her.*

"Ready to kill those million harpies?" he said. "Just you and me! It'll be romantic."

Elory blasted out fire at one of the creatures, knocking it back in the sky. "Shouldn't we leave some for the others?"

"To the Abyss with them." Lucem raised his claws, and his wings beat back clouds of icy fog. "Half a million for me, half a million for you. Let's keep score!"

They roared and flew together, charging into the enemy.

Dragons fell around them. Countless harpies hid the sky, driving toward them, flying in from all sides, shattering the forest, shattering the sky.

And Lucem knew that he would die here.

He knew that this was real, not a nightmare, but that Requiem herself had always been a dream, a brief moment of wonder, a reality they could never claim.

Requiem lived for a day, he thought. *And I am proud to die for her. A single day here in our land, fighting by Elory, is worth ten thousand days in a cave.*

The icicles slammed into him. The fog froze his wings, and the leathern membranes tore when he tried to flap them.

Talons tore at his dragon armor, and more harpies kept attacking, and more dragons kept falling. Elory cried out at his side, overcome by the creatures, her fire down to sparks, her claws bloody, her armor cracked.

"I love you, Elory," he said, blood on his scales, tears in his eyes.

"I love you, Lucem." She wept as she fought. "Always. In this Requiem and the Requiem beyond the stars."

The harpies slammed into Lucem, laughing, ripping at his scales, at his flesh, eating, drinking him. Great jaws closed around his leg, and pain washed over him. A dozen more harpies crashed into him, and he tried to claw them, and the teeth sank deeper into his leg.

It's here.

He convulsed, crying out.

This is the end. My death.

"Elory!" he cried. "Elory, look away. I love you. I lo—"

The jaws snapped shut tightly around his leg, tugging back, ripping off the limb, exposing and snapping the bone.

Lucem screamed.

He fell as a man.

Terror pulsed through him, but relief too. It was over. It was over . . .

His eyes darkened. He caught just a glimpse of lavender scales, of sputtering fire, heard Elory calling him . . . but then the harpies flowed across her, and she vanished in their cloud of feathers. And then Lucem saw and heard nothing more.

I love you, Elory. I love you more than Requiem and more than the sky.

He could no longer summon his magic. He could no longer fly. But he had found the sky of Requiem. He had flown in his kingdom for a day, flown with a woman he loved.

I will see you again, Elory, I know that I—

JAREN

Around him, they fell.

In the sky of their home, they died. The children of Requiem. Thousands falling like the rain.

Jaren flew through the battle, an old green dragon, scarred, weary, an old soul who had seen too much. Too much loss. Too much pain. Too much grief.

I was a healer, but how can I heal this? How can I heal a breaking nation?

The dragons fought around him, calling out hoarsely, sputtering their last sparks of fire. They fell around him, more and more. On the trees below they lay—butchered men, women, children. Babies, dead in the snow. Eyes staring skyward.

Lost.

Gone.

"I'm sorry," Jaren whispered. "I'm sorry I led you here. I'm sorry for everything."

They should have waited. They should have languished longer in chains. They could have lived. They had chased Requiem, and they had found their homeland—but only to die. Only a cursed victory. Only to perish so soon, to fall as bones onto the forest.

Live, Queen Gloriae had told him in his dream. *Live, son of Aeternum.*

Jaren reared in the sky, clawing at a harpy. He swiped his tail at another beast, suffering a gash to his side. More dragons fell around him, not soldiers now, mere children.

"What did I live for?" Jaren cried. "Why did you guide us here, stars? Only for death?"

He stared up at the sky, seeking those stars, but could see nothing but the harpies, their burning white eyes, their rotted wings, their hair of serpents. The sky was lost.

Jaren sneered and bared his fangs.

Then we will fight without our sky. We must survive.

"Requiem!" he bellowed. "Requiem, into the tunnels! The sky is lost. Fly down, fly down, into the underground!"

Around Jaren, they began to descend. Cut, frozen, some of them dying, thousands of dragons glided toward the forest. During the long night, waiting for the harpies, the Vir Requis had discovered three entrances to the catacombs beneath Requiem. Jaren now flew toward one opening—a stone archway half-hidden in soil, shaped as two rearing dragons, their top claws touching. Through the archway, a tunnel plunged underground. He landed, remained in dragon form, and cried out to the others.

"Vir Requis, into the tunnels! We fight underground. Soldiers—help the women and children in!"

Armored dragons roared above, blasting fire toward the setting sun, holding back the harpies. They formed a corridor of steel and scale, allowing the civilians—the older or younger dragons, no armor on them—to glide down to the forest.

The first dragon swooped toward the archway. Only yards away, a harpy burst between the trees, slammed into the dragon, and tore him apart. The dragon crashed onto the forest floor and returned to human form—an old greybeard. The harpy feasted on his flesh. Jaren plowed forward and blasted his fire, slamming the flames against the harpy, knocking the creature back, burning it until it fell.

"Requiem, to the tunnels!" he cried.

More dragons descended. A pair of young ones—no larger than horses—reached the forest floor and shifted into a boy and girl. They ran toward the archway.

Another harpy swooped. Jaren roared and shot upward, beating his wings, and knocked into the beast. Its hair of serpents bit him. Its teeth sank into his shoulder. Jaren blasted dragonfire, burning the creature, burning himself, shoving it back. He glanced down to see the boy and girl race into the tunnels, and more dragons kept diving.

Many nights among the huts of Tofet, Jaren had guided souls into death. Now he stood in a new land, guiding his people to life. One by one they descended. Broken. Limbs missing.

Bleeding. Some nearly frozen, pierced with icicles, skin white with frost. They stumbled into the tunnels beneath Requiem, seeking shelter from the storm.

And that storm roared with all its fury. The harpies seemed endless. For every one felled, ten dragons crashed down. They covered the sky. They swarmed through the forest, shattering trees. Their rot flowed across the land, and their cries shook the world. They danced around King's Column, hundreds of them, human limbs in their mouths, clutching severed heads in their talons. The Royal Army crumbled before them. Dragons crashed down, becoming men and women. Massive breastplates and helmets, the armor of dragons, slammed onto the trees. Dragonfire faded, and ice coated the world.

"Into the tunnels!" Jaren cried, voice hoarse, guiding them in. One by one. Children. Women. Wounded soldiers. A few other dragons stood with him, blasting fire, guarding the way in.

But more harpies attacked every moment.

They descended in the darkness, blowing their ice. The eyes of countless snakes blazed red in the night. The harpies flowed forth, ten emerging from the shadows for every one slain.

"They enter their tunnels, my harpies!" rose a voice above, and light flared through the darkness. "They flee underground like the cowardly maggots that they are. Shatter their hole! Slay them all."

The light grew brighter, blinding. A sickly halo blazed. Through the frozen fog he descended, wreathed in ice, his featherless wings spread wide. He wore a suit of gilded iron, not mere armor but a new skin, and a golden mask hid the ruined face within. In one hand, he held his lance, the blade bloody. In the other hand, he held a shield emblazoned with an eye within a sunburst.

He descended toward the tunnel, harpies dancing around him and cackling and snapping their teeth. Dragons fled before the unholy host. Ishtafel's lance thrust as he glided down, piercing a young dragon, then casting a girl toward the trees.

As Ishtafel landed before the tunnel, Jaren sneered. Still in dragon form, he walked up toward the seraph, placing the tunnel's entrance behind him.

"An aging, scarred dragon with sad eyes." Ishtafel's eyes, visible through the holes in his mask, crinkled with delight. "I do believe I stand before Jaren Aeternum, Priest of Requiem, the old man I knew from Tofet. The man who bedded my whore of a mother."

Jaren raised his head. He barely had any more fire to breathe. He was so weary he nearly lost his dragon form. But he let the last sparks fill his jaws, and he sneered, revealing his fangs.

"Your rule over Requiem has ended, Ishtafel." Jaren raised his spiked tail like a scorpion. "You will leave this hallowed ground. Return to your banishment across the sea, and never more set foot on our ancient land. Leave now, accursed one! Leave or you will burn in Requiem's fire."

Ishtafel spread out his arms, and his golden halo turned an ugly crimson color, crackling almost like fire. "Oh, but Requiem's fire has already burned me, peeling away my skin, my weakness, leaving me stronger, turning me into a god of gold and steel and retribution. But yes, weredragon king. I will leave this frozen land, and I will return to my palace in the south, but not before I cleanse my empire of weredragons. This place you call Requiem will be renamed Harash Es, land of the harpies. It will be their domain, and your bones will decorate their halls."

Ishtafel raised his lance—the lance that had slain countless Vir Requis. That had slain Jaren's wife, the kind Nala, the love of Jaren's life. With his other hand, Ishtafel raised his shield, and the eye engraved upon it blazed with light, and the sunburst crackled with true fire. The seraph rose several feet above the ground, and the air stormed around him with flame and ice, and the harpies danced. Dragons fled before the apparition.

"You have come here to your death, Ishtafel!" Jaren shouted over the storm. The frozen winds buffeted him. The flames burned him. But still the green dragon reared, hind feet on the soil of Requiem, front claws raised. "I offered you banishment. Now I will offer you only death. I am a priest, yes. And I am a healer. But I am also a warrior of starlight, a soldier of Requiem, an heir to a line of kings. Do not be fooled by my cracked scales, nor the grayness of my snout, nor the weight of many years upon me. I have shed the blood of many enemies.

Now I shall spill your blood on the soil of my ancestors and my children."

Lightning cleaved the sky, lighting the flying harpies and dragons. Thunder boomed. Rain came crashing down.

With a howl and blaze of light, Ishtafel charged.

Jaren leaped up to meet him.

The lance thrust, and Jaren swiped it aside with his claws. He blasted all the dragonfire that remained in him.

The blaze slammed into Ishtafel, white and blue in the center, flaring out to red. The flames washed across the seraph's armor, and Ishtafel laughed. His shield swung in an arc, ringed with light.

The metal disk slammed into Jaren's ribs with the force of a charging chariot.

Jaren heard a rib crack.

He fell to his side, lost his magic for an instant, returned to a man, then shifted into a dragon again in time to swipe aside another thrust of the lance. Above in the sky, the harpies held back any dragons who tried to fly near. Ishtafel and Jaren, King of Saraph and Priest of Requiem, battled in a cocoon of ice and steam.

"Already you fall, old one!" Ishtafel laughed. "And you are the great warrior guarding the halls of reptiles? You will die now, Aeternum, and die knowing this: the others will follow. Your son. Your daughters. All your people. I will slay them as I slew your wife."

Jaren roared and beat his wings. He charged toward Ishtafel, no more fire in his maw, but his claws lashed and teeth snapped.

And they fought.

It was not a dance, not a thing of grace and beauty like the duels of the young. Jaren's bones were too old, Ishtafel's flesh too raw. They were a beast of scales and a monster of metal. Clunky. Crying out hoarsely. Claws cut at armor, peeling back the gilt to reveal the steel within. Shield and lance slammed into scales, cracking them, cutting skin and muscle, shedding blood. Fire spurted and light flared and all around the harpies danced and sang and dragons died.

"She squealed like a hog in heat when I slew her." Ishtafel swung his shield, slamming it again into Jaren, cracking more scales, snapping another rib. "Your whore of a wife. Are you ready to meet her?"

Jaren tried to cut Ishtafel, but his claws only scraped against the seraph's armor, denting but not cracking the steel. The lance thrust into a wound on Jaren's shoulder, digging deeper into him.

Jaren lost his magic.

He fell to his knees, a man again, clad in burlap, his hair graying. Just an old priest.

"Yes," Ishtafel said, gliding down to place his feet on the ground. "Kneel before me, slave. Die like the rest of you will die."

I fly to join you now, Nala, he thought, burning in the glare of the unholy halo. *I rise now to our starlit halls, where I will fly forever at your side, my wife.*

Ishtafel hefted his lance and placed the tip against Jaren's chest.

"Will you beg me for your life, old man? Or will you simply squeal and weep as I take it?"

Jaren raised his eyes, but he did not look at the seraph. He stared beyond the light, beyond the cloud of harpies. In the distance, he saw them—thousands of dragons diving down, landing outside another entrance to the tunnels, the hole in the valley Elory had uncovered.

"Keep fighting, my children," Jaren whispered. "Fight them always. The world is good. The world is beautiful. Fight for it."

The lance drove forth.

The blade pierced Jaren's chest and emerged from his back.

Above him the smoke and ice seemed to part, and he saw them. The stars of his forebears. Not only the Draco constellation but millions of other stars, other lights, the souls of Vir Requis from the first king to his fallen wife. Waiting for him. Shining upon him.

Goodbye, my children, Jaren thought. *I love you. I love you always.*

The lance pulled back, and Jaren flew, rising, all his pain gone, until he saw nothing but starlight.

ISHTAFEL

Glory.

It was glory distilled, pure, sweeter than wine. A song of triumph. His greatest victory.

He was glad to have let the weredragons linger this long. He could have slain them in Tofet, but he had let them suffer. Let them dream. Let them flee here. Let them hope, feel some joy before the pain. What a fine place to end their race! Here, in sight of their precious column, he finally was slaying them, and here their bones would forever remain.

"See this death, Meliora!" he shouted. "Do you see how they die? I slew your father! Do you see?"

He laughed, lifted the corpse of the priest over his head, and tossed it into the air. Harpies grabbed the old man and ripped into the flesh, digging, feasting.

"See them tear your father apart!" he cried, laughing. "Hear the screams of those who still die. You will be the last, Meliora! The last weredragon. I will drag you back to my palace, but not before you hear every last scream."

Yet his sister did not answer. He beat his wings, rose higher, and scanned the sky, yet he could not see her. The coward must have fled into the tunnels. The worms hid there, as they had centuries ago. He had defeated them then in the darkness, and he would defeat them now.

"Come, my harpies!" He pointed his bloody lance at the archway leading into the tunnel. "Into the shadows."

He advanced toward the archway, walking over the frosted soil. He was only yards away when one's head emerged from within—a dragon lying in the tunnel, barely fitting, blowing dragonfire. Around Isthafel, harpies shrieked and fled the flames, but Ishtafel kept walking, shield held before him. The dragonfire slammed into the disk, melting the metal, heating his armor, but Ishtafel had been burned by dragonfire before. It could no longer hurt him. His pain was purified, his soul impossible to burn. He walked through the fire and thrust his lance, shoving it down the dragon's mouth and throat.

The beast lost its magic, returning to a man inside the tunnel, dead upon the lance. Ishtafel tugged his weapon free and entered the darkness.

And there again, after all this time—they awaited him.

The weredragons.

The beasts who had slain his lover.

"I return to you now," Ishtafel whispered, "to finish what I began here five hundred years ago."

The weredragons stood in human form, clad in their ancient armor, bearing swords. They howled and charged toward him, and Ishtafel danced.

He fought as he had never fought before. He was immortal, but his wounds had slowed him down, and his armor weighed heavily upon him, but his five hundred years of war had given him a ruthless expertise in killing. He beat his wings, rose to the top of the tunnel, and thrust his lance downward, skewering a man. His shield swung, the sharp edge tearing through helmets and skulls. The weredragons attacked him, lashing their swords, but the blades bounced off his armor, and his shield cut them down.

The tunnel was narrow; only three of the weredragons could fight abreast. He moved down the corridor, stepping on their corpses, slaying them as he had so many years ago—as he and Reehan had cut them together.

I still fight for you, Reehan.

In his memories, she seemed to float beside him, smiling as she slew, beautiful in the darkness, his lioness of Edinnu.

We will slay the reptiles together, my love!

Her voice echoed across the centuries, and her grin stretched at her cheeks, toothy, bright, her eyes shining with bloodlust and love for him.

"I still love you, Reehan," Ishtafel whispered as he shoved his lance through a mother and her babe, piercing them both with one blow. "I still fight our war."

Behind him, the harpies entered the tunnel too. They were so large they could only walk single file, hunched over, knees bent, their wings pulled close to their sides. When Ishtafel glanced over his shoulder, he saw their wrinkled, warty faces in the darkness, large as wagons, hissing and dripping saliva. Their bloated bodies scraped against the walls, boils bursting. Their mouths opened, and they shot icicles around Ishtafel, narrowly missing him and hitting weredragons ahead.

They moved deeper into the tunnels. The labyrinth soon split into many paths, and the harpies flowed down them all, biting, freezing, cutting, eating their enemies. Ishtafel had not been here for most of his life, yet he still remembered every twist and turn; he had been walking these tunnels in his dreams since that war long ago. He passed through chambers, mostly barren, a few still containing ancient metal vessels. A dragon roared in the library, not daring to blow fire and burn the books. Ishtafel beat his wings, rose high, and thrust his lance, piercing the creature's neck, sending it crashing down as a woman. The tunnels delved deeper, and soon Ishtafel passed a makeshift nursery, mothers and babes cowering in the shadows. He stabbed them as they begged. He moved onward, the harpies heeling him, feeding upon the corpses he made.

Five hundred years ago, I feared you, weredragons, Ishtafel thought as he stabbed a soldier, casting the man down. *No more.*

He gritted his teeth. He should have done this ages ago. Finally, after centuries, he faced his old demons. And he slew them. Each weredragon dead was another nightmare gone. Each corpse was redemption for his soul. He laughed as he fought that old war again, and always Reehan danced in his memories, fighting beside him as a spirit, eyes and smile bright.

They plunged deeper, and the tunnels grew narrow. Here were the darkest depths of Requiem.

Here is where she died.

The spirit of Reehan seemed to grow brighter at his side, but her smile died, and she cried out in pain. An astral sword cut through her, and she flickered . . . fading . . . becoming but a shadow.

Ishtafel raised his dripping lance, chest heaving, staring around at the craggy stone walls. It was here—this very place, this very spot where he stood. Here that she had died.

A tremble seized him. Suddenly Ishtafel could not breathe, and his wounds—the horrible burns that spread beneath his metal skin—blazed in agony, as if Tash were again bathing him with dragonfire. His heart pounded in his ears. Harpies crowded behind him, shrieking, licking their lips, sucking up last gobbets of flesh.

"I will finish this," Ishtafel hissed, lance trembling in his grip. "It ends here and now."

Several weredragon children cowered before him. He roared and ran toward them.

MELIORA

The forest burned below her.

The sky above froze.

The column rose through an inferno, a single tor in a sea of blood and death and light and shadow.

It ends here, Meliora thought as she flew through the storm. *In darkness our nation falls and our column cracks.*

The wind buffeted her, and she barely saw any more dragons flying. But the harpies were everywhere. Laughing. Feasting. Dancing in the dark sky. A million torturous creations, the bane of dragons.

"It was but a dream," Meliora whispered, flying through the storm of wind and rot. "We were but fools dreaming, praying, wishing for something that could never be. A dream that lasted but a day. And now it ends." Tears filled her eyes, and her fire blasted out, a white pillar piercing the clouds.

For thousands of years, we fought against those who rose up to destroy us, Meliora thought. *For thousands of years, we fell, burned, died . . . and rose again. In our primordial forests, we faced the rocs and the demons, and we withstood them. In our golden age, the griffins slew us, leaving only seven alive . . . yet we defeated our enemies, and we rose again. The phoenixes burned us in our halls, crumbling our cities, and we survived them, and we rebuilt. War after war, enemy after enemy, genocide after genocide, we rose again and again, never dying, remembering always our column. Remembering our sky. Remembering our name: Requiem.*

"Yet now it ends," she whispered. "Now this dream of a day—this dream of thousands of years—ends in ice."

They had never faced so many enemies—a million beasts covering the land, slaying all in their path. An enemy too strong for them. For here were no monsters, no demons, no men leading flying beasts—here were deities. Cruel immortals of Edinnu, beings of unholy gods.

Meliora lowered her head, ashamed of the ichor that flowed through her veins, for she was half of Edinnu, and that cruel blood burned her.

"I renounce you, Saraph!" she cried to the sky, rising through a storm of harpies, knocking them back with her tail and claws. "I renounce you, Eight Gods! I defy you, Ishtafel! I am Meliora Aeternum. I am an heiress of Requiem. I will fight for my column, for my people, for my stars."

She flew higher, faster, bursting through the enemies, rising through the clouds, until the sky opened up above her, dark and brilliant. And there they shone—the stars of Requiem. The Draco constellation. The gods of Requiem who had forever blessed the Vir Requis, who had given Meliora's people the strength to rise again and again, to overcome tragedy after tragedy.

The dragon's eye shone, and Meliora thought that she could hear a soft, high voice speak inside her.

Requiem is eternal.

"Requiem is eternal," Meliora whispered. "The line of Aeternum will never fall." She sneered and narrowed her eyes. "Not on my watch. Not so long as I draw breath."

She stared down toward the battle, and she saw that thousands of harpies were streaming into the tunnels like ants into a hive, forming three lines.

The tunnels of Requiem.

Meliora growled.

The place that had always haunted Ishtafel.

In her childhood, Meliora had heard Ishtafel screaming in his sleep, crying of weredragons in the tunnels. The guards and slaves would whisper of the ichor that had spilled there. Vir Requis told tales of Ishtafel slaying the king of Requiem in the darkness. Statues of Reehan—the great Lioness of Edinnu—still stood in the palace.

There Requiem's long night began, Meliora thought. *There it will end.*

Smoke blasting through her nostrils, Meliora swooped.

Harpies rose to meet her. She breathed her white fire, a humming pillar, a twin to King's Column, burning them down. Her claws tore through their flesh, severing the snakes on their heads. She kept diving. Her fire trailed across the land, burning trees, melting snow, melting boulders, crumpling seraphim like ants under a magnifying glass. Her flames exposed an archway leading into the tunnels, and Meliora dived down, roaring.

Her claws touched the ground, and her fire died down. At once harpies leaped toward her, each as large as her. Their talons reached out, cutting her scales. Meliora bellowed and reared, claws raised to her stars. She lashed her tail. She bit deep, tearing them apart, scattering their flesh. Their blood coated her, and she blew fire skyward.

"Requiem is eternal!" she cried.

Across the sky, the last few dragons who still fought echoed her cry. "Requiem is eternal! Fight for Requiem!"

Til Eleison still flew, an orange dragon blasting spinning flames. Vale flew higher above, rallying the last survivors, his claws bloody. But there were so few to rally. So little hope remained.

Surrounded by the corpses of harpies, Meliora released her magic. In her human form, she no longer wore the fine kalasiri and jewels of a princess. Nor did she wear the rough burlap and shackles of a slave. This night she stood in the ancient armor of Requiem, her breastplate engraved with the holy birch leaves, her green shield inlaid with silver stars. She drew her ancient longsword, the fabled Amerath, sword of her ancestor, Prince Relesar Aeternum.

If I die, I die free. I die as a warrior of Requiem.

She raced into the tunnels.

She ran through darkness.

She ran through a nightmare of harpies, her sword swinging, cutting into them. Hers was an ancient blade, the sword of Relesar himself, forged in dragonfire. The harpies were clumsy in the tunnels, unable to turn around, and Meliora was fast, agile, leaping between the chambers, her sword flashing. Once she would skip through the halls of a palace, but today she moved through darker, holier halls, the chambers of her true people. Today she filled these halls with the death of her enemies. Her halo crackled above her head, woven of fire, and the blood of her enemies coated her blade and armor.

"Requiem is eternal!" she cried out.

Across the tunnels, her fellow Vir Requis answered her call. "Requiem is eternal!"

They fought together, moving through the shadows. Many fell. The corpses of thousands fed the harpies. But still Meliora fought on.

Meliora did not know if her family still lived. She had not seen her father or sister since the first assault a night and day ago. But she knew that Requiem still lived—within those who still fought with her, within her own breast. Her blood perhaps was mixed but her heart was pure, and her sword sang but one song—a song of dragons.

She kept moving, stepping over corpses of Vir Requis and harpies, passing the armory, the library, the wine cellars, finally entering the deepest passageways, places where no foot had stepped for centuries.

And there ahead, cloaked in shadows and drenched in blood, he stood.

Her brother.

Ishtafel.

He stood over a pile of dead children, his back toward her. As Meliora stepped into the chamber, she saw him drive down his spear, slaying a girl. Only one child still lived here now—a little boy cowering in the corner. Just a single soul among so much death.

"Ishtafel!" Meliora said.

He tugged his lance free from the dead girl. Slowly, he turned toward her, armor creaking. No, not armor—new skin of metal to replace the true skin Tash had burned off. In the holes of his golden mask, his eyes narrowed in amusement. His wings spread out, dripping rot.

"Hello, my dear sister."

She trembled, but she forced herself to step forward, to raise her chin. A child still lived here. She would save him. She would save whoever she still could, even if it were just one soul.

"Ishtafel," she said. "As a daughter of Aeternum, as an heiress to Requiem, I banish you from this place. Leave now. Leave this land and I will spare your life." Meliora raised her sword, forcing herself to stare steadily into his eyes. "This is Amerath, the Amber Sword, the ancestral blade of my line, which slew many of my people's enemies. Retreat to the south lest it slay you too."

She did not wish him a life in luxury. She did not wish him to fester in the south, growing his forces. But Meliora knew that she could not defeat him. He was too strong, his forces too great. She could only hope against hope to scare him away, as a cat might scare a larger predator by bristling.

But Ishtafel only laughed.

"Your father offered me the same deal." He snorted. "The fool Jaren, the brute who had bedded our mother. Do you know how I answered him?" He hefted his lance. "With this blade." He stepped closer to Meliora, and his voice dropped to a dangerous hiss. "I carved him up, and I fed his corpse to the harpies."

Meliora stared at him, and the tunnels seemed to collapse around her.

Her heart seemed to stop beating.

Her world seemed to die.

No. Oh stars, no.

"It's true," Ishtafel said, as if able to read her thoughts. He tilted his head. "I just realized this means I killed both your parents. Interesting, isn't it?"

No. Stars, no.

Meliora's chest shook. She had to force herself to draw breath. Her eyes dampened. She knew he was telling the truth. She had always been able to tell when Ishtafel was lying.

My father is dead.

She wanted to rage. To scream. To race forward, swing her sword, cut him down.

But she could only force herself to whisper. "Why?" Her tears flowed. "Why, Ishtafel? You loved me once. I loved you. We played in the gardens. You read me stories. I rode on your back, and you taught me how to fish and . . . why do you do these things? Who have you become?"

He stepped closer to her. He now stood only a couple feet away. He towered above her, so much larger, made of metal and wounds.

"I am who I've always been," he said. "Who I've been for centuries. Long before you were born, I fought the weredragons in these tunnels. I stand now in the very place where Reehan died, where I vowed to enslave and torture the creatures. When you were a child, Meliora, I played with you in the gardens, then returned to slaughtering the barbarians of the east. I read you stories, then flew south to battle the giants. You never knew the true me. Not until you became a woman. And you are a woman now, and you know me, and we're going back home. Both of us. Never to return to Requiem. You will be my wife, Meliora, and we will rule the empire together."

She shook her head. "No."

He placed a hand on her shoulder. "We can end this, Meliora. We can end this war now, this youthful rebellion of yours. I am willing to forgive you. For many days now, I vowed to drag you home in chains. To sever your limbs and feed them to the harpies. To keep your torso and head in a cell, to impregnate you again and again, to keep you bringing me heirs for millennia. But I was wrathful. I am willing to forgive, to spare you that fate. To love you again. To see you love me as you once did. We can be as we were, my sister. To live again in the ziggurat. To play in the gardens. To laugh. To read stories. And to rule, to see our heirs rule."

Meliora trembled. She could end this. She could stop this war, this death. She could go home.

I can be as I once was, she thought. *A princess. A pampered girl who knows nothing of war, of death, of slavery, of conquest. I can sleep again in my old bed, and I can have my beloved brother back. All this can become but a bad dream.*

A small voice resisted inside her, but what choice did she have? To fight him? She would lose. To resist him? He would imprison her again, and this time there would be no Tash to save her.

She wanted to say yes. She wanted to forget all this pain, this death, this whole world outside of her palace.

But she still saw the starlight.

And still that voice whispered in her mind.

Requiem is eternal.

"No," Meliora whispered. "No, we cannot be as we were. You changed, Ishtafel. You're no longer a prince of seraphim. You've become a monster of metal. When you cut off my wings, you thought to hurt me, to shame me, but you purified me. I am no longer a seraph. I am no longer your sister. I can never be what I was, a beautiful princess in a palace. I am Vir Requis. I am the singer of an ancient song. I am a leaf in a forest of birches. I am heiress to a legacy too great, too holy, too strong for you to understand. Requiem's roots run deeper than you can reach, and though you may take our lives, you cannot silence our song. Requiem is eternal. I will fight for her, and I will die for her if I must."

His eyes narrowed, blazing with rage. "I will not allow you to die."

She raised her sword. "But I will allow you to."

He shouted and thrust his lance toward her.

Halo crackling, Meliora swung her blade, parrying the attack.

There was no room in this narrow chamber to become a dragon, not without the walls crushing her. Here Meliora would fight as a woman, bearing the ancient blade of her people.

"We once danced in a ballroom," Ishtafel said. "Now we dance with blades."

And they danced.

In the darkness underground, in the place where his lover had died, in Requiem—they danced.

Meliora had been a warrior for a season; Ishtafel had slain enemies for centuries. She was no match for him. She knew this. She could not defeat the seraph who had cleansed the world of so many. But she fought him nonetheless. She fought him for her kingdom. She fought him for the memory of her father. She fought him for Tash, slain in war. For her mother, slain in slavery. For sixty thousand decimated over the City of Kings, for countless more slain here in Requiem. For her stars. For the hopes and memories of an ancient race. For one child who cowered in the corner. For them all, she swung her sword, parrying his lance again and again, thrusting her blade, trying to kill him, knowing she could not.

Across Requiem, she knew, the great war still raged. And she knew that Requiem, like her, no longer had hope. That all dragons would perish under the harpies, as she would perish underground. And here—here in this chamber beat the heart of the war. A seraph. A Vir Requis. Brother. Sister. Master. Slave. Blade and blade. The old dance of her people.

His lance thrust, cracking the armor on her arm, cutting open the flesh, revealing the innards.

Meliora screamed and lashed her blade, slamming it against Ishtafel, but she could not dent his steel.

His lance thrust again, cutting through her armor, piercing her thigh. She cried out and nearly fell, swung her sword, knocked his lance aside, and brought her blade down hard onto his arm. Yet the steel would not even dent.

Again he attacked, this time swinging his shield. The sharp edge slammed into Meliora, cleaving through her steel armor as if it were tin, cutting into her side under the ribs. She cried out, voice weaker now, her blood dripping down her thigh and arm. His lance struck yet again, scraping across her cheek, and pain blazed, and more of her blood spilled.

"The blood of weredragons mixed with the ichor of the immortals," Ishtafel said. "Have you bled enough yet, Meliora? Are you ready to let the pain end? You can still live."

She screamed and charged, sword flying. She swung her blade down, and it scraped across his helmet, doing him no harm.

His shield drove forward and slammed into her face.

Meliora fell.

Even before she hit the ground, she felt teeth knocked out from her mouth, felt her nose shatter. She hit the stone floor, crying out in agony, tasting blood.

She lay on her back, dazed, consumed with more pain than she'd ever felt. Her vision blurred, but she could make him out standing above her. He raised his lance, placed it against her thigh, and stared down at her.

"Drop your sword," he said. "Or I take your leg. Then your other leg. Then both your arms."

She wanted to shift into a dragon, even if the chamber were too small, even if she slammed against the walls and crushed herself. But the child was still here, weeping in the corner. She could not crush him, not even to kill Ishtafel. She wanted to call to the child, to tell him to flee, but she could not speak. Blood and shattered teeth filled her mouth. Even if she wanted to, perhaps she was too weak to shift now, too hurt, dying.

I'm sorry, Requiem. I failed. I'm sorry.

She gave a wordless, gurgling cry and raised her sword.

The spear drove down, cleaving metal and flesh, driving through her thigh and into the floor.

She screamed. Her sword clanged uselessly against his armor, and Ishtafel grabbed the blade with his gauntlets, yanked the sword free, and tossed it again.

Meliora could barely cling to consciousness. The lance still pierced her thigh, pinning her to the floor. Ishtafel twisted the blade inside her, and Meliora screamed.

"I once pinned your brother to the ziggurat, you remember," he said. "I do enjoy pinning my precious little butterflies. Now that you're safe, I have a gift for you. Do you want to see?"

He reached for something that hung from his belt, tugged it free, and displayed it to her.

A collar.

A slave's collar.

No. Meliora's tears mingled with her blood. *Oh, stars of Requiem, no.*

He leaned down, pressed his knee against her belly, and closed the collar around her neck.

"Now you are my slave again." He kissed her bloody, shattered mouth and licked his lips. "Now you are mine forever."

"And . . ." She coughed, struggling to speak, just barely managing to push out the words. ". . . I . . . have a . . . gift . . . for . . . you."

She reached above her head.

When you cut off my wings, Ishtafel, my halo of pure godlight died. That day, a halo of dragonfire crackled to life around my brow. That day you gave me a weapon.

She closed her hand around the ring of fire.

It burned her palm but she did not scream.

She yanked her halo, tearing, ripping, severing. It felt like ripping off a limb, like cutting off her own scalp. She raised it before her—the same halo that had once burned Ishtafel's face—and smiled to see him recoil. She closed her second hand around the flaming ring, bent hard, and snapped the halo.

The flames shrieked as she tugged the halo, twisting the circle into a fiery horseshoe.

Requiem is eternal.

She screamed and shoved the dragonfire forth.

The two flaming prongs drove through the holes in Istafel's helmet, pierced his eyes, dug deep into his skull, and seared through the back of the helmet.

She released the halo and lifted her sword. Slowly, she rose to her feet.

Ishtafel fell to his knees, the broken halo embedded deep into his head. He was still alive. A hissing, horrible whine rose from him, an inhuman sound. He pawed at his metal mask and tore it free.

Meliora took a step back. He had no face left. Only raw, rotting muscle over bone, infected and dripping.

She cringed and shoved her sword forward. The ancient blade of Requiem drove into his neck and shattered within.

Light pulsed out from him, searing, blinding her, knocking her against the wall. His armor shattered, blasting out from him. The shards drove into Meliora, piercing her own armor, piercing her flesh, searing hot, melting inside her. The light turned black but still flowed, oozing out of Ishtafel like demons, cackling, slamming into her.

"I curse you!" rose his voice from the inferno. "I curse you, daughter of Aeternum! You will never see Requiem."

Only it was no longer his voice; it had become the voice of Leyleet, speaking in her memories.

Ishtafel shattered and fell, broken apart, his light gone dark, his halo fading to a wisp and vanishing. Meliora fell with him, her own halo gone, her own body broken. She still clutched the hilt of her bladeless sword.

And Meliora understood.

She knew now. She knew the meaning of the curse.

I saw the land of Requiem, and I saw King's Column rising from ruin. But I will not see Requiem reborn. I will not see her in peace. I will not see children running through the forest and flying above, laughing. I will not see my family grow old and our children holding our torch. I will not see spring in Requiem, and I will not see the marble halls rise anew.

Tears filled Meliora's eyes, and she smiled tremulously.

But I know now that Requiem will rise. That those columns and temples will stand again in the forest. That our kingdom will endure. I know that Requiem is eternal and that I will forever rest in her starlit halls.

Her eyes were going dark now. But as she lay on the ground, she could still turn her head, and she saw him there. The boy. He stared back at her, weeping, trembling. Living.

I saved at least one life. I saved a world entire. I brought light to this world, though I lived through much darkness. I sought righteousness though I saw much evil. I love you, Vale. I love you, Elory. I love you, Father. Always. Always. I will forever fly in the light you gave me.

Meliora Aeternum's eyes closed, and her world faded to starlight and a soothing end to pain.

VALE

He flew in the storm, bleeding, broken, close to death, when the harpies shrieked and the sky opened up to swallow them.

The bloated, feathered creatures spun in a maelstrom, eyes bugging out, talons scratching the sky.

"He is gone, he is gone!" they shrieked. "The master is gone!"

They flew in the wind, yanked backward, calling out in fear, hundreds of thousands of them. Their wings buzzed madly, shedding a rain of black, sticky feathers. Their voices rose in a deafening shriek, a sound that snapped the last trees below, that sent rocks tumbling, that cracked the earth itself. They rose from the tunnels below, sucked up into the sky, thousands and thousands emerging from the underground, all screeching in fear.

"He is dead! He is fallen! Ishtafel is no more!"

Vale flew on the wind with the last survivors of the Royal Army, a ragtag group of dragons—so few—with dented armor and bloodied claws. Til flew near him; the orange dragon's armor was cracked, her scales broken beneath it, and her eyes were haunted. Her brother flew with her, a black dragon, tears in his eyes. Only a handful of other warriors still flew. Most lay dead below.

The harpies no longer attacked. The warty creatures turned and tried to flee, to fly back south, but the storm caught them. The clouds churned above, darkening, flashing with lightning. An eye opened in the storm, revealing the sky. An eclipse burned above, the moon hiding the sun, forming a ring of fire like a halo.

"Our master is dead! Ishtafel is no more!"

The eclipse seemed to stare down through the storm, all-seeing, a great eye—the Eye of Saraph, staring from the lost realm of the gods. The harpies wailed as the storm caught them, pulling them upward toward that eye. They were as ants in water, drawn into a drain, but sucked upward, into the funnel, toward the waiting eye. Thousand by thousand, they rose, battling it, flapping their wings, clawing the sky, unable to resist as the gods reeled them upward. They kept emerging from the tunnels, from the forest, rising and rising, slamming into those dragons who still flew, then rising some more, vanishing into the hole in the sky. The wind shrieked. Broken branches and rocks flew through the air. Lightning slammed into the earth, and fire raced across the frozen soil of Requiem.

And then they were gone.

The last harpy vanished into the eye of the storm.

The maelstrom settled, and the clouds calmed. Rain began to fall, pattering against the dragons' armor and cleansing the earth of blood.

Vale looked around him at the sky. Several thousand dragons still flew here, some soldiers in armor, others civilians.

Far more Vir Requis lay dead below, their bodies shattered, torn apart, burnt, their light forever darkened.

"Father," Vale whispered. "Elory. Meliora."

He could not see them.

He cried out, "Father! Elory! Meliora!"

Across the rest of Requiem, a few cheers rose. A few voices sang in triumph. But more of the Vir Requis called out in pain, seeking their loved ones. Dragons flew above in circles, scanning the toppled forest, crying out the names of family and friends. Other Vir Requis ran through the forest in human form, moving between the bodies, weeping and seeking their loved ones—sometimes finding them dead.

Vale dived down.

He landed on the forest floor outside a tunnel's entrance—the archway shaped as two rearing dragons, claws touching. Many Vir Requis were emerging from the tunnels, clutching wounds, faces ashen.

Vale's heart thudded, and his fingers trembled.

Maybe they're in there, he thought. *Maybe my family made it into the tunnels, maybe they lived, maybe—*

Four soldiers came stepping out from the underground, carrying a makeshift litter made from a cloak and spears.

Vale's heart seemed to stop and shatter.

Before he even saw her, he knew.

The soldiers of Requiem walked toward him, faces grim, armor dented, eyes hard. The birch leaves and stars shone on their armor in the sunlight, but no beauty could fill the world this day. No light could shine through this darkness. Upon the litter she lay, her eyes closed, her face peaceful in death. Meliora Aeternum, Princess of Requiem.

My sister.

Vale fell to his knees, raised his head to the sky, and cried out in agony.

The storm above parted, revealing blue skies, and the sunlight shone on a ruined world.

ELORY

"Lucem!" she cried. "Lucem, where are you?"
Elory moved through the forest of the dead, back in human form, calling out his name. She wore dented, rusty armor. The wind blew ash into her hair. All around her spread the dead. Dead harpies, rotting in the sunlight, bloated bodies cut open. Dead soldiers of Requiem, armor cracked, eyes dark. Dead women, children, elders, some bodies unrecognizable. Countless dead. A victory drenched in blood. Hope buried under grief.

"Lucem!"

The trees lay fallen around her. Barely any still stood. Never had Elory seen such devastation, not even in Tofet. Perhaps Requiem would rise, perhaps Requiem had found its kingdom, its peace, its rededication, but here was a cursed victory. Here was a tragedy, not a triumph.

She limped across the hills, her wounds burning. Hundreds of others walked around her, calling out the names of their lost ones. King's Column rose a mile away, the sunlight shining on its marble, the dead piled up around its base, and even this ancient pillar—soaring so high, so bright—could not soothe the children of Requiem.

"Lucem!" she cried, tears in her eyes.

She had seen him fall. She had seen him vanish into smoke. It had been here! Right here! Yet she could not find him. Was he one of those bodies too burnt and ravaged to recognize? Had the harpies consumed him, or had—

"Elory."

A hoarse whisper.

Fresh tears flooded Elory's eyes.

She ran forward.

"Elory," rose the whisper again.

Several bodies lay ahead. Elory ran toward them, pulled the lifeless aside, and saw him there. Lying on the ground. Face gray as if coated with paste. Eyes sunken.

"Lucem," she said, voice trembling.

His leg was gone, and he clutched the stump. He had managed to pull off his belt, to fashion a tourniquet, but so much blood drenched the soil around him.

"I need a healer!" Elory cried, staring skyward. "A healer, please!"

Yet none answered. Few knew healing in Requiem, and those who did had too many to treat. She had to find her father, if he had lived. She had to find somebody who could pray, fix this, stop this bleeding.

"Elory," he whispered, reaching out a trembling, bloodless hand toward her. "Elory, be with me. Don't leave me."

"I won't." She knelt by him, caressed his cheek, and kissed his lips. Those lips were so cold. "I'm right here, Lucem. I'm right here. You stay with me. You don't leave me either."

He managed to smile—a weak, shaky smile. "We showed 'em, didn't we?"

She nodded, her tears splashing his face. "We did. We won, Lucem. Requiem is saved. You have to stay with me. You have to be with me when we rebuild. We have to build that little house, remember? The one with the garden. And have children. And grow old together."

"You'll have a house," he whispered. "And a garden. And children. Maybe not with me. I—"

"Hush!" She glared at him, still weeping. "You're going to live. You're going to be fine. I'm going to take care of you, I promise. I'm going to heal you."

He was fading. His blood kept dripping, his skin grew colder, his face more pale. Elory trembled and looked up to the sky.

She was no priestess. She was no healer. She had never heard the gods speak to her, as they had spoken to her father and to Vale.

"But I am a daughter of Aeternum," she whispered, staring at the sunlit sky. "If you can hear me even in the daylight, and if my name and my grief mean anything to you, please, stars of Requiem. Please, Issari. Let him live. I love him."

The sunlight was bright and she could not see the stars. She looked down at Lucem, and she placed a hand on his brow.

"Heal him, stars of Requiem," she whispered. "Don't let him leave me. He is the hero of Requiem. The first to resist. The man I love. And I need him. I can't fight on without him."

As she held his hand, his trembles eased, and he grew limp, and Elory sobbed, sure that his life was slipping away. She leaned down and kissed his lips.

"Live," she whispered.

And she felt his breath. It was shallow, but it was still there, steady, calm. Strong.

Ash rained from the sky, and dragons flew above, and Elory remained with him, holding his hand, praying, whispering to him, never letting him go.

VALE

It rained as they buried the dead.

The dragons labored through the day and night, digging graves, and at dawn they said their goodbyes. At dawn they wept. At dawn they beheld the price of their victory: row upon row of graves, stretching across the ravaged forest, hundreds of thousands of lost lights.

Most of the dead were never named. Some could no longer be recognized. Many others had lost all those who might have known their names. They had no tombstones. They lay nameless, no markers on their grave, yet perhaps in future springs new trees would grow here. Perhaps saplings would rise from these graves, pushing through the ash and shattered branches, and a forest would rise here again. A forest of the dead. A forest of new life. The forest of Requiem.

Yet there were still some tombstones in this land.

Upon a hill rose the ancient graves of Requiem's kings and queens. King Aeternum, founder of the nation, and Queen Laira, the Mother of Requiem. King Benedictus, who had fought the griffins. Queen Gloriae the Gilded, who had rebuilt Requiem from ruin. Queen Lyana who had slain phoenixes. King Valien Eleison and his wife, Queen Kaelyn Cadigus, who had healed a Requiem torn by civil war. Queen Fidelity, defeater of the Cured Temple, who raised the dragons again after their magic had nearly been lost. The names from the books. From the legends. From the old songs. The great heroes and heroines of Requiem's history, those souls who had fought so many enemies, who had led Requiem in war, who had rebuilt her halls so many times.

The graves of our past, Vale thought. *The graves of those who carried on a torch of starlight and dragonfire.*

It was here, upon the hill, that Vale buried his sister.

Not many came to the funeral. Most had lost too many of their own. Most were at other graves, grieving. A few hundred gathered here on the hill, standing silently. The rain died down to a drizzle, and the sun peeked between the clouds, and a rainbow shone above, flickering, struggling to form a bow. The last snows had melted, the ice was gone, and a few finches darted above, heralds of an early spring. Yet the day seemed too dark to Vale, and he did not know how spring could ever warm this land.

Elory stood at his side, clutching his hand. Lucem lay there on a litter, his stump bandaged, his face still pale. Til and Bim stood at his other side, faces stern.

But you're not here, Father, Vale thought, and the pain seemed unbearable. They would bury Meliora today, but they had never found Jaren's body, and it took all of Vale's strength to remain standing, not to kneel and weep.

Holding Elory's hand tightly, he looked down at Meliora.

She lay on a litter, clad in the polished armor of Requiem, her sword in her hands. Her face was pale, peaceful in death, her hair a soft gold, her eyes closed. For the first time, no halo shone above her head.

She was so beautiful, Vale thought. *She was so pure.*

Vale raised his eyes. Across the grave, the Vir Requis stared at him, more gathering from the valleys below. Vale spoke to them, voice deep, soft.

"Both the blood of Requiem and the ichor of Saraph flowed through her veins, but her heart was pure. Hers was a dragon's heart. She fought for Requiem, and she died for Requiem. She fought for her family, and she died for her family. She was too young. She was too pure. She was too righteous, too holy, too blessed to leave us so soon. Her soul has risen, and she rests now with our forebears among the stars of Requiem, yet that is little comfort for us, those who remain. Who miss her. Who mourn her. She was born to a queen of a foreign land, and she would have been queen of Requiem, and we would have been blessed by her grace." He placed his hand against her cheek. "Farewell, Meliora Aeternum, daughter of Requiem, my sister. May the stars light your final journey, guiding you to your sleep."

He draped a flag across her, which Kira—her former handmaiden—had sewn from fabrics collected from the camp, many taken from the fallen city of Keleshan. The flag was woven of rich green cotton, the color of birch leaves, and embroidered with silver stars shaped as the Draco constellation.

"Rest now in the kingdom that you loved," Vale whispered. "You're home now, Meliora. You're home."

He shifted into a dragon, and he lifted her gently. She felt so light in his grip. He placed her down in her grave, and finally he wept.

That day, after burying their dead, the survivors of Requiem found themselves facing life.

They never counted the dead, and some claimed that half of Requiem was gone, but hundreds of thousands still lived, for the first time facing a future, for the first time facing a life without chains, without battle, a life that seemed daunting. And they were afraid.

Many Vir Requis began to build crude huts from the felled trees. Others collected rain water and melted snow. Some dragons flew far to the north, where trees still stood, and hunted wild deer and boars that were emerging from their long winter. Kira and Talana were busy at the Chest of Plenty, duplicating food for the people.

There were no songs that day. No grand coronations. No dances or celebrations. One war had ended and another began— a struggle for simpler things. For food, water, shelter. Survival.

That day, Vale rose as a dragon, and he flew high and gazed down upon his kingdom.

Issari's words returned to him.

A great battle awaits you, son of Requiem, the Priestess in White had told him, healing him with her hands of starlight. *Live, child of Aeternum. Your war has not yet ended.*

For so long, Vale had wondered what battle she had meant. The battle against the seraphim in Shayeen? Perhaps the battle to retrieve the Chest of Plenty? Or maybe the great war against the harpies over Requiem?

And Vale knew now. He understood.

He looked up at the sky, and even though the sun shone, he could see it there. Issari's Star. A gleam in the sky, always guiding him.

"This is my battle," he spoke to that star. "A battle not against death but a battle for life. This is my great task: to lead my people. To build them a new home. To raise new halls of marble. To resurrect the lore of Requiem. Thank you, Issari Seran, Lady of Starlight. Thank you for guiding me here. For showing me your light."

The star shone, and he heard her voice in his mind.

Our light will always bless you, Vale Aeternum. You will never fly alone.

Vale lowered his head.

"I just wish you could fly here with me, Tash," he whispered. "I miss you."

"Vale?"

The voice spoke behind him, and Vale turned in the sky. He was so immersed in his thoughts he hadn't noticed her approach. An orange dragon flew before him, eyes green and sad.

"Til Eleison," he said.

"I found something," she said. "I want to show you. Will you fly with me?"

He narrowed his eyes, suddenly worried. Had she seen more enemies? Beasts attacking? Seraphim flying toward them? But there was no fear in Til's eyes, only sadness. He nodded and they flew together.

They flew for a long time, crossing the forests of Requiem, traveling north and leaving the column far behind. They flew silently, sometimes looking at each other, sharing a quick gaze, then flying onward.

The sun was low in the sky when they saw an escarpment ahead. The cliffs soared, stretching across Requiem, many miles long, and beyond them hills spread into the distance. A waterfall gushed down the cliff into a river.

Til led the way, gliding toward the escarpment. As they flew closer, Vale saw a canyon atop the shelf of stone. It was a small canyon, smaller than the limestone mine where he had worked back in Tofet. Several pillars of stone rose from it, naturally carved, topped with pine trees. Many more trees leaned atop the canyon and even grew, crooked and clinging, from its facades. Caves gaped open in the canyon walls, leading into shadows.

The two dragons glided into the canyon and landed on a floor strewn with boulders, some of them larger than men. Here they shifted back into human forms.

Til gazed around, eyes large. Her red hair billowed in a gust of wind. She had doffed her assortment of armored plates, remaining in her fur pelts, but her sword still hung from her belt.

"Do you know what this place is?" she whispered.

Vale nodded. "The escarpment. The place where, thousands of years ago, our ancestor—Jeid Aeternum—founded the kingdom of Requiem. Before we had a column, before we had a forest, before we had halls of marble and armor and swords, before our books and before our songs, we had a canyon. We had a cave. We had a dream."

Til nodded, reached out, and took his hands in hers. His were large hands, callused, hands that had spent years swinging a pickaxe. Hers were smaller hands, slender, pale, though hands that had swung her sword too many times.

"We stand on holy ground," she whispered. "A man and woman. Like King Aeternum and Queen Laira from the legends. We can do this again, Vale. Like they did. Build a kingdom. Raise halls of stone."

Her eyes shone, and Vale tried to imagine Tash standing here with him. She would smile at him crookedly, and the wind would play with her long brown hair and silken trousers, and the jewel in her navel would shine. She'd mock him, kiss him, and love him, and he would be happy—like the joy he had first felt with her, the only time he'd felt true joy.

And he thought of his father, the wisest, kindest man Vale had ever known. He wished Jaren could stand here with him, holding his staff, speaking of their old tales, granting him wisdom and strength.

He thought of Meliora, the sister he had known for less than a year, the sister he would always love. He wished she too were here, that she had lived to see Requiem reborn, that she had lived to be his sister in times of peace.

He thought of so many others—countless slain in the wars, sacrificing their lives so that others may live, so that the stars may shine upon them again. Each life—a world. Each life—worth as much as a nation. So many lights gone. So many who would never see their kingdom rise again.

"Your eyes are sad," Til said.

He looked at her. For perhaps the first time, Vale truly looked at her. Til Eleison. A woman who had suffered, who had fought, who stood with him on hallowed ground, vowing to forever fight with him. To share with him this battle Issari had commanded him to fight. To share with him this life.

"We lost so many," he said. "And I don't know how we can ever feel joy again."

Til embraced him, and when the wind blew again, her hair tickled his face, the same orange color as her dragon form. Her body was warm against his, soothing, soft.

"We will still feel joy." She touched his cheek. "Sadness will always fill us. Sadness does not always leave the souls of those who mourn. But that is not the same as never feeling joy again. Joy can always be found, even in wounded hearts, as flowers can still grow from ashen fields."

They rose from the canyon, and upon the escarpment, between the trees, they found a great stone statue, carved as a wild dragon—an ancient statue, perhaps carved by the very first Vir Requis, those who had lived wild in the forest before they had a kingdom.

Vale and Til sat on the dragon's head, both in human form, and held each other in the cold. Silently, they watched the sun set and the stars emerge, and for a brief few hours, here in the dark with her, Vale felt joy.

ELORY

The rain fell, and the sun set, and the sun rose, and the stars moved across the sky. And they lived. And they built.

Spring came to Requiem, and for the first time in five hundred years, leaves budded and flowers bloomed under a sky of dragons.

Throughout that spring, dragons toiled. For generations, they had toiled in Tofet, learning how to carve bricks, plow fields, raise great halls. They had worked under the whip there, but here they worked with joy. Now they plowed fields and sowed grains to feed themselves, not cruel masters. Now they built homes of stone to live in, not great temples to cruel gods. Slowly a city rose here from the ruins, and they named it Nova Vita, the same name as the ancient city that had once risen here. New life. New light.

Saplings rose in the ravaged forest. And new columns rose with them. One by one, the dragons raised them—great pillars of marble, twins to King's Column. It would be years, perhaps, before the palace of Requiem stood again in its old glory. But rise again it would, and a king once more would sit on its throne.

It was in this spring that they chose this king and crowned him.

The people of Requiem gathered before their marble columns that day, dressed in green and silver, the colors of their kingdom. Before them he stood, King's Column rising at his back—Vale Aeternum.

The heir of Requiem's ancient, royal dynasty wore silvery armor and a green cloak. A longsword hung at his side, its pommel shaped as a dragon's claw—a sword first borne by Queen Fidelity centuries ago. Vale's dark hair had grown longer, falling across his ears, and his beard was thick. No longer was he gaunt and haggard, for the spring had strengthened him, and he stood straight and strong before his people.

He looks like a great warrior king of old, Elory thought, gazing at her brother. *But this is a time of peace.*

She walked across the marble tiles they had lain out around King's Column. Her gown, woven of dark green velvet, whispered with every step. Around them, beyond the marble columns, rustled the young birches of King's Forest. Between the trees, spreading for miles, stood the children of Requiem in human forms, though many flew above as dragons too, gazing down upon them.

Elory approached her brother and stood at his side. She faced the crowd—the hundreds of thousands who stood before them. Suddenly Elory was afraid. She had never faced so many staring eyes before, never spoken to so many people. Sweat trickled down her back, and her pulse quickened.

Yet what have I to fear? she thought, feeling silly. *I faced armies in battle. I'm among friends.*

"Today we crown a new king!" she cried out. "We have chosen Vale Aeternum, son of Jaren, heir of our lost kings and queens, to wear a new crown, to sit upon a new throne. If anyone objects to his rule, speak now. For our time of tyranny has ended, and only one who is loved shall rule us."

They all stared, the nation of Requiem, silent for long moments.

Finally one voice rose.

"Long live Vale Aeternum!" cried a man.

Another joined the chant, then another, and soon thousands of voices rose together. "Long live Vale Aeternum!"

Elory blinked tears away from her eyes. She looked at her brother, smiling at him softly.

"Kneel, Vale, son of dragons."

He knelt before her on the marble tiles. In the light of King's Column, Elory placed a crown on his head. She had forged it herself in her dragonfire, had shaped it into many dragons flying together. She had made this crown from gold found in the mountains of Requiem, but she had mixed iron into it, taken from the shackles of a slave—a reminder of their enslavement, a memory they must never forget.

"Rise, King Vale Aeternum," she said.

He rose before her, King of Requiem, and turned toward the crowd.

They bowed, a nation, sweeping across the hills and valleys. Above in the sky, dragons sang their song. A prayer rose among the people, soft at first, rising louder.

Elory clasped her brother's hand, and they sang the prayer with their people.

"As the leaves fall upon our marble tiles, as the breeze rustles the birches beyond our columns, as the sun gilds the mountains above our halls—know, young child of the woods, you are home, you are home. Requiem! May our wings forever find your sky."

The sun set, and the sun rose. The rains fell, and snows covered the land, and spring rose again.

And they sang.

And they built.

And they lived.

Autumn came to Requiem, and grains swayed golden in the fields, and fruits and vegetables ripened, and ale brewed. There was a rich harvest that year, overflowing with squashes, sweet apples, and green peas. Some fields yielded only a handful of crops; these the Chest of Plenty quickly replicated. For the first time in centuries, the Vir Requis patted full bellies.

These were busy times, times of building, nurturing, remembering. But many days, Elory remained in her home, in the small brick house she had built with Lucem. Often she simply sat watching her husband as he walked through the garden on his wooden leg, inspecting the flowers, filling birdfeeders with seed, leaving lumps of bread on the fence for the squirrels. The hero of Requiem, the boy who had scaled the wall, who had slain the great bird Ziz and several archangels—he had become a gardener, and he had never seemed happier.

"I lost my ear," she would joke with him, "so you just had to lose your leg to one-up me."

He would smile at this joke—she told it every now and then—and always replied with, "Somewhere your ear met my leg and is feeling rather envious."

Yet there was always sadness to their smiles. And even in the beauty of autumn, as they sat together in their armchair, sharing hot cider, the sadness dwelled. Even as snow fell, glittering outside as a field of stars, and icicles gleamed as jewels, and many lanterns hung from trees and homes, the sadness remained.

Because we are broken, Elory thought. And she did not mean her ear or his leg. Something had broken inside them in the inferno of Tofet, something she knew could never mend. Something that a warm home, a nation at peace, a world of beauty could not heal.

"We are broken," she whispered to him one night, as they sat gazing out the window at the rain.

He held her in his arms. "Then let us make something whole."

Spring bloomed across Requiem, and the scent of flowers and song of birds filled the air, when Elory gave birth to her daughter. The child had her dark hair, Lucem's blue eyes, and tiny fingers that Elory loved to kiss.

"I name you Liora," she whispered to the babe, "for you're brave and beautiful like my sister."

The sun set and the sun rose. The dry leaves fell, and the snow glided down, and spring bloomed, and great halls of marble rose among the birches. The sound of laughter filled her house. And still the sadness lingered.

One autumn day, Elory took her daughter in her arms, and she walked through the woods of Requiem. It was a chilly day, and many dry leaves rustled among the birches, and the sounds of song and prayer rose from humble homes. Elory walked for a long time, leaving the city behind, and stepped onto the hill where they had buried her sister.

The wind played with her long brown hair. She stood, holding her daughter, gazing at Meliora's grave.

"I don't know how to go on," she whispered to her sister. "I don't know how to feel joy. I don't know how to forget."

Elory closed her eyes, cringing with sudden pain. Again she could feel it—the flaming whip against her back. Again she could see them—the bodies on the lances, a forest of dead in Tofet. Again she heard the cries of the harpies, and again she saw dragons falling like the rain. The pain felt too strong, the memories too real, and Elory's head spun and she could barely breathe.

Her baby gurgled in her arms, and Elory opened her eyes. Little Liora reached up and tugged at Elory's hair.

Tears streamed down Elory's cheeks. She gazed around at her homeland, at the forests of Requiem, the distant marble columns rising from among the birches, the blue mountains in the north.

"It's beautiful," she whispered, tasting her tears. "It's beautiful here, Liora. I did this for you. I fought for this land for you, for all the babes born here. This will never be my kingdom, Liora. My home will always be in Tofet. That is a land I cannot escape, that I cannot wrench out from within me. But you will never know such pain, Liora. I promise this to you. This will always be your home."

Liora smiled and giggled, a beautiful, innocent babe.

Elory kissed her. "May you know nothing but joy, sweet child. May you know nothing but peace. May your life be full of light, of family, of hope. May you always find Requiem's sky."

Footsteps sounded behind her, and she turned to see Lucem walking up the hill, wrapped in a warm cloak and holding a basket full of bread, cheese, and wine.

"Thought you'd be here," he said. "Figured we'd have a little meal, and . . ."

His voice faded when he saw her tears, and he hurried toward her. She embraced him. They stood together, holding each other, a family, watching the forests sway and the dragons fly above.

THE END

NOVELS BY DANIEL ARENSON

Dawn of Dragons:
Requiem's Song
Requiem's Hope
Requiem's Prayer

Song of Dragons:
Blood of Requiem
Tears of Requiem
Light of Requiem

Dragonlore:
A Dawn of Dragonfire
A Day of Dragon Blood
A Night of Dragon Wings

The Dragon War:
A Legacy of Light
A Birthright of Blood
A Memory of Fire

Requiem for Dragons:
Dragons Lost
Dragons Reborn
Dragons Rising

KEEP IN TOUCH

www.DanielArenson.com
Daniel@DanielArenson.com
Facebook.com/DanielArenson
Twitter.com/DanielArenson

CPSIA information can be obtained
at www.ICGtesting.com
Printed in the USA
BVOW08s0924020117

472333BV00003B/589/P